The Nemesis of Fire and Others

ALGERNON BLACKWOOD

The Nemesis of Fire and Others

Collected Short Fiction
Volume 2: 1908–1910

Edited by S. T. Joshi

Hippocampus Press

New York

Published by Hippocampus Press
P.O. Box 641, New York, NY 10156.
www.hippocampuspress.com

Cover illustration and design © 2023 by Jason Van Hollander.
Hippocampus Press logo designed by Anastasia Damianakos.

First edition
1 3 5 7 9 8 6 4 2

ISBN 978-1-61498-432-0 six-volume set
ISBN 978-1-61498-402-3 volume 2
ISBN 978-1-61498-430-6 ebook

Contents

Introduction...7

A Psychical Invasion..11

Ancient Sorceries 60

The Nemesis of Fire 105

Secret Worship 173

The Camp of the Dog...205

A Victim of Higher Space...271

The Secret...290

The Kit-Bag 295

Stodgman's Opportunity...306

The Boy Messenger 311

The Story Mr. Popkiss Told 319

Entrance and Exit 323

You *May* Telephone from Here...328

The Invitation..333

The Lease 338

Faith Cure on the Channel 343

Carlton's Drive..347

The Man Who Found Out 353

The Laying of a Red-Haired Ghost....................................369

Up and Down...380

The Face of the Earth 386

The Man Who Played upon the Leaf...................................395

The Terror of the Twins 412

Strange Disappearance of a Baronet...................................419

The Occupant of the Room 425

The Lock of Grey Hair 434
The South Wind 444
The Man from the "Gods" 447
If the Cap Fits— 459
Perspective 465
Special Delivery 484
The Lost Valley 494
Appendix 541
Author's Note [to *John Silence—Physician Extraordinary* (1942)] 543
Bibliography 545

Introduction

This volume of Algernon Blackwood's complete short fiction opens with the six stories he wrote about the psychic detective John Silence. The first five appeared in *John Silence—Physician Extraordinary* (1908) and are presented here in the order in which they appeared in that collection. But this is probably not the order in which the stories were written. It is apparent that Blackwood did not initially set out to write a series of stories revolving around a single detective-like figure; the impetus for such a series came from his publisher, Eveleigh Nash. Once Blackwood assented to a volume of this sort, he was obliged to rework some previously written tales so that they became "John Silence" stories. Mike Ashley, the leading authority on Blackwood, believes that "Ancient Sorceries" and "Secret Worship" had already been written before the idea of weaving them into the John Silence sequence occurred to Blackwood. It can be seen that in these tales John Silence's presence is something of an afterthought. They were probably written in the latter half of 1907, while the other four were apparently written in the winter of 1907–08. "The Camp of the Dog" was, by Blackwood's own testimony years later, the last one written.[1] "A Victim of Higher Space" was excluded from the collection because it was considered poorer than the other tales; in any event, the other five stories already constituted a large volume.

The unexpected success of *John Silence* allowed Blackwood to spend the next five years in relative economic independence, so that he could write what he wished without thought of earning an income from writing. However, most of the stories in this volume were probably written before Blackwood left England in January 1909 to spend the next half-decade in the Swiss Alps. Many of them were collected in

---

1. See, in general, Mike Ashley's discussion in *Starlight Man: The Extraordinary Life of Algernon Blackwood* (Eureka, CA: Stark House Press, 2019), 173–76.

his subsequent story collections: *The Lost Valley and Other Stories* (1910), *Pan's Garden: A Volume of Nature Stories* (1912), *Ten Minute Stories* (1914), and *Day and Night Stories* (1917); but a surprising number were uncollected, although they did appear in English periodicals of the period. Many of the collected and uncollected stories were published in the *Westminster Gazette*, a daily evening newspaper in London that habitually ran at least one short story every day. Its editor was John A. Spender, who was a colleague of Angus Hamilton, the man who had helped Blackwood land his first volume, *The Empty House* (1906), with Eveleigh Nash. Blackwood's first story for the *Westminster Gazette* was "The Secret" (7 November 1908); it was followed by forty more over the next fourteen years.

Blackwood's stories also appeared in popular English magazines of the day: *Nash's Magazine, Pall Mall Magazine, Lady's Realm, Country Life*. Only one story included here—"The Man from 'the Gods'"—did not receive periodical publication. A few of the stories in this book have been only recently discovered, such as "The Lock of Grey Hair" (published in the Christmas Supplement of the London newspaper, the *Observer*), "The Boy Messenger" (found in a newspaper in Nottinghamshire, although it probably appeared in other newspapers as well), "The Face of the Earth" (published in a weekly paper in Edinburgh), and "The Laying of a Red-Haired Ghost" (in the *Lady's Realm*).

The stories in this volume feature many of the major motifs that figure in Blackwood's entire corpus of weird fiction: ghosts and revenants; psychic experiences; nature worship; the baffling psychological fusion of twins. Although the stories in *John Silence* feature a diversity of locales (England, France, Sweden, Germany), most of the tales in this book are set in England and often deal with seemingly mundane experiences—a man taking some one else's hat ("If the Cap Fits—"), a train journey that hints at future disaster ("The Story Mr. Popkiss Told"), and the like. "The Man Who Played upon the Leaf" is Blackwood's first published story set in Switzerland; it appeared almost a year after the author settled in Bôle, in the canton of Neuchâtel, in the Jura Mountains. "The Occupant of the Room," "The South Wind," "Perspective," "Special Delivery," and "The Lost Valley" are also set in Switzerland. That last story is a complex one of twin brothers who fall in love with the same woman, with tragic consequences for one of them. A number of other tales are those that Mike Ashley refers to as "vague friend" stories,[2] where a man encounters a friend or acquaintance who tells a rambling account that may or may not veer into the strange or supernatural.

John Silence—Physician Extraordinary established Algernon Blackwood's reputation as a master storyteller and as one heavily invested in the weird—not merely for the sake of sending a shiver up one's spine, but in conveying messages about the interrelation of the human consciousness with the ethereal magic of the external world. Slight as some of the tales in this volume may be, they all emphasize the extent to which Blackwood believed in the possibility of a connection between the mind and the mysterious universe of which it is a part.

—S. T. JOSHI

---

2. See Mike Ashley, *Algernon Blackwood: A Bio-bibliography* (Westport, CT: Greenwood Press, 1987), 90–91.

A Psychical Invasion

And what is it makes you think I could be of use in this particular case?" asked Dr. John Silence, looking across somewhat sceptically at the Swedish lady in the chair facing him.

"Your sympathetic heart and your knowledge of occultism—"

"Oh, please—that dreadful word!" he interrupted, holding up a finger with a gesture of impatience.

"Well, then," she laughed, "your wonderful clairvoyant gift and your trained psychic knowledge of the processes by which a personality may be disintegrated and destroyed—these strange studies you've been experimenting with all these years—"

"If it's only a case of multiple personality I must really cry off," interrupted the doctor again hastily, a bored expression in his eyes.

"It's not that; now, please, be serious, for I want your help," she said; "and if I choose my words poorly you must be patient with my ignorance. The case I know will interest you, and no one else could deal with it so well. In fact, no ordinary professional man could deal with it at all, for I know of no treatment or medicine that can restore a lost sense of humour!"

"You begin to interest me with your 'case,'" he replied, and made himself comfortable to listen.

Mrs. Sivendson drew a sigh of contentment as she watched him go to the tube and heard him tell the servant he was not to be disturbed.

"I believe you have read my thoughts already," she said; "your intuitive knowledge of what goes on in other people's minds is positively uncanny."

Her friend shook his head and smiled as he drew his chair up to a convenient position and prepared to listen attentively to what she had to say. He closed his eyes, as he always did when he wished to absorb

11

the real meaning of a recital that might be inadequately expressed, for by this method he found it easier to set himself in tune with the living thoughts that lay behind the broken words.

By his friends John Silence was regarded as an eccentric, because he was rich by accident, and by choice—a doctor. That a man of independent means should devote his time to doctoring, chiefly doctoring folk who could not pay, passed their comprehension entirely. The native nobility of a soul whose first desire was to help those who could not help themselves, puzzled them. After that, it irritated them, and, greatly to his own satisfaction, they left him to his own devices.

Dr. Silence was a free-lance, though, among doctors, having neither consulting-room, bookkeeper, nor professional manner. He took no fees, being at heart a genuine philanthropist, yet at the same time did no harm to his fellow-practitioners, because he only accepted unremunerative cases, and cases that interested him for some very special reason. He argued that the rich could pay, and the very poor could avail themselves of organised charity, but that a very large class of ill-paid, self-respecting workers, often followers of the arts, could not afford the price of a week's comforts merely to be told to travel. And it was these he desired to help: cases often requiring special and patient study—things no doctor can give for a guinea, and that no one would dream of expecting him to give.

But there was another side to his personality and practice, and one with which we are now more directly concerned; for the cases that especially appealed to him were of no ordinary kind, but rather of that intangible, elusive, and difficult nature best described as psychical afflictions; and, though he would have been the last person himself to approve of the title, it was beyond question that he was known more or less generally as the "Psychic Doctor."

In order to grapple with cases of this peculiar kind, he had submitted himself to a long and severe training, at once physical, mental, and spiritual. What precisely this training had been, or where undergone, no one seemed to know,—for he never spoke of it, as, indeed, he betrayed no single other characteristic of the charlatan,—but the fact that it had involved a total disappearance from the world for five years, and that after he returned and began his singular practice no one ever dreamed of applying to him the so easily acquired epithet of quack, spoke much for the seriousness of his strange quest and also for the genuineness of his attainments.

For the modern psychical researcher he felt the calm tolerance of the "man who knows." There was a trace of pity in his voice—contempt he never showed—when he spoke of their methods.

"This classification of results is uninspired work at best," he said once to me, when I had been his confidential assistant for some years. "It leads nowhere, and after a hundred years will lead nowhere. It is playing with the wrong end of a rather dangerous toy. Far better, it would be, to examine the causes, and then the results would so easily slip into place and explain themselves. For the sources are accessible, and open to all who have the courage to lead the life that alone makes practical investigation safe and possible."

And towards the question of clairvoyance, too, his attitude was significantly sane, for he knew how extremely rare the genuine power was, and that what is commonly called clairvoyance is nothing more than a keen power of visualising.

"It connotes a slightly increased sensibility, nothing more," he would say. "The true clairvoyant deplores his power, recognising that it adds a new horror to life, and is in the nature of an affliction. And you will find this always to be the real test."

Thus it was that John Silence, this singularly developed doctor, was able to select his cases with a clear knowledge of the difference between mere hysterical delusion and the kind of psychical affliction that claimed his special powers. It was never necessary for him to resort to the cheap mysteries of divination; for, as I have heard him observe, after the solution of some peculiarly intricate problem—

"Systems of divination, from geomancy down to reading by tea-leaves, are merely so many methods of obscuring the outer vision, in order that the inner vision may become open. Once the method is mastered, no system is necessary at all."

And the words were significant of the methods of this remarkable man, the keynote of whose power lay, perhaps, more than anything else, in the knowledge, first, that thought can act at a distance, and, secondly, that thought is dynamic and can accomplish material results.

"Learn how to *think*," he would have expressed it, "and you have learned to tap power at its source."

To look at—he was now past forty—he was sparely built, with speaking brown eyes in which shone the light of knowledge and self-confidence, while at the same time they made one think of that wondrous gentleness seen most often in the eyes of animals. A close beard concealed the mouth without disguising the grim determination of lips and jaw, and the face somehow conveyed an impression of transparency, almost of light, so delicately were the features refined away. On the fine forehead was that indefinable touch of peace that comes from identifying the mind with what is permanent in the soul, and letting the impermanent slip by without power to wound or distress; while, from his manner,—so gentle, quiet, sympathetic,—few could have guessed the strength of purpose that burned within like a great flame.

"I think I should describe it as a psychical case," continued the Swedish lady, obviously trying to explain herself very intelligently, "and just the kind you like. I mean a case where the cause is hidden deep down in some spiritual distress, and—"

"But the symptoms first, please, my dear Svenska," he interrupted, with a strangely compelling seriousness of manner, "and your deductions afterwards."

She turned round sharply on the edge of her chair and looked him in the face, lowering her voice to prevent her emotion betraying itself too obviously.

"In my opinion there's only one symptom," she half whispered, as though telling something disagreeable—"fear—simply fear."

"Physical fear?"

"I think not; though how can I say? I think it's a horror in the psychical region. It's no ordinary delusion; the man is quite sane; but he lives in mortal terror of something—"

"I don't know what you mean by his 'psychical region,'" said the doctor, with a smile; "though I suppose you wish me to understand that his spiritual, and not his mental, processes are affected. Anyhow, try and tell me briefly and pointedly what you know about the man, his symptoms, his need for help, *my* peculiar help, that is, and all that seems vital in the case. I promise to listen devotedly."

"I am trying," she continued earnestly, "but must do so in my own words and trust to your intelligence to disentangle as I go along. He is a young author, and lives in a tiny house off Putney Heath somewhere.

He writes humorous stories—quite a genre of his own: Pender—you must have heard the name—Felix Pender? Oh, the man had a great gift, and married on the strength of it; his future seemed assured. I say 'had,' for quite suddenly his talent utterly failed him. Worse, it became transformed into its opposite. He can no longer write a line in the old way that was bringing him success—"

Dr. Silence opened his eyes for a second and looked at her.

"He still writes, then? The force has not gone?" he asked briefly, and then closed his eyes again to listen.

"He works like a fury," she went on, "but produces nothing"—she hesitated a moment—"nothing that he can use or sell. His earnings have practically ceased, and he makes a precarious living by book-reviewing and odd jobs—very odd, some of them. Yet, I am certain his talent has not really deserted him finally, but is merely—"

Again Mrs. Sivendson hesitated for the appropriate word.

"In abeyance," he suggested, without opening his eyes.

"Obliterated," she went on, after a moment to weigh the word, "merely obliterated by something else—"

"By some *one* else?"

"I wish I knew. All I can say is that he is haunted, and temporarily his sense of humour is shrouded—gone—replaced by something dreadful that writes other things. Unless something competent is done, he will simply starve to death. Yet he is afraid to go to a doctor for fear of being pronounced insane; and, anyhow, a man can hardly ask a doctor to take a guinea to restore a vanished sense of humour, can he?"

"Has he tried any one at all—?"

"Not doctors yet. He tried some clergymen and religious people; but they *know* so little and have so little intelligent sympathy. And most of them are so busy balancing on their own little pedestals—"

John Silence stopped her tirade with a gesture.

"And how is it that you know so much about him?" he asked gently.

"I know Mrs. Pender well—I knew her before she married him—"

"And is she a cause, perhaps?"

"Not in the least. She is devoted; a woman very well educated, though without being really intelligent, and with so little sense of humour herself that she always laughs at the wrong places. But she has nothing to do with the cause of his distress; and, indeed, has chiefly guessed it from observing him, rather than from what little he has told her. And he, you know, is a really lovable fellow, hard-working, patient—altogether worth saving."

Dr Silence opened his eyes and went over to ring for tea. He did not know very much more about the case of the humorist than when he first sat down to listen; but he realised that no amount of words from his Swedish friend would help to reveal the real facts. A personal interview with the author himself could alone do that.

"All humorists are worth saving," he said with a smile, as she poured out tea. "We can't afford to lose a single one in these strenuous days. I will go and see your friend at the first opportunity."

She thanked him elaborately, effusively, with many words, and he, with much difficulty, kept the conversation thenceforward strictly to the teapot.

And, as a result of this conversation, and a little more he had gathered by means best known to himself and his secretary, he was whizzing in his motor-car one afternoon a few days later up the Putney Hill to have his first interview with Felix Pender, the humorous writer who was the victim of some mysterious malady in his "psychical region" that had obliterated his sense of the comic and threatened to wreck his life and destroy his talent. And his desire to help was probably of equal strength with his desire to know and to investigate.

The motor stopped with a deep purring sound, as though a great black panther lay concealed within its hood, and the doctor—the "psychic doctor," as he was sometimes called—stepped out through the gathering fog, and walked across the tiny garden that held a blackened fir tree and a stunted laurel shrubbery. The house was very small, and it was some time before any one answered the bell. Then, suddenly, a light appeared in the hall, and he saw a pretty little woman standing on the top step begging him to come in. She was dressed in grey, and the gaslight fell on a mass of deliberately brushed light hair. Stuffed, dusty birds, and a shabby array of African spears, hung on the wall behind her. A hatrack, with a bronze plate full of very large cards, led his eye swiftly to a dark staircase beyond. Mrs. Pender had round eyes like a child's, and she greeted him with an effusiveness that barely concealed her emotion, yet strove to appear naturally cordial. Evidently she had been looking out for his arrival, and had outrun the servant girl. She was a little breathless.

"I hope you've not been kept waiting—I think it's *most* good of you to come—" she began, and then stopped sharp when she saw his face in the gaslight. There was something in Dr. Silence's look that did not encourage mere talk. He was in earnest now, if ever man was.

"Good evening, Mrs. Pender," he said, with a quiet smile that won confidence, yet deprecated unnecessary words, "the fog delayed me a little. I am glad to see you."

They went into a dingy sitting-room at the back of the house, neatly furnished but depressing. Books stood in a row upon the mantelpiece. The fire had evidently just been lit. It smoked in great puffs into the room.

"Mrs. Sivendson said she thought you might be able to come," ventured the little woman again, looking up engagingly into his face and betraying anxiety and eagerness in every gesture. "But I hardly dared to believe it. I think it is really too good of you. My husband's case is so peculiar that—well, you know, I am quite sure any *ordinary* doctor would say at once the asylum—"

"Isn't he in, then?" asked Dr. Silence gently.

"In the asylum?" she gasped. "Oh dear, no—not yet!"

"In the house, I meant," he laughed.

She gave a great sigh.

"He'll be back any minute now," she replied, obviously relieved to see him laugh; "but the fact is, we didn't expect you so early—I mean, my husband hardly thought you would come at all."

"I am always delighted to come—when I am really wanted, and can be of help," he said quickly; "and, perhaps, it's all for the best that your husband is out, for now that we are alone you can tell me something about his difficulties. So far, you know, I have heard very little."

Her voice trembled as she thanked him, and when he came and took a chair close beside her she actually had difficulty in finding words with which to begin.

"In the first place," she began timidly, and then continuing with a nervous incoherent rush of words, "he will be simply delighted that you've really come, because he said you were the only person he would consent to see at all—the only doctor, I mean. But, of course, he doesn't know how frightened I am, or how much I have noticed. He pretends with me that it's just a nervous breakdown, and I'm sure he doesn't realise all the odd things I've noticed him doing. But the main thing, I suppose—"

"Yes, the main thing, Mrs. Pender," he said encouragingly, noticing her hesitation.

"—is that he thinks we are not alone in the house. That's the chief thing."

"Tell me more facts—just facts."

"It began last summer when I came back from Ireland; he had been here alone for six weeks, and I thought him looking tired and queer—ragged and scattered about the face, if you know what I mean, and his manner worn out. He said he had been writing hard, but his inspiration had somehow failed him, and he was dissatisfied with his work. His sense of humour was leaving him, or changing into something else, he said. There was something in the house, he declared, that"—she emphasised the words—"prevented his feeling funny."

"Something in the house that prevented his feeling funny," repeated the doctor. "Ah, now we're getting to the heart of it!"

"Yes," she resumed vaguely, "that's what he kept saying."

"And what was it he *did* that you thought strange?" he asked sympathetically. "Be brief, or he may be here before you finish."

"Very small things, but significant it seemed to me. He changed his workroom from the library, as we call it, to the smoking-room. He said all his characters became wrong and terrible in the library; they altered, so that he felt like writing tragedies—vile, debased tragedies, the tragedies of broken souls. But now he says the same of the smoking-room, and he's gone back to the library."

"Ah!"

"You see, there's so little I can tell you," she went on, with increasing speed and countless gestures. "I mean it's only very small things he does and says that are queer. What frightens me is that he assumes there is some one else in the house all the time—some one I never see. He does not actually say so, but on the stairs I've seen him standing aside to let some one pass; I've seen him open a door to let some one in or out; and often in our bedrooms he puts chairs about as though for some one else to sit in. Oh—oh yes, and once or twice," she cried—"once or twice—"

She paused, and looked about her with a startled air.

"Yes?"

"Once or twice," she resumed hurriedly, as though she heard a sound that alarmed her, "I've heard him running—coming in and out of the rooms breathless as if something were after him—"

The door opened while she was still speaking, cutting her words off in the middle, and a man came into the room. He was dark and clean-shaven, sallow rather, with the eyes of imagination, and dark hair growing scantily about the temples. He was dressed in a shabby tweed suit, and wore an untidy flannel collar at the neck. The dominant expression of his face was startled—hunted; an expression that might any moment leap into the dreadful stare of terror and announce a total loss of self-control.

The moment he saw his visitor a smile spread over his worn features, and he advanced to shake hands.

"I hoped you would come; Mrs. Sivendson said you might be able to find time," he said simply. His voice was thin and reedy. "I am very glad to see you, Dr. Silence. It is 'Doctor,' is it not?"

"Well, I am entitled to the description," laughed the other, "but I rarely get it. You know, I do not practise as a regular thing; that is, I only take cases that specially interest me, or—"

He did not finish the sentence, for the men exchanged a glance of sympathy that rendered it unnecessary.

"I have heard of your great kindness."

"It's my hobby," said the other quickly, "and my privilege."

"I trust you will still think so when you have heard what I have to tell you," continued the author, a little wearily. He led the way across the hall into the little smoking-room where they could talk freely and undisturbed.

In the smoking-room, the door shut and privacy about them, Pender's attitude changed somewhat, and his manner became very grave. The doctor sat opposite, where he could watch his face. Already, he saw, it looked more haggard. Evidently it cost him much to refer to his trouble at all.

"What I have is, in my belief, a profound spiritual affliction," he began quite bluntly, looking straight into the other's eyes.

"I saw that at once," Dr. Silence said.

"Yes, you saw that, of course; my atmosphere must convey that much to any one with psychic perceptions. Besides which, I feel sure from all I've heard, that you are really a soul-doctor, are you not, more than a healer merely of the body?"

"You think of me too highly," returned the other; "though I prefer cases, as you know, in which the spirit is disturbed first, the body afterwards."

"I understand, yes. Well, I have experienced a curious disturbance in—*not* in my physical region primarily. I mean my nerves are all right, and my body is all right. I have no delusions exactly, but my spirit is tortured by a calamitous fear which first came upon me in a strange manner."

John Silence leaned forward a moment and took the speaker's hand and held it in his own for a few brief seconds, closing his eyes as he did so. He was not feeling his pulse, or doing any of the things that doctors ordinarily do; he was merely absorbing into himself the main note of the man's mental condition, so as to get completely his own point of view, and thus be able to treat his case with true sympathy. A very close observer might perhaps have noticed that a slight tremor ran through his frame after he had held the hand for a few seconds.

"Tell me quite frankly, Mr. Pender," he said soothingly, releasing the hand, and with deep attention in his manner, "tell me all the steps that led to the beginning of this invasion. I mean tell me what the particular drug was, and why you took it, and how it affected you—"

"Then you know it began with a drug!" cried the author, with undisguised astonishment.

"I only know from what I observe in you, and in its effect upon myself. You are in a surprising psychical condition. Certain portions of your atmosphere are vibrating at a far greater rate than others. This is the effect of a drug, but of no ordinary drug. Allow me to finish, please. If the higher rate of vibration spreads all over, you will become, of course, permanently cognisant of a much larger world than the one you know normally. If, on the other hand, the rapid portion sinks back to the usual rate, you will lose these occasional increased perceptions you now have."

"You amaze me!" exclaimed the author; "for your words exactly describe what I have been feeling—"

"I mention this only in passing, and to give you confidence before you approach the account of your real affliction," continued the doctor. "All perception, as you know, is the result of vibrations; and clair-voyance simply means becoming sensitive to an increased scale of vibrations. The awakening of the inner senses we hear so much about means no more than that. Your partial clairvoyance is easily explained. The only thing that puzzles me is how you managed to procure the drug, for it is not easy to get in pure form, and no adulterated tincture could have given you the terrific impetus I see you have acquired. But, please proceed now and tell me your story in your own way."

"This *Cannabis indica,*" the author went on, "came into my possession last autumn while my wife was away. I need not explain how I got it, for that has no importance; but it was the genuine fluid extract, and I could not resist the temptation to make an experiment. One of its effects, as you know, is to induce torrential laughter—"

"Yes; sometimes."

"—I am a writer of humorous tales, and I wished to increase my own sense of laughter—to see the ludicrous from an abnormal point of view. I wished to study it a bit, if possible, and—"

"Tell me!"

"I took an experimental dose. I starved for six hours to hasten the effect, locked myself into this room, and gave orders not to be disturbed. Then I swallowed the stuff and waited."

"And the effect?"

"I waited one hour, two, three, four, five hours. Nothing happened. No laughter came, but only a great weariness instead. Nothing in the room or in my thoughts came within a hundred miles of a humorous aspect."

"Always a most uncertain drug," interrupted the doctor. "We make very small use of it on that account."

"At two o'clock in the morning I felt so hungry and tired that I decided to give up the experiment and wait no longer. I drank some milk and went upstairs to bed. I felt flat and disappointed. I fell asleep at once and must have slept for about an hour, when I awoke suddenly with a great noise in my ears. It was the noise of my own laughter! I was simply shaking with merriment. At first I was bewildered and thought I had been laughing in dreams, but a moment later I remembered the drug, and was delighted to think that after all I had got an effect. It had been working all along, only I had miscalculated the time. The only unpleasant thing *then* was an odd feeling that I had not waked naturally, but had been wakened by some one else—deliberately. This came to me as a certainty in the middle of my noisy laughter and distressed me."

"Any impression who it could have been?" asked the doctor, now listening with close attention to every word, very much on the alert.

Pender hesitated and tried to smile. He brushed his hair from his forehead with a nervous gesture.

"You must tell me all your impressions, even your fancies; they are quite as important as your certainties."

"I had a vague idea that it was some one connected with my forgotten dream, some one who had been at me in my sleep, some one of great strength and great ability—of great force—quite an unusual personality—and, I was certain, too—a woman."

"A good woman?" asked John Silence quietly.

Pender started a little at the question and his sallow face flushed; it seemed to surprise him. But he shook his head quickly with an indefinable look of horror.

"Evil," he answered briefly, "appallingly evil, and yet mingled with the sheer wickedness of it was also a certain perverseness—the perversity of the unbalanced mind."

He hesitated a moment and looked up sharply at his interlocutor. A shade of suspicion showed itself in his eyes.

"No," laughed the doctor, "you need not fear that I'm merely humouring you, or think you mad. Far from it. Your story interests me exceedingly and you furnish me unconsciously with a number of clues as you tell it. You see, I possess some knowledge of my own as to these psychic byways."

"I was shaking with such violent laughter," continued the narrator, reassured in a moment, "though with no clear idea what was amusing me, that I had the greatest difficulty in getting up for the matches, and was afraid I should frighten the servants overhead with my explosions. When the gas was lit I found the room empty, of course, and the door locked as usual. Then I half dressed and went out on to the landing, my hilarity better under control, and proceeded to go downstairs. I wished to record my sensations. I stuffed a handkerchief into my mouth so as not to scream aloud and communicate my hysterics to the entire household."

"And the presence of this—this—?"

"It was hanging about me all the time," said Pender, "but for the moment it seemed to have withdrawn. Probably, too, my laughter killed all other emotions."

"And how long did you take getting downstairs?"

"I was just coming to that. I see you know all my 'symptoms' in advance, as it were; for, of course, I thought I should never get to the bottom. Each step seemed to take five minutes, and crossing the narrow hall at the foot of the stairs—well, I could have sworn it was half an hour's journey had not my watch certified that it was a few seconds. Yet I walked fast and tried to push on. It was no good. I walked apparently without advancing, and at that rate it would have taken me a week to get down Putney Hill."

"An experimental dose radically alters the scale of time and space sometimes—"

"But, when at last I got into my study and lit the gas, the change came horridly, and sudden as a flash of lightning. It was like a douche of icy water, and in the middle of this storm of laughter—"

"Yes; what?" asked the doctor, leaning forward and peering into his eyes.

"—I was overwhelmed with terror," said Pender, lowering his reedy voice at the mere recollection of it.

He paused a moment and mopped his forehead. The scared, hunted look in his eyes now dominated the whole face. Yet, all the time, the corners of his mouth hinted of possible laughter as though the recollection of that merriment still amused him. The combination of fear and laughter in his face was very curious, and lent great conviction to his story; it also lent a bizarre expression of horror to his gestures.

"Terror, was it?" repeated the doctor soothingly.

"Yes, terror; for, though the Thing that woke me seemed to have gone, the memory of it still frightened me, and I collapsed into a chair. Then I locked the door and tried to reason with myself, but the drug made my movements so prolonged that it took me five minutes to reach the door, and another five to get back to the chair again. The laughter, too, kept bubbling up inside me—great wholesome laughter that shook me like gusts of wind—so that even my terror almost made me laugh. Oh, but I may tell you, Dr. Silence, it was altogether vile, that mixture of fear and laughter, altogether vile!

"Then, all at once, the things in the room again presented their funny side to me and set me off laughing more furiously than ever. The bookcase was ludicrous, the arm-chair a perfect clown, the way the clock looked at me on the mantelpiece too comic for words; the arrangement of papers and inkstand on the desk tickled me till I roared and shook and held my sides and the tears streamed down my cheeks. And that footstool! Oh, that absurd footstool!"

He lay back in his chair, laughing to himself and holding up his hands at the thought of it, and at the sight of him Dr. Silence laughed, too.

"Go on, please," he said, "I quite understand. I know something myself of the hashish laughter."

The author pulled himself together and resumed, his face growing quickly grave again.

"So, you see, side by side with this extravagant, apparently causeless merriment, there was also an extravagant, apparently causeless terror. The drug produced the laughter, I knew; but what brought in the terror I could not imagine. Everywhere behind the fun lay the fear. It was terror masked by cap and bells; and I became the playground for two opposing emotions, armed and fighting to the death. Gradually, then, the impression grew in me that this fear was caused by the invasion—so you called it just now—of the 'person' who had wakened me: she was utterly evil; inimical to my soul, or at least to all in me that wished for good. There I stood, sweating and trembling, laughing at everything in the room, yet all the while with this white terror mastering my heart. And this creature was putting—putting her——"

He hesitated again, using his handkerchief freely.

"Putting what?"

"—putting ideas into my mind," he went on, glancing nervously about the room. "Actually tapping my thought-stream so as to switch off the usual current and inject her own. How mad that sounds! I know it, but it's true. It's the only way I can express it. Moreover, while the operation terrified me, the skill with which it was accomplished filled me afresh with laughter at the clumsiness of men by comparison. Our ignorant, bungling methods of teaching the minds of others, of inculcating ideas, and so on, overwhelmed me with laughter when I understood this superior and diabolical method. Yet my laughter seemed hollow and ghastly, and ideas of evil and tragedy trod close upon the heels of the comic. Oh, doctor, I tell you again, it was unnerving!"

John Silence sat with his head thrust forward to catch every word of the story which the other continued to pour out in nervous, jerky sentences and lowered voice.

"You *saw* nothing—no one—all this time?" he asked.

"Not with my eyes. There was no visual hallucination. But in my mind there began to grow the vivid picture of a woman—large, dark-skinned, with white teeth and masculine features, and one eye—the left—so drooping as to appear almost closed. Oh, such a face—!"

"A face you would recognise again?"

Pender laughed dreadfully.

"I wish I could forget it," he whispered, "I only wish I could forget it!" Then he sat forward in his chair suddenly, and grasped the doctor's hand with an emotional gesture.

"I *must* tell you how grateful I am for your patience and sympathy," he cried, with a tremor in his voice, "and—that you do not think me mad. I have told no one else a quarter of all this, and the mere freedom of speech—the relief of sharing my affliction with another—has helped me already more than I can possibly say."

Dr. Silence pressed his hand and looked steadily into the frightened eyes. His voice was very gentle when he replied.

"Your case, you know, is very singular, but of absorbing interest to me," he said, "for it threatens, not your physical existence, but the temple of your psychical existence—the inner life. Your mind would not be permanently affected here and now, in this world; but in the existence after the body is left behind, you might wake up with your spirit so twisted, so distorted, so befouled, that you would be *spiritually insane*—a far more radical condition than merely being insane here."

There came a strange hush over the room, and between the two men sitting there facing one another.

"Do you really mean—Good Lord!" stammered the author as soon as he could find his tongue.

"What I mean in detail will keep till a little later, and I need only say now that I should not have spoken in this way unless I were quite positive of being able to help you. Oh, there's no doubt as to that, believe me. In the first place, I am very familiar with the workings of this extraordinary drug, this drug which has had the chance effect of opening you up to the forces of another region; and, in the second, I have a firm belief in the reality of super-sensuous occurrences as well as considerable knowledge of psychic processes acquired by long and painful experiment. The rest is, or should be, merely sympathetic treatment and practical application. The hashish has partially opened another world to you by increasing your rate of psychical vibration, and thus rendering you abnormally sensitive. Ancient forces attached to this house have attacked you. For the moment I am only puzzled as to their precise nature; for were they of an ordinary character, I should myself be psychic enough to feel them. Yet I am conscious of feeling nothing as yet. But now, please continue, Mr. Pender, and tell me the rest of your wonderful story; and when you have finished, I will talk about the means of cure."

Pender shifted his chair a little closer to the friendly doctor and then went on in the same nervous voice with his narrative.

"After making some notes of my impressions I finally got upstairs again to bed. It was four o'clock in the morning. I laughed all the way up—at the grotesque banisters, the droll physiognomy of the staircase window, the burlesque grouping of the furniture, and the memory of that outrageous footstool in the room below; but nothing more happened to alarm or disturb me, and I woke late in the morning after a dreamless sleep, none the worse for my experiment except for a slight headache and a coldness of the extremities due to lowered circulation."

"Fear gone, too?" asked the doctor.

"I seemed to have forgotten it, or at least ascribed it to mere nervousness. Its reality had gone, anyhow for the time, and all that day I wrote and wrote and wrote. My sense of laughter seemed wonderfully quickened and my characters acted without effort out of the heart of true humour. I was exceedingly pleased with this result of my experiment. But when the stenographer had taken her departure and I came to read over the pages she had typed out, I recalled her sudden glances of surprise and the odd way she had looked up at me while I was dictating. I was amazed at what I read and could hardly believe I had uttered it."

"And why?"

"It was so distorted. The words, indeed, were mine so far as I could remember, but the meanings seemed strange. It frightened me. The sense was so altered. At the very places where my characters were intended to tickle the ribs, only curious emotions of sinister amusement resulted. Dreadful innuendoes had managed to creep into the phrases. There was laughter of a kind, but it was bizarre, horrible, distressing; and my attempt at analysis only increased my dismay. The story, as it read then, made me shudder, for by virtue of these slight changes it had come somehow to hold the soul of horror, of horror disguised as merriment. The framework of humour was there, if you understand me, but the characters had turned sinister, and their laughter was evil."

"Can you show me this writing?"

The author shook his head.

"I destroyed it," he whispered. "But, in the end, though of course much perturbed about it, I persuaded myself that it was due to some after-effect of the drug, a sort of reaction that gave a twist to my mind and made me read macabre interpretations into words and situations that did not properly hold them."

"And, meanwhile, did the presence of this person leave you?"

"No; that stayed more or less. When my mind was actively employed I forgot it, but when idle, dreaming, or doing nothing in particular, there she was beside me, influencing my mind horribly—"

"In what way, precisely?" interrupted the doctor.

"Evil, scheming thoughts came to me, visions of crime, hateful pictures of wickedness, and the kind of bad imagination that so far has been foreign, indeed impossible, to my normal nature—"

"The pressure of the Dark Powers upon the personality," murmured the doctor, making a quick note.

"Eh? I didn't quite catch—"

"Pray, go on. I am merely making notes; you shall know their purport fully later."

"Even when my wife returned I was still aware of this Presence in the house; it associated itself with my inner personality in most intimate fashion; and outwardly I always felt oddly constrained to be polite and respectful towards it—to open doors, provide chairs, and hold myself carefully deferential when it was about. It became very compelling at last, and, if I failed in any little particular, I seemed to know that it pursued me about the house, from one room to another, haunting my very soul in its inmost abode. It certainly came before my wife so far as my attentions were concerned.

"But, let me first finish the story of my experimental dose, for I took it again the third night, and underwent a very similar experience, delayed like the first in coming, and then carrying me off my feet when it did come with a rush of this false demon-laughter. This time, however, there was a reversal of the changed scale of space and time; it shortened instead of lengthened, so that I dressed and got downstairs in about twenty seconds, and the couple of hours I stayed and worked in the study passed literally like a period of ten minutes."

"That is often true of an overdose," interjected the doctor, "and you may go a mile in a few minutes, or a few yards in a quarter of an hour. It is quite incomprehensible to those who have never experienced it, and is a curious proof that time and space are merely forms of thought."

"This time," Pender went on, talking more and more rapidly in his excitement, "another extraordinary effect came to me, and I experienced a curious changing of the senses, so that I perceived external things through one large main sense-channel instead of through the five divisions known as sight, smell, touch, and so forth. You will, I know, understand me when I tell you that I *heard* sights and *saw* sounds. No language can make this comprehensible, of course, and I can only say, for instance, that the striking of the clock I saw as a visible picture in the air before me. I saw the sounds of the tinkling bell. And in precisely the same way I heard the colours in the room, especially the colours of those books in the shelf behind you. Those red bindings I heard in deep sounds, and the yellow covers of the French bindings next to them made a shrill, piercing note not unlike the chattering of starlings. That brown bookcase muttered, and those green curtains opposite kept up a constant sort of rippling sound like the lower notes of a wood-horn. But I only was conscious of these sounds when I looked steadily at the different objects, and thought about them. The room, you understand, was not full of a chorus of notes; but when I concentrated my mind upon a colour, I heard, as well as saw, it."

"That is a known, though rarely-obtained, effect of *Cannabis indi-ca*," observed the doctor. "And it provoked laughter again, did it?"

"Only the muttering of the cupboard-bookcase made me laugh. It was so like a great animal trying to get itself noticed, and made me think of a performing bear—which is full of a kind of pathetic humour, you know. But this mingling of the senses produced no confusion in my brain. On the contrary, I was unusually clear-headed and experienced an intensification of consciousness, and felt marvellously alive and keen-minded.

"Moreover, when I took up a pencil in obedience to an impulse to sketch—a talent not normally mine—I found that I could draw nothing but heads, nothing, in fact, but one head—always the same—the head of a dark-skinned woman, with huge and terrible features and a very drooping left eye; and so well drawn, too, that I was amazed, as you may imagine—"

"And the expression of the face—?"

Pender hesitated a moment for words, casting about with his hands in the air and hunching his shoulders. A perceptible shudder ran over him.

"What I can only describe as—*blackness*," he replied in a low tone; "the face of a dark and evil soul."

"You destroyed that, too?" queried the doctor sharply.

"No; I have kept the drawings," he said, with a laugh, and rose to get them from a drawer in the writing desk behind him.

"Here is all that remains of the pictures, you see," he added, pushing a number of loose sheets under the doctor's eyes; "nothing but a few scrawly lines. That's all I found the next morning. I had really drawn no heads at all—nothing but those lines and blots and wriggles. The pictures were entirely subjective, and existed only in my mind which constructed them out of a few wild strokes of the pen. Like the altered scale of space and time it was a complete delusion. These all passed, of course, with the passing of the drug's effects. But the other thing did not pass. I mean, the presence of that Dark Soul remained with me. It is here still. It is real. I don't know how I can escape from it."

"It is attached to the house, not to you personally. You must leave the house."

"Yes. Only I cannot afford to leave the house, for my work is my sole means of support, and—well, you see, since this change I cannot even write. They are horrible, these mirthless tales I now write, with their mockery of laughter, their diabolical suggestion. Horrible! I shall go mad if this continues."

He screwed his face up and looked about the room as though he expected to see some haunting shape.

"The influence in this house, induced by my experiment, has killed in a flash, in a sudden stroke, the sources of my humour, and though I still go on writing funny tales—I have a certain name, you know—my inspiration has dried up, and much of what I write I have to burn— yes, doctor, to burn, before any one sees it."

"As utterly alien to your own mind and personality?"

"Utterly! As though some one else had written it—"

"Ah!"

"And shocking!" He passed his hand over his eyes a moment and let the breath escape softly through his teeth. "Yet most damnably clever in the consummate way the vile suggestions are insinuated under cover of a kind of high drollery. My stenographer left me, of course— and I've been afraid to take another—"

John Silence got up and began to walk about the room leisurely without speaking; he appeared to be examining the pictures on the wall and reading the names of the books lying about. Presently he paused on the hearthrug, with his back to the fire, and turned to look his pa- tient quietly in the eyes. Pender's face was grey and drawn; the hunted expression dominated it; the long recital had told upon him.

"Thank you, Mr. Pender," he said, a curious glow showing about his fine, quiet face, "thank you for the sincerity and frankness of your account. But I think now there is nothing further I need ask you." He indulged in a long scrutiny of the author's haggard features, drawing purposely the man's eyes to his own and then meeting them with a look of power and confidence calculated to inspire even the feeblest soul with courage. "And, to begin with," he added, smiling pleasantly, "let me assure you without delay that you need have no alarm, for you are no more insane or deluded than I myself am—"

Pender heaved a deep sigh and tried to return the smile.

"—and this is simply a case, so far as I can judge at present, of a very singular psychical invasion, and a very sinister one, too, if you perhaps understand what I mean—"

"It's an odd expression; you used it before, you know," said the author wearily, yet eagerly listening to every word of the diagnosis, and deeply touched by the intelligent sympathy which did not at once indicate the lunatic asylum.

"Possibly," returned the other, "and an odd affliction, too, you'll allow, yet one not unknown to the nations of antiquity, nor to those moderns, perhaps, who recognise the freedom of action under certain pathogenic conditions between this world and another."

"And you think," asked Pender hastily, "that it is all primarily due to the *Cannabis?* There is nothing radically amiss with myself—nothing incurable, or—?"

"Due entirely to the overdose," Dr. Silence replied emphatically, "to the drug's direct action upon your psychical being. It rendered you ultra-sensitive and made you respond to an increased rate of vibration. And, let me tell you, Mr. Pender, that your experiment might have had results far more dire. It has brought you into touch with a somewhat singular class of Invisible, but of one, I think, chiefly human in character. You might, however, just as easily have been drawn out of human range altogether, and the results of such a contingency would have been exceedingly terrible. Indeed, you would not now be here to tell the tale. I need not alarm you on that score, but mention it as a warning you will not misunderstand or underrate after what you have been through.

"You look puzzled. You do not quite gather what I am driving at; and it is not to be expected that you should, for you, I suppose, are the nominal Christian with the nominal Christian's lofty standard of ethics, and his utter ignorance of spiritual possibilities. Beyond a somewhat childish understanding of 'spiritual wickedness in high places,' you probably have no conception of what is possible once you break down the slender gulf that is mercifully fixed between you and that Outer World. But my studies and training have taken me far outside these orthodox trips, and I have made experiments that I could scarcely speak to you about in language that would be intelligible to you."

He paused a moment to note the breathless interest of Pender's face and manner. Every word he uttered was calculated; he knew exactly the value and effect of the emotions he desired to waken in the heart of the afflicted being before him.

"And from certain knowledge I have gained through various experiences," he continued calmly, "I can diagnose your case as I said before to be one of psychical invasion."

"And the nature of this—er—invasion?" stammered the bewildered writer of humorous tales.

"There is no reason why I should not say at once that I do not yet quite know," replied Dr. Silence. "I may first have to make one or two experiments—"

"On me?" gasped Pender, catching his breath.

"Not exactly," the doctor said, with a grave smile, "but with your assistance, perhaps. I shall want to test the conditions of the house—to ascertain, if possible, the character of the forces, of this strange personality that has been haunting you—"

"At present you have no idea exactly who—what—why—" asked the other in a wild flurry of interest, dread, and amazement.

"I have a very good idea, but no proof rather," returned the doctor. "The effects of the drug in altering the scale of time and space, and merging the senses have nothing primarily to do with the invasion. They come to any one who is fool enough to take an experimental dose. It is the other features of your case that are unusual. You see, you are now in touch with certain violent emotions, desires, purposes, still active in this house, that were produced in the past by some powerful and evil personality that lived here. How long ago, or why they still persist so forcibly, I cannot positively say. But I should judge that they are merely forces acting automatically with the momentum of their terrific original impetus."

"Not directed by a living being, a conscious will, you mean?"

"Possibly not—but none the less dangerous on that account, and more difficult to deal with. I cannot explain to you in a few minutes the nature of such things, for you have not made the studies that would enable you to follow me; but I have reason to believe that on the dissolution at death of a human being, its forces may still persist and continue to act in a blind, unconscious fashion. As a rule they speedily dissipate themselves, but in the case of a very powerful personality they may last a long time. And, in some cases—of which I incline to think this is one—these forces may coalesce with certain non-human entities who thus continue their life indefinitely and increase their strength to an unbelievable degree. If the original personality was evil, the beings attracted to the left-over forces will also be evil. In this case, I think there has been an unusual and dreadful aggrandisement of the thoughts and purposes left behind long ago by a woman of consummate wickedness and great personal power of character and intellect. Now, do you begin to see what I am driving at a little?"

Pender stared fixedly at his companion, plain horror showing in his eyes. But he found nothing to say, and the doctor continued—

"In your case, predisposed by the action of the drug, you have experienced the rush of these forces in undiluted strength. They wholly obliterate in you the sense of humour, fancy, imagination,—all that makes for cheerfulness and hope. They seek, though perhaps automatically only, to oust your own thoughts and establish themselves in their place. You are the victim of a psychical invasion. At the same time, you have become clairvoyant in the true sense. You are also a clairvoyant victim."

Pender mopped his face and sighed. He left his chair and went over to the fireplace to warm himself.

"You must think me a quack to talk like this, or a madman," laughed Dr. Silence. "But never mind that. I have come to help you, and I can help you if you will do what I tell you. It is very simple: you must leave this house at once. Oh, never mind the difficulties; we will deal with those together. I can place another house at your disposal, or I would take the lease here off your hands, and later have it pulled down. Your case interests me greatly, and I mean to see you through, so that you have no anxiety, and can drop back into your old groove of work to-morrow! The drug has provided you, and therefore me, with a short-cut to a very interesting experience. I am grateful to you."

The author poked the fire vigorously, emotion rising in him like a tide. He glanced towards the door nervously.

"There is no need to alarm your wife or to tell her the details of our conversation," pursued the other quietly. "Let her know that you will soon be in possession again of your sense of humour and your health, and explain that I am lending you another house for six months. Meanwhile I may have the right to use this house for a night or two for my experiment. Is that understood between us?"

"I can only thank you from the bottom of my heart," stammered

Pender, unable to find words to express his gratitude.

Then he hesitated for a moment, searching the doctor's face anxiously.

"And your experiment with the house?" he said at length.

"Of the simplest character, my dear Mr. Pender. Although I am myself an artificially trained psychic, and consequently aware of the presence of discarnate entities as a rule, I have so far felt nothing here at all. This makes me sure that the forces acting here are of an unusual description. What I propose to do is to make an experiment with a view of drawing out this evil, coaxing it from its lair, so to speak, in order that it may *exhaust itself through me* and become dissipated for ever. I have already been inoculated," he added; "I consider myself to be immune."

"Heavens above!" gasped the author, collapsing onto a chair.

"Hell beneath! might be a more appropriate exclamation," the doctor laughed. "But, seriously, Mr. Pender, this is what I propose to do—with your permission."

"Of course, of course," cried the other, "you have my permission and my best wishes for success. I can see no possible objection, but—"

"But what?"

"I pray to heaven you will not undertake this experiment alone, will you?"

"Oh, dear, no; not alone."

"You will take a companion with good nerves, and reliable in case of disaster, won't you?"

"I shall bring two companions," the doctor said.

"Ah, that's better. I feel easier. I am sure you must have among your acquaintances men who—"

"I shall not think of bringing men, Mr. Pender."

The other looked up sharply.

"No, or women either; or children."

"I don't understand. Who will you bring, then?"

"Animals," explained the doctor, unable to prevent a smile at his companion's expression of surprise—"two animals, a cat and a dog."

Pender stared as if his eyes would drop out upon the floor, and then led the way without another word into the adjoining room where his wife was awaiting them for tea.

II

A few days later the humorist and his wife, with minds greatly relieved, moved into a small furnished house placed at their free disposal in another part of London; and John Silence, intent upon his approaching experiment, made ready to spend a night in the empty house on the top of Putney Hill. Only two rooms were prepared for occupation: the study on the ground floor and the bedroom immediately above it; all other doors were to be locked, and no servant was to be left in the house. The motor had orders to call for him at nine o'clock the following morning.

And, meanwhile, his secretary had instructions to look up the past history and associations of the place, and learn everything he could concerning the character of former occupants, recent or remote.

The animals, by whose sensitiveness he intended to test any unusual conditions in the atmosphere of the building, Dr. Silence selected with care and judgment. He believed (and had already made curious experiments to prove it) that animals were more often, and more truly, clairvoyant than human beings. Many of them, he felt convinced, possessed powers of perception far superior to that mere keenness of the senses common to all dwellers in the wilds where the senses grow specially alert; they had what he termed "animal clairvoyance," and from his experiments with horses, dogs, cats, and even birds, he had drawn certain deductions, which, however, need not be referred to in detail here.

Cats, in particular, he believed, were almost continuously conscious of a larger field of vision, too detailed even for a photographic camera, and quite beyond the reach of normal human organs. He had, further, observed that while dogs were usually terrified in the presence of such phenomena, cats on the other hand were soothed and satisfied. They welcomed manifestations as something belonging peculiarly to their own region.

He selected his animals, therefore, with wisdom, so that they might afford a differing test, each in its own way, and that one should not merely communicate its own excitement to the other. He took a dog and a cat.

The cat he chose, now full grown, had lived with him since kittenhood, a kittenhood of perplexing sweetness and audacious mischief. Wayward it was and fanciful, ever playing its own mysterious games in the corners of the room, jumping at invisible nothings, leaping sideways into the air and falling with tiny moccasined feet on to another part of the carpet, yet with an air of dignified earnestness which showed that the performance was necessary to its own well-being, and not done merely to impress a stupid human audience. In the middle of elaborate washing it would look up, startled, as though to stare at the approach of some Invisible, cocking its little head sideways and putting out a velvet pad to inspect cautiously. Then it would get absent-minded, and stare with equal intentness in another direction (just to confuse the onlookers), and suddenly go on furiously washing its body again, but in quite a new place. Except for a white patch on its breast it was coal black. And its name was—Smoke.

"Smoke" described its temperament as well as its appearance. Its movements, its individuality, its posing as a little furry mass of concealed mysteries, its elfin-like elusiveness, all combined to justify its name; and a subtle painter might have pictured it as a wisp of floating smoke, the fire below betraying itself at two points only—the glowing eyes.

All its forces ran to intelligence—secret intelligence, the wordless incalculable intuition of the Cat. It was, indeed, *the* cat for the business in hand.

The selection of the dog was not so simple, for the doctor owned many; but after much deliberation he chose a collie, called Flame from his yellow coat. True, it was a trifle old, and stiff in the joints, and even beginning to grow deaf, but, on the other hand, it was a very particular friend of Smoke's, and had fathered it from kittenhood upwards so that a subtle understanding existed between them. It was this that turned the balance in its favour, this and its courage. Moreover, though good-tempered, it was a terrible fighter, and its anger when provoked by a righteous cause was a fury of fire, and irresistible.

It had come to him quite young, straight from the shepherd, with the air of the hills yet in its nostrils, and was then little more than skin and bones and teeth. For a collie it was sturdily built, its nose blunter than most, its yellow hair stiff rather than silky, and it had full eyes, unlike the slit eyes of its breed. Only its master could touch it, for it ignored strangers, and despised their pattings—when any dared to pat it. There was something patriarchal about the old beast. He was in earnest, and went through life with tremendous energy and big things in view, as though he had the reputation of his whole race to uphold. And to watch him fighting against odds was to understand why he was terrible.

In his relations with Smoke he was always absurdly gentle; also he was fatherly; and at the same time betrayed a certain diffidence or shyness. He recognised that Smoke called for strong yet respectful management. The cat's circuitous methods puzzled him, and his elaborate pretences perhaps shocked the dog's liking for direct, undisguised action. Yet, while he failed to comprehend these tortuous feline mysteries, he was never contemptuous or condescending; and he presided over the safety of his furry black friend somewhat as a father, loving but intuitive, might superintend the vagaries of a wayward and talented child. And, in return, Smoke rewarded him with exhibitions of fascinating and audacious mischief.

And these brief descriptions of their characters are necessary for the proper understanding of what subsequently took place.

With Smoke sleeping in the folds of his fur coat, and the collie lying watchful on the seat opposite, John Silence went down in his motor after dinner on the night of November 15th.

And the fog was so dense that they were obliged to travel at quarter speed the entire way.

It was after ten o'clock when he dismissed the motor and entered the dingy little house with the latchkey provided by Pender. He found the hall gas turned low, and a fire in the study. Books and food had also been placed ready by the servant according to instructions. Coils of fog rushed in after him through the open door and filled the hall and passage with its cold discomfort.

The first thing Dr. Silence did was to lock up Smoke in the study with a saucer of milk before the fire, and then make a search of the house with Flame. The dog ran cheerfully behind him all the way while he tried the doors of the other rooms to make sure they were locked. He nosed about into corners and made little excursions on his own account. His manner was expectant. He knew there must be something unusual about the proceeding, because it was contrary to the habits of his whole life not to be asleep at this hour on the mat in front of the fire. He kept looking up into his master's face, as door after door was tried, with an expression of intelligent sympathy, but at the same time a certain air of disapproval. Yet everything his master did was good in his eyes, and he betrayed as little impatience as possible with all this unnecessary journeying to and fro. If the doctor was pleased to play this sort of game at such an hour of the night, it was surely not for him to object. So he played it too; and was very busy and earnest about it into the bargain.

After an uneventful search they came down again to the study, and here Dr. Silence discovered Smoke washing his face calmly in front of the fire. The saucer of milk was licked dry and clean; the preliminary examination that cats always make in new surroundings had evidently been satisfactorily concluded. He drew an arm-chair up to the fire, stirred the coals into a blaze, arranged the table and lamp to his satisfaction for reading, and then prepared surreptitiously to watch the animals. He wished to observe them carefully without their being aware of it.

Now, in spite of their respective ages, it was the regular custom of these two to play together every night before sleep. Smoke always made the advances, beginning with grave impudence to pat the dog's tail, and Flame played cumbrously, with condescension. It was his duty, rather than pleasure; he was glad when it was over, and sometimes he was very determined and refused to play at all.

And this night was one of the occasions on which he was firm.

The doctor, looking cautiously over the top of his book, watched the cat begin the performance. It started by gazing with an innocent expression at the dog where he lay with nose on paws and eyes wide open in the middle of the floor. Then it got up and made as though it meant to walk to the door, going deliberately and very softly. Flame's eyes followed it until it was beyond the range of sight, and then the cat turned sharply and began patting his tail tentatively with one paw. The tail moved slightly in reply, and Smoke changed paws and tapped it again. The dog, however, did not rise to play as was his wont, and the cat fell to parting it briskly with both paws. Flame still lay motionless.

This puzzled and bored the cat, and it went round and stared hard into its friend's face to see what was the matter. Perhaps some inarticulate message flashed from the dog's eyes into its own little brain, making it understand that the programme for the night had better not begin with play. Perhaps it only realised that its friend was immovable.

But, whatever the reason, its usual persistence thenceforward deserted it, and it made no further attempts at persuasion. Smoke yielded at once to the dog's mood; it sat down where it was and began to wash.

But the washing, the doctor noted, was by no means its real purpose; it only used it to mask something else; it stopped at the most busy and furious moments and began to stare about the room. Its thoughts wandered absurdly. It peered intently at the curtains; at the shadowy corners; at empty space above; leaving its body in curiously awkward positions for whole minutes together. Then it turned sharply and stared with a sudden signal of intelligence at the dog, and Flame at once rose somewhat stiffly to his feet and began to wander aimlessly and restlessly to and fro about the floor. Smoke followed him, padding quietly at his heels. Between them they made what seemed to be a deliberate search of the room.

And, here, as he watched them, noting carefully every detail of the performance over the top of his book, yet making no effort to interfere, it seemed to the doctor that the first beginnings of a faint distress betrayed themselves in the collie, and in the cat the stirrings of a vague excitement.

He observed them closely. The fog was thick in the air, and the tobacco smoke from his pipe added to its density; the furniture at the far end stood mistily, and where the shadows congregated in hanging clouds under the ceiling, it was difficult to see clearly at all; the lamplight only reached to a level of five feet from the floor, above which came layers of comparative darkness, so that the room appeared twice as lofty as it actually was. By means of the lamp and the fire, however, the carpet was everywhere clearly visible.

The animals made their silent tour of the floor, sometimes the dog leading, sometimes the cat; occasionally they looked at one another as though exchanging signals; and once or twice, in spite of the limited space, he lost sight of one or other among the fog and the shadows. Their curiosity, it appeared to him, was something more than the excitement lurking in the unknown territory of a strange room; yet, so far, it was impossible to test this, and he purposely kept his mind quietly receptive lest the smallest mental excitement on his part should communicate itself to the animals and thus destroy the value of their independent behaviour.

They made a very thorough journey, leaving no piece of furniture unexamined, or unsmelt. Flame led the way, walking slowly with lowered head, and Smoke followed demurely at his heels, making a transparent pretence of not being interested, yet missing nothing. And, at length, they returned, the old collie first, and came to rest on the mat before the fire. Flame rested his muzzle on his master's knee, smiling beatifically while he patted the yellow head and spoke his name; and Smoke, coming a little later, pretending he came by chance, looked from the empty saucer to his face, lapped up the milk when it was given him to the last drop, and then sprang upon his knees and curled round for the sleep it had fully earned and intended to enjoy.

Silence descended upon the room. Only the breathing of the dog upon the mat came through the deep stillness, like the pulse of time marking the minutes; and the steady drip, drip of the fog outside upon the window-ledges dismally testified to the inclemency of the night beyond. And the soft crashings of the coals as the fire settled down into the grate became less and less audible as the fire sank and the flames resigned their fierceness.

It was now well after eleven o'clock, and Dr. Silence devoted himself again to his book. He read the words on the printed page and took in their meaning superficially, yet without starting into life the correlations of thought and suggestion that should accompany interesting reading. Underneath, all the while, his mental energies were absorbed in watching, listening, waiting for what might come. He was not over sanguine himself, yet he did not wish to be taken by surprise. Moreover, the animals, his sensitive barometers, had incontinently gone to sleep.

After reading a dozen pages, however, he realised that his mind was really occupied in reviewing the features of Pender's extraordinary story, and that it was no longer necessary to steady his imagination by studying the dull paragraphs detailed in the pages before him. He laid down his book accordingly, and allowed his thoughts to dwell upon the features of the Case. Speculations as to the meaning, however, he rigorously suppressed, knowing that such thoughts would act upon his imagination like wind upon the glowing embers of a fire.

As the night wore on the silence grew deeper and deeper, and only at rare intervals he heard the sound of wheels on the main road a hundred yards away, where the horses went at a walking pace owing to the density of the fog. The echo of pedestrian footsteps no longer reached him, the clamour of occasional voices no longer came down the side street. The night, muffled by fog, shrouded by veils of ultimate mystery, hung about the haunted villa like a doom. Nothing in the house stirred. Stillness, in a thick blanket, lay over the upper storeys. Only the mist in the room grew more dense, he thought, and the damp cold more penetrating. Certainly, from time to time, he shivered.

The collie, now deep in slumber, moved occasionally—grunted, sighed, or twitched his legs in dreams. Smoke lay on his knees, a pool of warm, black fur, only the closest observation detecting the movement of his sleek sides. It was difficult to distinguish exactly where his head and body joined in that circle of glistening hair; only a black satin nose and a tiny tip of pink tongue betrayed the secret.

Dr. Silence watched him, and felt comfortable. The collie's breathing was soothing. The fire was well built, and would burn for another two hours without attention. He was not conscious of the least nervousness. He particularly wished to remain in his ordinary and normal state of mind, and to force nothing. If sleep came naturally, he would let it come—and even welcome it. The coldness of the room, when the fire died down later, would be sure to wake him again; and it would then be time enough to carry these sleeping barometers up to bed. From various psychic premonitions he knew quite well that the night would not pass without adventure; but he did not wish to force its arrival; and he wished to remain normal, and let the animals remain normal, so that, when it came, it would be unattended by excitement or by any straining of the attention. Many experiments had made him wise. And, for the rest, he had no fear.

Accordingly, after a time, he did fall asleep as he had expected, and the last thing he remembered, before oblivion slipped up over his eyes like soft wool, was the picture of Flame stretching all four legs at once, and sighing noisily as he sought a more comfortable position for his paws and muzzle upon the mat.

It was a good deal later when he became aware that a weight lay upon his chest, and that something was pencilling over his face and mouth. A soft touch on the cheek woke him. Something was patting him.

He sat up with a jerk, and found himself staring straight into a pair of brilliant eyes, half green, half black. Smoke's face lay level with his own; and the cat had climbed up with its front paws upon his chest.

The lamp had burned low and the fire was nearly out, yet Dr. Silence saw in a moment that the cat was in an excited state. It kneaded with its front paws into his chest, shifting from one to the other. He felt them prodding against him. It lifted a leg very carefully and patted his cheek gingerly. Its fur, he saw, was standing ridgewise upon its back; the ears were flattened back somewhat; the tail was switching sharply. The cat, of course, had wakened him with a purpose, and the instant he realised this, he set it upon the arm of the chair and sprang up with a quick turn to face the empty room behind him. By some curious instinct, his arms of their own accord assumed an attitude of defence in front of him, as though to ward off something that threatened his safety. Yet nothing was visible. Only shapes of fog hung about rather heavily in the air, moving slightly to and fro.

His mind was now fully alert, and the last vestiges of sleep gone. He turned the lamp higher and peered about him. Two things he became aware of at once: one, that Smoke, while excited, was *pleasurably* excited; the other, that the collie was no longer visible upon the mat at his feet. He had crept away to the corner of the wall farthest from the window, and lay watching the room with wide-open eyes, in which lurked plainly something of alarm.

Something in the dog's behaviour instantly struck Dr. Silence as unusual, and, calling him by name, he moved across to pat him. Flame got up, wagged his tail, and came over slowly to the rug, uttering a low sound that was half growl, half whine. He was evidently perturbed about something, and his master was proceeding to administer comfort when his attention was suddenly drawn to the antics of his other four-footed companion, the cat.

And what he saw filled him with something like amazement.

Smoke had jumped down from the back of the arm-chair and now occupied the middle of the carpet, where, with tail erect and legs stiff as ramrods, it was steadily pacing backwards and forwards in a narrow space, uttering, as it did so, those curious little guttural sounds of pleasure that only an animal of the feline species knows how to make expressive of supreme happiness. Its stiffened legs and arched back made it appear larger than usual, and the black visage wore a smile of beatific joy. Its eyes blazed magnificently; it was in an ecstasy.

At the end of every few paces it turned sharply and stalked back again along the same line, padding softly, and purring like a roll of little muffled drums. It behaved precisely as though it were rubbing against the ankles of some one who remained invisible. A thrill ran down the doctor's spine as he stood and stared. His experiment was growing interesting at last.

He called the collie's attention to his friend's performance to see whether he too was aware of anything standing there upon the carpet, and the dog's behaviour was significant and corroborative. He came as far as his master's knees and then stopped dead, refusing to investigate closely. In vain Dr. Silence urged him; he wagged his tail, whined a little, and stood in a half-crouching attitude, staring alternately at the cat and at his master's face. He was, apparently, both puzzled and alarmed, and the whine went deeper and deeper down into his throat till it changed into an ugly snarl of awakening anger.

Then the doctor called to him in a tone of command he had never known to be disregarded; but still the dog, though springing up in response, declined to move nearer. He made tentative motions, pranced a little like a dog about to take to water, pretended to bark, and ran to and fro on the carpet. So far there was no actual fear in his manner, but he was uneasy and anxious, and nothing would induce him to go within touching distance of the walking cat. Once he made a complete circuit, but always carefully out of reach; and in the end he returned to his master's legs and rubbed vigorously against him. Flame did not like the performance at all: that much was quite clear.

For several minutes John Silence watched the performance of the cat with profound attention and without interfering. Then he called to the animal by name.

"Smoke, you mysterious beastie, what in the world are you about?" he said, in a coaxing tone.

The cat looked up at him for a moment, smiling in its ecstasy, blinking its eyes, but too happy to pause. He spoke to it again. He called to it several times, and each time it turned upon him its blazing eyes, drunk with inner delight, opening and shutting its lips, its body large and rigid with excitement. Yet it never for one instant paused in its short journeys to and fro.

He noted exactly what it did: it walked, he saw, the same number of paces each time, some six or seven steps, and then it turned sharply and retraced them. By the pattern of the great roses in the carpet he measured it. It kept to the same direction and the same line. It behaved precisely as though it were rubbing against something solid. Undoubtedly, there was something standing there on that strip of carpet, something invisible to the doctor, something that alarmed the dog, yet caused the cat unspeakable pleasure.

"Smokie!" he called again, "Smokie, you black mystery, what is it excites you so?"

Again the cat looked up at him for a brief second, and then continued its sentry-walk, blissfully happy, intensely preoccupied. And, for an instant, as he watched it, the doctor was aware that a faint uneasiness stirred in the depths of his own being, focusing itself for the moment upon this curious behaviour of the uncanny creature before him.

There rose in him quite a new realisation of the mystery connected with the whole feline tribe, but especially with that common member of it, the domestic cat—their hidden lives, their strange aloofness, their incalculable subtlety. How utterly remote from anything that human beings understood lay the sources of their elusive activities. As he watched the indescribable bearing of the little creature mincing along the strip of carpet under his eyes, coquetting with the powers of darkness, welcoming, maybe, some fearsome visitor, there stirred in his heart a feeling strangely akin to awe. Its indifference to human kind, its serene superiority to the obvious, struck him forcibly with fresh meaning; so remote, so inaccessible seemed the secret purposes of its real life, so alien to the blundering honesty of other animals. Its absolute poise of bearing brought into his mind the opium-eater's words that "no dignity is perfect which does not at some point ally itself with the mysterious"; and he became suddenly aware that the presence of the dog in this foggy, haunted room on the top of Putney Hill was uncommonly welcome to him. He was glad to feel that Flame's dependable personality was with him. The savage growling at his heels was a pleasant sound. He was glad to hear it. That marching cat made him uneasy.

Finding that Smoke paid no further attention to his words, the doctor decided upon action. Would it rub against his leg, too? He would take it by surprise and see.

He stepped quickly forward and placed himself upon the exact strip of carpet where it walked.

But no cat is ever taken by surprise! The moment he occupied the space of the Intruder, setting his feet on the woven roses midway in the line of travel, Smoke suddenly stopped purring and sat down. It lifted up its face with the most innocent stare imaginable of its green eyes. He could have sworn it laughed. It was a perfect child again. In a single second it had resumed its simple, domestic manner; and it gazed at him in such a way that he almost felt Smoke was the normal being, and *his* was the eccentric behaviour that was being watched. It was consummate, the manner in which it brought about this change so easily and so quickly.

"Superb little actor!" he laughed in spite of himself, and stooped to stroke the shining black back. But, in a flash, as he touched its fur, the cat turned and spat at him viciously, striking at his hand with one paw. Then, with a hurried scutter of feet, it shot like a shadow across the floor and a moment later was calmly sitting over by the window-curtains washing its face as though nothing interested it in the whole world but the cleanness of its cheeks and whiskers.

John Silence straightened himself up and drew a long breath. He realised that the performance was temporarily at an end. The collie, meanwhile, who had watched the whole proceeding with marked disapproval, had now lain down again upon the mat by the fire, no longer growling. It seemed to the doctor just as though something that had entered the room while he slept, alarming the dog, yet bringing happiness to the cat, had now gone out again, leaving all as it was before. Whatever it was that excited its blissful attentions had retreated for the moment.

He realised this intuitively. Smoke evidently realised it, too, for presently he deigned to march back to the fireplace and jump upon his master's knees. Dr. Silence, patient and determined, settled down once more to his book. The animals soon slept; the fire blazed cheerfully; and the cold fog from outside poured into the room through every available chink and crannie.

For a long time silence and peace reigned in the room and Dr. Silence availed himself of the quietness to make careful notes of what had happened. He entered for future use in other cases an exhaustive analysis of what he had observed, especially with regard to the effect upon the two animals. It is impossible here, nor would it be intelligible to the reader unversed in the knowledge of the region known to a sci- entifically trained psychic like Dr. Silence, to detail these observations. But to him it was clear, up to a certain point—and for the rest he must still wait and watch. So far, at least, he realised that while he slept in the chair—that is, while his will was dormant—the room had suffered intrusion from what he recognised as an intensely active Force, and might later be forced to acknowledge as something more than merely a blind force, namely, a distinct personality.

So far it had affected himself scarcely at all, but had acted directly upon the simpler organisms of the animals. It stimulated keenly the centres of the cat's psychic being, inducing a state of instant happiness (intensifying its consciousness probably in the same way a drug or stimulant intensifies that of a human being); whereas it alarmed the less sensitive dog, causing it to feel a vague apprehension and distress.

His own sudden action and exhibition of energy had served to dis- perse it temporarily, yet he felt convinced—the indications were not lacking even while he sat there making notes—that it still remained near to him, conditionally if not spatially, and was, as it were, gathering force for a second attack.

And, further, he intuitively understood that the relations between the two animals had undergone a subtle change: that the cat had be- come immeasurably superior, confident, sure of itself in its own pecu- liar region, whereas Flame had been weakened by an attack he could not comprehend and knew not how to reply to. Though not yet afraid, he was defiant—ready to act against a fear that he felt to be approach- ing. He was no longer fatherly and protective towards the cat. Smoke held the key to the situation; and both he and the cat knew it.

Thus, as the minutes passed, John Silence sat and waited, keenly on the alert, wondering how soon the attack would be renewed, and at what point it would be diverted from the animals and directed upon himself.

The book lay on the floor beside him, his notes were complete. With one hand on the cat's fur, and the dog's front paws resting against his feet, the three of them dozed comfortably before the hot fire while the night wore on and the silence deepened towards midnight.

It was well after one o'clock in the morning when Dr. Silence turned the lamp out and lighted the candle preparatory to going up to bed. Then Smoke suddenly woke with a loud sharp purr and sat up. It neither stretched, washed, nor turned: it listened. And the doctor, watching it, realised that a certain indefinable change had come about that very moment in the room. A swift readjustment of the forces within the four walls had taken place—a new disposition of their personal equations. The balance was destroyed, the former harmony gone. Smoke, most sensitive of barometers, had been the first to feel it, but the dog was not slow to follow suit, for on looking down he noted that Flame was no longer asleep. He was lying with eyes wide open, and that same instant he sat up on his great haunches and began to growl.

Dr. Silence was in the act of taking the matches to re-light the lamp when an audible movement in the room behind made him pause. Smoke leaped down from his knee and moved forward a few paces across the carpet. Then it stopped and stared fixedly; and the doctor stood up on the rug to watch.

As he rose the sound was repeated, and he discovered that it was not in the room as he first thought, but outside, and that it came from more directions than one. There was a rushing, sweeping noise against the window-panes, and simultaneously a sound of something brushing against the door—out in the hall. Smoke advanced sedately across the carpet, twitching his tail, and sat down within a foot of the door. The influence that had destroyed the harmonious conditions of the room had apparently moved in advance of its cause. Clearly, something was about to happen.

For the first time that night John Silence hesitated; the thought of that dark narrow hall-way, choked with fog, and destitute of human comfort, was unpleasant. He became aware of a faint creeping of his flesh. He knew, of course, that the actual opening of the door was not necessary to the invasion of the room that was about to take place, since neither doors nor windows, nor any other solid barriers could interpose an obstacle to what was seeking entrance. Yet the opening of the door would be significant and symbolic, and he distinctly shrank from it.

But for a moment only. Smoke, turning with a show of impatience, recalled him to his purpose, and he moved past the sitting, watching creature, and deliberately opened the door to its full width.

What subsequently happened, happened in the feeble and flickering light of the solitary candle on the mantelpiece.

Through the opened door he saw the hall, dimly lit and thick with fog. Nothing, of course, was visible—nothing but the hat-stand, the African spears in dark lines upon the wall, and the high-backed wooden chair standing grotesquely underneath on the oilcloth floor. For one instant the fog seemed to move and thicken oddly; but he set that down to the score of the imagination. The door had opened upon nothing.

Yet Smoke apparently thought otherwise, and the deep growling of the collie from the mat at the back of the room seemed to confirm his judgment.

For, proud and self-possessed, the cat had again risen to his feet, and having advanced to the door, was now ushering some one slowly into the room. Nothing could have been more evident. He paced from side to side, bowing his little head with great *empressement* and holding his stiffened tail aloft like a flagstaff. He turned this way and that, mincing to and fro, and showing signs of supreme satisfaction. He was in his element. He welcomed the intrusion, and apparently reckoned that his companions, the doctor and the dog, would welcome it likewise.

The Intruder had returned for a second attack.

Dr. Silence moved slowly backwards and took up his position on the hearthrug, keying himself up to a condition of concentrated attention.

He noted that Flame stood beside him, facing the room, with body motionless, and head moving swiftly from side to side with a curious swaying movement. His eyes were wide open, his back rigid, his neck and jaws thrust forward, his legs tense and ready to leap. Savage, ready for attack or defence, yet dreadfully puzzled and perhaps already a little cowed, he stood and stared, the hair on his spine and sides positively bristling outwards as though a wind played through them. In the dim firelight he looked like a great yellow-haired wolf, silent, eyes shooting dark fire, exceedingly formidable. It was Flame, the terrible.

Smoke, meanwhile, advanced from the door towards the middle of the room, adopting the very slow pace of an invisible companion. A few feet away it stopped and began to smile and blink its eyes. There was something deliberately coaxing in its attitude as it stood there undecided on the carpet, clearly wishing to effect some sort of introduction between the Intruder and its canine friend and ally. It assumed its most winning manners, purring, smiling, looking persuasively from one to the other, and making quick tentative steps first in one direction and then in the other. There had always existed such perfect understanding between them in everything. Surely Flame would appreciate Smoke's intention now, and acquiesce.

But the old collie made no advances. He bared his teeth, lifting his lips till the gums showed, and stood stockstill with fixed eyes and heaving sides. The doctor moved a little farther back, watching intently the smallest movement, and it was just then he divined suddenly from the cat's behaviour and attitude that it was not only a single companion it had ushered into the room, but *several.* It kept crossing over from one to the other, looking up at each in turn. It sought to win over the dog to friendliness with them all. The original Intruder had come back with reinforcements. And at the same time he further realised that the Intruder was something more than a blindly acting force, impersonal though destructive. It was a Personality, and moreover a great personality. And it was accompanied for the purposes of assistance by a host of other personalities, minor in degree, but similar in kind.

He braced himself in the corner against the mantelpiece and waited, his whole being roused to defence, for he was now fully aware that the attack had spread to include himself as well as the animals, and he must be on the alert. He strained his eyes through the foggy atmosphere, trying in vain to see what the cat and dog saw; but the candlelight threw an uncertain and flickering light across the room and his eyes discerned nothing. On the floor Smoke moved softly in front of him like a black shadow, his eyes gleaming as he turned his head, still trying with many insinuating gestures and much purring to bring about the introductions he desired.

But it was all in vain. Flame stood riveted to one spot, motionless as a figure carved in stone.

Some minutes passed, during which only the cat moved, and then there came a sharp change. Flame began to back towards the wall. He moved his head from side to side as he went, sometimes turning to snap at something almost behind him. *They* were advancing upon him, trying to surround him. His distress became very marked from now onwards, and it seemed to the doctor that his anger merged into genuine terror and became overwhelmed by it. The savage growl sounded perilously like a whine, and more than once he tried to dive past his master's legs, as though hunting for a way of escape. He was trying to avoid something that everywhere blocked the way.

This terror of the indomitable fighter impressed the doctor enormously; yet also painfully; stirring his impatience; for he had never before seen the dog show signs of giving in, and it distressed him to witness it. He knew, however, that he was not giving in easily, and understood that it was really impossible for him to gauge the animal's sensations properly at all. What Flame felt, and saw, must be terrible indeed to turn him all at once into a coward. He faced something that made him afraid of more than his life merely. The doctor spoke a few quick words of encouragement to him, and stroked the bristling hair. But without much success. The collie seemed already beyond the reach of comfort such as that, and the collapse of the old dog followed indeed very speedily after this.

And Smoke, meanwhile, remained behind, watching the advance, but not joining in it; sitting, pleased and expectant, considering that all was going well and as it wished. It was kneading on the carpet with its front paws—slowly, laboriously, as though its feet were dipped in treacle. The sound its claws made as they caught in the threads was distinctly audible. It was still smiling, blinking, purring.

Suddenly the collie uttered a poignant short bark and leaped heavily to one side. His bared teeth traced a line of whiteness through the gloom. The next instant he dashed past his master's legs, almost upsetting his balance, and shot out into the room, where he went blundering wildly against walls and furniture. But that bark was significant; the doctor had heard it before and knew what it meant: for it was the cry of the fighter against odds and it meant that the old beast had found his courage again. Possibly it was only the courage of despair, but at any rate the fighting would be terrific. And Dr. Silence understood, too, that he dared not interfere. Flame must fight his own enemies in his own way.

But the cat, too, had heard that dreadful bark; and it, too, had understood. This was more than it had bargained for. Across the dim shadows of that haunted room there must have passed some secret signal of distress between the animals. Smoke stood up and looked swiftly about him. He uttered a piteous meow and trotted smartly away into the greater darkness by the windows. What his object was only those endowed with the spirit-like intelligence of cats might know. But, at any rate, he had at last ranged himself on the side of his friend. And the little beast meant business.

At the same moment the collie managed to gain the door. The doctor saw him rush through into the hall like a flash of yellow light. He shot across the oilcloth, and tore up the stairs, but in another second he appeared again, flying down the steps and landing at the bottom in a tumbling heap, whining, cringing, terrified. The doctor saw him slink back into the room again and crawl round by the wall towards the cat. Was, then, even the staircase occupied? Did *They* stand also in the hall? Was the whole house crowded from floor to ceiling?

The thought came to add to the keen distress he felt at the sight of the collie's discomfiture. And, indeed, his own personal distress had increased in a marked degree during the past minutes, and continued to increase steadily to the climax. He recognised that the drain on his own vitality grew steadily, and that the attack was now directed against himself even more than against the defeated dog, and the too much deceived cat.

It all seemed so rapid and uncalculated after that—the events that took place in this little modern room at the top of Putney Hill between midnight and sunrise—that Dr. Silence was hardly able to follow and remember it all. It came about with such uncanny swiftness and terror; the light was so uncertain; the movements of the black cat so difficult to follow on the dark carpet, and the doctor himself so weary and taken by surprise—that he found it almost impossible to observe accurately, or to recall afterwards precisely what it was he had seen or in what order the incidents had taken place. He never could understand what defect of vision on his part made it seem as though the cat had duplicated itself at first, and then increased indefinitely, so that there were at least a dozen of them darting silently about the floor, leaping softly on to chairs and tables, passing like shadows from the open door to the end of the room, all black as sin, with brilliant green eyes flashing fire in all directions. It was like the reflections from a score of mirrors placed round the walls at different angles. Nor could he make out at the time why the size of the room seemed to have altered, grown much larger, and why it extended away behind him where ordinarily the wall should have been. The snarling of the enraged and terrified collie sounded sometimes so far away; the ceiling seemed to have raised itself so much higher than before, and much of the furniture had changed in appearance and shifted marvellously.

It was all so confused and confusing, as though the little room he knew had become merged and transformed into the dimensions of quite another chamber, that came to him, with its host of cats and its strange distances, in a sort of vision.

But these changes came about a little later, and at a time when his attention was so concentrated upon the proceedings of Smoke and the collie, that he only observed them, as it were, subconsciously. And the excitement, the flickering candle-light, the distress he felt for the collie, and the distorting atmosphere of fog were the poorest possible allies to careful observation.

At first he was only aware that the dog was repeating his short dangerous bark from time to time, snapping viciously at the empty air, a foot or so from the ground. Once, indeed, he sprang upwards and forwards, working furiously with teeth and paws, and with a noise like wolves fighting, but only to dash back the next minute against the wall behind him. Then, after lying still for a bit, he rose to a crouching position as though to spring again, snarling horribly and making short half-circles with lowered head. And Smoke all the while meowed piteously by the window as though trying to draw the attack upon himself.

Then it was that the rush of the whole dreadful business seemed to turn aside from the dog and direct itself upon his own person. The collie had made another spring and fallen back with a crash into the corner, where he made noise enough in his savage rage to waken the dead before he fell to whining and then finally lay still. And directly afterwards the doctor's own distress became intolerably acute. He had made a half movement forward to come to the rescue when a veil that was denser than mere fog seemed to drop down over the scene, draping room, walls, animals, and fire in a mist of darkness and folding also about his own mind. Other forms moved silently across the field of vision, forms that he recognised from previous experiments, and welcomed not. Unholy thoughts began to crowd into his brain, sinister sug-

gestions of evil presented themselves seductively. Ice seemed to settle
about his heart, and his mind trembled. He began to lose memory—
memory of his identity, of where he was, of what he ought to do. The
very foundations of his strength were shaken. His will seemed paralysed.

And it was then that the room filled with this horde of cats, all
dark as the night, all silent, all with lamping eyes of green fire. The dimensions of the place altered and shifted. He was in a much larger
space. The whining of the dog sounded far away, and all about him the
cats flew busily to and fro, silently playing their tearing, rushing game
of evil, weaving the pattern of their dark purpose upon the floor. He
strove hard to collect himself and remember the words of power he
had made use of before in similar dread positions where his dangerous
practice had sometimes led; but he could recall nothing consecutively;
a mist lay over his mind and memory; he felt dazed and his forces scattered. The deeps within were too troubled for healing power to come
out of them.

It was glamour, of course, he realised afterwards, the strong glamour thrown upon his imagination by some powerful personality behind
the veil; but at the time he was not sufficiently aware of this and, as
with all true glamour, was unable to grasp where the true ended and
the false began. He was caught momentarily in the same vortex that
had sought to lure the cat to destruction through its delight, and
threatened utterly to overwhelm the dog through its terror.

There came a sound in the chimney behind him like wind booming and tearing its way down. The windows rattled. The candle flickered and went out. The glacial atmosphere closed round him with the
cold of death, and a great rushing sound swept by overhead as though
the ceiling had lifted to a great height. He heard the door shut. Far
away it sounded. He felt lost, shelterless in the depths of his soul. Yet
still he held out and resisted while the climax of the fight came nearer
and nearer. . . . He had stepped into the stream of forces awakened by
Pender and he knew that he must withstand them to the end or come
to a conclusion that it was not good for a man to come to. Something
from the region of utter cold was upon him.

And then quite suddenly, through the confused mists about him,
there slowly rose up the Personality that had been all the time directing
the battle. Some force entered his being that shook him as the tempest

shakes a leaf, and close against his eyes—clean level with his face—he found himself staring into the wreck of a vast dark Countenance, a countenance that was terrible even in its ruin.

For ruined it was, and terrible it was, and the mark of spiritual evil was branded everywhere upon its broken features. Eyes, face, and hair rose level with his own, and for a space of time he never could properly measure, or determine, these two, a man and a woman, looked straight into each other's visages and down into each other's hearts.

And John Silence, the soul with the good, unselfish motive, held his own against the dark discarnate woman whose motive was pure evil, and whose soul was on the side of the Dark Powers.

It was the climax that touched the depth of power within him and began to restore him slowly to his own. He was conscious, of course, of effort, and yet it seemed no superhuman one, for he had recognised the character of his opponent's power, and he called upon the good within him to meet and overcome it. The inner forces stirred and trembled in response to his call. They did not at first come readily as was their habit, for under the spell of glamour they had already been diabolically lulled into inactivity, but come they eventually did, rising out of the inner spiritual nature he had learned with so much time and pain to awaken to life. And power and confidence came with them. He began to breathe deeply and regularly, and at the same time to absorb into himself the forces opposed to him, and to *turn them to his own account*. By ceasing to resist, and allowing the deadly stream to pour into him unopposed, he used the very power supplied by his adversary and thus enormously increased his own.

For this spiritual alchemy he had learned. He understood that force ultimately is everywhere one and the same; it is the motive behind that makes it good or evil; and his motive was entirely unselfish. He knew—provided he was not first robbed of self-control—how vicariously to absorb these evil radiations into himself and change them magically into his own good purposes. And, since his motive was pure and his soul fearless, they could not work him harm.

Thus he stood in the main stream of evil unwittingly attracted by Pender, deflecting its course upon himself; and after passing through the purifying filter of his own unselfishness these energies could only add to his store of experience, of knowledge, and therefore of power.

And, as his self-control returned to him, he gradually accomplished this purpose, even though trembling while he did so.

Yet the struggle was severe, and in spite of the freezing chill of the air, the perspiration poured down his face. Then, by slow degrees, the dark and dreadful countenance faded, the glamour passed from his soul, the normal proportions returned to walls and ceiling, the forms melted back into the fog, and the whirl of rushing shadow-cats disappeared whence they came.

And with the return of the consciousness of his own identity John Silence was restored to the full control of his own will-power. In a deep, modulated voice he began to utter certain rhythmical sounds that slowly rolled through the air like a rising sea, filling the room with powerful vibratory activities that whelmed all irregularities of lesser vibrations in its own swelling tone. He made certain sigils, gestures, and movements at the same time. For several minutes he continued to utter these words, until at length the growing volume dominated the whole room and mastered the manifestation of all that opposed it. For just as he understood the spiritual alchemy that can transmute evil forces by raising them into higher channels, so he knew from long study the occult use of sound, and its direct effect upon the plastic region wherein the powers of spiritual evil work their fell purposes. Harmony was restored first of all to his own soul, and thence to the room and all its occupants.

And, after himself, the first to recognise it was the old dog lying in his corner. Flame began suddenly uttering sounds of pleasure, that "something" between a growl and a grunt that dogs make upon being restored to their master's confidence. Dr. Silence heard the thumping of the collie's tail against the ground. And the grunt and the thumping touched the depth of affection in the man's heart, and gave him some inkling of what agonies the dumb creature had suffered.

Next, from the shadows by the window, a somewhat shrill purring announced the restoration of the cat to its normal state. Smoke was advancing across the carpet. He seemed very pleased with himself, and smiled with an expression of supreme innocence. He was no shadow-cat, but real and full of his usual and perfect self-possession. He marched along, picking his way delicately, but with a stately dignity that suggested his ancestry with the majesty of Egypt. His eyes no longer glared; they shone steadily before him, they radiated, not excitement, but knowledge. Clearly he was anxious to make amends for the mischief to which he had unwittingly lent himself owing to his subtle and electric constitution.

Still uttering his sharp high purrings he marched up to his master and rubbed vigorously against his legs. Then he stood on his hind feet and pawed his knees and stared beseechingly up into his face. He turned his head towards the corner where the collie still lay, thumping his tail feebly and pathetically.

John Silence understood. He bent down and stroked the creature's living fur, noting the line of bright blue sparks that followed the motion of his hand down its back. And then they advanced together towards the corner where the dog was.

Smoke went first and put his nose gently against his friend's muzzle, purring while he rubbed, and uttering little soft sounds of affection in his throat. The doctor lit the candle and brought it over. He saw the collie lying on its side against the wall; it was utterly exhausted, and foam still hung about its jaws. Its tail and eyes responded to the sound of its name, but it was evidently very weak and overcome. Smoke continued to rub against its cheek and nose and eyes, sometimes even standing on its body and kneading into the thick yellow hair. Flame replied from time to time by little licks of the tongue, most of them curiously misdirected.

But Dr. Silence felt intuitively that something disastrous had happened, and his heart was wrung. He stroked the dear body, feeling it over for bruises or broken bones, but finding none. He fed it with what remained of the sandwiches and milk, but the creature clumsily upset the saucer and lost the sandwiches between its paws, so that the doctor had to feed it with his own hand. And all the while Smoke meowed piteously.

Then John Silence began to understand. He went across to the farther side of the room and called aloud to it.

"Flame, old man! come!"

At any other time the dog would have been upon him in an instant, barking and leaping to the shoulder. And even now he got up, though heavily and awkwardly, to his feet. He started to run, wagging his tail more briskly. He collided first with a chair, and then ran straight into a table. Smoke trotted close at his side, trying his very best to guide him. But it was useless. Dr. Silence had to lift him up into his own arms and carry him like a baby. For he was blind.

III

It was a week later when John Silence called to see the author in his new house, and found him well on the way to recovery and already busy again with his writing. The haunted look had left his eyes, and he seemed cheerful and confident.

"Humour restored?" laughed the doctor, as soon as they were comfortably settled in the room overlooking the Park.

"I've had no trouble since I left that dreadful place," returned Pender gratefully; "and thanks to you—"

The doctor stopped him with a gesture.

"Never mind that," he said, "we'll discuss your new plans afterwards, and my scheme for relieving you of the house and helping you settle elsewhere. Of course it must be pulled down, for it's not fit for any sensitive person to live in, and any other tenant might be afflicted in the same way you were. Although, personally, I think the evil has exhausted itself by now."

He told the astonished author something of his experiences in it with the animals.

"I don't pretend to understand," Pender said, when the account was finished, "but I and my wife are intensely relieved to be free of it all. Only I must say I should like to know something of the former history of the house. When we took it six months ago I heard no word against it."

Dr. Silence drew a typewritten paper from his pocket.

"I can satisfy your curiosity to some extent," he said, running his eye over the sheets, and then replacing them in his coat; "for by my secretary's investigations I have been able to check certain information obtained in the hypnotic trance by a 'sensitive' who helps me in such cases. The former occupant who haunted you appears to have been a woman of singularly atrocious life and character who finally suffered death by hanging, after a series of crimes that appalled the whole of England and only came to light by the merest chance. She came to her end in the year 1798, for it was not this particular house she lived in, but a much larger one that then stood upon the site it now occupies, and was then, of course, not in London, but in the country. She was a person of intellect, possessed of a powerful, trained will, and of consummate audacity, and I am convinced availed herself of the resources of the lower magic to attain her ends. This goes far to explain the virulence of the attack upon yourself, and why she is still able to carry on after death the evil practices that formed her main purpose during life."

"You think that after death a soul can still consciously direct—" gasped the author.

"I think, as I told you before, that the forces of a powerful personality may still persist after death in the line of their original momentum," replied the doctor; "and that strong thoughts and purposes can still react upon suitably prepared brains long after their originators have passed away.

"If you knew anything of magic," he pursued, "you would know that thought is dynamic, and that it may call into existence forms and pictures that may well exist for hundreds of years. For, not far removed from the region of our human life, is another region where floats the waste and drift of all the centuries, the limbo of the shells of the dead; a densely populated region crammed with horror and abomination of all descriptions, and sometimes galvanised into active life again by the will of a trained manipulator, a mind versed in the practices of lower magic. That this woman understood its vile commerce, I am persuaded, and the forces she set going during her life have simply been accumulating ever since, and would have continued to do so had they not been drawn down upon yourself, and afterwards discharged and satisfied through me.

"Anything might have brought down the attack, for, besides drugs, there are certain violent emotions, certain moods of the soul, certain spiritual fevers, if I may so call them, which directly open the inner being to a cognisance of this astral region I have mentioned. In your case it happened to be a peculiarly potent drug that did it.

"But now, tell me," he added, after a pause, handing to the perplexed author a pencil drawing he had made of the dark countenance that had appeared to him during the night on Putney Hill—"tell me if you recognise this face?"

Pender looked at the drawing closely, greatly astonished. He shuddered a little as he looked.

"Undoubtedly," he said, "it is the face I kept trying to draw—dark, with the great mouth and jaw, and the drooping eye. That is the woman."

Dr. Silence then produced from his pocket-book an old-fashioned woodcut of the same person which his secretary had unearthed from the records of the Newgate Calendar. The woodcut and the pencil drawing were two different aspects of the same dreadful visage. The men compared them for some moments in silence.

"It makes me thank God for the limitations of our senses," said Pender quietly, with a sigh; "continuous clairvoyance must be a sore affliction."

"It is indeed," returned John Silence significantly, "and if all the people nowadays who claim to be clairvoyant were really so, the statistics of suicide and lunacy would be considerably higher than they are. It is little wonder," he added, "that your sense of humour was clouded, with the mind-forces of that dead monster trying to use your brain for their dissemination. You have had an interesting adventure, Mr. Felix Pender, and, let me add, a fortunate escape."

The author was about to renew his thanks when there came a sound of scratching at the door, and the doctor sprang up quickly.

"It's time for me to go. I left my dog on the step, but I suppose—"

Before he had time to open the door, it had yielded to the pressure behind it and flew wide open to admit a great yellow-haired collie. The dog, wagging his tail and contorting his whole body with delight, tore across the floor and tried to leap up upon his owner's breast. And there was laughter and happiness in the old eyes; for they were clear again as the day.

Ancient Sorceries

I

There are, it would appear, certain wholly unremarkable persons, with none of the characteristics that invite adventure, who yet once or twice in the course of their smooth lives undergo an experience so strange that the world catches its breath—and looks the other way! And it was cases of this kind, perhaps, more than any other, that fell into the widespread net of John Silence, the psychic doctor, and, appealing to his deep humanity, to his patience, and to his great qualities of spiritual sympathy, led often to the revelation of problems of the strangest complexity, and of the profoundest possible human interest.

Matters that seemed almost too curious and fantastic for belief he loved to trace to their hidden sources. To unravel a tangle in the very soul of things—and to release a suffering human soul in the process—was with him a veritable passion. And the knots he untied were, indeed, often passing strange.

The world, of course, asks for some plausible basis to which it can attach credence—something it can, at least, pretend to explain. The adventurous type it can understand: such people carry about with them an adequate explanation of their exciting lives, and their characters obviously drive them into the circumstances which produce the adventures. It expects nothing else from them, and is satisfied. But dull, ordinary folk have no right to out-of-the-way experiences, and the world having been led to expect otherwise, is disappointed with them, not to say shocked. Its complacent judgment has been rudely disturbed.

"Such a thing happen to *that* man!" it cries—"a commonplace person like that! It is too absurd! There must be something wrong!"

Yet there could be no question that something did actually happen

to little Arthur Vezin, something of the curious nature he described to
Dr. Silence. Outwardly, or inwardly, it happened beyond a doubt, and
in spite of the jeers of his few friends who heard the tale, and observed
wisely that "such a thing might perhaps have come to Iszard, that
crack-brained Iszard, or to that odd fish Minski, but it could never
have happened to commonplace little Vezin, who was fore-ordained to
live and die according to scale."

But, whatever his method of death was, Vezin certainly did not
"live according to scale" so far as this particular event in his otherwise
uneventful life was concerned; and to hear him recount it, and watch
his pale delicate features change, and hear his voice grow softer and
more hushed as he proceeded, was to know the conviction that his
halting words perhaps failed sometimes to convey. He lived the thing
over again each time he told it. His whole personality became muffled
in the recital. It subdued him more than ever, so that the tale became a
lengthy apology for an experience that he deprecated. He appeared to
excuse himself and ask your pardon for having dared to take part in so
fantastic an episode. For little Vezin was a timid, gentle, sensitive soul,
rarely able to assert himself, tender to man and beast, and almost con-
stitutionally unable to say No, or to claim many things that should
rightly have been his. His whole scheme of life seemed utterly remote
from anything more exciting than missing a train or losing an umbrella
on an omnibus. And when this curious event came upon him he was
already more years beyond forty than his friends suspected or he cared
to admit.

John Silence, who heard him speak of his experience more than
once, said that he sometimes left out certain details and put in others;
yet they were all obviously true. The whole scene was unforgettably
cinematographed on to his mind. None of the details were imagined or
invented. And when he told the story with them all complete, the effect was undeniable. His appealing brown eyes shone, and much of the
charming personality, usually so carefully repressed, came forward and
revealed itself. His modesty was always there, of course, but in the telling he forgot the present and allowed himself to appear almost vividly
as he lived again in the past of his adventure.

He was on the way home when it happened, crossing northern
France from some mountain trip or other where he buried himself sol-

itary-wise every summer. He had nothing but an unregistered bag in the rack, and the train was jammed to suffocation, most of the passengers being unredeemed holiday English. He disliked them, not because they were his fellow-countrymen, but because they were noisy and obtrusive, obliterating with their big limbs and tweed clothing all the quieter tints of the day that brought him satisfaction and enabled him to melt into insignificance and forget that he was anybody. These English clashed about him like a brass band, making him feel vaguely that he ought to be more self-assertive and obstreperous, and that he did not claim insistently enough all kinds of things that he didn't want and that were really valueless, such as corner seats, windows up or down, and so forth.

So that he felt uncomfortable in the train, and wished the journey were over and he was back again living with his unmarried sister in Surbiton.

And when the train stopped for ten panting minutes at the little station in northern France, and he got out to stretch his legs on the platform, and saw to his dismay a further batch of the British Isles debouching from another train, it suddenly seemed impossible to him to continue the journey. Even *his* flabby soul revolted, and the idea of staying a night in the little town and going on next day by a slower, emptier train, flashed into his mind. The guard was already shouting *"en voiture"* and the corridor of his compartment was already packed when the thought came to him. And, for once, he acted with decision and rushed to snatch his bag.

Finding the corridor and steps impassable, he tapped at the window (for he had a corner seat) and begged the Frenchman who sat opposite to hand his luggage out to him, explaining in his wretched French that he intended to break the journey there. And this elderly Frenchman, he declared, gave him a look, half of warning, half of reproach, that to his dying day he could never forget; handed the bag through the window of the moving train; and at the same time poured into his ears a long sentence, spoken rapidly and low, of which he was able to comprehend only the last few words: *"à cause du sommeil et à cause des chats."*

In reply to Dr. Silence, whose singular psychic acuteness at once seized upon this Frenchman as a vital point in the adventure, Vezin admitted that the man had impressed him favourably from the beginning, though without being able to explain why. They had sat facing one another during the four hours of the journey, and though no conversation had passed between them—Vezin was timid about his stuttering French—he confessed that his eyes were being continually drawn to his face, almost, he felt, to rudeness, and that each, by a dozen nameless little politenesses and attentions, had evinced the desire to be kind. The men liked each other and their personalities did not clash, or would not have clashed had they chanced to come to terms of acquaintance. The Frenchman, indeed, seemed to have exercised a silent protective influence over the insignificant little Englishman, and without words or gestures betrayed that he wished him well and would gladly have been of service to him.

"And this sentence that he hurled at you after the bag?" asked John Silence, smiling that peculiarly sympathetic smile that always melted the prejudices of his patient, "were you unable to follow it exactly?"

"It was so quick and low and vehement," explained Vezin, in his small voice, "that I missed practically the whole of it. I only caught the few words at the very end, because he spoke them so clearly, and his face was bent down out of the carriage window so near to mine."

"'À cause du sommeil et à cause des chats'?" repeated Dr. Silence, as though half speaking to himself.

"That's it exactly," said Vezin; "which, I take it, means something like 'because of sleep and because of the cats,' doesn't it?"

"Certainly, that's how I should translate it," the doctor observed shortly, evidently not wishing to interrupt more than necessary.

"And the rest of the sentence—all the first part I couldn't understand, I mean—was a warning not to do something—not to stop in the town, or at some particular place in the town, perhaps. That was the impression it made on me."

Then, of course, the train rushed off, and left Vezin standing on the platform alone and rather forlorn.

The little town climbed in straggling fashion up a sharp hill rising out of the plain at the back of the station, and was crowned by the twin towers of the ruined cathedral peeping over the summit. From the station itself it looked uninteresting and modern, but the fact was that the mediæval position lay out of sight just beyond the crest. And once he reached the top and entered the old streets, he stepped clean out of modern life into a bygone century. The noise and bustle of the crowded train seemed days away. The spirit of this silent hill-town, remote from tourists and motor-cars, dreaming its own quiet life under the autumn sun, rose up and cast its spell upon him. Long before he recognised this spell he acted under it. He walked softly, almost on tip-toe, down the winding narrow streets where the gables all but met over his head, and he entered the doorway of the solitary inn with a depre-cating and modest demeanour that was in itself an apology for intrud-ing upon the place and disturbing its dream.

At first, however, Vezin said, he noticed very little of all this. The attempt at analysis came much later. What struck him then was only the delightful contrast of the silence and peace after the dust and noisy rattle of the train. He felt soothed and stroked like a cat.

"Like a cat, you said?" interrupted John Silence, quickly catching him up.

"Yes. At the very start I felt that." He laughed apologetically. "I felt as though the warmth and the stillness and the comfort made me purr. It seemed to be the general mood of the whole place—then."

The inn, a rambling ancient house, the atmosphere of the old coaching days still about it, apparently did not welcome him too warm-ly. He felt he was only tolerated, he said. But it was cheap and com-fortable, and the delicious cup of afternoon tea he ordered at once made him feel really very pleased with himself for leaving the train in this bold, original way. For to him it had seemed bold and original. He felt something of a dog. His room, too, soothed him with its dark pan-elling and low irregular ceiling, and the long sloping passage that led to it seemed the natural pathway to a real Chamber of Sleep—little dim cubby hole out of the world where noise could not enter. It looked upon the courtyard at the back. It was all very charming, and made him think of himself as dressed in very soft velvet somehow, and the floors seemed padded, the walls provided with cushions. The sounds of the streets could not penetrate there. It was an atmosphere of abso-lute rest that surrounded him.

On engaging the two-franc room he had interviewed the only per-son who seemed to be about that sleepy afternoon, an elderly waiter with Dundreary whiskers and a drowsy courtesy, who had ambled lazily towards him across the stone yard; but on coming downstairs again for a little promenade in the town before dinner he encountered the proprietress herself. She was a large woman whose hands, feet, and features seemed to swim towards him out of a sea of person. They emerged, so to speak. But she had great dark, vivacious eyes that counteracted the bulk of her body, and betrayed the fact that in reality she was both vigorous and alert. When he first caught sight of her she was knitting in a low chair against the sunlight of the wall, and something at once made him see her as a great tabby cat, dozing, yet awake, heavily sleepy, and yet at the same time prepared for instantaneous action. A great mouser on the watch occurred to him.

She took him in with a single comprehensive glance that was polite without being cordial. Her neck, he noticed, was extraordinarily supple in spite of its proportions, for it turned so easily to follow him, and the head it carried bowed so very flexibly.

"But when she looked at me, you know," said Vezin, with that little apologetic smile in his brown eyes, and that faintly deprecating gesture of the shoulders that was characteristic of him, "the odd notion came to me that really she had intended to make quite a different movement, and that with a single bound she could have leaped at me across the width of that stone yard and pounced upon me like some huge cat upon a mouse."

He laughed a little soft laugh, and Dr. Silence made a note in his book without interrupting, while Vezin proceeded in a tone as though he feared he had already told too much and more than we could believe.

"Very soft, yet very active she was, for all her size and mass, and I felt she knew what I was doing even after I had passed and was behind her back. She spoke to me, and her voice was smooth and running. She asked if I had my luggage, and was comfortable in my room, and then added that dinner was at seven o'clock, and that they were very early people in this little country town. Clearly, she intended to convey that late hours were not encouraged."

Evidently, she contrived by voice and manner to give him the impression that here he would be "managed," that everything would be arranged and planned for him, and that he had nothing to do but fall into the groove and obey. No decided action or sharp personal effort would be looked for from him. It was the very reverse of the train. He walked quietly out into the street feeling soothed and peaceful. He realised that he was in a *milieu* that suited him and stroked him the right way. It was so much easier to be obedient. He began to purr again, and to feel that all the town purred with him.

About the streets of that little town he meandered gently, falling deeper and deeper into the spirit of repose that characterised it. With no special aim he wandered up and down, and to and fro. The September sunshine fell slantingly over the roofs. Down winding alleyways, fringed with tumbling gables and open casements, he caught fairylike glimpses of the great plain below, and of the meadows and yellow copses lying like a dream-map in the haze. The spell of the past held very potently here, he felt.

The streets were full of picturesquely garbed men and women, all busy enough, going their respective ways; but no one took any notice of him or turned to stare at his obviously English appearance. He was even able to forget that with his tourist appearance he was a false note in a charming picture, and he melted more and more into the scene, feeling delightfully insignificant and unimportant and unself-conscious. It was like becoming part of a softly coloured dream which he did not even realise to be a dream.

On the eastern side the hill fell away more sharply, and the plain below ran off rather suddenly into a sea of gathering shadows in which the little patches of woodland looked like islands and the stubble fields like deep water. Here he strolled along the old ramparts of ancient fortifications that once had been formidable, but now were only vision-like with their charming mingling of broken grey walls and wayward vine and ivy. From the broad coping on which he sat for a moment, level with the rounded tops of clipped plane trees, he saw the esplanade far below lying in shadow. Here and there a yellow sunbeam crept in and lay upon the fallen yellow leaves, and from the height he looked down and saw that the townsfolk were walking to and fro in the cool of the evening. He could just hear the sound of their slow footfalls, and the murmur of their voices floated up to him through the gaps between the trees. The figures looked like shadows as he caught glimpses of their quiet movements far below.

He sat there for some time pondering, bathed in the waves of murmurs and half-lost echoes that rose to his ears, muffled by the leaves of the plane trees. The whole town, and the little hill out of which it grew as naturally as an ancient wood, seemed to him like a being lying there half asleep on the plain and crooning to itself as it dozed.

And, presently, as he sat lazily melting into its dream, a sound of horns and strings and wood instruments rose to his ears, and the town band began to play at the far end of the crowded terrace below to the accompaniment of a very soft, deep-throated drum. Vezin was very sensitive to music, knew about it intelligently, and had even ventured, unknown to his friends, upon the composition of quiet melodies with low-running chords which he played to himself with the soft pedal when no one was about. And this music floating up through the trees from an invisible and doubtless very picturesque band of the towns-people wholly charmed him. He recognised nothing that they played, and it sounded as though they were simply improvising without a conductor. No definitely marked time ran through the pieces, which ended and began oddly after the fashion of wind through an Æolian harp. It was part of the place and scene, just as the dying sunlight and faintly-breathing wind were part of the scene and hour, and the mellow notes of old-fashioned plaintive horns, pierced here and there by the sharper strings, all half smothered by the continuous booming of the deep drum, touched his soul with a curiously potent spell that was almost too engrossing to be quite pleasant.

There was a certain queer sense of bewitchment in it all. The music seemed to him oddly unartificial. It made him think of trees swept by the wind, of night breezes singing among wires and chimney-stacks, or in the rigging of invisible ships; or—and the simile leaped up in his thoughts with a sudden sharpness of suggestion—a chorus of animals, of wild creatures, somewhere in desolate places of the world, crying and singing as animals will, to the moon. He could fancy he heard the wailing, half-human cries of cats upon the tiles at night, rising and falling with weird intervals of sound, and this music, muffled by distance and the trees, made him think of a queer company of these creatures on some roof far away in the sky, uttering their solemn music to one another and the moon in chorus.

It was, he felt at the time, a singular image to occur to him, yet it expressed his sensation pictorially better than anything else. The instruments played such impossibly odd intervals, and the crescendos and diminuendos were so very suggestive of cat-land on the tiles at night, rising swiftly, dropping without warning to deep notes again, and all in such strange confusion of discords and accords. But, at the same time a plaintive sweetness resulted on the whole, and the discords of these half-broken instruments were so singular that they did not distress his musical soul like fiddles out of tune.

He listened a long time, wholly surrendering himself as his character was, and then strolled homewards in the dusk as the air grew chilly.

"There was nothing to alarm?" put in Dr. Silence briefly.

"Absolutely nothing," said Vezin; "but you know it was all so fantastical and charming that my imagination was profoundly impressed. Perhaps, too," he continued, gently explanatory, "it was this stirring of my imagination that caused other impressions; for, as I walked back, the spell of the place began to steal over me in a dozen ways, though all intelligible ways. But there were other things I could not account for in the least, even then."

"Incidents, you mean?"

"Hardly incidents, I think. A lot of vivid sensations crowded themselves upon my mind and I could trace them to no causes. It was just after sunset and the tumbled old buildings traced magical outlines against an opalescent sky of gold and red. The dusk was running down the twisted streets. All round the hill the plain pressed in like a dim sea, its level rising with the darkness. The spell of this kind of scene, you know, can be very moving, and it was so that night. Yet I felt that what came to me had nothing directly to do with the mystery and wonder of the scene."

"Not merely the subtle transformations of the spirit that come with beauty," put in the doctor, noticing his hesitation.

"Exactly," Vezin went on, duly encouraged and no longer so fearful of our smiles at his expense. "The impressions came from somewhere else. For instance, down the busy main street where men and women were bustling home from work, shopping at stalls and barrows, idly gossiping in groups, and all the rest of it, I saw that I aroused no interest and that no one turned to stare at me as a foreigner and stranger. I was utterly ignored, and my presence among them excited no special interest or attention.

"And then, quite suddenly, it dawned upon me with conviction that all the time this indifference and inattention were merely feigned. Everybody as a matter of fact was watching me closely. Every movement I made was known and observed. Ignoring me was all a pretence—an elaborate pretence."

He paused a moment and looked at us to see if we were smiling, and then continued, reassured—

"It is useless to ask me how I noticed this, because I simply cannot explain it. But the discovery gave me something of a shock. Before I got back to the inn, however, another curious thing rose up strongly in my mind and forced my recognition of it as true. And this, too, I may as well say at once, was equally inexplicable to me. I mean I can only give you the fact, as fact it was to me."

The little man left his chair and stood on the mat before the fire. His diffidence lessened from now onwards, as he lost himself again in the magic of the old adventure. His eyes shone a little already as he talked.

"Well," he went on, his soft voice rising somewhat with his excitement, "I was in a shop when it came to me first—though the idea must have been at work for a long time subconsciously to appear in so complete a form all at once. I was buying socks, I think," he laughed, "and struggling with my dreadful French, when it struck me that the woman in the shop did not care two pins whether I bought anything or not. She was indifferent whether she made a sale or did not make a sale. She was only pretending to sell.

"This sounds a very small and fanciful incident to build upon what follows. But really it was not small. I mean it was the spark that lit the line of powder and ran along to the big blaze in my mind.

"For the whole town, I suddenly realised, was something other than I so far saw it. The real activities and interests of the people were elsewhere and otherwise than appeared. Their true lives lay somewhere out of sight behind the scenes. Their busy-ness was but the outward semblance that masked their actual purposes. They bought and sold, and ate and drank, and walked about the streets, yet all the while the main stream of their existence lay somewhere beyond my ken, underground, in secret places. In the shops and at the stalls they did not care whether I purchased their articles or not; at the inn, they were indifferent to my staying or going; their life lay remote from my own, springing from hidden, mysterious sources, coursing out of sight, unknown. It was all a great elaborate pretence, assumed possibly for my benefit, or possibly for purposes of their own. But the main current of their energies ran elsewhere. I almost felt as an unwelcome foreign substance might be expected to feel when it has found its way into the human system and the whole body organises itself to eject it or to absorb it. The town was doing this very thing to me.

"This bizarre notion presented itself forcibly to my mind as I walked home to the inn, and I began busily to wonder wherein the true life of this town could lie and what were the actual interests and activities of its hidden life.

"And, now that my eyes were partly opened, I noticed other things too that puzzled me, first of which, I think, was the extraordinary silence of the whole place. Positively, the town was muffled. Although the streets were paved with cobbles the people moved about silently, softly, with padded feet, like cats. Nothing made noise. All was hushed, subdued, muted. The very voices were quiet, low-pitched like purring. Nothing clamorous, vehement, or emphatic seemed able to live in the drowsy atmosphere of soft dreaming that soothed this little hill-town into its sleep. It was like the woman at the inn—an outward repose screening intense inner activity and purpose.

"Yet there was no sign of lethargy or sluggishness anywhere about it. The people were active and alert. Only a magical and uncanny softness lay over them all like a spell."

Vezin passed his hand across his eyes for a moment as though the memory had become very vivid. His voice had run off into a whisper so that we heard the last part with difficulty. He was telling a true thing obviously, yet something that he both liked and hated telling.

"I went back to the inn," he continued presently in a louder voice, "and dined. I felt a new strange world about me. My old world of reality receded. Here, whether I liked it or no, was something new and incomprehensible. I regretted having left the train so impulsively. An adventure was upon me, and I loathed adventures as foreign to my nature. Moreover, this was the beginning apparently of an adventure somewhere deep within me, in a region I could not check or measure, and a feeling of alarm mingled itself with my wonder—alarm for the stability of what I had for forty years recognised as my 'personality.'

"I went upstairs to bed, my mind teeming with thoughts that were unusual to me, and of rather a haunting description. By way of relief I kept thinking of that nice, prosaic noisy train and all those wholesome, blustering passengers. I almost wished I were with them again. But my dreams took me elsewhere. I dreamed of cats, and soft-moving creatures, and the silence of life in a dim muffled world beyond the senses."

II

Vezin stayed on from day to day, indefinitely, much longer than he had intended. He felt in a kind of dazed, somnolent condition. He did nothing in particular, but the place fascinated him and he could not decide to leave. Decisions were always very difficult for him and he sometimes wondered how he had ever brought himself to the point of leaving the train. It seemed as though some one else must have arranged it for him, and once or twice his thoughts ran to the swarthy Frenchman who had sat opposite. If only he could have understood that long sentence ending so strangely with *"à cause du sommeil et à cause des chats."* He wondered what it all meant.

Meanwhile the hushed softness of the town held him prisoner and he sought in his muddling, gentle way to find out where the mystery lay, and what it was all about. But his limited French and his constitutional hatred of active investigation made it hard for him to buttonhole anybody and ask questions. He was content to observe, and watch, and remain negative.

The weather held on calm and hazy, and this just suited him. He wandered about the town till he knew every street and alley. The people suffered him to come and go without let or hindrance, though it became clearer to him every day that he was never free himself from observation. The town watched him as a cat watches a mouse. And he got no nearer to finding out what they were all so busy with or where the main stream of their activities lay. This remained hidden. The people were as soft and mysterious as cats.

But that he was continually under observation became more evident from day to day.

For instance, when he strolled to the end of the town and entered a little green public garden beneath the ramparts and seated himself upon one of the empty benches in the sun, he was quite alone—at first. Not another seat was occupied; the little park was empty, the paths deserted. Yet, within ten minutes of his coming, there must have been fully twenty persons scattered about him, some strolling aimlessly along the gravel walks, staring at the flowers, and others seated on the wooden benches enjoying the sun like himself. None of them appeared to take any notice of him; yet he understood quite well they had all come there to watch. They kept him under close observation. In the street they had seemed busy enough, hurrying upon various errands; yet these were suddenly all forgotten and they had nothing to do but loll and laze in the sun, their duties unremembered. Five minutes after he left, the garden was again deserted, the seats vacant. But in the crowded street it was the same thing again; he was never alone. He was ever in their thoughts.

By degrees, too, he began to see how it was he was so cleverly watched, yet without the appearance of it. The people did nothing *directly*. They behaved *obliquely*. He laughed in his mind as the thought thus clothed itself in words, but the phrase exactly described it. They looked at him from angles which naturally should have led their sight in another direction altogether. Their movements were oblique, too, so far as these concerned himself. The straight, direct thing was not their way evidently. They did nothing obviously. If he entered a shop to buy, the woman walked instantly away and busied herself with something at the farther end of the counter, though answering at once when he spoke, showing that she knew he was there and that this was only her way of attending to him. It was the fashion of the cat she followed. Even in the dining-room of the inn, the be-whiskered and courteous waiter, lithe and silent in all his movements, never seemed able to come straight to his table for an order or a dish. He came by zigzags, indirectly, vaguely, so that he appeared to be going to another table altogether, and only turned suddenly at the last moment, and was there beside him.

Vezin smiled curiously to himself as he described how he began to realise these things. Other tourists there were none in the hostel, but he recalled the figures of one or two old men, inhabitants, who took their *déjeuner* and dinner there, and remembered how fantastically they entered the room in similar fashion. First, they paused in the doorway, peering about the room, and then, after a temporary inspection, they came in, as it were, sideways, keeping close to the walls so that he wondered which table they were making for, and at the last minute making almost a little quick run to their particular seats. And again he thought of the ways and methods of cats.

Other small incidents, too, impressed him as all part of this queer, soft town with its muffled, indirect life, for the way some of the people appeared and disappeared with extraordinary swiftness puzzled him exceedingly. It may have been all perfectly natural, he knew, yet he could not make it out how the alleys swallowed them up and shot them forth in a second of time when there were no visible doorways or openings near enough to explain the phenomenon. Once he followed two elderly women who, he felt, had been particularly examining him from across the street—quite near the inn this was—and saw them turn the corner a few feet only in front of him. Yet when he sharply followed on their heels he saw nothing but an utterly deserted alley stretching in front of him with no sign of a living thing. And the only opening through which they could have escaped was a porch some fifty yards away, which not the swiftest human runner could have reached in time.

And in just such sudden fashion people appeared, when he never expected them. Once when he heard a great noise of fighting going on behind a low wall, and hurried up to see what was going on, what should he see but a group of girls and women engaged in vociferous conversation which instantly hushed itself to the normal whispering note of the town when his head appeared over the wall. And even then none of them turned to look at him directly, but slunk off with the most unaccountable rapidity into doors and sheds across the yard. And their voices, he thought, had sounded so like, so strangely like, the angry snarling of fighting animals, almost of cats.

The whole spirit of the town, however, continued to evade him as something elusive, protean, screened from the outer world, and at the same time intensely, genuinely vital; and, since he now formed part of its life, this concealment puzzled and irritated him; more—it began rather to frighten him.

Out of the mists that slowly gathered about his ordinary surface thoughts, there rose again the idea that the inhabitants were waiting for him to declare himself, to take an attitude, to do this, or to do that; and that when he had done so they in their turn would at length make some direct response, accepting or rejecting him. Yet the vital matter concerning which his decision was awaited came no nearer to him.

Once or twice he purposely followed little processions or groups of the citizens in order to find out, if possible, on what purpose they were bent; but they always discovered him in time and dwindled away, each individual going his or her own way. It was always the same: he never could learn what their main interest was. The cathedral was ever empty, the old church of St. Martin, at the other end of the town, deserted. They shopped because they had to, and not because they wished to. The booths stood neglected, the stalls unvisited, the little cafés desolate. Yet the streets were always full, the townsfolk ever on the bustle.

"Can it be," he thought to himself, yet with a deprecating laugh that he should have dared to think anything so odd, "can it be that these people are people of the twilight, that they live only at night their real life, and come out honestly only with the dusk? That during the day they make a sham though brave pretence, and after the sun is down their true life begins? Have they the souls of night-things, and is the whole blessed town in the hands of the cats?"

The fancy somehow electrified him with little shocks of shrinking and dismay. Yet, though he affected to laugh, he knew that he was beginning to feel more than uneasy, and that strange forces were tugging with a thousand invisible cords at the very centre of his being. Something utterly remote from his ordinary life, something that had not waked for years, began faintly to stir in his soul, sending feelers abroad into his brain and heart, shaping queer thoughts and penetrating even into certain of his minor actions. Something exceedingly vital to himself, to his soul, hung in the balance.

And, always when he returned to the inn about the hour of sunset, he saw the figures of the townsfolk stealing through the dusk from their shop doors, moving sentry-wise to and fro at the corners of the streets, yet always vanishing silently like shadows at his near approach. And as the inn invariably closed its doors at ten o'clock he had never yet found the opportunity he rather half-heartedly sought to see for himself what account the town could give of itself at night.

"—*à cause du sommeil et à cause des chats*"—the words now rang in his ears more and more often, though still as yet without any definite meaning.

Moreover, something made him sleep like the dead.

III

It was, I think, on the fifth day—though in this detail his story sometimes varied—that he made a definite discovery which increased his alarm and brought him up to a rather sharp climax. Before that he had already noticed that a change was going forward and certain subtle transformations being brought about in his character which modified several of his minor habits. And he had affected to ignore them. Here, however, was something he could no longer ignore; and it startled him.

At the best of times he was never very positive, always negative rather, compliant and acquiescent; yet, when necessity arose he was capable of reasonably vigorous action and could take a strongish decision. The discovery he now made that brought him up with such a sharp turn was that this power had positively dwindled to nothing. He found it impossible to make up his mind. For, on this fifth day, he realised that he had stayed long enough in the town and that for reasons he could only vaguely define to himself it was wiser *and safer* that he should leave.

And he found that he could not leave!

This is difficult to describe in words, and it was more by gesture and the expression of his face that he conveyed to Dr. Silence the state of impotence he had reached. All this spying and watching, he said, had as it were spun a net about his feet so that he was trapped and powerless to escape; he felt like a fly that had blundered into the intricacies of a great web; he was caught, imprisoned, and could not get away. It was a distressing sensation. A numbness had crept over his will till it had become almost incapable of decision. The mere thought of vigorous action—action towards escape—began to terrify him. All the currents of his life had turned inwards upon himself, striving to bring to the surface something that lay buried almost beyond reach, determined to force his recognition of something he had long forgotten—forgotten years upon years, centuries almost ago. It seemed as though a window deep within his being would presently open and reveal an entirely new world, yet somehow a world that was not unfamiliar. Beyond that, again, he fancied a great curtain hung; and when that too rolled up he would see still farther into this region and at last understand something of the secret life of these extraordinary people.

"Is this why they wait and watch?" he asked himself with rather a shaking heart, "for the time when I shall join them—or refuse to join them? Does the decision rest with me after all, and not with them?"

And it was at this point that the sinister character of the adventure first really declared itself, and he became genuinely alarmed. The stability of his rather fluid little personality was at stake, he felt, and something in his heart turned coward.

Why otherwise should he have suddenly taken to walking stealthily, silently, making as little sound as possible, for ever looking behind him? Why else should he have moved almost on tiptoe about the passages of the practically deserted inn, and when he was abroad have found himself deliberately taking advantage of what cover presented itself? And why, if he was not afraid, should the wisdom of staying indoors after sundown have suddenly occurred to him as eminently desirable? Why, indeed?

And, when John Silence gently pressed him for an explanation of these things, he admitted apologetically that he had none to give.

"It was simply that I feared something might happen to me unless I kept a sharp look-out. I felt afraid. It was instinctive," was all he could say. "I got the impression that the whole town was after me—wanted me for something; and that if it got me I should lose myself, or at least the Self I knew, in some unfamiliar state of consciousness. But I am not a psychologist, you know," he added meekly, "and I cannot define it better than that."

It was while lounging in the courtyard half an hour before the evening meal that Vezin made this discovery, and he at once went upstairs to his quiet room at the end of the winding passage to think it over alone. In the yard it was empty enough, true, but there was always the possibility that the big woman whom he dreaded would come out of some door, with her pretence of knitting, to sit and watch him. This had happened several times, and he could not endure the sight of her. He still remembered his original fancy, bizarre though it was, that she would spring upon him the moment his back was turned and land with one single crushing leap upon his neck. Of course it was nonsense, but then it haunted him, and once an idea begins to do that it ceases to be nonsense. It has clothed itself in reality.

He went upstairs accordingly. It was dusk, and the oil lamps had not yet been lit in the passages. He stumbled over the uneven surface of the ancient flooring, passing the dim outlines of doors along the corridor—doors that he had never once seen opened—rooms that seemed never occupied. He moved, as his habit now was, stealthily and on tiptoe.

Half-way down the last passage to his own chamber there was a sharp turn, and it was just here, while groping round the walls with outstretched hands, that his fingers touched something that was not wall—something that moved. It was soft and warm in texture, indescribably fragrant, and about the height of his shoulder; and he immediately thought of a furry, sweet-smelling kitten. The next minute he knew it was something quite different.

Instead of investigating, however,—his nerves must have been too overwrought for that, he said,—he shrank back as closely as possible against the wall on the other side. The thing, whatever it was, slipped past him with a sound of rustling, and retreating with light footsteps down the passage behind him, was gone. A breath of warm, scented air was wafted to his nostrils.

Vezin caught his breath for an instant and paused, stockstill, half leaning against the wall—and then almost ran down the remaining distance and entered his room with a rush, locking the door hurriedly behind him. Yet it was not fear that made him run: it was excitement, pleasurable excitement. His nerves were tingling, and a delicious glow made itself felt all over his body. In a flash it came to him that this was just what he had felt twenty-five years ago as a boy when he was in love for the first time. Warm currents of life ran all over him and mounted to his brain in a whirl of soft delight. His mood was suddenly become tender, melting, loving.

The room was quite dark, and he collapsed upon the sofa by the window, wondering what had happened to him and what it all meant. But the only thing he understood clearly in that instant was that something in him had swiftly, magically changed: he no longer wished to leave, or to argue with himself about leaving. The encounter in the passage-way had changed all that. The strange perfume of it still hung about him, bemusing his heart and mind. For he knew that it was a girl who had passed him, a girl's face that his fingers had brushed in the darkness, and he felt in some extraordinary way as though he had been actually kissed by her, kissed full upon the lips.

Trembling, he sat upon the sofa by the window and struggled to collect his thoughts. He was utterly unable to understand how the mere passing of a girl in the darkness of a narrow passage-way could communicate so electric a thrill to his whole being that he still shook with the sweetness of it. Yet, there it was! And he found it as useless to deny as to attempt analysis. Some ancient fire had entered his veins, and now ran coursing through his blood; and that he was forty-five instead of twenty did not matter one little jot. Out of all the inner turmoil and confusion emerged the one salient fact that the mere atmosphere, the merest casual touch, of this girl, unseen, unknown in the darkness, had been sufficient to stir dormant fires in the centre of his heart, and rouse his whole being from a state of feeble sluggishness to one of tearing and tumultuous excitement.

After a time, however, the number of Vezin's years began to assert their cumulative power; he grew calmer; and when a knock came at length upon his door and he heard the waiter's voice suggesting that dinner was nearly over, he pulled himself together and slowly made his way downstairs into the dining-room.

Every one looked up as he entered, for he was very late, but he took his customary seat in the far corner and began to eat. The trepidation was still in his nerves, but the fact that he had passed through the courtyard and hall without catching sight of a petticoat served to calm him a little. He ate so fast that he had almost caught up with the current stage of the table d'hôte, when a slight commotion in the room drew his attention.

His chair was so placed that the door and the greater portion of the long *salle à manger* were behind him, yet it was not necessary to turn round to know that the same person he had passed in the dark passage had now come into the room. He felt the presence long before he heard or saw any one. Then he became aware that the old men, the only other guests, were rising one by one in their places, and exchanging greetings with some one who passed among them from table to table. And when at length he turned with his heart beating furiously to ascertain for himself, he saw the form of a young girl, lithe and slim, moving down the centre of the room and making straight for his own table in the corner. She moved wonderfully, with sinuous grace, like a young panther, and her approach filled him with such delicious bewilderment that he was utterly unable to tell at first what her face was like, or discover what it was about the whole presentment of the creature that filled him anew with trepidation and delight.

"Ah, Ma'mselle est de retour!" he heard the old waiter murmur at his side, and he was just able to take in that she was the daughter of the proprietress, when she was upon him, and he heard her voice. She was addressing him. Something of red lips he saw and laughing white teeth, and stray wisps of fine dark hair about the temples; but all the rest was a dream in which his own emotion rose like a thick cloud before his eyes and prevented his seeing accurately, or knowing exactly what he did. He was aware that she greeted him with a charming little bow; that her beautiful large eyes looked searchingly into his own; that the perfume he had noticed in the dark passage again assailed his nostrils, and that she was bending a little towards him and leaning with one hand on the table at his side. She was quite close to him—that was the chief thing he knew—explaining that she had been asking after the comfort of her mother's guests, and now was introducing herself to the latest arrival—himself.

"M'sieur has already been here a few days," he heard the waiter say; and then her own voice, sweet as singing, replied—

"Ah, but M'sieur is not going to leave us just yet, I hope. My mother is too old to look after the comfort of our guests properly, but now I am here I will remedy all that." She laughed deliciously. "M'sieur shall be well looked after."

Vezin, struggling with his emotion and desire to be polite, half rose to acknowledge the pretty speech, and to stammer some sort of reply, but as he did so his hand by chance touched her own that was resting upon the table, and a shock that was for all the world like a shock of electricity, passed from her skin into his body. His soul wavered and shook deep within him. He caught her eyes fixed upon his own with a look of most curious intentness, and the next moment he knew that he had sat down wordless again on his chair, that the girl was already half-way across the room, and that he was trying to eat his salad with a dessert-spoon and a knife.

Longing for her return, and yet dreading it, he gulped down the remainder of his dinner, and then went at once to his bedroom to be alone with his thoughts. This time the passages were lighted, and he suffered no exciting contretemps; yet the winding corridor was dim with shadows, and the last portion, from the bend of the walls onwards, seemed longer than he had ever known it. It ran downhill like the pathway on a mountain side, and as he tiptoed softly down it he felt that by rights it ought to have led him clean out of the house into the heart of a great forest. The world was singing with him. Strange fancies filled his brain, and once in the room, with the door securely locked, he did not light the candles, but sat by the open window thinking long, long thoughts that came unbidden in troops to his mind.

IV

This part of the story he told to Dr. Silence, without special coaxing, it is true, yet with much stammering embarrassment. He could not in the least understand, he said, how the girl had managed to affect him so profoundly, and even before he had set eyes upon her. For her mere proximity in the darkness had been sufficient to set him on fire. He knew nothing of enchantments, and for years had been a stranger to anything approaching tender relations with any member of the opposite sex, for he was encased in shyness, and realised his overwhelming defects only too well. Yet this bewitching young creature came to him deliberately. Her manner was unmistakable, and she sought him out on every possible occasion. Chaste and sweet she was undoubtedly, yet frankly inviting; and she won him utterly with the first glance of her shining eyes, even if she had not already done so in the dark merely by the magic of her invisible presence.

"You felt she was altogether wholesome and good?" queried the doctor. "You had no reaction of any sort—for instance, of alarm?"

Vezin looked up sharply with one of his inimitable little apologetic smiles. It was some time before he replied. The mere memory of the adventure had suffused his shy face with blushes, and his brown eyes sought the floor again before he answered.

"I don't think I can quite say that," he explained presently. "I acknowledged certain qualms, sitting up in my room afterwards. A conviction grew upon me that there was something about her—how shall I express it?—well, something unholy. It is not impurity in any sense, physical or mental, that I mean, but something quite indefinable that gave me a vague sensation of the creeps. She drew me, and at the same time repelled me, more than—than—"

He hesitated, blushing furiously, and unable to finish the sentence.

"Nothing like it has ever come to me before or since," he concluded, with lame confusion. "I suppose it was, as you suggested just now, something of an enchantment. At any rate, it was strong enough to make me feel that I would stay in that awful little haunted town for years if only I could see her every day, hear her voice, watch her wonderful movements, and sometimes, perhaps, touch her hand."

"Can you explain to me what you felt was the source of her power?" John Silence asked, looking purposely anywhere but at the narrator.

"I am surprised that *you* should ask me such a question," answered Vezin, with the nearest approach to dignity he could manage. "I think no man can describe to another convincingly wherein lies the magic of the woman who ensnares him. I certainly cannot. I can only say this slip of a girl bewitched me, and the mere knowledge that she was living and sleeping in the same house filled me with an extraordinary sense of delight.

"But there's one thing I can tell you," he went on earnestly, his eyes aglow, "namely, that she seemed to sum up and synthesise in herself all the strange hidden forces that operated so mysteriously in the town and its inhabitants. She had the silken movements of the panther, going smoothly, silently to and fro, and the same indirect, oblique methods as the townsfolk, screening, like them, secret purposes of her own—purposes that I was sure had *me* for their objective. She kept me, to my terror and delight, ceaselessly under observation, yet so carelessly, so consummately, that another man less sensitive, if I may say so"—he made a deprecating gesture—"or less prepared by what had gone before, would never have noticed it at all. She was always still, always reposeful, yet she seemed to be everywhere at once, so that I never could escape from her. I was continually meeting the stare and laughter of her great eyes, in the corners of the rooms, in the passages, calmly looking at me through the windows, or in the busiest parts of the public streets."

Their intimacy, it seems, grew very rapidly after this first encounter which had so violently disturbed the little man's equilibrium. He was naturally very prim, and prim folk live mostly in so small a world that anything violently unusual may shake them clean out of it, and they therefore instinctively distrust originality. But Vezin began to forget his primness after awhile. The girl was always modestly behaved, and as her mother's representative she naturally had to do with the guests in the hotel. It was not out of the way that a spirit of camaraderie should spring up. Besides, she was young, she was charmingly pretty, she was French, and—she obviously liked him.

At the same time, there was something indescribable—a certain indefinable atmosphere of other places, other times—that made him try hard to remain on his guard, and sometimes made him catch his breath with a sudden start. It was all rather like a delirious dream, half delight, half dread, he confided in a whisper to Dr. Silence; and more than once he hardly knew quite what he was doing or saying, as though he were driven forward by impulses he scarcely recognised as his own.

And though the thought of leaving presented itself again and again to his mind, it was each time with less insistence, so that he stayed on from day to day, becoming more and more a part of the sleepy life of this dreamy mediæval town, losing more and more of his recognisable personality. Soon, he felt, the Curtain within would roll up with an awful rush, and he would find himself suddenly admitted into the secret purposes of the hidden life that lay behind it all. Only, by that time, he would have become transformed into an entirely different being.

And, meanwhile, he noticed various little signs of the intention to make his stay attractive to him: flowers in his bedroom, a more comfortable arm-chair in the corner, and even special little extra dishes on his private table in the dining room. Conversations, too, with "Mademoiselle Ilsé" became more and more frequent and pleasant, and although they seldom travelled beyond the weather, or the details of the town, the girl, he noticed, was never in a hurry to bring them to an end, and often contrived to interject little odd sentences that he never properly understood, yet felt to be significant.

And it was these stray remarks, full of a meaning that evaded him, that pointed to some hidden purpose of her own and made him feel uneasy. They all had to do, he felt sure, with reasons for his staying on in the town indefinitely.

"And has M'sieur not even yet come to a decision?" she said softly in his ear, sitting beside him in the sunny yard before *déjeuner,* the acquaintance having progressed with significant rapidity. "Because, if it's so difficult, we must all try together to help him!"

The question startled him, following upon his own thoughts. It was spoken with a pretty laugh, and a stray bit of hair across one eye, as she turned and peered at him half roguishly. Possibly he did not quite understand the French of it, for her near presence always confused his small knowledge of the language distressingly. Yet the words, and her manner, and something else that lay behind it all in her mind, frightened him. It gave such point to his feeling that the town was waiting for him to make his mind up on some important matter.

At the same time, her voice, and the fact that she was there so close beside him in her soft dark dress, thrilled him inexpressibly.

"It is true I find it difficult to leave," he stammered, losing his way deliciously in the depths of her eyes, "and especially now that Mademoiselle Ilsé has come."

He was surprised at the success of his sentence, and quite delighted with the little gallantry of it. But at the same time he could have bitten his tongue off for having said it.

"Then after all you like our little town, or you would not be pleased to stay on," she said, ignoring the compliment.

"I am enchanted with it, and enchanted with you," he cried, feeling that his tongue was somehow slipping beyond the control of his brain. And he was on the verge of saying all manner of other things of the wildest description, when the girl sprang lightly up from her chair beside him, and made to go.

"It is *soupe à l'oignon* to-day!" she cried, laughing back at him through the sunlight, "and I must go and see about it. Otherwise, you know, M'sieur will not enjoy his dinner, and then, perhaps, he will leave us!"

He watched her cross the courtyard, moving with all the grace and lightness of the feline race, and her simple black dress clothed her, he thought, exactly like the fur of the same supple species. She turned once to laugh at him from the porch with the glass door, and then stopped a moment to speak to her mother, who sat knitting as usual in her corner seat just inside the hall-way.

But how was it, then, that the moment his eye fell upon this ungainly woman, the pair of them appeared suddenly as other than they were? Whence came that transforming dignity and sense of power that enveloped them both as by magic? What was it about that massive woman that made her appear instantly regal, and set her on a throne in some dark and dreadful scenery, wielding a sceptre over the red glare of some tempestuous orgy? And why did this slender stripling of a girl, graceful as a willow, lithe as a young leopard, assume suddenly an air of sinister majesty, and move with flame and smoke about her head, and the darkness of night beneath her feet?

Vezin caught his breath and sat there transfixed. Then, almost simultaneously with its appearance, the queer notion vanished again, and the sunlight of day caught them both, and he heard her laughing to her mother about the *soupe à l'oignon,* and saw her glancing back at him over her dear little shoulder with a smile that made him think of a dew-kissed rose bending lightly before summer airs.

And, indeed, the onion soup was particularly excellent that day, because he saw another cover laid at his small table and, with fluttering heart, heard the waiter murmur by way of explanation that "Ma'mselle Ilsé would honor M'sieur to-day at *déjeuner,* as her custom sometimes is with her mother's guests."

So actually she sat by him all through that delirious meal, talking quietly to him in easy French, seeing that he was well looked after, mixing the salad-dressing, and even helping him with her own hand. And, later in the afternoon, while he was smoking in the courtyard, longing for a sight of her as soon as her duties were done, she came again to his side, and when he rose to meet her, she stood facing him a moment, full of a perplexing sweet shyness before she spoke—

"My mother thinks you ought to know more of the beauties of our little town, and I think so too! Would M'sieur like me to be his guide, perhaps? I can show him everything, for our family has lived here for many generations."

She had him by the hand, indeed, before he could find a single word to express his pleasure, and led him, all unresisting, out into the street, yet in such a way that it seemed perfectly natural she should do so, and without the faintest suggestion of boldness or immodesty. Her face glowed with the pleasure and interest of it, and with her short dress and tumbled hair she looked every bit the charming child of seventeen that she was, innocent and playful, proud of her native town, and alive beyond her years to the sense of its ancient beauty.

So they went over the town together, and she showed him what she considered its chief interest: the tumble-down old house where her forebears had lived; the sombre, aristocratic-looking mansion where her mother's family dwelt for centuries, and the ancient market-place where several hundred years before the witches had been burnt by the score. She kept up a lively running stream of talk about it all, of which he understood not a fiftieth part as he trudged along by her side, cursing his forty-five years and feeling all the yearnings of his early manhood revive and jeer at him. And, as she talked, England and Surbiton seemed very far away indeed, almost in another age of the world's history. Her voice touched something immeasurably old in him, something that slept deep. It lulled the surface parts of his consciousness to sleep, allowing what was far more ancient to awaken. Like the town, with its elaborate pretence of modern active life, the upper layers of his being became dulled, soothed, muffled, and what lay underneath began to stir in its sleep. That big Curtain swayed a little to and fro. Presently it might lift altogether. . . .

He began to understand a little better at last. The mood of the town was reproducing itself in him. In proportion as his ordinary external self became muffled, that inner secret life, that was far more real and vital, asserted itself. And this girl was surely the high-priestess of it all, the chief instrument of its accomplishment. New thoughts, with new interpretations, flooded his mind as she walked beside him through the winding streets, while the picturesque old gabled town, softly coloured in the sunset, had never appeared to him so wholly wonderful and seductive.

And only one curious incident came to disturb and puzzle him, slight in itself, but utterly inexplicable, bringing white terror into the child's face and a scream to her laughing lips. He had merely pointed to a column of blue smoke that rose from the burning autumn leaves and made a picture against the red roofs, and had then run to the wall and called her to his side to watch the flames shooting here and there through the heap of rubbish. Yet, at the sight of it, as though taken by surprise, her face had altered dreadfully, and she had turned and run like the wind, calling out wild sentences to him as she ran, of which he had not understood a single word, except that the fire apparently frightened her, and she wanted to get quickly away from it, and to get him away too.

Yet five minutes later she was as calm and happy again as though nothing had happened to alarm or waken troubled thoughts in her, and they had both forgotten the incident.

They were leaning over the ruined ramparts together listening to the weird music of the band as he had heard it the first day of his arrival. It moved him again profoundly as it had done before, and somehow he managed to find his tongue and his best French. The girl leaned across the stones close beside him. No one was about. Driven by some remorseless engine within he began to stammer something—he hardly knew what—of his strange admiration for her. Almost at the first word she sprang lightly off the wall and came up smiling in front of him, just touching his knees as he sat there. She was hatless as usual, and the sun caught her hair and one side of her cheek and throat.

"Oh, I'm *so* glad!" she cried, clapping her little hands softly in his face, "so very glad, because that means that if you like me you must also like what I do, and what I belong to."

Already he regretted bitterly having lost control of himself. Something in the phrasing of her sentence chilled him. He knew the fear of embarking upon an unknown and dangerous sea.

"You will take part in our real life, I mean," she added softly, with an indescribable coaxing of manner, as though she noticed his shrinking. "You will come back to us."

Already this slip of a child seemed to dominate him; he felt her power coming over him more and more; something emanated from her that stole over his senses and made him aware that her personality, for all its simple grace, held forces that were stately, imposing, august. He saw her again moving through smoke and flame amid broken and tempestuous scenery, alarmingly strong, her terrible mother by her side. Dimly this shone through her smile and appearance of charming innocence.

"You will, I know," she repeated, holding him with her eyes.

They were quite alone up there on the ramparts, and the sensation that she was overmastering him stirred a wild sensuousness in his blood. The mingled abandon and reserve in her attracted him furiously, and all of him that was man rose up and resisted the creeping influence, at the same time acclaiming it with the full delight of his forgotten youth. An irresistible desire came to him to question her, to summon what still remained to him of his own little personality in an effort to retain the right to his normal self.

The girl had grown quiet again, and was now leaning on the broad wall close beside him, gazing out across the darkening plain, her elbows on the coping, motionless as a figure carved in stone. He took his courage in both hands.

"Tell me, Ilsé," he said, unconsciously imitating her own purring softness of voice, yet aware that he was utterly in earnest, "what is the meaning of this town, and what is this real life you speak of? And why is it that the people watch me from morning to night? Tell me what it all means? And, tell me," he added more quickly with passion in his voice, "what you really are—yourself?"

She turned her head and looked at him through half-closed eyelids, her growing inner excitement betraying itself by the faint colour that ran like a shadow across her face.

"It seems to me,"—he faltered oddly under her gaze—"that I have some right to know—"

Suddenly she opened her eyes to the full. "You love me, then?" she asked softly.

"I swear," he cried impetuously, moved as by the force of a rising tide, "I never felt before—I have never known any other girl who—"

"Then you *have* the right to know," she calmly interrupted his confused confession; "for love shares all secrets."

She paused, and a thrill like fire ran swiftly through him. Her words lifted him off the earth, and he felt a radiant happiness, followed almost the same instant in horrible contrast by the thought of death. He became aware that she had turned her eyes upon his own and was speaking again.

"The real life I speak of," she whispered, "is the old, old life within, the life of long ago, the life to which you, too, once belonged, and to which you still belong."

A faint wave of memory troubled the deeps of his soul as her low voice sank into him. What she was saying he knew instinctively to be true, even though he could not as yet understand its full purport. His present life seemed slipping from him as he listened, merging his personality in one that was far older and greater. It was this loss of his present self that brought to him the thought of death.

"You came here," she went on, "with the purpose of seeking it, and the people felt your presence and are waiting to know what you decide, whether you will leave them without having found it, or whether—"

Her eyes remained fixed upon his own, but her face began to change, growing larger and darker with an expression of age.

"It is their thoughts constantly playing about your soul that makes you feel they watch you. They do not watch you with their eyes. The purposes of their inner life are calling to you, seeking to claim you. You were all part of the same life long, long ago, and now they want you back again among them."

Vezin's timid heart sank with dread as he listened; but the girl's eyes held him with a net of joy so that he had no wish to escape. She fascinated him, as it were, clean out of his normal self.

"Alone, however, the people could never have caught and held you," she resumed. "The motive force was not strong enough; it has faded through all these years. But I"—she paused a moment and looked at him with complete confidence in her splendid eyes—"I possess the spell to conquer you and hold you: the spell of old love. I can win you back again and make you live the old life with me, for the force of the ancient tie between us, if I choose to use it, is irresistible. And I do choose to use it. I still want you. And you, dear soul of my dim past"—she pressed closer to him so that her breath passed across his eyes, and her voice positively sang—"I mean to have you, for you love me and are utterly at my mercy."

Vezin heard, and yet did not hear; understood, yet did not understand. He had passed into a condition of exaltation. The world was beneath his feet, made of music and flowers, and he was flying somewhere far above it through the sunshine of pure delight. He was breathless and giddy with the wonder of her words. They intoxicated him. And, still, the terror of it all, the dreadful thought of death, pressed ever behind her sentences. For flames shot through her voice out of black smoke and licked at his soul.

And they communicated with one another, it seemed to him, by a process of swift telepathy, for his French could never have compassed all he said to her. Yet she understood perfectly, and what she said to him was like the recital of verses long since known. And the mingled pain and sweetness of it as he listened were almost more than his little soul could hold.

"Yet I came here wholly by chance—" he heard himself saying.

"No," she cried with passion, "you came here because I called to you. I have called to you for years, and you came with the whole force of the past behind you. You had to come, for I own you, and I claim you."

She rose again and moved closer, looking at him with a certain insolence in the face—the insolence of power.

The sun had set behind the towers of the old cathedral and the darkness rose up from the plain and enveloped them. The music of the band had ceased. The leaves of the plane trees hung motionless, but the chill of the autumn evening rose about them and made Vezin shiver. There was no sound but the sound of their voices and the occasional soft rustle of the girl's dress. He could hear the blood rushing in his ears. He scarcely realised where he was or what he was doing. Some terrible magic of the imagination drew him deeply down into the tombs of his own being, telling him in no unfaltering voice that her words shadowed forth the truth. And this simple little French maid, speaking beside him with so strange authority, he saw curiously alter into quite another being. As he stared into her eyes, the picture in his mind grew and lived, dressing itself vividly to his inner vision with a degree of reality he was compelled to acknowledge. As once before, he saw her tall and stately, moving through wild and broken scenery of forests and mountain caverns, the glare of flames behind her head and clouds of shifting smoke about her feet. Dark leaves encircled her hair, flying loosely in the wind, and her limbs shone through the merest rags of clothing. Others were about her too, and ardent eyes on all sides cast delirious glances upon her, but her own eyes were always for One only, one whom she held by the hand. For she was leading the dance in some tempestuous orgy to the music of chanting voices, and the dance she led circled about a great and awful Figure on a throne, brooding over the scene through lurid vapours, while innumerable other wild faces and forms crowded furiously about her in the dance. But the one she held by the hand he knew to be himself, and the monstrous shape upon the throne he knew to be her mother.

The vision rose within him, rushing to him down the long years of buried time, crying aloud to him with the voice of memory reawakened. . . . And then the scene faded away and he saw the clear circle of the girl's eyes gazing steadfastly into his own, and she became once more the pretty little daughter of the innkeeper, and he found his voice again.

"And you," he whispered tremblingly—"you child of visions and enchantment, how is it that you so bewitch me that I loved you even before I saw?"

She drew herself up beside him with an air of rare dignity.

"The call of the Past," she said; "and besides," she added proudly, "in the real life I am a princess—"

"A princess!" he cried.

"—and my mother is a queen!"

At this, little Vezin utterly lost his head. Delight tore at his heart and swept him into sheer ecstasy. To hear that sweet singing voice, and to see those adorable little lips utter such things, upset his balance beyond all hope of control. He took her in his arms and covered her unresisting face with kisses.

But even while he did so, and while the hot passion swept him, he felt that she was soft and loathsome, and that her answering kisses stained his very soul. . . . And when, presently, she had freed herself and vanished into the darkness, he stood there, leaning against the wall in a state of collapse, creeping with horror from the touch of her yielding body, and inwardly raging at the weakness that he already dimly realised must prove his undoing.

And from the shadows of the old buildings into which she disappeared there rose in the stillness of the night a singular, long-drawn cry, which at first he took for laughter, but which later he was sure he recognised as the almost human wailing of a cat.

V

For a long time Vezin leant there against the wall, alone with his surging thoughts and emotions. He understood at length that he had done the one thing necessary to call down upon him the whole force of this ancient Past. For in those passionate kisses he had acknowledged the tie of olden days, and had revived it. And the memory of that soft impalpable caress in the darkness of the inn corridor came back to him with a shudder. The girl had first mastered him, and then led him to the one act that was necessary for her purpose. He had been waylaid, after the lapse of centuries—caught, and conquered.

Dimly he realised this, and sought to make plans for his escape. But, for the moment at any rate, he was powerless to manage his thoughts or will, for the sweet, fantastic madness of the whole adventure mounted to his brain like a spell, and he gloried in the feeling that he was utterly enchanted and moving in a world so much larger and wilder than the one he had ever been accustomed to.

The moon, pale and enormous, was just rising over the sea-like plain, when at last he rose to go. Her slanting rays drew all the houses into new perspective, so that their roofs, already glistening with dew, seemed to stretch much higher into the sky than usual, and their gables and quaint old towers lay far away in its purple reaches.

The cathedral appeared unreal in a silver mist. He moved softly, keeping to the shadows; but the streets were all deserted and very silent; the doors were closed, the shutters fastened. Not a soul was astir. The hush of night lay over everything; it was like a town of the dead, a churchyard with gigantic and grotesque tombstones.

Wondering where all the busy life of the day had so utterly disappeared to, he made his way to a back door that entered the inn by means of the stables, thinking thus to reach his room unobserved. He reached the courtyard safely and crossed it by keeping close to the shadow of the wall. He sidled down it, mincing along on tiptoe, just as the old men did when they entered the *salle à manger*. He was horrified to find himself doing this instinctively. A strange impulse came to him, catching him somehow in the centre of his body—an impulse to drop upon all fours and run swiftly and silently. He glanced upwards and the idea came to him to leap up upon his window-sill overhead instead of going round by the stairs. This occurred to him as the easiest, and most natural way. It was like the beginning of some horrible transformation of himself into something else. He was fearfully strung up.

The moon was higher now, and the shadows very dark along the side of the street where he moved. He kept among the deepest of them, and reached the porch with the glass doors.

But here there was light; the inmates, unfortunately, were still about. Hoping to slip across the hall unobserved and reach the stairs, he opened the door carefully and stole in. Then he saw that the hall was not empty. A large dark thing lay against the wall on his left. At first he thought it must be household articles. Then it moved, and he thought it was an immense cat, distorted in some way by the play of light and shadow. Then it rose straight up before him and he saw that it was the proprietress.

What she had been doing in this position he could only venture a dreadful guess, but the moment she stood up and faced him he was aware of some terrible dignity clothing her about that instantly recalled the girl's strange saying that she was a queen. Huge and sinister she stood there under the little oil lamp; alone with him in the empty hall. Awe stirred in his heart, and the roots of some ancient fear. He felt that he must bow to her and make some kind of obeisance. The impulse was fierce and irresistible, as of long habit. He glanced quickly about him. There was no one there. Then he deliberately inclined his head towards her. He bowed.

"Enfin! M'sieur s'est donc décidé. C'est bien alors. J'en suis contente."

Her words came to him sonorously as through a great open space.

Then the great figure came suddenly across the flagged hall at him and seized his trembling hands. Some overpowering force moved with her and caught him.

"On pourrait faire un p'tit tour ensemble, n'est-ce pas? Nous y allons cette nuit et il faut s'exercer un peu d'avance pour cela. Ilsé, Ilsé, viens dans ici. Viens vite!"

And she whirled him round in the opening steps of some dance that seemed oddly and horribly familiar. They made no sound on the stones, this strangely assorted couple. It was all soft and stealthy. And presently, when the air seemed to thicken like smoke, and a red glare as of flame shot through it, he was aware that some one else had joined them and that his hand the mother had released was now tightly held by the daughter. Ilsé had come in answer to the call, and he saw her with leaves of vervain twined in her dark hair, clothed in tattered vestiges of some curious garment, beautiful as the night, and horribly, odiously, loathsomely seductive.

"To the Sabbath! to the Sabbath!" they cried. "On to the Witches' Sabbath!"

Up and down that narrow hall they danced, the women on each side of him, to the wildest measure he had ever imagined, yet which he dimly, dreadfully remembered, till the lamp on the wall flickered and went out, and they were left in total darkness. And the devil woke in his heart with a thousand vile suggestions and made him afraid.

Suddenly they released his hands and he heard the voice of the mother cry that it was time, and they must go. Which way they went he did not pause to see. He only realised that he was free, and he blundered through the darkness till he found the stairs and then tore up them to his room as though all hell was at his heels.

He flung himself on the sofa, with his face in his hands, and groaned. Swiftly reviewing a dozen ways of immediate escape, all equally impossible, he finally decided that the only thing to do for the moment was to sit quiet and wait. He must see what was going to happen. At least in the privacy of his own bedroom he would be fairly safe. The door was locked. He crossed over and softly opened the window which gave upon the courtyard and also permitted a partial view of the hall through the glass doors.

As he did so the hum and murmur of a great activity reached his ears from the streets beyond—the sound of footsteps and voices muffled by distance. He leaned out cautiously and listened. The moonlight was clear and strong now, but his own window was in shadow, the silver disc being still behind the house. It came to him irresistibly that the inhabitants of the town, who a little while before had all been invisible behind closed doors, were now issuing forth, busy upon some secret and unholy errand. He listened intently.

At first everything about him was silent, but soon he became aware of movements going on in the house itself. Rustlings and cheepings came to him across that still, moonlit yard. A concourse of living beings sent the hum of their activity into the night. Things were on the move everywhere. A biting, pungent odour rose through the air, coming he knew not whence. Presently his eyes became glued to the windows of the opposite wall where the moonshine fell in a soft blaze. The roof overhead, and behind him, was reflected clearly in the panes of glass, and he saw the outlines of dark bodies moving with long footsteps over the tiles and along the coping. They passed swiftly and silently, shaped like immense cats, in an endless procession across the pictured glass, and then appeared to leap down to a lower level where he lost sight of them. He just caught the soft thudding of their leaps. Sometimes their shadows fell upon the white wall opposite, and then he could not make out whether they were the shadows of human beings or of cats. They seemed to change swiftly from one to the other. The transformation looked horribly real, for they leaped like human beings, yet changed swiftly in the air immediately afterwards, and dropped like animals.

The yard, too, beneath him, was now alive with the creeping movements of dark forms all stealthily drawing towards the porch with the glass doors. They kept so closely to the wall that he could not determine their actual shape, but when he saw that they passed on to the great congregation that was gathering in the hall, he understood that these were the creatures whose leaping shadows he had first seen reflected in the window-panes opposite. They were coming from all parts of the town, reaching the appointed meeting-place across the roofs and tiles, and springing from level to level till they came to the yard.

Then a new sound caught his ear, and he saw that the windows all about him were being softly opened, and that to each window came a face. A moment later figures began dropping hurriedly down into the yard. And these figures, as they lowered themselves down from the windows, were human, he saw; but once safely in the yard they fell upon all fours and changed in the swiftest possible second into—cats— huge, silent cats. They ran in streams to join the main body in the hall beyond.

So, after all, the rooms in the house had not been empty and unoccupied.

Moreover, what he saw no longer filled him with amazement. For he remembered it all. It was familiar. It had all happened before just so, hundreds of times, and he himself had taken part in it and known the wild madness of it all. The outline of the old building changed, the yard grew larger, and he seemed to be staring down upon it from a much greater height through smoky vapours. And, as he looked, half remembering, the old pains of long ago, fierce and sweet, furiously assailed him, and the blood stirred horribly as he heard the Call of the Dance again in his heart and tasted the ancient magic of Ilsé whirling by his side.

Suddenly he started back. A great lithe cat had leaped softly up from the shadows below on to the sill close to his face, and was staring fixedly at him with the eyes of a human. "Come," it seemed to say, "come with us to the Dance! Change as of old! Transform yourself swiftly and come!" Only too well he understood the creature's soundless call.

It was gone again in a flash with scarcely a sound of its padded feet on the stones, and then others dropped by the score down the side of the house, past his very eyes, all changing as they fell and darting away rapidly, softly, towards the gathering point. And again he felt the dreadful desire to do likewise; to murmur the old incantation, and then drop upon hands and knees and run swiftly for the great flying leap into the air. Oh, how the passion of it rose within him like a flood, twisting his very entrails, sending his heart's desire flaming forth into the night for the old, old Dance of the Sorcerers at the Witches' Sabbath! The whirl of the stars was about him; once more he met the magic of the moon. The power of the wind, rushing from precipice and forest, leaping from cliff to cliff across the valleys, tore him away. . . . He heard the cries of the dancers and their wild laughter, and with this savage girl in his embrace he danced furiously about the dim Throne where sat the Figure with the sceptre of majesty. . . .

Then, suddenly, all became hushed and still, and the fever died down a little in his heart. The calm moonlight flooded a courtyard empty and deserted. They had started. The procession was off into the sky. And he was left behind—alone.

Vezin tiptoed softly across the room and unlocked the door. The murmur from the streets, growing momentarily as he advanced, met his ears. He made his way with the utmost caution down the corridor. At the head of the stairs he paused and listened. Below him, the hall where they had gathered was dark and still, but through opened doors and windows on the far side of the building came the sound of a great throng moving farther and farther into the distance.

He made his way down the creaking wooden stairs, dreading yet longing to meet some straggler who should point the way, but finding no one; across the dark hall, so lately thronged with living, moving things, and out through the opened front doors into the street. He could not believe that he was really left behind, really forgotten, that he had been purposely permitted to escape. It perplexed him.

Nervously he peered about him, and up and down the street; then, seeing nothing, advanced slowly down the pavement.

The whole town, as he went, showed itself empty and deserted, as though a great wind had blown everything alive out of it. The doors and windows of the houses stood open to the night; nothing stirred; moonlight and silence lay over all. The night lay about him like a cloak. The air, soft and cool, caressed his cheek like the touch of a great furry paw. He gained confidence and began to walk quickly, though still keeping to the shadowed side. Nowhere could he discover the faintest sign of the great unholy exodus he knew had just taken place. The moon sailed high over all in a sky, cloudless and serene.

Hardly realising where he was going, he crossed the open market-place and so came to the ramparts, whence he knew a pathway descended to the high road and along which he could make good his escape to one of the other little towns that lay to the northward, and so to the railway.

But first he paused and gazed out over the scene at his feet where the great plain lay like a silver map of some dream country. The still beauty of it entered his heart, increasing his sense of bewilderment and unreality. No air stirred, the leaves of the plane trees stood motionless, the near details were defined with the sharpness of day against dark shadows, and in the distance the fields and woods melted away into haze and shimmering mistiness.

But the breath caught in his throat and he stood stockstill as though transfixed when his gaze passed from the horizon and fell upon the near prospect in the depth of the valley at his feet. The whole lower slopes of the hill, that lay hid from the brightness of the moon, were aglow, and through the glare he saw countless moving forms, shifting thick and fast between the openings of the trees; while overhead, like leaves driven by the wind, he discerned flying shapes that hovered darkly one moment against the sky and then settled down with cries and weird singing through the branches into the region that was aflame.

Spellbound, he stood and stared for a time that he could not measure. And then, moved by one of the terrible impulses that seemed to control the whole adventure, he climbed swiftly upon the top of the broad coping, and balanced a moment where the valley gaped at his feet. But in that very instant, as he stood hovering, a sudden movement among the shadows of the houses caught his eye, and he turned to see the outline of a large animal dart swiftly across the open space behind him, and land with a flying leap upon the top of the wall a little lower down. It ran like the wind to his feet and then rose up beside him upon the ramparts. A shiver seemed to run through the moonlight, and his sight trembled for a second. His heart pulsed fearfully. Ilsé stood beside him, peering into his face.

Some dark substance, he saw, stained the girl's face and skin, shining in the moonlight as she stretched her hands towards him; she was dressed in wretched tattered garments that yet became her mightily; rue and vervain twined about her temples; her eyes glittered with unholy light. He only just controlled the wild impulse to take her in his arms and leap with her from their giddy perch into the valley below.

"See!" she cried, pointing with an arm on which the rags fluttered in the rising wind towards the forest aglow in the distance. "See where they await us! The woods are alive! Already the Great Ones are there, and the dance will soon begin! The salve is here! Anoint yourself and come!"

Though a moment before the sky was clear and cloudless, yet even while she spoke the face of the moon grew dark and the wind began to toss in the crests of the plane trees at his feet. Stray gusts brought the sounds of hoarse singing and crying from the lower slopes of the hill, and the pungent odour he had already noticed about the courtyard of the inn rose about him in the air.

"Transform, transform!" she cried again, her voice rising like a song. "Rub well your skin before you fly. Come! Come with me to the Sabbath, to the madness of its furious delight, to the sweet abandonment of its evil worship! See! the Great Ones are there, and the terrible Sacraments prepared. The Throne is occupied. Anoint and come! Anoint and come!"

She grew to the height of a tree beside him, leaping upon the wall with flaming eyes and hair strewn upon the night. He too began to change swiftly. Her hands touched the skin of his face and neck, streaking him with the burning salve that sent the old magic into his blood with the power before which fades all that is good.

A wild roar came up to his ears from the heart of the wood, and the girl, when she heard it, leaped upon the wall in the frenzy of her wicked joy.

"Satan is there!" she screamed, rushing upon him and striving to draw him with her to the edge of the wall. "Satan has come! The Sacraments call us! Come, with your dear apostate soul, and we will worship and dance till the moon dies and the world is forgotten!"

Just saving himself from the dreadful plunge, Vezin struggled to release himself from her grasp, while the passion tore at his reins and all but mastered him. He shrieked aloud, not knowing what he said, and then he shrieked again. It was the old impulses, the old awful habits instinctively finding voice; for though it seemed to him that he merely shrieked nonsense, the words he uttered really had meaning in them, and were intelligible. It was the ancient call. And it was heard below. It was answered.

The wind whistled at the skirts of his coat as the air round him darkened with many flying forms crowding upwards out of the valley. The crying of hoarse voices smote upon his ears, coming closer. Strokes of wind buffeted him, tearing him this way and that along the crumbling top of the stone wall; and Ilsé clung to him with her long shining arms, smooth and bare, holding him fast about the neck. But not Ilsé alone, for a dozen of them surrounded him, dropping out of the air. The pungent odour of the anointed bodies stifled him, exciting him to the old madness of the Sabbath, the dance of the witches and sorcerers doing honour to the personified Evil of the world.

"Anoint and away! Anoint and away!" they cried in wild chorus about him. "To the Dance that never dies! To the sweet and fearful fantasy of evil!"

Another moment and he would have yielded—and gone, for his will turned soft and the flood of passionate memory all but overwhelmed him, when—so can a small thing after the whole course of an adventure—he caught his foot upon a loose stone in the edge of the wall, and then fell with a sudden crash onto the ground below. But he fell towards the houses, in the open space of dust and cobble stones, and fortunately not into the gaping depth of the valley on the farther side.

And they, too, came in a tumbling heap about him, like flies upon a piece of food, but as they fell he was released for a moment from the power of their touch, and in that brief instant of freedom there flashed into his mind the sudden intuition that saved him. Before he could regain his feet he saw them scrabbling awkwardly back upon the wall, as though bat-like they could only fly by dropping from a height, and had no hold upon him in the open. Then, seeing them perched there in a row like cats upon a roof, all dark and singularly shapeless, their eyes like lamps, the sudden memory came back to him of Ilsé's terror at the sight of fire.

Quick as a flash he found his matches and lit the dead leaves that lay under the wall.

Dry and withered, they caught fire at once, and the wind carried the flame in a long line down the length of the wall, licking upwards as it ran; and with shrieks and wailings, the crowded row of forms upon the top melted away into the air on the other side, and were gone with a great rush and whirring of their bodies down into the heart of the haunted valley, leaving Vezin breathless and shaken in the middle of the deserted ground.

"Ilsé!" he called feebly; "Ilsé!" for his heart ached to think that she was really gone to the great Dance without him, and that he had lost the opportunity of its fearful joy. Yet at the same time his relief was so great, and he was so dazed and troubled in mind with the whole thing, that he hardly knew what he was saying, and only cried aloud in the fierce storm of his emotion. . . .

The fire under the wall ran its course, and the moonlight came out again, soft and clear, from its temporary eclipse. With one last shuddering look at the ruined ramparts, and a feeling of horrid wonder for the haunted valley beyond, where the shapes still crowded and flew, he turned his face towards the town and slowly made his way in the direction of the hotel.

And as he went, a great wailing of cries, and a sound of howling, followed him from the gleaming forest below, growing fainter and fainter with the bursts of wind as he disappeared between the houses.

VI

"It may seem rather abrupt to you, this sudden tame ending," said Arthur Vezin, glancing with flushed face and timid eyes at Dr. Silence sitting there with his notebook, "but the fact is—er—from that moment my memory seems to have failed rather. I have no distinct recollection of how I got home or what precisely I did.

"It appears I never went back to the inn at all. I only dimly recollect racing down a long white road in the moonlight, past woods and villages, still and deserted, and then the dawn came up, and I saw the towers of a biggish town and so came to a station.

"But, long before that, I remember pausing somewhere on the road and looking back to where the hill-town of my adventure stood up in the moonlight, and thinking how exactly like a great monstrous cat it lay there upon the plain, its huge front paws lying down the two main streets, and the twin and broken towers of the cathedral marking its torn ears against the sky. That picture stays in my mind with the utmost vividness to this day.

"Another thing remains in my mind from that escape—namely, the sudden sharp reminder that I had not paid my bill, and the decision I made, standing there on the dusty highroad, that the small baggage I had left behind would more than settle for my indebtedness.

"For the rest, I can only tell you that I got coffee and bread at a café on the outskirts of this town I had come to, and soon after found my way to the station and caught a train later in the day. That same evening I reached London."

"And how long altogether," asked John Silence quietly, "do you think you stayed in the town of the adventure?"

Vezin looked up sheepishly.

"I was coming to that," he resumed, with apologetic wrigglings of his body. "In London I found that I was a whole week out in my reckoning of time. I had stayed over a week in the town, and it ought to have been September 15th,—instead of which it was only September 10th!"

"So that, in reality, you had only stayed a night or two in the inn?" queried the doctor.

Vezin hesitated before replying. He shuffled upon the mat.

"I must have gained time somewhere," he said at length—

"somewhere or somehow. I certainly had a week to my credit. I can't explain it. I can only give you the fact."

"And this happened to you last year, since when you have never been back to the place?"

"Last autumn, yes," murmured Vezin; "and I have never dared to go back. I think I never want to."

"And, tell me," asked Dr. Silence at length, when he saw that the little man had evidently come to the end of his words and had nothing more to say, "had you ever read up the subject of the old witchcraft practices during the Middle Ages, or been at all interested in the subject?"

"Never!" declared Vezin emphatically. "I had never given a thought to such matters so far as I know—"

"Or to the question of reincarnation, perhaps?"

"Never—before my adventure; but I have since," he replied significantly.

There was, however, something still on the man's mind that he wished to relieve himself of by confession, yet could only with difficulty bring himself to mention; and it was only after the sympathetic tactfulness of the doctor had provided numerous openings that he at length availed himself of one of them, and stammered that he would like to show him the marks he still had on his neck where, he said, the girl had touched him with her anointed hands.

He took off his collar after infinite fumbling hesitation, and lowered his shirt a little for the doctor to see. And there, on the surface of the skin, lay a faint reddish line across the shoulder and extending a little way down the back towards the spine. It certainly indicated exactly the position an arm might have taken in the act of embracing. And on the other side of the neck, slightly higher up, was a similar mark, though not quite so clearly defined.

"That was where she held me that night on the ramparts," he whispered, a strange light coming and going in his eyes.

It was some weeks later when I again found occasion to consult John Silence concerning another extraordinary case that had come under my notice, and we fell to discussing Vezin's story. Since hearing it, the doctor had made investigations on his own account, and one of his secretaries had discovered that Vezin's ancestors had actually lived for generations in the very town where the adventure came to him. Two of them, both women, had been tried and convicted as witches, and had been burned alive at the stake. Moreover, it had not been difficult to prove that the very inn where Vezin stayed was built about 1700 upon the spot where the funeral pyres stood and the executions took place. The town was a sort of headquarters for all the sorcerers and witches of the entire region, and after conviction they were burnt there literally by scores.

"It seems strange," continued the doctor, "that Vezin should have remained ignorant of all this; but, on the other hand, it was not the kind of history that successive generations would have been anxious to keep alive, or to repeat to their children. Therefore I am inclined to think he still knows nothing about it.

"The whole adventure seems to have been a very vivid revival of the memories of an earlier life, caused by coming directly into contact with the living forces still intense enough to hang about the place, and, by a most singular chance too, with the very souls who had taken part with him in the events of that particular life. For the mother and daughter who impressed him so strangely must have been leading actors, with himself, in the scenes and practices of witchcraft which at that period dominated the imaginations of the whole country.

"One has only to read the histories of the times to know that these witches claimed the power of transforming themselves into various animals, both for the purposes of disguise and also to convey themselves swiftly to the scenes of their imaginary orgies. Lycanthropy, or the power to change themselves into wolves, was everywhere believed in, and the ability to transform themselves into cats by rubbing their bodies with a special salve or ointment provided by Satan himself, found equal credence. The witchcraft trials abound in evidences of such universal beliefs."

Dr. Silence quoted chapter and verse from many writers on the subject, and showed how every detail of Vezin's adventure had a basis in the practices of those dark days.

"But that the entire affair took place subjectively in the man's own consciousness, I have no doubt," he went on, in reply to my questions; "for my secretary who has been to the town to investigate, discovered his signature in the visitors' book, and proved by it that he had arrived on September 8th, and left suddenly without paying his bill. He left two days later, and they still were in possession of his dirty brown bag and some tourist clothes. I paid a few francs in settlement of his debt, and have sent his luggage on to him. The daughter was absent from home, but the proprietress, a large woman very much as he described her, told my secretary that he had seemed a very strange, absent-minded kind of gentleman, and after his disappearance she had feared for a long time that he had met with a violent end in the neighbouring forest where he used to roam about alone.

"I should like to have obtained a personal interview with the daughter so as to ascertain how much was subjective and how much actually took place with her as Vezin told it. For her dread of fire and the sight of burning must, of course, have been the intuitive memory of her former painful death at the stake, and have thus explained why he fancied more than once that he saw her through smoke and flame."

"And that mark on his skin, for instance?" I enquired.

"Merely the marks produced by hysterical brooding," he replied, "like the stigmata of the *religieuses,* and the bruises which appear on the bodies of hypnotised subjects who have been told to expect them. This is very common and easily explained. Only it seems curious that these marks should have remained so long in Vezin's case. Usually they disappear quickly."

"Obviously he is still thinking about it all, brooding, and living it all over again," I ventured.

"Probably. And this makes me fear that the end of his trouble is not yet. We shall hear of him again. It is a case, alas! I can do little to alleviate."

Dr. Silence spoke gravely and with sadness in his voice.

"And what do you make of the Frenchman in the train?" I asked further—"the man who warned him against the place, *à cause du sommeil et à cause des chats?* Surely a very singular incident?"

"A *very* singular incident indeed," he made answer slowly, "and one I can only explain on the basis of a highly improbable coincidence—"

"Namely?"

"That the man was one who had himself stayed in the town and undergone there a similar experience. I should like to find this man and ask him. But the crystal is useless here, for I have no slightest clue to go upon, and I can only conclude that some singular psychic affinity, some force still active in his being out of the same past life, drew him thus to the personality of Vezin, and enabled him to fear what might happen to him, and thus to warn him as he did.

"Yes," he presently continued, half talking to himself, "I suspect in this case that Vezin was swept into the vortex of forces arising out of the intense activities of a past life, and that he lived over again a scene in which he had often played a leading part centuries before. For strong actions set up forces that are so slow to exhaust themselves, they may be said in a sense never to die. In this case they were not vital enough to render the illusion complete, so that the little man found himself caught in a very distressing confusion of the present and the past; yet he was sufficiently sensitive to recognise that it was true, and to fight against the degradation of returning, even in memory, to a former and lower state of development.

"Ah yes!" he continued, crossing the floor to gaze at the darkening sky, and seemingly quite oblivious of my presence, "subliminal up-rushes of memory like this can be exceedingly painful, and sometimes exceedingly dangerous. I only trust that this gentle soul may soon escape from this obsession of a passionate and tempestuous past. But I doubt it, I doubt it."

His voice was hushed with sadness as he spoke, and when he turned back into the room again there was an expression of profound yearning upon his face, the yearning of a soul whose desire to help is sometimes greater than his power.

The Nemesis of Fire

I

By some means which I never could fathom, John Silence always contrived to keep the compartment to himself, and as the train had a clear run of two hours before the first stop, there was ample time to go over the preliminary facts of the case. He had telephoned to me that very morning, and even through the disguise of the miles of wire the thrill of incalculable adventure had sounded in his voice.

"As if it were an ordinary country visit," he called, in reply to my question; "and don't forget to bring your gun."

"With blank cartridges, I suppose?" for I knew his rigid principles with regard to the taking of life, and guessed that the guns were merely for some obvious purpose of disguise.

Then he thanked me for coming, mentioned the train, snapped down the receiver, and left me vibrating with the excitement of anticipation to do my packing. For the honour of accompanying Dr. John Silence on one of his big cases was what many would have considered an empty honour—and risky. Certainly the adventure held all manner of possibilities, and I arrived at Waterloo with the feelings of a man who is about to embark on some dangerous and peculiar mission in which the dangers he expects to run will not be the ordinary dangers to life and limb, but of some secret character difficult to name and still more difficult to cope with.

"The Manor House has a high sound," he told me, as we sat with our feet up and talked, "but I believe it is little more than an overgrown farmhouse in the desolate heather country beyond D———, and its owner, Colonel Wragge, a retired soldier with a taste for books, lives there practically alone, I understand, with an elderly invalid sister. So you need not look forward to a lively visit, unless the case provides some excitement of its own."

"Which is likely?"

By way of reply he handed me a letter marked "Private." It was dated a week ago, and signed "Yours faithfully, Horace Wragge."

"He heard of me, you see, through Captain Anderson," the doctor explained modestly, as though his fame were not almost world-wide; "you remember that Indian obsession case—"

I read the letter. Why it should have been marked private was difficult to understand. It was very brief, direct, and to the point. It referred by way of introduction to Captain Anderson, and then stated quite simply that the writer needed help of a peculiar kind and asked for a personal interview—a morning interview, since it was impossible for him to be absent from the house at night. The letter was dignified even to the point of abruptness, and it is difficult to explain how it managed to convey to me the impression of a strong man, shaken and perplexed. Perhaps the restraint of the wording, and the mystery of the affair had something to do with it; and the reference to the Anderson case, the horror of which lay still vivid in my memory, may have touched the sense of something rather ominous and alarming. But, whatever the cause, there was no doubt that an impression of serious peril rose somehow out of that white paper with the few lines of firm writing, and the spirit of a deep uneasiness ran between the words and reached the mind without any visible form of expression.

"And when you saw him—?" I asked, returning the letter as the train rushed clattering noisily through Clapham Junction.

"I have not seen him," was the reply. "The man's mind was charged to the brim when he wrote that; full of vivid mental pictures. Notice the restraint of it. For the main character of his case psychometry could be depended upon, and the scrap of paper his hand has touched is sufficient to give to another mind—a sensitive and sympathetic mind—clear mental pictures of what is going on. I think I have a very sound general idea of his problem."

"So there may be excitement after all?"

John Silence waited a moment before he replied.

"Something very serious is amiss there," he said gravely, at length. "Some one—not himself, I gather,—has been meddling with a rather dangerous kind of gunpowder. So—yes, there may be excitement, as you put it."

"And my duties?" I asked, with a decidedly growing interest. "Remember, I am your 'assistant.'"

"Behave like an intelligent confidential secretary. Observe everything, without seeming to. Say nothing—nothing that means anything. Be present at all interviews. I may ask a good deal of you, for if my impressions are correct this is—"

He broke off suddenly.

"But I won't tell you my impressions yet," he resumed after a moment's thought. "Just watch and listen as the case proceeds. Form your own impressions and cultivate your intuitions. We come as ordinary visitors, of course," he added, a twinkle showing for an instant in his eye; "hence, the guns."

Though disappointed not to hear more, I recognised the wisdom of his words and knew how valueless my impressions would be once the powerful suggestion of having heard his own lay behind them. I likewise reflected that intuition joined to a sense of humour was of more use to a man than double the quantity of mere "brains," as such.

Before putting the letter away, however, he handed it back, telling me to place it against my forehead for a few moments and then describe any pictures that came spontaneously into my mind.

"Don't deliberately look for anything. Just imagine you see the inside of the eyelid, and wait for pictures that rise against its dark screen."

I followed his instructions, making my mind as nearly a blank as possible. But no visions came. I saw nothing but the lines of light that pass to and fro like the changes of a kaleidoscope across the blackness. A momentary sensation of warmth came and went curiously.

"You see—what?" he asked presently.

"Nothing," I was obliged to admit disappointedly; "nothing but the usual flashes of light one always sees. Only, perhaps, they are more vivid than usual."

He said nothing by way of comment or reply.

"And they group themselves now and then," I continued, with painful candour, for I longed to see the pictures he had spoken of, "group themselves into globes and round balls of fire, and the lines that flash about sometimes look like triangles and crosses—almost like geometrical figures. Nothing more."

I opened my eyes again, and gave him back the letter.

"It makes my head hot," I said, feeling somehow unworthy for not seeing anything of interest. But the look in his eyes arrested my attention at once.

"That sensation of heat is important," he said significantly.

"It was certainly real, and rather uncomfortable," I replied, hoping he would expand and explain. "There was a distinct feeling of warmth—internal warmth somewhere—oppressive in a sense."

"That is interesting," he remarked, putting the letter back in his pocket, and settling himself in the corner with newspapers and books. He vouchsafed nothing more, and I knew the uselessness of trying to make him talk. Following his example I settled likewise with magazines into my corner. But when I closed my eyes again to look for the flashing lights and the sensation of heat, I found nothing but the usual phantasmagoria of the day's events—faces, scenes, memories,—and in due course I fell asleep and then saw nothing at all of any kind.

When we left the train, after six hours' travelling, at a little wayside station standing without trees in a world of sand and heather, the late October shadows had already dropped their sombre veil upon the landscape, and the sun dipped almost out of sight behind the moorland hills. In a high dogcart, behind a fast horse, we were soon rattling across the undulating stretches of an open and bleak country, the keen air stinging our cheeks and the scents of pine and bracken strong about us. Bare hills were faintly visible against the horizon, and the coachman pointed to a bank of distant shadows on our left where he told us the sea lay. Occasional stone farmhouses, standing back from the road among straggling fir trees, and large black barns that seemed to shift past us with a movement of their own in the gloom, were the only signs of humanity and civilisation that we saw, until at the end of a bracing five miles the lights of the lodge gates flared before us and we plunged into a thick grove of pine trees that concealed the Manor House up to the moment of actual arrival.

Colonel Wragge himself met us in the hall. He was the typical army officer who had seen service, real service, and found himself in the process. He was tall and well built, broad in the shoulders, but lean as a greyhound, with grave eyes, rather stern, and a moustache turning grey. I judged him to be about sixty years of age, but his movements showed a suppleness of strength and agility that contradicted the years. The face was full of character and resolution, the face of a man to be depended upon, and the straight grey eyes, it seemed to me, wore a veil of perplexed anxiety that he made no attempt to disguise. The whole appearance of the man at once clothed the adventure with gravity and importance. A matter that gave such a man cause for serious alarm, I felt, must be something real and of genuine moment.

His speech and manner, as he welcomed us, were like his letter, simple and sincere. He had a nature as direct and undeviating as a bullet. Thus, he showed plainly his surprise that Dr. Silence had not come alone.

"My confidential secretary, Mr. Hubbard," the doctor said, introducing me, and the steady gaze and powerful shake of the hand I then received were well calculated, I remember thinking, to drive home the impression that here was a man who was not to be trifled with, and whose perplexity must spring from some very real and tangible cause. And, quite obviously, he was relieved that we had come. His welcome was unmistakably genuine.

He led us at once into a room, half library, half smoking-room, that opened out of the low-ceilinged hall. The Manor House gave the impression of a rambling and glorified farmhouse, solid, ancient, comfortable, and wholly unpretentious. And so it was. Only the heat of the place struck me as unnatural. This room with the blazing fire may have seemed uncomfortably warm after the long drive through the night air; yet it seemed to me that the hall itself, and the whole atmosphere of the house, breathed a warmth that hardly belonged to well-filled grates or the pipes of hot air and water. It was not the heat of the greenhouse; it was an oppressive heat that somehow got into the head and mind. It stirred a curious sense of uneasiness in me, and I caught myself thinking of the sensation of warmth that had emanated from the letter in the train.

I heard him thanking Dr. Silence for having come; there was no preamble, and the exchange of civilities was of the briefest description. Evidently here was a man who, like my companion, loved action rather than talk. His manner was straightforward and direct. I saw him in a flash: puzzled, worried, harassed into a state of alarm by something he could not comprehend; forced to deal with things he would have preferred to despise, yet facing it all with dogged seriousness and making no attempt to conceal that he felt secretly ashamed of his incompetence.

"So I cannot offer you much entertainment beyond that of my own company, and the queer business that has been going on here, and is still going on," he said, with a slight inclination of the head towards me by way of including me in his confidence.

"I think, Colonel Wragge," replied John Silence impressively, "that we shall none of us find the time hang heavy. I gather we shall have our hands full."

The two men looked at one another for the space of some seconds, and there was an indefinable quality in their silence which for the first time made me admit a swift question into my mind; and I wondered a little at my rashness in coming with so little reflection into a big case of this incalculable doctor. But no answer suggested itself, and to withdraw was, of course, inconceivable. The gates had closed behind me now, and the spirit of the adventure was already besieging my mind with its advance guard of a thousand little hopes and fears.

Explaining that he would wait till after dinner to discuss anything serious, as no reference was ever made before his sister, he led the way upstairs and showed us personally to our rooms; and it was just as I was finishing dressing that a knock came at my door and Dr. Silence entered.

He was always what is called a serious man, so that even in moments of comedy you felt he never lost sight of the profound gravity of life, but as he came across the room to me I caught the expression of his face and understood in a flash that he was now in his most grave and earnest mood. He looked almost troubled. I stopped fumbling with my black tie and stared.

"It *is* serious," he said, speaking in a low voice, "more so even than I imagined. Colonel Wragge's control over his thoughts concealed a great deal in my psychometrising of the letter. I looked in to warn you to keep yourself well in hand—generally speaking."

"Haunted house?" I asked, conscious of a distinct shiver down my back.

But he smiled gravely at the question.

"Haunted House of Life more likely," he replied, and a look came into his eyes which I had only seen there when a human soul was in the toils and he was thick in the fight of rescue. He was stirred in the deeps.

"Colonel Wragge—or the sister?" I asked hurriedly, for the gong was sounding.

"Neither directly," he said from the door. "Something far older, something very, very remote indeed. This thing has to do with the ages, unless I am mistaken greatly, the ages on which the mists of memory have long lain undisturbed."

He came across the floor very quickly with a finger on his lips, looking at me with a peculiar searchingness of gaze.

"Are you aware yet of anything—odd here?" he asked in a whisper. "Anything you cannot quite define, for instance. Tell me, Hubbard, for I want to know all your impressions. They may help me."

I shook my head, avoiding his gaze, for there was something in the eyes that scared me a little. But he was so in earnest that I set my mind keenly searching.

"Nothing yet," I replied truthfully, wishing I could confess to a real emotion; "nothing but the strange heat of the place."

He gave a little jump forward in my direction.

"The heat again, that's it!" he exclaimed, as though glad of my corroboration. "And how would you describe it, perhaps?" he asked quickly, with a hand on the door knob.

"It doesn't seem like ordinary physical heat," I said, casting about in my thoughts for a definition.

"More a mental heat," he interrupted, "a glowing of thought and desire, a sort of feverish warmth of the spirit. Isn't that it?"

I admitted that he had exactly described my sensations.

"Good!" he said, as he opened the door, and with an indescribable gesture that combined a warning to be ready with a sign of praise for my correct intuition, he was gone.

I hurried after him, and found the two men waiting for me in front of the fire.

"I ought to warn you," our host was saying as I came in, "that my sister, whom you will meet at dinner, is not aware of the real object of your visit. She is under the impression that we are interested in the same line of study—folklore—and that your researches have led to my seeking acquaintance. She comes to dinner in her chair, you know. It will be a great pleasure to her to meet you both. We have few visitors."

So that on entering the dining-room we were prepared to find Miss Wragge already at her place, seated in a sort of bath-chair. She was a vivacious and charming old lady, with smiling expression and bright eyes, and she chatted all through dinner with unfailing spontaneity. She had that face, unlined and fresh, that some people carry through life from the cradle to the grave; her smooth plump cheeks were all pink and white, and her hair, still dark, was divided into two glossy and sleek halves on either side of a careful parting. She wore gold-rimmed glasses, and at her throat was a large scarab of green jasper that made a very handsome brooch.

Her brother and Dr. Silence talked little, so that most of the conversation was carried on between herself and me, and she told me a great deal about the history of the old house, most of which I fear I listened to with but half an ear.

"And when Cromwell stayed here," she babbled on, "he occupied the very rooms upstairs that used to be mine. But my brother thinks it safer for me to sleep on the ground floor now in case of fire."

And this sentence has stayed in my memory only because of the sudden way her brother interrupted her and instantly led the conversation on to another topic. The passing reference to fire seemed to have disturbed him, and thenceforward he directed the talk himself.

It was difficult to believe that this lively and animated old lady, sitting beside me and taking so eager an interest in the affairs of life, was practically, we understood, without the use of her lower limbs, and that her whole existence for years had been passed between the sofa, the bed, and the bath-chair in which she chatted so naturally at the dinner-table. She made no allusion to her affliction until the dessert was reached, and then, touching a bell, she made us a witty little speech about leaving us "like time, on noiseless feet," and was wheeled out of the room by the butler and carried off to her apartments at the other end of the house.

And the rest of us were not long in following suit, for Dr. Silence and myself were quite as eager to learn the nature of our errand as our host was to impart it to us. He led us down a long flagged passage to a room at the very end of the house, a room provided with double doors, and windows, I saw, heavily shuttered. Books lined the walls on every side, and a large desk in the bow window was piled up with volumes, some open, some shut, some showing scraps of paper stuck between the leaves, and all smothered in a general cataract of untidy foolscap and loose half sheets.

"My study and workroom," explained Colonel Wragge, with a delightful touch of innocent pride, as though he were a very serious scholar. He placed arm-chairs for us round the fire. "Here," he added significantly, "we shall be safe from interruption and can talk securely."

During dinner the manner of the doctor had been all that was natural and spontaneous, though it was impossible for me, knowing him as I did, not to be aware that he was subconsciously very keenly alert and already receiving upon the ultra-sensitive surface of his mind various and vivid impressions; and there was now something in the gravity of his face, as well as in the significant tone of Colonel Wragge's speech, and something, too, in the fact that we three were shut away in this private chamber about to listen to things probably strange, and certainly mysterious—something in all this that touched my imagination sharply and sent an undeniable thrill along my nerves. Taking the chair indicated by my host, I lit my cigar and waited for the opening of the attack, fully conscious that we were now too far gone in the adventure to admit of withdrawal, and wondering a little anxiously where it was going to lead.

What I expected precisely, it is hard to say. Nothing definite, perhaps. Only the sudden change was dramatic. A few hours before the prosaic atmosphere of Piccadilly was about me, and now I was sitting in a secret chamber of this remote old building waiting to hear an account of things that held possibly the genuine heart of terror. I thought of the dreary moors and hills outside, and the dark pine copses soughing in the wind of night; I remembered my companion's singular words up in my bedroom before dinner; and then I turned and noted carefully the stern countenance of the Colonel as he faced us and lit his big black cigar before speaking.

The threshold of an adventure, I reflected as I waited for the first words, is always the most thrilling moment—until the climax comes.

But Colonel Wragge hesitated—mentally—a long time before he began. He talked briefly of our journey, the weather, the country, and other comparatively trivial topics, while he sought about in his mind for an appropriate entry into the subject that was uppermost in the thoughts of all of us. The fact was he found it a difficult matter to speak of at all, and it was Dr. Silence who finally showed him the way over the hedge.

"Mr Hubbard will take a few notes when you are ready—you won't object," he suggested; "I can give my undivided attention in this way."

"By all means," turning to reach some of the loose sheets on the writing table, and glancing at me. He still hesitated a little, I thought. "The fact is," he said apologetically, "I wondered if it was quite fair to trouble you so soon. The daylight might suit you better to hear what I have to tell. Your sleep, I mean, might be less disturbed, perhaps."

"I appreciate your thoughtfulness," John Silence replied with his gentle smile, taking command as it were from that moment, "but really we are both quite immune. There is nothing, I think, that could prevent either of us sleeping, except—an outbreak of fire, or some such very physical disturbance."

Colonel Wragge raised his eyes and looked fixedly at him. This reference to an outbreak of fire I felt sure was made with a purpose. It certainly had the desired effect of removing from our host's manner the last signs of hesitancy.

"Forgive me," he said. "Of course, I know nothing of your methods in matters of this kind—so, perhaps, you would like me to begin at once and give you an outline of the situation?"

Dr. Silence bowed his agreement. "I can then take my precautions accordingly," he added calmly.

The soldier looked up for a moment as though he did not quite gather the meaning of these words; but he made no further comment and turned at once to tackle a subject on which he evidently talked with diffidence and unwillingness.

"It's all so utterly out of my line of things," he began, puffing out clouds of cigar smoke between his words, "and there's so little to tell with any real evidence behind it, that it's almost impossible to make a consecutive story for you. It's the total cumulative effect that is so—so disquieting." He chose his words with care, as though determined not to travel one hair's breadth beyond the truth.

"I came into this place twenty years ago when my elder brother died," he continued, "but could not afford to live here then. My sister, whom you met at dinner, kept house for him till the end, and during all these years, while I was seeing service abroad, she had an eye to the place—for we never got a satisfactory tenant—and saw that it was not allowed to go to ruin. I myself took possession, however, only a year ago.

"My brother," he went on, after a perceptible pause, "spent much of his time away, too. He was a great traveller, and filled the house with stuff he brought home from all over the world. The laundry—a small detached building beyond the servants' quarters—he turned into a regular little museum. The curios and things I have cleared away—they collected dust and were always getting broken—but the laundry-house you shall see to-morrow."

Colonel Wragge spoke with such deliberation and with so many pauses that this beginning took him a long time. But at this point he came to a full stop altogether. Evidently there was something he wished to say that cost him considerable effort. At length he looked up steadily into my companion's face.

"May I ask you—that is, if you won't think it strange," he said, and a sort of hush came over his voice and manner, "whether you have noticed anything at all unusual—anything queer, since you came into the house?"

Dr. Silence answered without a moment's hesitation.

"I have," he said. "There is a curious sensation of heat in the place."

"Ah!" exclaimed the other, with a slight start. "You *have* noticed it. This unaccountable heat—"

"But its cause, I gather, is not in the house itself—but outside," I was astonished to hear the doctor add.

Colonel Wragge rose from his chair and turned to unhook a framed map that hung upon the wall. I got the impression that the movement was made with the deliberate purpose of concealing his face.

"Your diagnosis, I believe, is amazingly accurate," he said after a moment, turning round with the map in his hands. "Though, of course, I can have no idea how you should guess—"

John Silence shrugged his shoulders expressively. "Merely my impression," he said. "If you pay attention to impressions, and do not allow them to be confused by deductions of the intellect, you will often find them surprisingly, uncannily, accurate."

Colonel Wragge resumed his seat and laid the map upon his knees. His face was very thoughtful as he plunged abruptly again into his story.

"On coming into possession," he said, looking us alternately in the face, "I found a crop of stories of the most extraordinary and impossible kind I had ever heard—stories which at first I treated with amused indifference, but later was forced to regard seriously, if only to keep my servants. These stories I thought I traced to the fact of my brother's death—and, in a way, I think so still."

He leant forward and handed the map to Dr. Silence.

"It's an old plan of the estate," he explained, "but accurate enough for our purpose, and I wish you would note the position of the plantations marked upon it, especially those near the house. That one," indicating the spot with his finger, "is called the Twelve Acre Plantation. It was just there, on the side nearest the house, that my brother and the head keeper met their deaths."

He spoke as a man forced to recognise facts that he deplored, and would have preferred to leave untouched—things he personally would rather have treated with ridicule if possible. It made his words peculiarly dignified and impressive, and I listened with an increasing uneasiness as to the sort of help the doctor would look to me for later. It seemed as though I were a spectator of some drama of mystery in which any moment I might be summoned to play a part.

"It was twenty years ago," continued the Colonel, "but there was much talk about it at the time, unfortunately, and you may, perhaps, have heard of the affair. Stride, the keeper, was a passionate, hot-tempered man, but I regret to say, so was my brother, and quarrels between them seem to have been frequent."

"I do not recall the affair," said the doctor. "May I ask what was the cause of death?" Something in his voice made me prick up my ears for the reply.

"The keeper, it was said, from suffocation. And at the inquest the doctors averred that both men had been dead the same length of time when found."

"And your brother?" asked John Silence, noticing the omission, and listening intently.

"Equally mysterious," said our host, speaking in a low voice with effort. "But there was one distressing feature I think I ought to mention. For those who saw the face—I did not see it myself—and though Stride carried a gun its chambers were undischarged—" He stammered and hesitated with confusion. Again that sense of terror moved between his words. He stuck.

"Yes," said the chief listener sympathetically.

"My brother's face, they said, looked as though it had been scorched. It had been swept, as it were, by something that burned—blasted. It was, I am told, quite dreadful. The bodies were found lying side by side, faces downwards, both pointing away from the wood, as though they had been in the act of running, and not more than a dozen yards from its edge."

Dr. Silence made no comment. He appeared to be studying the map attentively.

"I did not see the face myself," repeated the other, his manner somehow expressing the sense of awe he contrived to keep out of his voice, "but my sister unfortunately did, and her present state I believe to be entirely due to the shock it gave to her nerves. She never can be brought to refer to it, naturally, and I am even inclined to think that the memory has mercifully been permitted to vanish from her mind. But she spoke of it at the time as a face swept by flame—blasted."

John Silence looked up from his contemplation of the map, but with the air of one who wished to listen, not to speak, and presently Colonel Wragge went on with his account. He stood on the mat, his broad shoulders hiding most of the mantelpiece.

"They all centred about this particular plantation, these stories. That was to be expected, for the people here are as superstitious as Irish peasantry, and though I made one or two examples among them to stop the foolish talk, it had no effect, and new versions came to my ears every week. You may imagine how little good dismissals did, when I tell you that the servants dismissed themselves. It was not the house servants, but the men who worked on the estate outside. The keepers gave notice one after another, none of them with any reason I could accept; the foresters refused to enter the wood, and the beaters to beat in it. Word flew all over the countryside that Twelve Acre Plantation was a place to be avoided, day or night.

"There came a point," the Colonel went on, now well in his swing, "when I felt compelled to make investigations on my own account. I could not kill the thing by ignoring it; so I collected and analysed the stories at first hand. For this Twelve Acre Wood, you will see by the map, comes rather near home. Its lower end, if you will look, almost touches the end of the back lawn, as I will show you to-morrow, and its dense growth of pines forms the chief protection the house enjoys from the east winds that blow up from the sea. And in olden days, before my brother interfered with it and frightened all the game away, it was one of the best pheasant coverts on the whole estate."

"And what form, if I may ask, did this interference take?" asked Dr. Silence.

"In detail, I cannot tell you, for I do not know—except that I understand it was the subject of his frequent differences with the head keeper; but during the last two years of his life, when he gave up travelling and settled down here, he took a special interest in this wood, and for some unaccountable reason began to build a low stone wall round it. This wall was never finished, but you shall see the ruins to-morrow in the daylight."

"And the result of your investigations—these stories, I mean?" the doctor broke in, anxious to keep him to the main issues.

"Yes, I'm coming to that," he said slowly, "but the wood first, for this wood out of which they grew like mushrooms has nothing in any way peculiar about it. It is very thickly grown, and rises to a clearer part in the centre, a sort of mound where there is a circle of large boulders—old Druid stones, I'm told. At another place there's a small pond. There's nothing distinctive about it that I could mention—just an ordinary pine-wood, a very ordinary pine-wood—only the trees are a bit twisted in the trunks, some of 'em, and very dense. Nothing more.

"And the stories? Well, none of them had anything to do with my poor brother, or the keeper, as you might have expected; and they were all odd—such odd things, I mean, to invent or imagine. I never could make out how these people got such notions into their heads."

He paused a moment to relight his cigar.

"There's no regular path through it," he resumed, puffing vigorously, "but the fields round it are constantly used, and one of the gardeners whose cottage lies over that way declared he often saw moving lights in it at night, and luminous shapes like globes of fire over the tops of the trees, skimming and floating, and making a soft hissing sound—most of 'em said that, in fact—and another man saw shapes flitting in and out among the trees, things that were neither men nor animals, and all faintly luminous. No one ever pretended to see human forms—always queer, huge things they could not properly describe. Sometimes the whole wood was lit up, and one fellow—he's still here and you shall see him—has a most circumstantial yarn about having seen great stars lying on the ground round the edge of the wood at regular intervals—"

"What kind of stars?" put in John Silence sharply, in a sudden way that made me start.

"Oh, I don't know quite; ordinary stars, I think he said, only very large, and apparently blazing as though the ground was alight. He was too terrified to go close and examine, and he has never seen them since."

He stooped and stirred the fire into a welcome blaze—welcome for its blaze of light rather than for its heat. In the room there was already a strange pervading sensation of warmth that was oppressive in its effect and far from comforting.

"Of course," he went on, straightening up again on the mat, "this was all commonplace enough—this seeing lights and figures at night. Most of these fellows drink, and imagination and terror between them may account for almost anything. But others saw things in broad daylight. One of the woodmen, a sober, respectable man, took the shortcut home to his midday meal, and swore he was followed the whole length of the wood by something that never showed itself, but dodged from tree to tree, always keeping out of sight, yet solid enough to make the branches sway and the twigs snap on the ground. And it made a noise, he declared—but really"—the speaker stopped and gave a short laugh—"it's too absurd—"

"Please!" insisted the doctor; "for it is these small details that give me the best clues always."

"—it made a crackling noise, he said, like a bonfire. Those were his very words: like the crackling of a bonfire," finished the soldier, with a repetition of his short laugh.

"Most interesting," Dr. Silence observed gravely. "Please omit nothing."

"Yes," he went on, "and it was soon after that the fires began—the fires in the wood. They started mysteriously burning in the patches of coarse white grass that cover the more open parts of the plantation. No one ever actually saw them start, but many, myself among the number, have seen them burning and smouldering. They are always small and circular in shape, and for all the world like a picnic fire. The head keeper has a dozen explanations, from sparks flying out of the house chimneys to the sunlight focusing through a dewdrop, but none of them, I must admit, convince me as being in the least likely or probable. They are most singular, I consider, most singular, these mysterious fires, and I am glad to say that they come only at rather long intervals and never seem to spread.

"But the keeper had other queer stories as well, and about things that are verifiable. He declared that no life ever willingly entered the plantation; more, that no life existed in it at all. No birds nested in the trees, or flew into their shade. He set countless traps, but never caught so much as a rabbit or a weasel. Animals avoided it, and more than once he had picked up dead creatures round the edges that bore no obvious signs of how they had met their death.

"Moreover, he told me one extraordinary tale about his retriever chasing some invisible creature across the field one day when he was out with his gun. The dog suddenly pointed at something in the field at his feet, and then gave chase, yelping like a mad thing. It followed its imaginary quarry to the borders of the wood, and then went in—a thing he had never known it to do before. The moment it crossed the edge—it is darkish in there even in daylight—it began fighting in the most frenzied and terrific fashion. It made him afraid to interfere, he said. And at last, when the dog came out, hanging its tail down and panting, he found something like white hair stuck to its jaws, and brought it to show me. I tell you these details because—"

"They are important, believe me," the doctor stopped him. "And you have it still, this hair?" he asked.

"It disappeared in the oddest way," the Colonel explained. "It was curious looking stuff, something like asbestos, and I sent it to be analysed by the local chemist. But either the man got wind of its origin, or else he didn't like the look of it for some reason, because he returned it to me and said it was neither animal, vegetable, nor mineral, so far as he could make out, and he didn't wish to have anything to do with it. I put it away in paper, but a week later, on opening the package—it was gone! Oh, the stories are simply endless. I could tell you hundreds all on the same lines."

"And personal experiences of your own, Colonel Wragge?" asked John Silence earnestly, his manner showing the greatest possible interest and sympathy.

The soldier gave an almost imperceptible start. He looked distinctly uncomfortable.

"Nothing, I think," he said slowly, "nothing—er—I should like to rely on. I mean nothing I have the right to speak of, perhaps—yet."

His mouth closed with a snap. Dr. Silence, after waiting a little to see if he would add to his reply, did not seek to press him on the point:

"Well," he resumed presently, and as though he would speak contemptuously, yet dared not, "this sort of thing has gone on at intervals ever since. It spreads like wildfire, of course, mysterious chatter of this kind, and people began trespassing all over the estate, coming to see the wood, and making themselves a general nuisance. Notices of man-traps and spring-guns only seemed to increase their persistence; and—think of it," he snorted, "some local Research Society actually wrote and asked permission for one of their members to spend a night in the wood! Bolder fools, who didn't write for leave, came and took away bits of bark from the trees and gave them to clairvoyants, who invented in their turn a further batch of tales. There was simply no end to it all."

"Most distressing and annoying, I can well believe," interposed the doctor.

"Then suddenly the phenomena ceased as mysteriously as they had begun, and the interest flagged. The tales stopped. People got interested in something else. It all seemed to die out. This was last July. I can tell you exactly, for I've kept a diary more or less of what happened."

"Ah!"

"But now, quite recently, within the past three weeks, it has all revived again with a rush—with a kind of furious attack, so to speak. It has really become unbearable. You may imagine what it means, and the general state of affairs, when I say that the possibility of leaving has occurred to me."

"Incendiarism?" suggested Dr. Silence, half under his breath, but not so low that Colonel Wragge did not hear him.

"By Jove, sir, you take the very words out of my mouth!" exclaimed the astonished man, glancing from the doctor to me and from me to the doctor, and rattling the money in his pocket as though some explanation of my friend's divining powers were to be found that way.

"It's only that you are thinking very vividly," the doctor said quietly, "and your thoughts form pictures in my mind before you utter them. It's merely a little elementary thought-reading."

His intention, I saw, was not to perplex the good man, but to impress him with his powers so as to ensure obedience later.

"Good Lord! I had no idea—" He did not finish the sentence, and dived again abruptly into his narrative.

"I did not see anything myself, I must admit, but the stories of independent eye-witnesses were to the effect that lines of light, like streams of thin fire, moved through the wood and sometimes were seen to shoot out precisely as flames might shoot out—in the direction of this house. There," he explained, in a louder voice that made me jump, pointing with a thick finger to the map, "where the westerly fringe of the plantation comes up to the end of the lower lawn at the back of the house—where it links on to those dark patches, which are laurel shrubberies, running right up to the back premises—that's where these lights were seen. They passed from the wood to the shrubberies, and in this way reached the house itself. Like silent rockets, one man described them, rapid as lightning and exceedingly bright."

"And this evidence you spoke of?"

"They actually reached the sides of the house. They've left a mark of scorching on the walls—the walls of the laundry building at the other end. You shall see 'em to-morrow." He pointed to the map to indicate the spot, and then straightened himself and glared about the room as though he had said something no one could believe and expected contradiction.

"Scorched—just as the faces were," the doctor murmured, looking significantly at me.

"Scorched—yes," repeated the Colonel, failing to catch the rest of the sentence in his excitement.

There was a prolonged silence in the room, in which I heard the gurgling of the oil in the lamp and the click of the coals and the heavy breathing of our host. The most unwelcome sensations were creeping about my spine, and I wondered whether my companion would scorn me utterly if I asked to sleep on the sofa in his room. It was eleven o'clock, I saw by the clock on the mantelpiece. We had crossed the dividing line and were now well in the movement of the adventure. The fight between my interest and my dread became acute. But, even if turning back had been possible, I think the interest would have easily gained the day.

"I have enemies, of course," I heard the Colonel's rough voice break into the pause presently, "and have discharged a number of servants—"

"It's not that," put in John Silence briefly.

"You think not? In a sense I am glad, and yet—there are some things that can be met and dealt with—"

He left the sentence unfinished, and looked down at the floor with an expression of grim severity that betrayed a momentary glimpse of character. This fighting man loathed and abhorred the thought of an enemy he could not see and come to grips with. Presently he moved over and sat down in the chair between us. Something like a sigh escaped him. Dr. Silence said nothing.

"My sister, of course, is kept in ignorance, as far as possible, of all this," he said disconnectedly, and as if talking to himself. "But even if she knew, she would find matter-of-fact explanations. I only wish I could. I'm sure they exist."

There came then an interval in the conversation that was very significant. It did not seem a real pause, or the silence real silence, for both men continued to think so rapidly and strongly that one almost imagined their thoughts clothed themselves in words in the air of the room. I was more than a little keyed up with the strange excitement of all I had heard, but what stimulated my nerves more than anything else was the obvious fact that the doctor was clearly upon the trail of discovery. In his mind at that moment, I believe, he had already solved the nature of this perplexing psychical problem. His face was like a mask, and he employed the absolute minimum of gesture and words.

All his energies were directed inwards, and by those incalculable methods and processes he had mastered with such infinite patience and study, I felt sure he was already in touch with the forces behind these singular phenomena and laying his deep plans for bringing them into the open, and then effectively dealing with them.

Colonel Wragge meanwhile grew more and more fidgety. From time to time he turned towards my companion, as though about to speak, yet always changing his mind at the last moment. Once he went over and opened the door suddenly, apparently to see if any one were listening at the keyhole, for he disappeared a moment between the two doors, and I then heard him open the outer one. He stood there for some seconds and made a noise as though he were sniffing the air like a dog. Then he closed both doors cautiously and came back to the fireplace. A strange excitement seemed growing upon him. Evidently he was trying to make up his mind to say something that he found it difficult to say. And John Silence, as I rightly judged, was waiting patiently for him to choose his own opportunity and his own way of saying it. At last he turned and faced us, squaring his great shoulders, and stiffening perceptibly.

Dr. Silence looked up sympathetically.

"Your own experiences help me most," he observed quietly.

"The fact is," the Colonel said, speaking very low, "this past week there have been outbreaks of fire in the house itself. Three separate outbreaks—and all—in my sister's room."

"Yes," the doctor said, as if this was just what he had expected to hear.

"Utterly unaccountable—all of them," added the other, and then sat down. I began to understand something of the reason of his excitement. He was realising at last that the "natural" explanation he had held to all along was becoming impossible, and he hated it. It made him angry.

"Fortunately," he went on, "she was out each time and does not know. But I have made her sleep now in a room on the ground floor."

"A wise precaution," the doctor said simply. He asked one or two questions. The fires had started in the curtains—once by the window and once by the bed. The third time smoke had been discovered by the maid coming from the cupboard, and it was found that Miss Wragge's clothes hanging on the hooks were smouldering. The doctor listened attentively, but made no comment

"And now can you tell me," he said presently, "what your own feeling about it is—your general impression?"

"It sounds foolish to say so," replied the soldier, after a moment's hesitation, "but I feel exactly as I have often felt on active service in my Indian campaigns: just as if the house and all in it were in a state of siege; as though a concealed enemy were encamped about us—in ambush somewhere." He uttered a soft nervous laugh. "As if the next sign of smoke would precipitate a panic—a dreadful panic."

The picture came before me of the night shadowing the house, and the twisted pine trees he had described crowding about it, concealing some powerful enemy; and, glancing at the resolute face and figure of the old soldier, forced at length to his confession, I understood something of all he had been through before he sought the assistance of John Silence.

"And to-morrow, unless I am mistaken, is full moon," said the doctor suddenly, watching the other's face for the effect of his apparently careless words.

Colonel Wragge gave an uncontrollable start, and his face for the first time showed unmistakable pallor.

"What in the world—?" he began, his lip quivering.

"Only that I am beginning to see light in this extraordinary affair," returned the other calmly, "and, if my theory is correct, each month when the moon is at the full should witness an increase in the activity of the phenomena."

"I don't see the connection," Colonel Wragge answered almost savagely, "but I am bound to say my diary bears you out." He wore the most puzzled expression I have ever seen upon an honest face, but he abhorred this additional corroboration of an explanation that perplexed him.

"I confess," he repeated, "I cannot see the connection."

"Why should you?" said the doctor, with his first laugh that evening. He got up and hung the map upon the wall again. "But I do—because these things are my special study—and let me add that I have yet to come across a problem that is not natural, and has not a natural explanation. It's merely a question of how much one knows—and admits."

Colonel Wragge eyed him with a new and curious respect in his face. But his feelings were soothed. Moreover, the doctor's laugh and change of manner came as a relief to all, and broke the spell of grave suspense that had held us so long. We all rose and stretched our limbs, and took little walks about the room.

"I am glad, Dr. Silence, if you will allow me to say so, that you are here," he said simply, "very glad indeed. And now I fear I have kept you both up very late," with a glance to include me, "for you must be tired, and ready for your beds. I have told you all there is to tell," he added, "and to-morrow you must feel perfectly free to take any steps you think necessary."

The end was abrupt, yet natural, for there was nothing more to say, and neither of these men talked for mere talking's sake.

Out in the cold and chilly hall he lit our candles and took us upstairs. The house was at rest and still, every one asleep. We moved softly. Through the windows on the stairs we saw the moonlight falling across the lawn, throwing deep shadows. The nearer pine trees were just visible in the distance, a wall of impenetrable blackness.

Our host came for a moment to our rooms to see that we had everything. He pointed to a coil of strong rope lying beside the window, fastened to the wall by means of an iron ring. Evidently it had been recently put in.

"I don't think we shall need it," Dr. Silence said, with a smile.

"I trust not," replied our host gravely." I sleep quite close to you across the landing," he whispered, pointing to his door, "and if you— if you want anything in the night you will know where to find me."

He wished us pleasant dreams and disappeared down the passage into his room, shading the candle with his big muscular hand from the draughts.

John Silence stopped me a moment before I went.

"You know what it is?" I asked, with an excitement that even overcame my weariness.

"Yes," he said, "I'm almost sure. And you?"

"Not the smallest notion."

He looked disappointed, but not half as disappointed as I felt.

"Egypt," he whispered, "Egypt!"

II

Nothing happened to disturb me in the night——nothing, that is, except a nightmare in which Colonel Wragge chased me amid thin streaks of fire, and his sister always prevented my escape by suddenly rising up out of the ground in her chair——dead. The deep baying of dogs woke me once, just before the dawn, it must have been, for I saw the window frame against the sky; there was a flash of lightning, too, I thought, as I turned over in bed. And it was warm, for October oppressively warm.

It was after eleven o'clock when our host suggested going out with the guns, these, we understood, being a somewhat thin disguise for our true purpose. Personally, I was glad to be in the open air, for the atmosphere of the house was heavy with presentiment. The sense of impending disaster hung over all. Fear stalked the passages, and lurked in the corners of every room. It was a house haunted, but really haunted; not by some vague shadow of the dead, but by a definite though incalculable influence that was actively alive, and dangerous. At the least smell of smoke the entire household quivered. An odour of burning, I was convinced, would paralyse all the inmates. For the servants, though professedly ignorant by the master's unspoken orders, yet shared the common dread; and the hideous uncertainty, joined with this display of so spiteful and calculated a spirit of malignity, provided a kind of black doom that draped not only the walls, but also the minds of the people living within them.

Only the bright and cheerful vision of old Miss Wragge being pushed about the house in her noiseless chair, chatting and nodding briskly to every one she met, prevented us from giving way entirely to the depression which governed the majority. The sight of her was like a gleam of sunshine through the depths of some ill-omened wood, and just as we went out I saw her being wheeled along by her attendant into the sunshine of the back lawn, and caught her cheery smile as she turned her head and wished us good sport.

The morning was October at its best. Sunshine glistened on the dew-drenched grass and on leaves turned golden-red. The dainty messengers of coming hoar-frost were already in the air, asearch for permanent winter quarters. From the wide moors that everywhere swept up against the sky, like a purple sea splashed by the occasional grey of rocky clefts, there stole down the cool and perfumed wind of the west. And the keen taste of the sea ran through all like a master-flavour, borne over the spaces perhaps by the seagulls that cried and circled high in the air.

But our host took little interest in this sparkling beauty, and had no thought of showing off the scenery of his property. His mind was otherwise intent, and, for that matter, so were our own.

"Those bleak moors and hills stretch unbroken for hours," he said, with a sweep of the hand; "and over there, some four miles," pointing in another direction, "lies S—— Bay, a long, swampy inlet of the sea, haunted by myriads of seabirds. On the other side of the house are the plantations and pine-woods. I thought we would get the dogs and go first to the Twelve Acre Wood I told you about last night. It's quite near."

We found the dogs in the stable, and I recalled the deep baying of the night when a fine bloodhound and two great Danes leaped out to greet us. Singular companions for guns, I thought to myself, as we struck out across the fields and the great creatures bounded and ran beside us, nose to ground.

The conversation was scanty. John Silence's grave face did not encourage talk. He wore the expression I knew well—that look of earnest solicitude which meant that his whole being was deeply absorbed and preoccupied. Frightened, I had never seen him, but anxious often—it always moved me to witness it—and he was anxious now.

"On the way back you shall see the laundry building," Colonel Wragge observed shortly, for he, too, found little to say. "We shall attract less attention then."

Yet not all the crisp beauty of the morning seemed able to dispel the feelings of uneasy dread that gathered increasingly about our minds as we went.

In a very few minutes a clump of pine trees concealed the house from view, and we found ourselves on the outskirts of a densely-grown plantation of conifers. Colonel Wragge stopped abruptly, and, producing a map from his pocket, explained once more very briefly its position with regard to the house. He showed how it ran up almost to the walls of the laundry building—though at the moment beyond our actual view—and pointed to the windows of his sister's bedroom where the fires had been. The room, now empty, looked straight on to the wood. Then, glancing nervously about him, and calling the dogs to heel, he proposed that we should enter the plantation and make as thorough examination of it as we thought worth while. The dogs, he added, might perhaps be persuaded to accompany us a little way—and he pointed to where they cowered at his feet—but he doubted it. "Neither voice nor whip will get them very far, I'm afraid," he said. "I know by experience."

"If you have no objection," replied Dr. Silence, with decision, and speaking almost for the first time, "we will make our examination alone—Mr. Hubbard and myself. It will be best so."

His tone was absolutely final, and the Colonel acquiesced so politely that even a less intuitive man than myself must have seen that he was genuinely relieved.

"You doubtless have good reasons," he said.

"Merely that I wish to obtain my impressions uncoloured. This delicate clue I am working on might be so easily blurred by the thought-currents of another mind with strongly preconceived ideas."

"Perfectly. I understand," rejoined the soldier, though with an expression of countenance that plainly contradicted his words. "Then I will wait here with the dogs; and we'll have a look at the laundry on our way home."

I turned once to look back as we clambered over the low stone wall built by the late owner, and saw his straight, soldierly figure standing in the sunlit field watching us with a curiously intent look on his face. There was something to me incongruous, yet distinctly pathetic, in the man's efforts to meet all far-fetched explanations of the mystery with contempt, and at the same time in his stolid, unswerving investigation of it all. He nodded at me and made a gesture of farewell with his hand. That picture of him, standing in the sunshine with his big dogs, steadily watching us, remains with me to this day.

Dr. Silence led the way in among the twisted trunks, planted closely together in serried ranks, and I followed sharp at his heels. The moment we were out of sight he turned and put down his gun against the roots of a big tree, and I did likewise.

"We shall hardly want these cumbersome weapons of murder," he observed, with a passing smile.

"You are sure of your clue, then?" I asked at once, bursting with curiosity, yet fearing to betray it lest he should think me unworthy. His own methods were so absolutely simple and untheatrical.

"I am sure of my clue," he answered gravely. "And I think we have come just in time. You shall know in due course. For the present—be content to follow and observe. And think steadily. The support of your mind will help me."

His voice had that quiet mastery in it which leads men to face death with a sort of happiness and pride. I would have followed him anywhere at that moment. At the same time his words conveyed a sense of dread seriousness. I caught the thrill of his confidence; but also, in this broad light of day, I felt the measure of alarm that lay behind.

"You still have no strong impressions?" he asked. "Nothing happened in the night, for instance? No vivid dreamings?"

He looked closely for my answer, I was aware.

"I slept almost an unbroken sleep. I was tremendously tired, you know, and, but for the oppressive heat—"

"Good! You still notice the heat, then," he said to himself, rather than expecting an answer. "And the lightning?" he added, "that lightning out of a clear sky—that flashing—did you notice *that?*"

I answered truly that I thought I had seen a flash during a moment of wakefulness, and he then drew my attention to certain facts before moving on.

"You remember the sensation of warmth when you put the letter to your forehead in the train; the heat generally in the house last evening, and, as you now mention, in the night. You heard, too, the Colonel's stories about the appearances of fire in this wood and in the house itself, and the way his brother and the gamekeeper came to their deaths twenty years ago."

I nodded, wondering what in the world it all meant.

"And you get no clue from these facts?" he asked, a trifle surprised.

I searched every corner of my mind and imagination for some inkling of his meaning, but was obliged to admit that I understood nothing so far.

"Never mind; you will later. And now," he added, "we will go over the wood and see what we can find."

His words explained to me something of his method. We were to keep our minds alert and report to each other the least fancy that crossed the picture-gallery of our thoughts. Then, just as we started, he turned again to me with a final warning.

"And, for your safety," he said earnestly, "imagine *now*—and for that matter, imagine always until we leave this place—imagine with the utmost keenness, that you are surrounded by a shell that protects you. Picture yourself inside a protective envelope, and build it up with the most intense imagination you can evoke. Pour the whole force of your thought and will into it. Believe vividly all through this adventure that such a shell, constructed of your thought, will, and imagination, surrounds you completely, and that nothing can pierce it to attack."

He spoke with dramatic conviction, gazing hard at me as though to enforce his meaning, and then moved forward and began to pick his way over the rough, tussocky ground into the wood. And meanwhile, knowing the efficacy of his prescription, I adopted it to the best of my ability.

The trees at once closed about us like the night. Their branches met overhead in a continuous tangle, their stems crept closer and closer, the brambly undergrowth thickened and multiplied. We tore our trousers, scratched our hands, and our eyes filled with fine dust that made it most difficult to avoid the clinging, prickly network of branches and creepers. Coarse white grass that caught our feet like string grew here and there in patches. It crowned the lumps of peaty growth that stuck up like human heads, fantastically dressed, thrusting up at us out of the ground with crests of dead hair. We stumbled and floundered among them. It was hard going, and I could well conceive it impossible to find a way at all in the night-time. We jumped, when possible, from tussock to tussock, and it seemed as though we were springing among heads on a battlefield, and that this dead white grass concealed eyes that turned to stare as we passed.

Here and there the sunlight shot in with vivid spots of white light, dazzling the sight, but only making the surrounding gloom deeper by contrast. And on two occasions we passed dark circular places in the grass where fires had eaten their mark and left a ring of ashes. Dr. Silence pointed to them, but without comment and without pausing, and the sight of them woke in me a singular realisation of the dread that lay so far only just out of sight in this adventure.

It was exhausting work, and heavy going. We kept close together. The warmth, too, was extraordinary. Yet it did not seem the warmth of the body due to violent exertion, but rather an inner heat of the mind that laid glowing hands of fire upon the heart and set the brain in a kind of steady blaze. When my companion found himself too far in advance, he waited for me to come up. The place had evidently been untouched by hand of man, keeper, forester, or sportsman, for many a year; and my thoughts, as we advanced painfully, were not unlike the state of the wood itself—dark, confused, full of a haunting wonder and the shadow of fear.

By this time all signs of the open field behind us were hid. No single gleam penetrated. We might have been groping in the heart of some primeval forest. Then, suddenly, the brambles and tussocks and string-like grass came to an end; the trees opened out; and the ground began to slope upwards towards a large central mound. We had reached the middle of the plantation, and before us stood the broken Druid stones our host had mentioned. We walked easily up the little hill, between the sparser stems, and, resting upon one of the ivy-covered boulders, looked round upon a comparatively open space, as large, perhaps, as a small London Square.

Thinking of the ceremonies and sacrifices this rough circle of prehistoric monoliths might have witnessed, I looked up into my companion's face with an unspoken question. But he read my thought and shook his head.

"Our mystery has nothing to do with these dead symbols," he said, "but with something perhaps even more ancient, and of another country altogether."

"Egypt?" I said half under my breath, hopelessly puzzled, but recalling his words in my bedroom.

He nodded. Mentally I still floundered, but he seemed intensely preoccupied and it was no time for asking questions; so while his words circled unintelligibly in my mind I looked round at the scene before me, glad of the opportunity to recover breath and some measure of composure. But hardly had I time to notice the twisted and contorted shapes of many of the pine trees close at hand when Dr. Silence leaned over and touched me on the shoulder. He pointed down the slope. And the look I saw in his eyes keyed up every nerve in my body to its utmost pitch.

A thin, almost imperceptible column of blue smoke was rising among the trees some twenty yards away at the foot of the mound. It curled up and up, and disappeared from sight among the tangled branches overhead. It was scarcely thicker than the smoke from a small brand of burning wood.

"Protect yourself! Imagine your shell strongly," whispered the doctor sharply, "and follow me closely."

He rose at once and moved swiftly down the slope towards the smoke, and I followed, afraid to remain alone. I heard the soft crunching of our steps on the pine needles. Over his shoulder I watched the thin blue spiral, without once taking my eyes off it. I hardly know how to describe the peculiar sense of vague horror inspired in me by the sight of that streak of smoke pencilling its way upwards among the dark trees. And the sensation of increasing heat as we approached was phenomenal. It was like walking towards a glowing yet invisible fire.

As we drew nearer his pace slackened. Then he stopped and pointed, and I saw a small circle of burnt grass upon the ground. The tussocks were blackened and smouldering, and from the centre rose this line of smoke, pale, blue, steady. Then I noticed a movement of the atmosphere beside us, as if the warm air were rising and the cooler air rushing in to take its place: a little centre of wind in the stillness. Overhead the boughs stirred and trembled where the smoke disappeared. Otherwise, not a tree sighed, not a sound made itself heard. The wood was still as a graveyard. A horrible idea came to me that the course of nature was about to change without warning, *had* changed a little already, that the sky would drop, or the surface of the earth crash inwards like a broken bubble. Something, certainly, reached up to the citadel of my reason, causing its throne to shake.

John Silence moved forward again. I could not see his face, but his attitude was plainly one of resolution, of muscles and mind ready for vigorous action. We were within ten feet of the blackened circle when the smoke of a sudden ceased to rise, and vanished. The tail of the column disappeared in the air above, and at the same instant it seemed to me that the sensation of heat passed from my face, and the motion of the wind was gone. The calm spirit of the fresh October day resumed command.

Side by side we advanced and examined the place. The grass was smouldering, the ground still hot. The circle of burned earth was a foot to a foot and a half in diameter. It looked like an ordinary picnic fireplace. I bent down cautiously to look, but in a second I sprang back with an involuntary cry of alarm, for, as the doctor stamped on the ashes to prevent them spreading, a sound of hissing rose from the spot as though he had kicked a living creature. This hissing was faintly audible in the air. It moved past us, away towards the thicker portion of the wood in the direction of our field, and in a second Dr. Silence had left the fire and started in pursuit.

And then began the most extraordinary hunt of invisibility I can ever conceive.

He went fast even at the beginning, and, of course, it was perfectly obvious that he was following something. To judge by the poise of his head he kept his eyes steadily at a certain level—just above the height of a man—and the consequence was he stumbled a good deal over the roughness of the ground. The hissing sound had stopped. There was no sound of any kind, and what he saw to follow was utterly beyond me. I only know, that in mortal dread of being left behind, and with a biting curiosity to see whatever there was to be seen, I followed as quickly as I could, and even then barely succeeded in keeping up with him.

And, as we went, the whole mad jumble of the Colonel's stories ran through my brain, touching a sense of frightened laughter that was only held in check by the sight of this earnest, hurrying figure before me. For John Silence at work inspired me with a kind of awe. He looked so diminutive among these giant twisted trees, while yet I knew that his purpose and his knowledge were so great, and even in hurry he was dignified. The fancy that we were playing some queer, exaggerated game together met the fact that we were two men dancing upon the brink of some possible tragedy, and the mingling of the two emotions in my mind was both grotesque and terrifying.

He never turned in his mad chase, but pushed rapidly on, while I panted after him like a figure in some unreasoning nightmare. And, as I ran, it came upon me that he had been aware all the time, in his quiet, internal way, of many things that he had kept for his own secret consideration; he had been watching, waiting, planning from the very moment we entered the shade of the wood. By some inner, concentrated process of mind, dynamic if not actually magical, he had been in direct contact with the source of the whole adventure, the very essence of the real mystery. And now the forces were moving to a climax. Something was about to happen, something important, something possibly dreadful. Every nerve, every sense, every significant gesture of the plunging figure before me proclaimed the fact just as surely as the skies, the winds, and the face of the earth tell the birds the time to migrate and warn the animals that danger lurks and they must move.

In a few moments we reached the foot of the mound and entered the tangled undergrowth that lay between us and the sunlight of the field. Here the difficulties of fast travelling increased a hundredfold. There were brambles to dodge, low boughs to dive under, and countless tree trunks closing up to make a direct path impossible. Yet Dr. Silence never seemed to falter or hesitate. He went, diving, jumping, dodging, ducking, but ever in the same main direction, following a clean trail. Twice I tripped and fell, and both times, when I picked myself up again, I saw him ahead of me, still forcing a way like a dog after its quarry. And sometimes, like a dog, he stopped and pointed—human pointing it was, psychic pointing,—and each time he stopped to point I heard that faint high hissing in the air beyond us. The instinct of an infallible dowser possessed him, and he made no mistakes.

At length, abruptly, I caught up with him, and found that we stood at the edge of the shallow pond Colonel Wragge had mentioned in his account the night before. It was long and narrow, filled with dark brown water, in which the trees were dimly reflected. Not a ripple stirred its surface.

"Watch!" he cried out, as I came up. "It's going to cross. It's bound to betray itself. The water is its natural enemy, and we shall see the direction."

And, even as he spoke, a thin line like the track of a water-spider, shot swiftly across the shiny surface; there was a ghost of steam in the air above; and immediately I became aware of an odour of burning.

Dr. Silence turned and shot a glance at me that made me think of lightning. I began to shake all over.

"Quick!" he cried with excitement, "to the trail again! We must run round. It's going to the house!"

The alarm in his voice quite terrified me. Without a false step I dashed round the slippery banks and dived again at his heels into the sea of bushes and tree trunks. We were now in the thick of the very dense belt that ran round the outer edge of the plantation, and the field was near; yet so dark was the tangle that it was some time before the first shafts of white sunlight became visible. The doctor now ran in zig-zags. He was following something that dodged and doubled quite won-derfully, yet had begun, I fancied, to move more slowly than before.

"Quick!" he cried. "In the light we shall lose it!"

I still saw nothing, heard nothing, caught no suggestion of a trail; yet this man, guided by some interior divining that seemed infallible, made no false turns, though how we failed to crash headlong into the trees has remained a mystery to me ever since. And then, with a sud-den rush, we found ourselves on the skirts of the wood with the open field lying in bright sunshine before our eyes.

"Too late!" I heard him cry, a note of anguish in his voice. "It's out—and, by God, it's making for the house!"

I saw the Colonel standing in the field with his dogs where we had left him. He was bending double, peering into the wood where he heard us running, and he straightened up like a bent whip released. John Silence dashed passed, calling him to follow.

"We shall lose the trail in the light," I heard him cry as he ran. "But quick! We may yet get there in time!"

That wild rush across the open field, with the dogs at our heels, leaping and barking, and the elderly Colonel behind us running as though for his life, shall I ever forget it? Though I had only vague ideas of the meaning of it all, I put my best foot forward, and, being the youngest of the three, I reached the house an easy first. I drew up, panting, and turned to wait for the others. But, as I turned, something moving a little distance away caught my eye, and in that moment I swear I experienced the most overwhelming and singular shock of surprise and terror I have ever known, or can conceive as possible.

For the front door was open, and the waist of the house being nar-row, I could see through the hall into the dining-room beyond, and so out on to the back lawn, and there I saw no less a sight than the figure of Miss Wragge—running. Even at that distance it was plain that she had seen me, and was coming fast towards me, running with the frantic gait of a terror-stricken woman. She had recovered the use of her legs.

Her face was a livid grey, as of death itself, but the general expression was one of laughter, for her mouth was gaping, and her eyes, always bright shone with the light of a wild merriment that seemed the merriment of a child, yet was singularly ghastly. And that very second, as she fled past me into her brother's arms behind, I smelt again most unmistakably the odour of burning, and to this day the smell of smoke and fire can come very near to turning me sick with the memory of what I had seen.

Fast on her heels, too, came the terrified attendant, more mistress of herself, and able to speak—which the old lady could not do—but with a face almost, if not quite, as fearful.

"We were down by the bushes in the sun,"—she gasped and screamed in reply to Colonel Wragge's distracted questionings,—"I was wheeling the chair as usual when she shrieked and leaped—I don't know exactly—I was too frightened to see— Oh, my God! she jumped clean out of the chair—*and ran!* There was a blast of hot air from the wood, and she hid her face and jumped. She didn't make a sound—she didn't cry out, or make a sound. She just ran."

But the nightmare horror of it all reached the breaking point a few minutes later, and while I was still standing in the hall temporarily bereft of speech and movement; for while the doctor, the Colonel, and the attendant were half-way up the staircase, helping the fainting woman to the privacy of her room, and all in a confused group of dark figures, there sounded a voice behind me, and I turned to see the butler, his face dripping with perspiration, his eyes starting out of his head.

"The laundry's on fire!" he cried; "the laundry building's a-caught!"

I remember his odd expression "a-caught," and wanting to laugh, but finding my face rigid and inflexible.

"The devil's about again, s'help me Gawd!" he cried, in a voice thin with terror, running about in circles.

And then the group on the stairs scattered as at the sound of a shot, and the Colonel and Dr. Silence came down three steps at a time, leaving the afflicted Miss Wragge to the care of her single attendant.

We were out across the front lawn in a moment and round the

corner of the house, the Colonel leading, Silence and I at his heels, and the portly butler puffing some distance in the rear, getting more and more mixed in his addresses to God and the devil; and the moment we passed the stables and came into view of the laundry building, we saw a wicked-looking volume of smoke pouring out of the narrow windows, and the frightened women-servants and grooms running hither and thither, calling aloud as they ran.

The arrival of the master restored order instantly, and this retired soldier, poor thinker perhaps, but capable man of action, had the matter in hand from the start. He issued orders like a martinet, and, almost before I could realise it, there were streaming buckets on the scene and a line of men and women formed between the building and the stable pump.

"Inside," I heard John Silence cry, and the Colonel followed him through the door, while I was just quick enough at their heels to hear him add, "The smoke's the worst part of it. There's no fire yet, I think."

And, true enough, there was no fire. The interior was thick with smoke, but it speedily cleared and not a single bucket was used upon the floor or walls. The air was stifling, the heat fearful.

"There's precious little to burn in here; it's all stone," the Colonel exclaimed, coughing. But the doctor was pointing to the wooden covers of the great cauldron in which the clothes were washed, and we saw that these were smouldering and charred. And when we sprinkled half a bucket of water on them the surrounding bricks hissed and fizzed and sent up clouds of steam. Through the open door and windows this passed out with the rest of the smoke, and we three stood there on the brick floor staring at the spot and wondering, each in our own fashion, how in the name of natural law the place could have caught fire or smoked at all. And each was silent—myself from sheer incapacity and befuddlement, the Colonel from the quiet pluck that faces all things yet speaks little, and John Silence from the intense mental grappling with this latest manifestation of a profound problem that called for concentration of thought rather than for any words.

There was really nothing to say. The facts were indisputable.

Colonel Wragge was the first to utter.

"My sister," he said briefly, and moved off. In the yard I heard him sending the frightened servants about their business in an excellently matter-of-fact voice, scolding some one roundly for making such a big fire and letting the flues get over-heated, and paying no heed to the stammering reply that no fire had been lit there for several days. Then he dispatched a groom on horseback for the local doctor.

Then Dr. Silence turned and looked at me. The absolute control he possessed, not only over the outward expression of emotion by gesture, change of colour, light in the eyes, and so forth, but also, as I well knew, over its very birth in his heart, the mask-like face of the dead he could assume at will, made it extremely difficult to know at any given moment what was at work in his inner consciousness. But now, when he turned and looked at me, there was no sphinx-expression there, but rather the keen, triumphant face of a man who had solved a dangerous and complicated problem, and saw his way to a clean victory.

"*Now* do you guess?" he asked quietly, as though it were the simplest matter in the world, and ignorance were impossible.

I could only stare stupidly and remain silent. He glanced down at the charred cauldron-lids, and traced a figure in the air with his finger. But I was too excited, or too mortified, or still too dazed, perhaps, to see what it was he outlined, or what it was he meant to convey. I could only go on swing and shaking my puzzled head.

"A fire-elemental," he cried, "a fire-elemental of the most powerful and malignant kind—"

"A what?" thundered the voice of Colonel Wragge behind us, having returned suddenly and overheard.

"It's a fire-elemental," repeated Dr. Silence more calmly, but with a note of triumph in his voice he could not keep out, "and a fire-elemental enraged."

The light began to dawn in my mind at last. But the Colonel—who had never heard the term before, and was besides feeling considerably worked-up for a plain man with all this mystery he knew not how to grapple with—the Colonel stood, with the most dumfoundered look ever seen on a human countenance, and continued to roar, and stammer, and stare.

"And why," he began, savage with the desire to find something visible he could fight—"why, in the name of all the blazes—?" and then stopped as John Silence moved up and took his arm.

"There, my dear Colonel Wragge," he said gently, "you touch the heart of the whole thing. You ask 'Why.' That is precisely our problem." He held the soldier's eyes firmly with his own. "And that, too, I think, we shall soon know. Come and let us talk over a plan of action—that room with the double doors, perhaps."

The word "action" calmed him a little, and he led the way, without further speech, back into the house, and down the long stone passage to the room where we had heard his stories on the night of our arrival. I understood from the doctor's glance that my presence would not make the interview easier for our host, and I went upstairs to my own room—shaking.

But in the solitude of my room the vivid memories of the last hour revived so mercilessly that I began to feel I should never in my whole life lose the dreadful picture of Miss Wragge running—that dreadful human climax after all the non-human mystery in the wood—and I was not sorry when a servant knocked at my door and said that Colonel Wragge would be glad if I would join them in the little smoking-room.

"I think it is better you should be present," was all Colonel Wragge said as I entered the room. I took the chair with my back to the window. There was still an hour before lunch, though I imagine that the usual divisions of the day hardly found a place in the thoughts of any one of us.

The atmosphere of the room was what I might call electric. The Colonel was positively bristling; he stood with his back to the fire, fingering an unlit black cigar, his face flushed, his being obviously roused and ready for action. He hated this mystery. It was poisonous to his nature, and he longed to meet something face to face—something he could gauge and fight. Dr. Silence, I noticed at once, was sitting before the map of the estate which was spread upon a table. I knew by his expression the state of his mind. He was in the thick of it all, knew it, delighted in it, and was working at high pressure. He recognised my presence with a lifted eyelid, and the flash of the eye, contrasted with his stillness and composure, told me volumes.

"I was about to explain to our host briefly what seems to me afoot in all this business," he said without looking up, "when he asked that you should join us so that we can all work together." And, while signifying my assent, I caught myself wondering what quality it was in the calm speech of this undemonstrative man that was so full of power, so charged with the strange, virile personality behind it, and that seemed to inspire us with his own confidence as by a process of radiation.

"Mr. Hubbard," he went on gravely, turning to the soldier, "knows something of my methods, and in more than one—er—interesting situation has proved of assistance. What we want now"—and here he suddenly got up and took his place on the mat beside the Colonel, and looked hard at him—"is men who have self-control, who are sure of themselves, whose minds at the critical moment will emit positive forces, instead of the wavering and uncertain currents due to negative feelings—due, for instance, to fear."

He looked at us each in turn. Colonel Wragge moved his feet farther apart, and squared his shoulders; and I felt guilty but said nothing, conscious that my latent store of courage was being deliberately hauled to the front. He was winding me up like a clock.

"So that, in what is yet to come," continued our leader, "each of us will contribute his share of power, and ensure success for my plan."

"I'm not afraid of anything I can *see*," said the Colonel bluntly.

"I'm ready," I heard myself say, as it were automatically, "for anything," and then added, feeling the declaration was lamely insufficient, "and everything."

Dr. Silence left the mat and began walking to and fro about the room, both hands plunged deep into the pockets of his shooting-jacket. Tremendous vitality streamed from him. I never took my eyes off the small, moving figure; small, yes,—and yet somehow making me think of a giant plotting the destruction of worlds. And his manner was gentle, as always, soothing almost, and his words uttered quietly without emphasis or emotion. Most of what he said was addressed, though not too obviously, to the Colonel.

"The violence of this sudden attack," he said softly, pacing to and fro beneath the bookcase at the end of the room, "is due, of course, partly to the fact that to-night the moon is at the full"—here he glanced at me for a moment—"and partly to the fact that we have all been so deliberately concentrating upon the matter. Our thinking, our investigation, has stirred it into unusual activity. I mean that the intelligent force behind these manifestations has realised that some one is busied about its destruction. And it is now on the defensive: more, it is aggressive."

"But 'it'—what is 'it'?" began the soldier, fuming. "What, in the name of all that's dreadful, *is* a fire-elemental? "

"I cannot give you at this moment," replied Dr. Silence, turning to him, but undisturbed by the interruption, "a lecture on the nature and history of magic, but can only say that an Elemental is the active force behind the elements,—whether earth, air, water, *or fire,*—it is impersonal in its essential nature, but can be focused, personified, ensouled, so to say, by those who know how—by magicians, if you will—for certain purposes of their own, much in the same way that steam and electricity can be harnessed by the practical man of this century.

"Alone, these blind elemental energies can accomplish little, but governed and directed by the trained will of a powerful manipulator they may become potent activities for good or evil. They are the basis of all magic, and it is the motive behind them that constitutes the magic 'black' or 'white'; they can be the vehicles of curses or of blessings, for a curse is nothing more than the thought of a violent will perpetuated. And in such cases—cases like this—the conscious, directing will of the mind that is using the elemental stands always behind the phenomena—"

"You think that my brother—!" broke in the Colonel, aghast.

"Has nothing whatever to do with it—directly. The fire-elemental that has here been tormenting you and your household was sent upon its mission long before you, or your family, or your ancestors, or even the nation you belong to—unless I am much mistaken—was even in existence. We will come to that a little later; after the experiment I propose to make we shall be more positive. At present I can only say we have to deal now, not only with the phenomenon of Attacking Fire merely, but with the vindictive and enraged intelligence that is directing it from behind the scenes—vindictive and enraged,"—he repeated the words.

"That explains—" began Colonel Wragge, seeking furiously for words he could not find quickly enough.

"Much," said John Silence, with a gesture to restrain him.

He stopped a moment in the middle of his walk, and a deep silence came down over the little room. Through the windows the sunlight seemed less bright, the long line of dark hills less friendly, making me think of a vast wave towering to heaven and about to break and overwhelm us. Something formidable had crept into the world about us. For, undoubtedly, there was a disquieting thought, holding terror as well as awe, in the picture his words conjured up: the conception of a human will reaching its deathless hand, spiteful and destructive, down through the ages, to strike the living and afflict the innocent.

"But what *is* its object?" burst out the soldier, unable to restrain himself longer in the silence. "Why does it come from that plantation? And why should it attack us, or any one in particular?" Questions began to pour from him in a stream.

"All in good time," the doctor answered quietly, having let him run on for several minutes. "But I must first discover positively what, or who, it is that directs this particular fire-elemental. And, to do that, we must first"—he spoke with slow deliberation—"seek to capture—to confine by visibility—to limit its sphere in a concrete form."

"Good heavens almighty!" exclaimed the soldier, mixing his words in his unfeigned surprise.

"Quite so," pursued the other calmly; "for in so doing I think we can release it from the purpose that binds it, restore it to its normal condition of latent fire, and also"—he lowered his voice perceptibly—"also discover the face and form of the Being that ensouls it."

"The man behind the gun!" cried the Colonel, beginning to understand something, and leaning forward so as not to miss a single syllable.

"I mean that in the last resort, before it returns to the womb of potential fire, it will probably assume the face and figure of its Director, of the man of magical knowledge who originally bound it with his incantations and sent it forth upon its mission of centuries."

The soldier sat down and gasped openly in his face, breathing hard; but it was a very subdued voice that framed the question.

"And how do you propose to make it visible? How capture and confine it? What d'ye mean, Dr. John Silence?"

"By furnishing it with the materials for a form. By the process of materialisation simply. Once limited by dimensions, it will become slow, heavy, visible. We can then dissipate it. Invisible fire, you see, is dangerous and incalculable; locked up in a form we can perhaps manage it. We must betray it—to its death."

"And this material?" we asked in the same breath, although I think I had already guessed.

"Not pleasant, but effective," came the quiet reply; "the exhalations of freshly-spilled blood."

"Not human blood!" cried Colonel Wragge, starting up from his chair with a voice like an explosion. I thought his eyes would start from their sockets.

The face of Dr. Silence relaxed in spite of himself, and his spontaneous little laugh brought a welcome though momentary relief.

"The days of human sacrifice, I hope, will never come again," he explained. "Animal blood will answer the purpose, and we can make the experiment as pleasant as possible. Only, the blood must be freshly spilled and strong with the vital emanations that attract this peculiar class of elemental creature. Perhaps—perhaps if some pig on the estate is ready for the market—"

He turned to hide a smile; but the passing touch of comedy found no echo in the mind of our host, who did not understand how to change quickly from one emotion to another. Clearly he was debating many things laboriously in his honest brain. But, in the end, the earnestness and scientific disinterestedness of the doctor, whose influence over him was already very great, won the day, and he presently looked up more calmly, and observed shortly that he thought perhaps the matter could be arranged.

"There are other and pleasanter methods," Dr. Silence went on to explain, "but they require time and preparation, and things have gone much too far, in my opinion, to admit of delay. And the process need cause you no distress: we sit round the bowl and await results. Nothing more. The emanations of blood—which, as Levi says, is the first incarnation of the universal fluid—furnish the materials out of which the creatures of discarnate life, spirits if you prefer, can fashion themselves a temporary appearance. The process is old, and lies at the root of all blood sacrifice. It was known to the priests of Baal, and it is known to the modem ecstasy dancers who cut themselves to produce objective phantoms who dance with them. And the least gifted clairvoyant could tell you that the forms to be seen in the vicinity of slaughter-houses, or hovering above the deserted battlefield, are—well, simply beyond all description. I do not mean," he added, noticing the uneasy fidgeting of his host, "that anything in our laundry-experiment need appear to terrify us, for this case seems a comparatively simple one, and it is only the vindictive character of the intelligence directing this fire-elemental that causes anxiety and makes for personal danger."

"It is curious," said the Colonel, with a sudden rush of words, drawing a deep breath, and as though speaking of things distasteful to him, "that during my years among the Hill Tribes of Northern India I came across—personally came across—instances of the sacrifices of blood to certain deities being stopped suddenly, and all manner of disasters happening until they were resumed. Fires broke out in the huts, and even on the clothes, of the natives—and—and I admit I have read, in the course of my studies,"—he made a gesture towards his books and heavily laden table,—"of the Yezidis of Syria evoking phantoms by means of cutting their bodies with knives during their whirling dances—enormous globes of fire which turned into monstrous and terrible forms—and I remember an account somewhere, too, how the emaciated forms and pallid countenances of the spectres, that appeared to the Emperor Julian, claimed to be the true Immortals, and told him to renew the sacrifices of blood 'for the fumes of which, since the establishment of Christianity, they had been pining'—that these were in reality the phantoms evoked by the rites of blood."

Both Dr. Silence and myself listened in amazement, for this sudden speech was so unexpected, and betrayed so much more knowledge than we had either of us suspected in the old soldier.

"Then perhaps you have read, too," said the doctor, "how the Cosmic Deities of savage races, elemental in their nature, have been kept alive through many ages by these blood rites?"

"No," he answered; "that is new to me."

"In any case," Dr. Silence added, "I am glad you are not wholly unfamiliar with the subject, for you will now bring more sympathy, and therefore more help, to our experiment. For, of course, in this case, we only want the blood to tempt the creature from its lair and enclose it in a form—"

"I quite understand. And I only hesitated just now," he went on, his words coming much more slowly, as though he felt he had already said too much, "because I wished to be quite sure it was no mere curiosity, but an actual sense of necessity that dictated this horrible experiment."

"It is your safety, and that of your household, and of your sister, that is at stake," replied the doctor. "Once I have *seen*, I hope to discover whence this elemental comes, and what its real purpose is."

Colonel Wragge signified his assent with a bow.

"And the moon will help us," the other said, "for it will be full in the early hours of the morning, and this kind of elemental-being is always most active at the period of full moon. Hence, you see, the clue furnished by your diary."

So it was finally settled. Colonel Wragge would provide the materials for the experiment, and we were to meet at midnight. How he would contrive at that hour—but that was his business. I only know we both realised that he would keep his word, and whether a pig died at midnight, or at noon, was after all perhaps only a question of the sleep and personal comfort of the executioner.

"To-night, then, in the laundry," said Dr. Silence finally, to clinch the plan; "we three alone—and at midnight, when the household is asleep and we shall be free from disturbance."

He exchanged significant glances with our host, who, at that moment, was called away by the announcement that the family doctor had arrived, and was ready to see him in his sister's room.

For the remainder of the afternoon John Silence disappeared. I had my suspicions that he made a secret visit to the plantation and also to the laundry building; but, in any case, we saw nothing of him, and he kept strictly to himself. He preparing for the night, I felt sure, but the nature of his preparations I could only guess. There was movement in his room, I heard, and an odour like incense hung about the door, and knowing that he regarded rites as the vehicles of energies, my guesses were probably not far wrong.

Colonel Wragge, too, remained absent the greater part of the afternoon, and, deeply afflicted, had scarcely left his sister's bedside, but in response to my enquiry when we met for a moment at tea-time, he told me that although she had moments of attempted speech, her talk was quite incoherent and hysterical, and she was still quite unable to explain the nature of what she had seen. The doctor, he said, feared she had recovered the use of her limbs, only to lose that of her memory, and perhaps even of her mind.

"Then the recovery of her legs, I trust, may be permanent, at any rate," I ventured, finding it difficult to know what sympathy to offer. And he replied with a curious short laugh, "Oh yes; about that there can be no doubt whatever."

And it was due merely to the chance of my overhearing a fragment of conversation—unwillingly, of course—that a little further light was thrown upon the state in which the old lady actually lay. For, as I came out of my room, it happened that Colonel Wragge and the doctor were going downstairs together, and their words floated up to my ears before I could make my presence known by so much as a cough.

"Then you must find a way," the doctor was saying with decision; "for I cannot insist too strongly upon that—and at all costs she must be kept quiet. These attempts to go out must be prevented—if necessary, by force. This desire to visit some wood or other she keeps talking about is, of course, hysterical in nature. It cannot be permitted for a moment."

"It shall not be permitted," I heard the soldier reply, as they reached the hall below.

"It has impressed her mind for some reason—" the doctor went on, by way evidently of soothing explanation, and then the distance made it impossible for me to hear more.

At dinner Dr. Silence was still absent, on the public plea of a headache, and though food was sent to his room, I am inclined to believe he did not touch it, but spent the entire time fasting.

We retired early, desiring that the household should do likewise, and I must confess that at ten o'clock when I bid my host a temporary good-night, and sought my room to make what mental preparation I could, I realised in no very pleasant fashion that it was a singular and formidable assignation, this midnight meeting in the laundry building, and that there were moments in every adventure of life when a wise man, and one who knew his own limitations, owed it to his dignity to withdraw discreetly. And, but for the character of our leader, I probably should have then and there offered the best excuse I could think of, and have allowed myself quietly to fall asleep and wait for an exciting story in the morning of what had happened. But with a man like John Silence, such a lapse was out of the question, and I sat before my fire counting the minutes and doing everything I could think of to fortify my resolution and fasten my will at the point where I could be reasonably sure that my self-control would hold against all attacks of men, devils, or elementals.

III

At a quarter before midnight, clad in a heavy ulster, and with slippered feet, I crept cautiously from my room and stole down the passage to the top of the stairs. Outside the doctor's door I waited a moment to listen. All was still; the house in utter darkness; no gleam of light beneath any door; only, down the length of the corridor, from the direction of the sick-room, came faint sounds of laughter and incoherent talk that were not things to reassure a mind already half a-tremble, and I made haste to reach the hall and let myself out through the front door into the night.

The air was keen and frosty, perfumed with night smells, and exquisitely fresh; all the million candles of the sky were alight, and a faint breeze rose and fell with far-away sighings in the tops of the pine trees. My blood leaped for a moment in the spaciousness of the night, for the splendid stars brought courage; but the next instant, as I turned the corner of the house, moving stealthily down the gravel drive, my spirits sank again ominously. For, yonder, over the funereal plumes of the Twelve Acre Plantation, I saw the huge and yellow face of the full moon just rising in the east, staring down like some vast Being come to watch upon the progress of our doom. Seen through the distorting vapours of the earth's atmosphere, her face looked weirdly unfamiliar, her usual expression of benignant vacancy somehow a-twist. I slipped along by the shadows of the wall, keeping my eyes upon the ground.

The laundry-house, as already described, stood detached from the other offices, with laurel shrubberies crowding thickly behind it, and the kitchen-garden so close on the other side that the strong smells of soil and growing things came across almost heavily. The shadows of the haunted plantation, hugely lengthened by the rising moon behind them, reached to the very walls and covered the stone tiles of the roof with a dark pall. So keenly were my senses alert at this moment that I believe I could fill a chapter with the endless small details of the impression I received—shadows, odour, shapes, sounds—in the space of the few seconds I stood and waited before the closed wooden door.

Then I became aware of some one moving towards me through the moonlight, and the figure of John Silence, without overcoat and bareheaded, came quickly and without noise to join me. His eyes, I saw at once, were wonderfully bright, and so marked was the shining pallor of his face that I could hardly tell when he passed from the moonlight into the shade.

He passed without a word, beckoning me to follow, and then pushed the door open, and went in.

The chill air of the place met us like that of an underground vault; and the brick floor and whitewashed walls, streaked with damp and smoke, threw back the cold in our faces. Directly opposite gaped the black throat of the huge open fireplace, the ashes of wood fires still piled and scattered about the hearth, and on either side of the projecting chimney-column were the deep recesses holding the big twin cauldrons for boiling clothes. Upon the lids of these cauldrons stood the two little oil lamps, shaded red, which gave all the light there was, and immediately in front of the fireplace there was a small circular table with three chairs set about it. Overhead, the narrow slit windows, high up the walls, pointed to a dim network of wooden rafters half lost among the shadows, and then came the dark vault of the roof. Cheerless and unalluring, for all the red light, it certainly was, reminding me of some unused conventicle, bare of pews or pulpit, ugly and severe, and I was forcibly struck by the contrast between the normal uses to which the place was ordinarily put, and the strange and mediæval purpose which had brought us under its roof to-night.

Possibly an involuntary shudder ran over me, for my companion turned with a confident look to reassure me, and he was so completely master of himself that I at once absorbed from his abundance, and felt the chinks of my failing courage beginning to close up. To meet his eye in the presence of danger was like finding a mental railing that guided and supported thought along the giddy edges of alarm.

"I am quite ready," I whispered, turning to listen for approaching footsteps.

He nodded, still keeping his eyes on mine. Our whispers sounded hollow as they echoed overhead among the rafters.

"I'm glad you are here," he said. "Not all would have the courage. Keep your thoughts controlled, and imagine the protective shell round you—round your *inner* being."

"I'm all right," I repeated, cursing my chattering teeth.

He took my hand and shook it, and the contact seemed to shake into me something of his supreme confidence. The eyes and hands of a strong man can touch the soul. I think he guessed my thought, for a passing smile flashed about the corners of his mouth.

"You will feel more comfortable," he said, in a low tone, "when the chain is complete. The Colonel we can count on, of course. Remember, though," he added warningly, "he may perhaps become controlled—possessed—when the thing comes, because he won't know how to resist. And to explain the business to such a man—!" He shrugged his shoulders expressively. "But it will only be temporary, and I will see that no harm comes to him."

He glanced round at the arrangements with approval.

"Red light," he said, indicating the shaded lamps, "has the lowest rate of vibration. Materialisations are dissipated by strong light—won't form, or hold together—in rapid vibrations."

I was not sure that I approved altogether of this dim light, for in complete darkness there is something protective—the knowledge that one cannot be seen, probably—which a half-light destroys, but I remembered the warning to keep my thoughts steady, and forbore to give them expression.

There was a step outside, and the figure of Colonel Wragge stood in the doorway. Though entering on tiptoe, he made considerable noise and clatter, for his free movements were impeded by the burden he carried, and we saw a large yellowish bowl held out at arms' length from his body, the mouth covered with a white cloth. His face, I noted, was rigidly composed. He, too, was master of himself. And, as I thought of this old soldier moving through the long series of alarms, worn with watching and wearied with assault, unenlightened yet undismayed, even down to the dreadful shock of his sister's terror, and still showing the dogged pluck that persists in the face of defeat, I understood what Dr. Silence meant when he described him as a man "to be counted on."

I think there was nothing beyond this rigidity of his stern features, and a certain greyness of the complexion, to betray the turmoil of the emotions that was doubtless going on within; and the quality of these two men, each in his own way, so keyed me up that, by the time the door was shut and we had exchanged silent greetings, all the latent courage I possessed was well to the fore, and I felt as sure of myself as I knew I ever could feel.

Colonel Wragge set the bowl carefully in the centre of the table.

"Midnight," he said shortly, glancing at his watch, and we all three moved to our chairs.

There, in the middle of that cold and silent place, we sat, with the vile bowl before us, and a thin, hardly perceptible steam rising through the damp air from the surface of the white cloth and disappearing upwards the moment it passed beyond the zone of red light and entered the deep shadows thrown forward by the projecting wall of chimney.

The doctor had indicated our respective places, and I found myself seated with my back to the door and opposite the black hearth. The Colonel was on my left, and Dr. Silence on my right, both half facing me, the latter more in shadow than the former. We thus divided the little table into even sections, and sitting back in our chairs we awaited events in silence.

For something like an hour I do not think there was even the faintest sound within those four walls and under the canopy of that vaulted roof. Our slippers made no scratching on the gritty floor, and our breathing was suppressed almost to nothing; even the rustle of our clothes as we shifted from time to time upon our seats was inaudible. Silence smothered us absolutely—the silence of night, of listening, the silence of a haunted expectancy. The very gurgling of the lamps was too soft to be heard, and if light itself had sound, I do not think we should have noticed the silvery tread of the moonlight as it entered the high narrow windows and threw upon the floor the slender traces of its pallid footsteps.

Colonel Wragge and the doctor, and myself too for that matter, sat thus like figures of stone, without speech and without gesture. My eyes passed in ceaseless journeys from the bowl to their faces, and from their faces to the bowl. They might have been masks, however, for all the signs of life they gave; and the light steaming from the horrid contents beneath the white cloth had long ceased to be visible.

Then presently, as the moon rose higher, the wind rose with it. It sighed, like the lightest of passing wings, over the roof; it crept most softly round the walls; it made the brick floor like ice beneath our feet. With it I saw mentally the desolate moorland flowing like a sea about the old house, the treeless expanse of lonely bills, the nearer copses, sombre, and mysterious in the night. *The* plantation, too, in particular I

saw, and imagined I heard the mournful whisperings that must now be
a-stirring among its tree-tops as the breeze played down between the
twisted stems. In the depth of the room behind us the shafts of moonlight met and crossed in a growing network.

It was after an hour of this wearing and unbroken attention, and I
should judge about one o'clock in the morning, when the baying of the
dogs in the stable-yard first began, and I saw John Silence move suddenly in his chair and sit up in an attitude of attention. Every force in
my being instantly leaped into the keenest vigilance. Colonel Wragge
moved too, though slowly, and without raising his eyes from the table
before him.

The doctor stretched his arm out and took the white cloth from
the bowl.

It was perhaps imagination that persuaded me the red glare of the
lamps grew fainter and the air over the table before us thickened. I had
been expecting something for so long that the movement of my companions, and the lifting of the cloth, may easily have caused the momentary delusion that something hovered in the air before my face,
touching the skin of my cheeks with a silken run. But it was certainly
not a delusion that the Colonel looked up at the same moment and
glanced over his shoulder, as though his eyes followed the movements
of something to and fro about the room, and that he then buttoned his
overcoat more tightly about him and his eyes sought my own face first,
and then the doctor's. And it was no delusion that his face seemed
somehow to have turned dark, become spread as it were with a shadowy blackness. I saw his lips tighten and his expression grow hard and
stern, and it came to me then with a rush that, of course, this man had
told us but a part of the experiences he had been through in the house,
and that there was much more he had never been able to bring himself
to reveal at all. I felt sure of it. The way he turned and stared about
him betrayed a familiarity with other things than those he had described to us. It was not merely a sight of fire he looked for; it was a
sight of something alive, intelligent, something able to evade his
searching; it was *a person*. It was the watch for the ancient Being who
sought to obsess him.

And the way in which Dr. Silence answered his look—though it
was only by a glance of subtlest sympathy—confirmed my impression.

"We may be ready now," I heard him say in a whisper, and I understood that his words were intended as a steadying warning, and braced myself mentally to the utmost of my power.

Yet long before Colonel Wragge had turned to stare about the room, and long before the doctor had confirmed my impression that things were at last beginning to stir, I had become aware in most singular fashion that the place held more than our three selves. With the rising of the wind this increase to our numbers had first taken place. The baying of the hounds almost seemed to have signalled it. I cannot say how it may be possible to realise that an empty place has suddenly become—not empty, when the new arrival is nothing that appeals to any one of the senses; for this recognition of an "invisible," as of the change in the balance of personal forces in a human group, is indefinable and beyond proof. Yet it is unmistakable. And I knew perfectly well at what given moment the atmosphere within these four walls became charged with the presence of other living beings besides ourselves. And, on reflection, I am convinced that both my companions knew it too.

"Watch the light," said the doctor under his breath, and then I knew too that it was no fancy of my own that had turned the air darker, and the way he turned to examine the face of our host sent an electric thrill of wonder and expectancy shivering along every nerve in my body.

Yet it was no kind of terror that I experienced, but rather a sort of mental dizziness, and a sensation as of being suspended in some remote and dreadful altitude where things might happen, indeed were about to happen, that had never before happened within the ken of man. Horror may have formed an ingredient, but it was not chiefly horror, and in no sense ghostly horror.

Uncommon thoughts kept beating on my brain like tiny hammers, soft yet persistent, seeking admission; their unbidden tide began to wash along the far fringes of my mind, the currents of unwonted sensations to rise over the remote frontiers of my consciousness. I was aware of thoughts, and the fantasies of thoughts, that I never knew before existed. Portions of my being stirred that had never stirred before, and things ancient and inexplicable rose to the surface and beckoned me to follow. I felt as though I were about to fly off, at some immense tangent, into an outer space hitherto unknown even in dreams. And so singular was the result produced upon me that I was uncommonly glad to anchor my mind, as well as my eyes, upon the masterful personality of the doctor at my side, for there, I realised, I could draw always upon the forces of sanity and safety.

With a vigorous effort of will I returned to the scene before me, and tried to focus my attention, with steadier thoughts, upon the table, and upon the silent figures seated round it. And then I saw that certain changes had come about in the place where we sat.

The patches of moonlight on the floor, I noted, had become curiously shaded; the faces of my companions opposite were not so clearly visible as before; and the forehead and cheeks of Colonel Wragge were glistening with perspiration. I realised further, that an extraordinary change had come about in the temperature of the atmosphere. The increased warmth had a painful effect, not alone on Colonel Wragge, but upon all of us. It was oppressive and unnatural. We gasped figuratively as well as actually.

"You are the first to feel it," said Dr. Silence in low tones, looking across at him. "You are in more intimate touch, of course—"

The Colonel was trembling, and appeared to be in considerable distress. His knees shook, so that the shuffling of his slippered feet became audible. He inclined his head to show that he had heard, but made no other reply. I think, even then, he was sore put to it to keep himself in hand. I knew what he was struggling against. As Dr. Silence had warned me, he was about to be obsessed, and was savagely, though vainly, resisting.

But, meanwhile, a curious and whirling sense of exhilaration began to come over me. The increasing heat was delightful, bringing a sensation of intense activity, of thoughts pouring through the mind at high speed, of vivid pictures in the brain, of fierce desires and lightning energies alive in every part of the body. I was conscious of no physical distress, such as the Colonel felt, but only of a vague feeling that it might all grow suddenly too intense—that I might be consumed—that my personality, as well as my body, might become resolved into the flame of pure spirit. I began to live at a speed too intense to last. It was as if a thousand ecstasies besieged me—

"Steady!" whispered the voice of John Silence in my ear, and I looked up with a start to see that the Colonel had risen from his chair. The doctor rose too. I followed suit, and for the first time saw down into the bowl. To my amazement and horror I saw that the contents were troubled. The blood was astir with movement.

The rest of the experiment was witnessed by us standing. It came, too, with a curious suddenness. There was no more dreaming, for me at any rate.

I shall never forget the figure of Colonel Wragge standing there beside me, upright and unshaken, squarely planted on his feet, looking about him, puzzled beyond belief, yet full of a fighting anger. Framed by the white walls, the red glow of the lamps upon his streaming cheeks, his eyes glowing against the deathly pallor of his skin, breathing hard and making convulsive efforts of hands and body to keep himself under control, his whole being roused to the point of savage fighting, yet with nothing visible to get at anywhere—he stood there, immovable against odds. And the strange contrast of the pale skin and the burning face I had never seen before, or wish to seen again.

But what has left an even sharper impression on my memory was the blackness that then began crawling over his face, obliterating the features, concealing their human outline, and hiding him inch by inch from view. This was my first realisation that the process of materialisation was at work. His visage became shrouded. I moved from one side to the other to keep him in view, and it was only then I understood that, properly speaking, the blackness was not upon the countenance of Colonel Wragge, but that something had inserted itself between me and him, thus screening his face with the effect of a dark veil. Something that apparently rose through the floor was passing slowly into the air above the table and above the bowl. The blood in the bowl, moreover, was considerably less than before.

And, with this change in the air before us, there came at the same time a further change, I thought, in the face of the soldier. One-half was turned towards the red lamps, while the other caught the pale illumination of the moonlight falling aslant from the high windows, so that it was difficult to estimate this change with accuracy of detail. But it seemed to me that, while the features—eyes, nose, mouth—remained the same, the life informing them had undergone some profound transformation. The signature of a new power had crept into the face and left its traces there—an expression dark, and in some unexplained way, terrible.

Then suddenly he opened his mouth and spoke, and the sound of this changed voice, deep and musical though it was, made me cold and set my heart beating with uncomfortable rapidity. The Being, as he had dreaded, was already in control of his brain, using his mouth.

"I see a blackness like the blackness of Egypt before my face," said the tones of this unknown voice that seemed half his own and half another's. "And out of this darkness they come, they come."

I gave a dreadful start. The doctor turned to look at me for an instant, and then turned to centre his attention upon the figure of our host, and I understood in some intuitive fashion that he was there to watch over the strangest contest man ever saw—to watch over and, if necessary, to protect.

"He is being controlled—possessed," he whispered to me through the shadows. His face wore a wonderful expression, half triumph, half admiration.

Even as Colonel Wragge spoke, it seemed to me that this visible darkness began to increase, pouring up thickly out of the ground by the hearth, rising up in sheets and veils, shrouding our eyes and faces. It stole up from below—an awful blackness that seemed to drink in all the radiations of light in the building, leaving nothing but the ghost of a radiance in their place. Then, out of this rising sea of shadows, issued a pale and spectral light that gradually spread itself about us, and from the heart of this light I saw the shapes of fire crowd and gather. And these were not human shapes, or the shapes of anything I recognised as alive in the world, but outlines of fire that traced globes, triangles, crosses, and the luminous bodies of various geometrical figures. They grew bright, faded, and then grew bright again with an effect almost of pulsation. They passed swiftly to and fro through the air, rising and falling, and particularly in the immediate neighbourhood of the Colonel, often gathering about his head and shoulders, and even appearing to settle upon him like giant insects of flame. They were accompanied, moreover, by a faint sound of hissing—the same sound we had heard that afternoon in the plantation.

"The fire-elementals that precede their master," the doctor said in an undertone. "Be ready."

And while this weird display of the shapes of fire alternately flashed and faded, and the hissing echoed faintly among the dim rafters overhead, we heard the awful voice issue at intervals from the lips of the afflicted soldier. It was a voice of power, splendid in some way I cannot describe, and with a certain sense of majesty in its cadences, and, as I listened to it with quickly-beating heart, I could fancy it was some ancient voice of Time itself, echoing down immense corridors of stone, from the depths of vast temples, from the very heart of mountain tombs.

"I have seen my divine Father, Osiris," thundered the great tones. "I have scattered the gloom of the night. I have burst through the earth, and am one with the starry Deities!"

Something grand came into the soldier's face. He was staring fixedly before him, as though seeing nothing.

"Watch," whispered Dr. Silence in my ear, and his whisper seemed to come from very far away.

Again the mouth opened and the awesome voice issued forth.

"Thoth," it boomed, "has loosened the bandages of Set which fettered my mouth. I have taken my place in the great winds of heaven."

I heard the little wind of night, with its mournful voice of ages, sighing round the walls and over the roof.

"Listen!" came from the doctor at my side, and the thunder of the voice continued—

"I have hidden myself with you, O ye stars that never diminish. I remember my name—in—the—House—of—Fire!"

The voice ceased and the sound died away. Something about the face and figure of Colonel Wragge relaxed, I thought. The terrible look passed from his face. The Being that obsessed him was gone.

"The great Ritual," said Dr. Silence aside to me, very low, "the Book of the Dead. Now it's leaving him. Soon the blood will fashion it a body."

Colonel Wragge, who had stood absolutely motionless all this time, suddenly swayed, so that I thought he was going to fall,—and, but for the quick support of the doctor's arm, he probably would have fallen, for he staggered as in the beginning of collapse.

"I am drunk with the wine of Osiris," he cried,—and it was half with his own voice this time—"but Horus, the Eternal Watcher, is about my path—for—safety." The voice dwindled and failed, dying away into something almost like a cry of distress.

"Now, watch closely," said Dr. Silence, speaking loud, "for after the cry will come the Fire!"

I began to tremble involuntarily; an awful change had come without warning into the air; my legs grew weak as paper beneath my weight and I had to support myself by leaning on the table. Colonel Wragge, I saw, was also leaning forward with a kind of droop. The shapes of fire had vanished all, but his face was lit by the red lamps and the pale shifting moonlight rose behind him like mist.

We were both gazing at the bowl, now almost empty; the Colonel stooped so low I feared every minute he would lose his balance and drop into it; and the shadow, that had so long been in process of forming, now at length began to assume material outline in the air before us.

Then John Silence moved forward quickly. He took his place between us and the shadow. Erect, formidable, absolute master of the situation, I saw him stand there, his face calm and almost smiling, and fire in his eyes. His protective influence was astounding and incalculable. Even the abhorrent dread I felt at the sight of the creature growing into life and substance before us, lessened in some way so that I was able to keep my eyes fixed on the air above the bowl without too vivid a terror.

But as it took shape, rising out of nothing as it were, and growing momentarily more defined in outline, a period of utter and wonderful silence settled down upon the building and all it contained. A hush of ages, like the sudden centre of peace at the heart of the travelling cyclone, descended through the night, and out of this bush, as out of the emanations of the steaming blood, issued the form of the ancient being who had first sent the elemental of fire upon its mission. It grew and darkened and solidified before our eyes. It rose from just beyond the table so that the lower portions remained invisible, but I saw the outline limn itself upon the air, as though slowly revealed by the rising of a curtain. It apparently had not then quite concentrated to the normal proportions, but was spread out on all sides into space, huge, though rapidly condensing, for I saw the colossal shoulders, the neck, the lower portion of the dark jaws, the terrible mouth, and then the teeth and lips—and, as the veil seemed to lift further upon the tremendous face—I saw the nose and cheek bones. In another moment I should have looked straight into the eyes—

But what Dr. Silence did at that moment was so unexpected, and took me so by surprise, that I have never yet properly understood its nature, and he has never yet seen fit to explain in detail to me. He uttered some sound that had a note of command in it—and, in so doing, stepped forward and intervened between me and the face. The figure, just nearing completeness, he therefore hid from my sight—and I have always thought purposely hid from my sight.

"The fire!" he cried out. "The fire! Beware!"

There was a sudden roar as of flame from the very mouth of the pit, and for the space of a single second all grew light as day. A blinding flash passed across my face, and there was heat for an instant that seemed to shrivel skin, and flesh, and bone. Then came steps, and I heard Colonel Wragge utter a great cry, wilder than any human cry I have ever known. The heat sucked all the breath out of my lungs with a rush, and the blaze of light, as it vanished, swept my vision with it into enveloping darkness.

When I recovered the use of my senses a few moments later I saw that Colonel Wragge with a face of death, its whiteness strangely stained, had moved closer to me. Dr. Silence stood beside him, an expression of triumph and success in his eyes. The next minute the soldier tried to clutch me with his hand. Then he reeled, staggered, and, unable to save himself, fell with a great crash upon the brick floor.

After the sheet of flame, a wind raged round the building as though it would lift the roof off, but then passed as suddenly as it came. And in the intense calm that followed I saw that the form had vanished, and the doctor was stooping over Colonel Wragge upon the floor, trying to lift him to a sitting position.

"Light," he said quietly, "more light. Take the shades off."

Colonel Wragge sat up and the glare of the unshaded lamps fell upon his face. It was grey and drawn, still running heat, and there was a look in the eyes and about the corners of the mouth that seemed in this short space of time to have added years to its age. At the same time, the expression of effort and anxiety had left it. It showed relief.

"Gone!" he said, looking up at the doctor in a dazed fashion, and struggling to his feet. "Thank God! it's gone at last." He stared round the laundry as though to find out where he was. "Did it control me—take possession of me? Did I talk nonsense?" be asked bluntly. "After the heat came, I remember nothing—"

"You'll feel yourself again in a few minutes," the doctor said. To my infinite horror I saw that he was surreptitiously wiping sundry dark stains from the face. "Our experiment has been a success and—"

He gave me a swift glance to hide the bowl, standing between me and our host while I hurriedly stuffed it down under the lid of the nearest cauldron.

"—and none of us the worse for it," he finished.

"And fires?" he asked, still dazed, "there'll be no more fires?"

"It is dissipated—partly, at any rate," replied Dr. Silence cautiously.

"And the man behind the gun," he went on, only half realising what he was saying, I think; "have you discovered *that?*"

"A form materialised," said the doctor briefly. "I know for certain now what the directing intelligence was behind it all."

Colonel Wragge pulled himself together and got upon his feet. The words conveyed no clear meaning to him yet. But his memory was returning gradually, and he was trying to piece together the fragments into a connected whole. He shivered a little, for the place had grown suddenly chilly. The air was empty again, lifeless.

"You feel all right again now," Dr. Silence said, in the tone of a man stating a fact rather than asking a question.

"Thanks to you—both, yes." He drew a deep breath, and mopped his face, and even attempted a smile. He made me think of a man coming from the battlefield with the stains of fighting still upon him, but scornful of his wounds. Then he turned gravely towards the doctor with a question in his eyes. Memory had returned and he was himself again.

"Precisely what I expected," the doctor said calmly; "a fire-elemental sent upon its mission in the days of Thebes, centuries before Christ, and to-night, for the first time all these thousands of years, released from the spell that originally bound it."

We stared at him in amazement, Colonel Wragge opening his lips for words that refused to shape themselves.

"And, if we dig," he continued significantly, pointing to the floor where the blackness had poured up, "we shall find some underground connection——a tunnel most likely—leading to the Twelve Acre Wood. It was made by—your predecessor."

"A tunnel made by my brother!" gasped the soldier. "Then my sister should know—she lived here with him—" He stopped suddenly.

John Silence inclined his head slowly. "I think so," he said quietly. "Your brother, no doubt, was as much tormented as you have been," he continued after a pause in which Colonel Wragge seemed deeply preoccupied with his thoughts, "and tried to find peace by burying it in the wood, and surrounding the wood then, like a large magic circle, with the enchantments of the old formulæ. So the stars the man saw blazing—"

"But burying *what?*" asked the soldier faintly, stepping backwards towards the support of the wall.

Dr. Silence regarded us both intently for a moment before he replied. I think he weighed in his mind whether to tell us now, or when the investigation was absolutely complete.

"The mummy," he said softly, after a moment; "the mummy that your brother took from its resting-place of centuries, and brought home—here."

Colonel Wragge dropped down upon the nearest chair, hanging breathlessly on every word. He was far too amazed for speech.

"The mummy of some important person—a priest most likely—protected from disturbance and desecration by the ceremonial magic of the time. For they understood how to attach to the mummy, to lock up with it in the tomb, an elemental force that would direct itself even after ages upon any one who dared to molest it. In this case it was an elemental of fire."

Dr. Silence crossed the floor and turned out the lamps one by one. He had nothing more to say for the moment. Following his example, I folded the table together and took up the chairs, and our host, still dazed and silent, mechanically obeyed him and moved to the door.

We removed all traces of the experiment, taking the empty bowl back to the house concealed beneath an ulster.

The air was cool and fragrant as we walked to the house, the stars beginning to fade overhead and a fresh wind of early morning blowing up out of the east where the sky was already hinting of the coming day. It was after five o'clock.

Stealthily we entered the front hall and locked the door, and as we went on tiptoe upstairs to our rooms, the Colonel, peering at us over his candle as he nodded good-night, whispered that if we were ready the digging should be begun that very day.

Then I saw him steal along to his sister's room and disappear.

IV

But not even the mysterious references to the mummy, or the prospect of a revelation by digging, were able to hinder the reaction that followed the intense excitement of the past twelve hours, and I slept the sleep of the dead, dreamless and undisturbed. A touch on the shoulder woke me, and I saw Dr. Silence standing beside the bed, dressed to go out.

"Come," he said, "it's tea-time. You've slept the best part of a dozen hours."

I sprang up and made a hurried toilet, while my companion sat and talked. He looked fresh and rested, and his manner was even quieter than usual.

"Colonel Wragge has provided spades and pick-axes. We're going out to unearth this mummy at once," he said; "and there's no reason we should not get away by the morning train."

"I'm ready to go to-night, if you are," I said honestly.

But Dr. Silence shook his head.

"I must see this through to the end," he said gravely, and in a tone that made me think he still anticipated serious things, perhaps. He went on talking while I dressed.

"This is really typical of all stories of mummy-haunting, and none of them are cases to trifle with," he explained, "for the mummies of important people—kings, priests, magicians—were laid away with profoundly significant ceremonial, and were very effectively protected, as you have seen, against desecration, and especially against destruction.

"The general belief," he went on, anticipating my questions, "held, of course, that the perpetuity of the mummy guaranteed that of its Ka,—the owner's spirit,—but it is not improbable that the magical embalming was also used to retard reincarnation, the preservation of the body preventing the return of the spirit to the toil and discipline of earth-life; and, in any case, they knew how to attach powerful guardian-forces to keep off trespassers. And any one who dared to remove the mummy, or especially to unwind it—well," he added, with meaning, "you have seen—and you *will* see."

I caught his face in the mirror while I struggled with my collar. It was deeply serious. There could be no question that he spoke of what he believed and knew.

"The traveller-brother who brought it here must have been haunted too," he continued, "for he tried to banish it by burial in the wood, making a magic circle to enclose it. Something of genuine ceremonial he must have known, for the stars the man saw were of course the remains of the still flaming pentagrams he traced at intervals in the circle. Only he did not know enough, or possibly was ignorant that the mummy's guardian was a fire-force. Fire cannot be enclosed by fire, though, as you saw, it can be released by it."

'Then that awful figure in the laundry?" I asked, thrilled to find him so communicative.

"Undoubtedly the actual Ka of the mummy operating always behind its agent, the elemental, and most likely thousands of years old."

"And Miss Wragge—?" I ventured once more.

"Ah, Miss Wragge," he repeated with increased gravity, "Miss Wragge—"

A knock at the door brought a servant with word that tea was ready, and the Colonel had sent to ask if we were coming down. The thread was broken. Dr. Silence moved to the door and signed to me to follow. But his manner told me that in any case no real answer would have been forthcoming to my question.

"And the place to dig in," I asked, unable to restrain my curiosity, "will you find it by some process of divination or—?"

He paused at the door and looked back at me, and with that he left me to finish my dressing.

It was growing dark when the three of us silently made our way to the Twelve Acre Plantation; the sky was overcast, and a black wind came out of the east. Gloom hung about the old house and the air seemed full of sighings. We found the tools ready laid at the edge of the wood, and each shouldering his piece, we followed our leader at once in among the trees. He went straight forward for some twenty yards and then stopped. At his feet lay the blackened circle of one of the burned places. It was just discernible against the surrounding white grass.

"There are three of these," he said, "and they all lie in a line with one another. Any one of them will tap the tunnel that connects the laundry—the former Museum—with the chamber where the mummy now lies buried."

He at once cleared away the burnt grass and began to dig; we all began to dig. While I used the pick, the others shovelled vigorously. No one spoke. Colonel Wragge worked the hardest of the three. The soil was light and sandy, and there were only a few snake-like roots and occasional loose stones to delay us. The pick made short work of these. And meanwhile the darkness settled about us and the biting wind swept roaring through the trees overhead.

Then, quite suddenly, without a cry, Colonel Wragge disappeared up to his neck.

"The tunnel!" cried the doctor, helping to drag him out, red, breathless, and covered with sand and perspiration. "Now, let me lead the way." And he slipped down nimbly into the hole, so that a moment later we heard his voice, muffled by sand and distance, rising up to us.

"Hubbard, you come next, and then Colonel Wragge—if he wishes," we heard.

"I'll follow you, of course," he said, looking at me as I scrambled in.

The hole was bigger now, and I got down on all-fours in a channel not much bigger than a large sewer-pipe and found myself in total darkness. A minute later a heavy thud, followed by a cataract of loose sand, announced the arrival of the Colonel.

"Catch hold of my heel," called Dr. Silence, "and Colonel Wragge can take yours."

In this slow, laborious fashion we wormed our way along a tunnel that had been roughly dug out of the shifting sand, and was shored up clumsily by means of wooden pillars and posts. Any moment, it seemed to me, we might be buried alive. We could not see an inch before our eyes, but had to grope our way feeling the pillars and the walls. It was difficult to breathe, and the Colonel behind me made but slow progress, for the cramped position of our bodies was very severe.

We had travelled in this way for ten minutes, and gone perhaps as much as ten yards, when I lost my grasp of the doctor's heel.

"Ah!" I heard his voice, sounding above me somewhere. He was standing up in a clear space, and the next moment I was standing beside him. Colonel Wragge came heavily after, and he too rose up and stood. Then Dr. Silence produced his candles and we heard preparations for striking matches.

Yet even before there was light, an indefinable sensation of awe came over us all. In this hole in the sand, some three feet under ground, we stood side by side, cramped and huddled, struck suddenly with an overwhelming apprehension of something ancient, something formidable, something incalculably wonderful, that touched in each one of us a sense of the sublime and the terrible even before we could see an inch before our faces. I know not how to express in language this singular emotion that caught us here in utter darkness, touching no sense directly, it seemed, yet with the recognition that before us in the blackness of this underground night there lay something that was mighty with the mightiness of long past ages.

I felt Colonel Wragge press in closely to my side, and I understood the pressure and welcomed it. No human touch, to me at least, has ever been more eloquent.

Then the match flared, a thousand shadows fled on black wings, and I saw John Silence fumbling with the candle, his face lit up grotesquely by the flickering light below it.

I had dreaded this light, yet when it came there was apparently nothing to explain the profound sensations of dread that preceded it. We stood in a small vaulted chamber in the sand, the sides and roof shored with bars of wood, and the ground laid roughly with what seemed to be tiles. It was six feet high, so that we could all stand comfortably, and may have been ten feet long by eight feet wide. Upon the wooden pillars at the side I saw that Egyptian hieroglyphics had been rudely traced by burning.

Dr. Silence lit three candles and handed one to each of us. He placed a fourth in the sand against the wall on his right, and another to mark the entrance to the tunnel. We stood and stared about us, instinctively holding our breath.

"Empty, by God!" exclaimed Colonel Wragge. His voice trembled with excitement. And then, as his eyes rested on the ground, he added, "And footsteps—look—footsteps in the sand!"

Dr. Silence said nothing. He stooped down and began to make a search of the chamber, and as he moved, my eyes followed his crouching figure and noted the queer distorted shadows that poured over the walls and ceiling after him. Here and there thin trickles of loose sand ran fizzing down the sides. The atmosphere, heavily charged with faint yet pungent odours, lay utterly still, and the flames of the candles might have been painted on the air for all the movement they betrayed.

And, as I watched, it was almost necessary to persuade myself forcibly that I was only standing upright with difficulty in this little sand-hole of a modem garden in the south of England, for it seemed to me that I stood, as in vision, at the entrance of some vast rock-hewn Temple far, far down the river of Time. The illusion was powerful, and persisted. Granite columns, that rose to heaven, piled themselves about me, majestically uprearing, and a roof like the sky itself spread above a line of colossal figures that moved in shadowy procession along endless and stupendous aisles. This huge and splendid fantasy, borne I knew not whence, possessed me so vividly that I was actually obliged to concentrate my attention upon the small stooping figure of the doctor, as he groped about the walls, in order to keep the eye of imagination on the scene before me.

But the limited space rendered a long search out of the question, and his footsteps, instead of shuffling through loose sand, presently struck something of a different quality that gave forth a hollow and resounding echo. He stooped to examine more closely.

He was standing exactly in the centre of the little chamber when this happened, and he at once began scraping away the sand with his feet. In less than a minute a smooth surface became visible—the surface of a wooden covering. The next thing I saw was that he had raised it and was peering down into a space below. Instantly, a strong odour of nitre and bitumen, mingled with the strange perfume of unknown and powdered aromatics, rose up from the uncovered space and filled the vault, stinging the throat and making the eyes water and smart.

"The mummy!" whispered Dr. Silence, looking up into our faces over his candle; and as he said the word I felt the soldier lurch against me, and heard his breathing in my very ear.

"The mummy!" he repeated under his breath, as we pressed forward to look.

It is difficult to say exactly why the sight should have stirred in me so prodigious an emotion of wonder and veneration, for I have had not a little to do with mummies, have unwound scores of them, and even experimented magically with not a few. But there was something in the sight of that grey and silent figure, lying in its modern box of lead and wood at the bottom of this sandy grave, swathed in the bandages of centuries and wrapped in the perfumed linen that the priests of Egypt had prayed over with their mighty enchantments thousands of years before—something in the sight of it lying there and breathing its own spice-laden atmosphere even in the darkness of its exile in this remote land, something that pierced to the very core of my being and touched that root of awe which slumbers in every man near the birth of tears and the passion of true worship.

I remember turning quickly from the Colonel, lest he should see my emotion, yet fail to understand its cause, turn and clutch John Silence by the arm, and then fall trembling to see that he, too, had lowered his head and was hiding his face in his hands.

A kind of whirling storm came over me, rising out of I know not what utter deeps of memory, and in a whiteness of vision I heard the magical old chauntings from the Book of the Dead, and saw the Gods pass by in dim procession, the mighty, immemorial Beings who were yet themselves only the personified attributes of the true Gods, the God with the Eyes of Fire, the God with the Face of Smoke. I saw again Anubis, the dog-faced deity, and the children of Horus, eternal watcher of the ages, as they swathed Osiris, the first mummy of the world, in the scented and mystic bands, and I tasted again something of the ecstasy of the justified soul as it embarked in the golden Boat of Ra, and journeyed onwards to rest in the fields of the blessed.

And then, as Dr. Silence, with infinite reverence, stooped and touched the still face, so dreadfully staring with its painted eyes, there rose again to our nostrils wave upon wave of this perfume of thousands of years, and time fled backwards like a thing of naught, showing me in haunted panorama the most wonderful dream of the whole world.

A gentle hissing became audible in the air, and the doctor moved quickly backwards. It came close to our faces and then seemed to play about the walls and ceiling.

"The last of the Fire—still waiting for its full accomplishment," he muttered; but I heard both words and hissing as things far away, for I was still busy with the journey of the soul through the Seven Halls of Death, listening for echoes of the grandest ritual ever known to men.

The earthen plates covered with hieroglyphics still lay beside the mummy, and round it, carefully arranged at the points of the compass, stood the four jars with the heads of the hawk, the jackal, the cyno-cephalus, and man, the jars in which were placed the hair, the nail par-ings, the heart, and other special portions of the body. Even the amulets, the mirror, the blue clay statues of the Ka, and the lamp with seven wicks were there. Only the sacred scarabæus was missing.

"Not only has it been torn from its ancient resting-place," I heard Dr. Silence saying in a solemn voice as he looked at Colonel Wragge with fixed gaze, "but it has been partially unwound,"—he pointed to the wrappings of the breast,—"and—the scarabæus has been removed from the throat."

The hissing, that was like the hissing of an invisible flame, had ceased; only from time to time we heard it as though it passed back-wards and forwards in the tunnel; and we stood looking into each oth-er's faces without speaking.

Presently Colonel Wragge made a great effort and braced himself. I heard the sound catch in his throat before the words actually became audible.

"My sister," he said, very low. And then there followed a long pause, broken at length by John Silence.

"It must be replaced," he said significantly.

"I knew nothing," the soldier said, forcing himself to speak the words he hated saying. "Absolutely nothing."

"It must be returned," repeated the other," if it is not now too late. For I fear—I fear—"

Colonel Wragge made a movement of assent with his head.

"It shall be," he said.

The place was still as the grave.

I do not know what it was then that made us all three turn round with so sudden a start, for there was no sound audible to my ears, at least.

The doctor was on the point of replacing the lid over the mummy, when he straightened up as if he had been shot.

"There's something coming," said Colonel Wragge under his breath, and the doctor's eyes, peering down the small opening of the tunnel, showed me the true direction.

A distant shuffling noise became distinctly audible coming from a point about half-way down the tunnel we had so laboriously penetrated.

"It's the sand falling in," I said, though I knew it was foolish.

"No," said the Colonel calmly, in a voice that seemed to have the ring of iron, "I've heard it for some time past. It is something alive— and it is coming nearer."

He stared about him with a look of resolution that made his face almost noble. The horror in his heart was overmastering, yet he stood there prepared for anything that might come.

"There's no other way out," John Silence said.

He leaned the lid against the sand, and waited. I knew by the mask-like expression of his face, the pallor, and the steadiness of the eyes, that he anticipated something that might be very terrible— appalling.

The Colonel and myself stood on either side of the opening. I still held my candle and was ashamed of the way it shook, dripping the grease all over me; but the soldier had set his into the sand just behind his feet.

Thoughts of being buried alive, of being smothered like rats in a trap, of being caught and done to death by some invisible and merciless force we could not grapple with, rushed into my mind. Then I thought of fire—of suffocation—of being roasted alive. The perspiration began to pour from my face.

"Steady!" came the voice of Dr. Silence to me through the vault

For five minutes, that seemed fifty, we stood waiting, looking from each other's faces to the mummy, and from the mummy to the hole, and all the time the shuffling sound, soft and stealthy, came gradually nearer. The tension, for me at least, was very near the breaking point when at last the cause of the disturbance reached the edge. It was hidden for a moment just behind the broken rim of soil. A jet of sand, shaken by the close vibration, trickled down on to the ground; I have never in my life seen anything fall with such laborious leisure. The next second, uttering a cry of curious quality, it came into view.

And it was far more distressingly horrible than anything I had anticipated.

For the sight of some Egyptian monster, some god of the tombs, or even of some demon of fire, I think I was already half prepared; but when, instead, I saw the white visage of Miss Wragge framed in that round opening of sand, followed by her body crawling on all-fours, her eyes bulging and reflecting the yellow glare of the candles, my first instinct was to turn and run like a frantic animal seeking a way of escape.

But Dr. Silence, who seemed no whit surprised, caught my arm and steadied me, and we both saw the Colonel then drop upon his knees and come thus to a level with his sister. For more than a whole minute, as though struck in stone, the two faces gazed silently at each other: hers, for all the dreadful emotion in it, more like a gargoyle than anything human; and his, white and blank with an expression that was beyond either astonishment or alarm. She looked up; he looked down. It was a picture in a nightmare, and the candle, stuck in the sand close to the hole, threw upon it the glare of impromptu footlights.

Then John Silence moved forward and spoke in a voice that was very low, yet perfectly calm and natural.

"I am glad you have come," he said. "You are the one person whose presence at this moment is most required. And I hope that you may yet be in time to appease the anger of the Fire, and to bring peace again to your household, and," he added lower still so that no one heard it but myself, *"safety to yourself."*

And while her brother stumbled backwards, crushing a candle into the sand in his awkwardness, the old lady crawled farther into the vaulted chamber and slowly rose upon her feet.

At the sight of the wrapped figure of the mummy I was fully prepared to see her scream and faint, but on the contrary, to my complete amazement, she merely bowed her head and dropped quietly upon her knees. Then, after a pause of more than a minute, she raised her eyes to the roof and her lips began to mutter as in prayer. Her right hand, meanwhile, which had been fumbling for some time at her throat, suddenly came away, and before the gaze of all of us she held it out, palm upwards, over the grey and ancient figure outstretched below. And in it we beheld glistening the green jasper of the stolen scarabæus.

Her brother, leaning heavily against the wall behind, uttered a sound that was half cry, half exclamation, but John Silence, standing directly in front of her, merely fixed his eyes on her and pointed downwards to the staring face below.

"Replace it," he said sternly, "where it belongs."

Miss Wragge was kneeling at the feet of the mummy when this happened. We three men all had our eyes riveted on what followed. Only the reader who by some remote chance may have witnessed a line of mummies, freshly laid from their tombs upon the sand, slowly stir and bend as the heat of the Egyptian sun warms their ancient bodies into the semblance of life, can form any conception of the ultimate horror we experienced when the silent figure before us moved in its grave of lead and sand. Slowly, before our eyes, it writhed, and, with a faint rustling of the immemorial cerements, rose up, and, through sightless and bandaged eyes, stared across the yellow candle-light at the woman who had violated it

I tried to move—her brother tried to move—but the sand seemed to hold our feet. I tried to cry—her brother tried to cry—but the sand seemed to fill our lungs and throat. We could only stare—and, even so, the sand seemed to rise like a desert storm and cloud our vision. . . .

And when I managed at length to open my eyes again, the mummy was lying once more upon its back, motionless, the shrunken and painted face upturned towards the ceiling, and the old lady had tumbled forward and was lying in the semblance of death with her head and arms upon its crumbling body.

But upon the wrappings of the throat I saw the green jasper of the sacred scarabæus shining again like a living eye.

Colonel Wragge and the doctor recovered themselves long before I did, and I found myself helping them clumsily and unintelligently to raise the frail body of the old lady, while John Silence carefully replaced the covering over the grave and scraped back the sand with his foot, while he issued brief directions.

I heard his voice as in a dream; but the journey back along that cramped tunnel, weighted by a dead woman, blinded with sand, suffocated with heat, was in no sense a dream. It took us the best part of half an hour to reach the open air. And, even then, we had to wait a considerable time for the appearance of Dr. Silence. We carried her undiscovered into the house and up to her own room.

"The mummy will cause no further disturbance," I heard Dr. Silence say to our host later that evening as we prepared to drive for the night train, "provided always," he added significantly, "that you, and yours, cause *it* no disturbance."

It was in a dream, too, that we left.

"You did not see her face, I know," he said to me as we wrapped our rugs about us in the empty compartment. And when I shook my head, quite unable to explain the instinct that had come to me not to look, he turned towards me, his face pale, and genuinely sad.

"Scorched and blasted," he whispered.

Secret Worship

Harris, the silk merchant, was in South Germany on his way home from a business trip when the idea came to him suddenly that he would take the mountain railway from Strassbourg and run down to revisit his old school after an interval of something more than thirty years. And it was to this chance impulse of the junior partner in Harris Brothers of St. Paul's Churchyard that John Silence owed one of the most curious cases of his whole experience, for at that very moment he happened to be tramping these same mountains with a holiday knapsack, and from different points of the compass the two men were actually converging towards the same inn.

Now, deep down in the heart that for thirty years had been concerned chiefly with the profitable buying and selling of silk, this school had left the imprint of its peculiar influence, and, though perhaps unknown to Harris, had strongly coloured the whole of his subsequent existence. It belonged to the deeply religious life of a small Protestant community (which it is unnecessary to specify), and his father had sent him there at the age of fifteen, partly because he would learn the German requisite for the conduct of the silk business, and partly because the discipline was strict, and discipline was what his soul and body needed just then more than anything else.

The life, indeed, had proved exceedingly severe, and young Harris benefited accordingly; for though corporal punishment was unknown, there was a system of mental and spiritual correction which somehow made the soul stand proudly erect to receive it, while it struck at the very root of the fault and taught the boy that his character was being cleaned and strengthened, and that he was not merely being tortured in a kind of personal revenge.

That was over thirty years ago, when he was a dreamy and impressionable youth of fifteen; and now, as the train climbed slowly up the winding mountain gorges, his mind travelled back somewhat lovingly over the intervening period, and forgotten details rose vividly again before him out of the shadows. The life there had been very wonderful, it seemed to him, in that remote mountain village, protected from the tumults of the world by the love and worship of the devout Brotherhood that ministered to the needs of some hundred boys from every country in Europe. Sharply the scenes came back to him. He smelt again the long stone corridors, the hot pinewood rooms, where the sultry hours of summer study were passed with bees droning through open windows in the sunshine, and German characters struggling in the mind with dreams of English lawns—and then the sudden awful cry of the master in German—

"Harris, stand up! You sleep!"

And he recalled the dreadful standing motionless for an hour, book in hand, while the knees felt like wax and the head grew heavier than a cannon-ball.

The very smell of the cooking came back to him—the daily *Sauerkraut,* the watery chocolate on Sundays, the flavour of the stringy meat served twice a week at *Mittagessen;* and he smiled to think again of the half-rations that was the punishment for speaking English. The very odour of the milk-bowls,—the hot sweet aroma that rose from the soaking peasant-bread at the six-o'clock breakfast,—came back to him pungently, and he saw the huge *Speisesaal* with the hundred boys in their school uniform, all eating sleepily in silence, gulping down the coarse bread and scalding milk in terror of the bell that would presently cut them short—and, at the far end where the masters sat, he saw the narrow slit windows with the vistas of enticing field and forest beyond.

And this, in turn, made him think of the great barn-like room on the top floor where all slept together in wooden cots, and he heard in memory the clamour of the cruel bell that woke them on winter mornings at five o'clock and summoned them to the stone flagged *Waschkammer,* where boys and masters alike, after scanty and icy washing, dressed in complete silence.

From this his mind passed swiftly, with vivid picture-thoughts, to other things, and with a passing shiver he remembered how the loneliness of never being alone had eaten into him, and how everything— work, meals, sleep, walks, leisure—was done with his "division" of twenty other boys and under the eyes of at least two masters. The only solitude possible was by asking for half an hour's practice in the cell-like music rooms, and Harris smiled to himself as he recalled the zeal of his violin studies.

Then, as the train puffed laboriously through the great pine forests that cover these mountains with a giant carpet of velvet, he found the pleasanter layers of memory giving up their dead, and he recalled with admiration the kindness of the masters, whom all addressed as Brother, and marvelled afresh at their devotion in burying themselves for years in such a place, only to leave it, in most cases, for the still rougher life of missionaries in the wild places of the world.

He thought once more of the still, religious atmosphere that hung over the little forest community like a veil, barring the distressful world; of the picturesque ceremonies at Easter, Christmas, and New Year; of the numerous feast-days and charming little festivals. The *Beschehr-Fest,* in particular, came back to him,—the feast of gifts at Christmas,— when the entire community paired off and gave presents, many of which had taken weeks to make or the savings of many days to purchase. And then he saw the midnight ceremony in the church at New Year, with the shining face of the *Prediger* in the pulpit,—the village preacher who, on the last night of the old year, saw in the empty gallery beyond the organ loft the faces of all who were to die in the ensuing twelve months, and who at last recognised himself among them, and, in the very middle of his sermon, passed into a state of rapt ecstasy and burst into a torrent of praise.

Thickly the memories crowded upon him. The picture of the small village dreaming its unselfish life on the mountain-tops, clean, wholesome, simple, searching vigorously for its God, and training hundreds of boys in the grand way, rose up in his mind with all the power of an obsession. He felt once more the old mystical enthusiasm, deeper than the sea and more wonderful than the stars; he heard again the winds sighing from leagues of forest over the red roofs in the moonlight; he heard the Brothers' voices talking of the things beyond this life as though they had actually experienced them in the body; and, as he sat in the jolting train, a spirit of unutterable longing passed over his seared and tired soul, stirring in the depths of him a sea of emotions that he thought had long since frozen into immobility.

And the contrast pained him,—the idealistic dreamer then, the man of business now,—so that a spirit of unworldly peace and beauty known only to the soul in meditation laid its feathered finger upon his heart, moving strangely the surface of the waters.

Harris shivered a little and looked out of the window of his empty carriage. The train had long passed Hornberg, and far below the streams tumbled in white foam down the limestone rocks. In front of him, dome upon dome of wooded mountain stood against the sky. It was October, and the air was cool and sharp, wood-smoke and damp moss exquisitely mingled in it with the subtle odours of the pines. Overhead, between the tips of the highest firs, he saw the first stars peeping, and the sky was a clean, pale amethyst that seemed exactly the colour all these memories clothed themselves with in his mind.

He leaned back in his corner and sighed. He was a heavy man, and he had not known sentiment for years; he was a big man, and it took much to move him, literally and figuratively; he was a man in whom the dreams of God that haunt the soul in youth, though overlaid by the scum that gathers in the fight for money, had not, as with the majority, utterly died the death.

He came back into this little neglected pocket of the years, where so much fine gold had collected and lain undisturbed, with all his semi-spiritual emotions aquiver; and, as he watched the mountain-tops come nearer, and smelt the forgotten odours of his boyhood, something melted on the surface of his soul and left him sensitive to a degree he had not known since, thirty years before, he had lived here with his dreams, his conflicts, and his youthful suffering.

A thrill ran through him as the train stopped with a jolt at a tiny station and he saw the name in large black lettering on the grey stone building, and below it, the number of metres it stood above the level of the sea.

"The highest point on the line!" he exclaimed. "How well I remember it—Sommerau—Summer Meadow. The very next station is mine!"

And, as the train ran downhill with brakes on and steam shut off, he put his head out of the window and one by one saw the old familiar landmarks in the dusk. They stared at him like dead faces in a dream. Queer, sharp feelings, half poignant, half sweet, stirred in his heart.

"There's the hot, white road we walked along so often with the two Brüder always at our heels," he thought; "and there, by Jove, is the turn through the forest to *'Die Galgen,'* the stone gallows where they hanged the witches in olden days!"

He smiled a little as the train slid past.

"And there's the copse where the Lilies of the Valley powdered the ground in spring; and, I swear,"—he put his head out with a sudden impulse,—"if that's not the very clearing where Calame, the French boy, chased the swallow-tail with me, and Bruder Pagel gave us half-rations for leaving the road without permission, and for shouting in our mother tongues!" And he laughed again as the memories came back with a rush, flooding his mind with vivid detail.

The train stopped, and he stood on the grey gravel platform like a man in a dream. It seemed half a century since he last waited there with corded wooden boxes, and got into the train for Strassbourg and home after the two years' exile. Time dropped from him like an old garment and he felt a boy again. Only, things looked so much smaller than his memory of them; shrunk and dwindled they looked, and the distances seemed on a curiously smaller scale.

He made his way across the road to the little Gasthaus, and, as he went, faces and figures of former schoolfellows,—German, Swiss, Italian, French, Russian,—slipped out of the shadowy woods and silently accompanied him. They flitted by his side, raising their eyes questioningly, sadly, to his. But their names he had forgotten. Some of the Brothers, too, came with them, and most of these be remembered by name—Bruder Röst, Bruder Pagel, Bruder Schliemann, and the bearded face of the old preacher who had seen himself in the haunted gallery of those about to die—Bruder Gysin. The dark forest lay all about him like a sea that any moment might rush with velvet waves upon the scene and sweep all the faces away. The air was cool and wonderfully fragrant, but with every perfumed breath came also a pallid memory. . . .

Yet, in spite of the underlying sadness inseparable from such an experience, it was all very interesting, and held a pleasure peculiarly its own, so that Harris engaged his room and ordered supper feeling well pleased with himself, and intending to walk up to the old school that very evening. It stood in the centre of the community's village, some four miles distant through the forest, and he now recollected for the first time that this little Protestant settlement dwelt isolated in a section of the country that was otherwise Catholic. Crucifixes and shrines surrounded the clearing like the sentries of a beleaguring army. Once beyond the square of the village, with its few acres of field and orchard, the forest crowded up in solid phalanxes, and beyond the rim of trees began the country that was ruled by the priests of another faith. He vaguely remembered, too, that the Catholics had showed sometimes a certain hostility towards the little Protestant oasis that flourished so quietly and benignly in their midst. He had quite forgotten this. How trumpery it all seemed now with his wide experience of life and his knowledge of other countries and the great outside world. It was like stepping back, not thirty years, but three hundred.

There were only two others besides himself at supper. One of them, a bearded, middle-aged man in tweeds, sat by himself at the far end, and Harris kept out of his way because he was English. He feared he might be in business, possibly even in the silk business, and that he would perhaps talk on the subject. The other traveller, however, was a Catholic priest. He was a little man who ate his salad with a knife, yet so gently that it was almost inoffensive, and it was the sight of "the cloth" that recalled his memory of the old antagonism. Harris mentioned by way of conversation the object of his sentimental journey, and the priest looked up sharply at him with raised eyebrows and an expression of surprise and suspicion that somehow piqued him. He ascribed it to his difference of belief.

"Yes," went on the silk merchant, pleased to talk of what his mind was so full, "and it was a curious experience for an English boy to be dropped down into a school of a hundred foreigners. I well remember the loneliness and intolerable Heimweh of it at first." His German was very fluent.

The priest opposite looked up from his cold veal and potato salad and smiled. It was a nice face. He explained quietly that he did not belong here, but was making a tour of the parishes of Württemberg and Baden.

"It was a strict life," added Harris. "We English, I remember, used to call it *Gefängnisleben*—prison life!"

The face of the other, for some unaccountable reason, darkened.

After a slight pause, and more by way of politeness than because he wished to continue the subject, he said quietly—

"It was a flourishing school in those days, of course. Afterwards, I have heard—" He shrugged his shoulders slightly, and the odd look—it almost seemed a look of alarm—came back into his eyes. The sentence remained unfinished.

Something in the tone of the man seemed to his listener uncalled for—in a sense reproachful, singular. Harris bridled in spite of himself.

"It has changed?" he asked. "I can hardly believe—"

"You have not heard, then?" observed the priest gently, making a gesture as though to cross himself, yet not actually completing it. "You have not heard what happened there before it was abandoned—?"

It was very childish, of course, and perhaps he was overtired and overwrought in some way, but the words and manner of the little priest seemed to him so offensive—so disproportionately offensive—that he hardly noticed the concluding sentence. He recalled the old bitterness and the old antagonism, and for a moment he almost lost his temper.

"Nonsense," he interrupted with a forced laugh, "*Unsinn!* You must forgive me, sir, for contradicting you. But I was a pupil there myself. I was at school there. There was no place like it. I cannot believe that anything serious could have happened to—to take away its character. The devotion of the Brothers would be difficult to equal anywhere——"

He broke off suddenly, realising that his voice had been raised unduly and that the man at the far end of the table might understand German; and at the same moment he looked up and saw that this individual's eyes were fixed upon his face intently. They were peculiarly bright. Also they were rather wonderful eyes, and the way they met his own served in some way he could not understand to convey both a reproach and a warning. The whole face of the stranger, indeed, made a vivid impression upon him, for it was a face, he now noticed for the first time, in whose presence one would not willingly have said or done anything unworthy. Harris could not explain to himself how it was he had not become conscious sooner of its presence.

But he could have bitten off his tongue for having so far forgotten himself. The little priest lapsed into silence. Only once he said, looking up and speaking in a low voice that was not intended to be overheard, but that evidently *was* overheard, "You will find it different." Presently he rose and left the table with a polite bow that included both the others.

And, after him, from the far end rose also the figure in the tweed suit, leaving Harris by himself.

He sat on for a bit in the darkening room, sipping his coffee and smoking his fifteen-pfennig cigar, till the girl came in to light the oil lamps. He felt vexed with himself for his lapse from good manners, yet hardly able to account for it. Most likely, he reflected, he had been annoyed because the priest had unintentionally changed the pleasant character of his dream by introducing a jarring note. Later he must seek an opportunity to make amends. At present, however, he was too impatient for his walk to the school, and he took his stick and hat and passed out into the open air.

And, as he crossed before the Gasthaus, he noticed that the priest and the man in the tweed suit were engaged already in such deep conversation that they hardly noticed him as he passed and raised his hat.

He started off briskly, well remembering the way, and hoping to reach the village in time to have a word with one of the Brüder. They might even ask him in for a cup of coffee. He felt sure of his welcome, and the old memories were in full possession once more. The hour of return was a matter of no consequence whatever.

It was then just after seven o'clock, and the October evening was drawing in with chill airs from the recesses of the forest. The road plunged straight from the railway clearing into its depths, and in a very few minutes the trees engulfed him and the clack of his boots fell dead and echoless against the serried stems of a million firs. It was very black; one trunk was hardly distinguishable from another. He walked smartly, swinging his holly stick. Once or twice he passed a peasant on his way to bed, and the guttural "Gruss Got," unheard for so long, emphasised the passage of time, while yet making it seem as nothing. A fresh group of pictures crowded his mind. Again the figures of former schoolfellows flitted out of the forest and kept pace by his side, whispering of the doings of long ago. One reverie stepped hard upon the heels of another. Every turn in the road, every clearing of the forest, he knew, and each in turn brought forgotten associations to life. He enjoyed himself thoroughly.

He marched on and on. There was powdered gold in the sky till the moon rose, and then a wind of faint silver spread silently between the earth and stars. He saw the tips of the fir trees shimmer, and heard them whisper as the breeze turned their needles towards the light. The mountain air was indescribably sweet. The road shone like the foam of a river through the gloom. White moths flitted here and there like silent thoughts across his path, and a hundred smells greeted him from the forest caverns across the years.

Then, when he least expected it, the trees fell away abruptly on both sides, and he stood on the edge of the village clearing.

He walked faster. There lay the familiar outlines of the houses, sheeted with silver; there stood the trees in the little central square with the fountain and small green lawns; there loomed the shape of the church next to the Gasthof der Brüdergemeinde; and just beyond, dimly rising into the sky, he saw with a sudden thrill the mass of the huge school building, blocked castle-like with deep shadows in the moonlight, standing square and formidable to face him after the silences of more than a quarter of a century.

He passed quickly down the deserted village street and stopped close beneath its shadow, staring up at the walls that had once held him prisoner for two years—two unbroken years of discipline and homesickness. Memories and emotions surged through his mind; for the most vivid sensations of his youth had focused about this spot, and it was here he had first begun to live and learn values. Not a single footstep broke the silence, though lights glimmered here and there through cottage windows; but when he looked up at the high walls of the school, draped now in shadow, he easily imagined that well-known faces crowded to the windows to greet him—closed windows that really reflected only moonlight and the gleam of stars.

This, then, was the old school building, standing foursquare to the world, with its shuttered windows, its lofty, tiled roof, and the spiked lightning-conductors pointing like black and taloned fingers from the corners. For a long time he stood and stared. Then, presently, he came to himself again, and realised to his joy that a light still shone in the windows of the *Bruderstube*.

He turned from the road and passed through the iron railings; then climbed the twelve stone steps and stood facing the black wooden

door with the heavy bars of iron, a door he had once loathed and
dreaded with the hatred and passion of an imprisoned soul, but now
looked upon tenderly with a sort of boyish delight.

Almost timorously he pulled the rope and listened with a tremor of
excitement to the clanging of the bell deep within the building. And the
long-forgotten sound brought the past before him with such a vivid
sense of reality that he positively shivered. It was like the magic bell in
the fairy-tale that rolls back the curtain of Time and summons the figures from the shadows of the dead. He had never felt so sentimental in
his life. It was like being young again. And, at the same time, he began to
bulk rather large in his own eyes with a certain spurious importance. He
was a big man from the world of strife and action. In this little place of
peaceful dreams would he, perhaps, not cut something of a figure?

"I'll try once more," he thought after a long pause, seizing the iron
bell-rope, and was just about to pull it when a step sounded on the
stone passage within, and the huge door slowly swung open.

A tall man with a rather severe cast of countenance stood facing
him in silence.

"I must apologise—it is somewhat late," he began a trifle pomp-
ously, "but the fact is I am an old pupil. I have only just arrived and
really could not restrain myself." His German seemed not quite so fluent as usual. "My interest is so great. I was here in '70."

The other opened the door wider and at once bowed him in with a
smile of genuine welcome.

"I am Bruder Kalkmann," he said quietly in a deep voice. "I myself
was a master here about that time. It is a great pleasure always to welcome a former pupil." He looked at him very keenly for a few seconds,
and then added, "I think, too, it is splendid of you to come—very
splendid."

"It is a very great pleasure," Harris replied, delighted with his reception.

The dimly-lighted corridor with its flooring of grey stone, and the
familiar sound of a German voice echoing through it,—with the peculiar intonation the Brothers always used in speaking,—all combined to
lift him bodily, as it were, into the dream-atmosphere of long-forgotten
days. He stepped gladly into the building and the door shut with the
familiar thunder that completed the reconstruction of the past. He al-

most felt the old sense of imprisonment, of aching nostalgia, of having lost his liberty.

Harris sighed involuntarily and turned towards his host, who returned his smile faintly and then led the way down the corridor.

"The boys have retired," he explained, "and, as you remember, we keep early hours here. But, at least, you will join us for a little while in the *Bruderstube* and enjoy a cup of coffee." This was precisely what the silk merchant had hoped, and he accepted with an alacrity that he intended to be tempered by graciousness. "And to-morrow," continued the Bruder, "you must come and spend a whole day with us. You may even find acquaintances, for several pupils of your day have come back here as masters."

For one brief second there passed into the man's eyes a look that made the visitor start. But it vanished as quickly as it came. It was impossible to define. Harris convinced himself it was the effect of a shadow cast by the lamp they had just passed on the wall. He dismissed it from his mind.

"You are very kind, I'm sure," he said politely. "It is perhaps a greater pleasure to me than you can imagine to see the place again. Ah,"—he stopped short opposite a door with the upper half of glass and peered in—"surely there is one of the music rooms where I used to practise the violin. How it comes back to me after all these years!"

Bruder Kalkmann stopped indulgently, smiling, to allow his guest a moment's inspection.

"You still have the boys' orchestra? I remember I used to play *'zweite Geige'* in it. Bruder Schliemann conducted at the piano. Dear me, I can see him now with his long black hair and—and—" He stopped abruptly. Again the odd, dark look passed over the stern face of his companion. For an instant it seemed curiously familiar.

"We still keep up the pupils' orchestra," he said, "but Bruder Schliemann, I am sorry to say—" He hesitated an instant, and then added, "Bruder Schliemann is dead."

"Indeed, indeed," said Harris quickly. "I am sorry to hear it." He was conscious of a faint feeling of distress, but whether it arose from the news of his old music teacher's death, or—from something else— he could not quite determine. He gazed down the corridor that lost itself among shadows. In the street and village everything had seemed so much smaller than he remembered, but here, inside the school building, everything seemed so much bigger. The corridor was loftier and longer, more spacious and vast, than the mental picture he had preserved. His thoughts wandered dreamily for an instant.

He glanced up and saw the face of the Bruder watching him with a smile of patient indulgence.

"Your memories possess you," he observed gently, and the stern look passed into something almost pitying.

"You are right," returned the man of silk, "they do. This was the most wonderful period of my whole life in a sense. At the time I hated it—" He hesitated, not wishing to hurt the Brother's feelings.

"According to English ideas it seemed strict, of course," the other said persuasively, so that he went on.

"—Yes, partly that; and partly the ceaseless nostalgia, and the solitude which came from never being really alone. In English schools the boys enjoy peculiar freedom, you know."

Bruder Kalkmann, he saw, was listening intently.

"But it produced one result that I have never wholly lost," he continued self-consciously, "and am grateful for."

"*Ach! Wie so, denn?*"

"The constant inner pain threw me headlong into your religious life, so that the whole force of my being seemed to project itself towards the search for a deeper satisfaction—a real resting-place for the soul. During my two years here I yearned for God in my boyish way as perhaps I have never yearned for anything since. Moreover, I have never quite lost that sense of peace and inward joy which accompanied the search. I can never quite forget this school and the deep things it taught me."

He paused at the end of his long speech, and a brief silence fell between them. He feared he had said too much, or expressed himself clumsily in the foreign language, and when Bruder Kalkmann laid a hand upon his shoulder, he gave a little involuntary start.

"So that my memories perhaps do possess me rather strongly," he added apologetically; "and this long corridor, these rooms, that barred and gloomy front door, all touch chords that—that—" His German failed him and he glanced at his companion with an explanatory smile and gesture. But the brother had removed the hand from his shoulder and was standing with his back to him, looking down the passage.

"Naturally, naturally so," he said hastily without turning round. "*Es ist doch selbstverständlich.* We shall all understand."

Then he turned suddenly, and Harris saw that his face had turned most oddly and disagreeably sinister. It may only have been the shadows again playing their tricks with the wretched oil lamps on the wall, for the dark expression passed instantly as they retraced their steps down the corridor, but the Englishman somehow got the impression that he had said something to give offence, something that was not quite to the other's taste. Opposite the door of the *Bruderstube* they stopped. Harris realised that it was late and he had possibly stayed talking too long. He made a tentative effort to leave, but his companion would not hear of it.

"You must have a cup of coffee with us," he said firmly as though he meant it, "and my colleagues will be delighted to see you. Some of them will remember you, perhaps."

The sound of voices came pleasantly through the door, men's voices talking together. Bruder Kalkmann turned the handle and they entered a room ablaze with light and full of people.

"Ah,—but your name?" he whispered, bending down to catch the reply; "you have not told me your name yet."

"Harris," said the Englishman quickly as they went in. He felt nervous as he crossed the threshold, but ascribed the momentary trepidation to the fact that he was breaking the strictest rule of the whole establishment, which forbade a boy under severest penalties to come near this holy of holies where the masters took their brief leisure.

"Ah, yes, of course—Harris," repeated the other as though he remembered it. "Come in, Herr Harris, come in, please. Your visit will be immensely appreciated. It is really very fine, very wonderful of you to have come in this way."

The door closed behind them and, in the sudden light which made his sight swim for a moment, the exaggeration of the language escaped his attention. He heard the voice of Bruder Kalkmann introducing him. He spoke very loud, indeed, unnecessarily,—absurdly loud, Harris thought.

"Brothers," he announced, "it is my pleasure and privilege to introduce to you Herr Harris from England. He has just arrived to make us a little visit, and I have already expressed to him on behalf of us all the satisfaction we feel that he is here. He was, as you remember, a pupil in the year '70."

It was a very formal, a very German introduction, but Harris rather liked it. It made him feel important and he appreciated the tact that made it almost seem as though he had been expected.

The black forms rose and bowed; Harris bowed; Kalkmann bowed. Every one was very polite and very courtly. The room swam with moving figures; the light dazzled him after the gloom of the corridor; there was thick cigar smoke in the atmosphere. He took the chair that was offered to him between two of the Brothers, and sat down, feeling vaguely that his perceptions were not quite as keen and accurate as usual. He felt a trifle dazed perhaps, and the spell of the past came strongly over him, confusing the immediate present and making everything dwindle oddly to the dimensions of long ago. He seemed to pass under the mastery of a great mood that was a composite reproduction of all the moods of his forgotten boyhood.

Then he pulled himself together with a sharp effort and entered into the conversation that had begun again to buzz round him. Moreover, he entered into it with keen pleasure, for the Brothers—there were perhaps a dozen of them in the little room—treated him with a charm of manner that speedily made him feel one of themselves. This, again, was a very subtle delight to him. He felt that he had stepped out of the greedy, vulgar, self-seeking world, the world of silk and markets and profit-making—stepped into the cleaner atmosphere where spiritual ideals were paramount and life was simple and devoted. It all charmed him inexpressibly, so that he realised—yes, in a sense—the degradation of his twenty years' absorption in business. This keen atmosphere under the stars where men thought only of their souls, and of the souls of others, was too rarefied for the world he was now associated with. He found himself making comparisons to his own disadvantage,—comparisons with the mystical little dreamer that had stepped thirty years before from the stern peace of this devout community, and the man of the world that he had since become,—and the contrast made him shiver with a keen regret and something like self-contempt.

He glanced round at the other faces floating towards him through tobacco smoke—this acrid cigar smoke he remembered so well: how keen they were, how strong, placid, touched with the nobility of great aims and unselfish purposes. At one or two he looked particularly. He hardly knew why. They rather fascinated him. There was something so very stern and uncompromising about them, and something, too, oddly, subtly, familiar, that yet just eluded him. But whenever their eyes met his own they held undeniable welcome in them; and some held more—a kind of perplexed admiration, he thought, something that was between esteem and deference. This note of respect in all the faces was very flattering to his vanity.

Coffee was served presently, made by a black-haired Brother who sat in the comer by the piano and bore a marked resemblance to Bruder Schliemann, the musical director of thirty years ago. Harris exchanged bows with him when he took the cup from his white hands, which he noticed were like the hands of a woman. He lit a cigar, offered to him by his neighbour, with whom he was chatting delightfully, and who, in the glare of the lighted match, reminded him sharply for a moment of Bruder Pagel, his former room-master.

"Es ist wirklich merkwürdig," he said, "how many resemblances I see, or imagine. It is really *very* curious!"

"Yes," replied the other, peering at him over his coffee cup, "the spell of the place is wonderfully strong. I can well understand that the old faces rise before your mind's eye—almost to the exclusion of ourselves perhaps."

They both laughed pleasantly. It was soothing to find his mood understood and appreciated. And they passed on to talk of the mountain village, its isolation, its remoteness from worldly life, its peculiar fitness for meditation and worship, and for spiritual development—of a certain kind.

"And your coming back in this way, Herr Harris, has pleased us all so much," joined in the Bruder on his left. "We esteem you for it most highly. We honour you for it."

Harris made a deprecating gesture. "I fear, for my part, it is only a very selfish pleasure," he said a trifle unctuously.

"Not all would have had the courage," added the one who resembled Bruder Pagel.

"You mean," said Harris, a little puzzled, "the disturbing memories——?"

Bruder Pagel looked at him steadily, with unmistakable admiration and respect. "I mean that most men hold so strongly to life, and can give up so little for their beliefs," he said gravely.

The Englishman felt slightly uncomfortable. These worthy men really made too much of his sentimental journey. Besides, the talk was getting a little out of his depth. He hardly followed it.

"The worldly life still has *some* charms for me," he replied smilingly, as though to indicate that sainthood was not yet quite within his grasp.

"All the more, then, must we honour you for so freely coming," said the Brother on his left; "so unconditionally!"

A pause followed, and the silk merchant felt relieved when the conversation took a more general turn, although he noted that it never travelled very far from the subject of his visit and the wonderful situation of the lonely village for men who wished to develop their spiritual powers and practise the rites of a high worship. Others joined in, complimenting him on his knowledge of the language, making him feel utterly at his ease, yet at the same time a little uncomfortable by the excess of their admiration. After all, it was such a very small thing to do, this sentimental journey.

The time passed along quickly; the coffee was excellent, the cigars soft and of the nutty flavour he loved. At length, fearing to outstay his welcome, he rose reluctantly to take his leave. But the others would not hear of it. It was not often a former pupil returned to visit them in this simple, unaffected way. The night was young. If necessary they could even find him a corner in the great *Schlafzimmer* upstairs. He was easily persuaded to stay a little longer. Somehow he had become the centre of the little party. He felt pleased, flattered, honoured.

"And perhaps Bruder Schliemann will play something for us— now."

It was Kalkmann speaking, and Harris started visibly as he heard the name, and saw the black-haired man by the piano turn with a smile. For Schliemann was the name of his old music director, who was dead. Could this be his son? They were so exactly alike.

"If Bruder Meyer has not put his Amati to bed, I will accompany him," said the musician suggestively, looking across at a man whom Harris had not yet noticed, and who, he now saw, was the very image of a former master of that name.

Meyer rose and excused himself with a little bow, and the Englishman quickly observed that he had a peculiar gesture as though his neck had a false join on to the body just below the collar and feared it might break. Meyer of old had this trick of movement. He remembered how the boys used to copy it.

He glanced sharply from face to face, feeling as though some silent, unseen process were changing everything about him. All the faces seemed oddly familiar. Pagel, the Brother he had been talking with, was of course the image of Pagel, his former room-master; and Kalkmann, he now realised for the first time, was the very twin of another master whose name he had quite forgotten, but whom he used to dislike intensely in the old days. And, through the smoke, peering at him from the corners of the room, he saw that all the Brothers about him had the faces he had known and lived with long ago—Röst, Fluheim, Meinert, Rigel, Gysin.

He stared hard, suddenly grown more alert, and everywhere saw, or fancied he saw, strange likenesses, ghostly resemblances,—more, the identical faces of years ago. There was something queer about it all, something not quite right, something that made him feel uneasy. He shook himself, mentally and actually, blowing the smoke from before his eyes with a long breath, and as he did so he noticed to his dismay that every one was fixedly staring. They were watching him.

This brought him to his senses. As an Englishman, and a foreigner, he did not wish to be rude, or to do anything to make himself foolishly conspicuous and spoil the harmony of the evening. He was a guest, and a privileged guest at that. Besides, the music had already begun. Bruder Schliemann's long white fingers were caressing the keys to some purpose.

He subsided into his chair and smoked with half-closed eyes that yet saw everything.

But the shudder had established itself in his being, and, whether he would or not, it kept repeating itself. As a town, far up some inland river, feels the pressure of the distant sea, so he became aware that mighty forces from somewhere beyond his ken were urging themselves up against his soul in this smoky little room. He began to feel exceedingly ill at ease.

And as the music filled the air his mind began to clear. Like a lifted veil there rose up something that had hitherto obscured his vision. The words of the priest at the railway inn flashed across his brain unbidden: "You will find it different." And also, though why he could not tell, he saw mentally the strong, rather wonderful eyes of that other guest at the supper-table, the man who had overhead his conversation, and had later got into earnest talk with the priest. He took out his watch and stole a glance at it. Two hours had slipped by. It was already eleven o'clock.

Schliemann, meanwhile, utterly absorbed in his music, was playing a solemn measure. The piano sang marvellously. The power of a great conviction, the simplicity of great art, the vital spiritual message of a soul that had found itself—all this, and more, were in the chords, and yet somehow the music was what can only be described as impure—atrociously and diabolically impure. And the piece itself, although Harris did not recognise it as anything familiar, was surely the music of a Mass—huge, majestic, sombre? It stalked through the smoky room with slow power, like the passage of something that was mighty, yet profoundly intimate, and as it went there stirred into each and every face about him the signature of the enormous forces of which it was the audible symbol. The countenances round him turned sinister, but not idly, negatively sinister: they grew dark with purpose. He suddenly recalled the face of Bruder Kalkmann in the corridor earlier in the evening. The motives of their secret souls rose to the eyes, and mouths, and foreheads, and hung there for all to see like the black banners of an assembly of ill starred and fallen creatures. Demons— was the horrible word that flashed through his brain like a sheet of fire.

When this sudden discovery leaped out upon him, for a moment he lost his self-control. Without waiting to think and weigh his extraordinary impression, he did a very foolish but a very natural thing. Feeling himself irresistibly driven by the sudden stress to some kind of action, he sprang to his feet—and screamed! To his own utter amazement he stood up and shrieked aloud!

But no one stirred. No one, apparently, took the slightest notice of his absurdly wild behaviour. It was almost as if no one but himself had heard the scream at all—as though the music had drowned it and swallowed it up—as though after all perhaps he had not really screamed as loudly as he imagined, or had not screamed at all.

Then, as he glanced at the motionless, dark faces before him, something of utter cold passed into his being, touching his very soul. . . . All emotion cooled suddenly, leaving him like a receding tide. He sat down again, ashamed, mortified, angry with himself for behaving like a fool and a boy. And the music, meanwhile, continued to issue from the white and snake-like fingers of Bruder Schliemann, as poisoned wine might issue from the weirdly-fashioned necks of antique phials.

And, with the rest of them, Harris drank it in.

Forcing himself to believe that he had been the victim of some kind of illusory perception, he vigorously restrained his feelings. Then the music presently ceased, and every one applauded and began to talk at once, laughing, changing seats, complimenting the player, and behaving naturally and easily as though nothing out of the way had happened. The faces appeared normal once more. The Brothers crowded round their visitor, and he joined in their talk and even heard himself thanking the gifted musician.

But, at the same time, he found himself edging towards the door, nearer and nearer, changing his chair when possible, and joining the groups that stood closest to the way of escape.

"I must thank you all *tausendmal* for my little reception and the great pleasure—the very great honour you have done me," he began in decided tones at length, "but I fear I have trespassed far too long already on your hospitality. Moreover, I have some distance to walk to my inn."

A chorus of voices greeted his words. They would not hear of his going,—at least not without first partaking of refreshment. They produced pumpernickel from one cupboard, and rye-bread and sausage from another, and all began to talk again and eat. More coffee was made, fresh cigars lighted, and Bruder Meyer took out his violin and began to tune it softly.

"There is always a bed upstairs if Herr Harris will accept it," said one.

"And it is difficult to find the way out now, for all the doors are locked," laughed another loudly.

"Let us take our simple pleasures as they come," cried a third. "Bruder Harris will understand how we appreciate the honour of this last visit of his."

They made a dozen excuses. They all laughed, as though the politeness of their words was but formal, and veiled thinly—more and more thinly—a very different meaning.

"And the hour of midnight draws near," added Bruder Kalkmann with a charming smile, but in a voice that sounded to the Englishman like the grating of iron hinges.

Their German seemed to him more and more difficult to understand. He noted that they called him "Bruder" too, classing him as one of themselves.

And then suddenly he had a flash of keener perception, and realised with a creeping of his flesh that he had all along misinterpreted—grossly misinterpreted all they had been saying. They had talked about the beauty of the place, its isolation and remoteness from the world, its peculiar fitness for certain kinds of spiritual development and worship—yet hardly, he now grasped, in the sense in which he had taken the words. They had meant something different. Their spiritual powers, their desire for loneliness, their passion for worship, were not the powers, the solitude, or the worship that *he* meant and understood. He was playing a part in some horrible masquerade; he was among men who cloaked their lives with religion in order to follow their real purposes unseen of men.

What did it all mean? How had he blundered into so equivocal a situation? Had he blundered into it at all? Had he not rather been led into it, deliberately led? His thoughts grew dreadfully confused, and his confidence in himself began to fade. And why, he suddenly thought again, were they so impressed by the mere fact of his coming to revisit his old school? What was it they so admired and wondered at in his simple act? Why did they set such store upon his having the courage to come, to "give himself so freely," "unconditionally" as one of them had expressed it with such a mockery of exaggeration?

Fear stirred in his heart most horribly, and he found no answer to any of his questionings. Only one thing he now understood quite clearly: it was their purpose to keep him here. They did not intend that he should go. And from this moment he realised that they were sinister, formidable, and, in some way he had yet to discover, inimical to himself, inimical to his life. And the phrase one of them had used a moment ago—"this *last* visit of his"—rose before his eyes in letters of flame.

Harris was not a man of action, and had never known in all the course of his career what it meant to be in a situation of real danger. He was not necessarily a coward, though, perhaps, a man of untried nerve. He realised at last plainly that he was in a very awkward predicament indeed, and that he had to deal with men who were utterly in earnest. What their intentions were he only vaguely guessed. His mind, indeed, was too confused for definite ratiocination, and he was only able to follow blindly the strongest instincts that moved in him. It never occurred to him that the Brothers might all be mad, or that he himself might have temporarily lost his senses and be suffering under some terrible delusion. In fact, nothing occurred to him—he realised nothing—except that he meant to escape—and the quicker the better. A tremendous revulsion of feeling set in and overpowered him.

Accordingly, without further protest for the moment, he ate his pumpernickel and drank his coffee, talking meanwhile as naturally and pleasantly as he could, and when a suitable interval had passed, he rose to his feet and announced once more that he must now take his leave. He spoke very quietly, but very decidedly. No one hearing him could doubt that he meant what he said. He had got very close to the door by this time.

"I regret," he said, using his best German, and speaking to a hushed room, "that our pleasant evening must come to an end, but it is now time for me to wish you all good-night." And then, as no one said anything, he added, though with a trifle less assurance, "And I thank you all most sincerely for your hospitality."

"On the contrary," replied Kalkmann instantly, rising from his chair and ignoring the hand the Englishman had stretched out to him, "it is we who have to thank you; and we do so most gratefully and sincerely."

And at the same moment at least half a dozen of the Brothers took up their position between himself and the door.

"You are very good to say so," Harris replied as firmly as he could manage, noticing this movement out of the corner of his eye, "but really I had no conception that my little chance visit could have afforded you so much pleasure." He moved another step nearer the door, but Bruder Schliemann came across the room quickly and stood in front of him. His attitude was uncompromising. A dark and terrible expression had come into his face.

"But it was *not* by chance that you came, Bruder Harris," he said so that all the room could hear; "surely we have not misunderstood your presence here?" He raised his black eyebrows.

"No, no," the Englishman hastened to reply. "I was—I am delighted to be here. I told you what pleasure it gave me to find myself among you. Do not misunderstand me, I beg." His voice faltered a little, and he had difficulty in finding the words. More and more, too, he had difficulty in understanding *their* words.

"Of course," interposed Bruder Kalkmann in his iron bass, "*we* have not misunderstood. You have come back in the spirit of true and unselfish devotion. You offer yourself freely, and we all appreciate it. It is your willingness and nobility that have so completely won our veneration and respect." A faint murmur of applause ran round the room. "What we all delight in—what our great Master will especially delight in—is the value of your spontaneous and voluntary—"

He used a word Harris did not understand. He said *"Opfer."* The bewildered Englishman searched his brain for the translation, and searched in vain. For the life of him he could not remember what it meant. But the word, for all his inability to translate it, touched his soul with ice. It was worse, far worse, than anything he had imagined. He felt like a lost, helpless creature, and all power to fight sank out of him from that moment.

"It is magnificent to be such a willing—" added Schliemann, sidling up to him with a dreadful leer on his face. He made use of the same word—*"Opfer."*

"God! What could it all mean?" "Offer himself!" "True spirit of devotion!" "Willing," "unselfish," "magnificent!" *Opfer, Opfer, Opfer!* What in the name of heaven did it mean, that strange, mysterious word that struck such terror into his heart?

He made a valiant effort to keep his presence of mind and hold his nerves steady. Turning, he saw that Kalkmann's face was a dead white. Kalkmann! He understood that well enough. *Kalkmann* meant "Man of Chalk"; he knew that. But what did *"Opfer"* mean? That was the real key to the situation. Words poured through his disordered mind in an endless stream—unusual, rare words he had perhaps heard but once in his life—while *"Opfer,"* a word in common use, entirely escaped him. What an extraordinary mockery it all was!

Then Kalkmann, pale as death, but his face hard as iron, spoke a few low words that he did not catch, and the Brothers standing by the walls at once turned the lamps down so that the room became dim. In the half light he could only just discern their faces and movements.

"It is time," he heard Kalkmann's remorseless voice continue just behind him. "The hour of midnight is at hand. Let us prepare. He comes! He comes; Bruder Asmodelius comes!" His voice rose to a chant.

And the sound of that name, for some extraordinary reason, was terrible—utterly terrible; so that Harris shook from head to foot as he heard it. Its utterance filled the air like soft thunder, and a hush came over the whole room. Forces rose all about him, transforming the normal into the horrible, and the spirit of craven fear ran through all his being, bringing him to the verge of collapse.

Asmodelius! Asmodelius! The name was appalling. For he understood at last to whom it referred and the meaning that lay between its great syllables. At the same instant, too, he suddenly understood the meaning of that unremembered word. The import of the word *"Opfer"* flashed upon his soul like a message of death.

He thought of making a wild effort to reach the door, but the weakness of his trembling knees, and the row of black figures that stood between, dissuaded him at once. He would have screamed for help, but remembering the emptiness of the vast building, and the loneliness of the situation, he understood that no help could come that way, and he kept his lips closed. He stood still and did nothing. But he knew now what was coming.

Two of the brothers approached and took him gently by the arm.

"Bruder Asmodelius accepts you," they whispered; "are you ready?"

Then he found his tongue and tried to speak. "But what have I to do with this Bruder Asm—Asmo—?" he stammered, a desperate rush of words crowding vainly behind the halting tongue.

The name refused to pass his lips. He could not pronounce it as they did. He could not pronounce it at all. His sense of helplessness then entered the acute stage, for this inability to speak the name produced a fresh sense of quite horrible confusion in his mind, and he became extraordinarily agitated.

"I came here for a friendly visit," he tried to say with a great effort, but, to his intense dismay, he heard his voice saying something quite different, and actually making use of that very word they had all used: "I came here as a willing *Opfer,*" he heard his own voice say, "and *I am quite ready.*"

He was lost beyond all recall now! Not alone his mind, but the very muscles of his body had passed out of control. He felt that he was hovering on the confines of a phantom or demon world,—a world in which the name they had spoken constituted the Master-name, the word of ultimate power.

What followed he heard and saw as in a nightmare.

"In the half light that veils all truth, let us prepare to worship and adore," chanted Schliemann, who had preceded him to the end of the room.

"In the mists that protect our faces before the Black Throne, let us make ready the willing victim," echoed Kalkmann in his great bass.

They raised their faces, listening expectantly, as a roaring sound, like the passing of mighty projectiles, filled the air, far, far away, very wonderful, very forbidding. The walls of the room trembled.

"He comes! He comes! He comes!" chanted the Brothers in chorus.

The sound of roaring died away, and an atmosphere of still and utter cold established itself over all. Then Kalkmann, dark and unutterably stern, turned in the dim light and faced the rest.

"Asmodelius, our *Hauptbruder,* is about us," he cried in a voice that even while it shook was yet a voice of iron; "Asmodelius is about us. Make ready."

There followed a pause in which no one stirred or spoke. A tall Brother approached the Englishman; but Kalkmann held up his hand.

"Let the eyes remain uncovered," he said, "in honour of so freely giving himself." And to his horror Harris then realised for the first time that his hands were already fastened to his sides.

The Brother retreated again silently, and in the pause that followed all the figures about him dropped to their knees, leaving him standing alone, and as they dropped, in voices hushed with mingled reverence and awe, they cried softly, odiously, appallingly, the name of the Being whom they momentarily expected to appear.

Then, at the end of the room, where the windows seemed to have disappeared so that he saw the stars, there rose into view far up against the night sky, grand and terrible, the outline of a man. A kind of grey glory enveloped it so that it resembled a steel-cased statue, immense, imposing, horrific in its distant splendour; while, at the same time, the face was so spiritually mighty, yet so proudly, so austerely sad, that Harris felt as he stared, that the sight was more than his eyes could meet, and that in another moment the power of vision would fail him altogether, and he must sink into utter nothingness.

So remote and inaccessible hung this figure that it was impossible to gauge anything as to its size, yet at the same time so strangely close, that when the grey radiance from its mightily broken visage, august and mournful, beat down upon his soul, pulsing like some dark star with the powers of spiritual evil, he felt almost as though he were looking into a face no farther removed from him in space than the face of any one of the Brothers who stood by his side.

And then the room filled and trembled with sounds that Harris understood full well were the failing voices of others who had preceded him in a long series down the years. There came first a plain, sharp cry, as of a man in the last anguish, choking for his breath, and yet, with the very final expiration of it, breathing the name of the Worship—of the dark Being who rejoiced to hear it. The cries of the strangled; the short, running gasp of the suffocated; and the smothered gurgling of the tightened throat, all these, and more, echoed back and forth between the walls, the very walls in which he now stood a prisoner, a sacrificial victim. The cries, too, not alone of the broken bodies, but—far worse—of beaten, broken souls. And as the ghastly chorus rose and fell, there came also the faces of the lost and unhappy creatures to whom they belonged, and, against that curtain of pale grey light, he saw float past him in the air, an array of white and piteous human countenances that seemed to beckon and gibber at him as though he were already one of themselves.

Slowly, too, as the voices rose, and the pallid crew sailed past, that giant form of grey descended from the sky and approached the room that contained the worshippers and their prisoner. Hands rose and sank about him in the darkness, and he felt that he was being draped in other garments than his own; a circlet of ice seemed to run about his head, while round the waist, enclosing the fastened arms, he felt a girdle tightly drawn. At last, about his very throat, there ran a soft and silken touch which, better than if there had been full light, and a mirror held to his face, he understood to be the cord of sacrifice—and of death.

At this moment the Brothers, still prostrate upon the floor, began again their mournful, yet impassioned chanting, and as they did so a strange thing happened. For, apparently without moving or altering its position, the huge Figure seemed, at once and suddenly, to be inside the room, almost beside him, and to fill the space around him to the exclusion of all else.

He was now beyond all ordinary sensations of fear, only a drab feeling as of death—the death of the soul—stirred in his heart. His thoughts no longer even beat vainly for escape. The end was near, and he knew it.

The dreadfully chanting voices rose about him in a wave: "We worship! We adore! We offer!" The sounds filled his ears and hammered, almost meaningless, upon his brain.

Then the majestic grey face turned slowly downwards upon him, and his very soul passed outwards and seemed to become absorbed in the sea of those anguished eyes. At the same moment a dozen hands forced him to his knees, and in the air before him he saw the arm of Kalkmann upraised, and felt the pressure about his throat grow strong.

It was in this awful moment, when he had given up all hope, and the help of gods or men seemed beyond question, that a strange thing happened. For before his fading and terrified vision there slid, as in a dream of light,—yet without apparent rhyme or reason—wholly unbidden and unexplained,—the face of that other man at the supper table of the railway inn. And the sight, even mentally, of that strong, wholesome, vigorous English face, inspired him suddenly with a new courage.

It was but a flash of fading vision before he sank into a dark and terrible death, yet, in some inexplicable way, the sight of that face stirred in him unconquerable hope and the certainty of deliverance. It was a face of power, a face, he now realised, of simple goodness such as might have been seen by men of old on the shores of Galilee; a face, by heaven, that could conquer even the devils of outer space.

And, in his despair and abandonment, he called upon it, and called with no uncertain accents. He found his voice in this overwhelming moment to some purpose; though the words he actually used, and whether they were in German or English, he could never remember.

Their effect, nevertheless, was instantaneous. The Brothers understood, and that grey Figure of evil understood.

For a second the confusion was terrific. There came a great shattering sound. It seemed that the very earth trembled. But all Harris remembered afterwards was that voices rose about him in the clamour of terrified alarm—

"A man of power is among us! A man of God!"

The vast sound was repeated—the rushing through space as of huge projectiles—and he sank to the floor of the room, unconscious. The entire scene had vanished, vanished like smoke over the roof of a cottage when the wind blows.

And, by his side, sat down a slight, un-German figure,—the figure of the stranger at the inn,—the man who had the "rather wonderful eyes."

When Harris came to himself he felt cold. He was lying under the open sky, and the cool air of field and forest was blowing upon his face. He sat up and looked about him. The memory of the late scene was still horribly in his mind, but no vestige of it remained. No walls or ceiling enclosed him; he was no longer in a room at all. There were no lamps turned low, no cigar smoke, no black forms of sinister worshippers, no tremendous grey Figure hovering beyond the windows.

Open space was about him, and he was lying on a pile of bricks and mortar, his clothes soaked with dew, and the kind stars shining brightly overhead. He was lying, bruised and shaken, among the heaped-up débris of a ruined building.

He stood up and stared about him. There, in the shadowy distance, lay the surrounding forest, and here, close at hand, stood the outline of the village buildings. But, underfoot, beyond question, lay nothing but the broken heaps of stones that betokened a building long since crumbled to dust. Then he saw that the stones were blackened, and that great wooden beams, half burnt, half rotten, made lines through the general débris. He stood, then, among the ruins of a burnt and shattered building, the weeds and nettles proving conclusively that it had lain thus for many years.

The moon had already set behind the encircling forest, but the stars that spangled the heavens threw enough light to enable him to make quite sure of what he saw. Harris, the silk merchant, stood among these broken and burnt stones and shivered.

Then he suddenly became aware that out of the gloom a figure had risen and stood beside him. Peering at him, he thought he recognised the face of the stranger at the railway inn.

"Are *you* real?" he asked in a voice he hardly recognised as his own.

"More than real—I'm friendly," replied the stranger; "I followed you up here from the inn."

Harris stood and stared for several minutes without adding anything. His teeth chattered. The least sound made him start; but the simple words in his own language, and the tone in which they were uttered, comforted him inconceivably.

"You're English too, thank God," he said inconsequently. "These German devils—" He broke off and put a hand to his eyes. "But what's become of them all—and the room—and—and—" The hand travelled down to his throat and moved nervously round his neck. He drew a long, long breath of relief. "Did I dream everything—everything?" he said distractedly.

He stared wildly about him, and the stranger moved forward and took his arm. "Come," he said soothingly, yet with a trace of command in the voice, "we will move away from here. The high-road, or even the woods will be more to your taste, for we are standing now on one of the most haunted—and most terribly haunted—spots of the whole world."

He guided his companion's stumbling footsteps over the broken masonry until they reached the path, the nettles stinging their hands, and Harris feeling his way like a man in a dream. Passing through the twisted iron railing they reached the path, and thence made their way to the road, shining white in the night. Once safely out of the ruins, Harris collected himself and turned to look back.

"But, how is it possible?" he exclaimed, his voice still shaking. "How can it be possible? When I came in here I saw the building in the moonlight. They opened the door. I saw the figures and heard the voices and touched, yes touched their very hands, and saw their damned black faces, saw them far more plainly than I see you now." He was deeply bewildered. The glamour was still upon his eyes with a degree of reality stronger than the reality even of normal life. "Was I so utterly deluded?"

Then suddenly the words of the stranger, which he had only half heard or understood, returned to him.

"Haunted?" he asked, looking hard at him; "haunted, did you say?" He paused in the roadway and stared into the darkness where the building of the old school had first appeared to him. But the stranger hurried him forward.

"We shall talk more safely farther on," he said. "I followed you from the inn the moment I realised where you had gone. When I found you it was eleven o'clock—"

"Eleven o'clock," said Harris, remembering with a shudder.

"—I saw you drop. I watched over you till you recovered consciousness of your own accord and now—now I am here to guide you safely back to the inn. I have broken the spell—the glamour—"

"I owe you a great deal, sir," interrupted Harris again, beginning to understand something of the stranger's kindness, "but I don't understand it all. I feel dazed and shaken." His teeth still chattered, and spells of violent shivering passed over him from head to foot. He found that he was clinging to the other's arm. In this way they passed beyond the deserted and crumbling village and gained the high-road that led homewards through the forest.

"That school building has long been in ruins," said the man at his side presently; "it was burnt down by order of the Elders of the community at least ten years ago. The village has been uninhabited ever since. But the simulacra of certain ghastly events that took place under that roof in past days still continue. And the 'shells' of the chief participants still enact there the dreadful deeds that led to its final destruction, and to the desertion of the whole settlement. They were devil-worshippers!"

Harris listened with beads of perspiration on his forehead that did not come alone from their leisurely pace through the cool night. Although he had seen this man but once before in his life, and had never before exchanged so much as a word with him, he felt a degree of confidence and a subtle sense of safety and well-being in his presence that were the most healing influences he could possibly have wished after the experience he had been through. For all that, he still felt as if he were walking in a dream, and though he heard every word that fell from his companion's lips, it was only the next day that the full import of all he said became fully clear to him. The presence of this quiet stranger, the man with the wonderful eyes which he felt now, rather than saw, applied a soothing anodyne to his shattered spirit that healed him through and through. And this healing influence, distilled from the dark figure at his side, satisfied his first imperative need, so that he almost forgot to realise how strange and opportune it was that the man should be there at all.

It somehow never occurred to him to ask his name, or to feel any undue wonder that one passing tourist should take so much trouble on behalf of another. He just walked by his side, listening to his quiet words, and allowing himself to enjoy the very wonderful experience after his recent ordeal, of being helped, strengthened, blessed. Only once, remembering vaguely something of his reading of years ago, he turned to the man beside him, after some more than usually remarkable words, and heard himself, almost involuntarily it seemed, putting the question: "Then are you a Rosicrucian, sir, perhaps?" But the stranger had ignored the words, or possibly not heard them, for he continued with his talk as though unconscious of any interruption, and Harris became aware that another somewhat unusual picture had taken possession of his mind, as they walked there side by side through the cool reaches of the forest, and that he had found his imagination suddenly charged with the childhood memory of Jacob wrestling with an angel,—wrestling all night with a being of superior quality whose strength eventually became his own.

"It was your abrupt conversation with the priest at supper that first put me upon the track of this remarkable occurrence," he heard the man's quiet voice beside him in the darkness, "and it was from him I learned after you left the story of the devil worship that became secretly established in the heart of this simple and devout little community."

"Devil-worship! Here—!" Harris stammered, aghast.

"Yes—here;—conducted secretly for years by a group of Brothers before unexplained disappearances in the neighbourhood led to its discovery. For where could they have found a safer place in the whole wide world for their ghastly traffic and perverted powers than here, in the very precincts—under cover of the very shadow of saintliness and holy living?"

"Awful, awful!" whispered the silk merchant, "and when I tell you the words they used to me—"

"I know it all," the stranger said quietly. "I saw and heard everything. My plan first was to wait till the end and then to take steps for their destruction, but in the interest of your personal safety,"—he spoke with the utmost gravity and conviction,—"in the interest of the safety of your soul, I made my presence known when I did, and before the conclusion had been reached—"

"My safety! The danger, then, was real. They were alive and——" Words failed him. He stopped in the road and turned towards his companion, the shining of whose eyes he could just make out in the gloom.

"It was a concourse of the shells of violent men, spiritually-developed but evil men, seeking after death—the death of the body—to prolong their vile and unnatural existence. And had they accomplished their object you, in turn, at the death of your body, would have passed into their power and helped to swell their dreadful purposes."

Harris made no reply. He was trying hard to concentrate his mind upon the sweet and common things of life. He even thought of silk and St. Paul's Churchyard and the faces of his partners in business.

"For you came all prepared to be caught," he heard the other's voice like some one talking to him from a distance; "your deeply introspective mood had already reconstructed the past so vividly, so intensely, that you were *en rapport* at once with any forces of those days that chanced still to be lingering. And they swept you up all unresistingly."

Harris tightened his hold upon the stranger's arm as he heard. At the moment he had room for one emotion only. It did not seem to him odd that this stranger should have such intimate knowledge of his mind.

"It is, alas, chiefly the evil emotions that are able to leave their photographs upon surrounding scenes and objects," the other added, "and who ever heard of a place haunted by a noble deed, or of beautiful and lovely ghosts revisiting the glimpses of the moon? It is unfortunate. But the wicked passions of men's hearts alone seem strong enough to leave pictures that persist; the good are ever too lukewarm."

The stranger sighed as he spoke. But Harris, exhausted and shaken as he was to the very core, paced by his side, only half listening. He moved as in a dream still. It was very wonderful to him, this walk home under the stars in the early hours of the October morning, the peaceful forest all about them, mist rising here and there over the small clearings, and the sound of water from a hundred little invisible streams filling in the pauses of the talk. In after life he always looked back to it as something magical and impossible, something that had seemed too beautiful, too curiously beautiful, to have been quite true. And, though at the time he heard and understood but a quarter of what the stranger said, it came back to him afterwards, staying with him till the end of his days, and always with a curious, haunting sense of unreality, as though he had enjoyed a wonderful dream of which he could recall only faint and exquisite portions.

But the horror of the earlier experience was effectually dispelled; and when they reached the railway inn, somewhere about three o'clock in the morning, Harris shook the stranger's hand gratefully, effusively, meeting the look of those rather wonderful eyes with a full heart, and went up to his room, thinking in a hazy, dream-like way of the words with which the stranger had brought their conversation to an end as they left the confines of the forest—

"And if thought and emotion can persist in this way so long after the brain that sent them forth has crumbled into dust, how vitally important it must be to control their very birth in the heart, and guard them with the keenest possible restraint."

But Harris, the silk merchant, slept better than might have been expected, and with a soundness that carried him half-way through the day. And when he came downstairs and learned that the stranger had already taken his departure, he realised with keen regret that he had never once thought of asking his name.

"Yes, he signed in the visitors' book," said the girl in reply to his question.

And he turned over the blotted pages and found there, the last entry, in a very delicate and individual handwriting—

"*John Silence*, London."

The Camp of the Dog

I

Islands of all shapes and sizes troop northward from Stockholm by the hundred, and the little steamer that threads their intricate mazes in summer leaves the traveller in a somewhat bewildered state as regards the points of the compass when it reaches the end of its journey at Waxholm. But it is only after Waxholm that the true islands begin, so to speak, to run wild, and start up the coast on their tangled course of a hundred miles of deserted loveliness, and it was in the very heart of this delightful confusion that we pitched our tents for a summer holiday. A veritable wilderness of islands lay about us: from the mere round button of a rock that bore a single fir, to the mountainous stretch of a square mile, densely wooded, and bounded by precipitous cliffs; so close together often that a strip of water ran between no wider than a country lane, or, again, so far that an expanse stretched like the open sea for miles.

Although the larger islands boasted farms and fishing stations, the majority were uninhabited. Carpeted with moss and heather, their coast-lines showed a series of ravines and clefts and little sandy bays, with a growth of splendid pine-woods that came down to the water's edge and led the eye through unknown depths of shadow and mystery into the very heart of primitive forest.

The particular islands to which we had camping rights by virtue of paying a nominal sum to a Stockholm merchant lay together in a picturesque group far beyond the reach of the steamer, one being a mere reef with a fringe of fairy-like birches, and two others, cliff-bound monsters rising with wooded heads out of the sea. The fourth, which we selected because it enclosed a little lagoon suitable for anchorage, bathing, night-lines, and what-not, shall have what description is necessary as the story proceeds; but, so far as paying rent was concerned, we might equally well have pitched our tents on any one of a hundred others that clustered about us as thickly as a swarm of bees.

It was in the blaze of an evening in July, the air clear as crystal, the sea a cobalt blue, when we left the steamer on the borders of civilisation and sailed away with maps, compasses, and provisions for the little group of dots in the Skärgård that were to be our home for the next two months. The dinghy and my Canadian canoe trailed behind us, with tents and dunnage carefully piled aboard, and when the point of cliff intervened to hide the steamer and the Waxholm hotel we realised for the first time that the horror of trains and houses was far behind us, the fever of men and cities, the weariness of streets and confined spaces. The wilderness opened up on all sides into endless blue reaches, and the map and compasses were so frequently called into requisition that we went astray more often than not and progress was enchantingly slow. It took us, for instance, two whole days to find our crescent-shaped home, and the camps we made on the way were so fascinating that we left them with difficulty and regret, for each island seemed more desirable than the one before it, and over all lay the spell of haunting peace, remoteness from the turmoil of the world, and the freedom of open and desolate spaces.

And so many of these spots of world-beauty have I sought out and dwelt in, that in my mind remains only a composite memory of their faces, a true map of heaven, as it were, from which this particular one stands forth with unusual sharpness because of the strange things that happened there, and also, I think, because anything in which John Silence played a part has a habit of fixing itself in the mind with a living and lasting quality of vividness.

For the moment, however, Dr. Silence was not of the party. Some private case in the interior of Hungary claimed his attention, and it was not till later—the 15th of August, to be exact—that I had arranged to meet him in Berlin and then return to London together for our harvest of winter work. All the members of our party, however, were known to him more or less well, and on this third day as we sailed through the narrow opening into the lagoon and saw the circular ridge of trees in a gold and crimson sunset before us, his last words to me when we parted in London for some unaccountable reason came back very sharply to my memory, and recalled the curious impression of prophecy with which I had first heard them:

"Enjoy your holiday and store up all the force you can," he had said as the train slipped out of Victoria; "and we will meet in Berlin on the 15th—unless you should send for me sooner."

And now suddenly the words returned to me so clearly that it seemed I almost heard his voice in my ear: "Unless you should send for me sooner"; and returned, moreover, with a significance I was wholly at a loss to understand that touched somewhere in the depths of my mind a vague sense of apprehension that they had all along been intended in the nature of a prophecy.

In the lagoon, then, the wind failed us this July evening, as was only natural behind the shelter of the belt of woods, and we took to the oars, all breathless with the beauty of this first sight of our island home, yet all talking in somewhat hushed voices of the best place to land, the depth of water, the safest place to anchor, to put up the tents in, the most sheltered spot for the camp-fires, and a dozen things of importance that crop up when a home in the wilderness has actually to be made.

And during this busy sunset hour of unloading before the dark, the souls of my companions adopted the trick of presenting themselves very vividly anew before my mind, and introducing themselves afresh.

In reality, I suppose, our party was in no sense singular. In the conventional life at home they certainly seemed ordinary enough, but suddenly, as we passed through these gates of the wilderness, I saw them more sharply than before, with characters stripped of the atmosphere of men and cities. A complete change of setting often furnishes a startlingly new view of people hitherto held for well-known; they present another facet of their personalities. I seemed to see my own party almost as new people—people I had not known properly hitherto, people who would drop all disguises and henceforth reveal themselves as they really were. And each one seemed to say: "Now you will see me as I am. You will see me here in this primitive life of the wilderness without clothes. All my masks and veils I have left behind in the abodes of men. So, look out for surprises!"

The Reverend Timothy Maloney helped me to put up the tents, long practice making the process easy, and while he drove in pegs and tightened ropes, his coat off, his flannel collar flying open without a tie, it was impossible to avoid the conclusion that he was cut out for the life of a pioneer rather than the church. He was fifty years of age, muscular, blue-eyed, and hearty, and he took his share of the work, and more, without shirking. The way he handled the axe in cutting down saplings for the tent-poles was a delight to see, and his eye in judging the level was unfailing.

Bullied as a young man into a lucrative family living, he had in turn bullied his mind into some semblance of orthodox beliefs, doing the honours of the little country church with an energy that made one think of a coal-heaver tending china; and it was only in the past few years that he had resigned the living and taken instead to cramming young men for their examinations. This suited him better. It enabled him, too, to indulge his passion for spells of "wild life," and to spend the summer months of most years under canvas in one part of the world or another where he could take his young men with him and combine "reading" with open air.

His wife usually accompanied him, and there was no doubt she enjoyed the trips, for she possessed, though in less degree, the same joy of the wilderness that was his own distinguishing characteristic. The only difference was that while he regarded it as the real life, she regarded it as an interlude. While he camped out with his heart and mind, she played at camping out with her clothes and body. None the less, she made a splendid companion, and to watch her busy cooking dinner over the fire we had built among the stones was to understand that her heart was in the business for the moment and that she was happy even with the detail.

Mrs. Maloney at home, knitting in the sun and believing that the world was made in six days, was one woman; but Mrs. Maloney, standing with bare arms over the smoke of a wood fire under the pine trees, was another; and Peter Sangree, the Canadian pupil, with his pale skin, and his loose, though not ungainly figure, stood beside her in very unfavourable contrast as he scraped potatoes and sliced bacon with slender white fingers that seemed better suited to hold a pen than a knife. She ordered him about like a slave, and he obeyed, too, with willing pleasure, for in spite of his general appearance of debility he was as happy to be in camp as any of them.

But more than any other member of the party, Joan Maloney, the daughter, was the one who seemed a natural and genuine part of the landscape, who belonged to it all just in the same way that the trees and the moss and the grey rocks running out into the water belonged to it. For she was obviously in her right and natural setting, a creature of the wilds, a gipsy in her own home.

To any one with a discerning eye this would have been more or less apparent, but to me, who had known her during all the twenty-two years of her life and was familiar with the ins and outs of her primitive, utterly un-modern type, it was strikingly clear. To see her there made it impossible to imagine her again in civilisation. I lost all recollection of how she looked in a town. The memory somehow evaporated. This slim creature before me, flitting to and fro with the grace of the woodland life, swift, supple, adroit, on her knees blowing the fire, or stirring the frying-pan through a veil of smoke, suddenly seemed the only way I had ever really seen her. Here she was at home; in London she became some one concealed by clothes, an artificial doll overdressed and moving by clockwork, only a portion of her alive. Here she was alive all over.

I forget altogether how she was dressed, just as I forget how any particular tree was dressed, or how the markings ran on any one of the boulders that lay about the Camp. She looked just as wild and natural and untamed as everything else that went to make up the scene, and more than that I cannot say.

Pretty, she was decidedly not. She was thin, skinny, dark-haired, and possessed of great physical strength in the form of endurance. She had, too, something of the force and vigorous purpose of a man, tempestuous sometimes and wild to passionate, frightening her mother, and puzzling her easy-going father with her storms of waywardness, while at the same time she stirred his admiration by her violence. A pagan of the pagans she was besides, and with some haunting suggestion of old-world pagan beauty about her dark face and eyes. Altogether an odd and difficult character, but with a generosity and high courage that made her very lovable.

In town life she always seemed to me to feel cramped, bored, a devil in a cage, in her eyes a hunted expression as though any moment she dreaded to be caught. But up in these spacious solitudes all this disappeared. Away from the limitations that plagued and stung her, she would show at her best, and as I watched her moving about the Camp I repeatedly found myself thinking of a wild creature that had just obtained its freedom and was trying its muscles.

Peter Sangree, of course, at once went down before her. But she was so obviously beyond his reach, and besides so well able to take care of herself, that I think her parents gave the matter but little thought, and he himself worshipped at a respectful distance, keeping admirable control of his passion in all respects save one; for at his age the eyes are difficult to master, and the yearning, almost the devouring, expression often visible in them was probably there unknown even to himself. He, better than any one else, understood that he had fallen in love with something most hard of attainment, something that drew him to the very edge of life, and almost beyond it. It, no doubt, was a secret and terrible joy to him, this passionate worship from afar; only I think he suffered more than any one guessed, and that his want of vitality was due in large measure to the constant stream of unsatisfied yearning that poured for ever from his soul and body. Moreover, it seemed to me, who now saw them for the first time together, that there was an unnamable something—an elusive quality of some kind—that marked them as belonging to the same world, and that although the girl ignored him she was secretly, and perhaps unknown to herself, drawn by some attribute very deep in her own nature to some quality equally deep in his.

This, then, was the party when we first settled down into our two months' camp on the island in the Baltic Sea. Other figures flitted from time to time across the scene, and sometimes one reading man, sometimes another, came to join us and spend his four hours a day in the clergyman's tent, but they came for short periods only, and they went without leaving much trace in my memory, and certainly they played no important part in what subsequently happened.

The weather favoured us that night, so that by sunset the tents were up, the boats unloaded, a store of wood collected and chopped into lengths, and the candle-lanterns hung round ready for lighting on the trees. Sangree, too, had picked deep mattresses of balsam boughs for the women's beds, and had cleared little paths of brushwood from their tents to the central fireplace. All was prepared for bad weather. It was a cosy supper and a well-cooked one that we sat down to and ate under the stars, and, according to the clergyman, the only meal fit to eat we had seen since we left London a week before.

The deep stillness, after that roar of steamers, trains, and tourists, held something that thrilled, for as we lay round the fire there was no sound but the faint sighing of the pines and the soft lapping of the waves along the shore and against the sides of the boat in the lagoon. The ghostly outline of her white sails was just visible through the trees, idly rocking to and fro in her calm anchorage, her sheets flapping gently against the mast. Beyond lay the dim blue shapes of other islands floating in the night, and from all the great spaces about us came the murmur of the sea and the soft breathing of great woods. The odours of the wilderness—smells of wind and earth, of trees and water, clean, vigorous, and mighty—were the true odours of a virgin world unspoilt by men, more penetrating and more subtly intoxicating than any other perfume in the whole world. Oh!—and dangerously strong, too, no doubt, for some natures!

"Ahhh!" breathed out the clergyman after supper, with an indescribable gesture of satisfaction and relief. "Here there is freedom, and room for body and mind to turn in. Here one can work and rest and play. Here one can be alive and absorb something of the earth-forces that never get within touching-distance in the cities. By George, I shall make a permanent camp here and come when it is time to die!"

The good man was merely giving vent to his delight at being under canvas. He said the same thing every year, and he said it often. But it more or less expressed the superficial feelings of us all. And when, a little later, he turned to compliment his wife on the fried potatoes, and discovered that she was snoring, with her back against a tree, he grunted with content at the sight and put a ground-sheet over her feet, as if it were the most natural thing in the world for her to fall asleep after dinner, and then moved back to his own corner, smoking his pipe with great satisfaction.

And I, smoking mine too, lay and fought against the most delicious sleep imaginable, while my eyes wandered from the fire to the stars peeping through the branches, and then back again to the group about me. The Rev. Timothy soon let his pipe go out, and succumbed as his wife had done, for he had worked hard and eaten well. Sangree, also smoking, leaned against a tree with his gaze fixed on the girl, a depth of yearning in his face that he could not hide, and that really distressed me for him. And Joan herself, with wide staring eyes, alert, full of the new forces of the place, evidently keyed up by the magic of finding herself among all the things her soul recognised as "home," sat rigid by the fire, her thoughts roaming through the spaces, the blood stirring about her heart. She was as unconscious of the Canadian's gaze as she was that her parents both slept. She looked to me more like a tree, or something that had grown out of the island, than a living girl of the century; and when I spoke across to her in a whisper and suggested a tour of investigation, she started and looked up at me as though she heard a voice in her dreams.

Sangree leaped up and joined us, and without waking the others we three went over the ridge of the island and made our way down to the shore behind. The water lay like a lake before us still coloured by the sunset. The air was keen and scented, wafting the smell of the wooded islands that hung about us in the darkening air. Very small waves tumbled softly on the sand. The sea was sown with stars, and everywhere breathed and pulsed the beauty of the northern summer night. I confess I speedily lost consciousness of the human presences beside me, and I have little doubt Joan did too. Only Sangree felt otherwise, I suppose for presently we heard him sighing; and I can well imagine that he absorbed the whole wonder and passion of the scene into his aching heart, to swell the pain there that was more searching even than the pain at the sight of such matchless and incomprehensible beauty.

The splash of a fish jumping broke the spell.

"I wish we had the canoe now," remarked Joan; "we could paddle out to the other islands."

"Of course," I said; "wait here and I'll go across for it," and was turning to feel my way back through the darkness when she stopped me in a voice that meant what it said.

"No; Mr. Sangree will get it. We will wait here and cooee to guide him."

The Canadian was off in a moment, for she had only to hint of her wishes and he obeyed.

"Keep out from shore in case of rocks," I cried out as he went, "and turn to the right out of the lagoon. That's the shortest way round by the map."

My voice travelled across the still waters and woke echoes in the distant islands that came back to us like people calling out of space. It was only thirty or forty yards over the ridge and down the other side to the lagoon where the boats lay, but it was a good mile to coast round the shore in the dark to where we stood and waited. We heard him stumbling away among the boulders, and then the sounds suddenly ceased as he topped the ridge and went down past the fire on the other side.

"I didn't want to be left alone with him," the girl said presently in a low voice. "I'm always afraid he's going to say or do something—" She hesitated a moment, looking quickly over her shoulder towards the ridge where he had just disappeared—"something that might lead to unpleasantness." She stopped abruptly.

"*You* frightened, Joan!" I exclaimed, with genuine surprise. "This is a new light on your wicked character. I thought the human being who could frighten you did not exist." Then I suddenly realised she was talking seriously—looking to me for help of some kind—and at once I dropped the teasing attitude.

"He's very far gone, I think, Joan," I added gravely. "You must be kind to him, whatever else you may feel. He's exceedingly fond of you."

"I know, but I can't help it," she whispered, lest her voice should carry in the stillness; "there's something about him that—that makes me feel creepy and half afraid."

"But, poor man, it's not his fault if he is delicate and sometimes looks like death," I laughed gently, by way of defending what I felt to be a very innocent member of my sex.

"Oh, but it's not that I mean," she answered quickly; "it's something I feel about him, something in his soul, something he hardly knows himself, but that may come out if we are much together. It draws me, I feel, tremendously. It stirs what is wild in me—deep down—oh, very deep down,—yet at the same time makes me feel afraid."

"I suppose his thoughts are always playing about you," I said, "but he's nice-minded and—"

"Yes, yes," she interrupted impatiently, "I can trust myself absolutely with him. He's gentle and singularly pure-minded. But there's something else that—" She stopped again sharply to listen. Then she came up close beside me in the darkness, whispering—

"You know, Mr. Hubbard, sometimes my intuitions warn me a little too strongly to be ignored. Oh yes, you needn't tell me again that it's difficult to distinguish between fancy and intuition. I know all that. But I also know that there's something deep down in that man's soul that calls to something deep down in mine. And at present it frightens me. Because I cannot make out what it is; and I know, I *know,* he'll do something some day that—that will shake my life to the very bottom." She laughed a little at the strangeness of her own description.

I turned to look at her more closely, but the darkness was too great to show her face. There was an intensity, almost of suppressed passion, in her voice that took me completely by surprise.

"Nonsense, Joan," I said, a little severely; "you know him well. He's been with your father for months now."

"But that was in London; and up here it's different—I mean, I feel that it may be different. Life in a place like this blows away the restraints of the artificial life at home. I know, oh, I know what I'm saying. I feel all untied in a place like this; the rigidity of one's nature begins to melt and flow. Surely *you* must understand what I mean!"

"Of course I understand," I replied, yet not wishing to encourage her in her present line of thought, "and it's a grand experience—for a short time. But you're overtired to-night, Joan, like the rest of us. A few days in this air will set you above all fears of the kind you mention."

Then, after a moment's silence, I added, feeling I should estrange her confidence altogether if I blundered any more and treated her like a child—

"I think, perhaps, the true explanation is that you pity him for loving you, and at the same time you feel the repulsion of the healthy, vigorous animal for what is weak and timid. If he came up boldly and took you by the throat and shouted that he would force you to love him—well, then you would feel no fear at all. You would know exactly how to deal with him. Isn't it, perhaps, something of that kind?"

The girl made no reply, and when I took her hand I felt that it trembled a little and was cold.

"It's not his love that I'm afraid of," she said hurriedly, for at this moment we heard the dip of a paddle in the water, "it's something in his very soul that terrifies me in a way I have never been terrified before,—yet fascinates me. In town I was hardly conscious of his presence. But the moment we got away from civilisation, it began to come.

He seems so—so *real* up here. I dread being alone with him. It makes me feel that something must burst and tear its way out—that he would do something—or I should do something—I don't know exactly what I mean, probably,—but that I should let myself go and scream—"

"Joan!"

"Don't be alarmed," she laughed shortly; "I shan't do anything silly, but I wanted to tell you my feelings in case I needed your help. When I have intuitions as strong as this they are never wrong, only I don't know yet what it means exactly."

"You must hold out for the month, at any rate," I said in as matter-of-fact a voice as I could manage, for her manner had somehow changed my surprise to a subtle sense of alarm. "Sangree only stays the month, you know. And, anyhow, you are such an odd creature yourself that you should feel generously towards other odd creatures," I ended lamely, with a forced laugh.

She gave my hand a sudden pressure. "I'm glad I've told you at any rate," she said quickly under her breath, for the canoe was now gliding up silently like a ghost to our feet, "and I'm glad you're here too," she added as we moved down towards the water to meet it.

I made Sangree change into the bows and got into the steering seat myself, putting the girl between us so that I could watch them both by keeping their outlines against the sea and stars. For the intuitions of certain folk—women and children usually, I confess—I have always felt a great respect that has more often than not been justified by experience; and now the curious emotion stirred in me by the girl's words remained somewhat vividly in my consciousness. I explained it in some measure by the fact that the girl, tired out by the fatigue of many days' travel, had suffered a vigorous reaction of some kind from the strong, desolate scenery, and further, perhaps, that she had been treated to my own experience of seeing the members of the party in a new light—the Canadian, being partly a stranger, more vividly than the rest of us. But, at the same time, I felt it was quite possible that she had sensed some subtle link between his personality and her own, some quality that she had hitherto ignored and that the routine of town life had kept buried out of sight. The only thing that seemed difficult to explain was the fear she had spoken of, and this I hoped the wholesome effects of camp-life and exercise would sweep away naturally in the course of time.

We made the tour of the island without speaking. It was all too beautiful for speech. The trees crowded down to the shore to hear us pass. We saw their fine dark heads, bowed low with splendid dignity to watch us, forgetting for a moment that the stars were caught in the needled network of their hair. Against the sky in the west, where still lingered the sunset gold, we saw the wild toss of the horizon, shaggy with forest and cliff, gripping the heart like the motive in a symphony, and sending the sense of beauty all a-shiver through the mind—all these surrounding islands standing above the water like low clouds, and like them seeming to post along silently into the engulfing night. We heard the musical drip-drip of the paddle, and the little wash of our waves on the shore, and then suddenly we found ourselves at the opening of the lagoon again, having made the complete circuit of our home.

The Reverend Timothy had awakened from sleep and was singing to himself; and the sound of his voice as we glided down the fifty yards of enclosed water was pleasant to hear and undeniably wholesome. We saw the glow of the fire up among the trees on the ridge, and his shadow moving about as he threw on more wood.

"There you are!" he called aloud. "Good again! Been setting the night-lines, eh? Capital! And your mother's still fast asleep, Joan."

His cheery laugh floated across the water; he had not been in the least disturbed by our absence, for old campers are not easily alarmed.

"Now, remember," he went on, after we had told our little tale of travel by the fire, and Mrs. Maloney had asked for the fourth time exactly where her tent was and whether the door faced east or south, "every one takes their turn at cooking breakfast, and one of the men is always out at sunrise to catch it first. Hubbard, I'll toss you which you do in the morning and which I do!" He lost the toss. "Then I'll catch it," I said, laughing at his discomfiture, for I knew he loathed stirring porridge. "And mind you don't burn it as you did every blessed time last year on the Volga," I added by way of reminder.

Mrs. Maloney's fifth interruption about the door of her tent, and her further pointed observation that it was past nine o'clock, set us lighting lanterns and putting the fire out for safety.

But before we separated for the night the clergyman had a time-honoured little ritual of his own to go through that no one had the heart to deny him. He always did this. It was a relic of his pulpit habits.

He glanced briefly from one to the other of us, his face grave and earnest, his hands lifted to the stars and his eyes all closed and puckered up beneath a momentary frown. Then he offered up a short, almost inaudible prayer, thanking Heaven for our safe arrival, begging for good weather, no illness or accidents, plenty of fish, and strong sailing winds.

And then, unexpectedly—no one knew why exactly—he ended up with an abrupt request that nothing from the kingdom of darkness should be allowed to afflict our peace, and no evil thing come near to disturb us in the night-time.

And while he uttered these last surprising words, so strangely unlike his usual ending, it chanced that I looked up and let my eyes wander round the group assembled about the dying fire. And it certainly seemed to me that Sangree's face underwent a sudden and visible alteration. He was staring at Joan, and as he stared the change ran over it like a shadow and was gone. I started in spite of myself, for something oddly concentrated, potent, collected, had come into the expression usually so scattered and feeble. But it was all swift as a passing meteor, and when I looked a second time his face was normal and he was looking among the trees.

And Joan, luckily, had not observed him, her head being bowed and her eyes tightly closed while her father prayed.

"The girl has a vivid imagination indeed," I thought, half laughing, as I lit the lanterns, "if her thoughts can put a glamour upon mine in this way"; and yet somehow, when we said good-night, I took occasion to give her a few vigorous words of encouragement, and went to her tent to make sure I could find it quickly in the night in case anything happened. In her quick way the girl understood and thanked me, and the last thing I heard as I moved off to the men's quarters was Mrs. Maloney crying that there were beetles in her tent, and Joan's laughter as she went to help her turn them out.

Half an hour later the island was silent as the grave, but for the mournful voices of the wind as it sighed up from the sea. Like white sentries stood the three tents of the men on one side of the ridge, and on the other side, half hidden by some birches whose leaves just shivered as the breeze caught them, the women's tents, patches of ghostly grey, gathered more closely together for mutual shelter and protection. Something like fifty yards of broken ground, grey rock, moss, and lichen lay between, and over all lay the curtain of the night and the great whispering winds from the forests of Scandinavia.

And the very last thing, just before floating away on that mighty wave that carries one so softly off into the deeps of forgetfulness, I again heard the voice of John Silence as the train moved out of Victoria Station; and by some subtle connection that met me on the very threshold of consciousness there rose in my mind simultaneously the memory of the girl's half-given confidence, and of her distress. As by some wizardry of approaching dreams they seemed in that instant to be related; but before I could analyse the why and the wherefore, both sank away out of sight again, and I was off beyond recall.

"Unless you should send for me sooner."

II

Whether Mrs. Maloney's tent door opened south or east I think she never discovered, for it is quite certain she always slept with the flap tightly fastened; I only know that my own little "five by seven, all silk" faced due east, because next morning the sun, pouring in as only the wilderness sun knows how to pour, woke me early, and a moment later, with a short run over soft moss and a flying dive from the granite ledge, I was swimming in the most sparkling water imaginable.

It was barely four o'clock, and the sun came down a long vista of blue islands that led out to the open sea and Finland. Nearer by rose the wooded domes of our own property, still capped and wreathed with smoky trails of fast-melting mist, and looking as fresh as though it was the morning of Mrs. Maloney's Sixth Day and they had just issued, clean and brilliant, from the hands of the great Architect.

In the open spaces the ground was drenched with dew, and from the sea a cool salt wind stole in among the trees and set the branches trembling in an atmosphere of shimmering silver. The tents shone white where the sun caught them in patches. Below lay the lagoon, still dreaming of the summer night; in the open the fish were jumping busily, sending musical ripples towards the shore; and in the air hung the magic of dawn—silent, incommunicable.

I lit the fire, so that an hour later the clergyman should find good ashes to stir his porridge over, and then set forth upon an examination of the island, but hardly had I gone a dozen yards when I saw a figure standing a little in front of me where the sunlight fell in a pool among the trees.

It was Joan. She had already been up an hour, she told me, and had bathed before the last stars had left the sky. I saw at once that the new spirit of this solitary region had entered into her, banishing the fears of the night, for her face was like the face of a happy denizen of the wilderness, and her eyes stainless and shining. Her feet were bare, and drops of dew she had shaken from the branches hung in her loose-flying hair. Obviously she had come into her own.

"I've been all over the island," she announced laughingly, "and there are two things wanting."

"You're a good judge, Joan. What are they?"

"There's no animal life, and there's no—water."

"They go together," I said. "Animals don't bother with a rock like this unless there's a spring on it."

And as she led me from place to place, happy and excited, leaping adroitly from rock to rock, I was glad to note that my first impressions were correct. She made no reference to our conversation of the night before. The new spirit had driven out the old. There was no room in her heart for fear or anxiety, and Nature had everything her own way.

The island, we found, was some three-quarters of a mile from point to point, built in a circle, or wide horseshoe, with an opening of twenty feet at the mouth of the lagoon. Pine trees grew thickly all over, but here and there were patches of silver birch, scrub oak, and considerable colonies of wild raspberry and gooseberry bushes. The two ends of the horseshoe formed bare slabs of smooth granite running into the sea and forming dangerous reefs just below the surface, but the rest of the island rose in a forty-foot ridge and sloped down steeply to the sea on either side, being nowhere more than a hundred yards wide.

The outer shore-line was much indented with numberless coves and bays and sandy beaches, with here and there caves and precipitous little cliffs against which the sea broke in spray and thunder. But the inner shore, the shore of the lagoon, was low and regular, and so well protected by the wall of trees along the ridge that no storm could ever send more than a passing ripple along its sandy marges. Eternal shelter reigned there.

On one of the other islands, a few hundred yards away—for the rest of the party slept late this first morning, and we took to the canoe—we discovered a spring of fresh water untainted by the brackish flavour of the Baltic, and having thus solved the most important problem of the Camp, we next proceeded to deal with the second—fish. And in half an hour we reeled in and turned homewards, for we had no means of storage, and to clean more fish than may be stored or eaten in a day is no wise occupation for experienced campers.

And as we landed towards six o'clock we heard the clergyman singing as usual and saw his wife and Sangree shaking out their blankets in the sun, and dressed in a fashion that finally dispelled all memories of streets and civilisation.

"The Little People lit the fire for me," cried Maloney, looking natural and at home in his ancient flannel suit and breaking off in the middle of his singing, "so I've got the porridge going—and this time it's *not* burnt."

We reported the discovery of water and held up the fish.

"Good! Good again!" he cried. "We'll have the first decent breakfast we've had this year. Sangree'll clean 'em in no time, and the Bo'sun's Mate—"

"Will fry them to a turn," laughed the voice of Mrs. Maloney, appearing on the scene in a tight blue jersey and sandals, and catching up the frying-pan. Her husband always called her the Bo'sun's Mate in Camp, because it was her duty, among others, to pipe all hands to meals.

"And as for you, Joan," went on the happy man, "you look like the spirit of the island, with moss in your hair and wind in your eyes, and sun and stars mixed in your face." He looked at her with delighted admiration. "Here, Sangree, take these twelve, there's a good fellow, they're the biggest; and we'll have 'em in butter in less time than you can say Baltic island!"

I watched the Canadian as he slowly moved off to the cleaning pail. His eyes were drinking in the girl's beauty, and a wave of passionate, almost feverish, joy passed over his face, expressive of the ecstasy of true worship more than anything else. Perhaps he was thinking that he still had three weeks to come with that vision always before his eyes; perhaps he was thinking of his dreams in the night. I cannot say.

But I noticed the curious mingling of yearning and happiness in his eyes, and the strength of the impression touched my curiosity. Something in his face held my gaze for a second, something to do with its intensity. That so timid, so gentle a personality should conceal so virile a passion almost seemed to require explanation.

But the impression was momentary, for that first breakfast in Camp permitted no divided attentions, and I dare swear that the porridge, the tea, the Swedish "flatbread," and the fried fish flavoured with points of frizzled bacon, were better than any meal eaten elsewhere that day in the whole world.

The first clear day in a new camp is always a furiously busy one, and we soon dropped into the routine upon which in large measure the real comfort of every one depends. About the cooking-fire, greatly improved with stones from the shore, we built a high stockade consisting of upright poles thickly twined with branches, the roof lined with moss and lichen and weighted with rocks, and round the interior we made low wooden seats so that we could lie round the fire even in rain and eat our meals in peace. Paths, too, outlined themselves from tent to tent, from the bathing places and the landing stage, and a fair division of the island was decided upon between the quarters of the men and the women. Wood was stacked, awkward trees and boulders removed, hammocks slung, and tents strengthened. In a word, Camp was established, and duties were assigned and accepted as though we expected to live on this Baltic island for years to come and the smallest detail of the Community life was important.

Moreover, as the Camp came into being, this sense of a community developed, proving that we were a definite whole, and not merely separate human beings living for a while in tents upon a desert island. Each fell willingly into the routine. Sangree, as by natural selection, took upon himself the cleaning of the fish and the cutting of the wood into lengths sufficient for a day's use. And he did it well. The pan of water was never without a fish, cleaned and scaled, ready to fry for whoever was hungry; the nightly fire never died down for lack of material to throw on without going farther afield to search.

And Timothy, once reverend, caught the fish and chopped down the trees. He also assumed responsibility for the condition of the boat, and did it so thoroughly that nothing in the little cutter was ever found wanting. And when, for any reason, his presence was in demand, the first place to look for him was—in the boat, and there, too, he was usually found, tinkering away with sheets, sails, or rudder and singing as he tinkered.

Nor was the "reading" neglected; for most mornings there came a sound of droning voices from the white tent by the raspberry bushes, which signified that Sangree, the tutor, and whatever other man chanced to be in the party at the time, were hard at it with history or the classics.

And while Mrs. Maloney, also by natural selection, took charge of the larder and the kitchen, the mending and general supervision of the rough comforts, she also made herself peculiarly mistress of the megaphone which summoned to meals and carried her voice easily from one end of the island to the other; and in her hours of leisure she daubed the surrounding scenery on to a sketching block with all the honesty and devotion of her determined but unreceptive soul.

Joan, meanwhile, Joan, elusive creature of the wilds, became I know not exactly what. She did plenty of work in the Camp, yet seemed to have no very precise duties. She was everywhere and anywhere. Sometimes she slept in her tent, sometimes under the stars with a blanket. She knew every inch of the island and kept turning up in places where she was least expected—for ever wandering about, reading her books in sheltered corners, making little fires on sunless days to "worship by to the gods," as she put it, ever finding new pools to dive and bathe in, and swimming day and night in the warm and waveless lagoon like a fish in a huge tank. She went bare-legged and bare-footed, with her hair down and her skirts caught up to the knees, and if ever a human being turned into a jolly savage within the compass of a single week, Joan Maloney was certainly that human being. She ran wild.

So completely, too, was she possessed by the strong spirit of the place that the little human fear she had yielded to so strangely on our arrival seemed to have been utterly dispossessed. As I hoped and expected, she made no reference to our conversation of the first evening. Sangree bothered her with no special attentions, and after all they were very little together. His behaviour was perfect in that respect, and I, for my part, hardly gave the matter another thought. Joan was ever a prey to vivid fancies of one kind or another, and this was one of them. Mercifully for the happiness of all concerned, it had melted away before the spirit of busy, active life and deep content that reigned over the island. Every one was intensely alive, and peace was upon all.

Meanwhile the effect of the camp-life began to tell. Always a searching test of character, its results, sooner or later, are infallible, for it acts upon the soul as swiftly and surely as the hypo bath upon the negative of a photograph. A readjustment of the personal forces takes place quickly; some parts of the personality go to sleep, others wake up: but the first sweeping change that the primitive life brings about is that the artificial portions of the character shed themselves one after another like dead skins. Attitudes and poses that seemed genuine in the city drop away. The mind, like the body, grows quickly hard, simple, uncomplex. And in a camp as primitive and close to nature as ours was, these effects became speedily visible.

Some folk, of course, who talk glibly about the simple life when it is safely out of reach, betray themselves in camp by for ever peering about for the artificial excitements of civilisation which they miss. Some get bored at once; some grow slovenly; some reveal the animal in most unexpected fashion; and some, the select few, find themselves in very short order and are happy.

And, in our little party, we could flatter ourselves that we all belonged to the last category, so far as the general effect was concerned. Only there were certain other changes as well, varying with each individual, and all interesting to note.

It was only after the first week or two that these changes became marked, although this is the proper place, I think, to speak of them. For, having myself no other duty than to enjoy a well-earned holiday, I used to load my canoe with blankets and provisions and journey forth on exploration trips among the islands of several days together; and it was on my return from the first of these—when I rediscovered the party, so to speak—that these changes first presented themselves vividly to me, and in one particular instance produced a rather curious impression.

In a word, then, while every one had grown wilder, naturally wilder, Sangree, it seemed to me, had grown much wilder, and what I can only call unnaturally wilder. He made me think of a savage.

To begin with, he had changed immensely in mere physical appearance, and the full brown cheeks, the brighter eyes of absolute health, and the general air of vigour and robustness that had come to replace his customary lassitude and timidity, had worked such an improvement that I hardly knew him for the same man. His voice, too, was deeper and his manner bespoke for the first time a greater measure of confidence in himself. He now had some claims to be called nice-looking, or at least to a certain air of virility that would not lessen his value in the eyes of the opposite sex.

All this, of course, was natural enough, and most welcome. But, altogether apart from this physical change, which no doubt had also been going forward in the rest of us, there was a subtle note in his personality that came to me with a degree of surprise that almost amounted to shock.

And two things—as he came down to welcome me and pull up the canoe—leaped up in my mind unbidden, as though connected in some way I could not at the moment divine—first, the curious judgment formed of him by Joan; and secondly, that fugitive expression I had caught in his face while Maloney was offering up his strange prayer for special protection from heaven.

The delicacy of manner and feature—to call it by no milder term—which had always been a distinguishing characteristic of the man, had been replaced by something far more vigorous and decided, that yet utterly eluded analysis. The change which impressed me so oddly was not easy to name. The others—singing Maloney, the bustling Bo'sun's Mate, and Joan, that fascinating half-breed of undine and salamander—all showed the effects of a life so close to nature; but in their case the change was perfectly natural and what was to be expected, whereas with Peter Sangree, the Canadian, it was something unusual and unexpected.

It is impossible to explain how he managed gradually to convey to my mind the impression that something in him had turned savage, yet this, more or less, is the impression that he did convey. It was not that he seemed really less civilised, or that his character had undergone any definite alteration, but rather that something in him, hitherto dormant, had awakened to life. Some quality, latent till now—so far, at least, as we were concerned, who, after all, knew him but slightly—had stirred into activity and risen to the surface of his being.

And while, for the moment, this seemed as far as I could get, it was but natural that my mind should continue the intuitive process and acknowledge that John Silence, owing to his peculiar faculties, and the girl, owing to her singularly receptive temperament, might each in a different way have divined this latent quality in his soul, and feared its manifestation later.

On looking back to this painful adventure, too, it now seems equally natural that the same process, carried to its logical conclusion, should have wakened some deep instinct in me that, wholly without direction from my will, set itself sharply and persistently upon the watch from that very moment. Thenceforward the personality of Sangree was never far from my thoughts, and I was for ever analysing and searching for the explanation that took so long in coming.

"I declare, Hubbard, you're tanned like an aboriginal, and you look like one, too," laughed Maloney.

"And I can return the compliment," was my reply, as we all gathered round a brew of tea to exchange news and compare notes.

And later, at supper, it amused me to observe that the distinguished tutor, once clergyman, did not eat his food quite as "nicely" as he did at home—he devoured it; that Mrs. Maloney ate more, and, to say the least, with less delay, than was her custom in the select atmosphere of her English dining-room; and that while Joan attacked her tin plateful with genuine avidity, Sangree, the Canadian, bit and gnawed at his, laughing and talking and complimenting the cook all the while, and making me think with secret amusement of a starved animal at its first meal. While, from their remarks about myself, I judged that I had changed and grown wild as much as the rest of them.

In this and in a hundred other little ways the change showed, ways difficult to define in detail, but all proving—not the coarsening effect of leading the primitive life, but, let us say, the more direct and unvarnished methods that became prevalent. For all day long we were in the bath of the elements—wind, water, sun—and just as the body became insensible to cold and shed unnecessary clothing, the mind grew straightforward and shed many of the disguises required by the conventions of civilisation.

And in each, according to temperament and character, there stirred the life-instincts that were natural, untamed, and, in a sense—savage.

III

So it came about that I stayed with our island party, putting off my second exploring trip from day to day, and I think that this far-fetched instinct to watch Sangree was really the cause of my postponement.

For another ten days the life of the Camp pursued its even and delightful way, blessed by perfect summer weather, a good harvest of fish, fine winds for sailing, and calm, starry nights. Maloney's selfish prayer had been favourably received. Nothing came to disturb or perplex. There was not even the prowling of night animals to vex the rest of Mrs. Maloney; for in previous camps it had often been her peculiar affliction that she heard the porcupines scratching against the canvas, or the squirrels dropping fir-cones in the early morning with a sound of miniature thunder upon the roof of her tent. But on this island there was not even a squirrel or a mouse. I think two toads and a small and harmless snake were the only living creatures that had been discovered during the whole of the first fortnight. And these two toads in all probability were not two toads, but one toad.

Then, suddenly, came the terror that changed the whole aspect of the place—the devastating terror.

It came, at first, gently, but from the very start it made me realise the unpleasant loneliness of our situation, our remote isolation in this wilderness of sea and rock, and how the islands in this tideless Baltic ocean lay about us like the advance guard of a vast besieging army. Its entry, as I say, was gentle, hardly noticeable, in fact, to most of us: singularly undramatic it certainly was. But, then, in actual life this is often the way the dreadful climaxes move upon us, leaving the heart undisturbed almost to the last minute, and then overwhelming it with a sudden rush of horror. For it was the custom at breakfast to listen patiently while each in turn related the trivial adventures of the night—how they slept, whether the wind shook their tent, whether the spider on the ridge pole had moved, whether they had heard the toad, and so forth—and on this particular morning Joan, in the middle of a little pause, made a truly novel announcement:

"In the night I heard the howling of a dog," she said, and then flushed up to the roots of her hair when we burst out laughing. For the idea of there being a dog on this forsaken island that was only able to support a snake and two toads was distinctly ludicrous, and I remember Maloney, half-way through his burnt porridge, capping the announcement by declaring that he had heard a "Baltic turtle" in the lagoon, and his wife's expression of frantic alarm before the laughter undeceived her.

But the next morning Joan repeated the story with additional and convincing detail.

"Sounds of whining and growling woke me," she said, "and I distinctly heard sniffing under my tent, and the scratching of paws."

"Oh, Timothy! Can it be a porcupine?" exclaimed the Bo'sun's Mate with distress, forgetting that Sweden was not Canada.

But the girl's voice had sounded to me in quite another key, and looking up I saw that her father and Sangree were staring at her hard. They, too, understood that she was in earnest, and had been struck by the serious note in her voice.

"Rubbish, Joan! You are always dreaming something or other wild," her father said a little impatiently.

"There's not an animal of any size on the whole island," added Sangree with a puzzled expression.

He never took his eyes from her face.

"But there's nothing to prevent one swimming over," I put in briskly, for somehow a sense of uneasiness that was not pleasant had woven itself into the talk and pauses. "A deer, for instance, might easily land in the night and take a look round—"

"Or a bear!" gasped the Bo'sun's Mate, with a look so portentous that we all welcomed the laugh.

But Joan did not laugh. Instead, she sprang up and called to us to follow.

"There," she said, pointing to the ground by her tent on the side farthest from her mother's; "there are the marks close to my head. You can see for yourselves."

We saw plainly. The moss and lichen—for earth there was hardly any—had been scratched up by paws. An animal about the size of a large dog it must have been, to judge by the marks. We stood and stared in a row.

"Close to my head," repeated the girl, looking round at us. Her face, I noticed, was very pale, and her lip seemed to quiver for an instant. Then she gave a sudden gulp—and burst into a flood of tears.

The whole thing had come about in the brief space of a few minutes, and with a curious sense of inevitableness, moreover, as though it had all been carefully planned from all time and nothing could have stopped it. It had all been rehearsed before—had actually happened before, as the strange feeling sometimes has it; it seemed like the opening movement in some ominous drama, and that I knew exactly what would happen next. Something of great moment was impending.

For this sinister sensation of coming disaster made itself felt from the very beginning, and an atmosphere of gloom and dismay pervaded the entire Camp from that moment forward.

I drew Sangree to one side and moved away, while Maloney took the distressed girl into her tent, and his wife followed them, energetic and greatly flustered.

For thus, in undramatic fashion, it was that the terror I have spoken of first attempted the invasion of our Camp, and, trivial and unimportant though it seemed, every little detail of this opening scene is photographed upon my mind with merciless accuracy and precision. It happened exactly as described. This was exactly the language used. I see it written before me in black and white. I see, too, the faces of all concerned with the sudden ugly signature of alarm where before had been peace. The terror had stretched out, so to speak, a first tentative feeler towards us and had touched the hearts of each with a horrid directness. And from this moment the Camp changed.

Sangree in particular was visibly upset. He could not bear to see the girl distressed, and to hear her actually cry was almost more than he could stand. The feeling that he had no right to protect her hurt him keenly, and I could see that he was itching to do something to help, and liked him for it. His expression said plainly that he would tear in a thousand pieces anything that dared to injure a hair of her head.

We lit our pipes and strolled over in silence to the men's quarters, and it was his odd Canadian expression "Gee whiz!" that drew my attention to a further discovery.

"The brute's been scratching round my tent too," he cried, as he pointed to similar marks by the door and I stooped down to examine them. We both stared in amazement for several minutes without speaking.

"Only I sleep like the dead," he added, straightening up again, "and so heard nothing, I suppose."

We traced the paw-marks from the mouth of his tent in a direct line across to the girl's, but nowhere else about the Camp was there a sign of the strange visitor. The deer, dog, or whatever it was that had twice favoured us with a visit in the night, had confined its attentions to these two tents. And, after all, there was really nothing out of the way about these visits of an unknown animal, for although our own island was destitute of life, we were in the heart of a wilderness, and the mainland and larger islands must be swarming with all kinds of four-footed creatures, and no very prolonged swimming was necessary to reach us. In any other country it would not have caused a moment's interest—interest of the kind we felt, that is. In our Canadian camps the bears were for ever grunting about among the provision bags at night, porcupines scratching unceasingly, and chipmunks scuttling over everything.

"My daughter is overtired, and that's the truth of it," explained Maloney presently when he rejoined us and had examined in turn the other paw-marks. "She's been overdoing it lately, and camp-life, you know, always means a great excitement to her. It's natural enough. If we take no notice she'll be all right." He paused to borrow my tobacco pouch and fill his pipe, and the blundering way he filled it and spilled the precious weed on the ground visibly belied the calm of his easy language. "You might take her out for a bit of fishing, Hubbard, like a good chap; she's hardly up to the long day in the cutter. Show her some of the other islands in your canoe, perhaps. Eh?"

And by lunch-time the cloud had passed away as suddenly, and as suspiciously, as it had come.

But in the canoe, on our way home, having till then purposely ignored the subject uppermost in our minds, she suddenly spoke to me in a way that again touched the note of sinister alarm—the note that kept on sounding and sounding until finally John Silence came with his great vibrating presence and relieved it; yes, and even after he came, too, for a while.

"I'm ashamed to ask it," she said abruptly, as she steered me home, her sleeves rolled up, her hair blowing in the wind, "and ashamed of my silly tears too, because I really can't make out what caused them; but, Mr. Hubbard, I want you to promise me not to go off for your long expeditions—just yet. I beg it of you." She was so in earnest that she forgot the canoe, and the wind caught it sideways and made us roll dangerously. "I have tried hard not to ask this," she added, bringing the canoe round again, "but I simply can't help myself."

It was a good deal to ask, and I suppose my hesitation was plain; for she went on before I could reply, and her beseeching expression and intensity of manner impressed me very forcibly.

"For another two weeks only—"

"Mr. Sangree leaves in a fortnight," I said, seeing at once what she was driving at, but wondering if it was best to encourage her or not.

"If I knew you were to be on the island till then," she said, her face alternately pale and blushing, and her voice trembling a little, "I should feel so much happier."

I looked at her steadily, waiting for her to finish.

"And safer," she added almost in a whisper; "especially—at night, I mean."

"Safer, Joan?" I repeated, thinking I had never seen her eyes so soft and tender. She nodded her head, keeping her gaze fixed on my face.

It was really difficult to refuse, whatever my thoughts and judgment may have been, and somehow I understood that she spoke with good reason, though for the life of me I could not have put it into words.

"Happier—and safer," she said gravely, the canoe giving a dangerous lurch as she leaned forward in her seat to catch my answer. Perhaps, after all, the wisest way was to grant her request and make light of it, easing her anxiety without too much encouraging its cause.

"All right, Joan, you queer creature; I promise," and the instant look of relief in her face, and the smile that came back like sunlight to her eyes, made me feel that, unknown to myself and the world, I was capable of considerable sacrifice after all.

"But, you know, there's nothing to be afraid of," I added sharply; and she looked up in my face with the smile women use when they know we are talking idly, yet do not wish to tell us so.

"*You* don't feel afraid, I know," she observed quietly.

"Of course not; why should I?"

"So, if you will just humour me this once I—I will never ask anything foolish of you again as long as I live," she said gratefully.

"You have my promise," was all I could find to say. She headed the nose of the canoe for the lagoon lying a quarter of a mile ahead, and paddled swiftly; but a minute or two later she paused again and stared hard at me with the dripping paddle across the thwarts.

"You've not heard anything at night yourself, have you?" she asked.

"I never hear anything at night," I replied shortly, "from the moment I lie down till the moment I get up."

"That dismal howling, for instance," she went on, determined to get it out, "far away at first and then getting closer, and stopping just outside the Camp?"

"Certainly not."

"Because, sometimes I think I almost dreamed it."

"Most likely you did," was my unsympathetic response.

"And you don't think father has heard it either, then?"

"No. He would have told me if he had,"

This seemed to relieve her mind a little. "I know mother hasn't," she added, as if speaking to herself, "for she hears nothing—ever."

It was two nights after this conversation that I woke out of deep sleep and heard sounds of screaming. The voice was really horrible, breaking the peace and silence with its shrill clamour. In less than ten seconds I was half dressed and out of my tent. The screaming had stopped abruptly, but I knew the general direction, and ran as fast as the darkness would allow over to the women's quarters, and on getting close I heard sounds of suppressed weeping. It was Joan's voice. And just as I came up I saw Mrs. Maloney, marvellously attired, fumbling with a lantern. Other voices became audible in the same moment behind me, and Timothy Maloney arrived, breathless, less than half dressed, and carrying another lantern that had gone out on the way from being banged against a tree. Dawn was just breaking, and a chill wind blew in from the sea. Heavy black clouds drove low overhead.

The scene of confusion may be better imagined than described. Questions in frightened voices filled the air against this background of suppressed weeping. Briefly—Joan's silk tent had been torn, and the girl was in a state bordering upon hysterics. Somewhat reassured by our noisy presence, however,—for she was plucky at heart,—she pulled herself together and tried to explain what had happened; and her broken words, told there on the edge of night and morning upon this wild island ridge, were oddly thrilling and distressingly convincing.

"Something touched me and I woke," she said simply, but in a voice still hushed and broken with the terror of it, "something pushing against the tent; I felt it through the canvas. There was the same sniffing and scratching as before, and I felt the tent give a little as when wind shakes it. I heard breathing—very loud, very heavy breathing—and then came a sudden great tearing blow, and the canvas ripped open close to my face."

She had instantly dashed out through the open flap and screamed at the top of her voice, thinking the creature had actually got into the tent. But nothing was visible, she declared, and she heard not the faintest sound of an animal making off under cover of the darkness. The brief account seemed to exercise a paralysing effect upon us all as we listened to it. I can see the dishevelled group to this day, the wind blowing the women's hair, and Maloney craning his head forward to listen, and his wife, open-mouthed and gasping, leaning against a pine tree.

"Come over to the stockade and we'll get the fire going," I said; "that's the first thing," for we were all shaking with the cold in our scanty garments. And at that moment Sangree arrived wrapped in a blanket and carrying his gun; he was still drunken with sleep.

"The dog again," Maloney explained briefly, forestalling his questions; "been at Joan's tent. Torn it, by Gad! this time. It's time we did something." He went on mumbling confusedly to himself.

Sangree gripped his gun and looked about swiftly in the darkness. I saw his eyes flame in the glare of the flickering lanterns. He made a movement as though to start out and hunt—and kill. Then his glance fell on the girl crouching on the ground, her face hidden in her hands, and there leaped into his features an expression of savage anger that transformed them. He could have faced a dozen lions with a walking-stick at that moment, and again I liked him for the strength of his anger, his self-control, and his hopeless devotion.

But I stopped him going off on a blind and useless chase.

"Come and help me start the fire, Sangree," I said, anxious also to relieve the girl of our presence; and a few minutes later the ashes, still glowing from the night's fire, had kindled the fresh wood, and there was a blaze that warmed us well while it also lit up the surrounding trees within a radius of twenty yards.

"I heard nothing," he whispered; "what in the world do you think it is? It surely can't be only a dog!"

"We'll find that out later," I said, as the others came up to the grateful warmth; "the first thing is to make as big a fire as we can."

Joan was calmer now, and her mother had put on some warmer, and less miraculous, garments. And while they stood talking in low voices Maloney and I slipped off to examine the tent. There was little enough to see, but that little was unmistakable. Some animal had scratched up the ground at the head of the tent, and with a great blow of a powerful paw—a paw clearly provided with good claws—had struck the silk and torn it open. There was a hole large enough to pass a fist and arm through.

"It can't be far away," Maloney said excitedly. "We'll organise a hunt at once; this very minute."

We hurried back to the fire, Maloney talking boisterously about his proposed hunt. "There's nothing like prompt action to dispel alarm," he whispered in my ear; and then turned to the rest of us.

"We'll hunt the island from end to end at once," he said, with excitement; "that's what we'll do. The beast can't be far away. And the Bo'sun's Mate and Joan must come too, because they can't be left alone. Hubbard, you take the right shore, and you, Sangree, the left, and I'll go in the middle with the women. In this way we can stretch clean across the ridge, and nothing bigger than a rabbit can possibly escape us." He was extraordinarily excited, I thought. Anything affecting Joan, of course, stirred him prodigiously. "Get your guns and we'll start the drive at once," he cried. He lit another lantern and handed one each to his wife and Joan, and while I ran to fetch my gun I heard him singing to himself with the excitement of it all.

Meanwhile the dawn had come on quickly. It made the flickering lanterns look pale. The wind, too, was rising, and I heard the trees moaning overhead and the waves breaking with increasing clamour on the shore. In the lagoon the boat dipped and splashed, and the sparks from the fire were carried aloft in a stream and scattered far and wide.

We made our way to the extreme end of the island, measured our distances carefully, and then began to advance. None of us spoke. San-gree and I, with cocked guns, watched the shore-lines, and all within easy touch and speaking distance. It was a slow and blundering drive, and there were many false alarms, but after the best part of half an hour we stood on the farther end, having made the complete tour, and without putting up so much as a squirrel. Certainly there was no living creature on that island but ourselves.

"*I* know what it is!" cried Maloney, looking out over the dim ex-panse of grey sea, and speaking with the air of a man making a discov-ery; "it's a dog from one of the farms on the larger islands"—he pointed seawards where the archipelago thickened—"and it's escaped and turned wild. Our fires and voices attracted it, and it's probably half starved as well as savage, poor brute!"

No one said anything in reply, and he began to sing again very low to himself.

The point where we stood—a huddled, shivering group—faced the wider channels that led to the open sea and Finland. The grey dawn had broken in earnest at last, and we could see the racing waves with their angry crests of white. The surrounding islands showed up as dark masses in the distance, and in the east, almost as Maloney spoke, the sun came up with a rush in a stormy and magnificent sky of red and gold. Against this splashed and gorgeous background black clouds, shaped like fantastic and legendary animals, filed past swiftly in a tear-ing stream, and to this day I have only to close my eyes to see again that vivid and hurrying procession in the air. All about us the pines made black splashes against the sky. It was an angry sunrise. Rain, in-deed, had already begun to fall in big drops.

We turned, as by a common instinct, and, without speech, made our way back slowly to the stockade, Maloney humming snatches of his songs, Sangree in front with his gun, prepared to shoot at a mo-ment's notice, and the women floundering in the rear with myself and the extinguished lanterns.

Yet it was only a dog!

Really, it was most singular when one came to reflect soberly upon it all. Events, say the occultists, have souls, or at least that agglomerate life due to the emotions and thoughts of all concerned in them, so that cities, and even whole countries, have great astral shapes which may become visible to the eye of vision; and certainly here, the soul of this drive—this vain, blundering, futile drive—stood somewhere between ourselves and—laughed.

All of us heard that laugh, and all of us tried hard to smother the sound, or at least to ignore it. Every one talked at once, loudly, and with exaggerated decision, obviously trying to say something plausible against heavy odds, striving to explain naturally that might so easily conceal itself from us, or swim away before we had time to light upon its trail. For we all spoke of that "trail" as though it really existed, and we had more to go upon than the mere marks of paws about the tents of Joan and the Canadian. Indeed, but for these, and the torn tent, I think it would, of course, have been possible to ignore the existence of this beast intruder altogether.

And it was here, under this angry dawn, as we stood in the shelter of the stockade from the pouring rain, weary yet so strangely excited— it was here, out of this confusion of voices and explanations, that— very stealthily—the ghost of something horrible slipped in and stood among us. It made all our explanations seem childish and untrue; the false relation was instantly exposed. Eyes exchanged quick, anxious glances, questioning, expressive of dismay. There was a sense of won- der, of poignant distress, and of trepidation. Alarm stood waiting at our elbows. We shivered.

Then, suddenly, as we looked into each other's faces, came the long, unwelcome pause in which this new arrival established itself in our hearts.

And, without further speech, or attempt at explanation, Maloney moved off abruptly to mix the porridge for an early breakfast; Sangree to clean the fish; myself to chop wood and tend the fire; Joan and her mother to change their wet garments; and, most significant of all, to prepare her mother's tent for its future complement of two.

Each went to his duty, but hurriedly, awkwardly, silently; and this new arrival, this shape of terror and distress stalked, viewless, by the side of each.

"If only I could have traced that dog," I think was the thought in the minds of all.

*   *   *

But in Camp, where every one realises how important the individual contribution is to the comfort and well-being of all, the mind speedily recovers tone and pulls itself together.

During the day, a day of heavy and ceaseless rain, we kept more or less to our tents, and though there were signs of mysterious conferences between the three members of the Maloney family, I think that most of us slept a good deal and stayed alone with his thoughts. Certainly, I did, because when Maloney came to say that his wife invited us all to a special "tea" in her tent, he had to shake me awake before I realised that he was there at all.

And by supper-time we were more or less even-minded again, and almost jolly. I only noticed that there was an undercurrent of what is best described as "jumpiness," and that the merest snapping of a twig, or plop of a fish in the lagoon, was sufficient to make us start and look over our shoulders. Pauses were rare in our talk, and the fire was never for one instant allowed to get low. The wind and rain had ceased, but the dripping of the branches still kept up an excellent imitation of a downpour. In particular, Maloney was vigilant and alert, telling us a series of tales in which the wholesome humorous element was especially strong. He lingered, too, behind with me after Sangree had gone to bed, and while I mixed myself a glass of hot Swedish punch, he did a thing I had never known him do before—he mixed one for himself, and then asked me to light him over to his tent. We said nothing on the way, but I felt that he was glad of my companionship.

I returned alone to the stockade, and for a long time after that kept the fire blazing, and sat up smoking and thinking. I hardly knew why; but sleep was far from me for one thing, and for another, an idea was taking form in my mind that required the comfort of tobacco and a bright fire for its growth. I lay against a corner of the stockade seat, listening to the wind whispering and to the ceaseless drip-drip of the trees. The night, otherwise, was very still, and the sea quiet as a lake. I remember that I was conscious, peculiarly conscious, of this host of desolate islands crowding about us in the darkness, and that we were the one little spot of humanity in a rather wonderful kind of wilderness.

But this, I think, was the only symptom that came to warn me of highly strung nerves, and it certainly was not sufficiently alarming to destroy my peace of mind. One thing, however, did come to disturb my peace, for just as I finally made ready to go, and had kicked the embers of the fire into a last effort, I fancied I saw, peering at me round the farther end of the stockade wall, a dark and shadowy mass that might have been—that strongly resembled, in fact—the body of a large animal. Two glowing eyes shone for an instant in the middle of it. But the next second I saw that it was merely a projecting mass of moss and lichen in the wall of our stockade, and the eyes were a couple of wandering sparks from the dying ashes I had kicked. It was easy enough, too, to imagine I saw an animal moving here and there between the trees, as I picked my way stealthily to my tent. Of course, the shadows tricked me.

And though it was after one o'clock, Maloney's light was still burning, for I saw his tent shining white among the pines.

It was, however, in the short space between consciousness and sleep—that time when the body is low and the voices of the submerged region tell sometimes true—that the idea which had been all this while maturing reached the point of an actual decision, and I suddenly realised that I had resolved to send word to Dr. Silence. For, with a sudden wonder that I had hitherto been so blind, the unwelcome conviction dawned upon me all at once that some dreadful thing was lurking about us on this island, and that the safety of at least one of us was threatened by something monstrous and unclean that was too horrible to contemplate. And, again remembering those last words of his as the train moved out of the platform, I understood that Dr. Silence would hold himself in readiness to come.

"Unless you should send for me sooner," he had said.

I found myself suddenly wide awake. It is impossible to say what woke me, but it was no gradual process, seeing that I jumped from deep sleep to absolute alertness in a single instant. I had evidently slept for an hour and more, for the night had cleared, stars crowded the sky, and a pallid half-moon just sinking into the sea threw a spectral light between the trees.

I went outside to sniff the air, and stood upright. A curious impression that something was astir in the Camp came over me, and when I glanced across at Sangree's tent, some twenty feet away, I saw that it was moving. He too, then, was awake and restless, for I saw the canvas sides bulge this way and that as he moved within.

Then the flap pushed forward. He was coming out, like myself, to sniff the air; and I was not surprised, for its sweetness after the rain was intoxicating. And he came on all fours, just as I had done. I saw a head thrust round the edge of the tent.

And then I saw that it was not Sangree at all. It was an animal. And the same instant I realised something else too—it was *the* animal; and its whole presentment for some unaccountable reason was unutterably malefic.

A cry I was quite unable to suppress escaped me, and the creature turned on the instant and stared at me with baleful eyes. I could have dropped on the spot, for the strength all ran out of my body with a rush. Something about it touched in me the living terror that grips and paralyses. If the mind requires but the tenth of a second to form an impression, I must have stood there stockstill for several seconds while I seized the ropes for support and stared. Many and vivid impressions flashed through my mind, but not one of them resulted in action, because I was in instant dread that the beast any moment would leap in my direction and be upon me. Instead, however, after what seemed a vast period, it slowly turned its eyes from my face, uttered a low whining sound, and came out altogether into the open.

Then, for the first time, I saw it in its entirety and noted two things: it was about the size of a large dog, but at the same time it was utterly unlike any animal that I had ever seen. Also, that the quality that had impressed me first as being malefic, was really only its singular and original strangeness. Foolish as it may sound, and impossible as it is for me to adduce proof, I can only say that the animal seemed to me then to be—not real.

But all this passed through my mind in a flash, almost subconsciously, and before I had time to check my impressions, or even properly verify them; I made an involuntary movement, catching the tight rope in my hand so that it twanged like a banjo string, and in that instant the creature turned the corner of Sangree's tent and was gone into the darkness.

Then, of course, my senses in some measure returned to me, and I realised only one thing: it had been inside his tent!

I dashed out, reached the door in half a dozen strides, and looked in. The Canadian, thank God! lay upon his bed of branches. His arm was stretched outside, across the blankets, the fist tightly clenched, and the body had an appearance of unusual rigidity that was alarming. On his face there was an expression of effort, almost of painful effort, so far as the uncertain light permitted me to see, and his sleep seemed to be very profound. He looked, I thought, so stiff, so unnaturally stiff, and in some indefinable way, too, he looked smaller—shrunken.

I called to him to wake, but called many times in vain. Then I decided to shake him, and had already moved forward to do so vigorously when there came a sound of footsteps padding softly behind me, and I felt a stream of hot breath burn my neck as I stooped. I turned sharply. The tent door was darkened and something silently swept in. I felt a rough and shaggy body push past me, and knew that the animal had returned. It seemed to leap forward between me and Sangree—in fact, to leap upon Sangree, for its dark body hid him momentarily from view, and in that moment my soul turned sick and coward with a horror that rose from the very dregs and depth of life, and gripped my existence at its central source.

The creature seemed somehow to melt away into him, almost as though it belonged to him and were a part of himself, but in the same instant—that instant of extraordinary confusion and terror in my mind—it seemed to pass over and behind him, and, in some utterly unaccountable fashion, it was gone! And the Canadian woke and sat up with a start.

"Quick! You fool!" I cried, in my excitement, "the beast has been in your tent, here at your very throat while you sleep like the dead. Up, man! Get your gun! Only this second it disappeared over there behind your head. Quick! or Joan—!"

And somehow the fact that he was there, wide-awake now, to corroborate me, brought the additional conviction to my own mind that this was no animal, but some perplexing and dreadful form of life that drew upon my deeper knowledge, that much reading had perhaps assented to, but that had never yet come within actual range of my senses.

He was up in a flash, and out. He was trembling, and very white. We searched hurriedly, feverishly, but found only the traces of paw-marks passing from the door of his own tent across the moss to the women's. And the sight of the tracks about Mrs. Maloney's tent, where Joan now slept, set him in a perfect fury.

"Do you know what it is, Hubbard, this beast?" he hissed under his breath at me; "it's a damned wolf, that's what it is—a wolf lost among the islands, and starving to death—desperate. So help me God, I believe it's that!"

He talked a lot of rubbish in his excitement. He declared he would sleep by day and sit up every night until he killed it. Again his rage touched my admiration; but I got him away before he made enough noise to wake the whole Camp.

"I have a better plan than that," I said, watching his face closely. "I don't think this is anything we can deal with. I'm going to send for the only man I know who can help. We'll go to Waxholm this very morning and get a telegram through."

Sangree stared at me with a curious expression as the fury died out of his face and a new look of alarm took its place.

"John Silence," I said, "will know—"

"You think it's something—of that sort?" he stammered.

"I am sure of it."

There was a moment's pause. "That's worse, far worse than anything material," he said, turning visibly paler. He looked from my face to the sky, and then added with sudden resolution, "Come; the wind's rising. Let's get off at once. From there you can telephone to Stockholm and get a telegram sent without delay."

I sent him down to get the boat ready, and seized the opportunity myself to run and wake Maloney. He was sleeping very lightly, and sprang up the moment I put my head inside his tent. I told him briefly what I had seen, and he showed so little surprise that I caught myself wondering for the first time whether he himself had seen more going on than he had deemed wise to communicate to the rest of us.

He agreed to my plan without a moment's hesitation, and my last words to him were to let his wife and daughter think that the great psychic doctor was coming merely as a chance visitor, and not with any professional interest.

So, with frying-pan, provisions, and blankets aboard, Sangree and I sailed out of the lagoon fifteen minutes later, and headed with a good breeze for the direction of Waxholm and the borders of civilisation.

IV

Although nothing John Silence did ever took me, properly speaking, by surprise, it was certainly unexpected to find a letter from Stockholm waiting for me. "I have finished my Hungary business," he wrote, "and am here for ten days. Do not hesitate to send if you need me. If you telephone any morning from Waxholm I can catch the afternoon steamer."

My years of intercourse with him were full of "coincidences" of this description, and although he never sought to explain them by claiming any magical system of communication with my mind, I have never doubted that there actually existed some secret telepathic method by which he knew my circumstances and gauged the degree of my need. And that this power was independent of time in the sense that it saw into the future, always seemed to me equally apparent.

Sangree was as much relieved as I was, and within an hour of sunset that very evening we met him on the arrival of the little coasting steamer, and carried him off in the dinghy to the camp we had prepared on a neighbouring island, meaning to start for home early next morning.

"Now," he said, when supper was over and we were smoking round the fire, "let me hear your story." He glanced from one to the other, smiling.

"You tell it, Mr. Hubbard," Sangree interrupted abruptly, and went off a little way to wash the dishes, yet not so far as to be out of earshot. And while he splashed with the hot water, and scraped the tin plates with sand and moss, my voice, unbroken by a single question from Dr. Silence, ran on for the next half-hour with the best account I could give of what had happened.

My listener lay on the other side of the fire, his face half hidden by a big sombrero; sometimes he glanced up questioningly when a point needed elaboration, but he uttered no single word till I had reached the end, and his manner all through the recital was grave and attentive. Overhead, the wash of the wind in the pine branches filled in the pauses; the darkness settled down over the sea, and the stars came out in thousands, and by the time I finished the moon had risen to flood the scene with silver. Yet, by his face and eyes, I knew quite well that the doctor was listening to something he had expected to hear, even if he had not actually anticipated all the details.

"You did well to send for me," he said very low, with a significant glance at me when I finished; "very well,"—and for one swift second his eye took in Sangree,—"for what we have to deal with here is nothing more than a werewolf—rare enough, I am glad to say, but often very sad, and sometimes very terrible."

I jumped as though I had been shot, but the next second was heartily ashamed of my want of control; for this brief remark, confirming as it did my own worst suspicions, did more to convince me of the gravity of the adventure than any number of questions or explanations. It seemed to draw close the circle about us, shutting a door somewhere that locked us in with the animal and the horror, and turning the key. Whatever it was had now to be faced and dealt with.

"No one has been actually injured so far?" he asked aloud, but in a matter-of-fact tone that lent reality to grim possibilities.

"Good heavens, no!" cried the Canadian, throwing down his dishcloths and coming forward into the circle of firelight. "Surely there can be no question of this poor starved beast injuring anybody, can there?"

His hair straggled untidily over his forehead, and there was a gleam in his eyes that was not all reflection from the fire. His words made me turn sharply. We all laughed a little, short, forced laugh.

"I trust not, indeed," Dr. Silence said quietly. "But what makes you think the creature is starved?" He asked the question with his eyes straight on the other's face. The prompt question explained to me why I had started, and I waited with just a tremor of excitement for the reply.

Sangree hesitated a moment, as though the question took him by surprise. But he met the doctor's gaze unflinchingly across the fire, and with complete honesty.

"Really," he faltered, with a little shrug of the shoulders, "I can hardly tell you. The phrase seemed to come out of its own accord. I have felt from the beginning that it was in pain and—starved, though why I felt this never occurred to me till you asked."

"You really know very little about it, then?" said the other, with a sudden gentleness in his voice.

"No more than that," Sangree replied, looking at him with a puzzled expression that was unmistakably genuine. "In fact, nothing at all, really," he added, by way of further explanation.

"I am glad of that," I heard the doctor murmur under his breath, but so low that I only just caught the words, and Sangree missed them altogether, as evidently he was meant to do.

"And now," he cried, getting on his feet and shaking himself with a characteristic gesture, as though to shake out the horror and the mystery, "let us leave the problem till to-morrow and enjoy this wind and sea and stars. I've been living lately in the atmosphere of many people, and feel that I want to wash and be clean. I propose a swim and then bed. Who'll second me?" And two minutes later we were all diving from the boat into cool, deep water, that reflected a thousand moons as the waves broke away from us in countless ripples.

We slept in blankets under the open sky, Sangree and I taking the outside places, and were up before sunrise to catch the dawn wind. Helped by this early start we were half-way home by noon, and then the wind shifted to a few points behind us so that we fairly ran. In and out among a thousand islands, down narrow channels where we lost the wind, out into open spaces where we had to take in a reef, racing along under a hot and cloudless sky, we flew through the very heart of the bewildering and lonely scenery.

"A real wilderness," cried Dr. Silence from his seat in the bows where he held the jib sheet. His hat was off, his hair tumbled in the wind, and his lean brown face gave him the touch of an Oriental. Presently he changed places with Sangree, and came down to talk with me by the tiller.

"A wonderful region, all this world of islands," he said, waving his hand to the scenery rushing past us, "but doesn't it strike you there's something lacking?"

"It's—hard," I answered, after a moment's reflection. "It has a superficial, glittering prettiness, without—" I hesitated to find the word I wanted.

John Silence nodded his head with approval.

"Exactly," he said. "The picturesqueness of stage scenery that is not real, not alive. It's like a landscape by a clever painter, yet without true imagination. Soulless—that's the word you wanted."

"Something like that," I answered, watching the gusts of wind on the sails. "Not dead so much, as without soul. That's it."

"Of course," he went on, in a voice calculated, it seemed to me, not to reach our companion in the bows, "to live long in a place like this—long and alone—might bring about a strange result in some men."

I suddenly realised he was talking with a purpose and pricked up my ears.

"There's no life here. These islands are mere dead rocks pushed up from below the sea—not living land; and there's nothing really alive on them. Even the sea, this tideless, brackish sea, neither salt water nor fresh, is dead. It's all a pretty image of life without the real heart and soul of life. To a man with too strong desires who came here and lived close to nature, strange things might happen."

"Let her out a bit," I shouted to Sangree, who was coming aft. "The wind's gusty and we've got hardly any ballast."

He went back to the bows, and Dr. Silence continued—

"Here, I mean, a long sojourn would lead to deterioration, to degeneration. The place is utterly unsoftened by human influences, by any humanising associations of history, good or bad. This landscape has never awakened into life; it's still dreaming in its primitive sleep."

"In time," I put in, "you mean a man living here might become brutal?"

"The passions would run wild, selfishness become supreme, the instincts coarsen and turn savage probably."

"But—"

"In other places just as wild, parts of Italy for instance, where there are other moderating influences, it could not happen. The character might grow wild, savage too in a sense, but with a human wildness one could understand and deal with. But here, in a hard place like this, it might be otherwise." He spoke slowly, weighing his words carefully.

I looked at him with many questions in my eyes, and a precautionary cry to Sangree to stay in the fore part of the boat, out of earshot.

"First of all there would come callousness to pain, and indifference to the rights of others. Then the soul would turn savage, not from passionate human causes, or with enthusiasm, but by deadening down into a kind of cold, primitive, emotionless savagery—by turning, like the landscape, soulless."

"And a man with strong desires, you say, might change?"

"Without being aware of it, yes; he might turn savage, his instincts and desires turn animal. And if'—he lowered his voice and turned for a moment towards the bows, and then continued in his most weighty manner—"owing to delicate health or other predisposing causes, his Double—you know what I mean, of course—his etheric Body of Desire, or astral body, as some term it—that part in which the emotions, passions, and desires reside—if this, I say, were for some constitutional reason loosely joined to his physical organism, there might well take place an occasional projection—"

Sangree came aft with a sudden rush, his face aflame, but whether with wind or sun, or with what he had heard, I cannot say. In my surprise I let the tiller slip and the cutter gave a great plunge as she came sharply into the wind and flung us all together in a heap on the bottom. Sangree said nothing, but while he scrambled up and made the jib sheet fast my companion found a moment to add to his unfinished sentence the words, too low for any ear but mine—

"Entirely unknown to himself, however."

We righted the boat and laughed, and then Sangree produced the map and explained exactly where we were. Far away on the horizon, across an open stretch of water, lay a blue cluster of islands with our crescent-shaped home among them and the safe anchorage of the lagoon. An hour with this wind would get us there comfortably, and while Dr. Silence and Sangree fell into conversation, I sat and pondered over the strange suggestions that had just been put into my mind concerning the "Double," and the possible form it might assume when dissociated temporarily from the physical body.

The whole way home these two chatted, and John Silence was as gentle and sympathetic as a woman. I did not hear much of their talk, for the wind grew occasionally to the force of a hurricane and the sails and tiller absorbed my attention; but I could see that Sangree was pleased and happy, and was pouring out intimate revelations to his companion in the way that most people did—when John Silence wished them to do so.

But it was quite suddenly, while I sat all intent upon wind and sails, that the true meaning of Sangree's remark about the animal flared up in me with its full import. For his admission that he knew it was in pain and starved was in reality nothing more or less than a revelation of his deeper self. It was in the nature of a confession. He was speaking of something that he knew positively, something that was beyond question or argument, something that had to do directly with himself. "Poor starved beast" he had called it in words that had "come out of their own accord," and there had not been the slightest evidence of any desire to conceal or explain away. He had spoken instinctively— from his heart, and as though about his own self.

And half an hour before sunset we raced through the narrow opening of the lagoon and saw the smoke of the dinner-fire blowing here and there among the trees, and the figures of Joan and the Bo'sun's Mate running down to meet us at the landing-stage.

V

Everything changed from the moment John Silence set foot on that island; it was like the effect produced by calling in some big doctor, some great arbiter of life and death, for consultation. The sense of gravity increased a hundredfold. Even inanimate objects took upon themselves a subtle alteration, for the setting of the adventure—this deserted bit of sea with its hundreds of uninhabited islands—somehow turned sombre. An element that was mysterious, and in a sense dis- heartening, crept unbidden into the severity of grey rock and dark pine forest and took the sparkle from the sunshine and the sea.

I, at least, was keenly aware of the change, for my whole being shifted, as it were, a degree higher, becoming keyed up and alert. The figures from the background of the stage moved forward a little into the light—nearer to the inevitable action. In a word this man's arrival intensified the whole affair.

And, looking back down the years to the time when all this hap- pened, it is clear to me that he had a pretty sharp idea of the meaning of it from the very beginning. How much he knew beforehand by his strange divining powers, it is impossible to say, but from the moment he came upon the scene and caught within himself the note of what was going on amongst us, he undoubtedly held the true solution of the puzzle and had no need to ask questions. And this certitude it was that set him in such an atmosphere of power and made us all look to him instinctively; for he took no tentative steps, made no false moves, and while the rest of us floundered he moved straight to the climax. He was indeed a true diviner of souls.

I can now read into his behaviour a good deal that puzzled me at the time, for though I had dimly guessed the solution, I had no idea how he would deal with it. And the conversations I can reproduce almost verbatim, for, according to my invariable habit, I kept full notes of all he said.

To Mrs. Maloney, foolish and dazed; to Joan, alarmed, yet plucky; and to the clergyman, moved by his daughter's distress below his usual shallow emotions, he gave the best possible treatment in the best possible way, yet all so easily and simply as to make it appear naturally spontaneous. For he dominated the Bo'sun's Mate, taking the measure of her ignorance with infinite patience; he keyed up Joan, stirring her courage and interest to the highest point for her own safety; and the Reverend Timothy he soothed and comforted, while obtaining his implicit obedience, by taking him into his confidence, and leading him gradually to a comprehension of the issue that was bound to follow.

And Sangree—here his wisdom was most wisely calculated—he neglected outwardly because inwardly he was the object of his unceasing and most concentrated attention. Under the guise of apparent indifference his mind kept the Canadian under constant observation.

There was a restless feeling in the Camp that evening and none of us lingered round the fire after supper as usual. Sangree and I busied ourselves with patching up the torn tent for our guest and with finding heavy stones to hold the ropes, for Dr. Silence insisted on having it pitched on the highest point of the island ridge, just where it was most rocky and there was no earth for pegs. The place, moreover, was midway between the men's and women's tents, and, of course, commanded the most comprehensive view of the Camp.

"So that if your dog comes," he said simply, "I may be able to catch him as he passes across."

The wind had gone down with the sun and an unusual warmth lay over the island that made sleep heavy, and in the morning we assembled at a late breakfast, rubbing our eyes and yawning. The cool north wind had given way to the warm southern air that sometimes came up with haze and moisture across the Baltic, bringing with it the relaxing sensations that produced enervation and listlessness.

And this may have been the reason why at first I failed to notice that anything unusual was about, and why I was less alert than normally; for it was not till after breakfast that the silence of our little party struck me and I discovered that Joan had not yet put in an appearance. And then, in a flash, the last heaviness of sleep vanished and I saw that Maloney was white and troubled and his wife could not hold a plate without trembling.

A desire to ask questions was stopped in me by a swift glance from Dr. Silence, and I suddenly understood in some vague way that they were waiting till Sangree should have gone. How this idea came to me I cannot determine, but the soundness of the intuition was soon proved, for the moment he moved off to his tent, Maloney looked up at me and began to speak in a low voice.

"You slept through it all," he half whispered.

"Through what?" I asked, suddenly thrilled with the knowledge that something dreadful had happened.

"We didn't wake you for fear of getting the whole Camp up," he went on, meaning, by the Camp, I supposed, Sangree. "It was just before dawn when the screams woke me."

"The dog again?" I asked, with a curious sinking of the heart.

"Got right into the tent," he went on, speaking passionately but very low, "and woke my wife by scrambling all over her. Then she realised that Joan was struggling beside her. And, by God! the beast had torn her arm; scratched all down the arm she was, and bleeding."

"Joan injured?" I gasped.

"Merely scratched—this time," put in John Silence, speaking for the first time; "suffering more from shock and fright than actual wounds."

"Isn't it a mercy the doctor was here," said Mrs. Maloney, looking as if she would never know calmness again. "I think we should both have been killed."

"It has been a most merciful escape," Maloney said, his pulpit voice struggling with his emotion. "But, of course, we cannot risk another—we must strike Camp and get away at once—"

"Only poor Mr. Sangree must not know what has happened. He is so attached to Joan and would be so terribly upset," added the Bo'sun's Mate distractedly, looking all about in her terror.

"It is perhaps advisable that Mr. Sangree should not know what has occurred," Dr. Silence said with quiet authority, "but I think, for the safety of all concerned, it will be better not to leave the island just now." He spoke with great decision and Maloney looked up and followed his words closely.

"If you will agree to stay here a few days longer, I have no doubt we can put an end to the attentions of your strange visitor, and incidentally have the opportunity of observing a most singular and interesting phenomenon—"

"What!" gasped Mrs. Maloney, "a phenomenon?—you mean that you know what it is?"

"I am quite certain I know what it is," he replied very low, for we heard the footsteps of Sangree approaching, "though I am not so certain yet as to the best means of dealing with it. But in any case it is not wise to leave precipitately—"

"Oh, Timothy, does he think it's a devil—?" cried the Bo'sun's Mate in a voice that even the Canadian must have heard.

"In my opinion," continued John Silence, looking across at me and the clergyman, "it is a case of modern lycanthropy with other complications that may—" He left the sentence unfinished, for Mrs. Maloney got up with a jump and fled to her tent fearful she might hear a worse thing, and at that moment Sangree turned the corner of the stockade and came into view.

"There are footmarks all round the mouth of my tent," he said with excitement. "The animal has been here again in the night. Dr. Silence, you really must come and see them for yourself. They're as plain on the moss as tracks in snow."

But later in the day, while Sangree went off in the canoe to fish the pools near the larger islands, and Joan still lay, bandaged and resting, in her tent, Dr. Silence called me and the tutor and proposed a walk to the granite slabs at the far end. Mrs. Maloney sat on a stump near her daughter, and busied herself energetically with alternate nursing and painting.

"We'll leave you in charge," the doctor said with a smile that was meant to be encouraging, "and when you want us for lunch, or anything, the megaphone will always bring us back in time."

For, though the very air was charged with strange emotions, every one talked quietly and naturally as with a definite desire to counteract unnecessary excitement.

"I'll keep watch," said the plucky Bo'sun's Mate, "and meanwhile I find comfort in my work." She was busy with the sketch she had begun on the day after our arrival. "For even a tree," she added proudly, pointing to her little easel, "is a symbol of the divine, and the thought makes me feel safer." We glanced for a moment at a daub which was more like the symptom of a disease than a symbol of the divine—and then took the path round the lagoon.

At the far end we made a little fire and lay round it in the shadow of a big boulder. Maloney stopped his humming suddenly and turned to his companion. "And what do you make of it all?" he asked abruptly.

"In the first place," replied John Silence, making himself comfortable against the rock, "it is of human origin, this animal; it is undoubted lycanthropy."

His words had the effect precisely of a bombshell. Maloney listened as though he had been struck.

"You puzzle me utterly," he said, sitting up closer and staring at him.

"Perhaps," replied the other, "but if you'll listen to me for a few moments you may be less puzzled at the end—or more. It depends how much you know. Let me go further and say that you have underestimated, or miscalculated, the effect of this primitive wild life upon all of you."

"In what way?" asked the clergyman, bristling a trifle.

"It is strong medicine for any town-dweller, and for some of you it has been too strong. One of you has gone wild." He uttered these last words with great emphasis.

"Gone savage," he added, looking from one to the other.

Neither of us found anything to reply.

"To say that the brute has awakened in a man is not a mere metaphor always," he went on presently.

"Of course not!"

"But, in the sense I mean, may have a very literal and terrible significance," pursued Dr. Silence. "Ancient instincts that no one dreamed of, least of all their possessor, may leap forth—"

"Atavism can hardly explain a roaming animal with teeth and claws and sanguinary instincts," interrupted Maloney with impatience.

"The term is of your own choice," continued the doctor equably, "not mine, and it is a good example of a word that indicates a result while it conceals the process; but the explanation of this beast that haunts your island and attacks your daughter is of far deeper significance than mere atavistic tendencies, or throwing back to animal origin, which I suppose is the thought in your mind."

"You spoke just now of lycanthropy," said Maloney, looking bewildered and anxious to keep to plain facts evidently, "I think I have come across the word, but really—really—it can have no actual significance to-day, can it? These superstitions of mediæval times can hardly—"

He looked round at me with his jolly red face, and the expression of astonishment and dismay on it would have made me shout with laughter at any other time. Laughter, however, was never farther from my mind than at this moment when I listened to Dr. Silence as he carefully suggested to the clergyman the very explanation that had gradually been forcing itself upon my own mind.

"However mediæval ideas may have exaggerated the idea is not of much importance to us now," he said quietly, "when we are face to face with a modern example of what, I take it, has always been a profound fact. For the moment let us leave the name of any one in particular out of the matter and consider certain possibilities."

We all agreed with that at any rate. There was no need to speak of Sangree, or of any one else, until we knew a little more.

"The fundamental fact in this most curious case," he went on, "is that the 'Double' of a man—"

"You mean the astral body? I've heard of that, of course," broke in Maloney with a snort of triumph.

"No doubt," said the other, smiling, "no doubt you have;—that this Double, or fluidic body of a man, as I was saying, has the power under certain conditions of projecting itself and becoming visible to others. Certain training will accomplish this, and certain drugs likewise; illnesses, too, that ravage the body may produce temporarily the result that death produces permanently, and let loose this counterpart of a human being and render it visible to the sight of others.

"Every one, of course, knows this more or less to-day; but it is not so generally known, and probably believed by none who have not witnessed it, that this fluidic body can, under certain conditions, assume other forms than human, and that such other forms may be determined by the dominating thought and wish of the owner. For this Double, or astral body as you call it, is really the seat of the passions, emotions, and desires in the psychical economy. It is the Passion Body; and, in projecting itself, it can often assume a form that gives expression to the overmastering desire that moulds it; for it is composed of such tenuous matter that it lends itself readily to the moulding by thought and wish."

"I follow you perfectly," said Maloney, looking as if he would much rather be chopping firewood elsewhere and singing.

"And there are some persons so constituted," the doctor went on with increasing seriousness, "that the fluid body in them is but loosely associated with the physical, persons of poor health as a rule, yet often of strong desires and passions; and in these persons it is easy for the Double to dissociate itself during deep sleep from their system, and, driven forth by some consuming desire, to assume an animal form and seek the fulfilment of that desire."

There, in broad daylight, I saw Maloney deliberately creep closer to the fire and heap the wood on. We gathered in to the heat, and to each other, and listened to Dr. Silence's voice as it mingled with the swish and whirr of the wind about us, and the falling of the little waves.

"For instance, to take a concrete example," he resumed; "suppose some young man, with the delicate constitution I have spoken of, forms an overpowering attachment to a young woman, yet perceives that it is not welcomed, and is man enough to repress its outward manifestations. In such a case, supposing his Double be easily projected, the very repression of his love in the daytime would add to the intense force of his desire when released in deep sleep from the control of his will, and his fluidic body might issue forth in monstrous or animal shape and become actually visible to others. And, if his devotion were dog-like in its fidelity, yet concealing the fires of a fierce passion beneath, it might well assume the form of a creature that seemed to be half dog, half wolf——"

"A werewolf, you mean?" cried Maloney, pale to the lips as he listened.

John Silence held up a restraining hand. "A werewolf," he said, "is a true psychical fact of profound significance, however absurdly it may have been exaggerated by the imaginations of a superstitious peasantry in the days of unenlightenment, for a werewolf is nothing but the savage, and possibly sanguinary, instincts of a passionate man scouring the world in his fluidic body, his passion body, his body of desire. As in the case at hand, he may not know it—"

"It is not necessarily deliberate, then?" Maloney put in quickly, with relief.

"—It is hardly ever deliberate. It is the desires released in sleep from the control of the will finding a vent. In all savage races it has been recognised and dreaded, this phenomenon styled 'Wehr Wolf,' but to-day it is rare. And it is becoming rarer still, for the world grows tame and civilised, emotions have become refined, desires lukewarm, and few men have savagery enough left in them to generate impulses of such intense force, and certainly not to project them in animal form."

"By Gad!" exclaimed the clergyman breathlessly, and with increasing excitement, "then I feel I must tell you—what has been given to me in confidence—that Sangree has in him an admixture of savage blood—of Red Indian ancestry—"

"Let us stick to our supposition of a man as described," the doctor stopped him calmly, "and let us imagine that he has in him this admixture of savage blood; and further, that he is wholly unaware of his dreadful physical and psychical infirmity; and that he suddenly finds himself leading the primitive life together with the object of his desires; with the result that the strain of the untamed wild-man in his blood—"

"Red Indian, for instance," from Maloney.

"Red Indian, perfectly," agreed the doctor; "the result, I say, that this savage strain in him is awakened and leaps into passionate life. What then?"

He looked hard at Timothy Maloney, and the clergyman looked hard at him.

"The wild life such as you lead it here on this island, for instance, might quickly awaken his savage instincts—his buried instincts—and with profoundly disquieting results."

"You mean his Subtle Body, as you call it, might issue forth automatically in deep sleep and seek the object of its desire?" I said, coming to Maloney's aid, who was finding it more and more difficult to get words.

"Precisely;—yet the desire of the man remaining utterly unmalefic—pure and wholesome in every sense—"

"Ah!" I heard the clergyman gasp.

"The lover's desire for union run wild, run savage, tearing its way out in primitive, untamed fashion, I mean," continued the doctor, striving to make himself clear to a mind bounded by conventional thought and knowledge; "for the desire to possess, remember, may easily become importunate, and, embodied in this animal form of the Subtle Body which acts as its vehicle, may go forth to tear in pieces all that obstructs, to reach to the very heart of the loved object and seize it. *Au fond*, it is nothing more than the aspiration for union, as I said—the splendid and perfectly clean desire to absorb utterly into itself—"

He paused a moment and looked into Maloney's eyes.

"To bathe in the very heart's blood of the one desired," he added with grave emphasis.

The fire spurted and crackled and made me start, but Maloney found relief in a genuine shudder, and I saw him turn his head and look about him from the sea to the trees. The wind dropped just at that moment and the doctor's words rang sharply through the stillness.

"Then it might even kill?" stammered the clergyman presently in a hushed voice, and with a little forced laugh by way of protest that sounded quite ghastly.

"In the last resort it might kill," repeated Dr. Silence. Then, after another pause, during which he was clearly debating how much or how little it was wise to give to his audience, he continued: "And if the Double does not succeed in getting back to its physical body, that physical body would wake an imbecile—an idiot—or perhaps never wake at all."

Maloney sat up and found his tongue.

"You mean that if this fluid animal thing, or whatever it is, should be prevented getting back, the man might never wake again?" he asked, with shaking voice.

"He might be dead," replied the other calmly. The tremor of a positive sensation shivered in the air about us.

"Then isn't that the best way to cure the fool—the brute—?" thundered the clergyman, half rising to his feet.

"Certainly it would be an easy and undiscoverable form of murder," was the stern reply, spoken as calmly as though it were a remark about the weather.

Maloney collapsed visibly, and I gathered the wood over the fire and coaxed up a blaze.

"The greater part of the man's life—of his vital forces—goes out with this Double," Dr. Silence resumed, after a moment's consideration, "and a considerable portion of the actual material of his physical body. So the physical body that remains behind is depleted, not only of force, but of matter. You would see it small, shrunken, dropped together, just like the body of a materialising medium at a séance. Moreover, any mark or injury inflicted upon this Double will be found exactly reproduced by the phenomenon of repercussion upon the shrunken physical body lying in its trance—"

"An injury inflicted upon the one you say would be reproduced also on the other?" repeated Maloney, his excitement growing again.

"Undoubtedly," replied the other quietly; "for there exists all the time a continuous connection between the physical body and the Double—a connection of matter, though of exceedingly attenuated, possibly of etheric, matter. The wound *travels,* so to speak, from one to the other, and if this connection were broken the result would be death."

"Death," repeated Maloney to himself, "death!" He looked anxiously at our faces, his thoughts evidently beginning to clear.

"And this solidity?" he asked presently, after a general pause; "this tearing of tents and flesh; this howling, and the marks of paws? You mean that the Double—?"

"Has sufficient material drawn from the depleted body to produce physical results? Certainly!" the doctor took him up. "Although to explain at this moment such problems as the passage of matter through matter would be as difficult as to explain how the thought of a mother can actually break the bones of the child unborn."

Dr. Silence pointed out to sea, and Maloney, looking wildly about him, turned with a violent start. I saw a canoe, with Sangree in the stern-seat, slowly coming into view round the farther point. His hat was off, and his tanned face for the first time appeared to me—to us all, I think—as though it were the face of some one else. He looked like a wild man. Then he stood up in the canoe to make a cast with the rod, and he looked for all the world like an Indian. I recalled the expression of his face as I had seen it once or twice, notably on that occasion of the evening prayer, and an involuntary shudder ran down my spine.

At that very instant he turned and saw us where we lay, and his face broke into a smile, so that his teeth showed white in the sun. He looked in his element, and exceedingly attractive. He called out something about his fish, and soon after passed out of sight into the lagoon.

For a time none of us said a word.

"And the cure?" ventured Maloney at length.

"Is not to quench this savage force," replied Dr. Silence, "but to steer it better, and to provide other outlets. This is the solution of all these problems of accumulated force, for this force is the raw material of usefulness, and should be increased and cherished, not by separating it from the body by death, but by raising it to higher channels. The best and quickest cure of all," he went on, speaking very gently and with a hand upon the clergyman's arm, "is to lead it towards its object, provided that object is not unalterably hostile—to let it find rest where—"

He stopped abruptly, and the eyes of the two men met in a single glance of comprehension.

"Joan?" Maloney exclaimed, under his breath.

"Joan!" replied John Silence.

We all went to bed early. The day had been unusually warm, and after sunset a curious hush descended on the island. Nothing was audible but that faint, ghostly singing which is inseparable from a pine-wood even on the stillest day—a low, searching sound, as though the wind had hair and trailed it o'er the world.

With the sudden cooling of the atmosphere a sea-fog began to form. It appeared in isolated patches over the water, and then these patches slid together and a white wall advanced upon us. Not a breath of air stirred; the firs stood like flat metal outlines; the sea became as oil. The whole scene lay as though held motionless by some huge weight in the air; and the flames from our fire—the largest we had ever made—rose upwards, straight as a church steeple.

As I followed the rest of our party tent-wards, having kicked the embers of the fire into safety, the advance guard of the fog was creeping slowly among the trees, like white arms feeling their way. Mingled with the smoke was the odour of moss and soil and bark, and the peculiar flavour of the Baltic, half salt, half brackish, like the smell of an estuary at low water.

It is difficult to say why it seemed to me that this deep stillness masked an intense activity; perhaps in every mood lies the suggestion of its opposite, so that I became aware of the contrast of furious energy, for it was like moving through the deep pause before a thunderstorm, and I trod gently lest by breaking a twig or moving a stone I might set the whole scene into some sort of tumultuous movement. Actually, no doubt, it was nothing more than a result of overstrung nerves.

There was no more question of undressing and going to bed than there was of undressing and going to bathe. Some sense in me was alert and expectant. I sat in my tent and waited. And at the end of half an hour or so my waiting was justified, for the canvas suddenly shivered, and some one tripped over the ropes that held it to the earth. John Silence came in.

The effect of his quiet entry was singular and prophetic: it was just as though the energy lying behind all this stillness had pressed forward to the edge of action. This, no doubt, was merely the quickening of my own mind, and had no other justification; for the presence of John Silence always suggested the near possibility of vigorous action, and, as a matter of fact, he came in with nothing more than a nod and a significant gesture.

He sat down on a corner of my ground-sheet, and I pushed the blanket over so that he could cover his legs. He drew the flap of the tent after him and settled down, but hardly had he done so when the canvas shook a second time, and in blundered Maloney.

"Sitting in the dark?" he said self-consciously, pushing his head inside, and hanging up his lantern on the ridge-pole nail. "I just looked in for a smoke. I suppose—"

He glanced round, caught the eye of Dr. Silence, and stopped. He put his pipe back into his pocket and began to hum softly—that under-breath humming of a nondescript melody I knew so well and had come to hate.

Dr. Silence leaned forward, opened the lantern and blew the light out. "Speak low," he said, "and don't strike matches. Listen for sounds and movements about the Camp, and be ready to follow me at a moment's notice." There was light enough to distinguish our faces easily, and I saw Maloney glance again hurriedly at both of us.

"Is the Camp asleep?" the doctor asked presently, whispering.

"Sangree is," replied the clergyman, in a voice equally low. "I can't answer for the women; I think they're sitting up."

"That's for the best." And then he added: "I wish the fog would thin a bit and let the moon through; later—we may want it."

"It is lifting now, I think," Maloney whispered back. "It's over the tops of the trees already."

I cannot say what it was in this commonplace exchange of remarks that thrilled. Probably Maloney's swift acquiescence in the doctor's mood had something to do with it; for his quick obedience certainly impressed me a good deal. But, even without that slight evidence, it was clear that each recognised the gravity of the occasion, and understood that sleep was impossible and sentry duty was the order of the night.

"Report to me," repeated John Silence once again, "the least sound, and do nothing precipitately."

He shifted across to the mouth of the tent and raised the flap, fastening it against the pole so that he could see out. Maloney stopped humming and began to force the breath through his teeth with a kind of faint hissing, treating us to a medley of church hymns and popular songs of the day.

Then the tent trembled as though some one had touched it.

"That's the wind rising," whispered the clergyman, and pulled the flap open as far as it would go. A waft of cold damp air entered and made us shiver, and with it came a sound of the sea as the first wave washed its way softly along the shores.

"It's got round to the north," he added, and following his voice came a long-drawn whisper that rose from the whole island as the trees sent forth a sighing response. "The fog'll move a bit now. I can make out a lane across the sea already."

"Hush!" said Dr. Silence, for Maloney's voice had risen above a whisper, and we settled down again to another long period of watching and waiting, broken only by the occasional rubbing of shoulders against the canvas as we shifted our positions, and the increasing noise of waves on the outer coast-line of the island. And over all whirred the murmur of wind sweeping the tops of the trees like a great harp, and the faint tapping on the tent as drops fell from the branches with a sharp pinging sound.

We had sat for something over an hour in this way, and Maloney and I were finding it increasingly hard to keep awake, when suddenly Dr. Silence rose to his feet and peered out. The next minute he was gone.

Relieved of the dominating presence, the clergyman thrust his face close into mine. "I don't much care for this waiting game," he whispered, "but Silence wouldn't hear of my sitting up with the others; he said it would prevent anything happening if I did."

"He knows," I answered shortly.

"No doubt in the world about that," he whispered back; "it's this 'Double' business, as he calls it, or else it's obsession as the Bible describes it. But it's bad, whichever it is, and I've got my Winchester outside ready cocked, and I brought this too." He shoved a pocket Bible under my nose. At one time in his life it had been his inseparable companion.

"One's useless and the other's dangerous," I replied under my breath, conscious of a keen desire to laugh, and leaving him to choose. "Safety lies in following our leader—"

"I'm not thinking of myself," he interrupted sharply; "only, if anything happens to Joan to-night I'm going to shoot first—and pray afterwards!"

Maloney put the book back into his hip-pocket. and peered out of the doorway. "What is he up to now, in the devil's name, I wonder!" he added; "going round Sangree's tent and making gestures. How weird he looks disappearing in and out of the fog."

"Just trust him and wait," I said quickly, for the doctor was already on his way back. "Remember, he has the knowledge, and knows what he's about. I've been with him through worse cases than this."

Maloney moved back as Dr. Silence darkened the doorway and stooped to enter.

"His sleep is very deep," he whispered, seating himself by the door again. "He's in a cataleptic condition, and the Double may be released any minute now. But I've taken steps to imprison it in the tent, and it can't get out till I permit it. Be on the watch for signs of movement." Then he looked hard at Maloney. "But no violence, or shooting, remember, Mr. Maloney, unless you want a murder on your hands. Anything done to the Double acts by repercussion upon the physical body.

You had better take out the cartridges at once."

His voice was stern. The clergyman went out, and I heard him emptying the magazine of his rifle. When he returned he sat nearer the door than before, and from that moment until we left the tent he never once took his eyes from the figure of Dr. Silence, silhouetted there against sky and canvas.

And, meanwhile, the wind came steadily over the sea and opened the mist into lanes and clearings, driving it about like a living thing.

It must have been well after midnight when a low booming sound drew my attention; but at first the sense of hearing was so strained that it was impossible exactly to locate it, and I imagined it was the thunder of big guns far out at sea carried to us by the rising wind. Then Maloney, catching hold of my arm and leaning forward, somehow brought the true relation, and I realised the next second that it was only a few feet away.

"Sangree's tent," he exclaimed in a loud and startled whisper.

I craned my head round the corner, but at first the effect of the fog was so confusing that every patch of white driving about before the wind looked like a moving tent and it was some seconds before I discovered the one patch that held steady. Then I saw that it was shaking all over, and the sides, flapping as much as the tightness of the ropes allowed, were the cause of the booming sound we had heard. Something alive was tearing frantically about inside, banging against the stretched canvas in a way that made me think of a great moth dashing against the walls and ceiling of a room. The tent bulged and rocked.

"It's trying to get out, by Jupiter!" muttered the clergyman, rising to his feet and turning to the side where the unloaded rifle lay. I sprang up too, hardly knowing what purpose was in my mind, but anxious to be prepared for anything. John Silence, however, was before us both, and his figure slipped past and blocked the doorway of the tent. And there was some quality in his voice next minute when he began to speak that brought our minds instantly to a state of calm obedience.

"First—the women's tent," he said low, looking sharply at Maloney, "and if I need your help, I'll call."

The clergyman needed no second bidding. He dived past me and was out in a moment. He was labouring evidently under intense excitement. I watched him picking his way silently over the slippery ground, giving the moving tent a wide berth, and presently disappearing among the floating shapes of fog.

Dr. Silence turned to me. "You heard those footsteps about half an hour ago?" he asked significantly.

"I heard nothing."

"They were extraordinarily soft—almost the soundless tread of a wild creature. But now, follow me closely," he added, "for we must waste no time if I am to save this poor man from his affliction and lead his werewolf Double to its rest. And, unless I am much mistaken"—he peered at me through the darkness, whispering with the utmost distinctness—"Joan and Sangree are absolutely made for one another. And I think she knows it too—just as well as he does."

My head swam a little as I listened, but at the same time something cleared in my brain and I saw that he was right. Yet it was all so weird and incredible, so remote from the commonplace facts of life as commonplace people know them; and more than once it flashed upon me that the whole scene—people, words, tents, and all the rest of it—were delusions created by the intense excitement of my own mind somehow, and that suddenly the sea-fog would clear off and the world become normal again.

The cold air from the sea stung our cheeks sharply as we left the close atmosphere of the little crowded tent. The sighing of the trees, the waves breaking below on the rocks, and the lines and patches of mist driving about us seemed to create the momentary illusion that the whole island had broken loose and was floating out to sea like a mighty raft.

The doctor moved just ahead of me, quickly and silently; he was making straight for the Canadian's tent where the sides still boomed and shook as the creature of sinister life raced and tore about impatiently within. A little distance from the door he paused and held up a hand to stop me. We were, perhaps, a dozen feet away.

"Before I release it, you shall see for yourself," he said, "that the reality of the werewolf is beyond all question. The matter of which it is composed is, of course, exceedingly attenuated, but you are partially clairvoyant—and even if it is not dense enough for normal sight you will see something."

He added a little more I could not catch. The fact was that the curiously strong vibrating atmosphere surrounding his person somewhat confused my senses. It was the result, of course, of his intense concentration of mind and forces, and pervaded the entire Camp and all the persons in it. And as I watched the canvas shake and heard it boom and flap I heartily welcomed it. For it was also protective.

At the back of Sangree's tent stood a thin group of pine trees, but in front and at the sides the ground was comparatively clear. The flap was wide open and any ordinary animal would have been out and away without the least trouble. Dr. Silence led me up to within a few feet, evidently careful not to advance beyond a certain limit, and then stooped down and signalled to me to do the same. And looking over his shoulder I saw the interior lit faintly by the spectral light reflected from the fog, and the dim blot upon the balsam boughs and blankets signifying Sangree; while over him, and round him, and up and down him, flew the dark mass of "something" on four legs, with pointed muzzle and sharp ears plainly visible against the tent sides, and the occasional gleam of fiery eyes and white fangs.

I held my breath and kept utterly still, inwardly and outwardly, for fear, I suppose, that the creature would become conscious of my presence; but the distress I felt went far deeper than the mere sense of personal safety, or the fact of watching something so incredibly active and real. I became keenly aware of the dreadful psychic calamity it involved. The realisation that Sangree lay confined in that narrow space with this species of monstrous projection of himself—that he was wrapped there in the cataleptic sleep, all unconscious that this thing was masquerading with his own life and energies—added a distressing touch of horror to the scene. In all the cases of John Silence—and they were many and often terrible—no other psychic affliction has ever, before or since, impressed me so convincingly with the pathetic impermanence of the human personality, with its fluid nature, and with the alarming possibilities of its transformations.

"Come," he whispered, after we had watched for some minutes the frantic efforts to escape from the circle of thought and will that held it prisoner, "come a little farther away while I release it."

We moved back a dozen yards or so. It was like a scene in some impossible play, or in some ghastly and oppressive nightmare from which I should presently awake to find the blankets all heaped upon my chest.

By some method undoubtedly mental, but which, in my confusion and excitement, I failed to understand, the doctor accomplished his purpose, and the next minute I heard him say sharply under his breath, "It's out! Now, watch!"

At this very moment a sudden gust from the sea blew aside the mist, so that a lane opened to the sky, and the moon, ghastly and unnatural as the effect of stage limelight, dropped down in a momentary gleam upon the door of Sangree's tent, and I perceived that something had moved forward from the interior darkness and stood clearly defined upon the threshold. And, at the same moment, the tent ceased its shuddering and held still.

There, in the doorway, stood an animal, with neck and muzzle thrust forward, its head poking into the night, its whole body poised in that attitude of intense rigidity that precedes the spring into freedom, the running leap of attack. It seemed to be about the size of a calf, leaner than a mastiff, yet more squat than a wolf, and I can swear that I saw the fur ridged sharply upon its back. Then its upper lip slowly lifted, and I saw the whiteness of its teeth.

Surely no human being ever stared as hard as I did in those next few minutes. Yet, the harder I stared the clearer appeared the amazing and monstrous apparition. For, after all, it was Sangree—and yet it was not Sangree. It was the head and face of an animal, and yet it was the face of Sangree: the face of a wild dog, a wolf, and yet his face. The eyes were sharper, narrower, more fiery, yet they were his eyes—his eyes run wild; the teeth were longer, whiter, more pointed—yet they were his teeth, his teeth grown cruel; the expression was flaming, terrible, exultant—yet it was his expression carried to the border of savagery—his expression as I had already surprised it more than once, only dominant now, fully released from human constraint, with the mad yearning of a hungry and importunate soul. It was the soul of Sangree, the long suppressed, deeply loving Sangree, expressed in its single and intense desire—pure utterly and utterly wonderful.

Yet, at the same time, came the feeling that it was all an illusion. I suddenly remembered the extraordinary changes the human face can undergo in circular insanity, when it changes from melancholia to elation; and I recalled the effect of hashish, which shows the human countenance in the form of the bird or animal to which in character it most approximates; and for a moment I attributed this mingling of Sangree's face with a wolf to some kind of similar delusion of the senses. I was mad, deluded, dreaming! The excitement of the day, and this dim light of stars and bewildering mist combined to trick me. I had been amazingly imposed upon by some false wizardry of the senses. It was all absurd and fantastic; it would pass.

And then, sounding across this sea of mental confusion like a bell through a fog, came the voice of John Silence bringing me back to a consciousness of the reality of it all—

"Sangree—in his Double!"

And when I looked again more calmly, I plainly saw that it was indeed the face of the Canadian, but his face turned animal, yet mingled with the brute expression a curiously pathetic look like the soul seen sometimes in the yearning eyes of a dog,—the face of an animal shot with vivid streaks of the human.

The doctor called to him softly under his breath—

"Sangree! Sangree, you poor afflicted creature! Do you know me? Can you understand what it is you're doing in your 'Body of Desire'?"

For the first time since its appearance the creature moved. Its ears twitched and it shifted the weight of its body on to the hind legs. Then, lifting its head and muzzle to the sky, it opened its long jaws and gave vent to a dismal and prolonged howling.

But, when I heard that howling rise to heaven, the breath caught and strangled in my throat and it seemed that my heart missed a beat; for, though the sound was entirely animal, it was at the same time entirely human. But, more than that, it was the cry I had so often heard in the Western States of America where the Indians still fight and hunt and struggle—it was the cry of the Redskin!

"The Indian blood!" whispered John Silence, when I caught his arm for support; "the ancestral cry."

And that poignant, beseeching cry, that broken human voice, mingling with the savage howl of the brute beast, pierced straight to my very heart and touched there something that no music, no voice, passionate or tender, of man, woman, or child has ever stirred before or since for one second into life. It echoed away among the fog and the trees and lost itself somewhere out over the hidden sea. And some part of myself—something that was far more than the mere act of intense listening—went out with it, and for several minutes I lost consciousness of my surroundings and felt utterly absorbed in the pain of another stricken fellow-creature.

Again the voice of John Silence recalled me to myself.

"Hark!" he said aloud. "Hark!"

His tone galvanised me afresh. We stood listening side by side.

Far across the island, faintly sounding through the trees and brushwood, came a similar, answering cry. Shrill, yet wonderfully musical, shaking the heart with a singular wild sweetness that defies description, we heard it rise and fall upon the night air.

"It's across the lagoon," Dr. Silence cried, but this time in full tones that paid no tribute to caution. "It's Joan! She's answering him!"

Again the wonderful cry rose and fell, and that same instant the animal lowered its head, and, muzzle to earth, set off on a swift easy canter that took it off into the mist and out of our sight like a thing of wind and vision.

The doctor made a quick dash to the door of Sangree's tent, and, following close at his heels, I peered in and caught a momentary glimpse of the small, shrunken body lying upon the branches but half covered by the blankets—the cage from which most of the life, and not a little of the actual corporeal substance, had escaped into that other form of life and energy, the body of passion and desire.

By another of those swift, incalculable processes which at this stage of my apprenticeship I failed often to grasp, Dr. Silence reclosed the circle about the tent and body.

"Now it cannot return till I permit it," he said, and the next second was off at full speed into the woods, with myself close behind him. I had already had some experience of my companion's ability to run swiftly through a dense wood, and I now had the further proof of his power almost to see in the dark. For, once we left the open space about the tents, the trees seemed to absorb all the remaining vestiges of light, and I understood that special sensibility that is said to develop in the blind—the sense of obstacles.

And twice as we ran we heard the sound of that dismal howling drawing nearer and nearer to the answering faint cry from the point of the island whither we were going.

Then, suddenly, the trees fell away, and we emerged, hot and breathless, upon the rocky point where the granite slabs ran bare into the sea. It was like passing into the clearness of open day. And there, sharply defined against sea and sky, stood the figure of a human being. It was Joan.

I at once saw that there was something about her appearance that was singular and unusual, but it was only when we had moved quite close that I recognised what caused it. For while the lips wore a smile that lit the whole face with a happiness I had never seen there before, the eyes themselves were fixed in a steady, sightless stare as though they were lifeless and made of glass.

I made an impulsive forward movement, but Dr. Silence instantly dragged me back.

"No," he cried, "don't wake her!"

"What do you mean?" I replied aloud, struggling in his grasp.

"She's asleep. It's somnambulistic. The shock might injure her permanently."

I turned and peered closely into his face. He was absolutely calm. I began to understand a little more, catching, I suppose, something of his strong thinking.

"Walking in her sleep, you mean?"

He nodded. "She's on her way to meet him. From the very beginning he must have drawn her—irresistibly."

"But the torn tent and the wounded flesh?"

"When she did not sleep deep enough to enter the somnambulistic trance he missed her—he went instinctively and in all innocence to seek her out—with the result, of course, that she woke and was terrified—"

"Then in their heart of hearts they love?" I asked finally.

John Silence smiled his inscrutable smile "Profoundly," he answered, "and as simply as only primitive souls can love. If only they both come to realise it in their normal waking states his Double will cease these nocturnal excursions. He will be cured, and at rest."

The words had hardly left his lips when there was a sound of rustling branches on our left, and the very next instant the dense brushwood parted where it was darkest and out rushed the swift form of an animal at full gallop. The noise of feet was scarcely audible, but in that utter stillness I heard the heavy panting breath and caught the swish of the low bushes against its sides. It went straight towards Joan—and as it went the girl lifted her head and turned to meet it. And the same instant a canoe that had been creeping silently and unobserved round the inner shore of the lagoon, emerged from the shadows and defined itself upon the water with a figure at the middle thwart. It was Maloney.

It was only afterwards I realised that we were invisible to him where we stood against the dark background of trees; the figures of Joan and the animal he saw plainly, but not Dr. Silence and myself standing just beyond them. He stood up in the canoe and pointed with his right arm. I saw something gleam in his hand.

"Stand aside, Joan girl, or you'll get hit," he shouted, his voice ringing horribly through the deep stillness, and the same instant a pistol-shot cracked out with a burst of flame and smoke, and the figure of the animal, with one tremendous leap into the air, fell back in the shadows and disappeared like a shape of night and fog. Instantly, then, Joan opened her eyes, looked in a dazed fashion about her, and pressing both hands against her heart, fell with a sharp cry into my arms that were just in time to catch her.

And an answering cry sounded across the lagoon—thin, wailing, piteous. It came from Sangree's tent.

"Fool!" cried Dr. Silence, "you've wounded him!" and before we could move or realise quite what it meant, he was in the canoe and half-way across the lagoon.

Some kind of similar abuse came in a torrent from my lips too—though I cannot remember the actual words—as I cursed the man for his disobedience and tried to make the girl comfortable on the ground. But the clergyman was more practical. He was spreading his coat over her and dashing water on her face.

"It's not Joan I've killed at any rate," I heard him mutter as she turned and opened her eyes and smiled faintly up in his face. "I swear the bullet went straight."

Joan stared at him; she was still dazed and bewildered, and still imagined herself with the companion of her trance. The strange lucidity of the somnambulist still hung over her brain and mind, though outwardly she appeared troubled and confused.

"Where has he gone to? He disappeared so suddenly, crying that he was hurt," she asked, looking at her father as though she did not recognise him. "And if they've done anything to him—they have done it to me too—for he is more to me than—"

Her words grew vaguer and vaguer as she returned slowly to her normal waking state, and now she stopped altogether, as though suddenly aware that she had been surprised into telling secrets. But all the way back, as we carried her carefully through the trees, the girl smiled and murmured Sangree's name and asked if he was injured, until it finally became clear to me that the wild soul of the one had called to the wild soul of the other and in the secret depths of their beings the call had been heard and understood. John Silence was right. In the abyss of her heart, too deep at first for recognition, the girl loved him, and had loved him from the very beginning. Once her normal waking consciousness recognised the fact they would leap together like twin flames, and his affliction would be at an end; his intense desire would be satisfied; he would be cured.

And in Sangree's tent Dr. Silence and I sat up for the remainder of the night—this wonderful and haunted night that had shown us such strange glimpses of a new heaven and a new hell—for the Canadian tossed upon his balsam boughs with high fever in his blood, and upon each cheek a dark and curious contusion showed, throbbing with severe pain although the skin was not broken and there was no outward and visible sign of blood.

"Maloney shot straight, you see," whispered Dr. Silence to me after the clergyman had gone to his tent, and had put Joan to sleep beside her mother, who, by the way, had never once awakened. "The bullet must have passed clean through the face, for both cheeks are stained. He'll wear these marks all his life—smaller, but always there. They're the most curious scars in the world, these scars transferred by repercussion from an injured Double. They'll remain visible until just before his death, and then with the withdrawal of the subtle body they will disappear finally."

His words mingled in my dazed mind with the sighs of the troubled sleeper and the crying of the wind about the tent. Nothing seemed to paralyse my powers of realisation so much as these twin stains of mysterious significance upon the face before me.

It was odd, too, how speedily and easily the Camp resigned itself again to sleep and quietness, as though a stage curtain had suddenly dropped down upon the action and concealed it; and nothing contributed so vividly to the feeling that I had been a spectator of some kind of visionary drama as the dramatic nature of the change in the girl's attitude.

Yet, as a matter of fact, the change had not been so sudden and revolutionary as appeared. Underneath, in those remoter regions of consciousness where the emotions, unknown to their owners, do secretly mature, and owe thence their abrupt revelation to some abrupt psychological climax, there can be no doubt that Joan's love for the Canadian had been growing steadily and irresistibly all the time. It had now rushed to the surface so that she recognised it; that was all.

And it has always seemed to me that the presence of John Silence, so potent, so quietly efficacious, produced an effect, if one may say so, of a psychic forcing-house, and hastened incalculably the bringing together of these two "wild" lovers. In that sudden awakening had occurred the very psychological climax required to reveal the passionate emotion accumulated below. The deeper knowledge had leaped across and transferred itself to her ordinary consciousness, and in that shock the collision of the personalities had shaken them to the depths and shown her the truth beyond all possibility of doubt.

"He's sleeping quietly now," the doctor said, interrupting my reflections. "If you will watch alone for a bit I'll go to Maloney's tent and help him to arrange his thoughts." He smiled in anticipation of that "arrangement." "He'll never quite understand how a wound on the Double can transfer itself to the physical body, but at least I can persuade him that the less he talks and 'explains' to-morrow, the sooner the forces will run their natural course now to peace and quietness."

He went away softly, and with the removal of his presence Sangree, sleeping heavily, turned over and groaned with the pain of his broken head.

And it was in the still hour just before the dawn, when all the islands were hushed, the wind and sea still dreaming, and the stars visible through clearing mists, that a figure crept silently over the ridge and reached the door of the tent where I dozed beside the sufferer, before I was aware of its presence. The flap was cautiously lifted a few inches and in looked—Joan.

That same instant Sangree woke and sat up on his bed of branches. He recognised her before I could say a word, and uttered a low cry.

It was pain and joy mingled, and this time all human. And the girl too was no longer walking in her sleep, but fully aware of what she was doing. I was only just able to prevent him springing from his blankets.

"Joan, Joan!" he cried, and in a flash she answered him, "I'm here—I'm with you always now," and had pushed past me into the tent and flung herself upon his breast.

"I knew you would come to me in the end," I heard him whisper.

"It was all too big for me to understand at first," she murmured, "and for a long time I was frightened—"

"But not now!" he cried louder; "you don't feel afraid now of—of anything that's in me—"

"I fear nothing," she cried, "nothing, nothing!"

I led her outside again. She looked steadily into my face with eyes shining and her whole being transformed. In some intuitive way, surviving probably from the somnambulism, she knew or guessed as much as I knew.

"You must talk to-morrow with John Silence," I said gently, leading her towards her own tent. "He understands everything."

I left her at the door, and as I went back softly to take up my place of sentry again with the Canadian, I saw the first streaks of dawn lighting up the far rim of the sea behind the distant islands.

And, as though to emphasise the eternal closeness of comedy to tragedy, two small details rose out of the scene and impressed me so vividly that I remember them to this very day. For in the tent where I had just left Joan, all aquiver with her new happiness, there rose plainly to my ears the grotesque sounds of the Bo'sun's Mate heavily snoring, oblivious of all things in heaven or hell; and from Maloney's tent, so still was the night, where I looked across and saw the lantern's glow, there came to me, through the trees, the monotonous rising and falling of a human voice that was beyond question the sound of a man praying to his God.

A Victim of Higher Space

There's a hextraordinary gentleman to see you, sir," said the new man.

"Why 'extraordinary'?" asked Dr. Silence, drawing the tips of his thin fingers through his brown beard. His eyes twinkled pleasantly. "Why 'extraordinary,' Barker?" he repeated encouragingly, noticing the perplexed expression in the man's eyes.

"He's so—so thin, sir. I could hardly see 'im at all—at first. He was inside the house before I could ask the name," he added, remembering strict orders.

"And who brought him here?"

"He come alone, sir, in a closed cab. He pushed by me before I could say a word—making no noise not what I could hear. He seemed to move so soft like—"

The man stopped short with obvious embarrassment, as though he had already said enough to jeopardise his new situation, but trying hard to show that he remembered the instructions and warnings he had received with regard to the admission of strangers not properly accredited.

"And where is the gentleman now?" asked Dr. Silence, turning away to conceal his amusement.

"I really couldn't exactly say, sir. I left him standing in the 'all—"

The doctor looked up sharply. "But why in the hall, Barker? Why not in the waiting-room?" He fixed his piercing though kindly eyes on the man's face. "Did he frighten you?" he asked quickly.

"I think he did, sir, if I may say so. I seemed to lose sight of him, as it were—" The man stammered, evidently convinced by now that he had earned his dismissal. "He come in so funny, just like a cold wind," he added boldly, setting his heels at attention and looking his master full in the face.

The doctor made an internal note of the man's halting description;

he was pleased that the slight signs of psychic intuition which had induced him to engage Barker had not entirely failed at the first trial. Dr.
Silence sought for this qualification in all his assistants, from secretary
to serving man, and if it surrounded him with a somewhat singular
crew, the drawbacks were more than compensated for on the whole by
their occasional flashes of insight.

"So the gentleman made you feel queer, did he?"

"That was it, I think, sir," repeated the man stolidly.

"And he brings no kind of introduction to me—no letter or anything?" asked the doctor, with feigned surprise, as though he knew
what was coming.

The man fumbled, both in mind and pockets, and finally produced
an envelope.

"I beg pardon, sir," he said, greatly flustered; "the gentleman
handed me this for you."

It was a note from a discerning friend, who had never yet sent him
a case that was not vitally interesting from one point or another.

"Please see the bearer of this note," the brief message ran, "though
I doubt if even you can do much to help him."

John Silence paused a moment, so as to gather from the mind of
the writer all that lay behind the brief words of the letter. Then he
looked up at his servant with a graver expression than he had yet worn.

"Go back and find this gentleman," he said, "and show him into
the green study. Do not reply to his question, or speak more than actually necessary; but think kind, helpful, sympathetic thoughts as
strongly as you can, Barker. You remember what I told you about the
importance of *thinking,* when I engaged you. Put curiosity out of your
mind, and think gently, sympathetically, affectionately, if you can."

He smiled, and Barker, who had recovered his composure in the
doctor's presence, bowed silently and went out.

There were two different reception-rooms in Dr. Silence's house.
One (intended for persons who imagined they needed spiritual assistance when really they were only candidates for the asylum) had padded walls, and was well supplied with various concealed contrivances
by means of which sudden violence could be instantly met and overcome. It was, however, rarely used. The other, intended for the reception of genuine cases of spiritual distress and out-of-the-way afflictions

of a psychic nature, was entirely draped and furnished in a soothing deep green, calculated to induce calmness and repose of mind. And this room was the one in which Dr. Silence interviewed the majority of his "queer" cases, and the one into which he had directed Barker to show his present caller.

To begin with, the arm-chair in which the patient was always directed to sit, was nailed to the floor, since its immovability tended to impart this same excellent characteristic to the occupant. Patients invariably grew excited when talking about themselves, and their excitement tended to confuse their thoughts and to exaggerate their language. The inflexibility of the chair helped to counteract this. After repeated endeavours to drag it forward, or push it back, they ended by resigning themselves to sitting quietly. And with the futility of fidgeting there followed a calmer state of mind.

Upon the floor, and at intervals in the wall immediately behind, were certain tiny green buttons, practically unnoticeable, which on being pressed permitted a soothing and persuasive narcotic to rise invisibly about the occupant of the chair. The effect upon the excitable patient was rapid, admirable, and harmless. The green study was further provided with a secret spy-hole; for John Silence liked when possible to observe his patient's face before it had assumed that mask the features of the human countenance invariably wear in the presence of another person. A man sitting alone wears a psychic expression; and this expression is the man himself. It disappears the moment another person joins him. And Dr. Silence often learned more from a few moments' secret observation of a face than from hours of conversation with its owner afterwards.

A very light, almost a dancing, step followed Barker's heavy tread towards the green room, and a moment afterwards the man came in and announced that the gentleman was waiting. He was still pale and his manner nervous.

"Never mind, Barker," the doctor said kindly; "if you were not psychic the man would have had no effect upon you at all. You only need training and development. And when you have learned to interpret these feelings and sensations better, you will feel no fear, but only a great sympathy."

"Yes, sir; thank you, sir!" And Barker bowed and made his escape, while Dr. Silence, an amused smile lurking about the corners of his mouth, made his way noiselessly down the passage and put his eye to the spy-hole in the door of the green study.

This spy-hole was so placed that it commanded a view of almost the entire room, and, looking through it, the doctor saw a hat, gloves, and umbrella lying on a chair by the table, but searched at first in vain for their owner.

The windows were both closed and a brisk fire burned in the grate. There were various signs—signs intelligible at least to a keenly intuitive soul—that the room was occupied, yet so far as human beings were concerned, it was empty, utterly empty. No one sat in the chairs; no one stood on the mat before the fire; there was no sign even that a patient was anywhere close against the wall, examining the Böcklin reproductions—as patients so often did when they thought they were alone—and therefore rather difficult to see from the spy-hole. Ordinarily speaking, there was no one in the room. It was undeniable.

Yet Dr. Silence was quite well aware that a human being *was* in the room. His psychic apparatus never failed in letting him know the proximity of an incarnate or discarnate being. Even in the dark he could tell that. And he now knew positively that his patient—the patient who had alarmed Barker, and had then tripped down the corridor with that dancing footstep—was somewhere concealed within the four walls commanded by his spy-hole. He also realised—and this was most unusual—that this individual whom he desired to watch knew that he was being watched. And, further, that the stranger himself was also watching! In fact, that it was he, the doctor, who was being observed—and by an observer as keen and trained as himself.

An inkling of the true state of the case began to dawn upon him, and he was on the verge of entering—indeed, his hand already touched the door-knob—when his eye, still glued to the spy-hole, detected a slight movement. Directly opposite, between him and the fireplace, something stirred. He watched very attentively and made certain that he was not mistaken. An object on the mantelpiece—it was a blue vase—disappeared from view. It passed out of sight together with the portion of the marble mantelpiece on which it rested. Next, that part of the fire and grate and brass fender immediately below it vanished entirely, as though a slice had been taken clean out of them.

Dr. Silence then understood that something between him and these objects was slowly coming into being, something that concealed them and obstructed his vision by inserting itself in the line of sight between them and himself.

He quietly awaited further results before going in.

First he saw a thin perpendicular line tracing itself from just above the height of the clock and continuing downwards till it reached the woolly fire-mat. This line grew wider, broadened, grew solid. It was no shadow; it was something substantial. It defined itself more and more. Then suddenly, at the top of the line, and about on a level with the face of the clock, he saw a round luminous disc gazing steadily at him. It was a human eye, looking straight into his own, pressed there against the spy-hole. And it was bright with intelligence. Dr. Silence held his breath for a moment—and stared back at it.

Then, like some one moving out of deep shadow into light, he saw the figure of a man come sliding sideways into view, a whitish face following the eye, and the perpendicular line he had first observed broadening out and developing into the complete figure of a human being. It was the patient. He had apparently been standing there in front of the fire all the time. A second eye had followed the first, and both of them stared steadily at the spy-hole, sharply concentrated, yet with a sly twinkle of humour and amusement that made it impossible for the doctor to maintain his position any longer.

He opened the door and went in quickly. As he did so he noticed for the first time the sound of a German band coming in gaily through the open ventilators. In some intuitive, unaccountable fashion the music connected itself with the patient he was about to interview. This sort of prevision was not unfamiliar to him. It always explained itself later.

The man, he saw, was of middle age and of very ordinary appearance; so ordinary, in fact, that he was difficult to describe—his only peculiarity being his extreme thinness. Pleasant—that is, good—vibrations issued from his atmosphere and met Dr. Silence as he advanced to greet him, yet vibrations alive with currents and discharges betraying the perturbed and disordered condition of his mind and brain. There was evidently something wholly out of the usual in the state of his thoughts. Yet, though strange, it was not altogether dis-

tressing; it was not the impression that the broken and violent atmosphere of the insane produces upon the mind. Dr. Silence realised in a
flash that here was a case of absorbing interest that might require all
his powers to handle properly.

"I was watching you through my little peep-hole—as you saw," he
began, with a pleasant smile, advancing to shake hands. "I find it of the
greatest assistance sometimes—"

But the patient interrupted him at once. His voice was hurried and
had odd, shrill changes in it, breaking from high to low in unexpected
fashion. One moment it thundered, the next it almost squeaked.

"I understand without explanation," he broke in rapidly. "You get
the true note of a man in this way—when he thinks himself unobserved. I quite agree. Only, in my case, I fear, you saw very little. My
case, as you of course grasp, Dr. Silence, is extremely peculiar, uncomfortably peculiar. Indeed, unless Sir William had positively assured
me—"

"My friend has sent you to me," the doctor interrupted gravely,
with a gentle note of authority, "and that is quite sufficient. Pray, be
seated, Mr.—"

"Mudge—Racine Mudge," returned the other.

"Take this comfortable one, Mr. Mudge," leading him to the fixed
chair, "and tell me your condition in your own way and at your own
pace. My whole day is at your service if you require it."

Mr. Mudge moved towards the chair in question and then hesitated.

"You will promise me not to use the narcotic buttons," he said,
before sitting down. "I do not need them. Also I ought to mention
that anything you think of vividly will reach my mind. That is apparently part of my peculiar case." He sat down with a sigh and arranged
his thin legs and body into a position of comfort. Evidently he was
very sensitive to the thoughts of others, for the picture of the green
buttons had only entered the doctor's mind for a second, yet the other
had instantly snapped it up. Dr. Silence noticed, too, that Mr. Mudge
held on tightly with both hands to the arms of the chair.

"I'm rather glad the chair is nailed to the floor," he remarked, as
he settled himself more comfortably. "It suits me admirably. The fact
is—and this is my case in a nutshell—which is all that a doctor of your
marvellous development requires—the fact is, Dr. Silence, I am a victim

of Higher Space. That's what's the matter with me—Higher Space!"

The two looked at each other for a space in silence, the little patient holding tightly to the arms of the chair which "suited him admirably," and looking up with staring eyes, his atmosphere positively trembling with the waves of some unknown activity; while the doctor smiled kindly and sympathetically, and put his whole person as far as possible into the mental condition of the other.

"Higher Space," repeated Mr. Mudge, "that's what it is. Now, do you think you can help me with *that?*"

There was a pause during which the men's eyes steadily searched down below the surface of their respective personalities. Then Dr. Silence spoke.

"I am quite sure I can help," he answered quietly; "sympathy must always help, and suffering always owns my sympathy. I see you have suffered cruelly. You must tell me all about your case, and when I hear the gradual steps by which you reached this strange condition, I have no doubt I can be of assistance to you."

He drew a chair up beside his interlocutor and laid a hand on his shoulder for a moment. His whole being radiated kindness, intelligence, desire to help.

"For instance," he went on, "I feel sure it was the result of no mere chance that you became familiar with the terrors of what you term Higher Space; for Higher Space is no mere external measurement. It is, of course, a spiritual state, a spiritual condition, an inner development, and one that we must recognise as abnormal, since it is beyond the reach of the world at the present stage of evolution. Higher Space is a mythical state."

"Oh!" cried the other, rubbing his bird-like hands with pleasure, "the relief it is to be able to talk to some one who can understand! Of course what you say is the utter truth. And you are right that no mere chance led me to my present condition, but, on the other hand, prolonged and deliberate study. Yet chance in a sense now governs it. I mean, my entering the condition of Higher Space seems to depend upon the chance of this and that circumstance. For instance, the mere sound of that German band sent me off. Not that all music will do so, but certain sounds, certain vibrations, at once key me up to the requisite pitch, and off I go. Wagner's music always does it, and that band must have been playing a stray bit of Wagner. But I'll come to all that later. Only first, I must ask you to send away your man from the spy-hole."

John Silence looked up with a start, for Mr. Mudge's back was to the door, and there was no mirror. He saw the brown eye of Barker glued to the little circle of glass, and he crossed the room without a word and snapped down the black shutter provided for the purpose, and then heard Barker snuffle away along the passage.

"Now," continued the little man in the chair, "I can begin. You have managed to put me completely at my ease, and I feel I may tell you my whole case without shame or reserve. You will understand. But you must be patient with me if I go into details that are already familiar to you—details of Higher Space, I mean—and if I seem stupid when I have to describe things that transcend the power of language and are really therefore indescribable."

"My dear friend," put in the other calmly, "that goes without saying. To know Higher Space is an experience that defies description, and one is obliged to make use of more or less intelligible symbols. But, pray, proceed. Your vivid thoughts will tell me more than your halting words."

An immense sigh of relief proceeded from the little figure half lost in the depths of the chair. Such intelligent sympathy meeting him half-way was a new experience to him, and it touched his heart at once. He leaned back, relaxing his tight hold of the arms, and began in his thin, scale-like voice.

"My mother was a Frenchwoman, and my father an Essex barge-man," he said abruptly. "Hence my name—Racine and Mudge. My father died before I ever saw him. My mother inherited money from her Bordeaux relations, and when she died soon after, I was left alone with wealth and a strange freedom. I had no guardian, trustees, sisters, brothers, or any connection in the world to look after me. I grew up, therefore, utterly without education. This much was to my advantage; I learned none of that deceitful rubbish taught in schools, and so had nothing to unlearn when I awakened to my true love—mathematics, higher mathematics and higher geometry. These, however, I seemed to know instinctively. It was like the memory of what I had deeply studied before; the principles were in my blood, and I simply raced through the ordinary stages, and beyond, and then did the same with geometry.

Afterwards, when I read the books on these subjects, I understood how swift and undeviating the knowledge had come back to me. It was simply memory. It was simply *re-collecting* the memories of what I had known before in a previous existence and required no books to teach me."

In his growing excitement, Mr. Mudge attempted to drag the chair forward a little nearer to his listener, and then smiled faintly as he resigned himself instantly again to its immovability, and plunged anew into the recital of his singular "disease."

"The audacious speculations of Bolyai, the amazing theories of Gauss—that through a point more than one line could be drawn parallel to a given line; the possibility that the angles of a triangle are together *greater* than two right angles, if drawn upon immense curvatures—the breathless intuitions of Beltrami and Lobatchewsky—all these I hurried through, and emerged, panting but unsatisfied, upon the verge of my—my new world, my Higher Space possibilities—in a word, my disease!

"How I got there," he resumed after a brief pause, during which he appeared to be listening intently for an approaching sound, "is more than I can put intelligibly into words. I can only hope to leave your mind with an intuitive comprehension of the possibility of what I say.

"Here, however, came a change. At this point I was no longer absorbing the fruits of studies I had made before; it was the beginning of new efforts to learn for the first time, and I had to go slowly and laboriously through terrible work. Here I sought for the theories and speculations of others. But books were few and far between, and with the exception of one man—a 'dreamer,' the world called him—whose audacity and piercing intuition amazed and delighted me beyond description, I found no one to guide or help.

"You, of course, Dr. Silence, understand something of what I am driving at with these stammering words, though you cannot perhaps yet guess what depths of pain my new knowledge brought me to, nor why an acquaintance with a new development of space should prove a source of misery and terror."

Mr. Racine Mudge, remembering that the chair would not move, did the next best thing he could in his desire to draw nearer to the attentive man facing him, and sat forward upon the very edge of the cushions, crossing his legs and gesticulating with both hands as though he saw into this region of new space he was attempting to describe, and might any moment tumble into it bodily from the edge of the chair and disappear form view. John Silence, separated from him by three paces, sat with his eyes fixed upon the thin white face opposite, noting every word and every gesture with deep attention.

"This room we now sit in, Dr. Silence, has one side open to space—to Higher Space. A closed box only *seems* closed. There is a way in and out of a soap bubble without breaking the skin."

"You tell me no new thing," the doctor interposed gently.

"Hence, if Higher Space exists and our world borders upon it and lies partially in it, it follows necessarily that we see only portions of all objects. We never see their true and complete shape. We see their three measurements, but not their fourth. The new direction is concealed from us, and when I hold this book and move my hand all round it I have not really made a complete circuit. We only perceive those portions of any object which exist in our three dimensions; the rest escapes us. But, once we learn to see in Higher Space, objects will appear as they actually are. Only they will thus be hardly recognisable!

"Now, you may begin to grasp something of what I am coming to."

"I am beginning to understand something of what you must have suffered," observed the doctor soothingly, "for I have made similar experiments myself, and only stopped just in time—"

"You are the one man in all the world who can hear and understand, *and* sympathise," exclaimed Mr. Mudge, grasping his hand and holding it tightly while he spoke. The nailed chair prevented further excitability.

"Well," he resumed, after a moment's pause, "I procured the implements and the coloured blocks for practical experiment, and I followed the instructions carefully till I had arrived at a working conception of four-dimensional space. The tessaract, the figure whose boundaries are cubes, I knew by heart. That is to say, I knew it and saw it mentally, for my eye, of course, could never take in a new measurement, or my hands and feet handle it.

"So, at least, I thought," he added, making a wry face. "I had reached the stage, you see, when I could *imagine* in a new dimension. I was able to conceive the shape of that new figure which is intrinsically different to all we know—the shape of the tessaract. I could perceive in four dimensions. When, therefore, I looked at a cube I could see all its sides at once. Its top was not foreshortened, nor its farther side and base invisible. I saw the whole thing out flat, so to speak. And this tessaract was bounded by cubes! Moreover, I also saw its content—its insides."

"You were not yourself able to enter this new world," interrupted Dr. Silence.

"Not then. I was only able to conceive intuitively what it was like and how exactly it must look. Later, when I slipped in there and saw objects in their entirety, unlimited by the paucity of our poor three measurements, I very nearly lost my life. For, you see, space does not stop at a single new dimension, a fourth. It extends in all possible new ones, and we must conceive it as containing any number of new dimensions. In other words, there is no space at all, but only a spiritual condition. But, meanwhile, I had come to grasp the strange fact that the objects in our normal world appear to us only partially."

Mr. Mudge moved farther forward till he was balanced dangerously on the very edge of the chair. "From this starting point," he resumed, "I began my studies and experiments, and continued them for years. I had money, and I was without friends. I lived in solitude and experimented. My intellect, of course, had little part in the work, for intellectually it was all unthinkable. Never was the limitation of mere reason more plainly demonstrated. It was mystically, intuitively, spiritually that I began to advance. And what I learnt, and knew, and did is all impossible to put into language, since it all describes experiences transcending the experiences of men. It is only some of the results—what you would call the symptoms of my disease—that I can give you, and even these must often appear absurd contradictions and impossible paradoxes.

"I can only tell you, Dr. Silence"—his manner became exceedingly impressive—"that I reached sometimes a point of view whence all the great puzzle of the world became plain to me, and I understood what they call in the Yoga books 'The Great Heresy of Separateness'; why all great teachers have urged the necessity of man loving his neighbour as himself; how men are all really *one;* and why the utter loss of self is necessary to salvation and the discovery of the true life of the soul."

He paused a moment and drew breath.

"Your speculations have been my own long ago," the doctor said quietly. "I fully realise the force of your words. Men are doubtless not separate at all—in the sense they imagine—"

"All this about the very much Higher Space I only dimly, very dimly, conceived, of course," the other went on, raising his voice again by jerks; "but what did happen to me was the humbler accident of— the simpler disaster—oh, dear, how shall I put it—?"

He stammered and showed visible signs of distress.

"It was simply this," he resumed with a sudden rush of words, "that, accidentally, as the result of my years of experiment, I one day slipped bodily into the next world, the world of four dimensions, yet without knowing precisely how I got there, or how I could get back again. I discovered, that is, that my ordinary three-dimensional body was but an expression—a projection—of my higher four-dimensional body!

"Now you understand what I meant much earlier in our talk when I spoke of chance. I cannot control my entrance or exit. Certain people, certain human atmospheres, certain wandering forces, thoughts, desires even—the radiations of certain combinations of colour, and above all, the vibrations of certain kinds of music, will suddenly throw me into a state of what I can only describe as an intense and terrific inner vibration—and behold I am off! Off in the direction at right angles to all our known directions! Off in the direction the cube takes when it begins to trace the outlines of the new figure! Off into my breathless and semi-divine Higher Space! Off, *inside myself*, into the world of four dimensions!"

He gasped and dropped back into the depths of the immovable chair.

"And there," he whispered, his voice issuing from among the cushions, "there I have to stay until these vibrations subside, or until they do something which I cannot find words to describe properly or intelligibly to you—and then, behold, I am back again. First, that is, I disappear. Then I reappear."

"Just so," exclaimed Dr. Silence, "and that is why a few—"

"Why a few moments ago," interrupted Mr. Mudge, taking the words out of his mouth, "you found me gone, and then saw me return. The music of that wretched German band sent me off. Your intense thinking about me brought me back—when the band had stopped its Wagner. I saw you approach the peep-hole and I saw Barker's intention of doing so later. For me no interiors are hidden. I see inside.

When in that state the content of your mind, as of your body, is open to me as the day. Oh, dear, oh, dear, oh, dear!"

Mr. Mudge stopped and again mopped his brow. A light trembling ran over the surface of his small body like wind over grass. He still held tightly to the arms of the chair.

"At first," he presently resumed, "my new experiences were so vividly interesting that I felt no alarm. There was no room for it. The alarm came a little later."

"Then you actually penetrated far enough into that state to experience yourself as a normal portion of it?" asked the doctor, leaning forward, deeply interested.

Mr. Mudge nodded a perspiring face in reply.

"I did," he whispered, "undoubtedly I did. I am coming to all that. It began first at night, when I realised that sleep brought no loss of consciousness—"

"The spirit, of course, can never sleep. Only the body becomes unconscious," interposed John Silence.

"Yes, we know that—theoretically. At night, of course, the spirit is active elsewhere, and we have no memory of where and how, simply because the brain stays behind and receives no record. But I found that, while remaining conscious, I also retained memory. I had attained to the state of continuous consciousness, for at night I regularly, with the first approaches of drowsiness, entered *nolens volens* the four-dimensional world.

"For a time this happened regularly, and I could not control it; though later I found a way to regulate it better. Apparently sleep is unnecessary in the higher—the four-dimensional—body. Yes, perhaps. But I should infinitely have preferred dull sleep to the knowledge. For, unable to control my movements, I wandered to and fro, attracted, owing to my partial development and premature arrival, to parts of this new world that alarmed me more and more. It was the awful waste and drift of a monstrous world, so utterly different to all we know and see that I cannot even hint at the nature of the sights and objects and beings in it. More than that, I cannot even remember them. I cannot now picture them to myself even, but can recall only the *memory of the impression* they made upon me, the horror and devastating terror of it all. To be in several places at once, for instance—"

"Perfectly," interrupted John Silence, noticing the increase of the other's excitement, "I understand exactly. But now, please, tell me a little more of this alarm you experienced, and how it affected you."

"It's not the disappearing and reappearing *per se* that I mind," continued Mr. Mudge, "so much as certain other things. It's seeing people and objects in their weird entirety, in their true and complete shapes, that is so distressing. It introduces me to a world of monsters. Horses, dogs, cats, all of which I loved; people, trees, children; all that I have considered beautiful in life—everything, from a human face to a cathedral—appear to me in a different shape and aspect to all I have known before. I cannot perhaps convince you why this should be terrible, but I assure you that it is so. To hear the human voice proceeding from this novel appearance which I scarcely recognise as a human body is ghastly, simply ghastly. To see inside everything and everybody is a form of insight peculiarly distressing. To be so confused in geography as to find myself one moment at the North Pole, and the next at Clapham Junction—or possibly at both places simultaneously—is absurdly terrifying. Your imagination will readily furnish other details without my multiplying my experiences now. But you have no idea what it all means, and how I suffer."

Mr. Mudge paused in his panting account and lay back in his chair. He still held tightly to the arms as though they could keep him in the world of sanity and three measurements, and only now and again released his left hand in order to mop his face. He looked very thin and white and oddly unsubstantial, and he stared about him as though he saw into this other space he had been talking about.

John Silence, too, felt warm. He had listened to every word and had made many notes. The presence of this man had an exhilarating effect upon him. It seemed as if Mr. Racine Mudge still carried about with him something of that breathless Higher-Space condition he had been describing. At any rate, Dr. Silence had himself advanced sufficiently far along the legitimate paths of spiritual and psychic transformations to realise that the visions of this extraordinary little person had a basis of truth for their origin.

After a pause that prolonged itself into minutes, he crossed the room and unlocked a drawer in a bookcase, taking out a small book with a red cover. It had a lock to it, and he produced a key out of his pocket and proceeded to open the covers. The bright eyes of Mr. Mudge never left him for a single second.

"It almost seems a pity," he said at length, "to cure you, Mr. Mudge. You are on the way to discovery of great things. Though you may lose your life in the process—that is, your life here in the world of three dimensions—you would lose thereby nothing of great value— you will pardon my apparent rudeness, I know—and you might gain what is infinitely greater. Your suffering, of course, lies in the fact that you alternate between the two worlds and are never wholly in one or the other. Also, I rather imagine, though I cannot be certain of this from any personal experiments, that you have here and there penetrated even into space of more than four dimensions, and have hence experienced the terror you speak of."

The perspiring son of the Essex bargeman and the woman of Normandy bent his head several times in assent, but uttered no word in reply.

"Some strange psychic predisposition, dating no doubt from one of your former lives, has favoured the development of your 'disease'; and the fact that you had no normal training at school or college, no leading by the poor intellect into the culs-de-sac falsely called knowledge, has further caused your exceedingly rapid movement along the lines of direct inner experience. None of the knowledge you have foreshadowed has come to you through the senses, of course."

Mr. Mudge, sitting in his immovable chair, began to tremble slightly. A wind again seemed to pass over his surface and again to set it curiously in motion like a field of grass.

"You are merely talking to gain time," he said hurriedly, in a shaking voice. "This thinking aloud delays us. I see ahead what you are coming to, only please be quick, for something is going to happen. A band is again coming down the street, and if it plays—if it plays Wagner—I shall be off in a twinkling."

"Precisely. I will be quick. I was leading up to the point of how to effect your cure. The way is this: You must simply learn to *block the entrances*."

"True, true, utterly true!" exclaimed the little man, dodging about nervously in the depths of the chair. "But how, in the name of space, is that to be done?"

"By concentration. They are all within you, these entrances, although outer cases such as colour, music, and other things lead you towards them. These external things you cannot hope to destroy, but once the entrances are blocked, they will lead you only to bricked walls and closed channels. You will no longer be able to find the way."

"Quick, quick!" cried the bobbing figure in the chair. "How is this concentration to be effected?"

"This little book," continued Dr. Silence calmly, "will explain to you the way." He tapped the cover. "Let me now read out to you certain simple instructions, composed, as I see you divine, entirely from my own personal experiences in the same direction. Follow these instructions and you will no longer enter the state of Higher Space. The entrances will be blocked effectively."

Mr. Mudge sat bolt upright in his chair to listen, and John Silence cleared his throat and began to read slowly in a very distinct voice.

But before he had uttered a dozen words, something happened. A sound of street music entered the room through the open ventilators, for a band had begun to play in the stable mews at the back of the house—the March from *Tannhäuser*. Odd as it may seem that a German band should twice within the space of an hour enter the same mews and play Wagner, it was nevertheless the fact.

Mr. Racine Mudge heard it. He uttered a sharp, squeaking cry and twisted his arms with nervous energy round the chair. A piteous look that was not far from tears spread over his white face. Grey shadows followed it—the grey of fear. He began to struggle convulsively.

"Hold me fast! Catch me! For God's sake, keep me here! I'm on the rush already. Oh, it's frightful!" he cried in tones of anguish, his voice as thin as a reed.

Dr. Silence made a plunge forward to seize him, but in a flash, before he could cover the space between them, Mr. Racine Mudge, screaming and struggling, seemed to shoot past him into invisibility. He disappeared like an arrow from a bow propelled at infinite speed, and his voice no longer sounded in the external air, but seemed in some curious way to make itself heard somewhere within the depths of the doctor's own being. It was almost like a faint singing cry in his head, like a voice of dream, a voice of vision and unreality.

"Alcohol, alcohol!" it cried, "give me alcohol! It's the quickest way.

Alcohol, before I'm out of reach!"

The doctor, accustomed to rapid decisions and even more rapid action, remembered that a brandy flask stood upon the mantelpiece, and in less than a second he had seized it and was holding it out towards the space above the chair recently occupied by the visible Mudge. Then, before his very eyes, and long ere he could unscrew the metal stopper, he saw the contents of the closed glass phial sink and lessen as though some one were drinking violently and greedily of the liquor within.

"Thanks! Enough! It deadens the vibrations!" cried the faint voice in his interior, as he withdrew the flask and set it back upon the mantelpiece. He understood that in Mudge's present condition one side of the flask was open to space and he could drink without removing the stopper. He could hardly have had a more interesting proof of what he had been hearing described at such length.

But the next moment—the very same moment it almost seemed—the German band stopped midway in its tune—and there was Mr. Mudge back in his chair again, gasping and panting!

"Quick!" he shrieked, "stop that band! Send it away! Catch hold of me! Block the entrances! Block the entrances! Give me the red book! Oh, oh, oh-h-h-h!!!"

The music had begun again. It was merely a temporary interruption. The *Tannhäuser* March started again, this time at a tremendous pace that made it sound like a rapid two-step as though the instruments played against time.

But the brief interruption gave Dr. Silence a moment in which to collect his scattering thoughts, and before the band had got through half a bar, he had flung forward upon the chair and held Mr. Racine Mudge, the struggling little victim of Higher Space, in a grip of iron. His arms went all round his diminutive person, taking in a good part of the chair at the same time. He was not a big man, yet he seemed to smother Mudge completely.

Yet, even as he did so, and felt the wriggling form underneath him, it began to melt and slip away like air or water. The wood of the armchair somehow disentangled itself from between his own arms and those of Mudge. The phenomenon known as the passage of matter through matter took place. The little man seemed actually to get mixed up in his own being. Dr. Silence could just see his face beneath him. It puckered and grew dark as though from some great internal effort. He heard the thin, reedy voice cry in his ear to "Block the entrances, block the entrances!" and then—but how in the world describe what is indescribable?

John Silence half rose up to watch. Racine Mudge, his face distorted beyond all recognition, was making a marvellous inward movement, as though doubling back upon himself. He turned funnel-wise like water in a whirling vortex, and then appeared to break up somewhat as a reflection breaks up and divides in a distorting convex mirror. He went neither forward nor backwards, neither to the right nor the left, neither up nor down. But he went. He went utterly. He simply flashed away out of sight like a vanishing projectile.

All but one leg! Dr. Silence just had the time and the presence of mind to seize upon the left ankle and boot as it disappeared, and to this he held on for several seconds like grim death. Yet all the time he knew it was a foolish and useless thing to do.

The foot was in his grasp one moment, and the next it seemed—this was the only way he could describe it—inside his own skin and bones, and at the same time outside his hand and all round it. It seemed mixed up in some amazing way with his own flesh and blood. Then it was gone, and he was tightly grasping a draught of heated air.

"Gone! gone! gone!" cried a thick, whispering voice, somewhere deep within his own consciousness. "Lost! lost! lost!" it repeated, growing fainter and fainter till at length it vanished into nothing and the last signs of Mr. Racine Mudge vanished with it.

John Silence locked his red book and replaced it in the cabinet, which he fastened with a click, and when Barker answered the bell he enquired if Mr. Mudge had left a card upon the table. It appeared that he had, and when the servant returned with it, Dr. Silence read the address and made a note of it. It was in North London.

"Mr. Mudge has gone," he said quietly to Barker, noticing his expression of alarm.

"He's not taken his 'at with him, sir."

"Mr. Mudge requires no hat where he is now," continued the doctor, stooping to poke the fire. "But he may return for it—"

"And the humbrella, sir."

"And the umbrella."

"He didn't go out *my* way, sir, if you please," stuttered the amazed servant, his curiosity overcoming his nervousness.

"Mr. Mudge has his own way of coming and going, and prefers it. If he returns by the door at any time remember to bring him instantly to me, and be kind and gentle with him and ask no questions. Also, remember, Barker, to think pleasantly, sympathetically, affectionately of him while he is away. Mr. Mudge is a very suffering gentleman."

Barker bowed and went out of the room backwards, gasping and feeling round the inside of his collar with three very hot fingers of one hand.

It was two days later when he brought in a telegram to the study. Dr. Silence opened it, and read as follows:

"Bombay. Just slipped out again. All safe. Have blocked entrances. Thousand thanks. Address Cooks, London.—MUDGE."

Dr. Silence looked up and saw Barker staring at him bewilderingly. It occurred to him that somehow he knew the contents of the telegram.

"Make a parcel of Mr. Mudge's things," he said briefly, "and address them Thomas Cook & Sons, Ludgate Circus. And send them there exactly a month from to-day and marked 'To be called for.'"

"Yes, sir," said Barker, leaving the room with a deep sigh and a hurried glance at the waste-paper basket where his master had dropped the pink paper.

The Secret

I saw him walking down the floor of the A.B.C. shop where I was lunching. He was gazing about for a vacant seat with that vague stare of puzzled distress he always wore when engaged in practical affairs. Then he saw me and nodded. I pointed to the seat opposite; he sat down. There was a crumb in his brown beard, I noticed. There had been one a year ago, when I saw him last.

"What a long time since we met," I said, genuinely glad to see him. He was a most lovable fellow, though his vagueness was often perplexing to his friends.

"Yes—er—h'mmm—let me see—"

"Just about a year," I said .

He looked at me with an expression as though he did not see me. He was delving in his mind for dates and proofs. His fierce eyebrows looked exactly as though they were false—stuck on with paste—and I imagined how puzzled he would be if one of them suddenly dropped off into his soup. The eyes beneath, however, were soft and beaming; the whole face was tender, kind, gentle, and when he smiled he looked thirty instead of fifty.

"A year, is it?" he remarked, and then turned from me to the girl who was waiting to take his order. This ordering was a terrible affair. I marvelled at the patience of that never-to-be-tipped waitress in the dirty black dress. He looked with confusion from me to her, from her to the complicated bill of fare, and from this last to me again.

"Oh, have a cup of coffee and a bit of that lunch-cake," I said with desperation. He stared at me for a second, one eyebrow moving, the other still as the grave. I felt an irresistible desire to laugh.

All right," he murmured to the girl, "coffee and a bit of that lunch-cake." She went off wearily. "And a pat of butter," he whispered after her, but looking at the wrong waitress. "And a portion of that strawberry jam," he added, looking at another waitress.

Then he turned to talk with me.

"Oh no," he said, looking over his shoulder at the crowd of girls by the counter; "*not* the jam. I forgot I'd ordered that lunch-cake."

Again he switched round in his chair—he always perched on the edge like a bird—and made a great show of plunging into a long-deferred chat with me. I knew what would come. He was always writing books and sending them out among publishers and forgetting where they were at the moment.

"And how are *you?*" he asked. I told him.

"Writing anything these days?" I ventured boldly.

The eyebrows danced. "Well, the fact is, I've only just finished a book."

"Sent it anywhere?"

"It's gone off, yes. Let me see—it's gone to—er—" The coffee and lunch-cake arrived without the pat of butter, but with two lots of strawberry jam. "I won't have jam, thank you. And will you bring a pat of butter?" he muttered to the girl. Then, turning to me again—"Oh, I really forget for the moment. It's a good story, I think." His novels were, as a fact, extraordinarily good, which was the strange part of it all.

"It's about a woman, you see, who—" He proceeded to tell me the story in outline. Once he got beyond the confused openings of talk the man became interesting, but it took so long, and was so difficult to follow, that I remembered former experiences and cut him short with a lucky inspiration.

"Don't spoil it for me by telling it. I shan't enjoy it when it comes out."

He laughed, and both eyebrows dropped and hid his eyes. He busied himself with the cake and butter. A second crumb went to join the first. I thought of balls in golf bunkers, and laughed outright. For a time the conversation flagged. I became aware of a certain air of mystery about him. He was full of something besides the novel—something he wanted to talk about but had probably forgotten "for the moment." I got the impression he was casting about in the upper confusion of his mind for the cue.

"You're writing something else now?" I ventured.

The question hit the bull's-eye. Both eyebrows shot up, as though they would vanish next minute on wires and fly up into the wings. The cake in his hand would follow; and last of all he himself would go. The children's pantomime came vividly before me. Surely he was a made-up figure on his way to rehearsal.

"I am," he said; "but it's a *great* secret. "I've got a *magnificent* idea!"

"I promise not to tell. I'm safe as the grave. Tell me."

He fixed his kindly, beaming eyes on my face and smiled charmingly.

"It's a play," he murmured, and then paused for effect, hunting about on his plate for cake, where cake there was none.

"Another piece of that lunch-cake, please," he said in a sudden loud voice, addressed to the waitresses at large. "It came to me the other day in the London Library—er—very fine idea—"

"Something really original?"

"Well, I think so, perhaps." The cake came with a clatter of plates, but he pushed it aside as though he had forgotten about it, and leaned forward across the table. "I'll tell you. Of course you won't say anything. I don't want the idea to get about. There's money in a good play—and people do steal so, don't they?"

I made a gesture, as much as to say, "Do I look like a man who would repeat?" and he plunged into it with enthusiasm.

Oh! the story of that play! And those dancing eyebrows! And the bits of the plot he forgot and went back for! And the awful, wild confusion of names and scenes and curtains! And the way his voice rose and fell like a sound carried to and fro by a gusty wind! And the feeling that something was coming which would make it all clear—but which never came!

"The woman, you see,"—all his stories began that way,—"is one of those modern women who . . . and when she dies she tells on her death-bed how she knew all the time that Anna—"

"That's the heroine, I think?" I asked keenly, after ten minutes' exposition, hoping to heaven my guess was right.

"No, no, she's the widow, don't you remember, of the clergyman who went over to the Church of Rome to avoid marrying her sister—in the first act—or didn't I mention that?"

"You mentioned it, I think, but the explanation—"

"Oh, well, you see, the Anglican clergyman—he's Anglican in the first act—always suspected that Miriam had not died by her own hand, but had been poisoned. In fact, he finds the incriminating letter in the gas-pipe, and recognises the handwriting—"

"Oh, *he* finds the letter?"

"Rather. *He* finds the letter, don't you see? and compares it with the others, and makes up his mind who wrote it, and goes straight to Colonel Middleton with his discovery."

"So Middleton, of course, refuses to believe—"

"Refuses to believe that the second wife—oh, I forgot to mention that the clergyman had married again in his own Church; married a woman who turns out to be Anna's—no, I mean Miriam's—half-sister, who had been educated abroad in a convent,—refuses to believe, you see, that *his* wife had anything to do with it. Then Middleton has a splendid scene. He and the clergyman have the stage to themselves. Wyndham's the man for Middleton, of course. Well, he declares that he has the proof—proof that must convince everybody, and just as he waves it in the air in comes Miriam, who is walking in her sleep, from her sick-bed. They listen. She is talking in her sleep. By Jove, man, don't you see it? She is talking about the crime! She practically confesses it before their very eyes."

"Splendid!"

"And she never wakes up—I mean, not in that scene. She goes back to bed and has no idea next day what she has said and done."

"And the clergyman's honour is saved?" I hazarded, amazed at my rashness.

"No. *Anna* is saved. You see, I forgot to tell you that in the second act Miriam's brother, Sir John, had—"

The waitress brought the little paper checks.

"Let's go outside and finish. It's getting frightfully stuffy here," I suggested desperately, picking up the bills.

We walked out together, he still talking against time with the most terrible confusion of names and acts and scenes imaginable. He bumped into everybody who came in his way. His beard was full of crumbs. His eyebrows danced with excitement—I knew then positively they were false—and his voice ran up and down the scale like a buzz-saw at work on a tough board.

"By Jove, old man, that *is* a play!"

He turned to me with absolute happiness in his face.

"But for heaven's sake, don't let out a word of it. I must have a copyright performance first before it's really safe."

"Not a word, I promise."

"It's a dead secret—till I've finished it, I mean—then I'll come and tell you the *dénouement*. The last curtain is simply magnificent. You see, Middleton never hears—"

"I won't tell a living soul," I cried, running to catch a bus. "It's a secret—yours and mine!"

And the omnibus carried me away westwards.

Meanwhile the play remains to this day a "dead secret," known only to the man who thinks he told it, and to the other man who knows he heard it told.

The Kit-Bag

When the words "Not Guilty" sounded through the crowded court-room that dark December afternoon, Arthur Wilbraham, the great criminal K.C., and leader for the triumphant defence, was represented by his junior; but Johnson, his private secretary, carried the verdict across to his chambers like lightning.

"It's what we expected, I think," said the barrister, without emotion; "and, personally, I am glad the case is over." There was no particular sign of pleasure that his defence of John Turk, the murderer, on a plea of insanity, had been successful, for no doubt he felt, as everybody who had watched the case felt, that no man had ever better deserved the gallows.

"I'm glad too," said Johnson. He had sat in the court for ten days watching the face of the man who had carried out with callous detail one of the most brutal and cold-blooded murders of recent years.

The counsel glanced up at his secretary. They were more than employer and employed; for family and other reasons, they were friends. "Ah, I remember; yes," he said with a kind smile, "and you want to get away for Christmas? You're going to skate and ski in the Alps, aren't you? If I was your age I'd come with you."

Johnson laughed shortly. He was a young man of twenty-six, with a delicate face like a girl's. "I can catch the morning boat now," he said; "but that's not the reason I'm glad the trial is over. I'm glad it's over because I've seen the last of that man's dreadful face. It positively haunted me. That white skin, with the black hair brushed low over the forehead, is a thing I shall never forget, and the description of the way the dismembered body was crammed and packed with lime into that—"

"Don't dwell on it, my dear fellow," interrupted the other, looking at him curiously out of his keen eyes, "don't think about it. Such pictures have a trick of coming back when one least wants them." He paused a moment. "Now go," he added presently, "and enjoy your holiday. I shall want all your energy for my Parliamentary work when you get back. And don't break your neck ski-ing."

Johnson shook hands and took his leave. At the door he turned suddenly.

"I knew there was something I wanted to ask you," he said. "Would you mind lending me one of your kit-bags? It's too late to get one tonight, and I leave in the morning before the shops are open."

"Of course; I'll send Henry over with it to your rooms. You shall have it the moment I get home."

"I promise to take great care of it," said Johnson gratefully, delighted to think that within thirty hours he would be nearing the brilliant sunshine of the high Alps in winter. The thought of that criminal court was like an evil dream in his mind.

He dined at his club and went on to Bloomsbury, where he occupied the top floor in one of those old, gaunt houses in which the rooms are large and lofty. The floor below his own was vacant and unfurnished, and below that were other lodgers whom he did not know. It was cheerless, and he looked forward heartily to a change. The night was even more cheerless: it was miserable, and few people were about. A cold, sleety rain was driving down the streets before the keenest east wind he had ever felt. It howled dismally among the big, gloomy houses of the great squares, and when he reached his rooms he heard it whistling and shouting over the world of black roofs beyond his windows.

In the hall he met his landlady, shading a candle from the draughts with her thin hand. "This come by a man from Mr Wilbr'im's, sir."

She pointed to what was evidently the kit-bag, and Johnson thanked her and took it upstairs with him. "I shall be going abroad in the morning for ten days, Mrs. Monks," he said. "I'll leave an address for letters."

"And I hope you'll 'ave a merry Christmas, sir," she said, in a raucous, wheezy voice that suggested spirits, "and better weather than this."

"I hope so too," replied her lodger, shuddering a little as the wind went roaring down the street outside.

When he got upstairs he heard the sleet volleying against the window-panes. He put his kettle on to make a cup of hot coffee, and then set about putting a few things in order for his absence. "And now I must pack—such as my packing is," he laughed to himself, and set to work at once.

He liked the packing, for it brought the snow mountains so vividly before him, and made him forget the unpleasant scenes of the past ten days. Besides, it was not elaborate in nature. His friend had lent him the very thing—a stout canvas kit-bag, sack-shaped, with holes round the neck for the brass bar and padlock. It was a bit shapeless, true, and not much to look at, but its capacity was unlimited, and there was no need to pack carefully. He shoved in his waterproof coat, his fur cap and gloves, his skates and climbing boots, his sweaters, snow-boots, and ear-caps; and then on the top of these he piled his woollen shirts and underwear, his thick socks, puttees, and knickerbockers. The dress-suit came next, in case the hotel people dressed for dinner, and then, thinking of the best way to pack his white shirts, he paused a moment to reflect. "That's the worst of these kit-bags," he mused vaguely, standing in the centre of the sitting-room, where he had come to fetch some string.

It was after ten o'clock. A furious gust of wind rattled the windows as though to hurry him up, and he thought with pity of the poor Londoners whose Christmas would be spent in such a climate, whilst he was skimming over snowy slopes in bright sunshine, and dancing in the evening with rosy-checked girls— Ah! That reminded him; he must put in his dancing-pumps and evening socks. He crossed over from his sitting-room to the cupboard on the landing where he kept his linen.

And as he did so he heard some one coming softly up the stairs.

He stood still a moment on the landing to listen. It was Mrs. Monks's step, he thought; she must he coming up with the last post. But then the steps ceased suddenly, and he heard no more. They were at least two flights down, and he came to the conclusion they were too heavy to be those of his bibulous landlady. No doubt they belonged to a late lodger who had mistaken his floor. He went into his bedroom and packed his pumps and dress-shirts as best he could.

The kit-bag by this time was two-thirds full, and stood upright on its own base like a sack of flour. For the first time he noticed that it was old and dirty, the canvas faded and worn, and that it had obviously been subjected to rather rough treatment. It was not a very nice bag to have sent him—certainly not a new one, or one that his chief valued. He gave the matter a passing thought, and went on with his packing. Once or twice, however, he caught himself wondering who it could have been wandering down below, for Mrs. Monks had not come up with letters, and the floor was empty and unfurnished. From time to time, moreover, he was almost certain he heard a soft tread of some one padding about over the bare boards—cautiously, stealthily, as silently as possible—and, further, that the sounds had been lately coming distinctly nearer.

For the first time in his life he began to feel a little creepy. Then, as though to emphasise this feeling, an odd thing happened: as he left the bedroom, having, just packed his recalcitrant white shirts, he noticed that the top of the kit-bag lopped over towards him with an extraordinary resemblance to a human face. The canvas fell into a fold like a nose and forehead, and the brass rings for the padlock just filled the position of the eyes. A shadow—or was it a travel stain? for he could not tell exactly—looked like hair. It gave him rather a turn, for it was so absurdly, so outrageously, like the face of John Turk, the murderer.

He laughed, and went into the front room, where the light was stronger.

"That horrid case has got on my mind," he thought; "I shall be glad of a change of scene and air." In the sitting-room, however, he was not pleased to hear again that stealthy tread upon the stairs, and to realise that it was much closer than before, as well as unmistakably real. And this time he got up and went out to see who it could be creeping about on the upper staircase at so late an hour.

But the sound ceased; there was no one visible on the stairs. He went to the floor below, not without trepidation, and turned on the electric light to make sure that no one was hiding in the empty rooms of the unoccupied suite. There was not a stick of furniture large enough to hide a dog. Then he called over the banisters to Mrs. Monks, but there was no answer, and his voice echoed down into the dark vault of the house, and was lost in the roar of the gale that howled outside. Every one was in bed and asleep—every one except himself and the owner of this soft and stealthy tread.

"My absurd imagination, I suppose," he thought. "It must have been the wind after all, although—it seemed so *very* real and close, I thought." He went back to his packing. It was by this time getting on towards midnight. He drank his coffee up and lit another pipe—the last before turning in.

It is difficult to say exactly at what point fear begins, when the causes of that fear are not plainly before the eyes. Impressions gather on the surface of the mind, film by film, as ice gathers upon the surface of still water, but often so lightly that they claim no definite recognition from the consciousness. Then a point is reached where the accumulated impressions become a definite emotion, and the mind realises that something has happened. With something of a start, Johnson suddenly recognised that he felt nervous—oddly nervous; also, that for some time past the causes of this feeling had been gathering slowly in his mind, but that he had only just reached the point where he was forced to acknowledge them.

It was a singular and curious malaise that had come over him, and he hardly knew what to make of it. He felt as though he were doing something that was strongly objected to by another person, another person, moreover, who had some right to object. It was a most disturbing and disagreeable feeling, not unlike the persistent promptings of conscience: almost, in fact, as if he were doing something he knew to be wrong. Yet, though he searched vigorously and honestly in his mind, he could nowhere lay his finger upon the secret of this growing uneasiness, and it perplexed him. More, it distressed and frightened him.

"Pure nerves, I suppose," he said aloud with a forced laugh. "Mountain air will cure all that! Ah," he added, still speaking to himself, "and that reminds me—my snow-glasses."

He was standing by the door of the bedroom during this brief soliloquy, and as he passed quickly towards the sitting-room to fetch them from the cupboard he saw out of the corner of his eye the indistinct outline of a figure standing on the stairs, a few feet from the top. It was some one in a stooping position, with one hand on the banisters, and the face peering up towards the landing. And at the same moment he heard a shuffling footstep. The person who had been creeping about below all this time had at last come up to his own floor. Who in the world could it be? And what in the name of heaven did he want?

Johnson caught his breath sharply and stood stockstill. Then, after a few seconds' hesitation, he found his courage, and turned to investigate. The stairs, he saw to his utter amazement, were empty; there was no one. He felt a series of cold shivers run over him, and something about the muscles of his legs gave a little and grew weak. For the space of several minutes he peered steadily into the shadows that congregated about the top of the staircase where he had seen the figure, and then he walked fast—almost ran, in fact—into the light of the front room; but hardly had he passed inside the doorway when he heard some one come up the stairs behind him with a quick bound and go swiftly into his bedroom. It was a heavy, but at the same time a stealthy footstep—the tread of somebody who did not wish to be seen. And it was at this precise moment that the nervousness he had hitherto experienced leaped the boundary line, and entered the state of fear, almost of acute, unreasoning fear. Before it turned into terror there was a further boundary to cross, and beyond that again lay the region of pure horror. Johnson's position was an unenviable one.

"By Jove! That *was* some one on the stairs, then," he muttered, his flesh crawling all over; "and whoever it was has now gone into my bedroom." His delicate, pale face turned absolutely white, and for some minutes he hardly knew what to think or do. Then he realised intuitively that delay only set a premium upon fear; and he crossed the landing boldly and went straight into the other room, where, a few seconds before, the steps had disappeared.

"Who's there? Is that you, Mrs. Monks?" he called aloud, as he went, and heard the first half of his words echo down the empty stairs, while the second half fell dead against the curtains in a room that apparently held no other human figure than his own.

"Who's there?" he called again, in a voice unnecessarily loud and that only just held firm. "What do you want here?"

The curtains swayed very slightly, and, as he saw it, his heart felt as if it almost missed a beat; yet he dashed forward and drew them aside with a rush. A window, streaming with rain, was all that met his gaze. He continued his search, but in vain; the cupboards held nothing but rows of clothes, hanging motionless; and under the bed there was no sign of any one hiding. He stepped backwards into the middle of the room, and, as he did so, something all but tripped him up. Turning with a sudden spring of alarm he saw—the kit-bag.

"Odd!" he thought. "That's not where I left it!" A few moments before it had surely been on his right, between the bed and the bath; he did not remember having moved it. It was very curious. What in the world was the matter with everything? Were all his senses gone queer? A terrific gust of wind tore at the windows, dashing the sleet against the glass with the force of small gun-shot, and then fled away howling dismally over the waste of Bloomsbury roofs. A sudden vision of the Channel next day rose in his mind and recalled him sharply to realities.

"There's no one here at any rate; that's quite clear!" he exclaimed aloud. Yet at the time he uttered them he knew perfectly well that his words were not true and that he did not believe them himself. He felt exactly as though some one was hiding close about him, watching all his movements, trying to hinder his packing in some way. "And two of my senses," he added, keeping up the pretence, "have played me the most absurd tricks: the steps I heard and the figure I saw were both entirely imaginary."

He went back to the front room, poked the fire into a blaze, and sat down before it to think. What impressed him more than anything else was the fact that the kit-bag was no longer where he had left it. It had been dragged nearer to the door.

What happened afterwards that night happened, of course, to a man already excited by fear, and was perceived by a man that had not the full and proper control, therefore, of the senses. Outwardly, Johnson remained calm and master of himself to the end, pretending to the very last that everything he witnessed had a natural explanation, or was merely delusions of his tired nerves. But inwardly, in his very heart, he knew all along that some one had been hiding downstairs in the empty suite when he came in, that this person had watched his opportunity and then stealthily made his way up to the bedroom, and that all he saw and heard afterwards, from the moving of the kit-bag to—well, to the other things this story has to tell—were caused directly by the presence of this invisible person.

And it was here, just when he most desired to keep his mind and thoughts controlled, that the vivid pictures received day after day upon the mental plates exposed in the court-room of the Old Bailey, came strongly to light and developed themselves in the dark room of his inner vision. Unpleasant, haunting memories have a way of coming to life again just when the mind least desires them—in the silent watches of the night, on sleepless pillows, during the lonely hours spent by sick and dying beds. And so now, in the same way, Johnson saw nothing but the dreadful face of John Turk, the murderer, lowering at him from every corner of his mental field of vision; the white skin, the evil eyes, and the fringe of black hair low over the forehead. All the pictures of those ten days in court crowded back into his mind unbidden, and very vivid.

"This is all rubbish and nerves," he exclaimed at length, springing with sudden energy from his chair. "I shall finish my packing and go to bed. I'm overwrought, overtired. No doubt, at this rate I shall hear steps and things all night!"

But his face was deadly white all the same. He snatched up his field-glasses and walked across to the bedroom, humming a music-hall song as he went—a trifle too loud to be natural; and the instant he crossed the threshold and stood within the room something turned cold about his heart, and he felt that every hair on his head stood up.

The kit-bag lay close in front of him, several feet nearer to the door than he had left it, and just over its crumpled top he saw a head and face slowly sinking down out of sight as though some one were crouching behind it to hide, and at the same moment a sound like a long-drawn sigh was distinctly audible in the still air about him between the gusts of the storm outside.

Johnson had more courage and will-power than the girlish indecision of his face indicated; but at first such a wave of terror came over him that for some seconds he could do nothing but stand and stare. A violent trembling ran down his back and legs, and he was conscious of a foolish, almost a hysterical, impulse to scream aloud. That sigh seemed in his very ear, and the air still quivered with it. It was unmistakably a human sigh.

"Who's there?" he said at length, finding his voice; but though he meant to speak with loud decision, the tones came out instead in a faint whisper, for he had partly lost the control of his tongue and lips.

He stepped forward, so that he could see all round and over the kit-bag. Of course there was nothing there, nothing but the faded carpet and the bulging canvas sides. He put out his hands and threw open the mouth of the sack where it had fallen over, being only three parts full, and then he saw for the first time that round the inside, some six inches from the top, there ran a broad smear of dull crimson. It was an old and faded blood stain. He uttered a scream, and drew back his hands as if they had been burnt. At the same moment the kit-bag gave a faint, but unmistakable, lurch forward towards the door.

Johnson collapsed backwards, searching with his hands for the support of something solid, and the door, being farther behind him than he realised, received his weight just in time to prevent his falling, and shut to with a resounding bang. At the same moment the swinging of his left arm accidentally touched the electric switch, and the light in the room went out.

It was an awkward and disagreeable predicament, and if Johnson had not been possessed of real pluck he might have done all manner of foolish things. As it was, however, he pulled himself together, and groped furiously for the little brass knob to turn the light on again. But the rapid closing of the door had set the coats hanging on it a-swinging, and his fingers became entangled in a confusion of sleeves and pockets, so that it was some moments before he found the switch. And in those few moments of bewilderment and terror two things happened that sent him beyond recall over the boundary into the region of genuine horror—he distinctly heard the kit-bag shuffling heavily across the floor in jerks, and close in front of his face sounded once again the sigh of a human being.

In his anguished efforts to find the brass button on the wall he nearly scraped the nails from his fingers, but even then, in those frenzied moments of alarm—so swift and alert are the impressions of a man keyed up by a vivid emotion—he had time to realise that he dreaded the return of the light, and that it might be better for him to stay hidden in the merciful screen of darkness. It was but the impulse of a moment, however, and before he had time to act upon it he had yielded automatically to the original desire, and the room was flooded again with light.

But the second instinct had been right. It would have been better for him to have stayed in the shelter of the kind darkness. For there, close before him, bending over the half-packed kit-bag, clear as life in the merciless glare of the electric light, stood the figure of John Turk, the murderer. Not three feet from him the man stood, the fringe of black hair marked plainly against the pallor of the forehead, the whole horrible presentment of the scoundrel, as vivid as he had seen him day after day in the Old Bailey, when he stood there in the dock, cynical and callous, under the very shadow of the gallows.

In a flash Johnson realised what it all meant: the dirty and much-used bag; the smear of crimson within the top; the dreadful stretched condition of the bulging sides. He remembered how the victim's body had been stuffed into a canvas bag for burial, the ghastly, dismembered fragments forced with lime into this very bag; and the bag itself produced as evidence— It all came back to him as clear as day. . . .

Very softly and stealthily his hand groped behind him for the handle of the door, but before he could actually turn it the very thing that he most of all dreaded came about, and John Turk lifted his devil's face and looked at him. At the same moment that heavy sigh passed through the air of the room, formulated somehow into words: "It's my bag. And I want it."

Johnson just remembered clawing the door open, and then falling in a heap upon the floor of the landing, as he tried frantically to make his way into the front room.

He remained unconscious for a long time, and it was still dark when he opened his eyes and realised that he was lying, stiff and bruised, on the cold boards. Then the memory of what he had seen rushed back into his mind, and he promptly fainted again. When he woke the second time the wintry dawn was just beginning to peep in at the windows, painting the stairs a cheerless, dismal grey, and he managed to crawl into the front room, and cover himself with an overcoat in the arm-chair, where at length he fell asleep.

A great clamour woke him. He recognised Mrs. Monks's voice, loud and voluble.

"What! You ain't been to bed, sir! Are you ill, or has anything 'appened? And there's an urgent gentleman to see you, though it ain't seven o'clock yet, and—"

"Who is it?" he stammered. "I'm all right, thanks. Fell asleep in my chair, I suppose."

"Some one from Mr. Wilb'rim's, and he says he ought to see you quick before you go abroad, and I told him—"

"Show him up, please, at once," said Johnson, whose head was whirling, and his mind was still full of dreadful visions.

Mr. Wilbraham's man came in with many apologies, and explained briefly and quickly that an absurd mistake had been made, and that the wrong kit-bag had been sent over the night before.

"Henry somehow got hold of the one that came over from the court-room, and Mr. Wilbraham only discovered it when he saw his own lying in his room, and asked why it had not gone to you," the man said.

"Oh!" said Johnson stupidly.

"And he must have brought you the one from the murder case instead, sir, I'm afraid," the man continued, without the ghost of an expression on his face. "The one John Turk packed the dead body in. Mr. Wilbraham's awful upset about it, sir, and told me to come over first thing this morning with the right one, as you were leaving by the boat."

He pointed to a clean-looking kit-bag on the floor, which he had just brought. "And I was to bring the other one back, sir," he added casually.

For some minutes Johnson could not find his voice. At last he pointed in the direction of his bedroom. "Perhaps you would kindly unpack it for me. Just empty the things out on the floor."

The man disappeared into the other room, and was gone for five minutes. Johnson heard the shifting to and fro of the bag, and the rattle of the skates and boots being unpacked.

"Thank you, sir," the man said, returning with the bag folded over his arm. "And can I do anything more to help you, sir?"

"What is it?" asked Johnson, seeing that he still had something he wished to say.

The man shuffled and looked mysterious. "Beg pardon, sir, but knowing your interest in the Turk case, I thought you'd maybe like to know what's happened—"

"Yes."

"John Turk killed hisself last night with poison immediately on getting his release, and he left a note for Mr. Wilbraham saying as he'd be much obliged if they'd have him put away, same as the woman he murdered, in the old kit-bag."

"What time—did he do it?" asked Johnson.

"Ten o'clock last night, sir, the warder says."

Stodgman's Opportunity

Jonathan Stodgman was one of the writing fraternity. He was always talking about "placing" articles, getting "editors to look at my stuff," and all the rest of it. His "stuff" was good, too—of the solid and instructive kind. An article by Jonathan Stodgman was a guarantee of accuracy; and this was essential when its main interest depended upon the picturesque marshalling of facts, dates, measurements, and scientific data generally. Proof-readers had no trouble with Stodgman's "stuff."

But Stodgman himself would willingly have sacrificed the good-will of all the proof-readers in the world for a single pennyworth of a better quality than accuracy, and one of which he was utterly destitute. He had no imagination—not even enough to write a magazine story. And he knew it.

At the moment he was engaged upon a "paper" dealing with the "Soils of London." It was an "ordered" article for a technical journal, to run to about three thousand words, and he had just reached a point where definite practical information was necessary. On the stroke of seven o'clock he threw down his pen and went out, remembering that he was to dine at the club with several members of his craft. The sky was aflame with crimson, and exquisitely tinted clouds were reflected in puddles down the darkening street, but he never noticed flaming skies or clouds reflected in puddles. Purchasing a ticket for threepence—he lived some way out—he dived underground into one of the many pipes that burrow in a mysterious network below London, and was hurried away to his destination without delay.

In the train his mind dwelt exclusively upon clays, sands, loams, and gravel; he also reflected upon drainage, subsidence caused by moisture, and the porous qualities of sand. But, being weary and over-worked, his thoughts merely turned in a vicious circle. Stupid and heavy Stodgman felt.

"I must see those builders to-morrow," he reflected, "and get the actual facts about the area and depth—especially the depth—of the London clay." He sighed and lit a cigarette. Then he noticed the compartment was not "smoking," and he dropped the cigarette and ground his heel on it. His thoughts about the London clay continued dully.

The train roared and rattled meanwhile, and the stations flew by so fast that Stodgman suddenly realised with a jerk that he would forget to get out unless he kept his thoughts from wandering. He took the ticket out of his pocket and read it.

"But where in the world did I get *this?*" he exclaimed with surprise, examining the bit of pasteboard carefully. It was crimson, and the edges were fringed with neat little spots of shining gold like stars. "And what the dickens does it mean?"

His surprise increased suddenly very much indeed. But it was more than surprise. Something in it touched oddly upon the borders of alarm, and he became aware of a curious sensation of faintness, with an unpleasant sinking of the heart.

"That's queer," he thought, meaning partly the alarm and partly the card.

On it, in wee white letters, he read the words *"Pass one."*

He instantly fumbled through his pockets for the right ticket, but could not find it. His gloves turned thick and all his fingers were thumbs. He had a dim recollection that the booking-clerk had smiled curiously at him when he bought it. He searched furiously and got hot in the process. That tube ticket was nowhere to be found, and his hands stuck in his pockets as though they were full of clay. The train, meanwhile, began to slow down.

"The devil!" he exclaimed. "What's the matter with me?"

A strange sense of panic got hold of his mind. He felt like a fat woman with a dozen parcels climbing about in a bus. He began to breathe in a quick, flustered sort of way, and the breathing came a trifle hard.

Impulses, of course, were foreign to Stodgman's nature; but on this occasion he had one—a very strong one. He realised that he wanted to get out at once. He was in the wrong train. More—there was something uncommonly queer about the train itself!

It stopped with a lurch and a swagger, and Stodgman went to the door with the hop-skip-and-jump peculiar to tube travellers. The sooner he was out of it the better. A dreadful oppression came over him.

At the platform with the sliding doors, however, the conductor stopped him with menacing face. The man's face was positively dark.

"Can't get out now," he muttered. "You're too late. Everybody's out long ago—everybody but you and me. You've missed yer chance!"

Something in the voice, face, and manner of the conductor made him feel extraordinarily bewildered and afraid. He turned to look, and saw to his amazement that the whole compartment was empty. Already the carriage swayed from side to side as the train moved on again and got into its stride. Something in the queer way it moved, too, touched his sense of terror—like a thing of life, it moved—a living creature—an animal in a hurry!

A cold thing stirred in his heart, rising by jumps to his throat, making it difficult to get his words out. It was exactly like a nightmare. He remembered afterwards that he had wished it was only a nightmare.

"Let me out, you idiot!" he tried to shout angrily; "I've paid for my ticket." But his voice sounded weak and faint, hardly audible above the roar of the tunnel.

"Tickets ain't nothin'," the conductor roared. "You orter have a pass, not a ticket, to get out of *this* train."

"I have a pass, you ——!" Stodgman shrieked, now genuinely terrified.

"Too late now, any'ow," the man shouted above the din. "Too late now. We're fairly caught—both of us."

The train was rushing onwards, whistling as it went. Stodgman suddenly got the horrible impression that it was running on legs instead of on wheels—a hundred short iron legs—legs that raced along the sleepers; that it was some gigantic antediluvian beast come to life again after sleeping for centuries in the soil. The whistling and shrieking were just the sounds such a monster would make; they were not the noises of a train at all. He could feel it panting, leaping, struggling in its speed. And he was *inside it!*

"But what does it all mean? Where are we going to?" he cried in real anguish. "Tell me at once, you ——!" And in his heart he was dreadfully afraid—afraid of the answer the man would make. He felt he already know what it would be.

There came a sudden, complete hush when the carriages seemed to stop swaying and run on velvet and rubber. The roar ceased, the shrieking and whistling died away. The conductor left his post between the swinging doors and crept forward into the car. He put his lips to Stodgman's ear, with his hand up to help the sound.

"Shall I tell yer what it is?" he whispered in a way that made his hearer's flesh crawl. "I'll tell yet, then," he added, as Stodgman stared speechless in his eyes, finding no words.

The conductor drew himself up and caught a swinging strap over his head. His face was like death.

"We're lost!" he hissed, "lost in the clay; the London clay's got us at last! We're done for, we are!"

Stodgman sprang to his feet, a sudden raging fury taking the place of his terror. His hands seized the wretched conductor by the throat. He had just time to realise the throat was iron—when a voice behind him brought him to his senses with a violent start.

"——road Station! ——road Station!" it called, and Stodgman leaped to his feet and had exactly three seconds to dash out through the door before the train moved on again. It was the gradual stopping of the carriages that had produced the silence of his dream. He staggered out upon the platform, still thinking of gravels, loams, and clay, but chiefly amazed by the vividness of his four-minute nightmare.

"One's head invariably falls forward when one sleeps in a train," he reflected as he rose in a lift to the surface of the world. "I really must think up an article on that—'Curious Postures of the Head in Sleep,' or something of the kind, perhaps."

After dinner, in the smoking-room, Stodgman regaled his companions with an account of his dream. More or less bored, the majority barely listened to the end, so anxious was each to cap the dream with one of his own. Only one of them, the teller noticed, was silent; and *he* listened with rather a flushed face and attentive manner. Before they broke up for the night this fellow, whose name was O'Flynn, came up to Stodgman and asked a question or two on his own account.

"The pass was crimson, with a fringe of stars?" he asked; "and the train had turned alive with legs and wings that might have whipped you clean up into the sky? That's a capital idea, you know, for the beginning of a yarn."

"Capital," said Stodgman politely.

"Going to use it for anything?" asked O'Flynn.

"My dream? Oh, dear, no. There's no copy in a *dream* nowadays. By the bye, talking of copy, do you know any reliable builders or contractors who can tell me, &c.?"

It was a couple of months later, while engaged upon an article called "Great Bridges of the World," that Stodgman came across a gorgeously imaginative fantasy, charmingly illustrated, in the *Premier Magazine,* called "The Night Journey." It was all about the adventures of a man who found himself in a queer tram, and whose ticket turned out to be a pass to a most bewitching place outside London, where the writer took his reader and entertained him with much charm and power of imagination.

"Good yarn, by Jove, that!" Stodgman exclaimed after reading it through to the end. "How these fellows do invent, to be sure! I only wish I could do it myself; but such ideas never come to me."

Then he glanced at the signature of the author.

"Michael O'Flynn," he read; "let me see, now. I met a fellow of that name somewhere not so very long ago. I wonder where it was."

Then he dismissed the subject and switched back his mind on to the "Great Bridges of the World."

The Boy Messenger

It was the afternoon of Christmas Eve.

Partly by train, partly on foot, they had come to a charming village, not much more than a dozen miles from London Bridge, and were sitting at tea looking out upon the garden of the inn. The dusk, like a thin veil, gathered silently about them, and a curtain of wintry mist, half moisture from the near woodlands, half smoke from the village, hung over the tumbled cottage roofs and shrouded the crests of the elm trees that circled the green.

A few children played near the well, a line of white geese straggled over from the pond, and a typical village dog strayed dangerously near the hoofs of a typical village donkey that was trying its best to nibble grass where grass there was none. For the rest, the hamlet seemed deserted, the street peopled by shadows only, and the dishevelled yew-tree in the churchyard spread vaguely through the gloom till it embraced the church and most of the gravestones into the compass of its aged arms.

They were an unimaginative party. It is doubtful if any one of them possessed sufficient insight to appreciate the feelings of an untipped waiter—surely the least of tests—and yet, before the eyes of three of them, two girls and a man, this thing plainly happened. True, their accounts varied curiously when they came later to compare notes; but then accounts of the simplest occurrence—say, a rabbit running across a road—will vary amazingly when half a dozen persons who saw it run come to relate their impressions. So that proves nothing; the important thing is that something happened, and the observers started even. The rest remains to be told.

They were waiting for the arrival of another friend, who was to bicycle over and meet them at the inn, and then return for the Christmas Eve party, when they realised that the cold had grown suddenly much greater, and one of them—it was the younger girl—made the suggestion that they should go part of the way to meet him. The proposal was welcomed, and instantly acted upon, and the man and the two girls were up and away in a twinkling, leaving the others behind to nurse the tea against their speedy return.

"The moment we hear the bicycle bell we'll make tea," they shouted from the inn porch, as the three forms scattered into the darkness, the voices and footsteps making an unusual clamour in the peaceful little hamlet.

The road, winding like a white stream, and slippery with occasional ice, ran downhill out of the nest of cottages, and the trio followed its course headlong through the gloom, regardless of ruts or loose stones. A couple of villagers, walking briskly by, turned their heads to stare; a dog made a sudden run, barking shrilly; a cat shot silently across the road in front of them; and then, quite suddenly the village was left behind and the broad highway dwindled into a country lane. As they ran, the hedgerows flew past like palings with a level top, and the frosty evening air, keen with odours of ploughed fields and dead leaves, stung their cheeks sharply and whistled in their ears.

They had gone perhaps half a mile in this way, still urging the pace downhill, and they were running abreast along a clear stretch with nothing to obstruct, so that all had the same point of view, when suddenly—and this is where the accounts first begin to vary—they realised that something stood immediately in the road before them, something that brought them all up instinctively with a dead halt.

How they managed it, going at that pace downhill, is hard to understand—some things apparently possess the curious power of compelling a stop—for they came to a full halt as completely as though they had charged an invisible iron barrier breast-high across the road. Panting and speechless they drew up in line as by common instinct—drew up in presence of a fourth.

So far at least, they were all agreed—that it was a fourth.

Outlined against the white road where a moment before had been empty dusk, of indefinite shape in the mingling of the lights, stockstill, and bang in the centre of their path—the slang alone describes the uncompromising attitude of the thing—stood this fourth figure, facing them with a deliberate calmness of survey that seemed a little more than insolence, and only a little less than menace. Another second and their headlong rush would have sent them ploughing over it as an ocean liner ploughs over a fishing smack in the night. Moreover, so sudden was the appearance, and so abrupt the halt, that for more than a whole minute they merely stood in silence facing it, and staring back with no thought of doing anything. To each of them the idea came that it was not possible to get past it, that there was no available space. Though actually diminutive, it seemed to fill the entire road just as a mail cart might have done. And, quite apart from this singular deception of sight, each member confessed afterwards to an uncommon emotion, which warned them that to force a way past was somehow not exactly the right, or proper, or safe thing to do.

So at first they stood and stared rather helplessly—till at length their startled vision focussed itself better and the man of the party, finding his senses, expressed the relieved conviction of them all with a loud exclamation:

"Why, I declare, it's only a boy after all!" he cried, with a laugh.

Yet the words, as soon as uttered, had a false ring about them, for there was that about the figure of this little boy—this diminutive person dressed in clothes of dark green, oddly cut, with the white face and large blue eyes so wide apart in it—there was that about him which made it not difficult to imagine that, if he was something less than a man, he was at the same time something more than a boy. His self-possession was perfect. The manner in which he dominated the entire road, gazing so quietly and fixedly at them—peering it really was—produced an effect of privileged importance that was not calculated according to his mere size at any rate. Aided perhaps by the twilight and the background of dark woods, he certainly managed to convey an impression, strangely insistent, of being other than he was—other, at least, than these three saw him.

And, beyond question, each one saw him differently—at first. The picture varied astonishingly. For the elder girl thought it was a "woman or a shadow," and her sister said it looked like an animal on its hind legs, pausing to start in its flight across the road—a hare, for instance, magnified hugely by the dusk—while the man could have sworn, he declared, that at first he saw several figures, a whole line of them, indeed, which had then suddenly telescoped down into the single outline of this diminutive boy.

And the three accounts seem very suggestive of the curiously confusing effect produced upon their sense of sight from the very beginning.

For a time no one said a word, and up the spines of all three ran chills of various degrees. For the place had turned suddenly lonely; no habitation was in sight; dark woods lay close at hand, with mist creeping everywhere over the sombre landscape; and, immediately in front of them, this imp-thing with the glowing eyes and the confident manner, barring their way. It was eerie; though what there could be about a twilight country lane and an inquisitive little boy to make it so, no one of them could understand.

And then, while a stray breeze brought the dead leaves whirling about their feet in a little rustling eddy, the embarrassing silence was broken by the fourth itself, who in a thin, piping voice, like wind blowing through small reeds, ejaculated a sound that all heard differently.

"Surely it was my name that he called," was the thought in the mind of each.

This, however, they discovered afterwards when comparing notes, and discussing the singular affair from every possible point of view; for at the actual moment the man of the party, remembering the character of the friend they were come to meet, and his love of practical joking, thought to see his hand in the behaviour of the youngster, and cried again with laugh:

"But it's some elaborate trick of Harry's! He has sent the boy ahead to meet us. He is not far off himself at this very moment, and this is his messenger boy!"

But was it really a boy! Did it cast a shadow like the rest of them under the gathering stars? Was it unaccompanied truly, or were those merely shapes of mist that rose and melted so mysteriously into one another beside the hedge yonder? And how was it so vividly impressed upon the minds of all that the boy stood there with a definite purpose, a deliberate mission, and sought to spell some message to their brains? For, afterwards, it came out clearly, that it was this conception of the messenger—of some one come to tell something—that had impressed and perplexed the unimaginative three far more than the mere differences of sight and hearing.

"Let's go back," whispered the younger girl. "He frightens me."

It was the one who had most reason to wish for the arrival of the expected friend, and her voice gave utterance to a secret emotion that was beginning to stir in them all—an emotion of chill presentiment and fear. The imp, however, was far too fascinating for this course to recommend itself just then, and the others soon found their voices and began to ply the little fellow with questions. First of all they asked him who he was and where he lived; and without speaking, he pointed in a vague way, waving his hand generally to include sky and fields as though it were impossible more particularly to give his name or describe the place where he dwelt.

"He doesn't know who he is, or where he lives," cried the girl, who wanted the comforting lights of the Inn, and the comfortable presence of the one they awaited. "He's a goblin—of course, but a very nice goblin," she added quickly with an odd little forced laugh. The boy had turned his eyes upon her face. They seemed such old, old eyes, she declared afterwards by way of explanation.

"Do you live in the village?" asked the man next.

The boy shook his head with an indescribable gesture of contempt.

"Then where do you live?"

He opened his mouth so that they saw the white line of his teeth, and he began to utter a sound that was not unlike the throaty notes of a big bird. It continued for some seconds, but no words came. He stared at each of them in turn, the stream of sound broken at intervals by tiny explosions from the lips. It almost seemed as though speech were unfamiliar to him, something he could not manage and was struggling with for the first time. Then they discovered that the child had a dreadful stammer, but a stammer unlike anything they had ever heard before. It was fully a minute before he managed to produce the words, yet in the direction where he pointed finally there was nothing to be seen but ploughed fields looming darkly, and a few ragged and ungainly elms standing like broken pillars in the night.

"Over there—beyond," was what he seemed to say.

They began to realise somewhat vividly that it was a late December evening; the night gathered increasingly about them; in the tops of the high elms a faint wind stirred and whispered; the face of the world grew unfamiliar, as though they were plunged in some desolate region where human help availed not. The shadows had come forth in troops and taken possession of the landscape, somehow altering it. For the moment they forgot their immediate purpose of meeting a hungry bicycle-rider and hurrying back to tea at the Inn. The passage of time slipped back, as in dreams, to where it was of no account, and they stood there, half fascinated, half frightened by this imp of a creature who seemed to them about to lift a corner of the veil that hangs ever between the illusions of the broken senses and the realities that lie beyond.

But it was the boy himself who broke the spell by suddenly stepping forward and holding out his hands to them. A smile slipped out of his strange eyes and ran all over his face, making it shine.

"Come," he said, without any sign now of a stammer, "come, and I will show you where I live. Your friend is already there waiting."

And the imp mentioned him by name!

The younger girl—she who most looked forward to his coming—gave a perceptible start, and moved quickly backwards towards the hedge. Something clutched at her heart, and made her horribly afraid.

But at the mention of their friend's name, the man of the party burst into a cheery laugh.

"There!" he cried, "I told you it was Harry! It's his idea of a Christmas joke. He's gone on to the other Inn, the Black Horse, and sent this imp of darkness to waylay us. Now we shall have two teas to negotiate!" He clapped his hands, and turned to the girls behind him. "Come on," he said, "let's follow the youngster to the Black Horse, and then send him to fetch the others."

Yet the man's words seemed a sham, signifying nothing, or at most merely cheap bravado. They all stood stockstill and made no pretence of moving. Their real business was with this boy who hovered there before them between the dusk and the darkness, his hands still outstretched, an air of invitation in his face and manner. It was the boy's message they wanted, yet dreaded to hear, the real message not yet delivered. His eyes, there in the gloom, were so preternaturally steady, so compelling, so stern almost for a child, the younger girl thought. And they sought ever the one face, disregarding the other two. For each girl was positive he looked only into her own eyes, while the man afterwards declared that the boy looked only at him. To each the illusion was perfect.

Thus it seemed an act of inspiration, bringing relief to the uneasy feelings of them all, when the man walked forward towards the imp, and into those outstretched hands—dropped coppers.

Certainly it was a relief to see him pocket them without an instant's hesitation, for this was an eminently human proceeding. But the thin peal of elfin laughter that followed the action was not what they had expected, and the echoes that came from the leafless woods beyond, and prolonged the sound, made them all turn sharply about and try to face in every direction at once. The echoes had seemed so curiously like real voices.

Then the man, by way of protest against the increasing strangeness of it all, resolved to test the spell more vigorously.

"Come," he cried, laughing rather boisterously, "we'll play Puss in the Corner. You shall be Puss, and each time you get into a corner you shall have a halfpenny."

The boy made no audible reply, but danced about lightly in the twilight in the middle of the lane, while the smile flitted over his face like the reflections of an unseen lantern and the others ran wildly from corner to corner, till the imp had finally won sixpence. It was easy for him to win. The moment he made for a corner, its occupant fled screaming into the lane. It was impossible, they felt, to contest the points of a merely human game with such a creature of the shadows and the dusk.

Then occurred the strangest thing of all. The game was over and they were girding up their loins to follow the boy to the Black Horse first, and afterwards to their own inn, when, with a quick motion like the rush of a bird, he darted to the younger girl, flung down all the coppers into her hands, before she even guessed what he was about, whispered some words close to her face, uttered a shrill cry of laughter—and was gone!

"Oh, Oh!" she cried out, piteously—and this time there was real pain and terror in her voice. "Now I know! Now I know why I was afraid!"

She half fell backwards across a heap of broken stones, and the other two were swiftly at her side with sympathetic questions of alarm. But she was on her feet again in a second. She ran a few paces down the road to the spot where the boy had so mysteriously vanished.

None of them had seen exactly how he went, for one second he was there, and the next he was not there. That was all they knew.

The girl paused and held her hand to her side. She peered into the darkness.

"Harry!" she called faintly; and again with anguish in her voice, "Harry! Are you there?"

They were standing in the level space between the two sharp hills. In front of them, after an abrupt turn, the long white road seemed to run steeply into the sky. And it was down this hill that the coming bicyclist must shape his dangerous course.

"There!" she cried again suddenly, running to the side of the road where the hedge ceased, and an open gap led the sight as a single plunge into empty space. "Oh, I knew it, I knew it!"

And when the others joined her, and peered over the hedge they found themselves looking down into the chasm of a disused chalk pit, at the bottom of which in the faint glimmer of the lime and the starlight, lay the smashed bicycle, with the lifeless body of its rider outstretched beside it.

The Story Mr. Popkiss Told

Talking of railway accidents—"

"But we weren't," interrupted the prig.

"—and of narrow escapes," continued Mr. Popkiss, ignoring the contradictions, and looking like an offended parrot with its head on one side, "reminds me of one."

"Which?" enquired the prig smartly, "the railway accident or the narrow escape?" He was a small young man, with red eyes and a face like a weasel. He was also a "psychical student."

"Both," said Popkiss, looking at him over the top of his spectacles, and spreading out his coat-tails before the fire, so that he resembled more than ever a parrot, jaunty, yet slightly ruffled, swinging on its perch.

"Let's have the story," said Brown, in a tone of authority.

And the story began at once; for Brown was "the intellect" of the little party of newspaper men telling yarns round the club fireplace that deserted Christmas-week, when their duties held them in London after every one else had gone.

"It saved my life, so it *was* nearly an accident," continued Mr. Popkiss ambiguously, "and this is how it happened. *Most* odd, it was."

He buttoned his coat tightly, as though conscious that he resembled a bird, and anxious to dissemble the fact. He was a man of fifty, bald, shabby, timid, and kind-hearted—an unsuccessful solicitor.

"It was last year, on the Boxing Day after Christmas," he began in his high-pitched voice, "and I was in a third-class carriage, going down into Surrey for the New Year's week. I was alone, sitting by the window. It was after ten o'clock, and I was drowsy, but *not* asleep. The window streamed with rain. Outside, everything was black and raw and miserable—utterly cheerless. Just after leaving Wimbledon Station another train drew up alongside, and I watched it through the window of my corner-seat, trying to work up an interest, and wondering which would win. I imagined the two trains were racing—as one is apt to do at such times—and that all the passengers know it. But for a long time we ran an even race, neck and neck, and I remember thinking what a fool our engine-driver was not to put on steam and pull ahead.

"Faster and faster we went. It annoyed me that all these stupid passengers in the other train were so close to me, going to other destinations than mine. It seemed so dull and boring for them. You know the kind of foolish thoughts that wander up and down the mind at such time."

"Quite," said the psychical student; "quite!"

"And I was glad the windows were so blurred by rain that they couldn't see into my carriage—when, suddenly, I turned with a start and found that my own window was clear as crystal, and that I could see with the greatest ease into the carriage running close beside me. Something had sponged the windows clean. And in the corner-seat of that other carriage, so close to my elbow that I could have put my hand out and touched him, sat a man, huddled up in overcoats and rugs, just as I was."

Mr. Popkiss unbuttoned the top button of his coat to allow more freedom for possible gestures. The group of listeners stared with keen attention. The mind of the weasel-faced student was already busily searching for flaws by means of which he might tear the story to pieces the moment it was finished.

"Quite inexplicably," continued Mr. Popkiss, pitching his voice higher in key but lower in tone, "the figure of this man arrested my attention vividly—almost unpleasantly. The face was hidden by his hand, but there was something about him that made me reflect. It seemed to me that I knew who he was. Like myself, he was alone in an empty compartment. The curious idea entered my head that he was watching me through the fingers over his face; and a mysterious uneasiness I could not account for came over me.

"I made a movement forward to look at him through the middle window—and the man made a precisely similar movement. Through the middle windows of both carriages our eyes met, and in a flash I saw who it was—"

"You recognised him?" asked several voices together.

"I recognised him beyond all question: he was *myself!*" continued Mr. Popkiss, unfastening the second button of his coat; "absolutely myself!"

"Another Popkiss!" exclaimed the psychical student. "You mean a reflection, of course?"

"At first I thought it was a reflection, for the man copied exactly every movement I made—every single movement. I won't bore you with details; but everything I did in my carriage that man did also in his carriage. And yet"—Popkiss mopped his forehead and unfastened the last button—"there was something about him—something about that peering face with spectacles—about the silent movements and shadowy appearance—that woke a nameless terror in me. I began to perspire all over. And something in me, too, began to tremble. Each time I turned to look, there he stood, his arms placed precisely as mine were placed, his body in the same attitude exactly, and his spectacled eyes staring straight into my own."

His voice sank to the whisper as he said this. Every one listened breathlessly. "A projection of your own Double," murmured the student, "or a condition of hysteria inducing a vision"; but no one paid any attention to him.

"Yes, and this is how it happened," resumed Popkiss, passing a hand over his bald head, as though the world was so strange a place that it would not have surprised him to find unexpected tufts upon that marble surface, "and I never can persuade you how dreadfully queer I felt.

"Then, suddenly, an idea came to me just as the two trains were slowing down, still running neck and neck. I *opened the window!* The other man did the same. We put our heads out. There was no question of reflection then. I had to cling to the window-sides to prevent myself falling, so great was the shock. For, instead of disappearing, as a reflection must have disappeared, the face of this other man suddenly flamed up through the night in most amazing fashion; and, thrusting his head forward so that we almost touched one another, I heard his whisper fly sharply across to me through the darkness. The words came with a sense of most appalling reality, and it seemed to me that a wind of ice and snow passed over my cheeks.

"'*Leave this train!*' he said, above the rattle of the metals. '*Leave this train!*'

"And the very next second, before I could answer, or do anything at all, the lights in *his* carriage were extinguished and the train was running beside me in black darkness!

"But was it running beside me? That was the queer part of it. Was it still keeping up a neck-and-neck race with my own? For when I put my head further out to look, and as soon as my eyes got accustomed to the gloom, lo and behold, there was no train at all! Both in front and behind the lines were clear. There was no train, and no sign of one. . . . Five minutes later we ran into Woking Junction."

The psychical student longed to say something, but his mind was so confused with such phrases as "double personality," "veridical dreams," "subliminal consciousness," and the like, that before he could squeeze out a word Mr. Popkiss was at it again, finishing his story:

"It would be impossible to describe to you how, and why, the whole thing impressed me," he explained softly, "that I actually *did* leave the train at Woking Junction, although my destination was several stations further on. . . . All I can tell you is that the train itself—*my* train—ran off the metals before it had gone another mile down the line, and two people were killed outright and a dozen injured terribly. . . . I had to sleep at Woking and go on next day when the débris was cleared away. . . ."

He buttoned up his coat again very quickly, and touched the bell for the waiter.

"Queer, wasn't it?" he observed, looking round him with a thirsty sigh.

Involved discussion followed in a torrent, during the course of which the psychical student gave the group the benefit of much laboured explanation. A world in which he could not explain everything by the processes of his own acute little mind was intolerable to him. And when the others, led by Brown, made difficulties, he fell back upon the delightful generalisation that "to imagine such things at all was a sure sign of mental degeneration. . . ."

"What do you think of it yourself?" he asked at length of the story-teller.

"I?" said Popkiss deprecatingly; "oh, I don't think anything at all. It saved my life—and that's enough for me!"

He handed a cigarette to the student, who "didn't drink," and set back in his chair to listen to the next tale.

Entrance and Exit

These three—the old physicist, the girl, and the young Anglican parson who was engaged to her—stood by the window of the country house. The blinds were not yet drawn. They could see the dark clump of pines in the field, with crests silhouetted against the pale wintry sky of the February afternoon. Snow, freshly fallen, lay upon lawn and hill. A big moon was already lighting up.

"Yes, that's the wood," the old man said, "and it was this very day fifty years ago—February 13—the man disappeared from its shadows; swept in this extraordinary, incredible fashion into invisibility—*into some other place*. Can you wonder the grove is haunted?" A strange impressiveness of manner belied the laugh following the words.

"Oh, please tell us," the girl whispered; "we're all alone now." Curiosity triumphed; yet a vague alarm betrayed itself in the questioning glance she cast for protection at her younger companion, whose fine face, on the other hand, wore an expression that was grave and singularly "rapt." He was listening keenly.

"As though Nature," the physicist went on, half to himself, "here and there concealed vacuums, gaps, holes in space (his mind was always speculative; more than speculative, some said), through which a man might drop into invisibility—a new direction, in fact, at right angles to the three known ones—'higher space,' as Bolyai, Gauss, and Hinton might call it; and what you, with your mystical turn"—looking toward the young priest—"might consider a spiritual change of condition, into a region where space and time do not exist, and where all dimensions are possible—because they are *one*."

"But, *please,* the story," the girl begged, not understanding these dark sayings, "although I'm not sure that Arthur ought to hear it. He's much too interested in such queer things as it is!" Smiling, yet uneasy, she stood closer to his side, as though her body might protect his soul.

"Very briefly, then, you shall hear what I remember of this haunting, for I was barely ten years old at the time. It was evening—clear and cold like this, with snow and moonlight—when some one reported to my father that a peculiar sound, variously described as crying, singing, wailing, was being heard in the grove. He paid no attention until my sister heard it too, and was frightened. Then he sent a groom to investigate. Though the night was brilliant the man took a lantern. We watched from this very window till we lost his figure against the trees, and the lantern stopped swinging suddenly, as if he had put it down. It remained motionless. We waited half an hour, and then my father, curiously excited, I remember, went out quickly, and I, utterly terrified, went after him. We followed his tracks, which came to an end beside the lantern, the last step being a stride almost impossible for a man to have made. All around the snow was unbroken by a single mark, but the man himself had vanished. Then we heard him calling for help—above, behind, beyond us; from all directions at once, yet from none, came the sound of his voice; but though we called back he made no answer, and gradually his cries grew fainter and fainter, as if going into tremendous distance, and at last died away altogether."

"And the man himself?" asked both listeners.

"Never returned—from that day to this has never bear seen. . . . At intervals for weeks and months afterwards reports came in that he was still heard crying, always crying for help. With time, even these reports ceased—for most of us," he added under his breath; "and that is all I know. A mere outline, as you see."

The girl did not quite like the story, for the old man's manner made it too convincing. She was half disappointed, half frightened.

"See! there are the others coming home," she exclaimed, with a note of relief, pointing to a group of figures moving over the snow near the pine trees. "Now we can think of tea!" She crossed the room to busy herself with the friendly tray as the servant approached to fasten the shutters. The young priest, however, deeply interested, talked on with their host, though in a voice almost too low for her to hear. Only the final sentences reached her, making her uneasy—absurdly so, she thought—till afterwards.

"—for matter, as we know, interpenetrates matter," she heard, "and two objects may conceivably occupy the same space. The odd thing really is that one should hear, but not see; that air-waves should bring the voice, yet ether-waves fail to bring the picture."

And then the older man: "—as if certain places in Nature, yes, invited the change—places where these extraordinary forces stir from the earth as from the surface of a living Being with organs—places like islands, mountain-tops, pine-woods, especially pines isolated from their kind. You know the queer results of digging absolutely virgin soil, of course—and that theory of the earth's being *alive*—" The voice dropped again.

"States of mind also helping the forces of the place," she caught the priest's reply in part; "such as conditions induced by music, by intense listening, by certain moments in the Mass even—by ecstasy or—"

"I say, what *do* you think?" cried a girl's voice, as the others came in with welcome charter and odours of tweeds and open fields. "As we passed your old haunted pine-wood we heard *such* a queer noise. Like some one wailing or crying. Cæsar howled and ran; and Harry refused to go in and investigate. He positively funked it!" They all laughed. "More like a rabbit in a trap than a person crying," explained Harry, a blush kindly concealing his startling pallor. "I wanted my tea too much to bother about an old rabbit."

It was some time after tea when the girl became aware that the priest had disappeared, and putting two and two together, ran in alarm to her host's study. Quite easily, from the hastily opened shutters, they saw his figure moving across the snow. The moon was very bright over the world, yet he carried a lantern that shone pale yellow against the white

"Oh, for God's sake, quick!" she cried, pale with fear. "Quick! or we're too late! Arthur's simply wild about such things. Oh, I might have known—I might have guessed. And this is the very night. I'm terrified!"

By the time he had found his overcoat and slipped round the house with her from the back door, the lantern, they saw, was already swinging close to the pine-wood. The night was still as ice, bitterly cold. Breathlessly they ran, following the tracks. Half-way his steps diverged, and were plainly visible in the virgin snow by themselves. They heard the whispering of the branches ahead of them, for pines cry even when no airs stir. "Follow me close," said the old man sternly.

The lantern, he already saw, lay upon the ground unattended; no human figure was anywhere visible.

"See! The steps come to an end here," he whispered, stooping
down as soon as they reached the lantern. The tracks, hitherto so regular, showed an odd wavering—the snow curiously disturbed. Quite
suddenly they stopped. The final step was a very long one—a stride,
almost immense, "as though he was pushed forward from behind,"
muttered the old man, too low to be overheard, "or sucked forward
from in front—as in a fall."

The girl would have dashed forward but for his strong restraining
grasp. She clutched him, uttering a sudden dreadful cry. "Hark! I hear
his voice!" she almost sobbed. They stood still to listen. A mystery that
was more than the mystery of night closed about their hearts—a mystery that is beyond life and death, that only great awe and terror can
summon from the deeps of the soul. Out of the heart of the trees, fifty
feet away, issued a crying voice, half wailing, half singing, very faint.
"Help! help!" it sounded through the still night; "for the love of God,
pray for me!"

The melancholy rustling of the pines followed; and then again the
singular crying voice shot past above their heads, now in front of
them, now once more behind. It sounded everywhere. It grew fainter
and fainter, fading away, it seemed, into distance that somehow was
appalling. . . . The grove, however, was empty of all but the sighing
wind; the snow unbroken by any tread. The moon threw inky shadows; the cold bit; it was a terror of ice and death and this awful singing
cry. . . .

"But why *pray?*" screamed the girl, distracted, frantic with her bewildered terror. "Why *pray?* Let us *do* something to help—*do* something
. . . !" She swung round in a circle, nearly falling to the ground. Suddenly she perceived that the old man had dropped to his knees in the
snow beside her and was—praying.

"Because the forces of prayer, of thought, of the will to help, alone
can reach and succour him where he now is," was all the answer she
got. And a moment later both figures were kneeling in the snow, praying, so to speak, their very heart's life out. . . .

The search may be imagined—the steps taken by police, friends,
newspapers, by the whole country in fact. . . . But the most curious

part of this queer "Higher Space" adventure is the end of it—at least, the "end" so far as at present known. For after three weeks, when the winds of March were a-roar about the land, there crept over the fields towards the house the small dark figure of a man. He was thin, pallid as a ghost, worn and fearfully emaciated, but upon his face and in his eyes were traces of an astonishing radiance—a glory unlike anything ever seen. . . . It may, of course, have been deliberate, or it may have been a genuine loss of memory only; none could say—least of all the girl whom his return snatched from the gates of death; but, at any rate, what had come to pass during the interval of his amazing disappearance he has never yet been able to reveal.

"And you must never ask me," he would say to her—and repeat even after his complete and speedy restoration to bodily health—"for I simply cannot tell. I know no language, you see, that could express it. I was near you all the time. But I was also—elsewhere and otherwise . . ."

You *May* Telephone from Here

She sent the servant to bed at half-past ten, and sat up in the flat alone. "I'll let my cousin in," she explained; "she may be rather late." She read, knitted, began a letter, poked the fire, and examined her husband's photographs on the mantelpiece; but most of the time she looked about her nervously, sometimes going to the door to listen, sometimes lifting the corner of the blind to look out upon the lights of North Kensington struggling with the blackness. The fog was thicker than ever. A rumble of traffic feeling its way floated up to her from below.

But at last the door-bell rang sharply, and she ran to let in the cousin who had promised to spend the two nights with her during her husband's absence in Paris. They kissed. Both began talking at once.

"I thought you were *never* coming, Sybil—!"

"The play was out late—and the fog's bad. I sent on my box this afternoon on purpose."

"It came safely; and your room's quite ready. I do hope you'll manage all right without a maid. Oh, I'm *so* glad you've come, though!"

"Foolish little country mouse!"

"Oh, it's not that so much, though I admit that London still terrifies me at night rather; but you know this is the first time he's been away—and I suppose—"

"I know, dear; I understand perfectly." The cousin was brisk and cheerful. "You feel lonely, of course." They kissed again. "Just unhook me, will you?" she added, "and I'll get into my dressing-gown, and then we'll be cosy over the fire."

"I saw him off at Victoria at 8.45," said the little wife when the operation was over.

"Newhaven and Dieppe?"

"Yes. He gets to Paris at seven in the morning. He promised to telephone the first thing."

"You expensive little monkey!"

"Why?"

"It's ten shillings for three minutes, or something like that, and you have to go to the G.P.O. or the Mansion House or some such place, I believe."

"But I thought it was the usual long-distance thing direct here to the flat. He never told me all that."

"Probably you didn't give him the chance!"

They laughed, and went on chatting, with feet on the fender and skirts tucked up. The cousin lit her second cigarette. It was after midnight.

"I'm afraid I'm not the least bit sleepy," said the wife apologetically.

"Nor am I, dear. For once the play excited me." She began to describe it vigorously. Half-way through the recital the telephone sounded in the hall. It tinkled faintly, but gave no proper ring.

The other started. "There it is again! It's always doing that—ever since Harry put it in a week ago. I don't quite like it." She spoke in a hushed voice.

The cousin looked at her curiously. "Oh, you mustn't mind that," she laughed with a reassuring manner. "It's a little way they have when the line gets out of order. You're not used to playing the telephone game yet. You should call up the Exchange and complain. Always complain, you know, in this world if you want—"

"There it goes again," interrupted her friend nervously. "Oh, I do wish it would stop. It's so like some one standing out there in the hall and trying to talk—"

The cousin jumped up. They went into the hall together, and the experienced one briskly rang up the Exchange and asked if there was anybody trying to "get through." With fine indignation she complained that no one in the flat could sleep for the noise. After a brief conversation she turned, receiver in hand, to her companion.

"The operator says he's very sorry, but your line's a bit troublesome to-night for some reason. Got mixed, or something. He can't understand it. Advises you to leave the receiver unhooked till the morning. Then it can't possibly ring, you see!"

They left the receiver swinging, and went back to the fire.

"I'm sorry I'm such a timid donkey," the wife said, laughing a little;

"but I'm not used to it yet. There was no telephone at the farm, you know." She turned with a sudden start, as though she heard the bell again. "And to-night," she added in a lower voice, though with an obvious effort at self-control, "for some reason or other I feel uncomfortable, rather—excited, queer, I think."

"How? Queer?"

"I don't know exactly; almost as if there was some one else in the flat—some one besides ourselves and the servant, I mean."

The cousin moved abruptly. She switched on the electric lights in the wall beside her.

"Yes; but it's only imagination, *really*," she said with decision. "It's natural enough. It's the fog and the strangeness of London after the loneliness of your farm-life, and your husband being away, and—and all that. Once you analyse these queer feelings they always go—"

"Hark!" exclaimed the wife under her breath. "Wasn't that a step in the passage?" She sat bolt upright, her face pale, her eyes very bright. They listened a moment. The night was utterly still about them.

"Rubbish!" cried the cousin loudly. "It was my foot knocking the fender; like this—look!" She repeated the sound vigorously.

"I do believe it was," the other said, only half convinced. "But it *is* queer. You know I feel exactly as though some one had come into the flat—quite recently, since *you* came, I mean—just before that tinkling began, in fact."

"Come, come," laughed the cousin, "you'll give us both the jumps. At one o'clock in the morning it's easy to imagine anything. You'll be hearing elephants on the stairs next!" She looked sharply about her. "Let's brew our chocolate and get to bed," she added. "We shall sleep like tops."

"One o'clock already! Then Harry's half-way across by now," said the wife, smiling at her friend's language. "But I'm *so* glad, oh, *so* glad, you're here," she added; "and I think it's most awfully sweet of you to give up a comfy big house . . ." They kissed again and laughed. Soon afterwards, having scalded their throats with hot chocolate, they went to bed.

"It simply *can't* ring now!" remarked the cousin triumphantly as they passed the receiver dangling in mid-air.

"That's a relief," her friend said. "I feel less nervous. Really, I'm too ashamed of myself for anything."

"Fog's clearing, too," Sybil added, peering for a moment through the narrow window by the front door.

An hour later the little flat was still as the grave. No sound of traffic was heard. Even the tinkling of the telephone seemed a whole twenty-four hours away, when suddenly—it began again: first with little soft tentative noises, very faint, troubled, hurried, buried almost out of hearing inside the box; then louder and louder, with sharp jerks—finally with a challenging and alarming peal. And the wife, who had kept her door open, without pretence of sleep, heard it from the very beginning. In a moment she found herself in the passage, and Sybil, wakened by her cry, was at her heels. They turned up the lights and stood facing one another. The hall smelt—as things only smell at night—cold, musty . . .

"What's the matter? You frightened me. I heard you scream—!"

The telephone's ringing again—violently," the wife whispered, pale to the lips. "Don't you hear it? This time there's some one there—*really!*"

The cousin stared blankly at her. The laugh choked in her throat. "*I* hear nothing," she said defiantly, yet without confidence in her voice. "Besides, the thing's still disconnected. It *can't* ring—look!" She pointed to the hanging receiver motionless against the wall. "You're white as a ghost, though," she added, coming quickly forward. Her friend moved suddenly to the instrument and picked up the receiver. "It's some one for me," she said, with terror in her eyes. "It's some one who wants to talk to me! Oh, hark! hark how it rings!" Her voice shook. She placed the little disc to her ear and waited while her friend stood by and stared in amazement, uncertain what to do. *She* had heard no ringing!

"You, Harry!" whispered the wife into the telephone, with brief intervals of silence for the replies. "*You?* But how in the world so soon?—Yes, I can just hear, but very faintly. Miles and miles away your voice sounds—What?—A wonderful journey? And sooner than you expected!—*Not* in Paris? Where, then?—Oh! my darling boy—No, I don't quite hear; I can't catch it—I don't understand. . . . The pain of the sea is nothing—is *what?* . . . You know nothing of *what* . . . ?"

The cousin came boldly up. She took her arm. "But, child, there's no one there, bless you! You're dreaming—you're in fever or something—"

"Hush! For God's sake, hush!" She held up a hand. In her face and eyes was an expression indescribable—fear, love, bewilderment. Her body swayed a little, leaning against the wall. "Hush! I hear him still; but, oh! miles and miles away—He says—he's been trying for hours to find me. First he tried my brain direct, and then—then—oh! he says he may not get back again to me—only he can't understand, can't explain *why*—the cold, the awful cold, keeps his lips from— Oh!"

She screamed aloud as she flung the receiver down and dropped in a heap upon the floor. "I don't understand—it's death, death!" . . .

And the collision in the Channel that night, as they learned in due course, occurred a few minutes after one o'clock; while Harry himself, who remained unconscious for several hours after the boat picked him up, could only remember that his last desire as the wave caught him was an intense wish to communicate with his wife and tell her what had happened. . . . The next thing he knew was opening his eyes in a Dieppe hotel.

And the other curious detail was furnished by the man who came to repair the telephone next day. At the Exchange, he declared, the wire, from midnight till nearly three in the morning, had emitted sparks and flashes of light no one had been able to account for in any usual manner.

"Queer!" said the man to himself, after tinkering and tapping for ten minutes, "but there's nothing wrong with it at *this* end. It's the subscriber, most likely. It usually is!"

The Invitation

They bumped into one another by the swinging doors of the little Soho restaurant, and, recoiling sharply, each made a half-hearted pretence of lifting his hat (it was French manners, of course, *inside*). Then, discovering that they were English, and not strangers, they exclaimed, "Sorry!" and laughed.

"Hulloa! It's Smith!" cried the man with the breezy manner; "and when did *you* get back?" It sounded as though "Smith" and *"you"* were different persons. "I haven't seen you for months!" They shook hands cordially.

"Only last Saturday—on the *Rollitania*," answered the man with the pince-nez. They were acquaintances of some standing. Neither was aware of anything in the other he disliked. More positive cause for friendship there was none. They met, however, not infrequently.

"Last Saturday! Did you really?" exclaimed the breezy one; and, after an imperceptible pause which suggested nothing more vital, he added, "And had a good time in America, eh?"

"Oh! not bad, thanks—not bad at all." He likewise was conscious of a rather barren pause. "Awful crossing, though," he threw in a few seconds later with a slight grimace.

"Ah! At this time of year, you know—" said Breezy, shaking his head knowingly; "though *sometimes*, of course, one has better trips in winter than in summer. I crossed once in December when it was like a mill-pond the whole blessed way."

They moved a little to one side to let a group of Frenchmen enter the swinging doors.

"It's a good line," he added, in a voice that settled the reputation of the steamship company for ever. "By Jove, it's a good line."

"Oh! it's a good line, yes," agreed Pince-nez, gratified to find his choice approved. He shifted his glasses modestly. The discovery reflected glory upon his judgment. "*And* such an excellent table!"

Breezy agreed heartily. "I'd never cross now on any other," he declared, as though he meant the table. "You're right."

This happy little agreement about the food pleased them both; it showed their judgment to be sound; also it established a ground of common interest—a link—something that gave point to their little chat, and made it seem worth while to have stopped and spoken. They rose in one another's estimation. The chance meeting ought to lead to something, perhaps. Yet neither found the expected inspiration; for neither *au fond* had anything to say to the other beyond passing the time of day.

"Well," said Pince-nez, lingeringly but very pleasantly, making a movement towards the doors; "I suppose I must be going in. You—er—you've had lunch, of course? "

"Thanks, yes, I have," Breezy replied with a certain air of disappointment, as though the question had been an invitation. He moved a few steps backwards down the pavement. "But, now you're back," he added more cheerfully, "we must try and see something of one another."

"By all means. Do let's," said Pince-nez. His manner somehow suggested that he too expected an invitation, perhaps. He hesitated a moment, as though about to add something, but in the end said nothing.

"We must lunch together one day," observed Breezy, with his jolly smile. He glanced up at the restaurant.

"By all means—let's," agreed the other again, with one foot on the steps. "Any day you like. Next week, perhaps. You let me know." He nodded cordially, and half turned to enter.

"Lemme see, where are you staying?" called Breezy by way of afterthought.

"Oh! I'm at the X——," mentioning an obscure hostel in the W.C. district.

"Of course; yes, I remember. That's where you stopped before, isn't it? Up in Bloomsbury somewhere—?"

"Rooms ain't up to much, but the cooking's *quite* decent."

"Good. Then we'll lunch one day soon. What sort of time, by the bye, suits you?" The breezy one, for some obscure reason, looked vigorously at his watch.

"Oh! any time; one o'clock onwards, sort of thing, I suppose?"

with an air of "just let me know and I'll be there."

"Same here, yes," agreed the other, with slightly less enthusiasm.

"That's capital, then," from Pince-nez. He paused a moment, not finding precisely the suitable farewell phrase. Then, to his own undoing, he added carelessly, "There are one or two things—er—I should like to tell you about—"

"And luncheon *is* the best time," Breezy suggested at once, "for busy men like us. You might bespeak a table, in fact." He jerked his head towards the restaurant.

The two acquaintances, one on the pavement, the other on the steps, stood and stared at each other. The onus of invitation had somehow shifted insensibly from Breezy to Pince-nez. The next remark would be vital. Neither thought it worth while to incur the slight expense of a luncheon that involved an hour in each other's company. Yet it was nothing stronger than a dread of possible boredom that dictated the hesitancy.

"Not a bad idea," agreed Pince-nez vaguely. "But I doubt if they'll keep a table after one o'clock, you know."

"Never mind, then. You're on the telephone, I suppose, aren't you?" called Breezy down the pavement, still moving slowly backwards.

"Yes, you'll find it under the name of the hotel," replied the other, putting his head back round the door-post in the act of going in.

"My number's *not* in the book!" Breezy cried back; "but it's 0417 Westminster. Then you'll ring me up one day? That'll be very jolly indeed. *Don't forget the number!*" This shifting of telephonic responsibility, he felt, was a master-stroke.

"Right-O. I'll remember. So long, then, for the present," Pince-nez answered more faintly, disappearing into the restaurant.

"Decent fellow, that. I shall go to lunch if he asks me," was the thought in the mind of each. It lasted for perhaps half a minute, and then—oblivion.

Ten days later they ran across one another again about luncheon-time in Piccadilly; nodded, smiled, hesitated a second too long—and turned back to shake hands.

"How's everything?" asked the breezy one with gusto.

"First-rate, thanks. And how are *you?*"

"Jolly weather, isn't it?" Breezy said, looking about him generally, "this sunshine—by Jove—!"

"Nothing like it," declared Pince-nez, shifting his glasses to look at the sun, and concealing his lack of something to say by catching at the hearty manner.

"Nothing," agreed Breezy.

"In the world," echoed Pince-nez.

Again the topic was a link. The stream of pedestrians jostled them. They moved a few yards up Dover Street. Each was really on his way to luncheon. A pause followed the move.

"Still at—er—that hotel up there?" The name had escaped him. He jerked his head vaguely northwards.

"Yes; I thought you'd be looking in for lunch one day," a faint memory stirring in his brain.

"Delighted! Or—you'd better come to my Club, eh? Less out of the way, you know," declared Breezy.

"Very jolly. Thanks; that'd be first-rate." Both paused a moment. Breezy looked down the street as though expecting some one or something. They ignored that it was luncheon hour.

"You'll find me in the telephone book," observed Pince-nez presently.

"Under X—— Hotel, I suppose?" from Breezy. "All right."

"0995 Northern's the number, yes."

"And mine," said Breezy, "is 0417 Westminster; or the Club"— with an air of imparting valuable private information—"is 0866 Mayfair. Any day you like. Don't forget!"

"Rather not. Somewhere about one o'clock, eh?"

"Yes—or one-thirty." And off they went again—each to his solitary luncheon.

A fortnight passed, and once more they came together—this time in an A.B.C. shop.

"Hulloa! There's Smith," thought Breezy. "By Jove, I'll ask him to lunch with me."

"Why, there's that chap again," thought Pince-nez. "I'll invite him, I think."

They sat down at the same table. "But this is capital," exclaimed both; "you must lunch with me, of course!" And they laughed pleasantly. They talked of food and weather. They compared Soho with A.B.C. Each offered light excuses for being found in the latter.

"I was in a hurry to-day, and looked in by the merest chance for a cup of coffee," observed Breezy, ordering quite a lot of things at once, absent-mindedly, as it were.

"I like the butter here so awfully," mentioned Pince-nez later. "It's *quite* the best in London, and the freshest, I always think." As this was not *the* luncheon, they felt that only commonplace things were in order. The special things they had to discuss must wait, of course.

The waitress got their paper checks muddled somehow. "I've put a 'alfpenny of yours on 'is," she explained cryptically to Pince-nez.

"Oh," laughed Breezy, "that's nothing. This gentleman is lunching with me, anyhow."

"You'll 'ave to make it all right when you get outside, then," said the girl gravely.

They laughed over her reply. At the pay-desk both made vigorous search for money. Pince-nez, being nimbler, produced a florin first. "This is *my* lunch, of course. I asked you, remember," he said. Breezy demurred with a good grace.

"You can be host another time, if you insist," added Pince-nez, pocketing twopence change.

"Rather," said the other heartily. "You must come to the Club— any day you like, you know."

"I'll come to-morrow, then," said Pince-nez, quick as a flash. "I've got the telephone number."

"Do," cried Breezy, very, very heartily indeed. "I shall be delighted! One o'clock, remember."

The Lease

The other day I came across my vague friend again. Last time it was in an A.B.C. shop; this time it was in a bus. We always meet in humble places.

He was vaguer than ever, fuddled and distrait; but delightfully engaging. He had evidently not yet lunched, for he wore no crumb; but I had a shrewd suspicion that beneath his green Alpine hat there lurked a straw or two in his untidy hair. It would hardly have surprised me to see him turn with his childlike smile and say, "Would you mind *very much* taking them out for me? You know they *do* tickle so!"—half mumbled, half shouted.

Instead, he tried to shake hands, and his black eyebrows danced. He looked as loosely put together as a careless parcel. I imagined large bits of him tumbling out.

"You're off somewhere or other, I suppose?" he said; and the question was so characteristic it was impossible not to laugh.

I mentioned the City.

"I'm going that way too," he said cheerfully. He had come to the conclusion that he could not shake hands with safety; there were too many odds and ends about him—gloves, newspapers, half-open umbrella, parcels. Evidently he had left the house uncertain as to where he was going, and had brought all these things in case, like the White Knight, he might find a use for them on the way. His overcoat was wrongly buttoned, too, so that on one side the collar reached almost to his ear. From the pockets protruded large envelopes, white and blue. I marvelled again how he ever concentrated his mind enough to write plays and novels; for in both the action was quick and dramatic; the dialogue crisp, forcible, often witty.

"Going to the City!" I exclaimed. *"You?"* Museums, libraries, second-hand book-shops were his usual haunts—places where he could be vague and absent-minded without danger to any one. I felt genuinely curious. "Copy of some kind? Local colour for something, eh?" I laughed, hoping to draw him out.

A considerable pause followed, during which he rearranged several of his parcels, and his eyebrows shot up and down like two black-beetles dancing a hornpipe.

"I'm helping a chap with his lease," he replied, suddenly, in such a very loud voice that everybody in the bus heard and became interested.

He had this way of alternately mumbling and talking very loud—absurdly loud; picking out unimportant words with terrific emphasis. He also had this way of helping others. Indeed, it was difficult to meet him without suspecting an errand of kindness—rarely mentioned, however.

"Chap with his lease," he repeated in a kind of roar, as though he feared some one had not heard him—the driver, possibly!

We were in a white Putney bus, going East. The policeman just then held it up at Wellington Street.

"It's jolly stopping like this," he cried; "one can chat a bit without having to shout."

My curiosity about the lease, or rather about his part in it, prevented an immediate reply. How he could possibly help in such a complicated matter puzzled me exceedingly.

"Horrible things, leases!" I said at length. "Confusing, I mean, with their endless repetitions and absence of commas. Legal language seems so needlessly—"

"Oh, but this one is right enough," he interrupted. "You see, my pal hasn't signed it yet. He's in rather a muddle about it, to tell the truth, and I'm going to get it straightened out by my solicitor."

The bus started on with a lurch, and he rolled against me.

"It's a three-year lease," he roared, "with an option to renew, you know—oh no, I'm wrong there, by the bye," and he tapped my knee and dropped a glove, and, when it was picked up and handed to him, tried to stuff it up his sleeve as though it was a handkerchief—"I'm wrong there—that's the house he's in at present, and his wife wants to break *that* lease because she doesn't like it, and they've got more children than they expected (these words whispered), and there's no bath-room, and the kitchen stairs are absurdly narrow—"

"But the lease—you were just saying—?"

"Quite so; I was," and both eyebrows dropped so that the eyes were almost completely hidden, "but *that* lease *is* all right. It's the other one I was talking about just then—"

"The house he's in now, you mean, or—?" My head already swam. The attention of the people opposite had begun to wander.

My friend pulled himself together and clutched several parcels.

"No, no, no," he explained, smiling gently; "he likes *this* one. It's the other I meant—the one his wife doesn't approve of—the one with the narrow bathroom stairs and no kitchen—I mean the narrow kitchen stairs and no bathroom. It has so few cupboards, too, and the nursery chimneys smoke every time the wind's in the east. (Poor man! How devotedly he must have listened while it was being drummed into his good-natured ears!) So you see, Henry, my pal, thought of giving it up when the lease fell in and taking this other house—the one I was just talking about—and putting in a bathroom at his own expense, provided the landlord—"

A man opposite who had been listening intently got up to leave the bus with such a disappointed look that my friend thought it was the conductor asking for another fare, and fumbled for coppers. Seeing his mistake in time, he drew out instead a large blue envelope. Two other papers, feeling neglected, came out at the same time and dropped upon the floor. My friend and a working-man beside him stooped to pick them up and knocked their heads violently in the process.

"I *beg* your pardon," exclaimed the vague one, very loud, with a tremendous emphasis on the "beg."

"Oh, that's all right, guv'nor," said the working-man, handing over the papers. "Might 'appen to anybody, that!"

"I beg your pardon?" repeated my friend, not hearing him quite.

"I said a thing like that might 'appen to any one," repeated the other, louder.

He turned to me with his happy smile. "I suppose it might, yes," he said, very low. Then he opened the blue envelope and began to hunt.

"Oh no, that's the wrong envelope. It's the other," he observed vaguely. "What a bore, isn't it? This is merely a copy of his letters to—er—to—"

He looked distressingly about him through the windows, as though he hoped to find his words in the shop-letterings or among the advertisements.

"Where are we, I wonder? Oh yes; there's St. Paul's. Good!" His mind returned to the subject in hand. Several people got out, and swept the papers from his knee to the ground; and the next few minutes he spent gathering them up, stooping, clutching his coat, stuffing envelopes into his pockets, and exclaiming "I *beg* your pardon!" to the various folk he collided with in the process.

At last some sort of order was restored.

"—merely the letters," he resumed where he had left off, and in a voice that might suitably have addressed a public meeting, "the letters to his tenant. There's a tenant in the other house. I forgot to mention *that*, I think—"

"I think you did. But, I say, look here, my dear chap," I burst out, at length, in sheer self-preservation, "why in the world don't you let the fellow manage his own leases? It's giving you a dreadful lot of trouble. It's the most muddled-up thing I ever heard."

"That's because you've got no head for business," he whispered sweetly. "Besides, it's really a pleasure to me to help him. That's the best part of life, after all—helping people who get into muddles." He looked at me with his kindly smile. Then he turned and smiled at everybody in the bus—vaguely, happily, his black eyebrows very fierce. Several people, I fancied, smiled back at him.

"Let's see," he said, after a pause; " where was I?"

"You were saying something about a lease," I told him; "but, honestly, old man, I'm afraid I haven't quite followed it."

"That's my fault," he said; "all my fault. I feel a bit stupid to-day. I've got the 'flue, you know, and a touch of fever with it. But I promised Henry I would see to it for him, because he's awfully busy—"

"Is he really!" I wished I knew Henry. I felt a strong desire to say something to him.

"—packing up for a trip to Mexico, you know, or something; so, of course, he finds it difficult to—er—to—" He looked gently about him. "Where the deuce am I?" he asked in a very loud voice indeed.

Several people, myself among them, mentioned the Mansion House.

"Dear me!" he exclaimed, gathering up parcels, envelopes, and various loose parts of his body—his aching body, I'm afraid—"I must be getting out. I'm in the wrong bus. I wanted Essex Street—up there by the Law Courts, you know."

But I really couldn't stand it any longer. I took him by the arm and planted him, parcels, papers, and all, by my side in a taxi. We whizzed back along Queen Victoria Street, and on the way I sorted him out, buttoned his overcoat so that it no longer tickled his ear, rolled up his umbrella so that the points no longer got caught, and made him put on both gloves, so that he could not drop them any more. And I kept tight hold of him until we reached Essex Street. He talked leases the whole way.

"Thanks awfully," he said at the end, smiling; "you're always kind—if a little rough. But I'll keep on the taxi, I think, now. The fact is, I find I've left the right lease at home after all—you know, the one about the house without the———"

I heard the rest, alternately mumbled and shouted at me, as the taxi whirred off into the Strand, bound for some unknown destination in Chelsea. It was impossible to help him more. But I should like to have heard what he said to (*a*) the chauffeur at the end of his journey, (*b*) to the solicitor. I should also like to swear that when he got back to his rooms he found the right lease had been in his pocket all the time.

I met him again the following day, but I had not the courage to ask him anything.

Faith Cure on the Channel

A letter from my vague friend was always a source of difficulty: it allowed of so many interpretations—contradictory often. But this one was comparatively plain sailing:—

"You said you were going abroad about this time. So am I. Let's go as far as Paris together. Send me a line to above address at once. Thursday or Friday would suit me.—Yours, X. Y. Z.

" P.S.—I enclose P.O. for that 10s. I owe you."

I received this letter on a Wednesday morning.

It was written from the Club, but the Club address was carefully scored out and no other given.

The "P.O." was not enclosed.

In spite of these obstacles, however, we somehow met and arranged to start on Saturday; and the night before we dined together in that excellent little Soho restaurant—"there's nothing," my friend always said, "between its cooking and the Ritz, except prices"—and discussed our prospects, he going to finish a book at a Barbizon inn, I to inspect certain machinery in various Continental dairies.

His heart, it was plain, however, was neither in the cooking nor the book, nor in my wonderful machinery. Like a boy with a secret, he was mysterious about something hitherto unshared. Happy, too, for he kept smiling at nothing.

"The fact is," he observed at last over coffee, "I'm really a vile, simply a vile sailor."

"I remember," I said, for we had once been companions on the same yacht.

"And you," he added, holding the black eyebrows steady, "you—are another." When dealing with simple truths he was often brutally frank.

"What's the good of talking about it?"

"This," he replied, paying the bill and giving me the amount of the

" P.O.," "I'll show you."

He conducted me into a little box of a place bearing the legend outside "Foreign Chemist," and proceeded first to buy the most curious assortment of strange medicines I ever heard of. Weird indeed must have been his ailments. I had no time for reflection, however, on the point, for suddenly turning to me by way of introduction, and allowing the eyebrow next the chemist to dance and bristle so as to attract his attention, he mumbled, "This is my seasick friend. We're off to-morrow. If you've got the stuff ready we might take it now." And, before I had time to ask or argue, he had pocketed a little package and we were in the street again.

Never had I known him so brisk and practical. "It's a new seasick cure," he explained darkly as we went home; "something quite new— just invented, in fact; and that chap's asking a few of his special customers to try it and give their honest opinions. So I told him we were pretty bad—vile, in fact—and I've got this for nothing. He only wants vile sailors, you see, otherwise there's no test—"

"Know what's in it?"

He shook his head so violently that I was afraid for the eyebrows.

"But I believe in it. It's simply wonderful stuff; no bromide, he assured me, and no harmful drugs. Just a seasick cure; that's all!"

"I'll take it if you will," I laughed. "I could take poison with impunity before going on the Channel!"

He gave me one bottle. "Take a dose to-night," he explained, "another after breakfast in the morning, another in the train, and another the moment you go on board."

I gave my promise and we separated on his doorstep. It was a lot to promise, but as I have explained, I could drink tar or prussic acid before going on a steamer, and neither would have the time to work injury. I marvelled greatly, however, at my vague friend's fit of abnormal lucidity, and in the night I dreamed of him surrounded by all the medicine bottles he had bought to take abroad with him, swallowing their contents one by one, and smiling while he did so, with eyebrows grown to the size of hedges.

I took my doses faithfully, with the immediate result that in the train I became aware of symptoms that usually had the decency to wait for the steamer. My friend took his too. He was in excellent spirits, eyes bright, full of confidence. The bottles were wrapped in neat white paper, only the necks visible; and we drank our allotted quantity from the mouths, without glasses.

"Not much taste," I remarked.

"Wonderful stuff," he replied. "I believe in it absolutely. It's good for other things, too; it made me sleep like a top, and I had the appetite of a horse for breakfast. That chemist'll make his fortune when he brings it out. People will pay a pound a bottle, lots of 'em."

At Newhaven the sea was agitated—hideously so; even in the harbour the steamers rose and fell absurdly. Not all the fresh, salt winds in the world, nor all the jolly sunshine and sparkling waves, nor all that strong beauty that comes with the first glimpse of the sea and long horizons, could lessen the sinking dread that was in my—my heart. Truth to tell, I had no more belief in the elixir than if it had been chopped hay and treacle.

My friend, however, was confidence personified. "The fact is," he said, laughing at the wind and sea, "the real fact is *I believe in that chemist.* He told me this stuff was infallible; and I believe it is. The trouble with you is funk—sheer blue funk."

We stuck to our guns and swallowed the last prescribed dose just before the syren announced our departure—and fifteen minutes later. . . .

It was a degrading three hours; and the sting of it was that my friend, with a hideous cap tied down about his ears, a smile that was in the worst possible taste, and a jaunty confidence that was even more insulting than he intended it to be, walked up and down that loathsome, sliding, switchback deck the entire way. Not the entire way, though, for half-way across he disappeared into the dining-room, and returned in due course with that brown beard of his charged with bread-crumbs, and between his lips actually—a pipe. And, without so much as speaking to me, he paced to and fro before my chair, when a little of that imagination he put so delightfully into his books would have led him discreetly to pace the other deck where I could not see him. I thought out endless revenges, but the fact was I never had time to think out any single revenge properly to its conclusion. Something—something unspeakably vile—always came to interfere; and the sight of my friend, balancing up and down the rolling deck chatting to sailors, admiring the sea and sky, and puffing hard at his pipe all the time, was, I think, the most abominable thing I have ever seen.

"Simply marvellous, I call it," he told me in the *douane* at Dieppe. "The stuff is a revolutionary discovery. It's the first time I ever ate a meal on a steamer in my life. Sorry you suffered so. Can't understand it," he added, with a complacency that was insufferable. I was positively delighted to see the Customs officer open *all* his bags and litter his things about in glorious confusion. . . .

In Paris that night our little hotel was rather full, and we had to share a big two-bedded room. My friend groaned a good deal between two and three in the morning and kept me awake; and once, somewhere about five A.M., I saw him with a lighted candle fumbling at the table among a lot of little white paper packages which I recognised as his purchases from that criminal London chemist who had concocted the seasick cure.

It was at nine o'clock, however, while he was down at his bath, that I noticed something on the table by his bed that instantly arrested my attention. Regardless of morals, I investigated. It was unmistakable. It was his own bottle of the seasick cure. He had never taken it at all!

Then, just as his step sounded in the passage, it flashed across me. He had made one of his usual muddles. He had mistaken the bottle. He had swallowed the contents of some other phial instead.

Revenge is sweet; but I felt well again, and no longer harboured any spite. There was just time to hide the bottle in my hand when he entered.

"Awful headache I've got," he said. "Can't make out what's wrong with me. Such funny pains, too."

"After-effects of the seasick cure, probably. They'll pass in time," I suggested. But he remained in bed for a day and a night with all the symptoms of *mal de mer* on land.

It was many weeks later when I told him the truth, and showed the bottle to prove it—just in time to prevent his telling the chemist, "I have tried your seasick cure and found it absolutely efficacious," etc.

"What cured you," I said, "was far more wonderful than anything one can buy in bottles. It was faith, sheer faith!"

"I believe you're right," he replied meekly. "I believed in that stuff *absolutely.*" Then he added, " But, you know, I should like to find out what it was I *did* take."

Carlton's Drive

It is difficult, of course, to estimate the effect of such a thing upon another's temperament. The change seemed bewilderingly sudden; yet spiritual chemistry is a process incalculable, past finding out, and the results in this case were undeniable. Carlton had changed in the course of a brief year or two. And he dates it from that drive. He knows.

He told it to a few intimates only. Those who know his face as it is to-day, serene and strong, yet recall how it was scored and beaten with the ravages of dissipation a few years before (so that the human seemed almost to have dropped back into the beast), can scarcely credit his identity. *Now*—its calm austerity, softened by the greatest yearning known to men, the yearning to save, proclaim at a glance the splendid revolution; whereas *then*—! The memory is unpleasant; exceedingly wonderful the contrast. His life was inoffensive enough, negatively, at least, till the money came; then, with the inheritance, his innate sensuality broke out. Yet it seemed a prodigious step for a man to make in so brief a time: from that life of depravity that stained his face and smothered his soul, to the Brotherhood of Devotion he founded, and himself led full charge against the vice of the world! But not incomprehensible, perhaps. He did nothing by halves. It was the swing of the pendulum.

He was somewhere about thirty, his nerves shattered by the savagery of concentrated fast living, his system too exhausted to respond even to unusual stimulant, when he found himself one early spring morning on the pavement beside St. George's Hospital. He had been up all night, and was making his way homewards on foot, his pockets stuffed with the proceeds of lucky gambling; and how he happened to be standing at that particular spot, watching the traffic, at eight in the morning, is not clear. Probably, seduced by the sweetness of the air, he

347

had wandered, driven by gusts of mood as by gusts of wind. Though
he had drunk steadily since midnight he was not so much intoxicated
as fuddled—stupid. He was on the south corner, where the buses stop
in their journey westwards. The sun poured a flood of light down Piccadilly; the street was brisk with pedestrians going to work; the hospital
side-entrance behind him already astir. Across the road the trees in the
park shimmered in a wave of fluttering green. The pride of life was in
the June air. In his own heart, however, was a loathsome satiety—sign
of the first death.

In a line with the trees opposite stood a solitary hansom. A faint
surprise that it should be there at such an hour jostled in his sodden
brain with the idea that he might as well drive home—when, suddenly,
he became aware that the man perched on the box was looking at him
across the street with a fixity of manner that was both singular and offensive. Carlton felt his own gaze, blear-eyed and troubled, somehow
caught and held—uncomfortably. The other's eyes were fastened upon
his own—had been fastened for some time—sinisterly, and with a
purpose. Just at this moment, however, a sharp spasm of pain and
faintness, due to exhaustion and debauch, shot through him, so that he
reeled, half staggering, and, before he quite knew what he was doing,
he had nodded to the driver, and saw that the horse was already turning with clattering hoofs to cross the slippery street. A minute later he
had climbed heavily in, noticing vaguely that the driver wore all black,
the horse was black, and on the whip was a strip of crêpe that fluttered
in the breeze. As he got in, too, the effort strained him. But, more than
that, something that was cold and terrible—"like a hand of ragged steel,"
he described it afterwards—clutched at his heart. It puzzled him; but he
was too "done" to think; and he lurched back wearily on the cushions as
the horse started forward with the jerkiness of long habit.

"Same address, sir?" the man called down through the trap. His
voice was harsh "like iron"; and Carlton, supposing that he recognised
a fare, replied testily, "Of course, you fool! And let her rip—to the
devil!" The spasm of strange pain had passed. He only felt tired to
brokenness, sick with his corrupt and unsatisfying life, a dull, incomprehensible anger burning in him against the world, the driver—and
himself.

The hansom swung forwards over the smooth, uncrowded streets like a ship with a breeze behind her, for the horse was fresh, and the man drove well. He took off his opera hat and let the cool wind fan his face. That drive of a mile to his rooms was the most soothing and restful he had ever known. But, after a while, braced, perhaps, by the morning wind, he began to notice that they were following a strange route through streets he did not recognise. He had been lolling in the corner with half-closed eyes; now he sat up and looked about him. Time had passed. He ought to have reached home long ago. They were going at a tremendous and unholy pace, too. He poked open the trap sharply.

"Hi, hi!" he called out angrily; "are you drunk? Where, in the name of —— are you driving to?"

"It's all right, sir; it's the shortest way. The usual roads are closed."

The man's voice—deep, with a curious rumbling note—had such conviction and authority in it that Carlton accepted the explanation with a growl and flung himself back into his soft corner. Again, however, for a single second, that cold thing of steel moved horribly in his heart. He felt as if the "ragged hand" had given it another twist. Then it passed, and he gave himself up to the swinging motion of the drive. The hansom tore along now; it was delightful. Curious, though, that *all* the known streets should be "up"! Positively the houses were getting less, as though he was driving out into the country. Perhaps, too, the feeling of *laisser aller* that came over him was caused by some inhibition of the will due to prolonged excesses. Carlton admits it was unlike his normal self not to *force* the man to drive where he wanted; but he felt lulled, lazy, indifferent. "Let the fool take his own way!" his thought ran; "I shan't pay him any more for it!" . . .

Somebody was waving to him from the pavement with a coloured parasol—a girl he knew, one of his sort; gay and smiling, tripping along quickly. With a momentary surprise that she should be thus early astir, he smiled through the window and waved his hand. It gave him pleasure to see she was going in the same direction as himself. The instant he passed her the horse leaped forward with increased speed, so that the hansom rattled, shaking him a little as it lurched from side to side.

"Steady on, idiot!" he shouted, "or you'll smash me up before I get to the end!" And he was just going to bang open the trap and swear, when his attention was caught by another salutation from the pavement. It was a man this time—running hard; a man who played, drank, and the rest of it even harder than himself, a man who shared his trips to Paris. He was radiant and gesticulating. "Good journey, old man!" he heard him cry as the hansom shot past; "Hurry up! We're coming, too! We shall be there together!" Carlton did not quite like this greeting. It reminded him for a second that he was a bit uncertain where the mad driver was heading for. It gave him a passing uneasiness—almost immediately forgotten, however. The pace was too delicious to bring to an end just yet. Presently he would call the fellow to order with a vengeance, but meanwhile—"let her rip!" His friends were all going the same way; it must be all right. His thoughts, he admits, were somewhat mixed; for great speed destroys calm judgment; it exhilarated, but it also bewildered. The pace, assuredly, had something to do with his mental confusion, for it was terrific. Yet he saw on the pavement, from time to time, more friends and acquaintances, and somehow at the moment it did not strike him as *too* peculiar that they should be there, all moving hurriedly in the same direction. He had an odd feeling that they all knew of some destination agreed upon; that he, too, knew it; but that it was not "playing the game" to admit that he knew. Yet about some of them—their hurried steps, their gay faces, their waving hands—there was a queer fugitive suggestion of sadness, even of fear. One or two touched the source of horror in him even. It hardly surprised him that the horse, steaming and sweating, should start forward with a frightened leap as each figure in turn was sighted and left behind. Probably he was himself too much a part of the wild, exhilarating rush to realise how singular it was. Certainly, it seemed as though some faculty of his mind was suspended during that drive.

But at last, after passing another friend, the horse gave a leap that really frightened him, flinging him against the boards. It was a man, twice his own age, who more than any other had helped him in his evil living, not by doing likewise, but by smothering his first remorse with a smile and a sentence: "Of course, my boy, sow your wild oats! You'll settle down later. No man is worth his salt who hasn't sown his wild oats!" He was sliding along—a kind of crawl, with something loathsome in his motion that suggested the reptile. Carlton nodded to him. The same second the horse gave its terrible bound. The whip for the first time slashed down across its flanks. He saw the strip of crêpe, black against the green and sunny landscape. For by now all houses were left behind, and they were rushing at a mad pace along a broad country road, growing momentarily steeper, and—downhill.

At the same moment he caught his own face in the glass. To his utter horror he saw that a black veil, crêpe-like, hung over the upper part, already hiding the eyes, and that it was moving downwards, slowly creeping. The hand of steel turned again within him. He knew that it was Death.

Yet, most singular of all, he instantly found in himself the power to believe it was not there. His hand brushed it off. His face was young, clean, and smiling once more. . . . And now the hansom flew. The horse was running away; he heard the driver shouting to it, and the shouting sounded like a song. The man *was* drunk after all. Mingled with his song, too, came a confused murmur of voices behind—far away. What in the world did it all mean? Dashing aside the little curtain he looked back out of the window, and the first thing he saw was a face pressed close against the glass, staring straight into his eyes with a beseeching, pitiful expression. Good God! It was the face of his mother. He swore; the face melted away—and he then saw that the whole country behind him was black, and through it, down the darkened road, ran the figures he had passed. But how changed! The girl was no longer gay and smiling; her face was old, streaked with evil, and with one hand she clutched her heart as she ran—trying in vain to stop. Behind her were the others—worn and broken, with bloodshot eyes and toothless gums, all grinning dreadfully, all racing down the eversteepening descent, yet all trying frantically to stop. One or two, however, still ran with a brave show as if they wished to; debonair, holding themselves with a certain appearance of dignity and pleasure. And some—the old man of the "wild oats" sentence at their head—were close upon the hansom, *pushing it*. . . . The face of his mother slid once again upon the glass, between their evil, outstretched hands and himself, but less close, less visible than before. . . .

Carlton knew a spasm of pain that was terrible. He sat up. He flung open the doors, and his eyes measured the leap. But the faculty of mind that had all the time been in suspension returned a little, and he saw that to jump was—impossible. He smashed the trap open with his fist and cried out, "Stop! I tell you, stop!"

"Can't stop here, sir," the driver answered, peering down at him out of the square opening that let in—darkness. "It's not allowed. It's not usual, either."

"Stop, I say," thundered Carlton, trying to rise and strike him.

But the driver laughed through that square of blackness.

"Can't be done, sir. You told me 'same address.' There's no stopping now!"

Carlton's clenched fist was close to the man's eyes when the fingers grew limp and opened. He sank back upon the seat again. The face peering down upon him was—his own.

And in this supreme moment it was that some secret reserve of soul, hitherto untainted—stirred into life, he declares, by the sight of his mother's face at the window—rose and offered itself to him. He accepted it. *His will moved in its sleep and woke.*

"But I say you *shall* stop!" he cried, catching the reins in both hands, and, when they snapped, seizing the rims, and even the spokes, of the wheels. His great strength acted like a brake. The hansom reeled, shook, then slackened. It was a most curious thing, but the force that twisted his heart with its hand of "ragged steel" seemed to lend him its power. His will moved and gripped; the machinery groaned, but worked. Carlton did nothing by halves; he put his life into his efforts; the skin was torn like paper from his hands. The hansom stopped with a trembling jerk and flung him out upon his face in the mud. And the same second he saw the horse and driver, both torn from their fastenings, whirled past him overhead to disappear into a gulf that yawned dreadfully under his very eyes, blacker than night, deeper than all things. . . .

And when, at length, he rose to his feet, he found that he was tied with bands of iron to the shafts. Slowly, with vast efforts, groaning and sweating, he turned and began painfully to reclimb the huge and toilsome ascent, dragging the awful weight behind him . . . towards the Light.

For the glare that suddenly broke through the sky was the sunshine coming through the windows of the hospital room—St. George's Hospital—where they had carried him when he fainted on the pavement half-an-hour before.

The Man Who Found Out

(A Nightmare)

I

Professor Mark Ebor, the scientist, led a double life, and the only persons who knew it were his assistant, Dr. Laidlaw, and his publishers. But a double life need not always be a bad one, and, as Dr. Laidlaw and the gratified publishers well knew, the parallel lives of this particular man were equally good, and indefinitely produced would certainly have ended in a heaven somewhere that can suitably contain such strangely opposite characteristics as his remarkable personality combined.

For Mark Ebor, F.R.S., etc., etc., was that unique combination hardly ever met with in actual life, a man of science and a mystic.

As the first, his name stood in the gallery of the great, and as the second—but there came the mystery! For under the pseudonym of "Pilgrim" (the author of that brilliant series of books that appealed to so many), his identity was as well concealed as that of the anonymous writer of the weather reports in a daily newspaper. Thousands read the sanguine, optimistic, stimulating little books that issued annually from the pen of "Pilgrim," and thousands bore their daily burdens better for having read; while the Press generally agreed that the author, besides being an incorrigible enthusiast and optimist, was also—a woman; but no one ever succeeded in penetrating the veil of anonymity and discovering that "Pilgrim" and the biologist were one and the same person.

Mark Ebor, as Dr. Laidlaw knew him in his laboratory, was one man; but Mark Ebor, as he sometimes saw him after work was over, with rapt eyes and ecstatic face, discussing the possibilities of "union with God" and the future of the human race, was quite another.

"I have always held, as you know," he was saying one evening as he sat in the little study beyond the laboratory with his assistant and intimate, "that Vision should play a large part in the life of the awakened man—not to be regarded as infallible, of course, but to be observed and made use of as a guide-post to possibilities—"

"I am aware of your peculiar views, sir," the young doctor put in deferentially, yet with a certain impatience.

"For Visions come from a region of the consciousness where observation and experiment are out of the question," pursued the other with enthusiasm, not noticing the interruption, "and, while they should be checked by reason afterwards, they should not be laughed at or ignored. All inspiration, I hold, is of the nature of interior Vision, and all our best knowledge has come—such is my confirmed belief—as a sudden revelation to the brain prepared to receive it—"

"Prepared by hard work first, by concentration, by the closest possible study of ordinary phenomena," Dr. Laidlaw allowed himself to observe.

"Perhaps," sighed the other; "but by a process, none the less, of spiritual illumination. The best match in the world will not light a candle unless the wick be first suitably prepared."

It was Laidlaw's turn to sigh. He knew so well the impossibility of arguing with his chief when he was in the regions of the mystic, but at the same time the respect he felt for his tremendous attainments was so sincere that he always listened with attention and deference, wondering how far the great man would go and to what end this curious combination of logic and "illumination" would eventually lead him.

"Only last night," continued the elder man, a sort of light coming into his rugged features, "the vision came to me again—the one that has haunted me at intervals ever since my youth, and that will not be denied."

Dr. Laidlaw fidgeted in his chair.

"About the Tablets of the Gods, you mean—and that they lie somewhere hidden in the sands," he said patiently. A sudden gleam of interest came into his face as he turned to catch the professor's reply.

"And that I am to be the one to find them, to decipher them, and to give the great knowledge to the world—"

"Who will not believe," laughed Laidlaw shortly, yet interested in spite of his thinly-veiled contempt.

"Because even the keenest minds, in the right sense of the word, are hopelessly—unscientific," replied the other gently, his face positively aglow with the memory of his vision. "Yet what is more likely," he continued after a moment's pause, peering into space with rapt eyes that saw things too wonderful for exact language to describe, "than that there should have been given to man in the first ages of the world some record of the purpose and problem that had been set him to solve? In a word," he cried, fixing his shining eyes upon the face of his perplexed assistant, "that God's messengers in the far-off ages should have given to His creatures some full statement of the secret of the world, of the secret of the soul, of the meaning of life and death—the explanation of our being here, and to what great end we are destined in the ultimate fulness of things?"

Dr. Laidlaw sat speechless. These outbursts of mystical enthusiasm he had witnessed before. With any other man he would not have listened to a single sentence, but to Professor Ebor, man of knowledge and profound investigator, he listened with respect, because he regarded this condition as temporary and pathological, and in some sense a reaction from the intense strain of the prolonged mental concentration of many days.

He smiled, with something between sympathy and resignation as he met the other's rapt gaze.

"But you have said, sir, at other times, that you consider the ultimate secrets to be screened from all possible—"

"The *ultimate* secrets, yes," came the unperturbed reply; "but that there lies buried somewhere an indestructible record of the secret meaning of life, originally known to men in the days of their pristine innocence, I am convinced. And, by this strange vision so often vouchsafed to me, I am equally sure that one day it shall be given to me to announce to a weary world this glorious and terrific message."

And he continued at great length and in glowing language to describe the species of vivid dream that had come to him at intervals since earliest childhood, showing in detail how he discovered these very Tablets of the Gods, and proclaimed their splendid contents—whose precise nature was always, however, withheld from him in the vision—to a patient and suffering humanity.

"The *Scrutator*, sir, well described 'Pilgrim' as the Apostle of Hope," said the young doctor gently, when he had finished; "and now, if that reviewer could hear you speak and realise from what strange depths comes your simple faith—"

The professor held up his hand, and the smile of a little child broke over his face like sunshine in the morning.

"Half the good my books do would be instantly destroyed," he said sadly; "they would say that I wrote with my tongue in my cheek. But wait," he added significantly; "wait till I find these Tablets of the Gods! Wait till I hold the solutions of the old world-problems in my hands! Wait till the light of this new revelation breaks upon confused humanity, and it wakes to find its bravest hopes justified! Ah, then, my dear Laidlaw—"

He broke off suddenly; but the doctor, cleverly guessing the thought in his mind, caught him up immediately.

"Perhaps this very summer," he said, trying hard to make the suggestion keep pace with honesty; "in your explorations in Assyria—your digging in the remote civilisation of what was once Chaldea, you may find—what you dream of—"

The professor held up his hand, and the smile of a fine old face.

"Perhaps," he murmured softly, "perhaps!"

And the young doctor, thanking the gods of science that his leader's aberrations were of so harmless a character, went home strong in the certitude of his knowledge of externals, proud that he was able to refer his visions to self-suggestion, and wondering complaisantly whether in his old age he might not after all suffer himself from visitations of the very kind that afflicted his respected chief.

And as he got into bed and thought again of his master's rugged face, and finely shaped head, and the deep lines traced by years of work and self-discipline, he turned over on his pillow and fell asleep with a sigh that was half of wonder, half of regret.

II

It was in February, nine months later, when Dr. Laidlaw made his way to Charing Cross to meet his chief after his long absence of travel and exploration. The vision about the so-called Tablets of the Gods had meanwhile passed almost entirely from his memory.

There were few people in the train, for the stream of traffic was now running the other way, and he had no difficulty in finding the man he had come to meet. The shock of white hair beneath the low-crowned felt hat was alone enough to distinguish him by easily.

"Here I am at last!" exclaimed the professor, somewhat wearily, clasping his friend's hand as he listened to the young doctor's warm greetings and questions. "Here I am—a little older, and *much* dirtier than when you last saw me!" He glanced down laughingly at his travel-stained garments.

"And *much* wiser," said Laidlaw, with a smile, as he bustled about the platform for porters and gave his chief the latest scientific news.

At last they came down to practical considerations.

"And your luggage—where is that? You must have tons of it, I suppose?" said Laidlaw.

"Hardly anything," Professor Ebor answered. "Nothing, in fact, but what you see."

"Nothing but this hand-bag?" laughed the other, thinking he was joking.

"And a small portmanteau in the van," was the quiet reply. "I have no other luggage."

"You have no other luggage?" repeated Laidlaw, turning sharply to see if he were in earnest.

"Why should I need more?" the professor added simply.

Something in the man's face, or voice, or manner—the doctor hardly knew which—suddenly struck him as strange. There was a change in him, a change so profound—so little on the surface, that is—that at first he had not become aware of it. For a moment it was as though an utterly alien personality stood before him in that noisy, bustling throng. Here, in all the homely, friendly turmoil of a Charing Cross crowd, a curious feeling of cold passed over his heart, touching his life with icy finger, so that he actually trembled and felt afraid.

He looked up quickly at his friend, his mind working with startled and unwelcome thoughts.

"Only this?" he repeated, indicating the bag. "But where's all the stuff you went away with? And—have you brought nothing home—no treasures?"

"This is all I have," the other said briefly. The pale smile that went with the words caused the doctor a second indescribable sensation of uneasiness. Something was very wrong, something was very queer; he wondered now that he had not noticed it sooner.

"The rest follows, of course, by slow freight," he added tactfully, and as naturally as possible. "But come, sir, you must be tired and in want of food after your long journey. I'll get a taxi at once, and we can see about the other luggage afterwards."

It seemed to him he hardly knew quite what he was saying; the change in his friend had come upon him so suddenly and now grew upon him more and more distressingly. Yet he could not make out exactly in what it consisted. A terrible suspicion began to take shape in his mind, troubling him dreadfully.

"I am neither very tired, nor in need of food, thank you," the professor said quietly. "And this is all I have. There is no luggage to follow. I have brought home nothing—nothing but what you see."

His words conveyed finality. They got into a taxi, tipped the porter, who had been staring in amazement at the venerable figure of the scientist, and were conveyed slowly and noisily to the house in the north of London where the laboratory was, the scene of their labours of years.

And the whole way Professor Ebor uttered no word, nor did Dr. Laidlaw find the courage to ask a single question.

It was only late that night, before he took his departure, as the two men were standing before the fire in the study—that study where they had discussed so many problems of vital and absorbing interest—that Dr. Laidlaw at last found strength to come to the point with direct questions. The professor had been giving him a superficial and desultory account of his travels, of his journeys by camel, of his encampments among the mountains and in the desert, and of his explorations among the buried temples, and, deeper, into the waste of the prehistoric sands, when suddenly the doctor came to the desired point with a kind of nervous rush, almost like a frightened boy.

"And you found—" he began stammering, looking hard at the other's dreadfully altered face, from which every line of hope and cheerfulness seemed to have been obliterated as a sponge wipes markings from a slate—"you found—"

"I found," replied the other, in a solemn voice, and it was the voice of the mystic rather than the man of science—"I found what I went to seek. The vision never once failed me. It led me straight to the place like a star in the heavens. I found—the Tablets of the Gods."

Dr. Laidlaw caught his breath, and steadied himself on the back of a chair. The words fell like particles of ice upon his heart. For the first time the professor had uttered the well-known phrase without the glow of light and wonder in his face that always accompanied it.

"You have—brought them? " he faltered.

"I have brought them home," said the other, in a voice with a ring like iron; "and I have—deciphered them."

Profound despair, the gloom of outer darkness, the dead sound of a hopeless soul freezing in the utter cold of space seemed to fill in the pauses between the brief sentences. A silence followed, during which Dr. Laidlaw saw nothing but the white face before him alternately fade and return. And it was like the face of a dead man.

"They are, alas, indestructible," he heard the voice continue, with its even, metallic ring.

"Indestructible," Laidlaw repeated mechanically, hardly knowing what he was saying.

Again a silence of several minutes passed, during which, with a creeping cold about his heart, he stood and stared into the eyes of the man he had known and loved so long—aye, and worshipped, too; the man who had first opened his own eyes when they were blind, and had led him to the gates of knowledge, and no little distance along the difficult path beyond; the man who, in another direction, had passed on the strength of his faith into the hearts of thousands by his books.

"I may see them?" he asked at last, in a low voice he hardly recognised as his own. "You will let me know—their message?"

Professor Ebor kept his eyes fixedly upon his assistant's face as he answered, with a smile that was more like the grin of death than a living human smile.

"When I am gone," he whispered; "when I have passed away. Then you shall find them and read the translation I have made. And then, too, in your turn, you must try, with the latest resources of science at your disposal to aid you, to compass their utter destruction." He paused a moment, and his face grew pale as the face of a corpse. "Until that time," he added presently, without looking up, "I must ask you not to refer to the subject again—and to keep my confidence meanwhile—*ab—so—lute—ly*."

III

A year passed slowly by, and at the end of it Dr. Laidlaw had found it necessary to sever his working connection with his friend and one-time leader. Professor Ebor was no longer the same man. The light had gone out of his life; the laboratory was closed; he no longer put pen to paper or applied his mind to a single problem. In the short space of a few months he had passed from a hale and hearty man of late middle life to the condition of old age—a man collapsed and on the edge of dissolution. Death, it was plain, lay waiting for him in the shadows of any day—and he knew it.

To describe faithfully the nature of this profound alteration in his character and temperament is not easy, but Dr. Laidlaw summed it up to himself in three words: *Loss of Hope*. The splendid mental powers remained indeed undimmed, but the incentive to use them—to use them for the help of others—had gone. The character still held to its fine and unselfish habits of years, but the far goal to which they had been the leading strings had faded away. The desire for knowledge—knowledge for its own sake—had died, and the passionate hope which hitherto had animated with tireless energy the heart and brain of this splendidly equipped intellect had suffered total eclipse. The central fires had gone out. Nothing was worth doing, thinking, working for. There *was* nothing to work for any longer!

The professor's first step was to recall as many of his books as possible; his second to close his laboratory and stop all research. He gave no explanation, he invited no questions. His whole personality crumbled away, so to speak, till his daily life became a mere mechanical process of clothing the body, feeding the body, keeping it in good health so as to avoid physical discomfort, and, above all, doing nothing that could interfere with sleep. The professor did everything he could to lengthen the hours of sleep, and therefore of forgetfulness.

It was all clear enough to Dr. Laidlaw. A weaker man, he knew, would have sought to lose himself in one form or another of sensual indulgence—sleeping-draughts, drink, the first pleasures that came to hand. Self-destruction would have been the method of a little bolder type; and deliberate evil-doing, poisoning with his awful knowledge all he could, the means of still another kind of man. Mark Ebor was none of these. He held himself under fine control, facing silently and without complaint the terrible facts he honestly believed himself to have been unfortunate enough to discover. Even to his intimate friend and assistant, Dr. Laidlaw, he vouchsafed no word of true explanation or lament. He went straight forward to the end, knowing well that the end was not very far away.

And death came very quietly one day to him, as he was sitting in the arm-chair of the study, directly facing the doors of the laboratory— the doors that no longer opened. Dr. Laidlaw, by happy chance, was with him at the time, and was just able to reach his side in response to the sudden painful efforts for breath; just in time, too, to catch the murmured words that fell from the pallid lips like a message from the other side of the grave.

"Read them, if you must; and, if you can—destroy. But"—his voice sank so low that Dr. Laidlaw only just caught the dying syllables—"but—never, never—give them to the world."

And like a grey bundle of dust loosely gathered up in an old garment the professor sank back into his chair and expired.

But this was only the death of the body. His spirit had died two years before.

IV

The estate of the dead man was small and uncomplicated, and Dr. Laidlaw, as sole executor and residuary legatee, had no difficulty in settling it up. A month after the funeral he was sitting alone in his upstairs library, the last sad duties completed, and his mind full of poignant memories and regrets for the loss of a friend he had revered and loved, and to whom his debt was so incalculably great. The last two years, indeed, had been for him terrible. To watch the swift decay of the greatest combination of heart and brain he had ever known, and to realise he was powerless to help, was a source of profound grief to him that would remain to the end of his days.

At the same time an insatiable curiosity possessed him. The study of dementia was, of course, outside. his special province as a specialist, but he knew enough of it to understand how small a matter might be the actual cause of how great an illusion, and he had been devoured from the very beginning by a ceaseless and increasing anxiety to know what the professor had found in the sands of "Chaldea," what these precious Tablets of the Gods might be, and particularly—for this was the real cause that had sapped the man's sanity and hope—what the inscription was that he had believed to have deciphered thereon.

The curious feature of it all to his own mind was, that whereas his friend had dreamed of finding a message of glorious hope and comfort, he had apparently found (so far as he had found anything intelligible at all, and not invented the whole thing in his dementia) that the secret of the world, and the meaning of life and death, was of so terrible a nature that it robbed the heart of courage and the soul of hope. What, then, could be the contents of the little brown parcel the professor had bequeathed to him with his pregnant dying sentences?

Actually his hand was trembling as he turned to the writing-table and began slowly to unfasten a small old-fashioned desk on which the small gilt initials "M.E." stood forth as a melancholy memento. He put the key into the lock and half turned it. Then, suddenly, he stopped and looked about him. Was that a sound at the back of the room? It was just as though some one had laughed and then tried to smother the laugh with a cough. A slight shiver ran over him as he stood listening.

"This is absurd," he said aloud; "too absurd for belief—that I should be so nervous! It's the effect of curiosity unduly prolonged." He smiled a little sadly and his eyes wandered to the blue summer sky and the plane trees swaying in the wind below his window. "It's the reaction," he continued. "The curiosity of two years to be quenched in a single moment! The nervous tension, of course, must be considerable."

He turned back to the brown desk and opened it without further delay. His hand was firm now, and he took out the paper parcel that lay inside without a tremor. It was heavy. A moment later there lay on the table before him a couple of weather-worn plaques of grey stone—they looked like stone, although they felt like metal—on which he saw markings of a curious character that might have been the mere tracings of natural forces through the ages, or, equally well, the half-obliterated hieroglyphics cut upon their surface in past centuries by the more or less untutored hand of a common scribe.

He lifted each stone in turn and examined it carefully. It seemed to him that a faint glow of heat passed from the substance into his skin, and he put them down again suddenly, as with a gesture of uneasiness.

"A very clever, or a very imaginative man," he said to himself, "who could squeeze the secrets of life and death from such broken lines as those!"

Then he turned to a yellow envelope lying beside them in the desk, with the single word on the outside in the writing of the professor— the word *Translation.*

"Now," he thought, taking it up with a sudden violence to conceal his nervousness, "now for the great solution. Now to learn the meaning of the worlds, and why mankind was made, and why discipline is worth while, and sacrifice and pain the true law of advancement."

There was the shadow of a sneer in his voice, and yet something in him shivered at the same time. He held the envelope as though weighing it in his hand, his mind pondering many things. Then curiosity won the day, and he suddenly tore it open with the gesture of an actor who tears open a letter on the stage, knowing there is no real writing inside at all.

A page of finely written script in the late scientist's handwriting lay before him. He read it through from beginning to end, missing no word, uttering each syllable distinctly under his breath as he read.

The pallor of his face grew ghastly as he neared the end. He began to shake all over as with ague. His breath came heavily in gasps. He still gripped the sheet of paper, however, and deliberately, as by an intense effort of will, read it through a second time from beginning to end. And this time, as the last syllable dropped from his lips, the whole face of the man flamed with a sudden and terrible anger. His skin became deep, deep red, and he clenched his teeth. With all the strength of his vigorous soul he was struggling to keep control of himself.

For perhaps five minutes he stood there beside the table without stirring a muscle. He might have been carved out of stone. His eyes were shut, and only the heaving of the chest betrayed the fact that he was a living being. Then, with a strange quietness, he lit a match and applied it to the sheet of paper he held in his hand. The ashes fell slowly about him, piece by piece, and he blew them from the window-sill into the air, his eyes following them as they floated away on the summer wind that breathed so warmly over the world.

He turned back slowly into the room. Although his actions and movements were absolutely steady and controlled, it was clear that he was on the edge of violent action. A hurricane might burst upon the still room any moment. His muscles were tense and rigid. Then, suddenly, he whitened, collapsed, and sank backwards into a chair, like a tumbled bundle of inert matter. He had fainted.

In less than half an hour he recovered consciousness and sat up. As before, he made no sound. Not a syllable passed his lips. He rose quietly and looked about the room.

Then he did a curious thing.

Taking a heavy stick from the rack in the corner he approached the mantelpiece, and with a heavy shattering blow he smashed the clock to pieces. The glass fell in shivering atoms.

"Cease your lying voice for ever," he said, in a curiously still, even tone. "There is no such thing as *time!*"

He took the watch from his pocket, swung it round several times by the long gold chain, smashed it into smithereens against the wall with a single blow, and then walked into his laboratory next door, and hung its broken body on the bones of the skeleton in the corner of the room.

"Let one damned mockery hang upon another," he said smiling oddly. "Delusions, both of you, and cruel as false!"

He slowly moved back to the front room. He stopped opposite the bookcase where stood in a row the "Scriptures of the World," choicely bound and exquisitely printed, the late professor's most treasured possession, and next to them several books signed "Pilgrim."

One by one he took them from the shelf and hurled them through the open window.

"A devil's dreams! A devil's foolish dreams!" he cried, with a vicious laugh.

Presently he stopped from sheer exhaustion. He turned his eyes slowly to the wall opposite, where hung a weird array of Eastern swords and daggers, scimitars and spears, the collections of many journeys. He crossed the room and ran his finger along the edge. His mind seemed to waver.

"No," he muttered presently; "not that way. There are easier and better ways than that."

He took his hat and passed downstairs into the street.

V

It was five o'clock, and the June sun lay hot upon the pavement. He felt the metal door-knob burn the palm of his hand.

"Ah, Laidlaw, this is well met," cried a voice at his elbow; "I was in the act of coming to see you. I've a case that will interest you, and besides, I remembered that you flavoured your tea with orange leaves!—and I admit—"

It was Alexis Stephen, the great hypnotic doctor.

"I've had no tea to-day," Laidlaw said, in a dazed manner, after staring for a moment as though the other had struck him in the face. A new idea had entered his mind.

"What's the matter?" asked Dr. Stephen quickly. "Something's wrong with you. It's this sudden heat, or overwork. Come, man, let's go inside."

A sudden light broke upon the face of the younger man, the light of a heaven-sent inspiration. He looked into his friend's face, and told a direct lie.

"Odd," he said, "I myself was just coming to see you. I have something of great importance to test your confidence with. But in *your* house, please," as Stephen urged him towards his own door—"in your house. It's only round the corner, and I—I cannot go back there—to my rooms—till I have told you."

"I'm your patient—for the moment," he added stammeringly as soon as they were seated in the privacy of the hypnotist's sanctum, "and I want—er—"

"My dear Laidlaw," interrupted the other, in that soothing voice of command which had suggested to many a suffering soul that the cure for its pain lay in the powers of its own reawakened will, "I am always at your service, as you know. You have only to tell me what I can do for you, and I will do it." He showed every desire to help him out. His manner was indescribably tactful and direct.

Dr. Laidlaw looked up into his face.

"I surrender my will to you," he said, already calmed by the other's healing presence, "and I want you to treat me hypnotically—and at once. I want you to suggest to me"—his voice became very tense—"that I shall forget—forget till I die—everything that has occurred to me during the last two hours; till I die, mind," he added, with solemn emphasis, "till I die."

He floundered and stammered like a frightened boy. Alexis Stephen looked at him fixedly without speaking.

"And further," Laidlaw continued, "I want you to ask me no questions. I wish to forget for ever something I have recently discovered—something so terrible and yet so obvious that I can hardly understand why it is not patent to every mind in the world—for I have had a moment of absolute *clear vision*—of merciless clairvoyance. But I want no one else in the whole world to know what it is—least of all, old friend, yourself."

He talked in utter confusion, and hardly knew what he was saying. But the pain on his face and the anguish in his voice were an instant passport to the other's heart.

"Nothing is easier," replied Dr. Stephen, after a hesitation so slight that the other probably did not even notice it. "Come into my other room where we shall not be disturbed. I can heal you. Your memory of the last two hours shall be wiped out as though it had never been. You can trust me absolutely."

"I know I can," Laidlaw said simply, as he followed him in.

VI

An hour later they passed back into the front room again. The sun was already behind the houses opposite, and the shadows began to gather.

"I went off easily?" Laidlaw asked.

"You were a little obstinate at first. But though you came in like a lion, you went out like a lamb. I let you sleep a bit afterwards."

Dr. Stephen kept his eyes rather steadily upon his friend's face.

"What were you doing by the fire before you came here?" he asked, pausing, in a casual tone, as he lit a cigarette and handed the case to his patient.

"I? Let me see. Oh, I know; I was worrying my way through poor old Ebor's papers and things. I'm his executor, you know. Then I got weary and came out for a whiff of air." He spoke lightly and with perfect naturalness. Obviously he was telling the truth. "I prefer specimens to papers," he laughed cheerily.

"I know, I know," said Dr. Stephen, holding a lighted match for the cigarette. His face wore an expression of content. The experiment had been a complete success. The memory of the last two hours was wiped out utterly. Laidlaw was already chatting gaily and easily about a dozen other things that interested him. Together they went out into the street, and at his door Dr. Stephen left him with a joke and a wry face that made his friend laugh heartily.

"Don't dine on the professor's old papers by mistake," he cried, as he vanished down the street.

Dr. Laidlaw went up to his study at the top of the house. Half-way down he met his housekeeper, Mrs. Fewings. She was flustered and excited, and her face was very red and perspiring.

"There've been burglars here," she cried excitedly, "or something funny! All your things is just any'ow, sir. I found everything all about everywhere!" She was very confused. In this orderly and very precise establishment it was unusual to find a thing out of place.

"Oh, my specimens!" cried the doctor, dashing up the rest of the stairs at top speed. "Have they been touched or—"

He flew to the door of the laboratory. Mrs. Fewings panted up heavily behind him.

"The labatry ain't been touched," she explained, breathlessly, "but they smashed the libry clock and they've 'ung your gold watch, sir, on the skelinton's hands. And the books that weren't no value they flung out er the window just like so much rubbish. They must have been wild drunk, Dr. Laidlaw, sir!"

The young scientist made a hurried examination of the rooms. Nothing of value was missing. He began to wonder what kind of burglars they were. He looked up sharply at Mrs. Fewings standing in the doorway. For a moment he seemed to cast about in his mind for something.

"Odd," he said at length. "I only left here an hour ago and everything was all right then."

"Was it, sir? Yes, sir." She glanced sharply at him. Her room looked out upon the courtyard, and she must have seen the books come crashing down, and also have heard her master leave the house a few minutes later.

"And what's this rubbish the brutes have left?" he cried, taking up two slabs of worn grey stone, on the writing-table. "Bath brick, or something, I do declare."

He looked very sharply again at the confused and troubled house-keeper.

"Throw them on the dust heap, Mrs. Fewings, and—and let me know if anything is missing in the house, and I will notify the police this evening."

When she left the room he went into the laboratory and took his watch off the skeleton's fingers. His face wore a troubled expression, but after a moment's thought it cleared again. His memory was a complete blank .

"I suppose I left it on the writing-table when I went out to take the air," he said. And there was no one present to contradict him.

He crossed to the window and blew carelessly some ashes of burned paper from the sill, and stood watching them as they floated away lazily over the tops of the trees.

The Laying of a Red-Haired Ghost

It was a strange and incredible story, Jim thought, as he sat opposite his sister in the firelight, and listened to her nervous and disjointed telling of it. They held little in common, these two, and had not met for some years; she was greatly his senior, and when she had married Captain Blundell, who combined a love of spirits with a credulous belief in spiritualism, Jim sheered off altogether. He could not stand a man who came drunk to his own table, and who, in his sober moments, could talk of nothing but the vulgar claptrap of séances and spirit-rapping.

But now, six months after the funeral, Jim found himself summoned down by a pathetic little letter; and there he was after tea, in a corner of the big drawing-room, watching his sister's pale, emotional face in the firelight, and wondering how any woman could possibly believe all she was telling him.

In spite of this "wonder," however, he was beginning to feel conscious of a certain "creepiness" down the back, and several times he caught himself wishing that the footman would bring the lamps, and be quick about it.

"As you know, Jim, Harry was a tremendous spiritualist," she went on, with a little show of natural embarrassment. "He was always having séances and what he called 'experiments' in the house, up to the day of his seizure."

"Mediums?" asked Jim, feeling the old contempt stir in him.

She nodded, with a gesture imploring his patience.

"Every professional medium in the United Kingdom has slept in this house," she answered. "They came down, male and female, in endless succession for weekend visits, and for two years I kept a diary of all their phenomena."

Jim shuffled nervously, fearing a detailed account.

"But a few months before his death," she went on, "all this came to a sudden stop. He gave up having paid mediums—"

"You must have been glad," said Jim, with genuine sympathy.

"Because he said he had found something better. You see, our circles were made up of people staying in the house—always devout believers—and when there were not enough of these he brought in recruits from among the servants. First the upper servants, then anybody. Gardeners, grooms, upper housemaids, and even cooks have all sat at various times with us round the table or cabinet, watching hands, faces, and sometimes full-form figures flit about the room. Oh, it was very wonderful!"

Jim poked the fire, and lit another cigarette hastily. He believed nothing; but it was foolish, he considered, for nervous persons like his sister to talk of such things after dark, especially in a lonely country house with ill-lighted corridors and ghostly staircases. Moreover, she was always peering over her shoulder as though she saw something in the great darkened room behind her.

"It was on one of these occasions," she continued, lowering her voice, "he discovered that one of the servants was a medium of exceptional powers. After that no professional ever entered the house again."

"And this medium-servant—?" asked her brother impatiently.

"Was Masters."

"What?" he cried: "Masters, the old housekeeper?"

"Yes; she began by going into a trance at one of the séances, and my husband said she possessed most unusual powers and must sit for development."

"And you got the same results with that old woman?"

"Even better. Oh, Masters was extraordinary!" replied his sister with enthusiasm. "Simply extraordinary! But it's not that I want to tell you about. It's something very different."

Jim noticed her hesitation and embarrassment, and wondered what he was going to hear next. He suggested ringing for the lights, but his sister objected that she did not want the servants to overhear a single word. Her manner became more mysterious. She drew her chair closer, and began to speak in a hushed voice, but with great earnestness.

"It's what has gone on since—that I want to tell you," she whispered. "Since my husband's death, I mean—what goes on now—"

"Now!" repeated Jim, feeling more and more uncomfortable.

"And I sent for you because you are the only one of the family left. I could never speak to a stranger of this."

"Of course not," he said hurriedly. "You say things go on now, do you?" He glanced quickly at her face, and noted its sudden pallor and the unmistakable signs of fear in her manner. "Do you mean in this house?"

He got up to ring the bell for the lamps, but she drew him back into the chair.

"Wait till I've finished, please, Jim. You know, this is a very large house," she went on disconnectedly, still under her breath for fear of listeners. "And a very lonely one; and I've been living here since my husband died."

"Yes," he said emphatically.

"I only use a small part of it. The rest—his part—is shut up."

"Naturally."

"I have fewer servants too."

"Of course."

"And the greatest difficulty in keeping them. They won't stay. They are always hearing noises in the unused part of the house—his part. And some of them swear they have met IT on the stairs."

Jim looked up quickly; he was alarmed at her tone of voice.

"Met what?" he asked aloud.

"Him," she whispered back across the firelight. "He's been about all the time. He's always about now. He's not far from you and me at this very moment, probably."

Her brother sprang up, and faced the darkening room with his back to the fire. Her serious manner dismayed him a good deal.

"You mean—" he began.

"Harry still lives here—still comes here."

"Helen!" he said severely—"your nerves are unstrung. What in the world do you mean by talking in this way?"

"Exactly what I say, Jim. Harry is still in this house," she answered quietly, in a tone that sent the shivers down his back.

"The house is h—h—aunted, you mean!"

"I mean that Harry is still about in it," she whispered.

"But have you seen him?"

"Often," she went on, her excitement growing as she saw her brother's interest. "And he's always telling me to do things. He says his happiness depends on my doing them. He says this all the time. He comes at night to my room; and even when I don't see him, I hear his voice in the dark whispering at me."

Jim straightened himself up, and drew a long, deep breath. He was slowly forming his own conclusions. He knew a splendid nerve specialist in town, who would soon know how to put the matter right. He was not subtle-minded himself, and hardly knew how to deal with such a case, but the doctor would manage all that. So, for the moment, he said nothing, and schooled himself to listen with sympathy and patience. In spite of his conclusions, however, he regretted that his sister looked to him for protection in such a matter, and almost wished he had not come.

"Then, only a month ago," she went on, "Masters herself came to give warning. She cried a lot, and declared she really could not stand it any longer."

"Masters sees him too?"

"As often as I do nearly. The very night she gave notice he came into my room and said I must not let her go on any account, for she was such a wonderful medium, and he could not manifest at all without a medium. If Masters left he would be unable to come back, and he would suffer—and be very unhappy."

"So the wretched woman is still here?"

"I was obliged to double her wages before she'd consent to stay, and even now I'm always afraid she'll go out of her mind or do something dreadful like that."

The entrance of the footman with the much longed-for lamps put an end to their conversation for the moment, and the dressing-gong postponed it still further; but after a depressing *tête-à-tête* dinner, Jim asked to see Masters alone in the smoking-room. His sister was not there, for he did not wish her nerves to be further excited before going to bed.

He talked to Masters about family matters that interested them both, before approaching the topic of main interest. She volunteered little, but answered all his questions frankly, and he soon saw that she believed in it all even more implicitly than did his sister. She was less intelligent, and of course more credulous, and she told him some amazing bits of information about her late master which only confirmed Jim in his theory that these two hysterically inclined women were completely hypnotised into the belief that Captain Blundell had returned to the scene of his orgies and "experiments," and still walked the rooms and passages of the old family mansion. She mentioned that even with her higher wages she did not think she could stand it much longer.

Jim asked her particularly about the first séance at which she went into a trance.

"I simply felt kind of faint," she told him, "and then turned of a sudden all unconscious. That's all I knew till I woke up and they told me all what had 'appened while I was asleep. 'In a trance' the poor Captain called it. And after that I used to sit twice a week regular for him."

Jim felt sure she believed every word she uttered. Her descriptions of her meeting with the Captain since his death were very vivid, and she turned pale and trembled all over while she spoke of seeing his red head and bloated face bending over her bed in the night time. And when she told how she saw him moving silently down the corridors, sometimes overtaking and passing her without a word, and vanishing in the doorway of his old room, Jim was distinctly sorry that he had not waited for her recital until the morning.

But it did not in the least shake his belief that both women were entirely deluded, and his mind was already at work on a plan to send the foolish old housekeeper off on a holiday, while he got his sister up to London, and induced her to see a specialist.

He avoided further conversation on the subject that night—for his own sake as much as for theirs, and he felt quite angry with himself to note that his nerves gave an involuntary start when his sister led him to his lofty panelled bedroom, and informed him that this was the very room her husband had died in six months previously.

"There is far more chance of your seeing him if you sleep here," she explained, "and then you can judge for yourself. Masters, who sleeps just across the passage so as to be near me, tried hard to prevent my putting you here; but I knew you wouldn't feel the least afraid. But, do please remember, Jim," she added pleadingly, "if he comes, not to speak roughly or unkindly to him."

She was gone and the door closed behind her.

Jim's reflections for the next few minutes were very far from pleasant. He believed none of it, but he had nerves for all that; and to be put to sleep in the death-room, with a medium servant opposite and a hysterical sister a little farther up the passage—this was more than he had bargained for. His mind and imagination were alive with all the stories of the evil apparition he had heard; and even his bedroom, he noticed, was littered with spiritualist journals and cheap occult magazines, dealing with the marvellous and terrifying side of this class of things.

No wonder, he reflected, that these women, living alone in the country, their minds still dominated by the bluster and superstition of the bibulous Blundell—no wonder they still saw him walking the floors and whispering at them in the darkness of the night. It was matter for surprise they did not see and hear a great deal more.

And, although Jim possessed a strong will, and had soon reduced his imagination to order, it required considerable effort on his part to crawl between the sheets of old Blundell's bed and blow the candles out on the table beside him. And the last picture in his mind as he finally fell asleep took the form of this man as he had seen him at his sister's wedding years ago—with his flaming red hair, his bloated cheeks, and his small, pig-like eyes.

For all that, however, he slept undisturbed, and during the following day he tried to divert his sister's thoughts as much as possible to other things than spirits. He also contrived that Masters should never once see her alone.

For three days the household moved along normal and unexciting channels of ordinary country life, but the fourth morning Helen came down to breakfast pale and trembling, and declared her husband had appeared to her in the night, and had whispered that he could not come as before so long as Jim was in the house, and that he was suffering and very unhappy. Her brother's sceptical attitude, he said, destroyed the conditions, and made it almost impossible for him to materialise.

"That explains, you see, why he has not appeared to you," she said weepingly.

Jim did not care what the explanation might be, so long as the apparition did not actually come; and this only made him feel more than ever that his theory was correct, and that the whole story was a tissue of moonshine and hysteria.

But that very night something happened that compelled him to reconsider his theories, and, if possible, to readjust them.

It was after midnight when he came up from the smoking-room, where an interesting novel had detained him far beyond his usual hour. In order not to disturb his sister, whose room he had to pass, he took off his shoes and walked on tiptoe up the stairs. The house was dark and silent, and the great hall he had to pass through seemed unusually large. Its proportions seemed almost to have altered. To find his way he was obliged to keep his hand on the rail; but half-way up he became so confused as to his exact whereabouts that he decided to return to the smoking-room and get a candle.

It was at this very moment that his nerves signalled a warning to him. His heart suddenly began to beat very fast, and as he turned to grope his way downstairs he became aware that "something" had moved up directly in front of him out of the darkness.

Something, he felt positive, was standing within two feet, or less, of his person. In another second he would touch it. Everything was pitch-black; and at once his mind was flooded with the details of what his sister and Masters had seen. With terrible vividness the horrible stories came before him. The hair rose on his head, and he felt his knees shake. The theory about hypnotised and hysterical women, so convincing in the daylight, seemed in a second to have become inadequate and absurd. The frightened face of the housekeeper and his sister's pallor occurred to him with new meaning.

He tried hard to pull himself together, and began to fumble in his pocket for a match; but he only just had time to move a little to one side and get his back up against the wall, when the darkness before him grew faintly luminous, and he plainly saw a figure moving slowly past him down the stairs.

Jim felt the sweat trickling down his neck as he stared. Something with human shape passed him slowly, silently, with a sort of dim light of its own just sufficient to make it visible. It made absolutely no sound, but he felt the air stir on his cheek; and, just at the second when it was closest to him, it turned slowly round and showed him its face.

Jim almost screamed aloud. It was a man with bloated cheeks, small shining eyes, and red hair!

He thought every instant the figure would spring at him out of the darkness, and he almost fell forward on to it, and feared he would collapse on the floor from sheer fright. But, in the same second, it passed him and was gone; moving by with soundless feet as though his own presence had been quite unobserved.

His first thought was to rush to his sister or to Masters, and tell them what he had seen. But cooler thoughts followed quickly, when he reflected how mortified he would be to confess that he was too frightened to follow the figure and speak to it. Instead, his trembling fingers found a match, and he at once struck a light and peered about him.

The shadows ran away on all sides, and he saw a long empty corridor, lined with pictures, but devoid of all doors or furniture, and certainly destitute of any other human figure than his own. But it was not the passage he knew! Evidently he had taken the wrong turning in the dark. He ought to have gone up another flight of stairs before turning, and he forthwith began to retrace his steps by the light of the match, and happily reached his own door before its last flicker left him in the darkness again.

And, once within his own room, he locked the door, poked the fire into a blaze, lit every candle he could find—and then sat down to think it all over.

After thinking it over for half an hour, safe from the paralysing effects of fear, Jim realised honestly enough that his theories needed readjusting. He, therefore, readjusted them to the best of his ability—and then got into bed and slept peacefully till morning.

Next day he told his sister what he had seen, but assured her at the same time that he had a plan for making the unhappy spirit return to its grave and rest quietly.

"It was Harry, you see, as I told you."

"It gave me an awful turn," said Jim. "Eyes, face, hair, and all. It was exactly like him."

"And you really think you can stop it without making him unhappy?" she asked plaintively.

"I'll try. It won't make him unhappy, I promise that. Don't let Masters know I've seen him, or she'll have hysterics."

Jim arranged with his sister that he should slip into her room late that night, unobserved, and sleep on the sofa behind the curtains. She was to wake him when the apparition came, in case he was asleep. For the rest she must have confidence in him—and wait results.

At a few minutes past eleven Jim took up his position on the sofa behind the curtains, making himself comfortable with rugs and pillows. His sister was soon asleep. But he himself lay there with every sense alert, waiting for the first signs of the apparition. The room was in complete darkness, the house silent as the grave.

It was well after one o'clock when the sound of a door-handle being turned roused him out of a light doze and made his hand seek the dark lantern ready for use. Very cautiously and quietly the door was opened—and some one moved stealthily into the room.

The darkness was too great to allow him to see a vestige of anything, but from the sound of drapery brushing against the wardrobe he knew that the intruder was standing somewhere between him and the front of the bed.

An instant later he knew that this was correct, for the faint, pale, luminous glow he had seen the night before on the stairs made itself visible just where the bed ended, and Jim was able to make out by its aid the indistinct outline of a human head and shoulders.

At the same moment his sister moved uneasily in her sleep. The bed was being gently shaken; and almost immediately afterwards the jolting awakened her, and he heard her terrified voice from the bed-clothes:

"Harry, is that you, dear?"

A sepulchral whisper replied from the shape at the foot of the bed:

"It is. But I cannot come again while your brother is in the house."

The light shifted a little, and Jim plainly saw the mass of red hair on the figure's head.

"I will tell him," answered Helen, in a terrified whisper. "Please do not be angry with me."

"I am angry only because you do not obey me," continued the hoarse whisper. "You do not carry out what I say."

"But what have I not done?"

"The money I want left to my faithful old housekeeper is still not arranged for. You have not altered the will as I directed."

"But I will do so tomorrow, Harry dear—at once," said the other with a gulp of terror.

Meanwhile Jim had stealthily left his hiding-place on tiptoe and come close up to the apparition of Captain Blundell. He was almost touching it, and as his sister uttered these last words, he encircled the figure with his arms, and clapped his handkerchief over its mouth. There was a smothered cry, and a wild rush across the room in the darkness. Helen uttered a piercing scream, and when the door slammed behind him, Jim found himself out in the passage, with a very solid apparition struggling in his arms most violently.

"If you don't keep quiet, I'll stun you, d'ye hear?" he whispered.

The figure made no reply, and he dragged and carried the still struggling "Captain Blundell" down the passage into his own room. Once in, he produced the rope he had already provided in view of this very climax, and tied up the apparition so that it could not possibly move. Then he ran back to his sister's room as fast as his legs could carry him, first locking his door on the outside.

He found her with every candle alight, sobbing with terror, and in a condition certainly bordering on hysteria.

"Oh, Jim, did you see him that time? But what happened, and did he try to injure you? It was all so terrible. . . ."

"Come quickly," cried her brother. "Come to my room. I've laid the ghost. You never need be afraid again."

He dragged her by the hand, clad in a dressing-gown and shaking like a leaf, down the passage to his own room. He unlocked the door and they went in together. Silence and darkness met them.

"Now, Helen," he said, "I'll give you a light and you shall see the spirit better than you've ever seen it before."

There was a sound of heavy shuffling in the darkness. He turned his dark lantern on the scene at the same moment.

Helen gave a long scream and caught his arm for support. There, in front of them, leaning in a half-faint against the bed-post, just as Jim had left her, stood Masters, the old housekeeper! She had a villainous red wig on her head; her cheeks were rouged violently, and her eyes painted. And at her feet lay a faintly luminous slate, and the sheet she had used to wrap round her neck and shoulders.

Before releasing her, Jim insisted on Helen taking him at once to the woman's bedroom, where, as he suspected, they found further paraphernalia, consisting of a second red wig, grease paint, rubber hands, a couple of slates, and white sheets with loose arms carefully sewed on to them. She had learned all the tricks from the "professionals," and had played them at their own game and beaten them clean out of the market.

But Helen Blundell was never troubled again by the apparition of her late husband, and Masters, the faithful old housekeeper, had to seek another place without a character.

Up and Down

His vagueness, apparently, is only on the surface of his mind; down at the centre the pulses of life throb with unusual vigour and decision. And I think the explanation of his puzzled expression and dazed manner—to say nothing of his idiotic replies—when addressed upon ordinary topics is due to the fact that he prefers to live in that hot and very active centre. He dislikes being called out of it.

Down there his creative imagination is for ever at work: he sees clearly, thinks hard, acts even splendidly. But the moment you speak to him about trivial things the mists gather about his eyes, his voice hesitates, his hands make futile gestures, and he screws up his face into an expression of puzzled alarm. Up he comes to the best of his ability, but it is clear he is vexed at being disturbed.

"Oh yes, I think so—very," he replied the other day as we met on our way to the Club and I asked if he had enjoyed his holiday.

"Awful amount of rain, though, wasn't there?"

"Was there now? Yes, there must have been, of course. It *was* a wet summer."

He looked at me as though I were a comparative stranger, although our intimacy is of years' standing, and our talks on life, literature, and all the rest are a chief pleasure to each of us. We had not met for some months. I wanted to pierce through to that hot centre where the real man lived, and to find out what the real man had been doing during the interval. He came up slowly, however.

"You went to the mountains as usual, I suppose?" he asked, with his mind obviously elsewhere. He hopped along the pavement with his quick, bird-like motion.

"Mountains, yes. And you?"

He made no reply. From his face I could tell he had come about half-way up, but was already on the way down again. Once he got back to that centre of his I should get nothing out of him at all.

"And you?" I repeated louder. "Abroad, I suppose, somewhere?"

"Well—-er—not exactly," he mumbled. "That is to say—I—er—went to Switzerland somewhere—Austria, I mean—down there on the way towards Italy *beyond Bozen, you know.*" He ended the sentence very loud indeed, with quite absurd emphasis, as his way is when he knows he hasn't been listening. "I found a quiet inn out of the tourist track and did a rare lot of work there too." His face cleared and the brown eyes began to glow a little. It was like seeing the sun through opening mists. "Come in, and I'll tell you about it," he added, in an eager whisper, as we reached the Club doors.

At the same moment, however, the porter came down the steps and touched his hat, and my vague friend, recognising a face he felt he ought to know, stopped to ask him how he was, and whether So-and-so was back yet; and while the porter replied briefly and respectfully I saw to my dismay the mists settle down again upon the other's face. A moment later the porter touched his hat again and moved off down the street. My friend looked round at me as though I had but just arrived upon the scene.

"Here we are," he observed gently, "at the Club. I think I shall go in. What are *you* going to do?"

"I'm coming in too," I said.

"Good," he murmured; "let's go in together, then," his thoughts working away busily at something deep within him.

On our way to the hat-racks, and all up the winding stairs, he mumbled away about the wet summer, and tourists, and his little mountain inn, but never a word of the work I was so anxious to hear about, and he so anxious really to tell. In the reading-room I manœuvred to get two arm-chairs side by side before he could seize the heap of papers he smothered his lap with, but never read.

"And where have *you* been all the summer?" he asked, crossing his little legs and speaking in a voice loud enough to have been heard in the street. "Somewhere in the mountains, I suppose, as usual?"

"You were going to tell me about the work you got through up in your lonely inn," I insisted sharply. "Was it a play, or a novel, or criticism, or what?" He looked so small and lost in the big arm-chair that I felt quite ashamed of myself for speaking so violently. He turned round on the slippery leather and offered me a cigarette. The glow came back to his face.

"Well," he said, "as a matter of fact it was both. That is, I was preparing a stage version of my new novel." All the mist had gone now; he was alive at the centre, and thoroughly awake. He snapped his case to and put it away before I had taken my cigarette. But, of course, he did not notice that, and held out a lighted match to my lips as though there was something there to light.

"No, thanks," I said quickly, fearful that if I asked again for the cigarette the mists would instantly gather once more and the real man disappear.

"Won't you *really*, though?" he said, blowing the match out and forgetting to light his own cigarette at the same time. "I did the whole scenario, and most of the first act. There was nothing else to do. It rained all the time, and the place was quiet as the grave—"

A waiter brought him several letters on a tray. He took them automatically. The face clouded a bit.

"What'll you have?" he asked absent-mindedly, acting automatically upon the presence of the waiter.

"Nothing, thanks."

"Nor will I, then. Oh yes, I will, though—I'll have some dry ginger ale. Here, waiter! Bring me a small dry ginger ale."

The waiter, with the force of habit, bent his head questioningly for my order too.

"*You* said—?" asked my exasperating friend. He was right down in the mists now, and I knew I should never get him up again this side of lunch.

"I said nothing, thanks."

"Nothing, then, for this gentleman," he continued, gazing up at the waiter as though he were some monster seen for the first time, "and for me—a dry ginger ale, please."

"Yes, sir," said the man, moving off.

"Small," the other called after him.

"Yessir—small."

"And a slice of lemon in it."

The waiter inclined his head respectfully from the door. The other turned to me, searching in his perturbed mind—I could tell it by the way his eyes worked—for the trail of his vanished conversation. Before he got it, however, he slithered round again on the leather seat towards the door.

"A bit of ice too, don't forget!"

The waiter's head peeped round the corner, and from the movement of his lips I gathered he repeated the remark about the bit of ice.

"I *did* say 'dry'?" my friend asked, looking, anxiously at me; "didn't I?"

"You did."

"And a bit of lemon?"

"And a slice of lemon."

"And what are *you* going to have, then? Upon my word, old man, I forgot to ask you." He looked so distressed that it was impossible to show impatience.

"Nothing, thanks. You asked me, you know."

A pause fell between us. I gave it up. He would talk when he wanted to, but there was no forcing him. It struck me suddenly that he had a rather fagged and weary look for a man who had been spending several weeks at a mountain inn with work he loved. The pity and affection his presence always wakes in me ran a neck-and-neck race. At that "centre" of his, I knew full well, he was ever devising plans for the helping of others, quite as much as creating those remarkable things that issued periodically, ill-understood by a sensation-loving public, from the press. A sharp telepathic suspicion flashed through my mind, but before there was time to give it expression in words, up came the waiter with a long glass of ginger ale fizzing on a tray.

He handed it to my vague friend, and my vague friend took it and handed it to me.

"But it's yours, my dear chap," I suggested.

He looked puzzled for a second, and then his face cleared. "I forget what *you* ordered," he observed softly, looking interrogatively at the waiter and at me. We informed him simultaneously, "Nothing," and the waiter respectfully mentioned the price of the drink. My friend's left hand plunged into his trousers pocket, while his right carried the glass to his lips. Perhaps his left hand did not know what his right was about, or perhaps his mind was too far away to direct the motions of either with safety. Anyhow, the result was deplorable. He swallowed an uncomfortable gulp of air-bubbles and ginger—and choked—over me, over the waiter and tray, over his beard and clothes. The floating lump of ice bobbed up and hit his nose. I never saw a man look so surprised and distressed in my life. I took the glass from him, and when his left hand finally emerged with money he handed it first vaguely to me as though I were the waiter—for which there was no real excuse, since we were not in evening dress.

When, at length, order was restored and he was sipping quietly at the remains of the fizzing liquid, he looked up at me over the brim of his glass and remarked, with more concentration on the actual present than he had yet shown:

"By the way, you know, I'm going away to-morrow—going abroad for my holiday. Taking a lot of work with me, too—"

"But you've only just come back!" I expostulated, with a feeling very like anger in my heart.

He shook his head with decision. Evidently that choking had choked him into the living present. He was really "up" this time, and not likely to go down again.

"No, no," he replied; "I've been here all the summer in town looking after old Podger—"

"Old Podger!" I remembered a dirty, down-at-heel old man I once met at my friend's rooms—a poet who had "smothered his splendid talent" in drink, and who was always at starvation's door. "What in the world was the matter with Podger?"

"D.T. I've been nursing him through it. The poor devil nearly went under this time. I've got him into a home down in the country at last, but all August he was—well, we thought he was gone."

All August! So that was how my friend's summer had been spent. With never a word of thanks probably at that!

"But your mountain inn beyond Bozen! You said—"

"Did I? I must be wool-gathering," he laughed, with that beautifully tender smile that comes sometimes to his delicate, dreamy face. "That was *last* year. I spent my holidays last year up there. How stupid of me to get so absurdly muddled!" He plunged his nose into the empty glass, waiting for the last drop to trickle out, with his neck at an angle that betrayed the collar to be undone and the tie sadly frayed at the edges.

"But—all the work you said you did up there—the scenario and the first act and—and—"

He turned upon me with such sudden energy that I fairly jumped. Then, in a voice that mumbled the first half of his sentence, but shouted the end like a German officer giving instructions involving life or death, I heard:

"But, my dear good fellow, you don't half listen to what I say! All that work, as I told you just now, is what I expect and mean to do when I get up there. *Now*—have you got it clear at last?"

He looked me up and down with great energy. By biting the inner side of my lip I kept my face grave. Later we went down to lunch together, and I heard details of the weeks of unselfish devotion he had lavished upon "old Podger." I would give a great deal to possess some of the driving power for good that throbs and thrills at the real centre of my old friend with the vague manner and the absent-minded surface. But he is a singular contradiction, and almost always misunderstood. I should like to know, too, what Podger thinks.

The Face of the Earth

Finkelstein, like many another German, resembled a weak edition of Bismarck. A little way off the appearance was remarkable. Closer, of course, one saw the softness of eye and indecision of jaw that destroyed the illusion.

"I want you to fearful be—of nozzing," he said, looking the young man up and down.

"I am afraid of nothing," said Arthur Spinrobin, believing that the secretaryship was already his.

"Goot," said the old professor. "I take you on!"

And thus Arthur Spinrobin, orphan, penniless, the money provided for his Cambridge education just exhausted, began the high adventure of his life by a three months' engagement to Professor Adolf Finkelstein. The only qualification was that he should know German, have some knowledge of surveying, and be "afraid of nothing." Finkelstein, for reasons best known to himself, lived at the time in a little farmhouse of grey stone among the folds of the Dorsetshire hills; and thither Spinrobin, small, round, and active, with cheerful face and sanguine heart, betook himself, as agreed, on September 1.

"It may lead to something," he said to himself at the end of the first week; "but it's all jolly queer. I wonder if the old boy is a spy—or merely a lunatic." He remembered that he was expected to be afraid of nothing. Arrest, high treason, and other ominous words occurred to him; but in the end he rejected them all. "He's one of these Teutonic dreamers—transcendentalist and all that—gone a little bit cracky." Only the map-making puzzled him—uneasily.

For the life they led was not quite ordinary. They had a big sitting-room and a bedroom each in the farmhouse that was glad enough to take in a couple of boarders. The mornings they spent translating various German passages, beginning with authors like Novalis and Schlegel, and ending with more modern writers that Spinrobin had never heard of. While Finkelstein translated into French, Spinrobin did likewise into English—apparently with a view to simultaneous publication in both languages of some big Essay the German professor was at work on. This Essay was to include these passages, but Finkelstein did not take the secretary into his confidence concerning it. There was an air of mystery about the whole thing.

And the translated passages always had to do with one subject, viz., that the Earth was the body of a great Being—living, conscious; that it had organs and a physiognomy; that the beauty of nature was merely a revelation of its personality; and that human beings could no more realise this than a fly on an elephant could realise that it walked upon a living body differing from its own merely in size and habits.

"Some faces are too big to be seen as faces," Finkelstein said one morning to him. Then, leaning forward through the tobacco smoke above their work table, he suddenly touched Spinrobin's little turn-up nose with his thick finger. "The ten million microbes there dwelling," he said with an earnestness that made the secretary start, "do not know they are on a human face, *was?*" For he talked German and English indiscriminately.

The afternoons they walked together upon the hills, Spinrobin in normal shooting costume, and Finkelstein in baggy grey knickerbockers, elastic-side boots with nails, a loose jacket of Austrian Loden cloth, and a Tyrolese hat. A camera was swung round his shoulder, for he took frequent photographs, which he developed himself.

"Look," he said, pointing to the smooth, rounded hill-tops about them, treeless, with sheep and cattle feeding in groups. "The cheeks of a great face—see, I photograph it now, and later show you somezing your own little sight cannot take in. *Ach!* the camera is fine for that. *Wer weisst? Wer weisst?*" . . .

But the chalk pits drew him most, and he was for ever taking photographs or making sketches of them, and asking his secretary to draw accurate plans showing the exact relation they bore to one another; and poring over the results on paper at home till the smoke got too thick to see, and he would put them away with a sigh and discuss plans for the morrow. In particular there were two pits about a mile apart that interested him, with a third some hundreds of feet below them, very deep, with a ragged edge where gorse and furze bushes grew in a fringe along the lips.

"There, we have it, I think," he used to say in German, after wandering for hours from one to the other, and studying endless photographs and plans of them at home. "There, we have it. Wait and see if I am not right." All of which bewildered the secretary hopelessly, until one day, in his chief's absence, he peeped into his bedroom, and saw on the walls his own series of maps, distorted out of all truth or accuracy, with the pits marked in red, and the whole presenting different aspects of a mighty and very dreadful countenance. The two smaller pits were eyes, and the lower deep one with the bushes fringing it like hair, was a mouth—a huge, open, gaping mouth. The sight produced in him an unpleasant sense of alarm and disgust he was at a loss to account for. . . .

"*Ach,* not here! Do not stumble here!" the German cried one day when Spinrobin slipped near the edge of the bigger pit, and his face was so white that for a moment it seemed almost as if the depths of chalk below had shot up some curious message of reflected light upon his skin. And for some reason he never could explain quite to himself, the secretary always avoided that particular pit afterwards. A certain sense of personality pervaded it; and when the Professor told him the stories (corroborated in some measure, too, by the farmer) about the number of sheep and cattle it devoured yearly, the sense of dread— though he laughed at it—increased. One evening, too, coming home alone, he heard the wind whistling and booming round its white sides, polishing them to smoothness, and the sudden fancy leaped into his brain of a great purring throat. "Absurd!" he laughed, turning with a run in a safer direction; "this old Finkelstein with his crazy anthropomorphism has got into my imagination."

And that very night they translated long passages from Fechner— told with a bold power and originality that made it all unpleasantly real to the ordinarily cheerful, healthy-minded little secretary. "Like your own visionary, ze great Blake," exclaimed Finkelstein in the middle, curiously excited (and using a vigorous English phrase utterly incongruous to the professional type, and picked up heaven knows where!) "zis Fechner has a great imagination that bangs straight through into Reality!"

Thus there gradually grew up about the innocent Spinrobin a queer sense that the world was no longer quite the same as he had hitherto seen it. This Fechner, whom the Professor studied, laid a new spell upon him. The water for fish, the air for birds; the ether—well, the ether, too, in turn had its own denizens: worlds! The stars were alive; the planets great spiritual Beings; the earth on which he lived was the physical body of some vast Intelligence that boomed its mighty way through space just as he himself pattered with quick little footsteps across a field. Moreover, Finkelstein elaborated the theory of his fellow countryman with singular conviction.

"Ze worlds are ze true angels," he said, "and not imachination is ze music of the spheres. *Ach!* I will proof it to everypody when I gif out zis great book I write." Then, puffing his pipe voluminously into his secretary's face, he would become enthusiastic and more confidential. The worlds, he declared, were some kind of Beings superior to men and animals, but alive and conscious in the same sense. He dwelt upon the analogy till water came into his soft eyes, and his gesticulations threatened the crockery as well as Spinrobin's own astonished features. Arms and legs, he said, after all are only crutches to enable ill-constructed creatures to get about—whereas the worlds have no need for them, being round. Eyes are equally unnecessary, for they find their way through the ether without them infallibly. For lungs—their whole surface is in continual commerce with the winds; and for circulation, the rivers, springs, and rains are unceasing. Also all the worlds are in most delicate touch with one another, keenly sensitive to the last variation; and where they grow cold—they die.

"*Ach! Donnerwetter!* they starve!" he would cry with something between anger and laughter, as though his uncouth imaginations were really true.

And Spinrobin, hearing all this from morning till night, and having practical explanations given to him during their walks among the hills, reached a point before long where he became exceedingly uncomfortable. Those maps and tortured photographs haunted his dreams with their suggestions of Faces that it is not good for man to look upon. . . .

He kept incessant watch upon Finkelstein. It came to him somehow or other that the work, and the walks, and all the rest of it were a laboured pretence. The German dreamer had some very practical, matter-of-fact purpose behind all his imaginative writing and talking. It made him uneasy. Once or twice on the hills he caught Finkelstein looking at him with a singular expression in his eyes—an expression that made him inclined to run, or to cry for help, or do something to draw attention to themselves; and on more than one occasion he was certain he heard some one treading softly in the night about the door of his bedroom. And Spinrobin, though not a coward, was decidedly of the timid order. He did not like it! It bewildered his respectable and commonplace soul.

"There," exclaimed Finkelstein, in his native tongue, one November evening, when a first spray of snow had whitened the hills, "there you see it well. The snow helps to bring it out—the great whitened face with glorious features! *Ach! Ach!* In these desolate places where men have done little to obliterate or disturb, you can see more plainly." He indicated the curious configuration of the hills about them. From the high point on which they stood Spinrobin's awakened imagination easily permitted him to trace the "great whitened face" the enthusiastic German referred to. The pits marked the two eyes, now closed by the shadows of the dusk; and he saw the large, deep, capacious mouth, gaping wide open beneath its fringe of hair-like trees and bushes. It certainly bore a curious resemblance to a vast Face thrust up from below, the features outlined by the powdered snow.

The man came close to his side, and began to talk very rapidly. The secretary's knowledge of German was good, but the other talked so quickly, using such strange phrases and clipping his words with such guttural gymnastics, that he found it difficult to follow.

The only thing he gathered generally was that Finkelstein was indulging his imagination, aided by a grotesque humour, in describing the Death of the Earth. The snow and cold made him forecast the time when the body of the earth would be finally dead; and the cause, he declared—here came in the grotesque humour—was that she could no longer feed her internal fires. Mouths, channels, monstrous funnels to act as feeding pipes should be constructed, and the old earth should be kept alive for ever. Or she might even be fed through smaller holes like these very pits—he pointed to them, catching Spinrobin suddenly by the arm—just as human beings might be fed through the pores of the skin!

Spinrobin jumped away from his side in the middle of the strange outburst. They had approached nearer to the edge of the big pit than he cared about.

"My imachination runs me away!" cried the Professor. "Come, let us get home to supper. For it is our duty to feed our own bodies before we feed the earth"; and he laughed aloud as he followed his startled secretary down the stony hill path back to the farm.

During the next few days he made frequent reference, however, to this bizarre notion of feeding the dying earth through holes in her surface—pores in her skin. Spinrobin watched him more carefully than before.

Apparently he was not the only person who watched him, for one afternoon that same week the farmer came abruptly into the secretary's bedroom, and asked for a private word with him. Finkelstein was out. Briefly the man came with a warning. "You seem innocent like," explained he, "but you ain't the first secretary he's had down here, nor the first that's disappeared."

"But I've not disappeared!" gasped Spinrobin.

"You may do, though—in the cold weather."

The old man was cryptic and mysterious. He received a big price for his rooms, he explained, but—well, he could not help giving a warning to such a nice young fellow as Spinrobin.

The secretary felt his flesh begin to crawl, and a sudden light dawned upon him. The step of the German already sounded in the hall below, and he turned with a quick question to the friendly farmer. It was guesswork, but apparently it hit the bull's-eye.

"The sheep and cattle, then, that disappear—?"

"Oh! but he pays me big prices for them—"

The approaching steps of Finkelstein sent the farmer about his business, but Spinrobin went into his room and locked the door. He began to understand things better. His first quarter was up that week. He came to an abrupt decision. Finkelstein could get a new secretary! . . . and next day when he chose a discreet opportunity to announce his decision with plausible excuses, the Professor merely fixed his watery eyes on his face with the remark in German—"I regret it. You have been a patient and admirable secretary—just the material I want for my great—my great purpose." But the phrase "just the material" was ominous and stuck in Spinrobin's mind. Somehow he had come now to loathe the man—his voice, eyes, and gestures. His speculations no longer interested him as before. They touched secret springs of abhorrence and alarm in the depths of him. The figure with Tyrolese hat, baggy knickerbockers, and shapeless legs ending in the ridiculous elastic-side boots became cloaked with suggestions of a strange horror he could not in the least explain to himself.

And it was a week later—his last day, in fact—when a sound woke him at two in the morning, and he peeped out of his window and saw Finkelstein in the moonlight standing with the Loden cloak about his shoulders and throwing up small stones to attract his attention. The moon was reflected in his big spectacles. He carried a long stick. Grotesquely forbidding he looked.

"Come out," he whispered gutturally, holding up a finger to enjoin silence, "come out and see. It is too wonderful! *Ach!* it is too wonderful!" He was greatly excited, it seemed.

"What?" stammered little Spinrobin, half frightened. It was like a figure in a nightmare he felt, a figure he was compelled to obey, for his unlined young soul was very sensitive to suggestion, and this German undoubtedly exercised unconscious hypnotic influence over him.

"The pits are working!" continued the thick German voice. "Only once in a lifetime you see such a thing, perhaps. *Ach,* but quick, come quick. It is the feeding-time. I show you! *Was?* The feeding-time . . . !"

A crowd of conflicting emotions in the breast of the shivering Spinrobin—curiosity, fear, wonder, and a rash courage of youth that urged him to see this extraordinary adventure to its end—found their resultant expression (to this day he cannot quite explain how!) and brought him in a few minutes to the side of the German outside. They moved rapidly up the hill.

Moonlight lay over the whole tossed landscape of mountain and valley, and a gusty south-west wind from the sea boomed and echoed in the hollows. He heard it swish through the patches of long grass about their feet, and past his ears. The German, wrapped in his cloak, and holding his long stick partly concealed, led the way. His calves, thought Spinrobin, looked just like sausages. At any other time he could have laughed. . . . Instead, he pattered behind, shivering.

"Hark!" whispered Finkelstein, stopping a moment for breath, after a mile of silent climbing. "Now, you hear it." And the secretary heard in the distance that booming sound of the wind as it rushed like mighty breathing about the mouth of the big pit.

The same intense curiosity that had brought him out on this mad expedition overcame the instinct to turn and run—for his life. Finkelstein, he saw, was making sudden awkward movements under cover of his cloak. They were standing some fifty yards from the edge now. The great opening gaped there in the moonlight down the steep slope in front.

"It is the great cold," the German was crying, half to himself, "the cold that means death! She cries for food! Listen." He was very excited. "*Ach!* The great service you shall perhaps render!"

The wind rose with a wild roar about them, freezingly cold; it shouted horribly in the depths of the capacious opening in the hillside. It cried with shrill, swishing sounds as it rushed through the fringe of bushes that grew along the dizzy edge.

"She cried for you, for you, for you! *Ach!* You are so privileged as that!" called out Finkelstein, the "crise" of his mania full upon him, and fairly dancing with excitement. "It is only young food she wants. She refuses me again . . . !" And a lot more that Spinrobin did not understand.

The whole thing, and the ghastly dementia of this crazy German was very clear to him now!

He was an active, nimble-footed little fellow, but somehow or other he stumbled at the first step. The German's arm shot out, and the rope at the end of the long stick whistled dreadfully in the air as it flew towards him, and entangled itself about his legs. It flashed in the moonlight—death in its coils.

Spinrobin yelled and struggled. Finkelstein, breathing hard, came up along the shortening rope hand over hand towards him, pulling him nearer and nearer to the edge. They rolled and bumped down the precipitous slope, the German just managing to keep out of reach, and the mingled shouting of the two voices rose in wild clamour through the night.

"But why struggle?" cried the lunatic. "There will be no pain, no pain. And you are worth fifty sheep or cattle . . . !" The spectacled eyes shone like little lamps of silver.

"You shall come too, you brute!" shrieked Spinrobin, at last catching him by an elastic boot and dragging him down upon the ground with a crash.

They rolled a bit. Close to the brink, caught by the fringe of gorse bushes which tore and scratched him (though he only knew it afterwards when he saw the scars!), they stopped. The rope was hopelessly entangled about their feet. For a second the struggle ceased. Spinrobin heard a loosened stone drop past them, and land with a distant clatter far below. He made a tremendous effort. But the German wriggled free, and stood over him.

Spinrobin, dizzy and exhausted, closed his eyes. The wind rose with a booming roar, and to his terrified imagination it seemed like great arms that spread out a net to catch him as he fell.

"You feed her! You feed her! *Ach,* it is fine . . . !" The wind tore away with his words.

A moment later he would have toppled over to his death, when one of the gorse bushes, to his utter amazement, stood upright, struck the figure of the German a resounding blow in the chest that sent him spinning backwards to the ground, and at the same instant clutched Spinrobin's feet, and dragged him up into comparative safety.

It was the farmer, who had been disturbed by their leaving the house, and had followed them up the hill. But Spinrobin never knew quite how it happened. He fairly spun—mind and body.

How they managed between them to truss the maniac with the rope and stick, and carry him back, was not without humour; but the full meaning of the "secretaryship" (for which Spinrobin never received his salary) was only apparent some weeks later when the advertisement caused by the adventure drew out the whole facts.

For Finkelstein, it appeared, with his singular form of homicidal mania, was proved by the joint investigations of the English and German police to have been the author of at least three mysterious "disappearances" of young men who had acted as his secretaries; and his remarkable lunacy that imagined the Earth to be a living Being who required human sustenance to keep her alive (he, Finkelstein, being High Priest of the Ceremony), is now minutely recorded for all who care to read, in the Proceedings of the Psychological Societies of both countries.

The Man Who Played upon the Leaf

Where the Jura pine-woods push the fringe of their purple cloak down the slopes till the vineyards stop them lest they should troop into the lake of Neuchâtel, you may find the village where lived the Man Who Played upon the Leaf.

My first sight of him was genuinely prophetic—that spring evening in the garden café of the little mountain auberge. But before I saw him I heard him, and ever afterwards the sound and the sight have remained inseparable in my mind.

Jean Grospierre and Louis Favre were giving me confused instructions—the *vin rouge* of Neuchâtel is heady, you know—as to the best route up the Tête-de-Rang, when a thin, wailing music, that at first I took to be rising wind, made itself heard suddenly among the apple trees at the end of the garden, and riveted my attention with a thrill of I know not what.

Favre's description of the bridle path over Mont Racine died away; then Grospierre's eyes wandered as he, too, stopped to listen; and at the same moment a mongrel dog of indescribably forlorn appearance came whining about our table under the walnut tree.

"It's Perret 'Comment-va,' the man who plays on the leaf," said Favre.

"And his cursed dog," added Grospierre, with a shrug of disgust. And, after a pause, they fell again to quarrelling about my complicated path up the Tête-de-Rang.

I turned from them in the direction of the sound.

The dusk was falling. Through the trees I saw the vineyards sloping down a mile or two to the dark blue lake with its distant-shadowed shore and the white line of misty Alps in the sky beyond. Behind us the forests rose in folded purple ridges to the heights of Boudry and La Tourne, soft and thick like carpets of cloud. There was no one

about in the cabaret. I heard a horse's hoofs in the village street, a rattle of pans from the kitchen, and the soft roar of a train climbing the
mountain railway through gathering darkness towards France—and,
singing through it all, like a thread of silver through a dream, this sweet
and windy music.

But at first there was nothing to be seen. The Man Who Played on
the Leaf was not visible, though I stared hard at the place whence the
sound apparently proceeded. The effect, for a moment, was almost
ghostly.

Then, down there among the shadows of fruit trees and small
pines, something moved, and I became aware with a start that the little
sapin I had been looking at all the time was really not a tree, but a
man—hatless, with dark face, loose hair, and wearing a *pèlerine* over his
shoulders. How he had produced this singularly vivid impression and
taken upon himself the outline and image of a tree is utterly beyond me
to describe. It was, doubtless, some swift suggestion in my own imagination that deceived me. . . . Yet he was thin, small, straight, and his flying
hair and spreading *pèlerine* somehow pictured themselves in the network of dusk and background into the semblance, I suppose, of
branches.

I merely record my impression with the truest available words—
also my instant persuasion that this first view of the man was, after all,
significant and prophetic: his dominant characteristics presented themselves to me symbolically. I saw the man first as a tree; I heard his music first as wind.

Then, as he came slowly towards us, it was clear that he produced
the sound by blowing upon a leaf held to his lips between tightly
closed hands. And at his heel followed the mongrel dog.

"The inseparables!" sneered Grospierre, who did not appreciate
the interruption. He glanced contemptuously at the man and the dog,
his face and manner, it seemed to me, conveying a merest trace, however, of superstitious fear. "The tune your father taught you, *hein?*" he
added, with a cruel allusion I did not at the moment understand.

"Hush!" Favre said; "he plays thunderingly well all the same!" His
glass had not been emptied quite so often, and in his eyes as he listened there was a touch of something that was between respect and
wonder.

"The music of the devil," Grospierre muttered as he turned with the gesture of surly impatience to the wine and the rye bread. "It makes me dream at night. Ooua!"

The man, paying no attention to the gibes, came closer, continuing his leaf-music, and as I watched and listened the thrill that had first stirred in me grew curiously. To look at, he was perhaps forty, perhaps fifty; worn, thin, broken; and something seizingly pathetic in his appearance told its little wordless story into the air. The stamp of the outcast was mercilessly upon him. But the eyes were dark and fine. They proclaimed the possession of something that was neither worn nor broken, something that was proud to be outcast, and welcomed it.

"He's cracky, you know," explained Favre, "and half blind. He lives in that hut on the edge of the forest"—pointing with his thumb toward Côtendard—"and plays on the leaf for what he can earn."

We listened for five minutes perhaps while this singular being stood there in the dusk and piped his weird tunes; and if imagination had influenced my first sight of him it certainly had nothing to do with what I now heard. For it was unmistakable; the man played, not mere tunes and melodies, but the clean, strong, elemental sounds of Nature—especially the crying voices of wind. It was the raw material, if you like, of what the masters have used here and there—Wagner, and so forth—but by him heard closely and wonderfully, and produced with marvellous accuracy. It was now the notes of birds or the tinkle and rustle of sounds heard in groves and copses, and now the murmur of those airs that lose their way on summer noons among the tree tops; and then, quite incredibly, just as the man came closer and the volume increased, it grew to the crying of bigger winds and the whispering rush of rain among tossed branches. . . .

How he produced it passed my comprehension, but I think he somehow mingled his own voice with the actual notes of the vibrating edge of the leaf; perhaps, too, that the strange passion shaking behind it all in the depths of the bewildered spirit poured out and reached my mind by ways unknown and incalculable.

I must have momentarily lost myself in the soft magic of it, for I remember coming back with a start to notice that the man had stopped, and that his melancholy face was turned to me with a smile of comprehension and sympathy that passed again almost before I had time to recognise it, and certainly before I had time to reply. And this time I am ready to admit that it was my own imagination, singularly stirred, that translated his smile into the words that no one else heard—

"I was playing for you—because you understand."

Favre was standing up and I saw him give the man the half loaf of coarse bread that was on the table, offering also his own partly-emptied wine-glass. "I haven't the sou to-day," he was saying, "but if you're hungry, mon brave—" And the man, refusing the wine, took the bread with an air of dignity that precluded all suggestion of patronage or favour, and ought to have made Favre feel proud that he had offered it.

"And that for his son!" laughed the stupid Grospierre, tossing a cheese-rind to the dog, "or for his forest god!"

The music was about me like a net that still held my words and thoughts in a delicate bondage—which is my only explanation for not silencing the coarse guide in the way he deserved; but a few minutes later, when the men had gone into the inn, I crossed to the end of the garden, and there, where the perfumes of orchard and forest deliciously mingled, I came upon the man sitting on the grass beneath an apple-tree. The dog, wagging its tail, was at his feet, as he fed it with the best and largest portions of the bread. For himself, it seemed, he kept nothing but the crust, and—what I could hardly believe, had I not actually witnessed it—the cur, though clearly hungry, had to be coaxed with smiles and kind words to eat what it realised in some dear dog-fashion was needed even more by its master. A pair of outcasts they looked indeed, sharing dry bread in the back garden of the village inn; but in the soft, discerning eyes of that mangy creature there was an expression that raised it, for me at least, far beyond the ranks of common curdom; and in the eyes of the man, half-witted and pariah as he undoubtedly was, a look that set him somewhere in a lonely place where he heard the still, small voices of the world and moved with the elemental tides of life that are never outcast and that include the farthest suns.

He took the franc I offered; and, closer, I perceived that his eyes, for all their moments of fugitive brilliance, were indeed half sightless, and that perhaps he saw only well enough to know men as trees walking. In the village some said he saw better than most, that he saw in the dark, possibly even into the peopled regions beyond this world, and there were reasons—uncanny reasons—to explain the belief. I only know, at any rate, that from this first moment of our meeting he never failed to recognise me at a considerable distance, and to be aware of my whereabouts even in the woods at night; and the best explanation I ever heard, though of course unscientific, was Louis Favre's whispered communication that "he sees with the whole surface of his skin!"

He took the franc with the same air of grandeur that he took the bread, as though he conferred a favour, yet was grateful. The beauty of that gesture has often come back to me since with a sense of wonder for the sweet nobility that I afterwards understood inspired it. At the time, however, he merely looked up at me with the remark, *"C'est pour le Dieu*—merci!"

He did not say "le *bon* Dieu," as every one else did.

And though I had meant to get into conversation with him, I found no words quickly enough, for he at once stood up and began to play again on his leaf; and while he played his thanks and gratitude, or the thanks and gratitude of his God, that shaggy mongrel dog stopped eating and sat up beside him to listen. Both fixed their eyes upon me as the sounds of wind and birds and forest poured softly and wonderfully about my ears . . . so that, when it was over and I went down the quiet street to my *pension,* I was aware that some tiny sense of bewilderment had crept into the profounder regions of my consciousness and faintly disturbed my normal conviction that I belonged to the common world of men as of old. Some aspect of the village, especially of the human occupants in it, had secretly changed for me.

Those pearly spaces of sky, where the bats flew over the red roofs, seemed more alive, more exquisite than before; the smells of the open stables where the cows stood munching, more fragrant than usual of sweet animal life that included myself delightfully, keenly; the last chatterings of the sparrows under the eaves of my own *pension* more intimate and personal. . . .

Almost as if those strands of elemental music the man played on his leaf had for the moment made me free of the life of the earth, as distinct from the life of men. . . .

I can only suggest this, and leave the rest to the care of the imaginative reader; for it is impossible to say along what inner byways of fancy I reached the conclusion that when the man spoke of "the God," and not "the *good* God," he intended to convey his sense of some great woodland personality—some Spirit of the Forests whom he knew and loved and worshipped, and whom, he was intuitively aware, I also knew and loved and worshipped.

During the next few weeks I came to learn more about this poor, half-witted man. In the village he was known as Perret "Comment-va," the Man Who Plays on the Leaf; but when the people wished to be more explicit they described him as the man "without parents and without God." The origin of "Comment-va" I never discovered, but the other titles were easily explained—he was illegitimate and outcast. The mother had been a wandering Italian girl and the father a loose-living *bûcheron,* who was, it seems, a standing disgrace to the community. I think the villagers were not conscious of their severity; the older generation of farmers and *vignerons* had pity, but the younger ones and those of his own age were certainly guilty, if not of deliberate cruelty, at least of a harsh neglect and the utter withholding of sympathy. It was like the thoughtless cruelty of children, due to small unwisdom, and to that absence of charity which is based on ignorance. They could not in the least understand this crazy, picturesque being who wandered day and night in the forests and spoke openly, though never quite intelligibly, of worshipping another God than their own anthropomorphic deity. People looked askance at him because he was queer; a few feared him; one or two I found later—all women—felt vaguely that there was something in him rather wonderful, they hardly knew what, that lifted him beyond the reach of village taunts and sneers. But from all he was remote, alien, solitary—an outcast and a pariah.

It so happened that I was very busy at the time, seeking the seclusion of the place for my work, and rarely going out until the day was failing; and so it was, I suppose, that my sight of the man was always associated with a gentle dusk, long shadows and slanting rays of sunlight. Every time I saw that thin, straight, yet broken figure, every time the music of the leaf reached me, there came too, the inexplicable thrill of secret wonder and delight that had first accompanied his presence, and with it the subtle suggestion of a haunted woodland life, beautiful with new values. To this day I see that sad, dark face moving about the street, touched with melancholy, yet with the singular light of an inner glory that sometimes lit flames in the poor eyes. Perhaps—the fancy entered my thoughts sometimes when I passed him—those who are half out of their minds, as the saying goes, are at the same time half in another region whose penetrating loveliness has so bewildered and amazed them that they no longer can play their dull part in our commonplace world; and certainly for me this man's presence never failed to convey an awareness of some hidden and secret beauty that he knew apart from the ordinary haunts and pursuits of men.

Often I followed him up into the woods—in spite of the menacing growls of the dog, who invariably showed his teeth lest I should approach too close—with a great longing to know what he did there and how he spent his time wandering in the great forests, sometimes, I was assured, staying out entire nights or remaining away for days together. For in these Jura forests that cover the mountains from Neuchâtel to Yverdon, and stretch thickly up to the very frontiers of France, you may walk for days without finding a farm or meeting more than an occasional *bûcheron*. And at length, after weeks of failure, and by some process of sympathy he apparently communicated in turn to the dog, it came about that I was—*accepted*. I was allowed to follow at a distance, to listen and, if I could, to watch.

I make use of the conditional, because once in the forest this man had the power of concealing himself in the same way that certain animals and insects conceal themselves by choosing places instinctively where the colour of their surroundings merge into their outlines and obliterate them. So long as he moved all was well; but the moment he stopped and a chance dell or cluster of trees intervened I lost sight of him, and more than once passed within a foot of his presence without knowing it, though the dog was plainly there at his feet. And the instant I turned at the sound of the leaf, there he was, leaning against some dark tree-stem, part of a shadow perhaps, growing like a forest-thing out of the thick moss that hid his feet, or merging with extraordinary intimacy into the fronds of some drooping pine bough! Moreover, this concealment was never intentional, it seems, but instinctive. The life to which he belonged took him close to its heart, draping about the starved and wasted shoulders the cloak of kindly sympathy which the world of men denied him.

And, while I took my place some little way off upon a fallen stem, and the dog sat looking up into his face with its eyes of yearning and affection, Perret "Comment-va" would take a leaf from the nearest ivy, raise it between tightly pressed palms to his lips and begin that magic sound that seemed to rise out of the forest-voices themselves rather than to be a thing apart.

It was a late evening towards the end of May when I first secured this privilege at close quarters, and the memory of it lives in me still with the fragrance and wonder of some incredible dream. The forest just there was scented with wild lilies of the valley which carpeted the more open spaces with their white bells and big, green leaves; patches of violets and pale anemone twinkled down the mossy stairways of every glade; and through slim openings among the pine-stems I saw the shadowed blues of the lake beyond and the far line of the high Alps, soft and cloud-like in the sky. Already the woods were drawing the dusk out of the earth to cloak themselves for sleep, and in the east a rising moon stared close over the ground between the big trees, dropping trails of faint and yellowish silver along the moss. Distant cow-bells, and an occasional murmur of village voices, reached the ear. But a deep hush lay over all that mighty slope of mountain forest, and even the footsteps of ourselves and the dog had come to rest.

Then, as sounds heard in a dream, a breeze stirred the topmost branches of the pines, filtering down to us as from the wings of birds. It brought new odours of sky and sun-kissed branches with it. A moment later it lost itself in the darkening aisles of forest beyond; and out of the stillness that followed, I heard the strange music of the leaf rising about us with its extraordinary power of suggestion.

And, turning to see the face of the player more closely, I saw that it had marvellously changed, had become young, unlined, soft with joy. The spirit of the immense woods possessed him, and he was at peace. . . .

While he played, too, he swayed a little to and fro, just as a slender *sapin* sways in wind, and a revelation came to me of that strange beauty of combined sound and movement—trees bending while they sing, branches trembling and a-whisper, children that laugh while they dance. And, oh, the crying, plaintive notes of that leaf, and the pro-

found sense of elemental primitive sound that they woke in the pene-
tralia of the imagination, subtly linking simplicity to grandeur! Terribly
yet sweetly penetrating, how they searched the heart through, and
troubled the very sources of life! Often and often since have I wondered what it was in that singular music that made me *know* the distant
Alps listened in their sky-spaces, and that the purple slopes of Boudry
and Mont Racine bore it along the spires of their woods as though giant harp-strings stretched to the far summits of Chasseral and the arid
wastes of Tête de Rang.

In the music this outcast played upon the leaf there was something
of a wild, mad beauty that plunged like a knife to the home of tears,
and at the same time sang out beyond them—something coldly elemental, close to the naked heart of life. The truth, doubtless, was that
his strains, making articulate the sounds of Nature, touched deep,
primitive yearnings that for many are buried beyond recall. And between the airs, even between the bars, there fell deep weeping silences
when the sounds merged themselves into the sigh of wind or the
murmur of falling water, just as the strange player merged his body into the form and colour of the trees about him.

And when at last he ceased, I went close to him, hardly knowing
what it was I wanted so much to ask or say. He straightened up at my
approach. The melancholy dropped its veil upon his face instantly.

"But that was beautiful—unearthly!" I faltered. "You never have
played like that in the village—"

And for a second his eyes lit up as he pointed to the dark spaces of
forest behind us:

"In there," he said softly, "there is light!"

"You hear true music in these woods," I ventured, hoping to draw
him out; "this music you play—this exquisite singing of winds and
trees—?"

He looked at me with a puzzled expression and I knew, of course,
that I had blundered with my banal words. Then, before I could explain or alter, there floated to us through the trees a sound of church
bells from villages far away; and instantly, as he heard, his face grew
dark, as though he understood in some vague fashion that it was a
symbol of the faith of those parents who had wronged him, and of the
people who continually made him suffer. Something of this, I feel sure,

passed through his tortured mind, for he looked menacingly about him, and the dog, who caught the shadow of all his moods, began to growl angrily.

"My music," he said, with a sudden abruptness that was almost fierce, "is for my God."

"Your God of the Forests?" I said, with a real sympathy that I believe reached him.

"*Pour sûr! Pour sûr!* I play it all over the world"—he looked about him down the slopes of villages and vineyards—"and for those who understand—those who belong—to come."

He was, I felt sure, going to say more, perhaps to unbosom himself to me a little; and I might have learned something of the ritual this self-appointed priest of Pan followed in his forest temples—when, the sound of the bells swelled suddenly on the wind, and he turned with an angry gesture and made to go. Their insolence, penetrating even to the privacy of his secret woods, was too much for him.

"And you find many?" I asked.

Perret "Comment-va" shrugged his shoulders and smiled pityingly.

"Moi. Puis le chien—puis maintenant—*vous!*"

He was gone the same minute, as if the branches stretched out dark arms to draw him away among them, . . . and on my way back to the village, by the growing light of the moon, I heard far away in that deep world of a million trees the echoes of a weird, sweet music, as this unwitting votary of Pan piped and fluted to his mighty God upon an ivy leaf.

And the last thing I actually saw was the mongrel cur turning back from the edge of the forest to look at me for a moment of hesitation. He thought it was time now that I should join the little band of worshippers and follow them to the haunted spots of worship.

"Moi—puis le chien—puis maintenant—*vous!*"

From that moment of speech a kind of unexpressed intimacy between us came into being, and whenever we passed one another in the street he would give me a swift, happy look, and jerk his head significantly towards the forests. The feeling that, perhaps, in his curious lonely existence I counted for something important made me very careful with him. From time to time I gave him a few francs, and regularly twice a week when I knew he was away, I used to steal unobserved to his hut on the edge of the forest and put parcels of food inside the door— *salamé*, cheese, bread; and on one or two occasions when I had been extravagant with my own tea, pieces of plum-cake—what the Colombier baker called *plume-cak'!*

He never acknowledged these little gifts, and I sometimes wondered to what use he put them, for though the dog remained well favoured, so far as any cur can be so, he himself seemed to waste away more rapidly than ever. I found, too, that he did receive help from the village—official help—but that after the night when he was caught on the church steps with an oil can, kindling-wood, and a box of matches, this help was reduced by half, and the threat made to discontinue it altogether. Yet I feel sure there was no inherent maliciousness in the Man Who Played upon the Leaf, and that his hatred of an "alien" faith was akin to the mistaken zeal that in other days could send poor sinners to the stake for the ultimate safety of their souls.

Two things, moreover, helped to foster the tender belief I had in his innate goodness: first, that all the children of the village loved him and were unafraid, to the point of playing with him and pulling him about as though he were a big dog; and, secondly, that his devotion for the mongrel hound, his equal and fellow-worshipper, went to the length of genuine self-sacrifice. I could never forget how he fed it with the best of the bread, when his own face was pinched and drawn with hunger; and on other occasions I saw many similar proofs of his unselfish affection. His love for that mongrel, never uttered, in my presence at least, perhaps unrecognised as love even by himself, must surely have risen in some form of music or incense to sweeten the very halls of heaven.

In the woods I came across him anywhere and everywhere, sometimes so unexpectedly that it occurred to me he must have followed me stealthily for long distances. And once, in that very lonely stretch above the mountain railway, towards Montmollin, where the trees are spaced apart with an effect of cathedral aisles and Gothic arches, he caught me suddenly and did something that for a moment caused me a thrill of genuine alarm.

Wild lilies of the valley grow very thickly thereabouts, and the ground falls into a natural hollow that shuts it off from the rest of the forest with a peculiar and delightful sense of privacy; and when I came across it for the first time I stopped with a sudden feeling of quite bewildering enchantment—with a kind of childish awe that caught my breath as though I had slipped through some fairy door or blundered out of the ordinary world into a place of holy ground where solemn and beautiful things were the order of the day.

I waited a moment and looked about me. It was utterly still. The haze of the day had given place to an evening clarity of atmosphere that gave the world an appearance of having just received its finishing touches of pristine beauty. The scent of the lilies was overpoweringly sweet. But the whole first impression—before I had time to argue it away—was that I stood before some mighty chancel steps on the eve of a secret festival of importance, and that all was prepared and decorated with a view to the coming ceremony. The hush was the most delicate and profound imaginable—almost forbidding. I was a rude disturber.

Then, without any sound of approaching footsteps, my hat was lifted from my head, and when I turned with a sudden start of alarm, there before me stood Perret "Comment-va," the Man Who Played upon the Leaf.

An extraordinary air of dignity hung about him. His face was stern, yet rapt; something in his eyes genuinely impressive; and his whole appearance produced the instant impression—it touched me with a fleeting sense of awe—that here I had come upon him in the very act—had surprised this poor, broken being in some dramatic moment when his soul sought to find its own peculiar region, and to transform itself into loveliness through some process of outward worship.

He handed the hat back to me without a word, and I understood that I had unwittingly blundered into the secret place of his strange cult, some shrine, as it were, haunted doubly by his faith and imagination, perhaps even into his very Holy of Holies. His own head, as usual, was bared. I could no more have covered myself again than I could have put my hat on in Communion service of my own church.

"But—this wonderful place—this peace, this silence!" I murmured, with the best manner of apology for the intrusion I could muster on the instant. "May I stay a little with you, perhaps—and see?"

And his face passed almost immediately, when he realised that I understood, into that soft and happy expression the woods invariably drew out upon it—the look of the soul, complete and healed.

"Hush!" he whispered, his face solemn with the mystery of the listening trees; *"Vous êtes un pen en retard—mais pourtant . . ."*

And lifting the leaf to his lips he played a soft and whirring music that had for its undercurrent the sounds of running water and singing wind mingled exquisitely together. It was half chant, half song, solemn enough for the dead, yet with a strain of soaring joy in it that made me think of children and a perfect faith. The music *blessed* me, and the leagues of forest, listening, poured about us all their healing forces.

I swear it would not have greatly surprised me to see the shaggy flanks of Pan himself disappearing behind the moss-grown boulders that lay about the hollows, or to have caught the flutter of white limbs as the nymphs stepped to the measure of his tune through the mosaic of slanting sunshine and shadow beyond.

Instead, I saw only that picturesque madman playing upon his ivy leaf, and at his feet the faithful dog staring up without blinking into his face, from time to time turning to make sure that I listened and understood.

But the desolate places drew him most, and no distance seemed too great either for himself or his dog.

In this part of the Jura there is scenery of a sombre and impressive grandeur that, in its way, is quite as majestic as the revelation of far bigger mountains. The general appearance of soft blue pine-woods is deceptive. The Boudry cliffs, slashed here and there with inaccessible couloirs, are undeniably grand, and in the sweep of the Creux du Van precipices there is a splendid terror quite as solemn as that of the Matterhorn itself. The shadows of its smooth, circular walls deny the sun all day, and the winds, caught within the 700-ft. sides of its huge amphitheatre, as in the hollow of some awful cup, boom and roar with the crying of lost thunders.

I often met him in these lonely fastnesses, wearing that half-bewildered, half-happy look of the wandering child; and one day in particular, when I risked my neck scrambling up the most easterly of the Boudry couloirs, I learned afterwards that he had spent the whole time—four hours and more—on the little Champ de Trémont at the bottom, watching me with his dog till I arrived in safety at the top. His fellow-worshippers were few, he explained, and worth keeping; though it was ever inexplicable to me how his poor damaged eyes performed the marvels of sight they did.

And another time, at night, when, I admit, no sane man should have been abroad, and I had lost my way coming home from a climb along the torn and precipitous ledges of La Tourne, I heard his leaf thinly piercing the storm, always in front of me yet never overtaken, a sure though invisible guide. The cliffs on that descent are sudden and treacherous. The torrent of the Areuse, swollen with the melting snows, thundered ominously far below; and the forests swung their vast wet cloaks about them with torrents of blinding rain and clouds of darkness—yet all fragrant with warm wind as a virgin world answering to its first spring tempest. There he was, the outcast with his leaf, playing to his God amid all these crashings and bellowings. . . .

In the night, too, when skies were quiet and stars a-gleam, or in the still watches before the dawn, I would sometimes wake with the sound of clustered branches combing faint music from the gently-rising wind, and figure to myself that strange, lost creature wandering with his dog and leaf, his *pélerine,* his flying hair, his sweet, rapt expression of an inner glory, out there among the world of swaying trees he loved so well. And then my first soft view of the man would come back to me when I had seen him in the dusk as a tree; as though by some queer optical freak my outer and my inner vision had mingled so that I perceived both his broken body and his soul of magic.

For the mysterious singing of the leaf, heard in such moments from my window while the world slept, expressed absolutely the inmost cry of that lonely and singular spirit, damaged in the eyes of the village beyond repair, but in the sight of the wood-gods he so devoutly worshipped, made whole with their own peculiar loveliness and fashioned after the image of elemental things.

The spring wonder was melting into the peace of the long summer days when the end came. The vineyards had begun to dress themselves in green, and the forest in those soft blues when individual trees lose their outline in the general body of the mountain. The lake was indistinguishable from the sky; the Jura peaks and ridges gone a-soaring in-

to misty distances; the white Alps withdrawn into inaccessible and remote solitudes of heaven. I was making reluctant preparations for leaving—dark London already in my thoughts—when the news came. I
forget who first put it into actual words. It had been about the village
all the morning, and something of it was in every face as I went down
the street. But the moment I came out and saw the dog on my doorstep, looking up at me with puzzled and beseeching eyes, I knew that
something untoward had happened; and when he bit at my boots and
caught my trousers in his teeth, pulling me in the direction of the forest, a sudden sense of poignant bereavement shot through my heart
that I found it hard to explain, and that must seem incredible to those
who have never known how potent may be the conviction of a sudden
intuition.

I followed the forlorn creature whither it led, but before a hundred
yards lay behind us I had learned the facts from half-a-dozen mouths.
That morning, very early, before the countryside was awake, the first
mountain train, swiftly descending the steep incline below Chambre-
lien, had caught Perret "Comment-va" just where the Mont Racine *sen-
tier* crosses the line on the way to his best-beloved woods, and in one
swift second had swept him into eternity. The spot was in the direct
line he always took to that special woodland shrine—his Holy Place.

And the manner of his death was characteristic of what I had divined in the man from the beginning; for he had given up his life to
save his dog—this mongrel and faithful creature that now tugged so
piteously at my trousers. Details, too, were not lacking; the engine-
driver had not failed to tell the story at the next station, and the news
had travelled up the mountain-side in the way that all such news travels—swiftly. Moreover, the woman who lived at the hut beside the
crossing, and lowered the wooden barriers at the approach of all trains,
had witnessed the whole sad scene from the beginning.

And it is soon told. Neither she nor the engine-driver knew exactly
how the dog got caught in the rails, but both saw that it *was* caught,
and both saw plainly how the figure of the half-witted wanderer, hatless as usual and with cape flying, moved deliberately across the line to
release it. It all happened in a moment. The man could only have saved
himself by leaving the dog to its fate. The shrieking whistle had as little
effect upon him as the powerful breaks had upon the engine in those

few available moments. Yet, in the fraction of a second before the engine caught them, the dog somehow leapt free, and the soul of the Man Who Played upon the Leaf passed into the presence of his God—singing.

As soon as it realised that I followed willingly, the beastie left me and trotted on ahead, turning every few minutes to make sure that I was coming. But I guessed our destination without difficulty. We passed the Pontarlier railway first, then climbed for half-an-hour and crossed the mountain line about a mile above the scene of the disaster, and so eventually entered the region of the forest, still quivering with innumerable flowers, where in the shaded heart of trees we approached the spot of lilies that I knew—the place where a few weeks before the devout worshipper had lifted the hat from my head because the earth whereon I stood was holy ground. We stood in the pillared gateway of his Holy of Holies. The cool airs, perfumed beyond belief, stole out of the forest to meet us on the very threshold, for the trees here grew so thickly that only patches of the summer blaze found an entrance. And this time I did not wait on the outskirts, but followed my four-footed guide to a group of mossy boulders that stood in the very centre of the hollow.

And there, as the dog raised its eyes to mine, soft with the pain of its great unanswerable question, I saw in a cleft of the grey rock the ashes of many hundred fires; and, placed about them in careful array, an assortment of the sacrifices he had offered, doubtless in sharp personal deprivation, to his deity:—bits of mouldy bread, half-loaves, untouched portions of cheese, *salamé* with the skin uncut—most of it exactly as I had left it in his hut; and last of all, wrapped in the original white paper, the piece of Colombier *plume-cak'*, and a row of ten silver francs round the edge. . . .

I learned afterwards, too, that among the almost unrecognisable remains on the railway, untouched by the devouring terror of the iron, they had found a hand—tightly clasping in its dead fingers a crumpled ivy leaf. . . .

My efforts to find a home for the dog delayed my departure, I remember, several days; but in the autumn when I returned it was only to hear that the creature had refused to stay with any one, and finally had escaped into the forest and deliberately starved itself to death.

They found its skeleton, Louis Favre told me, in a rocky hollow on the lower slopes of Mont Racine in the direction of Montmollin. But Louis Favre did not know, as I knew, that this hollow had received other sacrifices as well, and was consecrated ground.

And somewhere, if you search well the Jura slopes between Champ du Moulin, where Jean-Jacques Rousseau had his temporary house, and Côtendard where he visited Lord Wemyss when "Milord Maréchal Keith" was Governor of the Principality of Neuchâtel under Frederic II, King of Prussia—if you look well these haunted slopes, somewhere between the vineyards and the gleaming limestone heights, you shall find the forest glade where lie the bleached bones of the mongrel dog, and the little village cemetery that holds the remains of the Man Who Played upon the Leaf to the honour of the Great God Pan.

The Terror of the Twins

That the man's hopes had built upon a son to inherit his name and estates—a single son, that is—was to be expected; but no one could have foreseen the depth and bitterness of his disappointment, the cold, implacable fury, when there arrived instead—twins. For, though the elder legally must inherit, that other ran him so deadly close. A daughter would have been a more reasonable defeat. But twins—! To miss his dream by so feeble a device—!

The complete frustration of a hope deeply cherished for years may easily result in strange fevers of the soul, but the violence of the father's hatred, existing as it did side by side with a love he could not deny, was something to set psychologists thinking. More than unnatural, it was positively uncanny. Being a man of rigid self-control, however, it operated inwardly, and doubtless along some morbid line of weakness little suspected even by those nearest to him, preying upon his thought to such dreadful extent that finally the mind gave way. The suppressed rage and bitterness deprived him, so the family decided, of his reason, and he spent the last years of his life under restraint. He was possessed naturally of immense forces—of will, feeling, desire; his dynamic value truly tremendous, driving through life like a great engine; and the intensity of this concentrated and buried hatred was guessed by few. The twins themselves, however, knew it. They divined it, at least, for it operated ceaselessly against them side by side with the genuine soft love that occasionally sweetened it, to their great perplexity. They spoke of it only to each other, though.

"At twenty-one," Edward, the elder, would remark sometimes, unhappily, "we shall know more." "Too much," Ernest would reply, with a rush of unreasoning terror the thought never failed to evoke—*in him*. "Things father said always happened—in life." And they paled perceptibly. For the hatred, thus compressed into a veritable bomb of

412

psychic energy, had found at the last a singular expression in the cry of the father's distraught mind. On the occasion of their final visit to the asylum, preceding his death by a few hours only, very calmly, but with an intensity that drove the words into their hearts like points of burning metal, he had spoken. In the presence of the attendant, at the door of the dreadful padded cell, he said it: "You are not two, but *one*. I still regard you as one. And at the coming of age, by h——, you shall find it out!"

The lads perhaps had never fully divined that icy hatred which lay so well concealed against them, but that this final sentence was a curse, backed by all the man's terrific force, they quite well realised; and accordingly, almost unknown to each other, they had come to dread the day inexpressibly. On the morning of that twenty-first birthday—their father gone these five years into the Unknown, yet still sometimes so strangely close to them—they shared the same biting, inner terror, just as they shared all other emotions of their life—intimately, without speech. During the daytime they managed to keep it at a distance, but when the dusk fell about the old house they knew the stealthy approach of a kind of panic sense. Their self-respect weakened swiftly . . . and they persuaded their old friend, and once tutor, the vicar, to sit up with them till midnight. . . . He had humoured them to that extent, willing to forgo his sleep, and at the same time more than a little interested in their singular belief—that before the day was out, before midnight struck, that is, the curse of that terrible man would somehow come into operation against them.

Festivities over and the guests departed, they sat up in the library, the room usually occupied by their father, and little used since. Mr. Curtice, a robust man of fifty-five, and a firm believer in spiritual principalities and powers, dark as well as good, affected (for their own good) to regard the youths' obsession with a kindly cynicism. "I do not think it likely for one moment," he said gravely, "that such a thing would be permitted. All spirits are in the hands of God, and the violent ones more especially." To which Edward made the extraordinary reply: "Even if father does not come himself he will—*send!*" And Ernest agreed: "All this time he's been making preparations for this very day. We've both known it for a long time—by odd things that have happened, by our dreams, by nasty little dark hints of various kinds, and by these persistent attacks of terror that come from nowhere, especially of late. Haven't we, Edward?" Edward assenting with a shudder: "Father has been *at us* of late with renewed violence. To-night it will be a regular assault upon our lives, or minds, or souls!"

"Strong personalities *may* possibly leave behind them forces that continue to act," observed Mr. Curtice with caution, while the brothers replied almost in the same breath: "That's exactly what we feel so curiously. Though—nothing has actually happened yet, you know, and it's a good many years now since—"

This was the way the twins spoke of it all. And it was their profound conviction that had touched their old friend's sense of duty. The experiment should justify itself—and cure them. Meanwhile none of the family knew. Everything was planned secretly.

The library was the quietest room in the house. It had shuttered bow-windows, thick carpets, heavy doors. Books lined the walls, and there was a capacious open fireplace of brick in which the wood-logs blazed and roared, for the autumn night was chilly. Round this the three of them were grouped, the clergyman reading aloud from the Book of Job in low tones; Edward and Ernest, in dinner-jackets, occupying deep leather arm-chairs, listening. They looked exactly what they were—Cambridge "undergrads," their faces pale against their dark hair, and alike as two peas. A shaded lamp behind the clergyman threw the rest of the room into shadow. The reading voice was steady, even monotonous, but something in it betrayed an underlying anxiety, and although the eyes rarely left the printed page, they took in every movement of the young men opposite, and noted every change upon their faces. It was his aim to produce an unexciting atmosphere, yet to miss nothing; if anything did occur to see it from the very beginning. Not to be taken by surprise was his main idea. . . . And thus, upon this falsely peaceful scene, the minutes passed the hour of eleven and slipped rapidly along towards midnight.

The novel element in his account of this distressing and dreadful occurrence seems to be that what happened—happened without the slightest warning or preparation. There was no gradual presentment of any horror; no strange blast of cold air; no dwindling of heat or light; no shaking of windows or mysterious tapping upon furniture. Without preliminaries it fell with its black trappings of terror upon the scene.

The clergyman had been reading aloud for some considerable time, one or other of the twins—Ernest usually—making occasional remarks, which proved that his sense of dread was disappearing. As the time grew short and nothing happened they grew more at their ease. Edward, indeed, actually nodded, dozed, and finally fell asleep. It was a few minutes before midnight. Ernest, slightly yawning, was stretching himself in the big chair. "Nothing's going to happen," he said aloud, in a pause. "Your good influence has prevented it." He even laughed now. "What superstitious asses we've been, sir; haven't we—?"

Curtice, then, dropping his Bible, looked hard at him under the lamp. For in that second, even while the words sounded, there had come about a most abrupt and dreadful change; and so swiftly that the clergyman, in spite of himself, was taken utterly by surprise and had no time to think. There had swooped down upon the quiet library—so he puts it—an immense hushing silence, so profound that the peace already reigning there seemed clamour by comparison; and out of this enveloping stillness there rose through the space about them a living and abominable Invasion—soft, motionless, terrific. It was as though vast engines, working at full speed and pressure, yet too swift and delicate to be appreciable to any definite sense, had suddenly dropped down upon them—from nowhere. "It made me think," the vicar used to say afterwards, "of the *Mauretania* machinery compressed into a nutshell, yet losing none of its awful power."

". . . haven't we?" repeated Ernest, still laughing. And Curtice, making no audible reply, heard the true answer in his heart: "Because everything has *already happened*—even as you feared."

Yet, to the vicar's supreme astonishment, Ernest still noticed—nothing!

"Look," the boy added, "Eddy's sound asleep—sleeping like a pig. Doesn't say much for your reading, you know, sir!" And he laughed again—lightly, even foolishly. But that laughter jarred, for the clergyman understood now that the sleep of the elder twin was either feigned—or *unnatural*.

And while the easy words fell so lightly from his lips, the monstrous engines worked and pulsed against him and against his sleeping brother, all their huge energy concentrated down into points fine as

Suggestion, delicate as Thought. The Invasion affected everything. The very objects in the room altered incredibly, revealing suddenly behind their normal exteriors horrid little hearts of darkness. It was truly amazing, this vile metamorphosis. Books, chairs, pictures, all yielded up their pleasant aspect, and betrayed, as with silent mocking laughter, their inner soul of blackness—their *decay*. This is how Curtice tries to body forth in words what he actually witnessed. . . . And Ernest, yawning, talking lightly, half foolishly—still noticed nothing!

For all this, as described, came about in something like ten seconds; and with it swept into the clergyman's mind, like a blow, the memory of that sinister phrase used more than once by Edward: "If father doesn't come, he will certainly—*send*." And Curtice understood that he had done both—both sent and come himself. . . . That violent mind, released from its spell of madness in the body, yet still retaining the old implacable hatred, was now directing the terrible, unseen assault. This silent room, so hushed and still, was charged to the brim. The horror of it, as he said later, "seemed to peel the very skin from my back." . . . And, while Ernest noticed nothing, Edward slept! . . . The soul of the clergyman, strong with the desire to help or save, yet realising that he was alone against a Legion, poured out in wordless prayer to his Deity. The clock just then, whirring before it struck, made itself audible.

"By Jove! It's all right, you see!" exclaimed Ernest, his voice oddly fainter and lower than before. "There's midnight—and nothing's happened. Bally nonsense, all of it!" His voice had dwindled curiously in volume. "I'll get the whisky and soda from the hall." His relief was great and his manner showed it. But in him somewhere was a singular change. His voice, manner, gestures, his very tread as he moved over the thick carpet towards the door, all showed it. He seemed less *real*, less alive, reduced somehow to littleness, the voice without timbre or quality, the appearance of him diminished in some fashion quite ghastly. His presence, if not actually shrivelled, was at least impaired. Ernest had suffered a singular and horrible *decrease*. . . .

The clock was still whirring before the strike. One heard the chain running up softly. Then the hammer fell upon the first stroke of midnight.

"I'm off," he laughed faintly from the door; "it's all been pure funk—on my part, at least . . . !" He passed out of sight into the hall.

The Power that throbbed so mightily about the room followed him out. Almost at the same moment Edward woke up. But he woke with a tearing and indescribable cry of pain and anguish on his lips: "Oh, oh, oh! But it hurts! It hurts! I can't hold you; leave me. It's breaking me asunder—"

The clergyman had sprung to his feet, but in the same instant everything had become normal once more—the room as it was before, the horror gone. There was nothing he could do or say, for there was no longer anything to put right, to defend, or to attack. Edward was speaking; his voice, deep and full as it never had been before: "By Jove, how that sleep has refreshed me! I feel twice the chap I was before—twice the chap. I feel quite splendid. Your voice, sir, must have hypnotised me to sleep. . . ." He crossed the room with great vigour. "Where's—er—where's—Ernie, by the bye?" he asked casually, hesitating—almost searching—for the name. And a shadow as of a vanished memory crossed his face and was gone. The tone conveyed the most complete indifference where once the least word or movement of his twin had wakened solicitude, love. "Gone away, I suppose—gone to bed, I mean, of course."

Curtice has never been able to describe the dreadful conviction that overwhelmed him as he stood there staring, his heart in his mouth—the conviction, the positive certainty, that Edward had changed interiorly, had suffered an incredible accession to his existing personality. But he *knew* it as he watched. His mind, spirit, soul had most wonderfully increased. Something that hitherto the lad had known from the outside only, or by the magic of loving sympathy, had now passed, to be incorporated with his own being. And, being himself, it required no expression. Yet this visible increase was somehow terrible. Curtice shrank back from him. The instinct—he has never grasped the profound psychology of *that,* nor why it turned his soul dizzy with a kind of nausea—the instinct to strike him where he stood, passed, and a plaintive sound from the hall, stealing softly into the room between them, sent all that was left to him of self-possession into his feet. He turned and ran. Edward followed him—very leisurely.

They found Ernest, or what had been Ernest, crouching behind the table in the hall, weeping foolishly to himself. On his face lay blackness. The mouth was open, the jaw dropped; he dribbled hopelessly; and from the face had passed all signs of intelligence—of spirit.

For a few weeks he lingered on, regaining no sign of spiritual or mental life before the poor body, hopelessly disorganised, released what was left of him, from pure inertia—from complete and utter loss of vitality.

And the horrible thing—so the distressed family thought, at least—was that all those weeks Edward showed an indifference that was singularly brutal and complete. He rarely even went to visit him. I believe, too, it is true that he only once spoke of him by name; and that was when he said—

"Ernie? Oh, but Ernie is much better and happier where he is—!"

Strange Disappearance of a Baronet

His intrinsic value before the Eternities was exceedingly small, but he possessed most things the world sets store by—presence, name, wealth—and, above all, that high opinion of himself which saves it the bother of a separate and troublesome valuation. Outside these possessions he owned nothing of permanent value, or that could decently claim to be worthy of immortality. The fact was he had never even experienced that expansion of self commonly known as generosity. No apology, however, is necessary for his amazing adventure, for these same Eternities who judged him have made their affidavit that it was They who stripped him bare and showed himself—to himself.

It all began with the receipt of that shattering letter from his solicitors. He read and re-read it in his comfortable first-class compartment as the express hurried him to town, exceedingly comfortable among his rugs and furs, exceedingly distressed and ill at ease in his mind. And in his private sitting-room of the big hotel that same evening Mr. Smirles, more odious even than his letter, informed him plainly that this new and unexpected claimant to his title and estates was likely to be exceedingly troublesome—"even dangerous, Sir Timothy! I am bound to say, since you ask me, that it might be wise to regard the future—er—with a different scale of vision than the one you have been accustomed to."

Sir Timothy practically collapsed. Instinctively he perceived that the lawyer's manner already held less respect: the reflection was a shock to his vain and fatuous personality. "After all, then, it wasn't *me* he worshipped, but my position, and so forth . . . !" If this nonsense continued he would be no longer "Sir Timothy," but simply "Mister" Puffe, poor, a nobody. He seemed to shrink in size as he gazed at himself in the mirror of the gorgeous, flamboyantly decorated room. "It's too pre-

posterous and absurd! There's nothing in it! Why, the whole County
would go to pieces without me!" He even thought of making his secretary draft a letter to the *Times*—a letter of violent, indignant protest.

He was a handsome, portly man, with a full-blown vanity justified
by no single item of soul or mind; not unkind, so much as empty; created and kept alive by the small conventions and the ceaseless contemplation of himself, the withdrawal of which might be expected to leave him
flat as a popped balloon. . . . Such a mass of pompous conceit obscured
his vision that he only slowly took in the fact that his very existence
was at stake. His thoughts rumbled on without direction, the sense of
loss, however, dreadfully sharp and painful all the time, till at length he
sought relief in something he could *really* understand. He changed for
dinner! He would dine in his sitting-room alone. And, meanwhile, he
rang for the remainder of his voluminous luggage. But it was vastly
annoying to his diminishing pride to discover that the gorgeous Head
Porter (he remembered now having vaguely recognised him in the hall)
was the same poor relation to whom he had denied help a year ago.
The vicissitudes of life were indeed preposterous. He ought to have
been protected from so ridiculous an encounter. For the moment, of
course, he merely pretended not to see him—certainly he did not
commend the excellently quick delivery of the luggage. And to praise
the young fellow's pluck never occurred to him for one single instant.

"The house valet, please," he asked of the waiter who answered
the bell soon afterwards—and then directed somewhat helplessly the
unpacking of his emporium of exquisite clothes. "Yes, take everything
out—everything," he said in reply to the man's question—rather an
extraordinary, almost insolent question when he came to reflect upon it,
surely: "Is it worth while, perhaps, sir . . . ?" It flashed across his dazed
mind that the Head Porter had made the very same remark to his sub-
ordinate in the passage when he asked if "everything" was to come in.
With a shrug of his gold-braided shoulders that poor relation had replied, "Seems hardly worth while, but they may as well all go in, yes."

And, with the double rejoinder perplexingly in his mind, Sir Timothy turned sharply upon the valet.

But the thing he was going to say faded on his lips. The man, holding out in his arms a heap of clothes, suits, and what not, seemed so
much taller than before. Sir Timothy had looked down upon him a

moment ago, whereas now their eyes stared level. It was passing strange.

"Will you want these, sir?"

"Not to-night, of course."

"Want them at all, I meant, sir?"

Sir Timothy gasped. "Want them at all? Of course! What in the world are you talking about?"

"Beg pardon, sir. Didn't know if it was worth while now," the man said, with a quick flush. And, before the pompous and amazed baronet could get any words between his quivering lips, the man was gone. The waiter, Head Waiter it was, answered the bell almost immediately, and Sir Timothy found consolation for his injured feelings in discussing food and wine. He ordered an absurdly sumptuous meal for a man dining alone. He did so with a vague feeling that it would spite somebody, perhaps; he hardly knew whom. "The Pol Roger well iced, mind," he added with a false importance as the clever servant withdrew. But at the door the man paused and turned, as though he had not heard. "*Large* bottle, I said," repeated the other. The Head Waiter made an extraordinary gesture of indifference. "As you wish, Sir Timothy, as you wish!" And he was gone in his turn. But it was only the man's adroitness that had chosen the words instead of those others: "Is it really worth while?"

And at that very moment, while Sir Timothy stood there fuming inwardly over the extraordinary words and ways of these people—veiled insolence, *he* called it—the door opened, and a tall young woman poked her head inside, then followed it with her person. She was dignified, smart even for a hotel like this, and uncommonly pretty. It was the upper housemaid. Full in the eye she looked at him. In her face was a kind of swift sympathy and kindness; but her whole presentment betrayed more than anything else—terror.

"Make an effort, make an effort!" she whispered earnestly. "Before it's too late, make an effort!" And *she* was gone. Sir Timothy, hardly knowing what he meant to do, opened the door to dash after her and make her explain this latest insolence. But the passage was dark, and he heard the swish of skirts far away—too far away to overtake; while running along the walls, as in a whispering gallery, came the words, "Make an effort, make an effort!"

"Confound it all, then, I will!" he exclaimed to himself, as he stumbled back into the room, feeling horribly bewildered. "I will make an effort." And he dressed to go downstairs and show himself in the halls and drawing-rooms, give a few pompous orders, assert himself, and fuss about generally. But that process of dressing without his valet was chiefly and weirdly distressing because he had so amazingly— dwindled. His sight was, of course, awry; disordered nerves had played tricks with vision, proportion, perspective; something of the sort must explain why he seemed so small to himself in the reflection. The pier-glass, which showed him full length, he turned to the wall. But, none the less, to complete his toilet, he had to stand upon a footstool before the other mirror above the mantelpiece.

And go downstairs he did, his heart working with a strange and increasing perplexity. Yet, wherever he went, there came that poor relation, the Head Porter, to face him. Always big, he now looked bigger than ever. Sir Timothy Puffe felt somehow ridiculous in his presence. The young fellow had character, pluck, some touch of intrinsic value. For all his failure in life, the Eternities considered him *real*. He towered rather dreadfully in his gold braid and smart uniform—towered in his great height all about the hall, like some giant in his own palace. The other's head scarcely came up to his great black belt where the keys swung and jangled.

The Baronet went upstairs again to his room, strangely disconcerted. The first thing he did as he left the lift was to stumble over the step. The liftman picked him up as though he were a boy. Down the passage, now well lighted, he went quickly, his feet almost pattering, his tread light, and—so oddly short. His importance had gone. A voice behind each door he passed whispered to him through the narrow crack as it cautiously opened, "Make an effort, make an effort! Be yourself, be real, be alive before it's too late!" But he saw no one, and the first thing he did on entering his room was to hide the smaller mirror by turning it against the wall, just as he had done to the pier-glass. He was so painfully little and insignificant now. As the externals and the possessions dropped away one by one in his thoughts, the revelation of the tiny little centre of activity within was horrible. He puffed himself out in thought as of old, but there was no response. was degrading.

The fact was—he began to understand it now—his mind had been pursuing possible results of his loss of title and estates to their logical conclusion. The idea in all its brutal nakedness, of course, hardly reached him—namely, that, without possessions, he was practically—nil! All he grasped was that he was—*less*. Still, the notion did prey upon him atrociously. He followed the advice of the strange housemaid and "made an effort," but without marked success. So empty, indeed, was his life that, once stripped of the possessions, he would stand there as useless and insignificant as an ownerless street dog. And the thought appalled him. He had not even enough real interest in others to hold him upright, and certainly not enough sufficiency of self, good or evil, to stand alone before any tribunal. The discovery shocked him inexpressibly. But what distressed him still more was to find a fixed mirror in his sitting-room that he could *not* take down, for in its depths he saw himself shrunken and dwindled to the proportions of a . . .

The knock at the door and the arrival of his dinner broke the appalling train of thought, but rather than be seen in his present diminutive appearance—later, of course, he would surely grow again—he ran into the bedroom. And when he came out again after the waiter's departure he found that his dinner shared the same abominable change. The food upon the dishes was reduced to the minutest proportions—the toast like children's, the soup an egg-cupful, the tenderloin a little slice the size of a visiting-card, and the bird not much larger than a black-beetle. And yet more than he could eat; more than sufficient! He sat in the big chair positively lost, his feet dangling. Then, mortified, frightened, and angry beyond expression, he undressed and concealed himself beneath the sheets and blankets of his bed.

"Of course I'm going mad—that's what it all means," he exclaimed. "I'm no longer of any account in the world. I could never go into my Club, for instance, *like this!*"—and he surveyed the small outline that made a little lump beneath the surface of the bed-clothes—"or read the lessons having to stand upon a chair to reach the lectern." And tears of bleeding vanity and futile wrath mingled upon his pillow. . . . The humiliation was agonising.

In the middle of which the door opened and in came the hotel valet, bearing before him upon a silver salver what at first appeared to be small, striped sandwiches, darkish in hue, but upon closer inspection were seen to be several wee suits of clothes, neatly pressed and folded for wearing. Glancing round the room and perceiving no one, the man proceeded to put them away in the chest of drawers, soliloquising from time to time as he did so.

"So the old buffer did go out after all!" he reflected, as he smoothed the tiny trousers in the drawer. "'E's nothing but a gas-bag, anyway! Close with the coin, too—always was that!" He whistled, spat in the grate, hunted about for a cigarette, and again found relief in speech. "My little dawg's worth two of 'im all the time, and lots to spare. Tim's *real* . . . !" And other things, too, he said in similar vein. He was utterly oblivious of Sir Timothy's presence—serenely unconscious that the thin, fading line beneath the sheets *was* the very individual he was talking about. "Even hides his cigarettes, does he? He's right, though. Take away what he's got and there wouldn't be enough left over to stand upright at a poultry show!" And he guffawed merrily to himself. But what brought the final horror into that vanishing Personality on the bed was the singular fact that the valet made no remark about the absurd and horrible size of those tiny clothes. *This, then, was how others—even a hotel valet—saw him!*

All night long, it seemed, he lay in atrocious pain, the darkness mercifully hiding him, though never from himself, and only towards daylight did he pass off into a condition of unconsciousness. He must have slept very late indeed, too, for he woke to find sunlight in the room, and the housemaid—that tall, dignified girl who had tried to be kind—dusting and sweeping energetically. He screamed to her, but his voice was too feeble to make itself heard above the sweeping. The high-pitched squeak was scarcely audible even to himself. Presently she approached the bed and flung the sheets back. "That's funny," she observed, "could've sworn I saw something move!" She gave a hurried look, then went on sweeping. But in the process she had tossed his person, now no larger than a starved mouse, out on to the carpet. He cried aloud in his anguish, but the squeak was too faint to be audible. "Ugh!" exclaimed the girl, jumping to one side, "there's that 'orrid mouse again! Dead, too, I do declare!" And then, without being aware of the fact, she swept him up with the dust and bits of paper into her pan.

Whereupon Sir Timothy awoke with a bad start, and perceived that his train was running somewhat uneasily into King's Cross, and that he had slept nearly the whole way.

The Occupant of the Room

He arrived late at night by the yellow diligence, stiff and cramped after the toilsome ascent of three slow hours. The village, a single mass of shadow, was already asleep. Only in front of the little hotel was there noise and light and bustle—for a moment. The horses, with tired, slouching gait, crossed the road and disappeared into the stable of their own accord, their harness trailing in the dust; and the lumbering diligence stood for the night where they had dragged it—the body of a great yellow-sided beetle with broken legs.

In spite of his physical weariness the schoolmaster, revelling in the first hours of his ten-guinea holiday, felt exhilarated. For the high Alpine valley was marvellously still; stars twinkled over the torn ridges of the Dent du Midi where spectral snows gleamed against rocks that looked like solid ink; and the keen air smelt of pine forests, dewsoaked pastures, and freshly sawn wood. He took it all in with a kind of bewildered delight for a few minutes, while the other three passengers gave directions about their luggage and went to their rooms. Then he turned and walked over the coarse matting into the glare of the hall, only just able to resist stopping to examine the big mountain map that hung upon the wall by the door.

And, with a sudden disagreeable shock, he came down from the ideal to the actual. For at the inn—the only inn—there was no vacant room. Even the available sofas were occupied. . . .

How stupid he had been not to write! Yet it had been impossible, he remembered, for he had come to the decision suddenly that morning in Geneva, enticed by the brilliance of the weather after a week of rain.

They talked endlessly, this gold-braided porter and the hard-faced old woman—her face was hard, he noticed—gesticulating all the time, and pointing all about the village with suggestions that he ill understood, for his French was limited and their *patois* was fearful.

"There!"—he might find a room, "or *there!* But we are, *hélas,* full—more full than we care about. To-morrow, perhaps—if So-and-so give up their rooms—!" And then, with much shrugging of shoulders, the hard-faced old woman stared at the gold-braided porter, and the porter stared sleepily at the schoolmaster.

At length, however, by some process of hope he did not himself understand, and following directions given by the old woman that were utterly unintelligible, he went out into the street and walked towards a dark group of houses she had pointed out to him. He only knew that he meant to thunder at a door and ask for a room. He was too weary to think out details. The porter half made to go with him, but turned back at the last moment to speak with the old woman. The houses sketched themselves dimly in the general blackness. The air was cold. The whole valley was filled with the rush and thunder of falling water. He was thinking vaguely that the dawn could not be very far away, and that he might even spend the night wandering in the woods, when there was a sharp noise behind him and he turned to see a figure hurrying after him. It was the porter—running.

And in the little hall of the inn there began again a confused three-cornered conversation, with frequent muttered colloquy and whispered asides in *patois* between the woman and the porter—the net result of which was that, "If Monsieur did not object—there *was* a room, after all, on the first floor—only it was in a sense 'engaged.' That is to say—"

But the schoolmaster took the room without enquiring too closely into the puzzle that had somehow provided it so suddenly. The ethics of hotel-keeping had nothing to do with him. If the woman offered him quarters it was not for him to argue with her whether the said quarters were legitimately hers to offer.

But the porter, evidently a little thrilled, accompanied the guest up to the room and supplied in a mixture of French and English details omitted by the landlady—and Minturn, the schoolmaster, soon shared the thrill with him, and found himself in the atmosphere of a possible tragedy.

All who know the peculiar excitement that belongs to lofty mountain valleys where dangerous climbing is a chief feature of the attractions, will understand a certain faint element of high alarm that goes with the picture. One looks up at the desolate, soaring ridges and thinks involuntarily of the men who find their pleasure for days and nights together scaling perilous summits among the clouds, and conquering inch by inch the icy peaks that for ever shake their dark terror in the sky. The atmosphere of adventure, spiced with the possible horror of a very grim order of tragedy, is inseparable from any imaginative contemplation of the scene; and the idea Minturn gleaned from the half-frightened porter lost nothing by his ignorance of the language. This Englishwoman, the real occupant of the room, had insisted on going without a guide. She had left just before daybreak two days before—the porter had seen her start—and . . . she had not returned! The route was difficult and dangerous, yet not impossible for a skilled climber, even a solitary one. And the Englishwoman was an experienced mountaineer. Also, she was self-willed, careless of advice, bored by warnings, self-confident to a degree. Queer, moreover; for she kept entirely to herself, and sometimes remained in her room with locked doors, admitting no one, for days together; a "crank," evidently, of the first water.

This much Minturn gathered clearly enough from the porter's talk while his luggage was brought in and the room set to rights; further, too, that the search party had gone out and *might*, of course, return at any moment. In which case— Thus the room was empty, yet still hers. "If Monsieur did not object—if the risk he ran of having to turn out suddenly in the night—" It was the loquacious porter who furnished the details that made the transaction questionable; and Minturn dismissed the loquacious porter as soon as possible, and prepared to get into the hastily arranged bed and snatch all the hours of sleep he could before he was turned out.

At first, it must be admitted, he felt uncomfortable—distinctly uncomfortable. He was in some one else's room. He had really no right to be there. It was in the nature of an unwarrantable intrusion; and while he unpacked he kept looking over shoulder as though some one were watching him from corners. Any moment, it seemed, he would hear a step in the passage, a knock would come at the door, the door would open, and there he would see this vigorous Englishwoman looking him up and down with anger. Worse still—he would hear her voice asking him what he was doing in her room—her bedroom. Of course, he had an adequate explanation, but still—!

Then, reflecting that he was already half undressed, the humour of it flashed for a second across his mind, and he laughed—*quietly*. And at once, after that laughter, under his breath, came the sudden sense of tragedy he had felt before. Perhaps, even while he smiled, her body lay broken and cold upon those awful heights, the wind of snow playing over her hair, her glazed eyes staring sightless up to the stars. . . . It made him shudder. The sense of this woman whom he had never seen, whose name even he did not know, became extraordinarily real. Almost he could imagine that she was somewhere in the room with him, hidden, observing all he did.

He opened the door softly to put his boots outside, and when he closed it again he turned the key. Then he finished unpacking and distributed his few things about the room. It was soon done; for, in the first place, he had only a small Gladstone and a knapsack, and secondly, the only place where he could spread his clothes was the sofa. There was no chest of drawers, and the cupboard, an unusually large and solid one, was locked. The Englishwoman's things had evidently been hastily put away in it. The only sign of her recent presence was a bunch of faded *Alpenrosen* standing in a glass jar upon the washhand stand. This, and a certain faint perfume, were all that remained. In spite, however, of these very slight evidences, the whole room was pervaded with a curious sense of occupancy that he found exceedingly distasteful. One moment the atmosphere seemed subtly charged with a "just left" feeling; the next it was a queer awareness of "still here" that made him turn and look hurriedly behind him.

Altogether, the room inspired him with a singular aversion, and the strength of this aversion seemed the only excuse for his tossing the faded flowers out of the window, and then hanging his mackintosh upon the cupboard door in such a way as to screen it as much as possible from view. For the sight of that big, ugly cupboard, filled with the clothing of a woman who might then be beyond any further need of covering—thus his imagination insisted on picturing it—touched in him a startled sense of the Incongruous that did not stop there, but crept through his mind gradually till it merged somehow into a sense of a rather grotesque horror. At any rate, the sight of that cupboard was offensive, and he covered it almost instinctively. Then, turning out the electric light, he got into bed.

But the instant the room was dark he realised that it was more than he could stand; for, with the blackness, there came a sudden rush of cold that he found it hard to explain. And the odd thing was that, when he lit the candle beside his bed, he noticed that his hand trembled.

This, of course, was too much. His imagination was taking liberties and must be called to heel. Yet the way he called it to order was significant, and its very deliberateness betrayed a mind that has already admitted fear. And fear, once in, is difficult to dislodge. He lay there upon his elbow in bed and carefully took note of all the objects in the room—with the intention, as it were, of taking an inventory of everything his senses perceived, then drawing a line, adding them up finally, and saying with decision, "That's all the room contains! I've counted every single thing. There is nothing more. *Now*—I may sleep in peace!"

And it was during this absurd process of enumerating the furniture of the room that the dreadful sense of distressing lassitude came over him that made it difficult even to finish counting. It came swiftly, yet with an amazing kind of violence that overwhelmed him softly and easily with a sensation of enervating weariness hard to describe. And its first effect was to banish fear. He no longer possessed enough energy to feel really afraid or nervous. The cold remained, but the alarm vanished. And into every corner of his usually vigorous personality crept the insidious poison of a *muscular* fatigue—at first—that in a few seconds, it seemed, translated itself into *spiritual* inertia. A sudden consciousness of the foolishness, the crass futility of life, of effort, of fighting—of all that makes life worth living, oozed into every fibre of his being, and left him utterly weak. A spirit of black pessimism that was not even vigorous enough to assert itself, invaded the secret chambers of his heart. . . .

Every picture that presented itself to his mind came dressed in grey shadows: those bored and sweating horses toiling up the ascent to—nothing! that hard-faced landlady taking so much trouble to let her desire for gain conquer her sense of morality—for a few francs! that gold-braided porter, so talkative, fussy, energetic, and so anxious to tell all he knew! What was the use of them all? And for himself, what in the world was the good of all the labour and drudgery he went through in that preparatory school where he was junior master? What could it lead to? Wherein lay the value of so much uncertain toil, when the ultimate secrets of life were hidden and no one knew the final goal? How foolish was effort, discipline, work! How vain was pleasure! How trivial the noblest life! . . .

With a fearful jump that nearly upset the candle Minturn pulled himself together. Such vicious thoughts were usually so remote from his normal character that the sudden vile invasion produced a swift reaction. Yet, only for a moment. Instantly, again, the depression descended upon him like a wave. His work—it could lead to nothing but the dreary labour of a small headmastership after all—seemed as vain and foolish as his holiday in the Alps. What an idiot he had been, to be sure, to come out with a knapsack merely to work himself into a state of exhaustion climbing over toilsome mountains that led to nowhere—resulted in nothing. A dreariness of the grave possessed him. Life was a ghastly fraud! Religion a childish humbug! Everything was merely a trap—a trap of death; a coloured toy that Nature used as a decoy! But a decoy for what? For nothing! There was no meaning in anything. The only real thing was—DEATH. And the happiest people were those who found it soonest.

Then why wait for it to come?

He sprang out of bed, thoroughly frightened. This was horrible. Surely mere physical fatigue could not produce a world so black, an outlook so dismal, a cowardice that struck with such sudden hopelessness at the very roots of life? For, normally, he was cheerful and strong, full of the tides of healthy living; and this appalling lassitude swept the very basis of his personality into nothingness and the desire for death. It was like the development of a Secondary Personality. He had read, of course, how certain persons who suffered shocks developed thereafter entirely different characteristics, memory, tastes, and so forth. It had all rather frightened him. Though scientific men vouched for it, it was hardly to be believed. Yet here was a similar thing taking place in his own consciousness. He was, beyond question, experiencing all the mental variations of—*some one else!* It was un-moral. It was awful. It was—well, after all, at the same time, it was uncommonly interesting.

And this interest he began to feel was the first sign of his returned normal Self. For to feel interest is to live, and to love life.

He sprang into the middle of the room—then switched on the

electric light. And the first thing that struck his eye was—the big cupboard.

"Hallo! There's that—beastly cupboard!" he exclaimed to himself, involuntarily, yet aloud. It held all the clothes, the swinging skirts and coats and summer blouses of the dead woman. For he knew now—somehow or other—that she *was* dead. . . .

At that moment, through the open windows, rushed the sound of falling water, bringing with it a vivid realisation of the desolate, snow-swept heights. He saw her—positively *saw* her!—lying where she had fallen, the frost upon her cheeks, the snow-dust eddying about her hair and eyes, her broken limbs pushing against the lumps of ice. For a moment the sense of spiritual lassitude—of the emptiness of life—vanished before this picture of broken effort—of a small human force battling pluckily, yet in vain, against the impersonal and pitiless Potencies of Inanimate Nature—and he found himself again, his normal self. Then, instantly, returned again that terrible sense of cold, nothingness, emptiness. . . .

And he found himself standing opposite the big cupboard where her clothes were. He suddenly wanted to see those clothes—things she had used and worn. Quite close he stood, almost touching it. The next second he had touched it. His knuckles struck upon the wood.

Why he knocked is hard to say. It was an instinctive movement probably. Something in his deepest self dictated it—ordered it. He knocked at the door. And the dull sound upon the wood into the stillness of that room brought—horror. Why it should have done so he found it as hard to explain to himself as why he should have felt impelled to knock. The fact remains that when he heard the faint reverberation inside the cupboard, it brought with it so vivid a realisation of the woman's presence that he stood there shivering upon the floor with a dreadful sense of anticipation: he almost expected to hear an answering knock from within—the rustling of the hanging skirts perhaps—or, worse still, to see the locked door slowly open towards him.

And from that moment, he declares that in some way or other he must have partially lost control of himself, or at least of his better judgment; for he became possessed by such an overmastering desire to tear open that cupboard door and see the clothes within, that he tried every key in the room in the vain effort to unlock it, and then, finally, before he quite realised what he was doing—rang the bell!

But, having rung the bell for no obvious or intelligent reason at two o'clock in the morning, he then stood waiting in the middle of the floor for the servant to come, conscious for the first time that something outside his ordinary self had pushed him towards the act. It was almost like an internal voice that directed him . . . and thus, when at last steps came down the passage and he faced the cross and sleepy chambermaid, amazed at being summoned at such an hour, he found no difficulty in the matter of what he should say. For the same power that insisted he should open the cupboard door also impelled him to utter words over which he apparently had no control.

"It's not *you* I rang for!" he said with decision and impatience. "I want a man. Wake the porter and send him up to me at once—hurry! I tell you, hurry—!"

And when the girl had gone, frightened at his earnestness, Minturn realised that the words surprised himself as much as they surprised her. Until they were out of his mouth he had not known what exactly he was saying. But now he understood that some force foreign to his own personality was using his mind and organs. The black depression that had possessed him a few moments before was also part of it. The powerful mood of this vanished woman had somehow momentarily taken possession of him—communicated, possibly, by the atmosphere of things in the room still belonging to her. But even now, when the porter, without coat or collar, stood beside him in the room, he did not understand *why* he insisted, with a positive fury admitting no denial, that the key of that cupboard must be found and the door instantly opened.

The scene was a curious one. After some perplexed whispering with the chambermaid at the end of the passage, the porter managed to find and produce the key in question. Neither he nor the girl knew clearly what this excited Englishman was up to, or why he was so passionately intent upon opening the cupboard at two o'clock in the morning. They watched him with an air of wondering what was going to happen next. But something of his curious earnestness, even of his late fear, communicated itself to them, and the sound of the key grating in lock made them both jump.

They held their breath as the creaking door swung slowly open. All heard the clatter of that other key as it fell against the wooden floor—within. The cupboard had been locked *from the inside*. But it was the scared housemaid, from her position in the corridor, who first saw—and with a wild scream fell crashing against the banisters.

The porter made no attempt to save her. The schoolmaster and himself made a simultaneous rush towards the door, now wide open. They, too, had seen.

There were no clothes, skirts, or blouses on the pegs, but, all by itself, from an iron hook in the centre, they saw the body of the Englishwoman hanging by the neck, the head bent horribly forwards, the tongue protruding. Jarred by the movement of unlocking, the body swung slowly round to face them. . . . Pinned upon the inside of the door was a hotel envelope with the following words penciled in straggling writing:

"Tired—unhappy—hopelessly depressed. . . . I cannot face life any longer. . . . All is black. I must put an end to it. . . . I meant to do it on the mountains, but was afraid. I slipped back to my room unobserved. This way is easiest and best. . . ."

The Lock of Grey Hair

It hung so conspicuously there amid the surrounding mop of fine dark hair that it piqued the curiosity of Dr. Blane's friends more than any other detail of his very distinguished appearance. Grief, said a good number, had caused it; anxiety, declared others; but the majority, including servants and women, plumped of course for love. He was successful, and he was unmarried: the evidence was unanswerable. I believe, however, that I am the only living person who holds the true secret.

"Most people who have really lived," he used to say, "possess some singular experience or other that they do not care about telling indiscriminately. And this is mine. I'm a little ashamed of it," he added, "for nowadays we explain everything—or confess ourselves unscientific. Besides,"—he shrugged his shoulders—"my conduct, I always feel, was not strictly professional perhaps in the best sense. And, also,—it was the only time in my life when I was obliged to acknowledge a sense of unreasoning fear;—and yield to it!"

And the story, it must be confessed, certainly would have claimed belief more readily in those picturesque times when "Possession," diabolical or otherwise, was a prevalent superstition, and when the post-mortem activity of a disembodied spirit was held to be often exceedingly lively.

It happened before the days when Dr. Blane's skill had earned for him the honours of knighthood, together with the privilege of Inspectorship of Royal Diseases. This, somewhat, is as he told it to me shortly before his own death:

With an intimate friend, it appears, he was revisiting a little village in the Swiss Jura where had been to learn French as a boy, when the friend incontinently was laid low with diphtheria, and he stayed out perforce to nurse him. Both men had their meals in the cosy little Pension de La Poste, where twenty years before they had studied grammar and irregular verbs together; but Dr. Blane, who wanted quiet, had his work- and bed-room in Michaud's new house at the other end of the village where the vineyards begin.

Now, the epidemic, it so happened, was a severe one, and two other persons—but for whom this thing might not have come about—were also laid low: one, the village aesculapius, Dr. Ducommun, the other, Mlle. Udriet, a wealthy but avaricious old woman whose personality was of dark and sinister odour throughout the whole countryside, and who on account of her intense miserliness was known generally as *'la mauvaise riche.'* And she was well named, for village wit has a way hitting the nail on the head. She was an evil woman, with great force of individuality, dreaded by all; and her fear of spending money went to amazing lengths. It was even reported of her that she enticed her neighbours' cats into her big house, slew and cooked them with her own hands, and ate them to save a butcher's bill. Her long finger-nails, and certain other unappetising peculiarities, were evidence, the village held, for anything and everything.

And Dr. Blane, who was sent for to prescribe in the temporary absence of Dr. Ducommun, admits that the moment he crossed the threshold of the ill-smelling room and saw the old miser staring fixedly at him from her bed, he was inspired by an instant and singularly powerful aversion for her. The face he always described as truly venomous, and her thin fingers lying on the coverlet were "taloned and be-clawed," he used to declare with a shuddering laugh, "like the feet of a great bird of prey." Here, for the first time in his life, was a patient, he hinted afterwards, whom he would rather have helped to die than to live.

Though ashamed of his revulsion, he could not quite conceal it. The fact that she would never pay his fees was nothing. It was the woman herself. "She was like some great loathsome insect in that dark room," he said; "some insect whose sting was death!"

The situation at first was merely unpleasant, but a little later it became more awkward and furnished Dr. Blane with the excuse for what he terms his unprofessional attitude. For the village doctor got better —well enough to crawl out and see his pet patients—and *la mauvaise riche* got steadily worse. Moreover, she insisted on sending for Dr. Blane because she preferred his greater skill, and Dr. Blane as often as possible shelved the unpleasant responsibility upon the shoulders of the local practitioner.

Plainly put, he avoided seeing her—even refused point blank to do so, and the old woman, when she found that he no longer came, suffered paroxysms of rage that were positively terrifying in their concentrated fury.

It was one night towards the end of March when the matter came to a climax. Earlier in the evening Mlle. Udriet, apparently at her crisis, had sent him an imperious summons, and Dr. Blane, not without pricks of conscience, had passed on the summons by messenger to his colleague at the other end of the village. Dr. Ducommun, however, was delayed for several hours, with the unfortunate result that *la mauvaise riche* lay neglected to the end.

The Englishman, of course, knew nothing of this. He was in the *pension* sitting by the bedside of his friend, reading. It was ten o'clock. Shaded candles stood on the little table and the sick man was sleeping peacefully the sleep of recovery. For twenty-four hours there had been no return of the delirium. At the end the darkened room Mme. Favre, who owned the *pension* and had proved herself a devoted helper, was in the act of mixing a tumbler of Thé St. Germain—her invariable remedy for all complaints—when suddenly two things—two surprising things—happened simultaneously: the sick man sat bolt upright in bed with startling abruptness, stared fixedly into the dim room in front of him, and pointed; while Mme. Favre let fall her tumbler with a crash upon the floor and cried in a voice of genuine alarm, "Who is it? Somebody pushed past me! There's some one else in the room!"

The singular way these two persons acted on the same instant impressed Dr. Blane unpleasantly—curiously. He was conscious at once of a disagreeable thrill—of something that brought the water with a rush to his eyes and made the skin of his back crawl. Yet, of course, he never for one moment believed that any one had really entered the room through the closed doors.

"A return of the delirium," he said quietly, as his friend continued to glare about him and to point. And then added more sternly. "There's no need for alarm, Mme. Favre, I assure you"; for the old lady was leaning, pale and terrified, against the cupboard, and staring towards the bed as though her eyes would drop out.

But the patient, of course, absorbed his immediate attention. To the doctor there could be nothing very unusual about a scene of delirium; yet about this particular scene of delirium, he became sharply and unpleasantly aware, there was something very unusual indeed. It was convincingly and horribly real. To begin with, though the sick man had forgotten his French almost to the simplest phrases, he was now gabbling the language with a speed and fluency that were positively uncanny; and at the same time with a vehemence, a passion, a fury that had characterised none of his former attacks: moreover—most disquieting of all—with a thin, whispering voice that was beyond question not his own.

But of the whole wild torrent, all he, and for that matter all Mme. Favre, could catch before it subsided again into abrupt silence were the short phrases, uttered with eyes fixed upon the doctor and a hand pointing into his very face: "You passed me by. But now I am out— and I shall not pass you by!"

The singular thing however—and it was this that gave the good woman the *crise de nerfs* that ended in a fainting fit—the singular and horrible thing was that as the changed voice poured out of the sick man, his face altered visibly as well, altered too into the lineaments of another visage that they both knew. How the eyes and mouth of a man could slip into the expression of a woman—an evil, vindictive woman—is beyond the power of description, yet the calm, experienced Dr. Blane as well as the frightened old lady at the end of the room both recognised beyond possibility of discussion that voice, face, and manner belonged to the evil personality of that perverted old woman, *la mauvaise riche*. In the eyes, perhaps, the resemblance lay chiefly. It was unmistakable. It was weirdly impressive.

Then it all passed as quickly as it came. The sick man slept peacefully once more. Mme. Favre pulled herself together, assisted by the judicious aid of cold water, and half an hour later Dr. Blane, battling already with vivid sensations of alarm such as he had never known before in his life, left the *pension* to go back his own rooms.

His shortest way lay down the village street, past the house ot Mlle. Udriet, and so home. Yet the doctor deliberately chose the longer route. He admits it frankly. He did not wish to pass the woman's house. "I was curiously nervous, almost frightened," he said; "though exactly of what I could not tell. I came out of La Poste into the night all trembling. It was the most unaccountable sensation I have ever known. Rather than pass the door of that woman's house I'd have walked a mile."

So he went home by a roundabout way of perhaps fifteen minutes. The village was utterly deserted, and the night air swept about him with the scents of early spring from the surrounding forests. In his mind however he still saw his friend's changed face and heard the whispered words so vindictively uttered, "You passed me by. Now I'm out. I shan't pass you by!" And do what he might he could not dismiss them. The words kept time with the echo of his feet on the hard road.

A little more than half-way his path joined the main street by the fountain and then turned to the right and ran between low stone walls to Michaud's house. Beyond the walls were vineyards with hundreds of bare sticks already planted in the earth.

And it was here, as he passed the fountain, that he first heard a noise that sent the blood tingling about his ears. The mountain water splashes there all the year round with a steady fall, but what he heard had nothing to do with that. It was the sound of small feet pattering along under the deep shadow of the houses.

Something was following him. "It's a dog," he said, yet at the same time he knew quite well that it was not a dog. It was on two feet, not on four. Fear dropped cold and wet over his face.

The road slopes the whole way to where the Michaud house stands isolated from the rest of the village among the vineyards, and Dr. Blane quickened his pace almost to a run. He found the excuse that he was cold, though he was perfectly well aware that the cold he felt was not the common cold of night.

For a time he resisted the desire to look round, but before he was half-way down the hill the moon emerged from the clouds, and at last, with a sudden movement as though he expected to be attacked from behind—he stopped short and turned.

The village street in the pale wintry moonlight was empty. Black shadows lined its sides; the church pierced the sky; far above gleamed the spectral snows on the heights of Mont Racine, and the great mountain of Boudry with its dark army of pines hung, immense and forbidding, in the air. Nothing moved. But from the spaces of open moonlit road close behind him came the sound of light pattering. The steps still followed him.

The way this creeping fear had begun to master him was beyond all things strange. He pulled himself together with a great effort of will and continued his way, this time without undue haste; for to run, he realised, was to admit that terror was in his heart. Yet, along some dark byway, it had undoubtedly established itself already in his blood beyond all reach of argument. He walked with firm and measured steps, and as result he at once noticed that the sounds were no longer audible. The moment he asserted his will, apparently, they ceased. The whole thing was, of course, imaginary, born of the night, of the deep wintry silence, and of the unpleasant memory that vivid scene in the sick-room had marked on his brain: in a word, nerves!

Leaving the village behind him he entered the section of road where low walls separated it from the vineyards on either side. But, before he had gone a dozen yards, he became aware that something was running stealthily among the serried ranks of vinesticks over the wall on his left. The soft pattering on the earth was distinctly audible. The thing was keeping pace with him still, yet always a little behind. It was holding him in view—watching. waiting.

"This," he says, "I realised above all else—that I was being followed with some sinister purpose."

Keeping to the middle of the road, however, Dr. Blane refused now to quicken his steps. It was remarkable how dead, how deserted the mountain village seemed. No one was about; lights were out in every house. Wind, the night, and the timid mood with her fugitive gleams held possession of the world. And those swift, pattering footsteps, making their way without a single false tread between thousands of upright stakes, was ever beside him on the other side of the low wall.

At last the outline the house loomed welcome before him, and he entered the iron gates, slowly, still master of himself, and fumbled in the lock with his key. A space of gravel path led up to the door, and as he stooped to insert the key he was positive that he heard something leap the wall and land with a kind of hushed shuffle on the shingly path close behind him. He turned with an exclamation, half cry, half curse,—again with the instinctive idea of protecting himself from attack, when suddenly a light shone through the door and Michaud, his landlord, opened it from the inside.

The sounds ceased, Dr. Blane passed hurriedly in. Never was light or human presence more welcome.

"I'll close after you," said Michaud, a little man with a jolly, smiling, fat face. "I knew your step."

Before shutting the door he peered out into the night.

"Tiens!" he said, looking about him, "I thought I heard some one!"

"It's a dog or something that followed me down the road," said the doctor. He was glad to be with another man—uncommonly glad.

Michaud closed the door and locked it, but as he did so Dr. Blane got the curious impression that something darted in past his legs like a swift shadow into the house. At the same moment the lantern standing on the steps behind fell with crash, as though knocked over, and the light was extinguished. Michaud laughed as he struck a match to relight it. He looked rather closely at his lodger for a moment. Dr. Blane declares that to the end he could never be certain that he had not himself stumbled against the lantern and so kicked it over.

"They've been here several times to fetch you," the man said the moment the door was fastened. "But I told them you were out."

"Who came?" asked the other with an odd catch in his voice.

"I couldn't see. I called down from the window, but didn't recognise the voice—some woman, I think. It was too dark to see. I told them to get Dr. Ducommun. She's dead, you know," he added abruptly. "Gone to her account at last."

"Who—who is dead?"

Michaud's voice was curiously hushed as he replied.

"La mauvaise riche." He shrugged his shoulders.

Presently they said good-night and Dr. Blane went up to his room to work or to sleep. They were alone in the house, these two, for Mme. Michaud was away visiting her mother at La Chaux-de-Fonds, and there were no other occupants. He heard the little man thumping about for a space in his bedroom below. Then, presently, all sounds ceased.

Dr. Blane's room was on the top floor—an attic room really. There were double windows, a cupboard, a bed in one corner with a mountainous duvet, hot-air pipes, a wash-hand stand opposite, and in the centre his work-table with two lighted candles. By the bed and table two strips of carpet—the rest pine boards, not even stained. It was all very primitive.

At first he tried to work—in vain. Then, turning his thoughts inwards, he deliberately attacked the problem with a view to solving it and recovering his normal state of balance. He brought to bear upon it all the force of his acute mind, together with his great medical knowledge and experience. But analysis only confirmed things: he was suffering from a singular invasion of utterly unreasoning fear. He was afraid in the depths of his soul; cold and perspiring in turns; horribly creepy about the skin; and his hair ready at the least sound to rise upon his head. Yet, in his search, he could find nothing that seemed an adequate cause. His neglect of a patient, not even properly his, he admitted was not wholly pardonable, but, after all—! His mind, in spite of all efforts, came back always to the thought of that horrible changed expression in his friend's face—the expression of that evil woman's eyes, and to the whispered words that had seemed like a curse. "I'm out. You passed me by. I shall not pass you by!"

Finally, to steady his mind and possibly find a measure of relief in expression, he sat down to put an analysis of his mental state on paper. He worked hard. But presently he paused and looked about him. He heard the wind. It had changed and *la bise* was blowing up over the Lake of Neuchâtel. Now and again it rose to a wild, whistling cry that made him shiver. The clocks of Colombier struck one in the morning.

At length, in a calmer state of mind, Dr. Blane, half wondering, half laughing, but still strangely nervous, put out the candles and got into bed.

And the moment the room was dark the noise began again.

There was no interval of guesswork; he knew at once what it was. Something was scratching at the door—outside. And the curious part of it was that the instant he heard it he realised that the door was no sort of protection. That it was locked was all a useless pretence. The thing could, and would, get in to him. And the next minute, with a nauseous rush of terror, he knew that it was in. It had somehow squeezed itself underneath the door—and was pattering across the bare boards to the side of his bed. And as he heard it, that vile pattering seemed inside him—on the very substance of his heart.

The actual distance between door and bed was small enough, but in those few seconds of intense horror it stretched into a hundred yards, and he knew all the prolonged agony of the steady, merciless approach that a man fastened to the rails must know when in the distance he hears the first rumble of the coming train. For a kind of paralysis crept over him so that he could not move. His heart dropped like lead. The perspiration that drenched him froze instantly into ice.

Then the steps quickened for a running leap; there was a sound of rushing through the air; a gust of glacial wind; and something dropped heavily upon the bed by his feet—and then began to climb quickly upwards towards his face.

Dr. Blane says he tried furiously to shout, but could get no sound out above a whisper.

The sensation of the footsteps treading up the whole length of his paralysed body was the most horrible thing he had known. But his climax of terror brought with it at least a certain power of movement, and he was just able to bury his face beneath a pile of clothes and pillows when the thing settled down with a clinging grip like wire netting upon his head and there began the most dreadful struggle imaginable in the thick darkness.

But it was an unequal fight. His hands were so moist with the clamminess of fear that the sheets slipped through fingers, and inch by inch the strength of his adversary succeeded in uncovering his face. First he felt it against the skin of his neck where thin fingers that gripped like cold iron caught him behind in a suddenly exposed place. The rest went swiftly; for that touch of ice somehow seemed to paralyse all the nerve centres at a stroke and bereft him of any power he had left. In a moment the clothes were torn from off him and he lay there helpless and motionless on his back, his face at last wholly uncovered.

And then, so close to his ear that the breath touched him as though the *bise* had forced its way in through the open window, he heard a thin whisper of words: "You passed me by. Now I'm out. I shall not pass you by!" and immediately after it came a smothering sensation over eyes and mouth as though a weight of snow had fallen to suffocate him, while creeping through it a stinging pain moved slowly down the sides of his face towards the throat. It was like claws of iron entering his flesh.

The freezing air of night blowing upon his face revived him after what must have been a long period of unconsciousness, for the grey light of early morning was in the room when he opened his eyes again and there was a sound of movement in the house below. With the precision of a strong mind accustomed to quick reflection and decision Dr. Blane at once realised the situation. There was no groping of memory. It all came back vividly, and in that very first minute of returning consciousness he was aware clearly of two things: first, that it had all been real and no dream; secondly, that the terror had passed completely from his soul.

Wholly master of himself, yet with a feeling that he was bruised and battered, he got out of bed and examined the room. And to his amazement he noticed for the first time that the double-windows were wide open and the *bise* was blowing straight into the room.

Wondering greatly—for they had been closed and fastened when he went to bed—he shut them tight. Then he crossed the floor to turn on the supply of hot air in the radiator. It was on his way back that he caught the reflection of his face in the mirror that hung by the window. The morning light fell full upon it. Down both cheeks ran dull red lines that ended in marks round the neck like the marks of the rope that he had known years before as prison doctor on the neck of a hanged man. There was no blood—merely a dull contusion under the skin; and almost as he looked the lines faded away and were gone.

But above them, signature of his great terror, was something else that did not fade, and that remained to the day of his death. A lock of hair over the right temple had turned grey in a single night.

The South Wind

It is impossible to say through which sense, or combination of senses, I knew that Some one was approaching—was already near; but most probably it was the deep underlying "mother-sense" including them all that conveyed the delicate warning. At any rate, the scene-shifters of my moods knew it too, for very swiftly they prepared the stage; then, ever soft-footed and invisible, stood aside to wait.

As I went down the village street on my way to bed after midnight, the high Alpine valley lay silent in its frozen stillness. For days it had now lain thus, even the mouths of its cataracts stopped with ice; and for days, too, the dry, tight cold had drawn up the nerves of the humans in it to a sharp, thin pitch of exhilaration that at last began to call for the gentler comfort of relaxation. The key had been a little too high, the inner tautness too prolonged. The tension of that implacable north-east wind, the *bise noire,* had drawn its twisted wires too long through our very entrails. We all sighed for some loosening of the bands—the comforting touch of something damp, soft, less penetratingly acute.

And now, as I turned, midway in the little journey from the inn to my room above La Poste, this sudden warning that Some one was approaching repeated its silent wireless message, and I paused to listen and to watch.

Yet at first I searched in vain. The village street lay empty—a white ribbon between the black walls of the big-roofed châlets; there were no lights in any of the houses; the hotels stood gaunt and ugly with their myriad shuttered windows; and the church, topped by the Crown of Savoy in stone, was so engulfed by the shadows of the mountains that it seemed almost a part of them.

Beyond, reared the immense buttresses of the Dent du Midi, terrible and stalwart against the sky, their feet resting among the crowding pines, their streaked precipices tilting up at violent angles towards the stars. The bands of snow, belting their enormous flanks, stretched for miles, faintly gleaming, like Saturn's rings. To the right I could just make out the pinnacles of the Dents Blanches, cruelly pointed; and, still farther, the Dent de Bonnaveau, as of iron and crystal, running up its gaunt and dreadful pyramid into relentless depths of night. Everywhere in the hard, black-sparkling air was the rigid spell of winter. It seemed as if this valley could never melt again, never know currents of warm wind, never taste the sun, nor yield its million flowers.

And now, dipping down behind me out of the reaches of the darkness, the New Comer moved close, heralded by this subtle yet compelling admonition that had arrested me in my very tracks. For, just as I turned in at the door, kicking the crunched snow from my boots against the granite step, I *knew* that, from the heart of all this tightly frozen winter's night, the "Some one" whose message had travelled so delicately in advance was now, quite suddenly, at my very heels. And while my eyes lifted to sift their way between the darkness and the snow I became aware that It was already coming down the village street. It ran on feathered feet, pressing close against the enclosing walls, yet at the same time spreading from side to side, brushing the window-panes, rustling against the doors, and even including the shingled roofs in its enveloping advent. It came, too—*against the wind.* . . .

It flew up close and passed me, very faintly singing, running down between the châlets and the church, very swift, very soft, neither man nor animal, neither woman, girl, nor child, turning the corner of the snowy road beyond the *Curé's* house with a rushing, cantering motion, that made me think of a Body of water—something of fluid and generous shape, too mighty to be confined in common forms. And, as it passed, it touched me—touched me through all skin and flesh upon the naked nerves, loosening, relieving, setting free the congealed sources of life which the *bise* so long had mercilessly bound, so that magic currents, flowing and released, washed down all the secret byways of the spirit and flooded again with full tide into a thousand dried-up cisterns of the heart.

The thrill I experienced is quite incommunicable in words. I ran upstairs and opened all my windows wide, knowing that soon the Messenger would return with a million others—only to find that already it had been there before me. Its taste was in the air, fragrant and alive; in my very mouth—and all the currents of the inner life ran sweet again, and

full. Nothing in the whole village was quite the same as it had been before. The deeply slumbering peasants, even behind their shuttered windows and barred doors; the *Curé*, the servants at the inn, the consumptive
man opposite, the children in the house behind the church, the horde of
tourists in the caravanserai—all knew—more or less, according to the
delicacy of their receiving apparatus—that Something charged with
fresh and living force had swept on viewless feet down the village street,
passed noiselessly between the cracks of doors and windows, touched
nerves and eyelids, and—set them free. In response to the great Order
of Release that the messenger left everywhere behind her, even the
dreams of the sleepers had shifted into softer and more flowing keys. . . .

And the Valley—the Valley also knew! For, as I watched from my
window, something loosened about the trees and stones and boulders;
about the massed snows on the great slopes; about the roots of the
hanging icicles that fringed and sheeted the dark cliffs; and down in the
deepest beds of the killed and silent streams. Far overhead, across
those desolate bleak shoulders of the mountains, ran some sudden
softness like the rush of awakening life . . . and was gone. A touch,
lithe yet dewy, as of silk and water mixed, dropped softly over all . . .
and, silently, without resistance, the *bise noire,* utterly routed, went back
to the icy caverns of the north and east, where it sleeps, hated of men,
and dreams its keen black dreams of death and desolation. . . .

. . . And some five hours later, when I woke and looked towards
the sunrise, I saw those strips of pearly grey, just tinged with red, the
Messenger had been to summon . . . charged with the warm moisture
that brings relief. On the wings of a rising South Wind they came
down hurriedly to cap the mountains and to unbind the captive forces
of life; then moved with flying streamers up our own valley, sponging
from the thirsty woods their richest perfume. . . .

And farther down, in soft, wet fields, stood the leafless poplars,
with little pools of water gemming the grass between and pouring their
musical overflow through runnels of dark and sodden leaves to join
the rapidly increasing torrents descending from the mountains. For
across the entire valley ran magically that sweet and welcome message
of relief which Job knew when he put the whole delicious tenderness
and passion of it into less than a dozen words: *"He comforteth the earth
with the south wind."*

The Man from the "Gods"

That there was something wrong with all his work Le Maistre well knew. Words and music, as the critics never failed to remind him, "just missed" that nameless "something" which would have made them good—perhaps great. Moreover, he was sane enough to realise that the blame lay not with an uncomprehending public, but simply with himself. The spark of inspiration that was beyond question in all his work never gathered to the flame stage. Thus his productions warmed people, but did not light them. He understood well enough what was lacking—and that no amount of mere painstaking "work" could put it right.

But on one occasion Le Maistre achieved a singular and startling success. As a sober record of fact, concealed by initials, it was reported in the Proceedings of the French Psychological Society for that year; and people who believed in the Subliminal Self, the Higher Ego, and all that consoling teaching about an attainable God within, made great havoc with the facts.

The way it came about, moreover, probably has a profound psychical significance. In any case, the result remains as the very best kind of tangible proof; for it was the only great thing he ever really achieved—this Fairy Play (so called); and its beauty was absolutely arresting.

He was something over fifty when he wrote it in its original form. The central idea came to him with the quick flash of a genuine inspiration; so did most of the music; but, in the working out of both, the fire had become smothered. The spark had never gathered into flame. The result was mediocrity. Yet, like so many artists, he confused what was in his mind and imagination with what he had actually set down upon paper; for, when he went over the score to himself, he heard the original beauty in his thoughts and believed he had transferred into his work his own memory of that beauty. The music and words themselves, however, had *not* caught it. Thus, those who heard the preliminary recital in his rooms were more or less bored according to their powers of divination.

"It's fine; it's original," they remarked, shaking their heads as they went home after the performance; "but just misses it!"

The transformation that changed the common lead into gold as by some mysterious process of spiritual alchemy came about as follows:—

The little play was finished, and Le Maistre, having his eye upon a certain manager, went to that particular theatre one night in order to study the "feel" of it—to catch the flavour of the house, the size of the stage, and any other details he could. The management had given him a dress circle box, and he saw admirably. It was characteristic of the man, rather, that he put himself to this far-fetched kind of trouble. During the performance his mind was keenly at work. Yet he saw nothing of what was going on before his eyes; he had come with a definite purpose; he saw his own play all the time, heard his own music; watched his own creatures come on and go off among his own scenery.

At the same time the music, light, and colour provided a stimulus that acted upon his own imagination, and set all the finer machinery of his own creative genius working. Subconsciously he revised his own work, with the illuminating result that a white light shone through his mind and showed up all the flaws, all the places where he had "missed it"; all the passages where he had trailed off into banality. And a tremendous desire went crashing through his being to revise his work in the light of this knowledge. "I felt," he said, "as though a great prayer had gone out of me—a cry, as it were, to my higher self to come to my assistance. Never in my life have I wished anything so intensely before."

Then, in that curious fashion with which many artists must be familiar, it all faded again, and the reaction set in. The effort had no doubt exhausted him. He turned his attention to the actual performances on the stage before him, and lost the power to visualise his own piece. But the play—trivial, vulgar, and untrue to life—wearied him; and he withdrew into the back of the box, and incontinently—fell asleep upon the little plush sofa!

When a considerable time later he woke up, the entire theatre was dark and empty; the piece was over; the audience had gone home to a man; and the building was deserted.

Le Maistre at once realised what had happened, though he could not understand why the final applause had not waked him, and hurried into his overcoat. A faint glimmer pervaded the vast auditorium, for as he leaned over the edge he could just make out the rows of empty stalls, the scattered white patches where the discarded programmes lay, the music-stands of the orchestra, and the exit doors of glass where the pit began. The air still smelt unpleasantly of a crowd—wraps, furs, stale scent, and cigarettes.

Then he struck a match and saw by his watch that it was two o'clock in the morning. He had slept three hours!

He pushed open the door and passed out into the passage, his one idea being how he could get out into the street, or how he would spend the time if he did not get out. He felt hungry, stiff, and a trifle chilly. Feeling his way along by the backs of the upper circle seats, he advanced slowly and carefully, his footsteps making no sound upon the soft carpet, and so came at last to the first exit door. It was locked and barred. He tried the next door with the same result. There was no other exit—nothing but that narrow semi-circular gangway between the wall and the seats, a box at either end, and pillars at intervals to mark the distance. "Like the exercise-walk in a prison-yard," he thought to himself, laughing. No single light was left burning anywhere in the building. Even the hall was in darkness. He saw the gilt-framed pictures of actors and actresses on the walls; a faint rumble from the streets reached him too—voices, traffic, footsteps, wind. Then he turned back into the theatre and carefully made his way down the aisle to the front, feeling the steps first with his toe, and peered over into the body of the house. A sea of shadows swam to and fro below him. Here and there certain stalls picked themselves out of the general gloom almost as though they were occupied; he could easily imagine he saw figures still sitting in them. . . .

And it was here, just at this point, he said, that he began for the first time to feel a little uneasy. A slight tremor of the nerves passed over him, and sitting down in one of the front-row seats he considered the situation carefully and deliberately. There was not much to consider. He was shut in for the rest of the night; the dress circle seemed to be the limits of his prison; he could get neither up nor down; there was no escape till the morning. The prospect was not pleasant; still, it was not very terrible, and his sense of humour would easily have carried him through with credit, but for one thing—this curiously disturbing sense of something he could not quite define: of something that was *going to happen*, it seemed. . . .

It was too vague, too remote for him to deal with squarely. His mind, always keenly imaginative and pictorial, preferred to see it in the terms of a picture. He thought of the Thames as he had sometimes seen it from the Chelsea Embankment in the dusk when dark barges, too far for their outline to be defined, come looming up through the mist. In this way thoughts lie in the depths of the mind; in this way they rise gradually before the consciousness; in this way the cause of his present discomfort would presently reach the point where he would recognise it and understand. In similar fashion, he felt this "something" that moved at the back of his mind, coming slowly forward.

A sudden idea came to him—

"If I could climb down to the auditorium floor I might find a door open somewhere, or escape by way of the orchestra, perhaps!"

And the idea of action was pleasant; though how he climbed over the edge of the box in the dark and swarmed down the slippery pillar, landing with a crash upon the rim of the stage box below, he never quite understood. With a plunge he dropped backwards into the dark space, kicking over as he did so a couple of chairs, which fell with a loud clatter and woke resounding echoes all through the empty building. That clatter seemed prodigious. He held his breath for several seconds to listen, standing motionless against the wall with the distinct idea that all this noise would attract attention to himself, and that if, after all, there was any one watching him—that if among those shadows some one—

"Ah!" he exclaimed quickly. "Now I've got it! There *is* some one watching me in another part of the building. That's why I felt uneasy—"

That tumble into the box had shaken the thought up to the surface of his mind. The picture had emerged from the mist, and he recognised the cause of his uneasiness. All this time, though none of his senses had yet proved it to him, the mind of another person, perhaps the eyes too, had been focused upon him. He was not alone.

Le Maistre felt no alarm, he said, but rather a definite thrill of exhilaration, as though the idea of this other person came to him with a sense of pleasurable excitement. His first instinct to sit concealed in the corner of the box and await events he dismissed almost at once in favour of some kind of prompt action. Stumbling in the gloom, he made his way down to the orchestra, and while groping cautiously among the crowded easels, his hand touched a tiny knob, and a dozen lights that bent over the music folios, like little heads screened under black bonnets, sprang into brilliance. The first thing he noticed was that the fire curtain was down, closing the cavernous mouth of the stage.

The shaded lights, however, were so carefully arranged that they fell only upon the music, and the main body of the theatre still yawned in comparative darkness behind him. Vast and unfriendly it seemed; charged to the brim with faint shufflings and whispers as though an audience sat there stealthily turning over programmes. The stalls faced him like fixed but living beings; the balconies frowned down upon him; the boxes—especially the upper ones—had an air of concealing people behind their curtains. Far overhead, glimmered a huge skylight; he heard the wind sighing across it like wind in the rigging of a ship. And, more than once, he fancied he caught the faint tread of footsteps moving about among the stalls and gangways.

Regretting that he had turned the lights up (they made himself so conspicuous, so easily visible!), he made an instinctive movement to turn them out again; but he touched the wrong knob, so that a row of lights flashed out up under the roof. In that topmost gallery of all, known as "the gods," a little line of starry lights leaped into being, and the first thing he noticed as he looked up was the figure of a man leaning over the edge of the railing—watching him.

The same moment he saw that this figure was making a movement of some kind—a gesture. It beckoned to him. So his feeling that some one was in the theatre with him was justified. There had been a man in the gods all the time.

Le Maistre admitted frankly that, in his first surprise, he collapsed backwards upon the stool usually occupied by the second 'cello. But his alarm passed with a strange swiftness, and gave place almost immediately to a peculiar and deep-seated thrill. The instant he perceived this dim figure of a man up there under the roof his heart leaped with an emotion that was partly delight, partly pleasurable anticipation, and partly—most curious of all—*awe*. And in a voice that was unlike his own, and that carried across the intervening space, for all its faintness, with perfect ease, he heard the words driven out of him as if by command of some deeper instinct than he understood—yet the very last words that he could have imagined as appropriate—

"You're up there in the gods!" he called out. "Won't you come down to me here?"

And then the figure withdrew, and he heard the sound of the footsteps descending the winding passages and stairs behind, as their owner obeyed him and came.

Alarmed, yet curiously exultant, Le Maistre stood up among the music-easels to await his coming. He was extraordinarily alert, prepared. He fumbled again with the little switch-board under the conductor's desk, for he wished to see the man face to face in full light—not to be gradually approached in darkness. But the only thing that came of the button he pressed was a creaking noise behind him, and when he turned quickly to examine, lo and behold, he saw the huge fire-curtain rising slowly and majestically into the air. And, as it rose, revealing the stage beyond, he got the distinct impression that this very stage, now empty, had a moment before been crowded with a throng of living people, and that even now they were there concealed among the wings within a few feet of where he stood, waiting the summons to appear.

Moreover, this discovery, far from causing him the kind of amazement that might have been expected, only communicated, for the second time within the space of a few minutes, another thrill of delight. Again this lightning sense of exhilaration swept him from head to foot.

The footsteps, meanwhile, came nearer; sometimes disappearing behind a thickness of walls that rendered them inaudible, and at other times starting suddenly into greater clearness as they came down from floor to floor. Le Maistre, unable to endure the suspense any longer, felt impelled to go forward and meet them half-way. An intense desire to see this stranger face to face came upon him. He climbed awkwardly over the orchestra railing and made his way past the first rows of the stalls. Already the steps sounded upon the same floor as himself. Hardly a dozen yards, to judge by the fall of these oddly cushioned footsteps, could now separate them. He moved more slowly, and the stranger moved more slowly too—entering at last the gangway in which he stood.

"And it is from this point," to use the words of the report he afterwards wrote for the society, "that my memory begins to fade somewhat, or rather, that the sense of bewilderment grew so astonishingly disturbing that I find it difficult to look back and recall with accuracy the true sequence of what followed. My normal measurement of the passage of time changed too, I think; all went so swiftly, almost as in a dream, though at the time it did not appear to me to be short or hurried. But—describe the sense of glory, wonder, and happiness that enveloped me as in a cloud, I simply cannot. As well might a hashish-eater attempt during the dulness of next morning to reconstruct the phantasmal wonder of all he experienced the night before. Only, this was no phantasy; it was real and actual, and more palpitatingly vivid than any other experience of my life.

"I stood waiting in the gangway while this other person—the stranger—came towards me along the narrow space between the wall and the main body of seats. The footsteps were unhurried and regular. It was very dark; all I could see were two faint patches of light where the exit doors of the pit glimmered beyond. First one patch of light, then the other, was temporarily obscured as he passed in front of these doors. Down he moved steadily towards me through the gloom, and at the barrier of velvet rope that separated the stalls from the pit, he stopped—just near enough for me to distinguish the head and shoulders of a man about my own height and about my own size. He stood facing me there, some ten or twelve feet away.

"For a few seconds there was complete silence—like the silence in a mine, I remember thinking—and I instinctively clenched my fists, almost expecting something violent to happen. But the next instant the man spoke; and the moment I heard his voice all traces of fear left me, and I felt nothing but this peculiarly delightful sense of exhilaration I have already mentioned. It ran through me like the flush of a generous wine, rousing all my faculties, critical and imaginative, to their highest possible power, yet at the same time so bewildering me for the moment that I scarcely realised what I was saying, doing, or thinking. From this point I went through the whole scene without hesitation or dismay—certainly without a thought of disobeying. I mean, it was a pleasure to me to help it all forward, rather than to seek to prevent.

"'Here I am,' said the man in a voice wholly wonderful. 'You called me down, and I have come!'

"'You have come from up there—from the gods,' I heard myself reply.

"'I have come from up there—from the gods,' he answered; and his sentence seemed to mean so much more than mine did, although we used identical words.

"I held on to the back of the stall nearest to me. I could think for the moment of nothing further to say. The idea of what was coming thrilled me inexpressibly, though I could only hazard wild guesses as to its character.

"'Are you ready then?' he asked.

"'Ready! Ready for what?'

"'For the rehearsal,' he said, 'the secret rehearsal.'

"'The secret rehearsal—?' I stammered, pretending, as a child pretends in order to heighten its joy, that I did not understand.

"'—of your play, you know; your fairy play,' he finished the sentence.

"Then he moved towards me a few steps, and, hardly knowing why, I retreated. It was still impossible to see his face. The curious idea came to me that there was something odd about the man that prevented, and that would always prevent, me getting closer to him, and that perhaps I should never see his face completely at all. I cannot point to anything definite that caused this impression; I can merely report that it was so.

"'Look!' he went on, 'every one is ready and waiting. The moment the music starts we can begin. You will find a violin down there; the rehearsal can go on at once.'

"And although it struck me at the time as most curious he should be aware of the fact, it seemed quite natural, because I do play the violin, and in fact compose all my melodies first on that instrument before I put a pen to paper. At the same time I can remember faintly protesting—

"'I?' I remember asking; 'I'm to play?'

"'Certainly,' replied this soft-spoken figure among the shadows. 'You're to play. Who else, pray? And see! Every one is ready and waiting.'

"I was far too happily bewildered to object further; there seemed, indeed, no time for reflection at all; I felt impelled, driven forward as it were, to go through with the adventure and to ask no questions. Besides, I wanted to go through with it. I felt the old power of the first inspiration upon me—only heightened; I felt in me the supreme and splendid confidence that I could do it all better than I had ever dreamed—do it perfectly as it should be done. I was borne forwards upon a wave of inspiration that nothing in the whole world could interfere with.

"And, as I turned to obey, I saw for the first time that the stage was brilliantly lighted; that the scenery was the scenery already chosen by my mind; that the performers thronged the wings, and the opening characters were actually standing in their places waiting for the signal of the music to begin. The performers, moreover, I perceived, were identical in figure, feature, and bearing with those ideal performers who had already enacted the play upon the inner stage of my imagination. It was all, in fact, precisely as the original inspiration had come to me weeks ago before the fires of beauty had faded during the wearisome toil of working it all out in limited terms upon the paper.

"The power that drove me forward, and at the same time filled me with this splendour of untrammelled creation, refused me, however, the least moment for consideration. I could only make my way into the orchestra and pick up the first violin-case that came to hand, belonging, doubtless, to some member of the band I had listened to earlier in the evening; and all eyes were fixed upon me from the stage as I clambered into the conductor's seat and drew the bow across the strings to tune the instrument. At the first sound I realised that my fingers, accustomed to the harsh tones of my own cheaper fiddle, were now feeling their way over the exquisite nervous system of a genuine Guarnierius that responded instantly to the lightest touch; and that the bow in my right hand was so perfectly balanced that even the best Tourte ever made could only seem like a strip of raw, unfinished wood by comparison. For the bow 'swam' over the strings, the sound streamed, smooth as honey, past my ears, and my fingers found the new intervals as easily as if they had never known any other key-board. Harmonics, double-stopping, and arpeggios issued from my efforts as perfectly as trills from the throat of a bird.

"In that moment I *lived;* I understood much; I heard my soul singing within me. . . . I finished tuning, and tapped sharply on the back of the violin to indicate that I was ready, and in the slight pause that ensued before I actually played the opening bars, I became aware that the stalls behind me, the boxes, the dress circle, and the whole house in fact right up to the 'gods,' were crowded with eager listeners; and, further, that the stranger—that man among the shadows in the background—standing ever beyond the reach of the light, still remained in some mysterious and potent fashion intimately in touch with my inner self, directing, helping, inspiring the performance from beginning to end.

"And, in front of me, upon the conductor's desk, lay the score of my own music in clearest manuscript, no longer crossed out and corrected as it lay in my rooms after all the first passion of beauty had been ground out of it, but lovely and perfect as the original inspiration had rushed flame-like into my soul months before.

"The whole performance from that moment—'rehearsal' seems no adequate word to describe it—went with the smoothness of a dream from beginning to end. Just as the music was my own music made perfect, so the words and songs were the mature expression of the original conception before my blundering efforts had confined them, stammering and incomplete, in broken form. Moreover—more wonderful still—I noticed the very places in my score where I had floundered, and where, in the laborious process of composition, the first inspiration had failed me and I had filled in with what was mediocre and banal. It was as if a master pointed out to me with the simplicity of true power the passages where the commonplace might pass—could—*did* pass—by deft, inspired touches into what was fine, moving, noble. . . . The lesson was a sublime one; at the time, however, it all seemed so ridiculously simple and easy that I felt I could never again write anything that was not great and splendid.

"Moreover, the acting, speaking, and dancing provided the perfect medium for my ideas; and the whole performance was the consummate representation of my first conception; even the scenery shifted swiftly and noiselessly, and the intervals between the acts were hardly noticeable. . . .

"And the end came with a curious abruptness, bringing me to myself—my limited, stammering, caged little self, as, it seemed, after these moments of intoxicating expression—with a sharp sense of pain that all was over; and I became aware that, without hurry, without noise, the entire audience that filled the huge building had risen to their feet like one man, and that thousands of hands were clapping *silently* the measure of their intense appreciation. From floor to ceiling, and from wall to wall, flew a great wave of emotion that swept their praise into me, gathered and focused into a single mighty draught of applause. It was, I remember thinking, all their thoughts of joy, their feelings of gratitude, beating in upon my soul in that form of praise which is the artist's only adequate reward; and it reminded me of nothing so much as the whirring of innumerable soft wings all rising through the air at the same moment. Pictorially, in this fashion, it came before my mind.

"Violin in hand, I rose too, and turned to face the auditorium, for I realised that they were calling for the author—for him who had ministered so adequately to their pleasure—and that I must be prepared to say something in reply. I had, indeed, made my first bow, and was already casting about in my mind for suitable words, when, for the first time during the whole adventure—something in me *hesitated*. Either it was that the sea of glimmering faces frightened me, or that I was obeying instinctively some faint warning that it was not myself, but some other, who was the true author of the play, and that it was for him these thousands before me clamoured and called.

"But when, still hesitating in confusion, I turned again towards the stage, I saw that the great fire curtain had meanwhile descended and that a footstep, regular and unhurried, was at that very moment coming forward towards the footlights. I heard the tread. I knew at once who it was. The stranger from the shadows behind me who had directed the entire performance was now moving to the front. It was he for whom the audience clamoured; it was he who was the true author of the play!

"And instantly I clamoured with them, forgetting my own small pain in a kind of delightful exultation that I, too, owed this man everything, and that I should at last see him face to face and join my thanks and gratitude to theirs.

"Almost that same instant he appeared and stood before the centre of the curtains, the glare of the footlights casting upwards into his face. And he looked, not at the great throng behind and beyond me, but down into *my own* face, into *my own* eyes, smiling, approving, his expression radiant with a glory I have never seen before or since upon any human countenance.

"And the stranger, I then realised—*was myself!*

"What happened next is so difficult to describe—though I scarcely know why it should be so—that I cannot hope to convey the reality of it properly, or paint the instantaneous manner in which he vanished and was gone. He neither faded nor moved. But in a second that seemed to have no perceptible duration he was beside me—with me—*in* me; and this swift way he became suddenly merged into myself has always seemed to me the most amazing thing I have ever witnessed. The wave of delight and exultation swept into me anew. I felt for one brief moment that I was as a god—with a god's power of perfect expression.

"But for one second only; for, at once, a new sound, terrible and overwhelming, rose in a flood and tore me away from all that I had ever known. And the sound was ugly and distressing . . . and darkness followed it. . . .

"It was real clapping this time, the clapping of human hands . . . and an indifferent orchestra was playing a noisy march just below me with a great blare of brass out of tune. The lights were up all over the theatre; the audience, busy with wraps and overcoats and applause, were hurrying out. I saw the actors and actresses of the play bowing and scraping before the curtain; and the sight of the perspiration trickling down over the grease-paint of the leading man directly beneath my box struck me like a blow in the face. Then came the frantic whistling for broughams and taxicabs and the hoarse shouting from the street where men cried the evening papers in the roar of the outer world. I picked up my opera-hat, which had rolled into the middle of the floor while I had slept upon the sofa, scrambled into my overcoat, rushed out into the street, and told the driver of the first taxicab I found to drive for his life at double rates. . . .

"And all that night, before the memory of the wonder and the glory faded, I worked upon my score of words and music, striving to get down on the paper something at least of what had been shown to me. How much, or how little I succeeded it is now impossible to say. As I have already explained in this report, the memory faded with distressing swiftness. But I did my best. I hope—I believe—I am told, at least—that there is something in the work that people like. . . ."

If the Cap Fits—

Field-Martin, the naturalist, sat in his corner arm-chair at the Club and watched them—this group of men that had drifted together round the table just opposite and begun to talk. He did not wish to listen, but was too near to help himself. The newspaper over which he had dozed lay at his feet, and he bent forward to pick it up and make it crackle with a pretence of reading.

"Then what *is* psychometry?" was the question that first caught his attention. It was Slopkins who asked it, the man with the runaway chin and over-weighted, hooked nose, that seemed to bring forward all the top of his face and made him resemble a large codfish for ever in the act of rising to some invisible bait.

"Something to do with soul measuring, I suppose, unless my Greek has gone utterly to pot," said the jovial man beside him, pouring out his tea from a height, as a waiter pours out flat beer when he wants to force it to froth in the glass.

"Like those Yankee doctors, don't you remember," put in some one else, with the irrelevance of casual conversation, "who weighed a human body just before it died and just after, and made an affidavit that the difference in ounces represented the weight of the soul."

Several laughed. Field-Martin wheeled up his chair with vigorous strokes of his heels and joined the group, accepting the offer of an extra cup out of that soaring teapot. The particular subject under discussion bored him, but he liked to sit and watch men talking, just as he liked to sit and watch birds or animals in the open air, studying their movements, learning their little habits, and the rest. The conversation flowed on in desultory fashion in the way conversations usually do flow on, one or two talkers putting in occasional real thoughts, the majority merely repeating what they have heard others say.

"Yes, but what *is* psychometry really?" repeated the codfish man, after an interval during which the talk had drifted into an American story that grew apparently out of the reference to American doctors. For that particular invisible bait still hovered above the surface of his slow mental stream, and he was making a second shot at it, after the manner of his ilk.

The question was so obviously intended to be answered seriously that this time no one guffawed or exercised his wit. For a moment, indeed, no one answered at all. Then a man at the back of the group, a man with a deep voice and a rather theatrical and enthusiastic manner, spoke.

"Psychometry, I take it," he said with conviction, "is the quality possessed by everything, even by inanimate objects, of sending out vibrations which—which can put certain sensitive persons *en rapport*, pictorially as it were, with all the events that have ever happened within the ken of such objects—"

"Persons known as psychometrists, I suppose?" from the codfish man, who seemed to like things labelled carefully.

The other nodded. "Psychometrist, I believe," he continued, "is the name of that very psychical and imaginative type that can 'sense' such infinitely delicate vibrations. In reality, I suppose, they are receptive folk who correspond to the sensitive photographic plate that records vibrations of light in a similar way and results in a visible picture."

A man dropped his teaspoon with a clatter; another splashed noisily in his cup, stirring it; a third plunged at the buttered toast of his neighbour; and Field-Martin, the naturalist, gave an impatient kick with his leg against the arm-chair opposite. He loathed this kind of talk. The speaker evidently was one of those who knew by heart the "patter" of psychical research, or what passes for it among credulous and untrained minds—master of that peculiar jargon, quasi-scientific, about vibrations and the rest, that such persons affect. But he was too lazy to interrupt or disagree. Wondering vaguely who the speaker might be, he drank his tea, and listened with laughter and disgust about equally mingled in his mind. Others, besides the codfish, were asking questions. Answers were not behindhand.

"You remember Denton's experiments—Professor Denton, of Cambridge, Mass.," the enthusiastic man was saying, "who found that his wife was a psychometrist, and how she had only to hold a thing in her hand, with eyes blindfolded, to get pictures of scenes that had passed before it. A bit of stone he gave her brought vivid and gorgeous pictures of processions and pageants before her inner eye, I remember, and at the end of the experiment her husband told her what the stone was."

"By Jove! And what was it?" asked codfish.

"A fragment from an old temple at Thebes," was the reply.

"Telepathy," suggested some one.

"Quite possible," was the reply. "But, another time, when he gave her something wrapped up in a bit of paper, taken from a tray covered with objects similarly wrapped up so that he could not know what particular one he held at the moment, she took it for a second, then screamed out that she was rushing, tearing, falling through space, and let it drop with a gasp of breathless excitement—"

"And—?" asked one or two.

"It was a piece of meteorite," was the answer. "You see, she had psychometrised the sensations of the falling star. I know, for instance, another woman who is so sensitive to the atmospheres of things and people, that she can tell you every blessed thing about a stranger whose just-vacated chair she sits down in. I've known her leave a bus, too, when certain people have got in and sat next to her, because—"

Field-Martin paid for his neighbour's tea by mistake and moved away, hoping his contempt was not too clearly marked for politeness.

"—everything, you see, has an atmosphere charged with its own individual associations. An object can communicate an emotion it has borrowed by contact with some one living—" was a fragment of the last sentence he heard as he left the room and went downstairs, spitting fire internally against the speaker and all his kidney. He seized his hat and hurried away. He walked home to his Chelsea flat, fuming inwardly, wondering vaguely if there was any other club he could join where he could have his tea without being obliged to listen to such stuff. . . . He walked through the Park, meaning to cut through *via* Queensgate, and as he went he followed his usual custom of thinking out details of his work: the next day, for instance, he was to lecture upon "English Birds of Prey," and in his mind he reviewed carefully the form and substance of what he would say. He skirted the Serpentine, watching the sea-gulls wheeling through the graceful figures of their evening dance against the saffron sky. The exquisite tilt and balance of their bodies fascinated him as usual. He stopped a moment to watch it. To a mind like his it was full of suggestion, and instinctively he began comparing the method of flight with that of the hawks; one or two points occurred to him that he could make good use of in his lecture . . . when he became aware that something drew his attention down from the sky to the water, and that the interest he felt in the birds was being usurped by thoughts of another kind. Without apparent reason, reflections of a very different order passed into the stream of his consciousness—somewhat urgently. Sea-gulls, hawks, birds of prey, and the rest faded from his mental vision; wings and details of flight departed; his eye, and with it his thought, dropped from the sky to the surface of the water, shimmering there beneath the last tints of the sunset. The emotion of the "naturalist," stirred into activity by the least symbol of his lifelong study—a bird, an animal, an insect—had been curiously replaced; and the transition was abrupt enough to touch him with a sense of surprise—almost, perhaps, of shock.

Now, vigorous imagination, the kind that creates out of next to nothing, was not an ingredient of his logical and "scientific" cast of mind, and Field-Martin, slightly puzzled, was at a loss to explain this irregular behaviour of his usually methodical system. He stepped back farther from the brink where the little waves splashed . . . yet, even as he did so, he realised that the force dictating the impulse was of a protective character, guiding, directing, almost warning. In words, had he been a writer, he might have transposed it thus: "Be careful of that water!" For the truth was it had suddenly made him *shrink*.

He continued his way, puzzled and disturbed. Of the mutinous forces that lie so thinly screened behind life, dropping from time to time their faint, wireless messages upon the soul, Field-Martin hardly discerned the existence. And this passing menace of the water was disquieting—all the more so because his temperament furnished him with no possible instrument of measurement. A sense of deep water, cold, airless, still, invaded his mind; he thought of its suffocating mass lying over mouth and ears; he realised something of the struggle for breath, and the frantic efforts to reach the surface and keep afloat that a drowning man—

"But what nonsense is this? Where do these thoughts suddenly come from?" he exclaimed, hurrying along. He had crossed the road

now, so as to put a greater distance, and a stretch of wholesome human traffic, between him and that sheet of water lying like painted
glass beneath the fading sky. Yet it pulled and drew him back again to
the shore, inviting him with a curious, soft insistence that rendered
necessary a distinct effort of will to resist it successfully. Birds were utterly forgotten. His very being was steeped in water—to the neck, to
the eyes, his lungs filled, his ears charged with the rushing noises of
singing and drumming that come to complete the dread bewilderment
of the drowning man. Field-Martin shook and trembled as he crossed
the bridge by Kensington Gardens. . . . That impulse to throw himself
over the parapet was the most outrageous and unaccountable thing that
had ever come upon him . . . and as he hurried down Queensgate he
tried to calculate whether there was time for him to see his doctor that
very night before dinner, or whether he must postpone it to the first
thing in the morning. For, assuredly, this passing disorder of his brain
must have immediate attention; such results of overwork could not be
seen to quickly enough. If necessary, he would take a holiday at once. . . .

He decided to say nothing to his wife . . . and yet the odd thing
was that before dinner was half over the whole mood had vanished so
completely, and his normal wholesome balance of mind recovered
such perfect control, that he could afford to laugh at the whole thing,
and *did* laugh at it—what was more, even made his wife laugh at it too.
The fact remained to puzzle and perplex, but the reality of it was gone.

But that night, when he went to the Club, the hall-porter stopped
him:

"Beg pardon, sir, but Mr. Finsen thought you might have taken his
hat by mistake last night?"

"His hat?" The name "Finsen" was unknown to him.

"He wears a green felt hat like yours, sir, and they were on adjoining pegs."

Field-Martin took off his head-covering and discovered his mistake. Finsen's name was inside in small gold letters. He explained matters with the porter, and left the necessary directions for the exchange
to be effected. Upstairs he ran into Slopkins.

"That chap Finsen was asking for you," he remarked; "it seems
you exchanged hats last night by mistake, and the porter thought possibly—"

"Who is Finsen?"

"You remember, he was talking so wonderfully last night about psychometry—"

"Oh, is *that* Finsen?"

"Yes," replied the other. "Interesting man, but a bit queer, you know. Gets melancholia and that sort of thing, I believe. It was only a week or two ago, don't you remember, that he tried to drown himself?"

"Indeed," said Field-Martin dryly, and went upstairs to look at the evening papers.

Perspective

I

The amount of duty and pleasure combined in Alpine summer chaplaincies of a month each just suited the Rev. Phillip Ambleside. He was still young enough to climb—carefully; and genuine enough to enjoy seeing the crowd of holiday-makers having a good time. As a rule he was on the Entertainment Committee that organised the tennis, dances, and gymkhanas. During the week one would hardly have guessed his calling. On Sundays he appeared a bronzed, lean, vigorous figure in the pulpit of the hot little wooden church, and people liked to see him. His sermons, never over ten minutes, were the same four every year: one for each Sunday of the month; and when he passed on to another month's duty in the next place he repeated them. The surroundings suggested them obviously: Beauty, Rest, Power, Majesty; and they were more like little confidential talks than sermons. Moreover, incidents from the life of the place—the escape of a tourist, the accident to a guide, and what not, usually came ready to hand to point a moral. One summer, however, there occurred a singular adventure that he has never yet been able to introduce into a sermon. Only in private conversation with souls full of faith himself does he ever mention it. And the short recital always begins with a sentence more or less follows—

". . . Talking of the wondrous ways of God, and the little understanding of the children of men, I am always struck by the huge machinery He sometimes adopts to accomplish such delicate and apparently insignificant ends. I remember once when I was doing summer 'duty' in a Swiss resort high up among the mountains of the Valais . . ."

And then follows the curious occurrence I was once privileged to hear, and have obtained permission to re-tell, duly disguised.

In the particular mountain village where he was taking a month's duty at the time, his church was full every Sunday, so full indeed that twice a week he held afternoon services for those who cared to worship more quietly. And to these little ceremonies, beloved of his own heart, came two persons regularly who attracted his attention in spite of himself. They sat together at the back; shared the same books, although there was no necessity to do so; courted the shadowy corners of the pews: in a word, they came to worship one another, not to worship God.

But the clergyman took a broad view. Courtships fostered in the holy atmosphere of the sacred building were more likely to be true than those fanned to flame in the feverish surroundings of the dance-room. And true love is ever an offering to God. He knew the couple, too. The man, quiet, earnest, well over forty; the girl, young, dashing, spirited, leader in mischief, hard to believe sincere, flirting with more than one. In spite of the careful concealment with which she covered their proceedings, choosing the deserted afternoon service rather than the glare of the garden or ball-room for their talks, the couple were marked. The difference in their ages, characters, and appearance singled them out, as much as the general knowledge that she was rich, vain, flighty, while he was poor, strenuous, living a life of practical charity in London, that precluded gaiety or pleasure, so called.

"What *can* she see in that dull man twice her age?" the elder women said to one another—the answer generally being that it probably amused the girl to turn him so easily round her little finger.

"What a chance for her fortune to be well spent," reflected one or two. While the men, when they said anything at all, contented themselves with: "Pretty hard hit, isn't he? A fine fellow though! Hope he gets her!"

It is always somewhat pathetic to see a man of real value fall before the conquering beauty of an ordinary young girl of the world. The clergyman, however, with an eye for spiritual values, even deeply hidden, divined that beneath her lightness and love for conquest's sake there lay the desire for something more real. And he guessed, though at first the wish may have been father to the thought only, that it was the elder man's fine zeal and power that attracted the butterfly in spite of herself towards a life that was more worth living. Hers, after all, he felt, was a soul worth "saving"; and this middle-aged man, perhaps, was the force God brought into her life to provide her with the opportunity of escape—could she but seize it.

So far Ambleside's story runs along ordinary lines enough. One sees his man and girl without further detail. From this point, however, it slips into a stride where the sense of proportion seems somehow lost, or else "man's little understanding" is too close to the thing to obtain the proper perspective. If any one but this devout and clear-headed clergyman told the tale, one might say "Fancy," "Delusion," or any other description that seemed suitable. But to hear him tell it, with that air of conviction and truth, in those short, abrupt, even jerky sentences, that left so much to the imagination, and with that pallor of the skin that threw into such vivid contrast the fire burning in his far-seeing blue eyes—to sit close to him and hear the story grow in that tense low voice, was to know beyond all question that he spoke of something real and actual, in the same sense that a train or St. Paul's Cathedral are real and actual.

What he saw, he really saw: though the sight may have been of a kind unfamiliar to the majority. He was used as a real pawn in a real game. The girl's life and soul were rescued, so to speak, by the marriage brought about, and her forces of mind and spirit lifted bodily for what they were worth into the scheme that God had ordained for them from the beginning of the world. Only—the machinery brought to bear upon the end in view seemed so prodigious, so extraordinary, so unnecessary. . . . One thinks of the sentence with which Ambleside always began his tale. One wonders. But no one who heard the tale ever asked questions at its close. There was absolutely nothing to say.

Even to the smallest details the affair seemed thought out and planned, for that particular Tuesday Ambleside started without the guide-porter who usually carried his telescope, camera, and lunch. He went off at six A.M., with merely an ice-axe and a small knapsack containing food and Shetland vest for the summit.

It was one of those days towards the end of August when some quality in the atmosphere—usually sign of approaching rain—brings the mountains uncannily close, yet, at the same time, sets out every detail of pinnacle, precipice, and ridge with a terror of size and grandeur that makes one realise their true and gigantic scale. They press up close, yet at the same time stand away in the depths of the sky like unattainable masses in some dream world. This mingling of proximity and distance has a confusing effect upon the eye. When Ambleside toiled up the zigzags without actually looking beyond, he felt that the towering *massif* of the Valais Alps all about him loomed very close; but when he stopped for breath and raised his eyes steadily into their detail, he felt that their distance was too great to be conquered by any little two-legged being like himself merely taking steps. And as he rose out of the valley into the clearer strata of air this effect increased. The whole scale of the chain of Alps about him seemed raised to an immeasurably higher power than he had ever known. He felt like an insect crawling over the craters of the moon. The prodigious splendours of the scenery all round oppressed him more than ever before with his own futile littleness, yet at the same time made him conscious of the grandeur of his soul before the God who had set him and his kind above all this chaos of tumbled planet.

He thought of the mountains as part of the "garment of God," and of nature as expressing some portion of the Deity not intended to be expressed by man—all part of His purpose, alive with His informing will. This glory of the inanimate Alps linked on to some stranger glory in himself that interpreted for him, as in a mystical revelation, God's thundering message and purpose known in the great forms and moods of nature. Closely in touch with the spirit of the mountains he was; glad to be alone.

This, in a sentence, expresses his mood: that the mountains accepted him. Forces in his deepest being that were akin to the life of the planet on which he made his tiny track rose up and triumphed. Over the treacherous Pas d'Iliez, where he usually felt giddy and unsafe, he felt this morning only exhilaration. The gulf yawning at his feet touched him with its splendour, not its terror.

Thus, feeling inclined to shout and run, he eventually reached the desolate valley of rock and shale that lies, unrelieved by a single blade of grass, between the glacier-covered slopes that shut it in impassably on three sides. The bed of this valley lies some 7,000 feet above the sea. The peaks and ridges that rear about it reach 12,000 feet. Here, being a good climber, he rested for the first time at the end of two hours' steady ascent. The air nipped. The loneliness and desolation were very impressive. Beyond him hung the glaciers like immense thick blankets of blue-white upon the steep slopes, dropping from time to time lumps of ice into the shale-strewn valley below. For the sun shining in a cloudless sky was fierce. The clergyman, before attacking the long snow-field that began at his very feet, took out his blue spectacles and disentangled the cord. He ate some chocolate, and took the dried prunes from his knapsack, knowing that thirst would soon be upon him, and that ice-water was not for drinking.

"What a mite I am, to be sure, amid all this appalling wilderness!" he exclaimed; "and how splendid to be able to hold my own!"

And then it was, just as he stood up to arrange the glasses on his forehead, ready to pull down at a moment's notice, that he became aware of something that was strange—unaccustomed. Through the giant splendours of the scorching August day, across all this stupendous scenery of desolation and loneliness, something fine as a needle, delicate as a hair, had begun picking at his mind. The idea came to him that he was no longer alone. Like a man who hears his name called out of darkness he turned instinctively to find the speaker; almost as though some one had been calling to him for a considerable time, and he had only just had his attention drawn to it. He looked keenly up and down the immense, deserted valley.

In every direction, however, he saw nothing but miles of rock, dazzling snow-fields, dark precipices, and endless peaks cutting the blue sky overhead with teeth that gleamed like burnished steel. It was desolation everywhere. The gentle wind that fanned his cheek made no sound against the stones. There was neither tree nor grass for it to rustle through. No bird's wing whirred the air; and the far-off falling of a hundred cascades was of too regular and monotonous a character to have taken on the quality of a voice or the rhythm of uttered words. He examined, so far as he could, the enormous sides of mountain about him, and the great soaring ridges. It was just possible some climber in distress had spied him out, and shouted down upon him from the heights. But he searched in vain. There was no moving human figure. The sound, if sound it had been, was not repeated; only he was no longer alone, as before. That, at least, was certain. . . . He nibbled more chocolate, put a couple of sour prunes into his mouth to suck, arranged the blue snow-glass over his eyes, and started on again for a steady pull up to the next ridge.

And as he rose the scale of the surrounding mountains rose appallingly with him. The true distance of the peaks proclaimed itself; the tremendous reaches that from below appeared telescoped up into a little space opened up and stretched themselves. The hour grew into two. It was considerably after twelve before he reached the *arête* where he had promised himself lunch. And all the way, without ceasing, the idea that he was being accompanied remained insistent in his mind. It troubled and perplexed him. Perhaps it frightened him a little, too. More than once it came close enough to make him pause and consider whether he should continue or turn back.

For the curious part of it was that this idea exercised a direct and deliberate effect upon him. By a hundred little details that seemed to be spontaneous until he examined them, it kept suggesting somehow that he should change his route. Something in his consciousness grew that had not been there before. He thought of a bird bringing tiny morsels of grass and twig until a nest formed. In this way the steady stream of thoughts from somewhere outside himself came nesting in his brain until at length they acquired the consistency of an impression, next of a distinct desire, lastly, the momentum of a definite intention. They acted upon his volition, stirring softly among the roots of his will. Before he realised how it had quite come about he had *changed his mind.*

"Instead of going on to the top as I intended," he said to himself, as he sat on the dizzy ledge munching hard-boiled eggs and sugar sandwiches, "I shall strike off to the left and find my way back into the valley again. That, I think, would be—nicer!"

He had no real reason; he invented none.

And the moment he said it there was a sense of pressure removed, a consciousness of relief, the knowledge, in a word, that he was following a route that it was desired he should follow.

To a man, of course, whose habit it was to seek often the will of a personal Deity he worshipped, there was nothing very out of the way in all this, although he never remembered to have felt any guidance so distinctly and forcibly indicated before. The feeling that he was being "guided" now became a certainty, and in order to follow instructions as well as possible he made his will of no account and opened himself to receive the slightest token this other Directing Agency might care to vouchsafe.

After lunch, therefore, he struck out a diagonal course across a steep snow-slope that would eventually bring him down again to the valley a little nearer its head. And before he had gone a hundred yards he ran into the track of another climber. The marks were a couple of days old, perhaps, for in their hollows lay little heaps of fine snow-dust, freshly blown. Judging by the size there had been two men. He noted the trace of the ice-axe and the occasional streak of the trailing rope. The men had made straight for the valley far below. Here and there they had glissaded. Here and there, too, they had also tumbled gloriously, for the snow was tossed about by their floundering. Yet there was no danger; no precipices intervened; the snow sloped without a break right down into the shale below.

"I'll follow their example," said the Rev. Phillip Ambleside. He strapped on the extra leather seat he carried for sliding and sat down. A moment later he was rushing at high speed over the hard surface. There were hollows of softer snow, however, which stopped him from time to time, drifts as it were into which he plunged, and from which he emerged, wet and shivering. Then he stood up and leaned on his axe, trying to glissade on his feet. For this, however, the surface was not smooth enough. The result was he tumbled, rolled, slid, sat down, and took immense gliding strides. It was very exhilarating. He revelled in it.

But all the while he kept his eyes sharply about him, for in his heart he felt that he was obeying that guiding Influence so strongly impressed upon him—the Power that had persuaded him to change his route, and was now leading him to some particular point with some particular purpose. Now, too, for the first time a vague sense of calamity touched him. Once introduced, it grew. Soon it amounted to a positive foreboding, a presentiment of disaster almost. He could not avoid the idea that he was being led by supernatural means to the scene of some catastrophe where he was to prove of use—a rescue, an arrival in the nick of time to save some one. He actually looked about him already for—yes, for the body. And through his subconscious mind, with the force of habit, ran the magnificent use he could make of it all in a future sermon.

Yet nothing came. The tracks of the other men stretched clear and unbroken into the valley of rocks below. He traced the wavering thin line the whole way down.

"It's nothing to do with *these* men, at any rate," he said to himself, as he sat down for the final slide that should take him to the bottom of the slope. "No accident could possibly have happened here. The snow's too soft, and there are no rocks to fall over or—"

The sentence, or the thought, remained unfinished, for the mouth of the Rev. Phillip was stopped temporarily with wet snow as he lost his balance and rushed sideways with an undignified plunge into a drifted hollow. His eyes were blinded, his feet twisted, the skin of his back drenched and icy. He rose spluttering and gasping. Luckily his axe had a leather loop, or he would have lost it; as it was, his slouch hat was already a hundred feet below, sliding and turning like a top on its way to the followed by the snow-goggles.

And in the act of brushing himself free of snow the truth came to him. It was as though a hand had struck him on the back and pointed—as though a voice had uttered the five words: *"This is the place. Look!"*

Swiftly, searchingly, keenly he looked, and saw—nothing; nothing, at least, that explained the impression of disaster that had possessed him. There was no body certainly, nor any sign of an accident; no place, indeed, where an accident could possibly have come about. He dug quickly in the loose snow with his axe, but the snow was barely two feet deep in this particular hollow, and all round it was a hard surface of smoothly and tightly-packed stuff that was almost ice. Nothing bigger than a cat could have lain buried there!

"This is the place! Look well!" the words seemed to ring in his ears.

Yet the more he looked and saw nothing, the more strongly beat this message upon his brain. This was the place where he was to come, where he was to fulfil some purpose, to find something, do something, accomplish the end intended by the Will that had so carefully guided him all day. The feeling was positive; not to be denied. It was, at the same time, distressingly vast—mighty.

Fixing himself securely against his axe, he stood and stared. The sun beat back into his face from the glittering snow on all sides. Tremendous black precipices towered not far behind him; to his left rolled the frozen mass of the huge glacier, its pinnacles of tottering ice catching the afternoon sun; to his right stretched into bewildering distance the interminable and desolate reaches of shale and moraine till the eye rested upon summits of a dozen peaks that literally swam in the sky where white clouds streamed westwards. There was no sound but falling water, no sign of humanity except the single track of those other climbers, no indication of any disturbance upon the vast face of nature that spread all about him, immense, still, terrific.

Then, piercing the monotony of the falling water, a faint sound of fluttering, heard for the first time, reached his ear. He turned as at the sound of a pistol-shot in the direction whence it came—but again saw nothing. The sound ceased. From the slope below came a breath of icy wind that made him shiver, and with it, he fancied, came the faint hissing noise of his sliding hat and spectacles. This, perhaps, was the sound he had heard as "fluttering."

At length after prolonged and vain searching, the clergyman decided there was nothing for him to do but continue his journey, for the sun was getting low, and he had a long way to go before dusk could be regarded with equanimity. He felt exhausted, wearied, impatient too if the truth were told, yet ashamed of his impatience.

"If this is all *real*," he argued under his breath, "why isn't it made clear what I'm to do?"

And immediately upon the heels of the thought came again that faint and curious sound of something fluttering.

Now, there can be no question that he understood perfectly well that this sound of fluttering had a direct connection with the whole purpose of the day—that it was the clue to his presence in this particular spot, and that he had been forced to halt here by means of his fall in order that he might investigate something or other on this very spot. He knew it; he felt it. But he was too impatient, too cold, too weary to spend any further time over it all. Alarm, too, was plucking uneasily at his reins.

So this time he affected to ignore the sound. Leaning back on his axe he threw his body into position for sliding down to the bottom of the slope. In another second he would have started—when something that froze him into the immobility of a terror worse than death arrested him with a power beyond anything he had ever known before in his life—a Power that seemed to carry behind it the pressure of the entire universe.

There, close beside him in this mountain wilderness, had risen up suddenly a Face—close as the handle of the ice-axe he so tightly grasped, yet at the same time so far away, so immense, so stupendous in scale that he has never understood to this day how it was he could have perceived that it was—a Face. Yet a face it undoubtedly was, a living face; and its eyes—its regard, at any rate, for eyes he divined rather than saw—were focussed upon some object that lay at his very feet.

Clammy with fear, his heart thumping dreadfully, he dropped back upon the snow. Without looking at any particular detail he became aware that the entire world of giant scenery about him was involved in the building up of this appalling Countenance, whose gaze was directed upon a tiny point immediately. before him—the point, he now perceived, whence proceeded that familiar little sound of fluttering.

Words obviously fail him when he attempts to describe the terror of this Visage that rose about him through the day. Pallid and immense, it seemed to stretch itself against the wastes of grey rock, with entire slopes of snow upon the cheeks, ridged and furrowed by precipice and cliff, with torn clouds of flying hair that streaked the blue, and the expanse of glaciers for the splendid brows. Across it the dark line of two moraines tilted for eyebrows, and the massive columns of compressed strata embedded in the whole structure of the mountain chain bulged for the muscles of the awful neck. . . . Moreover, the shoulders upon which it all rested—the vast framework of body that he divined below—the dizzy drop in space where such fearful limbs must seek their resting-place—!

His mind went reeling. The titanic proportions of this Countenance of splendour threatened in some horrible way to overwhelm his life. Its calmness, its iron immobility, its remorseless fixity of mien petrified him. The thought that he had dared to question it, to put himself in opposition to its purpose, even to be impatient with it—this turned all his soul within him soft and dead with a kind of ultimate terror that bereft him of any clear memory, perhaps momentarily, too, of consciousness.

The clergyman *thinks* he fainted. Exactly what happened, probably, he never knew nor realised. All that he can say in attempting to describe it is that he found his own eyes caught up and carried away in the gigantic stream of vision that this Face of Mountains poured upon the ground—caught up and directed upon a tiny little white object that fluttered in the wind at his very feet.

He saw what the Face was looking at and wished him to look at. It made him see what it saw.

For there, in front of him, unnoticed hitherto, lay a scrap of paper half embedded in the snow. Automatically he stooped and picked it up. It was an envelope bearing the printed inscription of an hotel in the village. It was sealed. On the outside in a fine handwriting, he read the Christian name of a man. Opening the corner he saw inside a small lock of dark-coloured hair. And this was all . . . !

Then it was just this moment that the snow where his feet rested gave way, and he started off at full speed to slide to the bottom of the slope, where he only just stopped himself in time to prevent shooting with a violent collision into a mass of shale and loose stones.

In less than thirty seconds it had all happened . . . and the swift descent and tumble had shaken him back as it were into a normal state of mind. But the oppression that had burdened him all day was gone. The mountains looked as usual. An indescribable sense of relief came over him. He felt a free agent once more—no longer guided, pushed, directed. He had fulfilled the purpose.

Putting the little envelope in his inside pocket he picked up his slouch hat and snow-goggles, ate some chocolate and dried prunes, and started off at a brisk pace for his return journey of three hours to the village and—dinner. And the whole way home the grandeur of that face, with its splendid pallor, and its expression of majesty, haunted him with indescribable sensations. With it, however, all the time ran the accompanying thought: "What a tremendous business for so small a result! All that vast manœuvring, all that terror of the imagination, and all that complex pressure upon my insignificant spirit merely in the end to find a wisp of girl's hair in an envelope evidently fallen from the pocket of some careless climber!"

The more the Rev. Phillip Ambleside thought about it, the more bewildered he felt. He was uncommonly glad, however, to get in before dark. The memory of that Mountain Countenance was no agreeable companion for the forest paths and lonely slopes through which his way led in the dusk.

II

That same night it so happened, before he was able to take any steps to trace the owner of the little envelope, there was a Bal de Têtes at the principal hotel. Although the clergyman was on the Entertainment Committee which organised the simple gaieties of the place, he held that honorary position only as a personal compliment to himself; he did not at a rule take an active part in the detail, nor did he as a general rule attend the balls.

This particular night, however, he strolled down to the hotel, and after a little conversation with one or two friends in the hall he made his way to a secluded corner of the glass gallery where the dancers sat out between times, and lit his pipe for a quiet smoke. From behind the shelter of a large sham palm he was able to see all he wanted of the ball-room, to hear the music, and to take in the pleasant sight of all the people enjoying themselves. And the sight did him good. He liked to see it. A number were in costume, which added to the picturesqueness of the scene. Perhaps he sat more in the shadows than he knew, or perhaps the dancers who came to "sit out" near him in the gallery did not realise how their voices carried. Several couples, as the evening advanced, came so close to him that, had he wished, he could have overheard easily every word they uttered. He did not wish, however. His mind was busy with thoughts of its own. That haunting scene of desolation in the mountains obsessed him still; and about ten o'clock, his pipe being finished, he was on the point of getting up to leave, when two dancers came and sat down immediately behind him and began to talk in such very distinct tones that it was impossible to avoid hearing every single word they uttered.

The clergyman pushed his chair aside to make room to go, when, in doing so, he threw a passing glance at the couple—and instantly recognised them. The girl, a Carmen, and a very becoming Carmen, was the one who frequented his afternoon services, and the man, who wore simple evening dress and was not in costume at all, was the middle-aged Englishman who had been at her heels like a slave all the summer. They were absorbed in one another, and evidently unaware of his presence.

To say that he hesitated would not be true. Some force beyond himself simply took him by the shoulders and pushed him back into the chair. Against his own will—for Mr. Ambleside was no eavesdropper—he remained there deliberately to listen.

In telling the story he tells it just like this, making no excuses for conduct that was certainly dishonourable. He declares he could not help himself; the instinct was too imperious to be disobeyed. Again, as in the afternoon, he understood that he was merely being used as a pawn in the game, a game of great importance to some Intelligence that saw through to the distant end.

The man was quiet, but tremendously in earnest, with the kind of steady manner that no woman likes unless she finds it in her to respond with a similar sincerity. Under the bronze his skin showed pale a little. He began to speak the instant they sat down; and in his voice was passion.

"I want you, and I want your money, and I want your life and soul—everything," he said, evidently continuing a conversation; "your youth and energy, your talents, your will, all that is you and yours—*all*." His voice was pitched very low, yet without tremor. He was playing the whole stake, as a strong man of middle age plays it when he is utterly in earnest. "For my scheme, for *our* scheme, for God's scheme I want you; and no one else but you will do. I want you to awake, and change your life, and be your true, fine self. We can make a success, you and I, a success for ourselves and for others. I shall never give you up until—until you give yourself to the world, or"—his voice dropped very low—"to another."

The clergyman waited breathlessly for the answer. The man's words vibrated with such suppressed fire that only a serious reply could be forthcoming. But for a space Carmen merely toyed with her fan, the little red spangled fan that swung from a single finger. Behind the black domino her eyes sparkled, but the expression of her face was hidden.

"The difference in age is nothing," he continued almost sternly. "For me, you are *the* woman, and for you I will prove that I am *the* man. I see clean through to the great soul hidden in you. I can bring it out. I can make you *real*—a soul of value in the big order of God's purposes. What can these boys ever be, or do, for you? I've got a big, useful, practical scheme that can use you, just as it can use me. And my great unselfish love has picked you out of the whole world as the one woman necessary. Will you come to me?"

Still the girl was silent. She tapped him on the knee two or three times, would-be playfully, with the tip of her fan. Her head was bent down a little.

"And I'm strong," he went on earnestly; "I'm a man. The power in me recognises and calls to the power in you. Let me hold you and mould you, and let's take the fine, high life together. Drop this life of child's play you've been leading. Come to me; my arms are hungry for you! But I want you for a higher purpose than my own happiness— though I swear I can make you happy as no woman in this world has ever before been happy. And without you," he added more softly after a slight pause, "this splendid scheme of mine, of ours, can come to nothing. For I cannot do it alone—and there is only one *You* in the world. Answer me now. It was to-night, remember, you promised. I leave to-morrow, and London days lie far ahead. Give me your answer to go back with."

It was a curious way to make love. The reverend gentleman thought he had never heard anything quite like it. An ordinarily frivolous girl, of course, would have been impatient long ago. But the fine passion of the man broke everywhere through his rather lame words, and set something in the air about them aflame. The violins sounded thin and trashy compared to the rhythm of this earnest voice; all the glitter of the ball-room seemed cheap—the costume of Carmen absurdly incongruous. Mr. Ambleside slipped back somehow into the key of the afternoon when Cosmic Powers had held direct communion with his soul. He understood that he was meant to listen. Something big was in progress, something important in a high sense. He did listen—to every word. It was Carmen speaking now; but her voice marred the picture. It was thin, trifling, even affected.

"It's very flattering," she simpered, "but—don't you see—it means the end of all my fun and enjoyment in life. You're so fearfully in earnest. You'd exhaust me in the first week!" She cocked her pretty head on one side, holding the fan against her cheek. Something, nevertheless, belied the lightness of her words, the listener felt.

"But I'll teach you a different kind of happiness," replied the man eagerly, "so that you'll never again want this passing excitement, this 'unrest which men miscall delight.' Give me your answer—now. I see it in your eyes. Let me go away to-morrow with this great new happiness in my heart." He leaned forward. "Let your real self speak out once for all!" He took her fan away and she made no resistance. She clasped her hands in her lap, still looking at him mischievously through her mask.

"Let's wait till we meet later in town," she sighed at length prettily, coaxingly. "I shall be able to enjoy myself here then for the rest of the summer first—I feel so young for such a programme."

But the man cut her short.

"Now," he said, holding her steadily with his eyes. "You said that to me a year ago, remember. I have waited ever since. It is your youth I want."

The girl played with him for another ten minutes, while the clergyman listened, wondering greatly at the other's patience Clearly, she delighted to feel his great love beating up against the citadel she meant in the end to yield. The lighter side of her was vastly interested and amused by it; but all the time the deeper part was ready with its answer. It was only that the "child" in her wanted to enjoy itself a little longer before it capitulated for ever to the strength that should take her captive, and lead her by sharp ways of sacrifice to the high *rôle* she was meant to fill.

It would all have vexed and wearied Mr. Ambleside exceedingly, but for this singular feeling that it was part of some much larger scheme of which he might never know the whole perhaps, but in which he was playing his little part with a secret thrill. Through the tawdry glitter of that scented ball-room he saw again that terrible white-lipped Face, and felt the measure of this great purpose rolling past him—immense, remorseless—which, for all its splendour, could include even so small a thing as this vain and silly girl. The tide of it rose about him with a flood of power. He glanced at the small black domino of the Carmen opposite him . . . he saw the little flashing eyes, the pert lips and mouth—thinking with something like a shudder of that other Countenance in the hollow of whose eyes hid tempests, yet which could look down upon a tiny fluttering paper, because that paper was an item of importance in its great scheme of which both beginning and end were nevertheless veiled. . . .

His thoughts must have wandered for a time. The conversation, at any rate, had meanwhile taken a singular turn. The girl was on her feet, the man facing her.

"Then what is this test of yours?" he was saying, half serious, half laughing—"this test which you say will prove how much I care?"

The girl put back between her lips the small red rose that was part of the Carmen costume. Either it was that the stalk made her lisp a little, or else that a sudden rush of the violins in the waltz drowned her words. The Reverend Phillip, standing there trembling—he never quite understood why he should have awaited her answer so nervously—only caught the second half of her phrase.

". . . that I gave you in this very room six weeks ago, and that you promised to carry about with you always?" he heard the end of her sentence, in a voice that for the first time that evening was serious; "because, if you've kept your word in a small thing like that I can trust you to keep it in bigger things. It was a part of myself, you know, that little bit of hair!" She laughed deliciously in his face, raising herself on tiptoe with her hands behind her back. "You said so yourself, didn't you? You promised it should never, *never* leave you."

The man made a curiously sudden gesture as though a pain beyond his control passed through him. His hands were on the back of a chair. The chair squeaked audibly along the polished floor beneath a violent momentary pressure. He looked straight into his companion's eyes, but made no immediate reply.

Carmen's gaze behind the black mask became hard. With a truly feminine idiocy she was obviously playing this whim as a serious move in the game.

"For if you have lost *that*," she continued, her face flushing beneath the paint, "how can you expect to keep the rest of me, the important part of me?" She spoke as though she believed that he, too, was half-playing—that the next minute he would put his hand into his pocket and produce it. His delay, his awkwardness, above all his silence, angered her. For the surface of her self-contradictory character was obviously—minx.

After a pause that seemed interminable the man spoke, and for the first time his deep voice shook a little.

"This time to-morrow night you shall have it," he said.

"But you're leaving, you said, in the morning!" The tone was piqued and shrill.

"I shall stay another day—on purpose." A pause followed.

"Then you really have lost it—envelope and all—with your name in *my* writing on the outside, and *my* hair for all to recognise who find it—and to sneer."

Her eyes flashed as she said it. The girl was disappointed, incensed, furious. It was all silly enough, of course, and utterly out of proportion. But how silly and childish real life is apt to be at such moments, only those who have reached middle age and have observed closely can know. At the time, to the clergyman who stood there listening and observing, it seemed genuinely poignant, even tragic.

"Until the day before yesterday it had never left me for a single instant," he said at length. "I was in the mountains—glissading with your brother. It fell out of my pocket with a lot of other papers. I lost it on the upper snow slopes of the Dents Blanches—"

The rest of his words were drowned by an inrush of people, for the band was beginning a two-step and couples were sorting themselves and seeking their partners. A Frenchman, dressed as Napoleon, came up to claim his dance. Carmen was swept away. Scornfully, angrily, with concentrated resentment in her voice and manner, she turned upon her heel and from the lips that bit the stalk of the small red rose came the significant words—

"And with it you have also lost—*me!*"

She was gone. Perhaps the Reverend Phillip Ambleside only imagined the tears in her voice. He never knew, and had no time to think, for he found himself looking straight into the eyes of the lover, thus absurdly rejected, and who now became aware of his close presence for the first time. Even then the absurdity of the whole situation did not wholly reveal itself. It came later with reflection. At the moment he felt that it was all like a vivid and singular dream in which the values and proportions were oddly exaggerated, yet in which the sense of tragedy was distressingly real. His heart went out to the faithful and patient man who was being so trifled with, yet who might be in danger of losing by virtue of his very simplicity what was to be of real value in his life—and scheme.

"It's *my* move now," was the thought in his mind as he took a step forward.

The other, embarrassed and annoyed to discover that the whole scene had probably been overheard, made an awkward movement to withdraw, but before he could do so, the clergyman approached him. Only one step was necessary. He moved up from behind a palm, and drawing his hand from an inner pocket, he handed across to him a white envelope bearing the printed name of the hotel and a neat inscription in feminine writing just below it.

"I found this on the snow slopes of the Dents Blanches this afternoon," he said courteously. The other stared him steadily in the face—his colour coming and going quickly. "Take it to her and say that after all it was you—you, who were applying the test—that you wished to see if for so small a thing she was ready to reject so true a love. And, pray, pardon this interference which—er—chance has placed in my power. The matter, I need hardly say, is entirely between yourself and me."

The man took the paper awkwardly, a soft smile of gratitude and comprehension dawning in his eyes. He began to stammer a few words, but the clergyman did not stay to listen. He bowed politely and left him.

He went out of the hotel into the night, and a wind from the surrounding snow slopes brushed his face with its touch of great spaces. He looked up and saw the crowding stars, brilliant as in winter. The mountains in this faint light seemed incredibly close. Slowly he walked up the village street to his rooms in the châlet by the church.

And suddenly the true proportion of normal things in this little life returned to him, and with it a sharp realisation of the triviality of the scene he had been forced to witness—and of the horrible grandeur of the means by which he had been dragged, by the scruff of his priestly neck as it were, so awkwardly into the middle of it all: merely to provide a scrap of evidence the loss of which threatened to bring about a foolish estrangement, and might conceivably have prevented a marriage of apparently insignificant importance.

He felt as though the machinery of the entire solar system had been employed to help a pair of ants carry a pine-needle too heavy for them to the top of the nest.

And then a moment's reflection brought to him another thought. For who could say what the result of this marriage might be? Who could say that from just the exact combination of those two forces—the earnest man, and the lighter girl—a son might not be born who should shake the world and lead some cherished purpose of Deity to completion? For, truly, of the threads which weave into the pattern of life and out again, men see but the tiny section immediately beneath their eyes. The majority focus their gaze upon some detail—thus losing the view of the whole. The beginning and the end are for ever hidden; and what appears insignificant and out of proportion when caught alone at close quarters, may reveal all the splendour of the Eternal Purpose when surveyed with the proper perspective—of the Infinite. The Reverend Phillip Ambleside felt as if for a moment he had been lifted to a height whence he had caught perhaps a glimpse of these larger horizons.

With his faith vastly strengthened, but his nerves considerably shaken, the clergyman went to bed and slept the sleep of a just man who has done his duty by chance as it were. He had helped forward a purpose of which he really understood nothing, but which, he somehow felt, was bigger than anything with which he had so far been connected in his life. Some day—his faith whispered it next morning while he was preparing his sermon—he would see the matter with proper perspective, and would understand.

Special Delivery

Meiklejohn, the curate, was walking through the Jura when this thing happened to him. There is only his word to vouch for it, for the inn and its proprietor are now both of the past, and the local record of the occurrence has long since assumed the proportions of a picturesque but inaccurate legend. As a true story, however, it stands out from those of its kidney by the fact that there seems to have been a deliberate intention in it. It saved a life—a life the world had need of. And this singular rescue of a man of value to the best order of things makes one feel that there was some sense, even logic, in the affair.

Moreover, Meiklejohn asserts that it was the only psychic experience he ever knew. Things of the sort were not a "habit" with him. His rescue, thus, not one of those meaningless interventions that puzzle the man in the street while they exhilarate the psychologist. It was a deliberate and very determined affair.

Meiklejohn found himself that hot August night in one of the valleys that slip like blue shadows hidden among pine-woods between the Swiss frontier and France. He had passed Ste. Croix earlier in the day; Les Rasses had been left behind about four o'clock; Buttes, and the Val de Travers, where the cement of many a London street comes from, was his goal. But the light failed long before he reached it, and he stopped at an inn that appeared unexpectedly round a corner of the dusty road, built literally against the great cliffs that formed one wall of the valley. He was so footsore, and his knapsack so heavy, that he turned in without more ado.

Le Guillaume Tell was the name of the inn—dirty white walls, with thin, almost mangy vines scrambling over the door, and the stream brawling beneath shuttered windows with green and white stripes all patched by sun and rain. His room was sevenpence, his dinner of soup, omelette, fruit, cheese, and coffee, a franc. The prices suited his pocket and made him feel comfortable and at home. Immediately behind the hotel—the only house visible, except the sawmill across the road, rose the ever-crumbling ridges and precipices that formed the flanks of Chasseront and ran on past La Sagne towards the grey Aiguilles de Baulmes. He was in the Jura fastnesses where tourists rarely penetrate.

Through the low doorway of the inn he carried with him the strong atmosphere of thoughts that had accompanied him all day— dreams of how he intended to spend his life, plans of sacrifice and effort. For his hopes of great achievement, even then at twenty-five, were a veritable passion in him, and his desire to spend himself for humanity a devouring flame. So occupied, indeed, was his mind with the emotions belonging to this line of thinking, that he hardly noticed the singular, though exceedingly faint, sense of alarm that stirred somewhere in the depths of his being as he passed within that doorway where the drooping vine-leaves clutched at his hat. He remembered it a little later. The sense of danger had been touched in him. He felt at the moment only a hint of discomfort, too vague to claim definite recognition. Yet it was there—the instant he stepped within the threshold—and afterwards he distinctly recalled its sudden and unaccountable advent.

His bedroom, though stuffy, as from windows long unopened, was clean; carpetless, of course, and primitive, with white pine floor and walls, and the short bed, smothered under its duvet, very creaky. And very short! For Meiklejohn was well over six feet.

"I shall have to curl up, as usual, in a knot," was his reflection as he measured the bed with his eye; "though to-night I think—after my twenty miles in this air—"

The thought refused to complete itself. He was going to add that he was tired enough to have slept on a stone floor, but for some undefined reason the same sense of alarm that had tapped him on the shoulder as he entered the inn returned now when he contemplated the bed. A sharp repugnance for that bed, as sudden and unaccountable as it was curious, swept into him—and was gone again before he had time to seize it wholly. It was in reality so slight that he dismissed it immediately as the merest fancy; yet, at the same time, he was aware that he would rather have slept on another bed, had there been one in the room—and then the queer feeling that, after all, perhaps, he would *not* sleep there in the end at all. How this idea came to him he never knew. He records it, however, as part of the occurrence.

After eight o'clock a few peasants, and workmen from the sawmill, came in to drink their *demi-litre* of red wine in the common room downstairs, to stare at the unexpected guest, and to smoke their vile tobacco. They were neither picturesque nor amusing—simply dirty and slightly malodorous. At nine o'clock Meiklejohn knocked the ashes from his briar pipe upon the limestone window-ledge, and went upstairs, overpowered with sleep. The sense of alarm had utterly disappeared; his mind was busy once more with his great dreams of the future—dreams that materialised themselves, as all the world knows, in the famous Meiklejohn Institutes. . . .

Berthoud, the proprietor, short and sturdy, with faded brown coat and no collar, slightly confused with red wine and a "tourist" guest, showed him the way up. For, of course, there was no *femme de chambre*.

"You have the corridor all to yourself," the man said; showed him the best corner of the landing to shout from in case he wanted anything—there being no bell—eyed his knapsack, and flask with considerable curiosity, wished him good-night, and was gone. He went downstairs with a noise like a horse, thought the curate, as he locked the door after him.

The windows had been open now for a couple of hours, and the room smelt sweet with the odours of sawn wood and shavings, the resinous perfume of the surrounding hosts of pines, and the sharp, delicate touch of a lonely mountain valley where civilisation has not yet tainted the air. Whiffs of coarse tobacco, pungent without being offensive, came invisibly through the cracks of the floor. Primitive and simple it all was—a sort of vigorous "backwoods" atmosphere. Yet, once again, as he turned to examine the room after Berthoud's steps had blundered down below into the passage, something rose faintly within him to set his nerves mysteriously a-quiver.

Out of these perfectly simple conditions, without the least apparent cause, the odd feeling again came over him that he was—in danger.

The curate was not much given to analysis. He was a man of action pure and simple, as a rule. But to-night, in spite of himself, his thoughts went plunging, searching, asking. For this singular message of dread that emanated as it were from the room, or from some article of furniture in the room perhaps—that bed still touched his mind with a peculiar repugnance—demanded somewhat insistently for an explanation. And the only explanation that suggested itself to his unimaginative mind was that the forces of nature hereabouts were— overpowering; that, after the slum streets and factory chimneys of the last twelve months, these towering cliffs and smothering pine-forests communicated to his soul a word of grandeur that amounted to awe. Inadequate and far-fetched as the explanation seems, it was the only one that occurred to him; and its value in this remarkable adventure lies in the fact that he connected his sense of danger partly with the bed and partly with the mountains.

"I felt once or twice," he said afterwards, "as though some powerful agency of a spiritual kind were all the time trying to beat into my stupid brain a message of warning." And this way of expressing it is more true and graphic than many paragraphs of attempted analysis.

Meiklejohn hung his clothes by the open window to air, washed, read his Bible, looked several times over his shoulder without apparent cause, and then knelt down to pray. He was a simple and devout soul; his Self lost in the yearning, young but sincere, to live for humanity. He prayed, as usual, with intense earnestness that his life might be preserved for use in the world, when in the middle of his prayer—there came a knocking at the door.

Hastily rising from his knees, he opened. The sound of rushing water filled the corridor. He heard the voices of the workmen below in the drinking-room. But only darkness stood in the passages, filling the house to the very brim. No one was there. Here turned to his interrupted devotions.

"I imagined it," he said to himself. He continued his prayers, however, longer than usual. At the back of his thoughts, dim, vague, half-defined only, lay this lurking sense of uneasiness—that he was in danger. He prayed earnestly and simply, as a child might pray, for the preservation of his life. . . .

Again, just as he prepared to get into bed, struggling to make the heaped-up duvet spread all over, came that knocking at the bedroom door. It was soft, wonderfully soft, and something within him thrilled curiously in response. He crossed the floor to open—then hesitated. Suddenly he understood that that knocking at the door was connected with the sense of danger in his heart. In the region of subtle intuitions the two were linked. With this realisation there came over him, he declares, a singular mood in which, as in a revelation, he knew that Nature held forces that might somehow communicate directly and positively with—human beings. This thought rushed upon him out of the night, as it were. It arrested his movements. He stood there upon the bare pine boards, hesitating to open the door.

The delay thus described lasted actually only a few seconds, but in those few seconds these thoughts tore rapidly and like fire through his mind. The beauty of this lost and mysterious valley was certainly in his veins. He felt the strange presence of the encircling forests, soft and splendid, their million branches sighing in the night airs. The crying of the falling water touched him. He longed to transfer their peace and power to the hearts of suffering thousands of men and women and children. The towering precipices that literally dropped their pale walls over the roof of the inn lifted his thoughts to their own wind-swept heights; he longed to convey their message of inflexible strength to the weak-kneed folk in the slums where he worked. He was peculiarly conscious of the presence of these forces of Nature—the irresistible powers that regenerate as easily as they destroy.

All this, and far more, swept his soul like a huge wind as he stood there, waiting to open the door in answer to that mysterious soft knocking.

And there, when at length he opened, stood the figure of a man— staring at him and smiling.

Disappointment seized him instantly. He had expected, almost believed, that he would see something un-ordinary; and instead, there stood a man who had merely mistaken the door of his room, and was now bowing his apology for the interruption. Then, to his amazement, he saw that the man beckoned: the figure was some one who sought to draw him out.

"Come with me," it seemed to say.

But Meiklejohn only realised this afterwards, he says, when it was too late and he had already shut the door in the stranger's face. For the man had withdrawn into the darkness a little, and the curate had taken the movement for a mere acknowledgment of his mistake instead of—as he afterwards felt—a sign that he should follow.

"And the moment the door was shut," he says, "I felt that it would have been better for me to have gone out into the passage to see what he wanted. It came over me that the man had something important to say to me. I had missed it."

For some seconds, it seemed, he resisted the inclination to go after him. He argued with himself; then turned to his bed, pulled back the sheets and heavy duvet, and was met sharply again with the sense of repugnance, almost of fear, as before. It leaped out upon him—as though the drawing back of the blankets had set free some cold blast of wind that struck him across the face and made him shiver.

At the same moment a shadow fell from behind his shoulder and dropped across the pillow and upper half of the bed. It may, of course, have been the magnified shadow of the moth that buzzed about the pale-yellow electric light in the ceiling. He does not pretend to know. It passed swiftly, however, and was gone; and Meiklejohn, feeling less sure of himself than ever before in his life, crossed the floor quickly, almost running, and opened the door to go after the man who had knocked—twice. For in reality less than half a minute had passed since the shutting of the door and its reopening.

But the corridor was empty. He marched down the pine-board floor for some considerable distance. Below he saw the glimmer of the hall, and heard the voices of the peasants and workmen from the sawmill as they still talked and drank their red wine in the public room. That sound of falling water, as before, filled the air. Darkness reigned. But the person—the *messenger*—who had twice knocked at his door was gone utterly. . . . Presently a door opened downstairs, and the peasants clattered out noisily. He turned and went back to bed. The electric light switched off below. Silence fell. Conquering his strange repugnance, Meiklejohn, with a prayer on his lips, got into bed, and in less than ten minutes was sound asleep.

"I admit," he says, in telling the story, "that what happened afterwards came so swiftly and so confusingly, yet with such a storm of overwhelming conviction of its reality, that its sequence may be somewhat blurred in my memory, while, at the same time, I see it after all these years as though it was a thing of yesterday. But in my sleep, first of all, I again heard that soft, mysterious tapping—not in the course of a dream of any sort, but sudden and alone out of the dark blank of forgetfulness. I tried to wake. At first, however, the bonds of unconsciousness held me tight. I had to struggle in order to return to the waking world. There was a distinct effort before I opened my eyes; and in that slight interval I became aware that the person who had knocked at the door had meanwhile opened it and passed into the room. I had left the lock unturned. The person was close beside me in the darkness—not in utter darkness, however, for a rising three-quarter moon shed its faint silver upon the floor in patches, and, as I sprang swiftly from the bed, I noticed something alive moving towards me across the carpetless boards. Upon the edges of a patch of moonlight, where the fringe of silver and shadow mingled, it stopped. Three feet away from it I, too, stopped, shaking in every muscle. It lay there crouching at my very feet, staring up at me. But was it man or was it animal? For at first I took it certainly for a human being on all fours; but the next moment, with a spasm of genuine terror that half stopped my breath, it was borne in upon me that the creature was—nothing human. Only in this way can I describe it. It was identical with the human figure who had knocked before and beckoned to me to follow, but it was another presentation of that figure.

"And it held (or brought, if you will) some tremendous message for me—some message of tremendous importance, I mean. The first time I had argued, resisted, refused to listen. Now it had returned in a form that ensured obedience. Some quite terrific power emanated from it—a power that I understood instinctively belonged to the mountains and the forests and the untamed elemental forces of Nature. Amazing as it may sound in cold blood, I can only say that I felt as though the towering precipices outside had sent me a direct warning—that my life was in immediate danger.

"For a space that seemed minutes, but was probably less than a few seconds, I stood there trembling on the bare boards, my eyes riveted upon the dark, uncouth shape that covered all the floor beyond. I saw no limbs or features, no suggestion of outline that I could connect with any living form I know, animate or inanimate. Yet it moved and stirred all the time—*whirled within itself*, describes it best; and into my mind sprang a picture of an immense dark wheel, turning, spinning, whizzing so rapidly that it appears motionless, and uttering that low and ominous thunder that fills a great machinery-room of a factory. Then I thought of Ezekiel's vision of the Living Wheels. . . .

"And it must have been at this instant, I think, that the muttering and deep note that issued from it formed itself into words within me. At any rate, I heard a voice that spoke with unmistakable intelligence:

"'Come!' it said. 'Come out—at once!' And the sense of power that accompanied the Voice was so splendid that my fear vanished and I obeyed instantly without thinking more. I followed; it led. It altered in shape. The door *was* open. It ran silently in a form that was more like a stream of deep black water than anything else I can think of— out of the room, down the stairs, across the hall, and up to the deep shadows that lay against the door leading into the road. There I lost sight of it."

Meiklejohn's only desire, he says, then was to rush after it—to escape. This he did. He understood that somehow it passed through the door into the open air. Ten seconds later, perhaps even less, he, too, was in the open air. He acted almost automatically; reason, reflection, logic all swept away. Nowhere, however, in the soft moonlight about him was any sign of the extraordinary apparition that had succeeded in drawing him out of the inn, out of his bedroom, out of his—bed. He stared in a dazed way at everything—just beginning to get control of his faculties a bit—wondering what in the world it all meant. That huge spinning form, he felt convinced, lay hidden somewhere close beside him, waiting for the end. The danger it had enabled him to avoid was close at hand. . . . He *knew* that, he says. . . .

There lay the meadows, touched here and there with wisps of floating mist; the stream roared and tumbled down its rocky bed to his left; across the road the sawmill lifted its skeleton-like outline, moonlight shining on the dew-covered shingles of the roof, its lower part hidden in shadow. The cold air of the valley was exquisitely scented.

To the right, where his eye next wandered, he saw the thick black woods rising round the base of the precipices that soared into the sky, sheeted with silvery moonlight. His gaze ran up them to the far ridges that seemed to push the very stars farther into the heavens. Then, as he saw those stars crowding the night, he staggered suddenly backwards, seizing the wall of the road for support, and catching his breath. For the top of the cliff, he fancied, moved. A group of stars was for a fraction of a second—hidden. The earth—the scenery of the valley, at least—turned about him. Something prodigious was happening to the solid structure of the world. The precipices seemed to bend over upon the valley. The far, uppermost ridge of those beetling cliffs shifted downwards. Meiklejohn declares that the way its movement hid momentarily a group of stars was the most startling—for some reason horrible—thing he had ever witnessed.

Then came the roar and crash and thunder as the mass toppled, slid, and finally—took the frightful plunge. How long the forces of rain and frost had been chiselling out the slow detachment of the giant slabs that fell, or whence came the particular extra little push that drove the entire mass out from the parent rock, no one can know. Only one thing is certain: that it was due to no chance, but to the nicely and exactly calculated results of balanced cause and effect. From the beginning of time it had been known—it might have been accurately calculated, rather—that this particular thousand tons of rock would break away from the crumbling tops of the precipices and crash downwards with the roar of many tempests into the lost and mysterious mountain valley where Meiklejohn the curate spent such and such a night of such and such a holiday. It was just as sure as the return of Halley's comet.

"I watched it," he says, "because I couldn't do anything else. I would far rather have run—I was so frightfully close to it all—but I couldn't move a muscle. And in a few seconds it was over. A terrific wind knocked me backwards against the stone wall; there was a vast clattering of smaller stones, set rolling down the neighbouring couloirs; a steady roll of echoes ran thundering up and down the valley; and then all was still again exactly as it had been before. And the curious thing was—ascertained a little later, as you may imagine, and not at once—that the inn, being so closely built up against the cliffs, had almost entirely escaped. The great mass of rock and trees had taken a leap farther out, and filled the meadows, blocked the road, crushed the sawmill like a matchbox, and dammed up the stream; but the inn itself was almost untouched.

"*Almost*—for a single block of limestone, about the size of a grand piano, had dropped straight upon one corner of the roof and smashed its way through my bedroom, carrying everything it contained down to the level of the cellar, so terrific was the momentum of its crushing journey. Not a stick of the furniture was afterwards discoverable—as such. The bed seems to have been caught by the very middle of the fallen mass."

The confusion in Meiklejohn's mind may be imagined—the rush of feeling and emotion that swept over him. Berthoud and the peasants mustered in less than a dozen minutes, talking, crying, praying. Then the stream, dammed up by the accumulation of rock, carried off the debris of the broken roof and walls in less than half an hour. The rock, however, that swept the room and the *empty* bed of Meiklejohn the curate into dust, still lies in the valley where it fell.

"The only other thing that I remember," he says, in telling the story, "is that, as I stood there, shaking with excitement and the painful terror of it all, before Berthoud and the peasants had come to count over their number and learn that no one was missing—while I stood there, leaning against the wall of the road, something rose out of the white dust at my feet, and, with a noise like the whirring of some immense projectile, passed swiftly and invisibly away up into space—so far as I could judge, towards the distant ridges that reared their motionless outline in moonlight beneath the stars."

The Lost Valley

Mark and Stephen, twins, were remarkable even of their kind: they were not so much one soul split in twain, as two souls fashioned in precisely the same mould. Their characters were almost identical—tastes, hopes, fears, desires, everything. They even liked the same food, wore the same kind of hats, ties, suits; and, strongest link of all, of course disliked the same things too. At the age of thirty-five neither had married, for they invariably liked the same woman; and when a certain type of girl appeared upon their horizon they talked it over frankly, agreed it was impossible to separate, and together turned their backs upon her for a change of scene before she could endanger their peace.

For their love for one another was unbounded—irresistible as a force of nature, tender beyond words—and their one keen terror was that they might one day be separated.

To look at, even for twins, they were uncommonly alike. Even their eyes were similar: that grey-green of the sea that sometimes changes to blue, and at night becomes charged with shadows. And both faces were of the same strong type with aquiline noses, stern-lipped mouths, and jaws well marked. They possessed imagination, real imagination of the winged kind, and at the same time the fine controlling will without which such a gift is apt to prove a source of weakness. Their emotions, too, were real and living: not the sort that merely tickle the surface of the heart, but the sort that plough.

Both had private means, yet both had studied medicine because it interested them, Mark specialising in diseases of eye and ear, Stephen in mental and nervous cases; and they carried on a select, even a distinguished, practice in the same house in Wimpole Street with their names on the brass plate thus: Dr. Mark Winters, Dr. Stephen Winters.

In the summer of 1900 they went abroad together as usual for the months of July and August. It was their custom to explore successive ranges of mountains, collecting the folklore and natural history of the region into small volumes, neatly illustrated with Stephen's photographs. And this particular year they chose the Jura, that portion of it, rather, that lies between the Lac de Joux, Baulmes, and Fleurier. For, obviously, they could not exhaust a whole range in a single brief holiday. They explored it in sections, year by year. And they invariably chose for their head-quarters quiet, unfashionable places where there was less danger of meeting attractive people who might break in upon the happiness of their profound brotherly devotion—the incalculable, mystical devotion of twins.

"For abroad, you know," Mark would say, "people have an insinuating way with them that is often hard to withstand. The chilly English reserve disappears. Acquaintanceship becomes intimacy before one has time to weigh it."

"Exactly," Stephen added. "The conventions that protect one at home suddenly wear thin, don't they? And one becomes soft and open to attack—unexpected attack."

They looked up and laughed, reading each other's thoughts like trained telepathists. What each meant was the dread that one should, after all, be taken and the other left—by a woman.

"Though at our age, you know, one is almost immune," Mark observed; while Stephen smiling agreed philosophically—

"Or *ought* to be."

"*Is,*" quoth Mark decisively. For by common consent Mark played the *rôle* of the elder brother. His character, if anything, was a shade more practical. He was slightly more critical of life, perhaps, Stephen being ever more apt to accept without analysis, even without reflection. But Stephen had that richer heritage of dreams which comes from an imagination loved for its own sake.

II

In the peasant's châlet, where they had a sitting-room and two bedrooms, they were very comfortable. It stood on the edge of the forests that run along the slopes of Chasseront, on the side of Les Rasses farthest from Ste Croix. Marie Petavel provided them with the simple cooking they liked; and they spent their days walking, climbing, exploring, Mark collecting legend and folklore, Stephen making his natural history studies, with the little maps and surveys he drew so cleverly. Even this was only a division of labour, for each was equally interested in the occupation of the other; and they shared results in the long evenings, when expeditions brought them back in time, smoking in the rickety wooden balcony, comparing notes, shaping chapters, happy as two children. They brought the enthusiasm of boys to all they did, and they enjoyed the days apart almost as much as those they spent together. After separate expeditions each invariably returned with surprises which awakened the other's interest—even amazement.

Thus, the life of the foreign element in the hotels—unpicturesque in the daytime, noisy and overdressed at night—passed them by. The glimpses they caught as they passed these caravansarais, when gaieties were the order of the evening, made them value their peaceful retreat among the skirts of the forest. They brought no evening dress with them, not even "le smoking."

"The atmosphere of these huge hotels simply poisons the mountains," quoth Stephen. "All that 'haunted' feeling goes."

"Those people," agreed Mark, with scorn in his eyes, "would be far happier at Trouville or Dieppe, gambling, flirting, and the rest."

Feeling, thus, secure from that jealousy which lies so terribly close to the surface of all giant devotions where the entire life depends upon exclusive possession, the brothers regarded with indifference the signs of this gayer world about them. In that throng there was no one who could introduce an element of danger into their lives—no woman, at least, either of them could like would be found *there!*

For this thought must be emphasised, though not exaggerated. Certain incidents in the past, from which only their strength of will had made escape possible, proved the danger to be a real one. (Usually, too, it was some un-English woman: to wit, the Budapesth adventure, or the incident in London with the Greek girl who was first Mark's patient and then Stephen's.) Neither of them made definite reference to the danger, though undoubtedly it was present in their minds more or less vividly whenever they came to a new place: this singular dream that one day a woman would carry off one, and leave the other lonely.

It was instinctive, probably, just as the dread of the wolf is instinctive in the deer. The curious fact, though natural enough, was that each brother feared for the other and not for himself. Had any one told Mark that some day he would marry, Mark would have shrugged his shoulders with a smile, and replied, "No; but I'm awfully afraid Stephen may!" And *vice versâ*.

III

Then, out of a clear sky, the bolt fell—upon Stephen. Catching him utterly unawares, it sent him fairly reeling. For Stephen, even more than his brother, possessed that glorious yet fatal gift, common to poets and children, by which out of a few insignificant details the soul builds for itself a whole sweet heaven to dwell in.

It was at the end of their first month, a month of unclouded happiness together. Since their exploration of the Abruzzi, two years before, they had never enjoyed anything so much. And not a soul had come to disturb their privacy. Plans were being mooted for moving their head-quarters some miles farther towards the Val de Travers and the Creux du Van; only the day of departure, indeed, remained to be fixed, when Stephen, coming home from an afternoon of photography alone, saw, with bewildering and arresting suddenness—a Face. And with the effect of a blow full upon the heart it literally struck him.

How such a thing can come upon a strong man, a man of balanced mind, healthy in nerves and spirit, and in a single moment change his serenity into a state of feverish and passionate desire for possession, is a mystery that lies too deep for philosophy or science to explain. It turned him dizzy with a sudden and tempestuous delight—a veritable sickness of the soul, wondrous sweet as it was deadly. Rare enough, of course, such instances may be, but that they happen is undeniable.

He was making his way home in the dusk somewhat wearily. The sun had already dipped below the horizon of France behind him. Across the open country that stretched away to the distant mountains of the Rhone Valley, the moonlight climbed with wings of ghostly radiance that fanned their way into the clefts and pine-woods of the Jura all about him. Cool airs of night stirred and whispered; lights twinkled through the openings among the trees, and all was scented like a garden.

He must have strayed considerably from the right trail—path there was none—for instead of striking the mountain road that led straight to his châlet, he suddenly emerged into a pool of electric light that shone round one of the smaller wooden hotels by the borders of the forest. He recognised it at once, because he and his brother always avoided it deliberately. Not so gay or crowded as the larger caravansa-rais, it was nevertheless full of people of the kind they did not care about. Stephen was a good half-mile out of his way.

When the mind is empty and the body tired it would seem that the system is sensitive to impressions with an acuteness impossible when these are vigorously employed. The face of this girl, framed against the glass of the hotel verandah, rushed out towards him with a sudden in-vading glory, and took the most complete imaginable possession of this temporary unemployment of his spirit. Before he could think or act, accept or reject, it had lodged itself eternally at the very centre of his being. He stopped, as before an unexpected flash of lightning, caught his breath—and stared.

A little apart from the throng of "dressy" folk who sat there in the glitter of the electric light, this face of melancholy dark splendour rose close before his eyes, all soft and wondrous as though the beauty of the night—of forest, stars, and moon-rise—had dropped down and focussed itself within the compass of a single human countenance. Framed within a corner pane of the big windows, peering sideways in-to the darkness, the vision of this girl, not twenty feet from where he stood, produced upon him a shock of the most convincing delight he had ever known. It was almost as though he saw some one who had dropped down among all these hotel people from another world. And from another world, in a sense, she undoubtedly was; for her face held in it nothing that belonged to the European countries he knew. She was of the East. The magic of other suns swept into his soul with the vision; the pageantry of other skies flashed brilliantly and was gone. Torches flamed in recesses of his being hitherto dark.

The incongruous surroundings unquestionably deepened the con-trast to her advantage, but what made this first sight of her so extraordi-narily arresting was the curious chance that where she sat the glare of the electric light did not touch her. She was in shadow from the shoulders downwards. Only, as she leaned backwards against the window, the face and neck turned slightly, there fell upon her exquisite Eastern features the soft glory of the rising moon. And comely she was in Stephen's eyes as nothing in his life had hitherto seemed comely. Apart from the vulgar throng as an exotic is apart from the weeds that choke its growth, this face seemed to swim towards him along the pathway of the slanting moonbeams. And, with it, came literally herself. Some released projection of his consciousness flew forth to meet her. The sense of nearness took his breath away with the faintness of too great happiness. She was in his arms, and his lips were buried in her scented hair. The sensation was vivid with pain and joy, as an ecstasy. And of the nature of true ecstasy, perhaps, it was: for he stood, it seemed, *outside himself.*

He remained there riveted in the patch of moonlight at the forest edge, for perhaps a whole minute, perhaps two, before he realised what had happened. Then came a second shock that was even more conquering than the first, for the girl, he saw, was not only gazing into his very face, she was also rising, as with an incipient gesture of recognition. As though she knew him, the little head bent itself forward gently, gracefully, and the dear eyes positively smiled.

The impetuous yearning that leaped full-fledged into his blood taught him in that instant the spiritual secret that pain and pleasure are fundamentally the same force. His attempt at self-control, made instinctively, was utterly overwhelmed. Something flashed to him from her eyes that melted the very roots of resolve; he staggered backwards, catching at the nearest tree for support, and in so doing left the patch of moonlight and stood concealed from view within the deep shadows behind.

Incredible as it must seem in these days of starved romance, this man of strength and firm character, who had hitherto known of such attacks only vicariously from the description of others, now reeled back against the trunk of a pine tree, knowing all the sweet faintness of an overpowering love at first sight.

"For that, by God, I'd let myself waste utterly to death! To bring her an instant's happiness I'd suffer torture for a century—!"

For the words, with their clumsy, concentrated passion, were out before he realised what he was saying, what he was doing; but, once out, he knew how pitifully inadequate they were to express a tithe of what was in him like a rising storm. All words dropped away from him;

the breath that came and went so quickly clothed no further speech.

With his retreat into the shadows the girl had sat down again, but she still gazed steadily at the place where he had stood. Stephen, who had lost the power of further movement, also stood and stared. The picture, meanwhile, was being traced with hot iron upon plastic deeps in his soul of which he had never before divined the existence. And, again, with the magic of this master-yearning, it seemed that he drew her out from that horde of hotel guests till she stood close before his eyes, warm, perfumed, caressing. The delicate, sharp splendour of her face, already dear beyond all else in life, flamed there within actual touch of his lips. He turned giddy with the joy, wonder and mystery of it all. The frontiers of his being melted—then extended to include her.

From the words a lover fights among to describe the face he worships one divines only a little of the picture; these dimly-coloured symbols conceal more beauty than they reveal. And of this dark, young oval face, first seen sideways in the moonlight, with drooping lids over the almond-shaped eyes, soft cloudy hair, all enwrapped with the haunting and penetrating mystery of love, Stephen never attempted to analyse the ineffable secret. He just accepted it with a plunge of utter self-abandonment. He only realised vaguely by way of detail that the little nose, without being Jewish, curved singularly down towards a chin daintily chiselled in firmness; that the mouth held in its lips the invitation of all womankind as expressed in another race, a race alien to his own—an Eastern race; and that something untamed, almost savage, in the face was corrected by the exquisite tenderness of the large dreamy, brown eyes. The mighty revolution of love spread its soft tide into every corner of his being.

Moreover, that gesture of welcome, so utterly unexpected yet so spontaneous (so natural, it seemed to him now!), the smile of recognition that had so deliciously perplexed him, he accepted in the same way. The girl had felt what he had felt, and had betrayed herself even as he had done by a sudden, uncontrollable movement of revelation and delight; and to explain it otherwise by any vulgar standard of worldly wisdom, would be to rob it of all its dear modesty, truth, and wonder. She yearned to know him, even as he yearned to know her.

And all this in the little space, as men count time, of two minutes, even less.

How he was able at the moment to restrain all precipitate and impulsive action, Stephen has never properly understood. There was a fight, and it was short, painful, and confused. But it ended on a note of triumphant joy—the rapture of happiness to come. . . .

With a great effort he remembers that he found the use of his feet and continued his journey homewards, passing out once more into the moonlight. The girl in the verandah followed his disappearing figure with her turning head; she craned her neck to watch till he disappeared beyond the angle of vision; she even waved her little dark hand.

"I shall be late," ran the thought sharply through Stephen's mind. It was cold; vivid with keen pain. "Mark will wonder what in the world has become of me—!"

For, with swift and terrible reaction, the meaning of it all—the possible consequences of The Face—swept over his heart and drowned it in a flood of icy water. In estimating his brotherly love, even the love of the twin, he had never conceived such a thing as this—had never reckoned with the possibility of a force that could make all else in the world seem so trivial. . . .

Mark, had he been there, with his more critical attitude to life, might have analysed something of it away. But Mark was not there. And Stephen had—*seen*.

Those mighty strings of life upon which, as upon an instrument, the heart of man lies stretched had been set powerfully a-quiver. The new vibrations poured and beat through him. Something within him swiftly disintegrated; in its place something else grew marvellously. The Face had established dominion over the secret places of his soul; thenceforward the process was automatic and inevitable.

IV

Then, spectre-like and cold, the image of his brother rose before his inner vision. The profound brotherly love of the twin confronted him in the path.

He stumbled among the roots and stones, searching for the means of self-control, but finding them with difficulty. Windows had opened everywhere in his soul; he looked out through them upon a new world, immense and gloriously coloured. Behind him in the shadows, as his

vision searched and his heart sang, reared the single thought that hitherto had dominated his life: his love for Mark. It had already grown in-
disputably dim.

For both passions were genuine and commanding, the one built up
through thirty-five years of devotion cemented by ten thousand associations and sacrifices, the other dropping out of heaven upon him with
a suddenness simply appalling. And from the very first instant he understood that both could not live. One must die to feed the other. . . .

On the staircase was the perfume of a strange tobacco, and, to his
surprise and intense relief, when he entered the châlet he found that
his brother for the first time was not alone. A small, dark man stood
talking earnestly with him by the open window—the window where
Mark had obviously been watching with anxiety for his arrival. Before
introducing him to the stranger, Mark at once gave expression to his
relief.

"I was beginning to be afraid something had happened to you," he
said quietly enough, but in a way that the other understood. And after
a moment's pause, in which he searched Stephen's face keenly, he added, "but we didn't wait supper as you see, and old Petavel has kept
yours all hot and ready for you in the kitchen."

"I—er—lost my way," Stephen said quickly, glancing from Mark
to the stranger, wondering vaguely who he was. "I got confused somehow in the dusk—"

Mark, remembering his manners now that his anxiety was set at
rest, hastened to introduce him—a Professor in a Russian University,
interested in folklore and legend, who had read their book on the
Abruzzi and discovered quite by chance that they were neighbours
here in the forest. He was staying in a little hotel at Les Rasses, and
had ventured to come up and introduce himself. Stephen was far too
occupied trying to conceal his new battling emotions to notice that
Mark and the stranger seemed on quite familiar terms. He was so fearful lest the perturbations of his own heart should betray him that he
had no power to detect anything subtle or unusual in anybody else.

"Professor Samarianz comes originally from Tiflis," Mark was explaining, "and has been telling me the most fascinating things about
the legends and folklore of the Caucasus. We really must go there another year, Stephen. . . . Mr. Samarianz most kindly has promised me

letters to helpful people. . . . He tells me, too, of a charming and exquisite legend of a 'Lost Valley' that exists hereabouts, where the spirits of all who die by their own hands, or otherwise suffer violent deaths, find perpetual peace—the peace denied them by all the religions, that is. . . ."

Mark went on talking for some minutes while Stephen took off his knapsack and exchanged a few words with their visitor, who spoke excellent English. He was not quite sure what he said, but hoped he talked quietly and sensibly enough, in spite of the passions that waged war so terrifically in his breast. He noticed, however, that the man's face held an unusual charm, though he could not detect wherein its secret specifically lay. Presently, with excuses of hunger, he went into the kitchen for his supper, hugely relieved to find the opportunity to collect his thoughts a little; and when he returned twenty minutes later he found that his brother was alone. Professor Samarianz had taken his leave. In the room still lingered the perfume of his peculiarly flavoured cigarettes.

Mark, after listening with half an ear to his brother's description of the day, began pouring out his new interest; he was full of the Caucasus, and its folklore, and of the fortunate chance that had brought the stranger their way. The legend of the "Lost Valley" in the Jura, too, particularly interested him, and he spoke of his astonishment that he had hitherto come across no trace anywhere of the story.

"And fancy," he exclaimed, after a recital that lasted half-an-hour, "the man came up from one of those little hotels on the edge of the forest—that noisy one we have always been so careful to avoid. You never know where your luck hides, do you?" he added, with a laugh.

"You never do, indeed," replied Stephen quietly, now wholly master of himself, or, at least, of his voice and eyes.

And, to his secret satisfaction and delight, it was Mark who provided the excuses for staying on in the châlet, instead of moving further down the valley as they had intended. Besides, it would have been unnatural and absurd to leave without investigating so picturesque a legend as the "Lost Valley."

"We're uncommonly happy here," Mark added quietly; "why not stay on a bit?"

"Why not, indeed?" answered Stephen, trusting that the fearful inner storm instantly roused again by the prospect did not betray itself.

"You're not very keen, perhaps, old fellow?" suggested Mark gently.

"On the contrary—I am, *very*," was the reply.

"Good. Then we'll stay."

The words were spoken after a pause of some seconds. Stephen, who was down at the end of the room sorting his specimens by the lamp, looked up sharply. Mark's face, where he sat on the window-ledge in the dusk, was hardly visible. It must have been something in his voice that had shot into Stephen's heart with a flash of sudden warning.

A sensation of cold passed swiftly over him and was gone. Had he already betrayed himself? Was the subtle, almost telepathic sympathy between the twins developed to such a point that emotions could be thus transferred with the minimum of word or gesture, within the very shades of their silence even? And another thought: Was there some-thing different in Mark too—something in him also that had changed? Or was it merely his own raging, heaving passion, though so sternly repressed, that distorted his judgment and made him imaginative?

What stood so darkly in the room—between them?

A sudden and fearful pain seared him inwardly as he realised, prac-tically, and with cruelly acute comprehension, that one of these two loves in his heart must inevitably die to feed the other; and that it might have to be—Mark. The complete meaning of it came home to him. And at the thought all his deep love of thirty years rose in a tide within him, flooding through the gates of life, seeking to overwhelm and merge in itself all obstacles that threatened to turn it aside. Unshed tears burned behind his eyes. He ached with a degree of actual, physical pain.

After a moment of savage self-control he turned and crossed the room; but before he had covered half the distance that separated him from the window where his brother sat smoking, the rush of burning words—were they to have been of confession, of self-reproach, or of renewed devotion?—swept away from him, so that he wholly forgot them. In their place came the ordinary dead phrases of convention. He hardly heard them himself, though his lips uttered them.

"Come along, Mark, old chap," he said, conscious that his voice trembled, and that another face slipped imperiously in front of the one his eyes looked upon; "it's time to go to bed. I'm dead tired like your-self."

"You are right," Mark replied, looking at him steadily as he turned towards the lamplight. "Besides, the night air's getting chilly—and we've been sitting in a draught, you know, all along."

For the first time in their lives the eyes of the two brothers could not quite find each other. Neither gaze hit precisely the middle of the other. It was as though a veil hung down between them and a deliberate act of focus was necessary. They looked one another straight in the face as usual, but with an effort—with momentary difficulty. The room, too, as Mark had said, was cold, and the lamp, exhausted of its oil, was beginning to smell. Both light and heat were going. It was certainly time for bed.

The brothers went out together; arm in arm, and the long shadows of the pines, thrown by the rising moon through the window, fell across the floor like arms that waved. And from the black branches outside, the wind caught up a shower of sighs and dropped them about the roofs and walls as they made their way to their bedrooms on opposite sides of the little corridor.

V

Four hours later, when the moon was high overhead and the room held but a single big shadow, the door opened softly and in came—Stephen. He was dressed. He crossed the floor stealthily, unfastened the windows, and let himself out upon the balcony. A minute afterwards he had disappeared into the forest beyond the strip of vegetable garden at the back of the châlet.

It was two o'clock in the morning, and no sleep had touched his eyes. For his heart burned, ached, and fought within him, and he felt the need of open spaces and the great forces of the night and mountains. No such battle had he ever known before. He remembered his brother saying years ago, with a laugh half serious, half playful, ". . . for if ever one of us comes a cropper in love, old fellow, it will be time for the other to—go!" And by "go" they both understood the ultimate meaning of the word.

Through the glades of forest, sweet-scented by the night, he made his way till he reached the spot where that Face of soft splendour had first blessed his soul with its mysterious glory. There he sat down and, with his back against the very tree that had supported him a few hours ago, he drove his thoughts forward into battle with the whole strength of his will and character behind him. Very quietly, and with all the care, precision, and steadiness of mind that he would have brought to bear upon a difficult "case" at Wimpole Street, he faced the situation and wrestled with it. The emotions during four hours' tossing upon a sleepless bed had worn themselves out a little. He was, in one sense of the word, calm, master of himself. The facts, with the huge issue that lay in their hands, he saw naked. And, as he thus saw them, he discerned how very, very far he had already travelled down the sweet path that led him towards the girl—and away from his brother.

Details about her, of course, he knew none; whether she was free even; for he only knew that he loved, and that his entire life was already breaking with the yearning to sacrifice itself for that love. That was the naked fact. The problem bludgeoned him. Could he do anything to hold back the flood still rising, to arrest its terrific flow? Could he divert its torrent, and take it, girl and all, to offer upon the altar of that other love—the devotion of the twin for its twin, the mysterious affinity that hitherto had ruled and directed all the currents of his soul?

There was no question of undoing what had already been done. Even if he never saw that face again, or heard the accents of those beloved lips; if he never was to know the magic of touch, the perfume of close thought, or the strange blessedness of telling her his burning message and hearing the murmur of her own—the fact of love was already accomplished between them. That was ineradicable. He had seen. The sensitive plate had received its undying picture.

For this was no foolish passion arising from the mere propinquity that causes so many of the world's misfit marriages. It was a profound and mystical union already accomplished, psychical in the utter sense, inevitable as the marriage of wind and fire. He almost heard his soul laugh as he thought of the revolution effected in an instant of time by the message of a single glance. What had science, or his own special department of science, to say to this tempest of force that invaded him, and swept with its beautiful terrors of wind and lightning the furthest recesses of his being? This whirlwind that so shook him, that so deliciously wounded him, that already made the thought of sacrificing his brother seem sweet—what was there to say to it, or do with it, or think of it?

Nothing, nothing, nothing! . . . He could only lie in its arms and rest, with that peace, deeper than all else in life, which the mystic knows when he is conscious that the everlasting arms are about him and that his union with the greatest force of the world is accomplished.

Yet Stephen struggled like a lion. His will rose up and opposed itself to the whole invasion . . . and in the end his will of steel, trained as all men of character train their wills against the difficulties of life, did actually produce a certain, definite result. This result was almost a *tour de force*, perhaps, yet it seemed valid. By its aid Stephen forced himself into a position he felt intuitively was an impossible one, but in which nevertheless he determined, by a deliberate act of almost incredible volition, that he would remain fixed. He decided to conquer his obsession, and to remain true to Mark. . . .

The distant ridges of the dim blue Jura were tipped with the splendours of the coming dawn when at length he rose, chilly and exhausted, to retrace his steps to the châlet.

He realised fully the meaning of the resolve he had come to. And the knowledge of it froze something within him into a stiffness that was like the stiffness of death. The pain in his heart battling against the resolution was atrocious. He had estimated, or thought so, at least, the meaning of his sacrifice. As a matter of fact his decision was entirely artificial, of course, and his resolve dictated by a moral code rather than by the living forces that direct life and can alone make its changes permanent. Stephen had in him the stuff of the hero; and, having said that, one has said all that language can say.

On the way home in the cool white dawn, as he crossed the open spaces of meadow where the mist rose and the dew lay like rain, he suddenly thought of her lying dead—dead, that is, as he had thus decided she was to be dead—for him. And instantly, as by a word of command, the entire light went out of the landscape and out of the world. His soul turned wintry, and all the sweetness of his life went bleak. For it was the ancient soul in him that loved, and to deny it was to deny life itself. He had pronounced upon himself a sentence of death by starvation—a lingering and prolonged death accompanied by tortures of the most exquisite description. And along this path he really believed at the moment his little human will could hold him firm.

He made his way through the dew-drenched grass with the elation caused by so vast a sacrifice singing curiously in his blood. The splendour of the mountain sunrise and all the vital freshness of the dawn was in his heart. He was upon the châlet almost before he knew it, and there on the balcony, waiting to receive him, his grey dressing-gown wrapped about his ears in the sharp air, stood—Mark!

And, somehow or other, at the sight, all this false elation passed and dropped. Stephen looked up at him, standing suddenly still there in his tracks, as he might have looked up at his executioner. The picture had restored him most abruptly, with sharpest pain, to reality again.

"Like me, you couldn't sleep, eh?" Mark called softly, so as not to waken the peasants who slept on the ground floor.

"Have *you* been lying awake, too?" Stephen replied.

"All night. I haven't closed an eye." Then Mark added, as his brother came up the wooden steps towards him, "I knew you were awake I felt it. I knew, too—you had gone out."

A silence passed between them. Both had spoken quietly, naturally, neither expressing surprise.

"Yes," Stephen said slowly at length; "we always reflect each other's pai—each other's moods—" He stopped abruptly, leaving the sentence unfinished.

Their eyes met as of old. Stephen knew an instant of quite freezing terror in which he felt that his brother had divined the truth. Then Mark took his arm and led the way indoors on tiptoe.

"Look here, Stevie, old fellow," he said, with extraordinary tenderness, "there's no good saying anything, but I know perfectly well that you're unhappy about something; and so, of course, I am unhappy too." He paused, as though searching for words. Under ordinary circumstances Stephen would have caught his precise thought, but now the tumult of suppressed emotion in him clouded his divining power. He felt his arm clutched in a sudden vice. They drew closer to one another. Neither spoke. Then Mark, low and hurriedly, said—he almost mumbled it—"It's all my fault *really,* all my fault—dear old boy!"

Stephen turned in amazement and stared. What in the world did his brother mean? What was he talking about? Before he could find speech, however, Mark continued, speaking distinctly now, and with evidences of strong emotion in his voice—

"I'll tell you what we'll do," he exclaimed, with sudden decision; "we'll go away; we'll leave! We've stayed here a bit too long, perhaps. Eh? What d'you say to that?"

Stephen did not notice how sharply Mark searched his face. At the thought of separation all his mighty resolution dropped like a house of cards. His entire life seemed to melt away and run in a stream of impetuous yearning towards the Face.

But he answered quietly, sustaining his purpose artificially by a force of will that seemed to break and twist his life at the source with extraordinary pain. He could not have endured the strain for more than a few seconds. His voice sounded strange and distant.

"All right; at the end of the week," he said—the faintness in him was dreadful, filling him with cold—"and that'll give us just three days to make our plans, won't it?"

Mark nodded his head. Both faces were lined and drawn like the faces of old men; only there was no one there to remark upon it—nor upon the fixed sternness that had dropped so suddenly upon their eyes and lips.

Arm in arm they entered the châlet and went to their bedrooms without another word. The sun, as they went, rose close over the tree-tops and dropped its first rays upon the spot where they had just stood.

VI

They came down in dressing-gowns to a very late breakfast. They were quiet, grave, and slightly preoccupied. Neither made the least reference to their meeting at sunrise. New lines had graved themselves upon their faces, identical lines it seemed, drawing the mouth down at the corners with a touch of grimness where hitherto had been merely firmness.

And the eyes of both saw new things, new distances, new terrors. Something, feared till now only as a possibility, had come close, and stood at their elbows for the first time as an actuality. Sleep, in which changes offered to the soul during the day are confirmed and ratified, had established this new element in their personal equation. They had changed—if not towards one another, then towards something else.

But Stephen saw the matter only from his own point of view. For the first time in his memory he seemed to have lost the intuitive sympathy which enabled him to see things from his brother's point of view as well. The change, he felt positive, was in himself, not in Mark.

"He knows—he feels—something in me has altered dreadfully, but he doesn't yet understand what," his thoughts ran. "Pray to God he need never know—at least until I have utterly conquered it!"

For he still held with all the native tenacity of his strong will to the course he had so heroically chosen. The degree of self-deception his imagination brought into the contest seemed incredible when his mind looked back upon it all from the calmness of the end. But at the time he genuinely hoped, wished, intended to conquer, even *believed* that he would conquer.

Mark, he noticed, reacted in little ways that curiously betrayed his mental perturbation, and at any other time might have roused his brother's suspicions. He put sugar in Stephen's coffee, for instance; he forgot to bring him a cigarette when he went to the cupboard to get one for himself; he said and did numerous little things that were contrary to his habits, or to the habits of his twin.

In all of which, however, Stephen saw only the brotherly reaction to the change he was conscious of in himself. Nothing happened to convince him that anything in Mark had suffered revolution. With the mystical devotion peculiar to the twin he was too keenly aware of his own falling away to imagine the falling away of the other. He, Stephen, was the guilty one, and he suffered atrociously. Moreover, the pain of his renunciation was heightened by the sense that his ideal love for Mark had undergone a change—that he was making this fatal sacrifice, therefore, for something that perhaps no longer existed. This, however, he did not realise yet as an accomplished fact. Even if it were true, the resolution he had come to, acted by way of hypnotic suggestion to conceal it. At the same time it added enormously to the confusion and perplexity of his mind.

That day for the brothers was practically a *dies non*. They spent what was left of the morning over many aimless and unnecessary little duties, somewhat after the way of women. Although neither referred to the decision to leave at the end of the week, both acted upon it in desultory fashion, almost as though they wished to make a point of proving to one another that it was *not* forgotten—not wholly forgotten, at any rate. They made a brave pretence of collecting various things with a view to ultimate packing. No word was spoken, however, that bore more closely upon it than occasional phrases such as, "When the time comes to go"—"when we leave"—"better put *that* out, or it will be forgotten, you know."

The sentences dropped from their mouths alternately at long intervals, the only one deceived being the utterer. It was not unlike the pretence of school-boys, only more elaborate and infinitely more clumsy and ill-done. Stephen, at any other time, would probably have laughed aloud. Yet the curious thing was that he noticed the pretence only in his own case. Mark, he thought, was genuine, though perhaps not too eager. "He's agreed to leave, the dear old chap, because he thinks I want it, and not for himself," he said. And the idea of the small brotherly sacrifice pleased, yet pained him horribly at the same time. For it tended to rehabilitate the old love which stood in the way of the new one.

He began, however, to take less trouble to sort and find his things for packing; he wrote letters, put out photographs to print in the sun, even studied his maps for expeditions, making occasional remarks thereon aloud which Mark did not negative. Presently, he forgot altogether about packing. Mark said nothing. Mark followed his example, however.

During the afternoon both lay down and slept, meeting again for tea at five. It was rare that they found themselves in for tea. Mark today made a special little ritual of it; he made it over their own spirit-lamp—almost tenderly, looking after his brother's wants like a woman. And the little meal was hardly over when a boy in hotel livery arrived with a note—an invitation from Professor Samarianz.

"He has looked up a lot of his papers," observed Mark carelessly as he tossed the note down, "and suggests my coming in for dinner, so that he can show me everything afterwards without hurry."

"I should accept," said Stephen. "It might be valuable for us if we go to the Caucasus later."

Mark hesitated a minute or two, telling the boy to wait in the kitchen. "I think I'll go in *after* dinner instead," he decided presently. There was a trace of eagerness in his manner which Stephen, however, did not notice.

"Take your notebook and pump the old boy dry," Stephen added, with a slight laugh. "I shall go to bed early myself probably." And Mark, stuffing the note into his pocket, laughed back and consented, to the other's great relief.

It was very late when Mark returned from the visit, but his brother did not hear him come, having taken a draught to ensure sleeping. And next morning Mark was so full of the interesting information he had collected, and would continue to collect, that the question of leaving at the end of the week dropped of its own accord without further ado. Neither of the brothers made the least pretence of packing. Both wished and intended to stay on where they were.

"I shall look up Samarianz again this afternoon," Mark said casually during the morning, "and—if you've no objection—I might bring him back to supper. He's the most obliging fellow I've ever met, and crammed with information."

Stephen, signifying his agreement, took his camera, his specimen-tin, and his geological hammer and went out with bread and chocolate in his knapsack for the rest of the afternoon by himself.

VII

Moreover, he not only set out bravely, but for many hours held true, keeping so rigid a control over his feelings that it seemed literally to cost him blood. All the time, however, a passionate yearning most craftily attacked him, and the very memory he strove to smother rose with a persistence that ridiculed repression. Like snowflakes, whose individual weight is inappreciable but their cumulative burden irresistible, the thoughts of *her* gathered behind his spirit, ready at a given moment to overwhelm; and it was on the way home again in the evening that the temptation came upon him like a tidal wave that made the mere idea of resistance seemed utterly absurd.

He remembered wondering with a kind of wild delight whether it could be possible for any human will to withstand such a tempest of pressure as that which took him by the shoulders and literally pushed him out of his course towards the little hotel on the edge of the forest.

It was utterly inconsistent, of course, and he made no pretence of argument or excuse. He hardly knew, indeed, what he expected to see or do; his mind, at least, framed no definite idea. But far within him that deep heart which refused to be stifled cried out for a drop of the living water that was now its very life. And, chiefly, he wanted to *see*. If only he could see her once again—even from a distance—the merest glimpse—! With one more sight of her that should charge his memory to the brim for life he might face the future with more courage perhaps. Ah! that *perhaps!* . . . For she was drawing him with those million invisible cords of love that persuade a man he is acting of his own volition when actually he is but obeying the inevitable forces that bind the planets and the suns.

And this time there was no hurry; there was a good hour before Mark would expect him home for supper; he could sit among the shadows of the wood, and wait.

In his pocket were the field-glasses, and he realised with a sudden secret shame that it was not by accident that they were there. He stumbled, even before he got within a quarter of a mile of the place, for the idea that perhaps he would see her again made him ridiculously happy, and like a school-boy he positively trembled, tripping over roots and misjudging the distance of his steps. It was all part of a great whirling dream in which his soul sang and shouted the first delirious nonsense that came into his head. The possibility of his eyes again meeting hers produced a sensation of triumph and exultation that only one word describes—intoxication.

As he approached the opening in the trees whence the hotel was so easily visible, he went more slowly, moving even on tiptoe. It was instinctive; for he was nearing a place made holy by his love. Picking his way almost stealthily, he found the very tree; then leaned against it while his eyes searched eagerly for a sign of her in the glass verandah. The swiftness and accuracy of sight at such a time may be cause for wonder, but it is beyond question that in less than a single second he knew that the throng of moving figures did not contain the one he sought. She was not among them.

And he was just preparing to make himself comfortable for an extended watch when a sound or movement, perhaps both, somewhere among the trees on his right attracted his attention. There was a faint rustling; a twig snapped.

Stephen turned sharply. Under a big spruce, not half-a-dozen yards away, something moved—then rose up. At first, owing to the gloom, he took it for an animal of some kind, but the same second he saw that it was a human figure. It was *two* human figures, standing close together. Then one moved apart from the other; he saw the outline of a man against a space of sky between the trees. And a voice spoke—a voice charged with great tenderness, yet driven by high passion—

"But it's nothing, nothing! I shall not be gone two minutes. And to save you an instant's discomfort you know that I would run the whole circle of the earth! Wait here for me—!"

That was all; but the voice and figure caused Stephen's heart to stop beating as though it had been suddenly plunged into ice, for they were the voice and the figure of his brother Mark.

Quickly running down the slope towards the hotel, Mark disappeared.

The other figure, leaning against the tree, was the figure of a girl; and Stephen, even in that first instant of fearful bewilderment, understood why it was that the face of the man Samarianz had so charmed him. For this, of course, was his daughter. And then the whole thing flashed mercilessly clear upon his inner vision, and he knew that Mark, too, had been swept from his feet, and was undergoing the same fierce tortures, and fighting the same dread battle, as himself. . . .

There seemed to be no conscious act of recognition. The fire that flamed through him and set his frozen heart so fearfully beating again, hammering against his ribs, left him apparently without volition or any power of cerebral action at all. *She* stood there, not half-a-dozen yards away from where he sat all huddled upon the ground, stood there in all her beauty, her mystery, her wonder, near enough for him to have taken her almost with a single leap into his arms;—stood there, veiled a little by the shadows of the dusk—waiting for the return of—Mark!

He remembers what happened with the blurred indistinctness common to moments of overwhelming passion. For in the next few seconds, that mocked all scale of time, he lived through a series of concentrated emotions that burned his brain too vividly for precise recollection. He rose to his feet unsteadily, his hand upon the rough bark of the tree. Absurd details only seem to remain of these few moments: that a foot was "asleep" with pins and needles up to the knee, and that his slouch hat fell from his head, filling him with fury because it hid her from him for the fraction of a second. These odd details he remembers.

And then, as though the driving-power of the universe had deliberately pushed him from behind, he was advancing slowly, with short, broken steps, towards the tree where the girl stood with her back half turned against him.

He did not know her name, had never heard her voice, had never even stood close enough to "feel" her atmosphere; yet, so deeply had his love and imagination already prepared the little paths of intimacy within him, that he felt he was moving towards some one whom he had known ever since he could remember, and who belonged to him as utterly as if from the beginning of time his possession of her had been absolute. Had they shared together a whole series of previous lives, the sensation could not have been more convincing and complete.

And out of all this whirlwind and tumult two small actions, he remembers, were delivered: a confused cry that was no definite word came from his lips, and—he opened his arms to take her to his heart. Whereupon, of course, she turned with a quick start, and became for the first time aware of his near presence.

"Oh, oh! But how so softly quick you return!" she cried falteringly, looking into his eyes with a smile both of welcome and alarm. "You a little frightened me, I tell you."

It was just the voice he had known would come, with the curiously slow, dragging tone of its broken English, the words lingering against the lips as if loath to leave, the soft warmth of their sound in the throat like a caress. The next instant he held her smothered in his arms, his face buried in the scented hair about her neck.

There was an unbelievable time of forgetfulness in which touch, perfume, and a healing power that emanated from her blessed the depths of his soul with a peace that calmed all pain, stilled all tumult— a moment in which Time itself for once stopped its remorseless journey, and the very processes of life stood still to watch. Then there was a frightened cry, and she had pushed him from her. She stood there, her soft eyes puzzled and surprised, looking hard at him; panting a little, her breast heaving.

And Stephen understood then, if he had not already understood before. The gesture of recognition in the hotel verandah two days ago, and this glorious realisation of it that now seemed to have happened a century ago, shared a common origin. They were intended for another, and on both occasions the girl had taken him for his brother Mark.

And, turning sharply, almost falling with the abruptness of it all, as the girl's lips uttered that sudden cry, he saw close beside them the very person for whom they were intended. Mark had come up the slope behind them unobserved, carrying upon his arm the little red cloak he had been to fetch.

It was as though a wind of ice had struck him in the face. The revulsion of feeling with which Stephen saw the return of his brother passed rapidly into a state of numbness where all emotion whatsoever ebbed like the tides of death. He lost momentarily the power of realisation. He forgot who he was, what he was doing there. He was dazed by the fact that Mark had so completely forestalled him. His life shook and tottered upon its foundations. . . .

Then the face and figure of his brother swayed before his eyes like the branch of a tree, as an attack of passing dizziness seized him. It may have been a mere hazard that led his fingers to close, moist and clammy, upon the geological hammer at his belt. Certainly, he let it go again almost at once. . . . And, when the tide of emotion returned upon him with the dreadful momentum it had gathered during the interval, the possibility of his yielding to wild impulse and doing something mad or criminal, was obviated by the swift enactment of an exceedingly poignant little drama that made both brothers forget themselves in their desire to save the girl.

In sweetest bewilderment, like a frightened little child or animal, the girl looked from one brother to the other. Her eyes shone in the dusk. Strangely appealing her loveliness was in that moment of seeking some explanation of the double vision. She made a movement first towards Mark—turned half-way in her steps and ran, startled, upon Stephen—then, with a sharp scream of fear, dropped in a heap to the ground midway between the two.

Her indecision of half-a-second, however, seemed to Stephen to have lasted many minutes. Had she fallen finally into the arms of his brother, he felt nothing on earth could have prevented his leaping upon him with the hands of a murderer. As it was—mercifully—the singular beauty of her little Eastern face, touched as it was by the white terror of her soul, momentarily arrested all other feeling in him. A shudder of fearful admiration passed through him as he saw her sway and fall. Thus might have dropped some soft angel from the skies. . . .

It was Mark, however, with his usual decision, who brought some possibility of focus back to his mind; and he did it with an action and a sentence so utterly unexpected, so incongruous amid this whirlwind of passion, that had he seen it on the stage or read it in a novel, he must surely have burst out laughing. For, in that very second after the dear form swayed and fell, while the eyes of the brothers met across her in one swift look that held the possibilities of the direst results, Mark, his face abruptly clearing to calmness, stooped down beside the prostrate girl, and, looking up at Stephen steadily, said in a gentle voice, but with his most deliberate professional manner—

"Stephen, old fellow, this is—*my* patient. One of us, perhaps, had better—go."

He bent down to loosen the dress at the throat and chafe the cold hands, and Stephen, uncertain exactly what he did, and trembling like a child, turned and disappeared among the thick trees in the direction of their little house. For he understood only one thing clearly in that awful moment: that he must either kill—or not see. And his will, well-nigh breaking beneath the pressure, was just able to take the latter course.

"*Go!*" it said peremptorily.

And the little word sounded through the depths of his soul like the tolling of a last bell.

VIII

"*This is my patient!*" The dreadful comedy of the phrase, the grim mockery of the professional manner, the contrast between the words that some one *ought* to have uttered and the words Mark actually *had* uttered—all this had the effect of restoring Stephen to some measure of sanity. No one but his brother, he felt, could have said the thing so exactly calculated to relieve the choking passion of the situation. It was an inspiration—yet horrible in its bizarre mingling of true and false.

"But it's all like a thing in a dream," he heard an inner voice murmur as he stumbled homewards without once looking back; "the kind of thing people say and do in the rooms of strange sleep-houses. We are all surely in a dream, and presently I shall wake up—!"

The voice continued talking, but he did not listen. A web of confusion began to spin itself about his thoughts, and there stole over him an odd sensation of remoteness from the actual things of life. It was surely one of those vivid, haunting dreams he sometimes had when his spirit seemed to take part in real scenes, with real people, only far, far away, and on quite another scale of time and values.

"I shall find myself in my bed at Wimpole Street!" he exclaimed. He even tried to escape from the pain closing about him like a vice— tried to escape by waking up, only to find, of course, that the effort drove him more closely to the reality of his position.

Yet the texture of a dream certainly ran through the whole thing; the outlandish proportions of dream-events showed themselves everywhere; the tiny causes and prodigious effects: the terrific power of the Face upon his soul; the uncanny semi-quenching of his love for Mark; the ridiculous way he had come upon these two in the forest, with the nightmare discovery that they had known one another for days; and then the sight of that dear, magical face dropping through the dusky forest air between the two of them. Moreover—just when the dream ought to have ended with his sudden awakening, it had taken this abrupt and inconsequent turn, and Mark had uttered the language of—well, the impossible and rather horrible language of the nightmare world—

"This is my patient. . . ."

Moreover, his face of ice as he said it; yet, at the same time, the wisdom, the gentleness of the decision that lay behind the words: the desire to relieve an impossibly painful situation. And then—the other words, meant kindly, even meant nobly, but charged for all that with the naked cruelty of life—

"One of us, perhaps, had better—go."

And he had gone—fortunately, he had gone. . . .

Yet an hour later, after lying motionless upon his bed seeking with all his power for a course of action his will could follow and his mind approve, it was no dream-voice that called softly to him through the keyhole—

"Stevie, old fellow . . . she is well . . . she is all right now. She leaves in the morning with her father . . . the first thing . . . very early. . . ."

And then, after a pause in which Stephen said nothing lest he should at the same time say all—

". . . and it is best, perhaps . . . we should not see one another . . . you and I . . . for a bit. Let us go our ways . . . till to-morrow night. Then we shall be . . . alone together again . . . you and I . . . as of old. . . ."

The voice of Mark did not tremble; but it sounded far away and unreal, almost like wind in the keyhole, thin, reedy, sighing; oddly broken and interrupted.

". . . I'm yours, Stevie, old fellow, always yours," it added far down the corridor, more like the voice of dream again than ever.

But, though he made no reply at the moment, Stephen welcomed and approved both the proposal and the spirit in which it was made; and next day, soon after sunrise, he left the châlet very quietly and went off alone into the mountains with his thoughts, and with the pain that all night long had simply been eating him alive.

IX

It is impossible to know precisely what he felt all that morning in the mountains. His emotions charged like wild bulls to and fro. He seemed conscious only of two master-feelings: first, that his life now belonged beyond possibility of change or control—to another; yet, secondly, that his will, tried and tempered weapon of steel that it was, held firm.

Thus his powerful feelings flung him from one wall of his dreadful prison to another without possible means of escape. For his position involved a fundamental contradiction: the new love owned him, yet his will cried, "I love Mark; I hold true to that; in the end I shall conquer!" He refused, that is, to capitulate, or rather to acknowledge that he had capitulated. And meanwhile, even while he cried, his inmost soul listened, watched, and laughed, well content to abide the issue.

But if his feelings were in too great commotion for clear analysis, his thoughts, on the other hand, were painfully definite—some of them, at least; and, as the physical exercise lessened the assaults of emotion, these stood forth in sharp relief against the confusion of his inner world. It was now clear as the day, for instance, that Mark had been through a battle similar to his own. The chance meeting with the Professor had led to the acquaintance with his daughter. Then, swiftly and inevitably, just as it would have happened to Stephen in his place, love had accomplished its full magic. And Mark had been afraid to tell him. The twins had travelled the same path, only personal feeling having clouded their usual intuition, neither had divined the truth.

Stephen saw it now with pitiless clarity: his brother's frequent visits to the hotel, omitting to mention that the notes of invitation probably also included himself; the desire, nay, the intention to stay on; the delay in packing—and a dozen other details stood out clearly. He remembered, too, with a pang how Mark had not slept that memorable night; he recalled their enigmatical conversation on the balcony as the sun rose . . . and all the rest of the miserable puzzle.

And, as he realised from his own torments what Mark must also have suffered—be suffering now—he was conscious of a strengthening of his will to conquer. The thought linked him fiercely again to his twin; for nothing in their lives had yet been separate, and the chain of their spiritual intimacy was of incalculably vast strength. They would win—win back to one another's side again. Mark would conquer her. He, Stephen, would also in the end conquer . . . her . . . !

But with the thought of her lying thus dead to him, and his life cold and empty without her, came the inevitable revulsion of feeling. It was the anarchy of love. The Face, the perfume, the rushing power of her melancholy dear eyes, with their singular touch of proud languor— in a word, all the amazing magic that had swept himself and Mark from their feet, tore back upon him with such an invasion of entreaty and command, that he sat down upon the very rocks where he was and buried his face in his hands, literally groaning with the pain of it. For the thought lacerated within. To give her up was a sheer impossibility; . . . to give up his brother was equally inconceivable. The weight of thirty-five years' love and associations thus gave battle against the telling blow of a single moment. Behind the first lay all that life had built into the woof of his personality hitherto, but *beyond* the second lay the potent magic, the huge seductive invitation of what he might become in the future—with her.

The contest, in the nature of the forces engaged, was an unequal one. Yet all that morning as he wandered aimlessly over ridge and summit, and across the high Jura pastures above the forests, meeting no single human being, he fought with himself as only men with innate energy of soul know how to fight—bitterly, savagely, blindly. He did not stop to realise that he was somewhat in the position of a fly that strives to push from its appointed course the planet on which it rides through space. For the tides of life itself bore him upon their crest, and at thirty-five these tides are at the full.

Thus, gradually it was, then, as the hopelessness of the struggle became more and more apparent, that the door of the only alternative opened slightly and let him peer through. Once ajar, however, it seemed the same second wide open; he was through; and it was closed—behind him.

For a different nature the alternative might have taken a different form. As has been seen, he was too strong a man to drift merely; a definite way out that could commend itself to a man of action had to be found; and, though the raw material of heroism may have been in him, he made no claim to a martyrdom that should last as long as life itself. And this alternative dawned upon him now as the grey light of a last morning must dawn upon the condemned prisoner: given Stephen, and given this particular problem, it was the only way out.

He envisaged it thus suddenly with a kind of ultimate calmness and determination that was characteristic of the man. And in every way it *was* characteristic of the man, for it involved the precise combination of courage and cowardice, weakness and strength, selfishness and sacrifice, that expressed the true resultant of all the forces at work in his soul. To him, at the moment of his rapid decision, however, it seemed that the dominant motive was the sacrifice to be offered upon the altar of his love for Mark. The twisted notion possessed him that in this way he might atone in some measure for the waning of his brotherly devotion. His love for the girl, her possible love for him—both were to be sacrificed to obtain the happiness—the eventual happiness—of these other two. Long, long ago Mark had himself said that under such circumstances one or other of them would have to—*go*. And the decision Stephen had come to was that the one to "go" was—himself.

This day among the woods and mountains should be his last on earth. By the evening of the following day Mark should be free.

"I'll give my life for him."

His face was grey and set as he said it. He stood on the high ridge, bathed by sun and wind. He looked over the fair world of wooded vales and mountains at his feet, but his eyes, turned inwards, saw only his brother—and that sweet Eastern face—then darkness.

"He will understand—and perforce accept it—and with time, yes, with time, the new happiness shall fill his soul utterly—and hers. It is for her, too, that I give it. It *must*—under these unparalleled circumstances be right . . . !"

And although there was no single cloud in the sky, the landscape at his feet suddenly went dark and sunless from one horizon to the other.

X

Then, having come into the gloom of this terrible decision, his imaginative nature at once bounded to the opposite extreme, and a kind of exaltation possessed him. The stereotyped verdict of a coroner's jury might in this instance have been true. The prolonged stress of emotion under which he had long been labouring had at last produced a condition of mind that could only be considered—unsound.

A cool wind swept his face as he let his tired eyes wander over the leagues of silent forest below. The blue Jura with its myriad folded valleys lay about him like the waves of a giant sea ready to swallow up the little atom of his life within its deep heart of forgetfulness. Clear away into France he saw on the one side where, beyond the fortress of Pontarlier, white clouds sailed the horizon before a westerly wind; and, on the other, towards the white-robed Alps rising mistily through the haze of the autumn sunshine. Between these extreme distances lay all that world of a hundred intricate valleys, curiously winding, deeply wooded, little inhabited—a region of soft, confusing loveliness where a traveller might well lose himself for days together before he discovered a way out of so vast a maze.

And, as he gazed, there passed across his mind, like the dim memory of something heard in childhood, that legend of the "Lost Valley" in which the souls of the unhappy dead find the deep peace that is denied to them by all the religions—and to which hundreds, who have not yet the sad right of entry, seek to find the mournful forest gates. The memory was vivid, but swiftly engulfed by others and forgotten. They chased each other in rapid succession across his mind, as clouds at sunset pass before a high wind, merging on the horizon in a common mass.

Then, slowly, at length, he turned and made his way down the mountain-side in the direction of the French frontier for a last journey upon the sweet surface of the world he loved. In his soul was the one dominant feeling: this singular exaltation arising from the knowledge that in the long run his great sacrifice must ensure the happiness of the two beings he loved more than all else in life.

At the solitary farm where an hour later he had his lunch of bread and cheese and milk, he learned that he had wandered many miles out of the routes with which he was more or less familiar. He had been walking faster than he knew all these hours of battle. A physical weariness came upon him that made him conscious of every muscle in his body as he realised what a long road over mountain and valley he had to retrace. But, with the heaviness of fatigue, ran still that sense of interior spiritual exaltation. Something in him walked on air with springs of steel—something that was independent of the dragging limbs and the aching back. For the rest, his sensations seemed numb. His great Decision stood black before him, blocking the way. Thoughts and feelings forsook him as rats leave a sinking ship. The time for these was past. Two overmastering desires, however, clung fast: one, to see Mark again, and be with him; the other, to be once more—with her. These two desires left no room for others. With the former, indeed, it was almost as though Mark had called aloud to him by name.

He stood a moment where the depth of the valley he had to thread lay like a twisting shadow at his feet; it ran, soft and dim, through the slanting sunshine. From the whole surface of the woods rose a single murmur; like the whirring of voices heard in a dream, he thought. The individual purring of separate trees was merged. Peace, most ancient and profound, lay in it, and its hushed whisper soothed his spirit.

He hurried his pace a little. The cool wind that had swept his face on the heights earlier in the afternoon followed him down, urging him forwards with deliberate pressure, as though a thousand soft hands were laid upon his back. And there were spirits in the wind that day. He heard their voices; and far below he traced by the motion of the tree-tops where they coiled upwards to him through miles of forest. His way, meanwhile, dived down through dense growths of spruce and pine into a region unfamiliar. There was an aspect of the scenery that almost suggested it was unknown—an undiscovered corner of the world. The countless signs that mark the passage of humanity were absent, or at least did not obtrude themselves upon him. Something remote from life, alien, at any rate, to the normal life he had hitherto known, began to steal gently over his burdened soul. . . .

In this way, perhaps, the effect of his dreadful Decision already showed its influence upon his mind and senses. So very soon now he would be—*going!*

The sadness of autumn lay all about him, and the loneliness of this secluded vale spoke to him of the melancholy of things that die—of vanished springs, of summers unfulfilled, of things for ever incomplete and unsatisfying. Human effort, he felt, this valley had never known. No hoofs had ever pressed the mossy turf of these forest clearings; no traffic of peasants or woodsmen won echoes from these limestone cliffs. All was hushed, lonely, deserted.

And yet—? The depths to which it apparently plunged astonished him more and more. Nowhere more than a half-mile across, each turn of the shadowy trail revealed new distances below. With spots of a haunting, fairy loveliness too: for here and there, on isolated patches of lawn-like grass, stood wild lilac bushes, rounded by the wind; willows from the swampy banks of the stream waved pale hands; firs, dark and erect, guarded their eternal secrets on the heights. In one little opening, standing all by itself, he found a lime-tree; while beyond it, shining among the pines, was a group of shimmering beeches. And, although there was no wild life, there were flowers; he saw clumps of them— tall, graceful, blue flowers whose name he did not know, nodding in dream across the foaming water of the little torrent.

And his thoughts ran incessantly to Mark. Never before had he been conscious of so imperious a desire to see him, to hear his voice, to stand at his side. At moments it almost obliterated that other great desire. . . . Again he increased his pace. And the path plunged more and more deeply into the heart of the mountains, sinking ever into deeper silence, ever into an atmosphere of deeper peace. For no sound could reach him here without first passing along great distances that were cushioned with soft wind, and padded, as it were, with a million feathery pine-tops. A sense of peace that was beyond reach of all possible disturbance began to cover his breaking life with a garment as of softest shadows. Never before had he experienced anything approaching the wonder and completeness of it. It was a peace, still as the depths of the sea which are motionless because they *cannot* move— cannot even tremble. It was a peace unchangeable—what some have called, perhaps, the Peace of God. . . .

"Soon the turn *must* come," he thought, yet without a trace of impatience or alarm, "and the road wind upwards again to cross the last ridge!" But he cared little enough; for this enveloping peace drowned him, hiding even the fear of death.

And still the road sank downwards into the sleep-laden atmosphere of the crowding trees, and with it his thoughts, oddly enough, sank deeper and deeper into dim recesses of his own being. As though a secret sympathy lay between the path that dived and the thoughts that plunged. Only, from time to time, the thought of his brother Mark brought him back to the surface with a violent rush. Dreadfully, in those moments, he wanted him—to feel his warm, strong hand within his own—to ask his forgiveness—perhaps, too, to grant his own . . . he hardly knew.

"But is there no end to this delicious valley?" he wondered, with something between vagueness and confusion in his mind. "Does it never stop, and the path climb again to the mountains beyond?" Drowsily, divorced from any positive interest, the question passed through his thoughts. Underfoot the grass already grew thickly enough to muffle the sound of his footsteps. The trail even had vanished, swallowed by moss. His feet sank in.

"I wish Mark were with me now—to see and feel all this—"

He stopped short and looked keenly about him for a moment, leaving the thought incomplete. A deep sighing, instantly caught by the wind and merged in the soughing of the trees, had sounded close beside him. Was it perhaps himself that sighed—unconsciously? His heart was surely charged enough! . . .

A faint smile played over his lips—instantly frozen, however, as another sigh, more distinct than the first, and quite obviously external to himself, passed him closely in the darkening air. More like deep breathing, though, it was, than sighing. . . . It was nothing but the wind, of course. Stephen hurried on again, not surprised that he had been so easily deceived, for this valley was full of sighings and breathings—of trees and wind. It ventured upon no louder noise. Noise of any kind, indeed, seemed impossible and forbidden in this muted vale. And so deeply had he descended now, that the sunshine, silver rather than golden, already streamed past far over his head along the ridges, and no gleam found its way to where he was. The shadows, too, no longer blue and purple, had changed to black, as though woven of some delicate substance that had definite thickness, like a veil. Across the opposite slope, one of the mountain summits in the western sky already dropped its monstrous shadow fringed with pines. The day was rapidly drawing in.

XI

And here, very gradually, there began to dawn upon his overwrought mind certain curious things. They pierced clean through the mingled gloom and exaltation that characterised his mood. And they made the skin upon his back a little to—stir and crawl.

For he now became distinctly aware that the emptiness of this lonely valley was only apparent. It is impossible to say through what sense, or combination of senses, this singular certainty was brought to him that the valley was not really as forsaken and deserted as it seemed—that, on the contrary, it was the very reverse. It came to him suddenly—as a certainty. The valley as a matter of fact was—full. Packed, thronged, and crowded it was to the very brim of its mighty wooded walls—with life. It was now borne in upon him, with an inner conviction that left no room for doubt, that on all sides living things—persons—were jostling him, rubbing elbows, watching all his movements, and only waiting till the darkness came to reveal themselves.

Moreover, with this eerie discovery came also the further knowledge that a vast multitude of others, again, with pallid faces and yearning eyes, with arms outstretched and groping feet, were searching everywhere for the way of entrance that he himself had found so easily. All about him, he felt, were people by the hundred, by the thousand, seeking with a kind of restless fever for the narrow trail that led down into the valley, longing with an intensity that beat upon his soul in a million waves, for the rest, the calm silence of the place—but most of all for its strange, deep, and unalterable peace.

He, alone of all these, had found the Entrance; he, *and one other.*

For out of this singular conviction grew another even more singular: his brother Mark was also somewhere in this valley with him. Mark, too, was wandering like himself in and out among its intricate dim turns. He had said but a short time ago, "I wish Mark were here!" Mark *was* here. And it was precisely then—while he stood still a moment, trying to face these overwhelming obsessions and deal with them—that the figure of a man, moving swiftly through the trees, passed him with a great gliding stride, and with averted face. Stephen started horribly, catching his breath. In an instant the man was gone again, swallowed up by the crowding pines.

With a quick movement of pursuit and a cry that should make the man turn, he sprang forward—but stopped again almost the same moment, realising that the extraordinary speed at which the man had shot past him rendered pursuit out of the question. He had been going downhill into the valley; by this time he was already far, far ahead. But in that momentary glimpse of him he had seen enough to know. The face was turned away, and the shadows under the trees were heavy, but the figure was beyond question the figure of—his brother Mark.

It was his brother, yet not his brother. It was Mark—but Mark altered. And the alteration was in some way—awful; just as the silent speed at which he had moved—the impossible speed in so dense a forest—was likewise awful. Then, still shaking inwardly with the suddenness of it all, Stephen realised that when he called aloud he had uttered certain definite words. And these words now came back to him—

"Mark, Mark! Don't go yet! Don't go—without me!"

Before, however, he could act, a most curious and unaccountable sensation of deadly faintness and pain came upon him, without cause, without explanation, so that he dropped backwards in momentary collapse, and but for the closeness of the tree stems would have fallen full length to the ground. From the centre of the heart it came, spreading thence throughout his whole being like a swift and dreadful fever. All the muscles of his body relaxed; icy perspiration burst forth upon his skin; the pulses of life seemed suddenly reduced to the threshold beyond which they stop. There was a thick, rushing sound in his ears and his mind went utterly blank.

These were the sensations of death by suffocation. He knew this as certainly as though another doctor stood by his side and labelled each spasm, explained each successive sinking of the vital flame. He was passing through the last throes of a dying man. And then into his mind, thus deliberately left blank, rushed at lightning speed a whole series of the pictures of his past life. Even while his breath failed, he saw his thirty-five years pictorially, successively, yet in some queer fashion *at once,* pass through the lighted chambers of his brain. In this way, it is said, they pass through the brain of a drowning man during the last seconds before death.

Childhood rose about him with its scenes, figures, voices; the Kentish lawns where he had played with Mark in stained overalls; the summer-house where they had tea, the hay-fields where they romped. The scent of lime and walnut, of garden pinks, and roses by the tumbled rockery came back to his nostrils. . . . He heard the voices of grown-ups in the distance . . . faint barking of dogs . . . the carriage wheels upon the gravel drive . . . and then the sharp summons from the opened window—"Time to come in now! Time to come in!" . . .

Time to come in now. It all drove before him as of yesterday on the scented winds of childhood's summer days. . . . He heard his brother's voice—dreadfully faint and far away—calling him by name in the shrill accents of the boy: "Stevie—I say, you *might* shut up . . . and play properly. . . ."

And then followed the panorama of the thirty years, all the chief events drawn in steel-like lines of white and black, vivid in sunshine, alive—right down to the present moment with the portentous dark shadow of his terrible Decision closing the series like a cloud.

Yes, like a smothering black cloud that blocked the way. There was nothing visible beyond it. There, for him, life ceased—

Only, as he gazed with inward-turned eyes that could not close even if they would, he saw to his amazement that the black cloud suddenly opened, and into a space of clear light there swam the vision, radiant as morning, of that dark young Eastern face—the face that held for him all the beauty in the world. The eyes instantly found his own, and smiled. Behind her, moreover, and beyond, before the moving vapours closed upon it, he saw a long vista of brilliance, crowded with pictures he could but half discern—as though, in spite of himself and his Decision, life continued—as though, too, it *continued with her.*

And instantly, with the sight and thought of her, the consuming faintness passed; strength returned to his body with the glow of life; the pain went; the pictures vanished; the cloud was no more. In his blood the pulses of life once again beat strong, and the blackness left his soul. The smile of those beloved eyes had been charged with the invitation to live. Although his determination remained unshaken, there shone behind it the joy of this potent magic: life with her. . . .

With a strong effort, at length he recovered himself and continued on his way. More or less familiar, of course, with the psychology of vision, he dimly understood that his experiences had been in some measure subjective—within himself. To find the line of demarcation, however, was beyond him. That Mark had wandered out to fight his own battle upon the mountains, and so come into this same valley, was well within the bounds of coincidence. But the nameless and dreadful alteration discerned in that swift moment of his passing—that remained inexplicable. Only he no longer thought about it. The glory of that sweet vision had bewildered him beyond any possibility of reason or analysis.

His watch told him that the hour was past five o'clock—ten minutes past, to be exact. He still had several hours before reaching the country he was familiar with nearer home. Following the trail at an increased pace, he presently saw patches of meadow glimmering between the thinning trees, and knew that the bottom of the valley was at last in sight.

"And Mark, God bless him, is down there too—somewhere!" he exclaimed aloud. "I shall surely find him." For, strange to say, nothing could have persuaded him that his twin was not wandering among the shadows of this peaceful and haunted valley with himself, and—that he would shortly find him.

XII

And a few minutes later he passed from the forest as through an open door and found himself before a farmhouse standing in a patch of bright green meadow against the mountain-side. He was in need both of food and information.

The châlet, less lumbering and picturesque than those found in the

Alps, had, nevertheless, the appearance of being exceedingly ancient. It was not toy-like—as the Jura châlets sometimes are. Solidly built, its balcony and overhanging roof supported by immense beams of deeply stained wood, it stood so that the back walls merged into the mountain slope behind, and the arms of pine, spruce, and fir seemed stretched out to include it among their shadows. A last ray of sunshine, dipping between two far summits overhead, touched it with pale gold, bringing out the rich beauty of the heavily-dyed beams. Though no one was visible at the moment, and no smoke rose from the shingled chimney, it had the appearance of being occupied, and Stephen approached it with the caution due to the first evidence of humanity he had come across since he entered the valley.

Under the shadow of the broad balcony roof he noticed that the door, like that of a stable, was in two parts, and, wondering rather to find it closed, he knocked firmly upon the upper half. Under the pressure of a second knock this upper half yielded slightly, though without opening. The lower half, however, evidently barred and bolted, remained unmoved.

The third time he knocked with more force than he intended, and the knock sounded loud and clamorous as a summons. From within, as though great spaces stretched beyond, came a murmur of voices, faint and muffled, and then almost immediately—the footsteps of some one coming softly up to open.

But, instead of the heavy brown door opening, there came a voice. He heard it, petrified with amazement. For it was a voice he knew—hushed, soft, lingering. His heart, hammering atrociously, seemed to leave its place, and cut his breath away.

"Stephen!" it murmured, calling him by name, "what are *you* doing here so soon? And what is it that you want?"

The knowledge that only this dark door separated him from her, at first bereft him of all power of speech or movement; and the possible significance of her words escaped him. Through the sweet confusion that turned his spirit faint he only remembered, flash-like, that she and her father were indeed to have left the hotel that very morning. After that his thought stopped dead.

Then, also flash-like, swept back upon him the memory of the figure that had passed him with averted face—and, with it, the clear conviction that at this moment Mark, too, was somewhere in this very valley, even close beside him. More: Mark was in this châlet—with her.

The torrent of speech that instantly crowded to his lips was almost too thick for utterance.

"Open, open, open!" was all he heard intelligibly from the throng of words that poured out. He raised his hands to push and force; but her reply again stopped him.

"Even if I open—*you* may not enter yet," came the whisper through the door. And this time he could almost have sworn that it sounded within himself rather than without.

"I must enter," he cried. "Open to me, I say!"

"But you are trembling—"

"Open to me, O my life! Open to me!"

"But your heart—it is shaking."

"Because you—you are so near," came in passionate, stammering tones. "Because you stand there beside me!" And then, before she could answer, or his will control the words, he had added: "And because Mark—my brother—is in there—with you—"

"Hush, hush!" came the soft, astonishing reply. "He is in here, true; but he is not with me. And it is for my sake that he has come—for my sake and for yours. My soul, alas! has led him to the gates . . ."

But Stephen's emotions had reached the breaking-point, and the necessity for action was upon him like a storm. He drew back a pace so as to fling himself better against the closed door, when to his utter surprise, it moved. The upper half swung slowly outwards, and he—saw.

He was aware of a vast room, with closely shuttered windows, that seemed to stretch beyond the walls into the wooded mountain-side, thronged with moving figures, like forms of life gently gliding to and fro in some huge darkened tank; and there, framed against this opening—the girl herself. She stood, visible to the waist, radiant in the solitary beam of sunshine that reached the châlet, smiling down wondrously into his face with the same exquisite beauty in her eyes that he had seen before in the vision of the cloud: with, too, that supreme invitation in them—the invitation to live.

The loveliness blinded him. He could see the down upon her little dark cheeks where the sunlight kissed them; there was the cloud of hair upon her neck where his lips had lain; there, too, the dear, slight breast that not twenty-four hours ago had known the pressure of his arms. And, once again, driven forward by the love that triumphed over all obstacles, real or artificial, he advanced headlong with outstretched arms to take her.

"Katýa!" he cried, never thinking how passing strange it was that he knew her name at all, much more the endearing and shortened form of it. "Katýa!"

But the young girl held up her little brown hand against him with a gesture that was more strong to restrain than any number of bolted doors.

"Not here," she murmured, with her grave smile, while behind the words he caught in that darkened room the alternate hush and sighing as of a thousand sleepers. "Not here! You cannot see him now; for these are the Reception Halls of Death and here I stand in the Vestibule of the Beyond. Our way . . . your way and mine . . . lies farther yet . . . traced there since the beginning of the world . . . together. . . ."

In quaintly broken English it was spoken, but his mind remembers the singular words in their more perfect form. Even this, however, came later. At the moment he only felt the twofold wave of love surge through him with a tide of power that threatened to break him asunder: he *must* hold her to his heart; he *must* come instantly to his brother's side, meet his eyes, have speech with him. The desire to enter that great darkened room and force a path through the dimly gliding forms to his brother became irresistible, while tearing upon its heels came like a fever of joy the meaning of the words she had just uttered, and especially of that last word: *"Together!"*

Then, for an instant, all the forces in his being turned negative so that his will refused to act. The excess of feeling numbed him. A flying interval of knowledge, calm and certain, came to him. The exaltation of spirit which produced the pictures of all this spiritual clairvoyance moved a stage higher, and he realised that he witnessed an order of things pertaining to the world of eternal causes rather than of temporary effects. Some one had lifted the Veil.

With a feeling that he could only wait and let things take their extraordinary course, he stood still. For an instant, even less, he must have hidden his eyes in his hand, for when, a moment later, he again looked up, he saw that the half of the swinging door which had been open, was now closed. He stood alone upon the balcony. And the sunshine had faded entirely from the scene.

It was here, it seems, that the last vestige of self-control disappeared. He flung himself against the door; and the door met his assault like a wall of solid rock. Crying aloud alternately the names of his two loved ones, he turned, scarcely knowing what he did, and ran into the meadow. Dusk was about the châlet, drawing the encircling forests closer. Soon the true darkness would stalk down the slopes. The walls of the valley reared, it seemed, up to heaven.

Still calling, he ran about the walls, searching wildly for a way of entrance, his mind charged with bewildering fragments of what he had heard: "The Reception Halls of Death"—"The Vestibule of the Beyond"—"You cannot see him now"—"Our way lies farther—*and together!*" . . .

And, on the far side of the châlet, by the corner that touched the trees, he suddenly stopped, feeling his gaze drawn upwards, and there, pressed close against the window-pane of an upper room, saw that some one was peering down upon him.

With a sensation of freezing terror he realised that he was staring straight into the eyes of his brother Mark. Bent a little forward with the effort to look down, the face, pale and motionless, gazed into his own, but without the least sign of recognition. Not a feature moved: and although but a few feet separated the brothers, the face wore the dim, misty appearance of great distance. It was like the face of a man called suddenly from deep sleep—dazed, perplexed; nay, more—frightened and horribly distraught.

What Stephen read upon it, however, in that first moment of sight, was the signature of the great, eternal question men have asked since the beginning of time, yet never heard the answer. And into the heart of the twin the pain of it plunged like a sword.

"Mark!" he stammered, in that low voice the valley seemed to exact; "Mark! Is that really *you?*" Tears swam already in his eyes, and yearning in a flood choked his utterance.

And Mark, with a dreadful, steady stare that still held no touch of recognition, gazed down upon him from the closed window of that upper chamber, motionless, unblinking as an image of stone. It was almost like an imitation figure of himself—only with the effect of some added alteration. For alteration certainly there was—awful and unknown alteration—though Stephen was utterly unable to detect wherein it lay. And he remembered how the figure had passed him in the woods with averted face.

He made then, it seems, some violent sign or other, in response to which his brother at last moved—slowly opening the window. He leaned forward, stooping with lowered head and shoulders over the sill, while Stephen ran up against the wall beneath and craned up towards him. The two faces drew close; their eyes met clean and straight. Then the lips of Mark moved, and the distraught look half vanished within the borders of a little smile of puzzled and affectionate wonder.

"Stevie, old fellow," issued a tiny, far-away voice; "but where are you? I see you—so dimly?"

It was like a voice crying faintly down half-a-mile of distance. He shuddered to hear it.

"I'm here, Mark—close to you," he whispered.

"I hear your voice, I feel your presence," came the reply like a man talking in his sleep, "but I see you—as through a glass darkly. And I want to see you all clear, and close—"

"But *you!* Where are *you?*" interrupted Stephen, with anguish.

"Alone; quite alone—over here. And it's cold, oh, so cold!" The words came gently, half veiling a complaint. The wind caught them and ran round the walls towards the forest, wailing as it went.

"But how did you come, how did you come?" Stephen raised himself on tiptoe to catch the answer. But there was no answer. The face receded a little, and as it did so the wind, passing up the walls again, stirred the hair on the forehead. Stephen saw it move. He thought, too, the head moved with it, shaking slightly to and fro.

"Oh, but tell me, my dear, dear brother! Tell me—!" he cried, sweating horribly, his limbs shaking.

Mark made a curious gesture, withdrawing at the same time a little farther into the room behind, so that he now stood upright, half in shadow by the window. The alteration in him proclaimed itself more plainly, though still without betraying its exact nature. There was something about him that was terrible. And the air that came from the open window upon Stephen was so freezing that it seemed to turn the perspiration on his face into ice.

"I do not know; I do not remember," he heard the tiny voice inside the room, ever withdrawing. "Besides—I may not speak with you—yet; it is so difficult—and it hurts."

Stephen stretched out his body, the arms scraping the wooden walls above his head, trying to climb the smooth and slippery surface.

"For the love of God!" he cried with passion, "tell me what it all means and what you are doing here—you and—and—oh, and *all three of us?*" The words rang out through the silent valley.

But the other stood there motionless again by the window, his face distraught and dazed as though the effort of speech had already been too much for him. His image had begun to fade a little. He seemed, without moving, yet to be retreating into some sort of interior distance. Presently, it seemed, he would disappear altogether.

"I don't know," came the voice at length, fainter than before, half muffled. "I have been asleep, I think. I have just waked up, and come across from somewhere elsewhere we were all together, you and I and—and—"

Like his brother, he was unable to speak the name. He ended the sentence a moment later in a whisper that was only just audible. "But I cannot tell you *how* I came," he said, "for I do not know the words."

Stephen, then, with a violent leap tried to reach the window-sill and pull himself up. The distance was too great, however, and he fell back upon the grass, only just keeping his feet.

"I'm coming in to you," he cried out very loud. "Wait there for me! For the love of heaven, wait till I come to you. I'll break the doors in—!"

Once again Mark made that singular gesture; again he seemed to recede a little farther into a kind of veiled perspective that caused his appearance to fade still more; and, from an incredible distance—a distance that somehow conveyed an idea of appalling height—his thin, tiny voice floated down upon his brother from the fading lips of shadow.

"Old fellow, don't you come! You are not ready—and it is too cold here. I shall wait, Stevie, I shall wait for you. Later—I mean farther from here—we shall one day all three be together.... Only you cannot understand now. I am here for your sake, old fellow, and for hers. She loves us both, but ... it is ... you ... she loves ... the best...."

The whispering voice rose suddenly on these last words into a long high cry that the wind instantly caught away and buried far in the smothering silences of the woods. For, at the same moment, Mark had come with a swift rush back to the window, had leaned out and stretched both hands towards his brother underneath. And his face had cleared and smiled. Caught within that smile, the awful change in him had vanished.

Stephen turned and made a mad rush round the châlet to find the door he would batter in with his hands and feet and body. He searched in vain, however, for in the shadows the supporting beams of the building were indistinguishable from the stems of the trees behind; the roof sank away, blotted out by the gloom of the branches, and the darkness now wove forest, sky, and mountain into a uniform black sheet against which no item was separately visible.

There was no châlet any longer. He was simply battering with bruised hands and feet upon the solid trunks of pines and spruces in his path; which he continued to do, calling ever aloud for Mark, until finally he grew dizzy with exhaustion and fell to the ground in a state of semi-consciousness.

And for the best part of half-an-hour he lay there motionless upon the moss, while the vast hands of Night drew the cloak of her softest darkness over valley and mountain, covering his small body with as much care as she covered the sky, the hemisphere, and all those leagues of velvet forest.

XIII

It was not long before he came to himself again—shivering with cold, for the perspiration had dried upon him where he lay. He got up and ran. The night was now fairly down, and the keen air stung his cheeks. But, with a sure instinct not to be denied, he took the direction of home.

He travelled at an extraordinary pace, considering the thickness of the trees and the darkness. How he got out of the valley he does not remember; nor how he found his way over the intervening ridges that lay between him and the country he knew. At the back of his mind crashed and tumbled the loose fragments of all he had seen and heard, forming as yet no coherent pattern. For himself, indeed, the details were of small interest. He was a man under sentence of death. His determination, in spite of everything, remained unshaken. In a few short hours he would be gone.

Yet, with the habit of the professional mind, he tried a little to sort out things. During that state of singular exaltation, for instance, he understood vaguely that his deep longings had somehow translated themselves into act and scene. For these longings were life; his decision negatived them; hence, they dramatised themselves pictorially with what vividness his imagination allowed.

They were dramatised inventions, singularly elaborate, of the emotions that burned so fiercely within. All were projections of his consciousness, maimed and incomplete, masquerading as persons before his inner vision. It began with the singular sensations of death by drowning he had experienced. From that moment the other forces at work in the problem had taken their cue and played their part more or less convincingly, according to their strength. . . .

He thought and argued a great deal as he hurried homewards through the night. But all the time he knew that it was untrue. He had no real explanation at all!

From the high ridges, cold and bleak under the stars, swept by the free wind of night, he ran almost the entire way. It was downhill. And during that violent descent of nearly an hour the details of his "going" shaped themselves. Until then he had formed no definite plans. Now he settled everything. He chose the very pool where the water coiled and bubbled as in a cauldron just where the little torrent made a turn above their house; he decided upon the very terms of the letter he would leave behind. He would put it on the kitchen table so that they should know where to find him.

He urged his pace tremendously, for the idea that his brother would have left—that he would find him gone—haunted him. It grew, doubtless, out of that singular, detailed vision that had come upon him in his great weakness in the valley. He was terrified that he would not see his brother again—that he had already gone deliberately—after her. . . .

"I *must* see Mark once more. I *must* get home before he leaves!" flashed the strong thought continually in his mind, making him run like a deer down the winding trail.

It was after ten o'clock when he reached the little clearing behind the châlet, panting with exhaustion, blinded with perspiration. There was no light visible; all the windows were dark; but presently he made out a figure moving to and fro below the balcony. It was *not* Mark—he saw that in a flash. It moved oddly. A sound of moaning reached him at the same time. And then he saw that it was the figure of the peasant woman who cooked for them, Marie Petavel.

And the instant he saw who it was, and heard her moaning, he knew what had happened. Mark had left a letter to explain—and gone: gone after the girl. His heart sank into death.

The woman came forward heavily through the darkness, the dew-drenched grass swishing audibly against her skirts. And the words he heard were precisely what he had expected to hear, though patois and excitement rendered them difficult—

"Your brother—oh, your poor brother, Monsieur le Docteur—he—has gone!"

And then he saw the piece of white paper glimmering in her hands as she stood quite close. He took it mechanically from her. It was the letter Mark had left behind to explain.

But before Stephen had time to read it, a man with a lantern came out of the barn that stood behind the house. It was her husband. He came slowly towards them.

"We searched for you, oh, we searched," he said in a thick voice, "my son went as far as Buttes even, and hasn't come back yet. You've been long, too long away—"

He stopped short and glanced down at his wife, telling her roughly to cease her stupid weeping. Stephen, shaking inwardly, with an icy terror in his blood, began to feel that things were not precisely as he had anticipated. Something else was the matter. The expression in the face of the peasant as the lantern's glare fell upon it came to him suddenly with the shock of a revelation.

"You have told monsieur—all?" the man whispered, stooping to his wife. She shook her head; and her husband led the way without another word. The interval of a few seconds seemed endless to Stephen; he was trembling all over like a man with the ague. Behind them the old woman floundered through the wet grass, moaning to herself.

"No one would have believed it could have happened—anything of *that* sort," the man mumbled. The lantern was unsteady in his hand. The next minute the barn, like some monstrous animal, rose against the stars, and the huge wooden doors gaped wide before them.

The peasant, uncovering his head, went first, and Stephen, following with stumbling footsteps, saw the shadows of the beams and posts shift across the boarded floor. Against the wall, whither the man led, was a small littered heap of hay, and upon this, covered by a white sheet, was stretched a human body. The peasant drew back the sheet gently with his heavy brown hand, stooping close over it so that the lantern threw its light full upon the act.

And Stephen, tumbling forward, scarcely knowing what he did, without further warning or preparation, looked down upon the face of his brother Mark. The eyes stared fixedly into—nothing; the features wore the distraught expression he had seen upon them a few hours before through the window-pane of that upper chamber.

"We found him in that deep pool just where the stream makes the quick turn above the house," the peasant whispered. "He left a bit of paper on the kitchen table to say where he would be. It was after dark when we got there. His watch had stopped, though, long before—" He muttered on unintelligibly.

Stephen looked up at the man, unable to utter a word, and the man replied to the unspoken question—"At ten minutes past five the watch had stopped," he said. "That was when the water reached it."

By the flicker of the lantern, then, sitting beside that still figure covered with the sheet, Stephen read the letter Mark had left for him—

> "Stevie, old fellow, one of us, you know, has got to—go; and it is better, I think, that it should not be you. I know all you have been through, for I have fought and suffered every step with you. I have been along the same path, loving her too much for you, and you too much for her. And I leave her to you, boy, because I am convinced she now loves you even as she first believed she loved me. But all that evening she cried incessantly for you. More I cannot explain to you now; she will do that. And she need never know more than that I have withdrawn in your favour: she need never know *how*. Perhaps, one day, when there is no marriage or giving in marriage, we may all three be together, and happy. I have often wondered, as you know . . ."

The remainder of the sentence was scratched out and illegible.

". . . And, if it be possible, old fellow, of course *I shall wait.*"

Then came more words blackened out.

". . . I am now going, within a few minutes of writing this last word to you of blessing and forgiveness (for I know you will want that, although there is nothing, *nothing* to forgive!)—going down into that Lost Valley her father told us about—the Valley hidden among these mountains we love—the Lost Valley where even the unhappy dead find peace. There I shall wait for you both.—MARK."

.   .   .   .

Several weeks later, before he took the train eastwards, Stephen retraced his steps to the farmhouse where he had bought milk and asked for directions. Thence for some distance he followed the path he well remembered. At a point, however, the confusion of the woods grew strangely upon him. The mountains, true to the map, were not true to his recollections. The trail stopped; high, unknown ridges intervened; and no such deep and winding valley as he had travelled that afternoon for so many hours was anywhere to be found. The map, the peasants, the very configuration of the landscape even, denied its existence.

Appendix

Author's Note [to *John Silence— Physician Extraordinary* (1942)]

The re-issue of these stories has a peculiar interest for their author. They first appeared some thirty-five years ago, and I vividly recall (about 1908) watching the horse-buses lumbering along Piccadilly with the big red letters "JOHN SILENCE" challenging attention on the "knife-board" advertisement space. This was the original idea of the astute and enterprising Eveleigh Nash; but, for me personally, they stood for liberty. Why? Because the reception of the book suggested a possibility that I might make a modest livelihood by writing—in other words, live where I liked and be independent of a boss.

At the time I was in the dried-milk business, an intimate working associate of the man who owned the original dried-milk patents. Glaxo and other brands were on the way; big business lay in the offing; we had just run a horse, Azote, in the Derby after two years' exclusive diet of dried milk to convince the sceptical doctors that its bones were well made. Very big money lay just round the corner. Dared I, at the age of thirty-seven, throw up the security of a lucrative, yet utterly uncongenial, career, and take the vagabond's trail? After a week of careful reflection, I left dried milk and went off to a mountain village abroad to try my hand at further books.

How these stories came into being may possibly be of interest to a reader. They were originally separate imaginative studies of various "psychic" themes, and it was on the suggestion of Mr. Nash, who had already published two books for me, that I grouped them under the common leadership of a single man, Dr. John Silence. The title was due to a chance question he put to his intelligent and gifted "reader," Maude ffoulkes, as we sat at dinner one night discussing the stories and searching for a good title: "Wasn't there somebody or other in your family," he asked, "with the name of Silence?" This is my recollection of that dinner-table talk thirty-five years ago. Anyhow, the name was born.

The stories are, like most stories, the dramatised emotions I registered in certain places. "Ancient Sorceries" derives from a night in Laon, a place much in the news last year. The picturesque little town, perched on its hill, had an extraordinary atmosphere, and though I dare not pretend that the inhabitants turned into cats, they certainly betrayed all the feline characteristics I have tried to describe: it was an unholy and mysterious spot, and the Hostelry de la Hure possibly still exists. I recall writing the story on the backs of envelopes in that old-world inn, so vividly did the place possess my imagination. "Secret Worship" owns a different birth—a Moravian school at Koenigsfeld in the Black Forest, where, after leaving Wellington, I spent rather an unhappy eighteen months in learning German, and where talking English was punished by half-rations at breakfast. Revisiting it many years later, the disgust at the over-strict, semi-military discipline revived strongly. This Moravian settlement had actually almost a saintly atmosphere, the schoolmasters being honest, upstanding Christians, yet some mysterious law of compensation apparently operated in me, so that I pitched my story into the heart of mediæval Satan-Worship.

The Vampire theme, I felt, needed a new twist to make it palatable, and an island in the Baltic provided the *mise en scène* for the "Camp of the Dog." Having hired the ten-acre island from the Swedish Government for £1 a week, our party of six, equipped with tents and tinned food, procured boats in Stockholm and made our way north to the wild island where we spent two months of holiday. Though none of our six was a "vampire," the story came to me as we sat talking round our camp-fire. The "Nemesis of Fire" needs no pedigree or explanation, and the opening story in this collection is just a treatment of the possible effects of an otherworldly atmosphere upon members, respectively, of the feline and canine family.

Bibliography

I. Collections

John Silence—Physician Extraordinary. London: Eveleigh Nash, 1908. Boston: John W. Luce, 1909. New York: Brentano's, 1910. London: Macmillan, 1912. London: George Newnes, 1913. New York: Vaughan & Gomme, 1914. New York: D. C. Vaughan, 1915. New York: Knopf, 1917. New York: Dutton, 1920. London: T. Fisher Unwin, 1922. London: Eveleigh Nash & Grayson, 1929. London: Richards Press, 1942. [*Contents:* A Psychical Invasion; Ancient Sorceries; The Nemesis of Fire; Secret Worship; The Camp of the Dog.]

The Lost Valley and Other Stories. London: Eveleigh Nash, 1910. London: G. Bell & Sons, 1910. New York: Vaughan & Gomme, 1914. New York: Knopf, 1917. London: Eveleigh Nash & Grayson, 1931. [*Contents:* The Lost Valley; The Wendigo; Old Clothes; Perspective; The Terror of the Twins; The Man from the "Gods"; The Man Who Played upon the Leaf; The Price of Wiggin's Orgy; Carlton's Drive; The Eccentricity of Simon Parnacute.]

Pan's Garden: A Volume of Nature Stories. London: Macmillan, 1912. New York: Macmillan, 1912. [*Contents:* The Man Whom the Trees Loved; The South Wind; The Sea Fit; The Attic; The Heath Fire; The Messenger; The Glamour of the Snow; The Return; Sand; The Transfer; Clairvoyance; The Golden Fly; Special Delivery; The Destruction of Smith; The Temptation of the Clay.]

Ten Minute Stories. London: John Murray, 1914. New York: Dutton, 1914. [*Contents:* Accessory Before the Fact; The Deferred Appointment; The Prayer; Strange Disappearance of a Baronet; The Secret; The Lease; Up and Down; Faith Cure on the Channel; The Goblin's Collection; Imagination; The Invitation; The Impulse; Her Birthday; Two in One;

Ancient Lights; Dream Trespass; Let Not the Sun—; Entrance and Exit; You *May* Telephone from Here; The Whisperers; Violence; The House of the Past; Jimbo's Longest Day; If the Cap Fits—; News *v.* Nourishment; Wind; Pines; The Winter Alps; The Second Generation.]

Day and Night Stories. London: Cassell, 1917. New York: E. P. Dutton, 1917. [*Contents:* The Tryst; The Touch of Pan; The Wings of Horus; A Bit of Wood; Initiation; A Desert Episode; Transition; The Other Wing; The Occupant of the Room; Cain's Atonement; An Egyptian Hornet; By Water; H.S.H.; The Tradition; A Victim of Higher Space.]

Ancient Sorceries and Other Tales. London: Collins, 1927. [*Contents:* Ancient Sorceries; The Willows; The Return; Running Wolf; The Man Whom the Trees Loved; The Man Who Played upon the Leaf.]

The Dance of Death and Other Tales. London: Herbert Jenkins, 1927. New York: Lincoln MacVeagh/Dial Press, 1928. [*Contents:* The Dance of Death; A Psychical Invasion; The Old Man of Visions; The South Wind; The Touch of Pan; The Valley of the Beasts.]

Strange Stories. London: Heinemann, 1929. [*Contents:* The Man Whom the Trees Loved; The Sea Fit; The Glamour of the Snow; The Tryst; Transition; The Occupant of the Room; The Wings of Horus; By Water; Malahide and Forden; Alexander Alexander; The Man Who Was Milligan; The Little Beggar; The Pikestaff Case; Accessory Before the Fact; The Deferred Appointment; Ancient Lights; You *May* Telephone from Here; the Goblin's Collection; Running Wolf; The Valley of the Beasts; The Decoy; Confession; A Descent into Egypt; The Damned; The Willows; Ancient Sorceries.]

The Willows and Other Queer Tales. London: Collins, 1932. [*Contents:* The Willows; Ancient Sorceries; The Return; Running Wolf; The Man Whom the Trees Loved; The Man Who Played upon the Leaf; The Tryst; By Water; The Occupant of the Room; The Decoy; Dream Trespass.]

Tales of Algernon Blackwood. London: Martin Secker, 1938. New York: Dutton, 1939. [*Contents:* The Empty House; A Case of Eavesdropping; Strange Adventures of a Private Secretary; With Intent to Steal; Keeping His Promise; The Wood of the Dead; A Suspicious Gift; The Listener; Max Hensig; The Willows; The Insanity of Jones; The Dance of Death; May Day Eve; The Woman's Ghost Story; A Psychical Invasion; Ancient Sorceries; The Nemesis of Fire; Secret Worship; The Camp of the Dog; The Man from the "Gods"; The Wendigo.]

Selected Tales of Algernon Blackwood. Harmondsworth, UK: Penguin, 1942. [*Contents:* The Empty House; Strange Adventures of a Private Secretary; Keeping His Promise; The Woman's Ghost Story; Ancient Sorceries; The Camp of the Dog.]

Selected Short Stories of Algernon Blackwood. New York: Editions for the Armed Services, [1945]. [*Contents:* The Willows; The Wendigo; A Psychical Invasion; The Woman's Ghost Story; Max Hensig; The Wood of the Dead; The Listener.]

Tales of the Uncanny and Supernatural. London: Peter Nevill, 1949. [*Contents:* The Doll; Running Wolf; The Little Beggar; The Occupant of the Room; The Man Whom the Trees Loved; The Valley of the Beasts; The South Wind; The Man Who Was Milligan; The Trod; The Terror of the Twins; The Deferred Appointment; Accessory Before the Fact; The Glamour of the Snow; The House of the Past; The Decoy; The Tradition; The Touch of Pan; Entrance and Exit; The Pikestaffe Case; The Empty Sleeve; Violence; The Lost Valley.]

II. First Appearances of Individual Stories

"Ancient Sorceries." In *John Silence* (1908), *Ancient Sorceries* (1927), *Strange Stories* (1929), *The Willows* (1932), *Tales* (1938), *Selected Tales* (1942).

"The Boy Messenger." *Nottinghamshire Weekly Guardian* [Nottingham] (7 December 1908).

"The Camp of the Dog." In *John Silence* (1908), *Tales* (1938), *Selected Tales* (1942).

"Carlton's Drive." *Westminster Gazette* (17 July 1909): 2–3. In *The Lost Valley* (1910).

"Entrance and Exit." *Westminster Gazette* (13 February 1909): 5 (with subtitle: "(A Special Adventure)"). In *Ten Minute Stories* (1914), *Tales of the Uncanny and Supernatural* (1949).

"The Face of the Earth." *Weekly Scotsman* [Edinburgh] (11 October 1909).

"Faith Cure on the Channel." *Westminster Gazette* (19 June 1909): 3. In *Ten Minute Stories* (1914).

"If the Cap Fits——." *Westminster Gazette* (12 February 1910): 3. In *Ten Minute Stories* (1914).

"The Invitation." *Westminster Gazette* (3 April 1909): 6. In *Ten Minute Stories* (1914).

"The Kit-Bag." *Pall Mall Magazine* 42 (December 1908): 699–705.

"The Laying of a Red-Haired Ghost." *Lady's Realm* 26 (September 1909): 457–64.

"The Lease." *Westminster Gazette* (22 May 1909): 7. In *Ten Minute Stories* (1914).

"The Lock of Grey Hair." *Observer* (London) (Christmas Supplement, 8 December 1911): 3.

"The Lost Valley." In *The Lost Valley* (1910), *Tales of the Uncanny and Supernatural* (1949).

"The Man from the 'Gods.'" In *The Lost Valley* (1910), *Tales* (1938).

"The Man Who Found Out." *Lady's Realm* (June 1909). *Canadian Magazine* 40, No. 2 (December 1912): 129–38. *All-Story Weekly* 71, No. 1 (12 May 1917): 25–34. In *The Wolves of God* (1921).

"The Man Who Played upon the Leaf." *Country Life* (26 (30 October 1909): 591–93; (6 November 1909): 627–28. In *The Lost Valley* (1910), *Ancient Sorceries* (1927), *The Willows* (1932).

"The Nemesis of Fire." In *John Silence* (1908), *Tales* (1938).

"The Occupant of the Room." *Nash's Magazine* 2, No. 9 (December 1909): 123–28. In *Day and Night Stories* (1917), *Strange Stories* (1929), *The Willows* (1932), *Tales of the Uncanny and Supernatural* (1949).

"Perspective." *Pall Mall Magazine* 45 (March 1910): 407–18. In *The Lost Valley* (1910).

"A Psychical Invasion." In *John Silence* (1908), *The Dance of Death* (1927), *Tales* (1938), *Selected Short Stories* (1945).

"The Secret." *Westminster Gazette* (7 November 1908): 7. In *Ten Minute Stories* (1914).

"Secret Worship." In *John Silence* (1908), *Tales* (1938).

"The South Wind." *Westminster Gazette* (29 January 1910): 3 (as "The Messenger at Midnight"). In *Pan's Garden* (1912), *The Dance of Death* (1927), *Tales of the Uncanny and Supernatural* (1949).

"Special Delivery." *Pall Mall Magazine* 45 (May 1910): 780–86. In *Pan's Garden* (1912).

"Stodgman's Opportunity." *Westminster Gazette* (5 December 1908): 9.

"The Story Mr. Popkiss Told." *Westminster Gazette* (24 December 1908): 3.

"The Strange Disappearance of a Baronet." *Westminster Gazette* (27 November 1909): 17. In *Ten Minute Stories* (1914).

"The Terror of the Twins." *Westminster Gazette* (6 November 1909): 9. In *The Lost Valley* (1910), *Tales of the Uncanny and Supernatural* (1949).

"Up and Down." *Westminster Gazette* (9 October 1909): 7. In *Ten Minute Stories* (1914).

"A Victim of Higher Space." *Occult Review* 20, No. 6 (December 1914): 318–35. In *Day and Night Stories* (1917).

"You *May* Telephone from Here." *Westminster Gazette* (27 February 1909): 2–3 (as "A 'Trunk Call'"). *Ten Minute Stories* (1914), *Strange Stories* (1929).

www.ingramcontent.com/pod-product-compliance
Lightning Source LLC
Chambersburg PA
CBHW070354030726
47504CB00001B/181